The Republic
of Dreams

The Republic of Dreams

of Dreams

a novel by

Nélida Piñon

Translated from the Portuguese by Helen Lane

19  89

Alfred A. Knopf   New York

This translation has been made possible in part through a grant
from the Wheatland Foundation.

Library of Congress Cataloging-in-Publication Data
Piñon, Nélida.
[República dos sonhos.   English]
The republic of dreams : a novel / by Nélida Piñon ;
translated from the Portuguese by Helen Lane.—1st American ed.
p.   cm.
Translation of: A república dos sonhos.
ISBN 0-394-55525-2
I. Title
PQ9698.26.I5R413   1989
869.3—dc19   88-8290   CIP

Manufactured in the United States of America
First American Edition

To those who came . . .

The Republic
of Dreams

Eulália started to die on Tuesday. Having forgotten the last Sunday dinner, when the family had gathered together around the long table specially made so as to have room enough to receive children and grandchildren as guests. At the head, Madruga presided over the festivities and customs that had been a solid tradition in his house ever since his arrival in America. So he listened to those present with a certain boredom, demanding of them their life's blood and appreciation for the platters heaped with fancily garnished dishes.

Eulália allowed her husband to share discrete portions of herself, eager to be off to her room, followed as always by Odete, her faithful maidservant. Or to church, still fasting, arriving in time to attend the first Mass, which she never missed, not even for one day.

Near the altar, absorbed in the beads of her rosary and the scent of the lighted candles, she would little by little make the saints and the gold and silver objects part of a reality shaped by her dreams and foreign to ordinary eyes. And when some diffuse and nameless voice was about to suffocate her heart, Eulália hastened to receive, along with the host, memories of Galicia, to which she had not returned for years now. Faint, almost colorless memories, and the words with which to fix them missing. With deep sadness, then, Eulália fortified herself with prayer and her shy smile.

A ritual repeated automatically. On certain days, however, she seemed to be at the theater, as if figures were moving before her, their masks corresponding to dead kinfolk. Without this being a terrifying vision. Simply because, for a long time now, she had taken the dead as a standard for her feelings. It seemed to her that, from afar, they looked at life with the benevolence of those who have all eternity before them. Simply by being extraordinarily appreciative of everything that had been left behind. Quite different from the living, who expressed their happiness in a boisterous way that bordered on falsehood and senility. And hence taking no notice of the stories that she occasionally tried to tell them in her eagerness to preserve the memory of her father, Dom Miguel.

Eulália had recently taken to gazing at Madruga as though she found the duty of sharing everyday life with her husband a burden. While he, sensing his wife's feelings, felt that Eulália's gaze accused him of having given in forever to the shadow of his own overbearing nature.

At such moments, Madruga was careful to speak in a tone of voice that would not sound metallic. And even careful about the expression on his face, easily distorted by intense emotions, almost invariably of suspect origin. At this point particularly, he did not want to stir up unnecessary trouble within the walls of the house. He was certain that Eulália would not come to his aid as she once had, to provide him with an explanation of his inexplicable acts.

From his rocking chair on the broad veranda of the house in Leblon, Madruga looked out over the sea. As, sitting there woolgathering, he dreamed that he was approaching Africa, on the other side. In old age, practically freed of the responsibilities of watching over his fortune and other people's lives, time hung on his hands. Besides Breta, only one or another of his sons would come out to him at the end of the afternoon, presumably to test whether he still had the same business acumen as in the old days.

After his morning stroll in the garden or along the beach walk, he would settle down to contemplate the Atlantic. In an effort to wring legends from an ocean that he had loved since he was just a lad and that inspired in him the same respect owed divinities. And when he gazed out over this sea crossed by ships, adventurers, and immigrants, he was able, now and again, to bring the past back to life.

His memory took him straight back to Galicia, the setting of his childhood. Through which he moved like someone chasing butterflies. Not forgetting, however, to call on Grandfather Xan. The first person to give him wings, to offer him adventure.

From Grandfather Xan's house, in Sobreira, there could be seen the mountains that the Celts too had worshiped in the past. A landscape that gave the village an air of splendor. That great mass of stones piled one atop the other serving to tone the muscles of the village workers, who clambered up the steep slopes, the peaks of the range, the goat paths.

Despite the charms of Sobreira, and of Grandfather Xan, Madruga had chosen America, though he did not share his secret with his family. Despite his misgivings about the dubious hospitality of the American continent. A welcome that would surely take the form of stale bread, a hard cot in a cheap boardinghouse, salty food bound to ruin a person's digestion. This pessimistic vision of America had not been enough, however, to dissuade him from casting his anchor on the shore of Brazil, just because he so wanted to see with his own eyes its outlandish flora and fauna, the lurking dangers of malaria and rattlesnake bite notwithstanding.

From the veranda, Madruga watched the ever-changing sea. The turbulent waters gave him the impression that he had never crossed the Atlantic, when in fact he had traversed it any number of times. The first of them a memorable one, when he was still a youngster, coming across from Galicia.

A first voyage that filled his heart at one and the same time with a feeling of chaos and of discovery. Not knowing, back then, what to expect next during the crossing. One that dragged on for weeks. Subject each day to the abuses of the English sailors, who blocked the passageways with arrogant gestures so as to bar access to the deck. Thus restricting the poor immigrants to the sweltering steerage, with bunks crowded together every which way.

After a night of fitful sleep down there, Madruga would lie waiting for dawn. He knew that they would be landing in Rio de Janeiro almost any moment now. And was all set to descend upon a city seething with lust and peopled by strange creatures who'd been the subject of many a hair-raising story. On that continent he was about to find himself confronted with a predominantly Indian culture, where whites were a minority. Not to mention the difficulty of communication. Since he would have to master a new language, through intuition alone. And in order to do so, having to destroy a system of fantasies and defenses that would stubbornly resist.

The rocking chair, reserved for Madruga's exclusive use, made him feel as though he were in a drifting boat. The movements back and forth, faster and faster, muddled his thoughts. Forcing him to reflect on death, at a time when he would still prefer to explain life. And above all else, to sharpen his memory and leave it to Breta as an inheritance.

In recent months, relatively depressed, Madruga had found himself suddenly surrounded by a thick fog that kept him from being able to make out the reality round about him. As if he were a passenger on an ocean liner being buffeted by enormous waves, whales, and the wreckage of other boats immediately swallowed up by the wake of foam following after them, along which the shipwreck victims were walking. He would then seem to hear, from a long way away, the mournful whistle of a ship that refused to come closer so as to give Madruga a good look at the passengers on deck, leaning disconsolately on the rail, watching time go by. Emitting stammered sounds that no one on Madruga's ship understood. Warnings, perhaps, that there was no navigation chart aboard, and thus no way to know what port to make for.

While still in this state of mind, Madruga would experience a sudden change of scene. He was at a circus, and in the ring before him a number of old men were acting out past episodes in their own lives, yet their performance was arousing no reaction on the part of the audience. At the same time tongues of flame were leaping from the canvas, which the circus ring, the boxes, and even the tiers of seats were successfully withstanding.

At times, when subjected to her husband's intense scrutiny, Eulália would discreetly thread her way amid the furniture to the living room, clasping a book to her bosom. The life of Teresa de Ávila, for instance, printed in block letters, always upset her. Within that Spanish saint was a seething vortex that exceeded the ardor of flames licking a parched forest. But what could be the source of a fervor such that reality itself appeared to capitulate to it? Could God possibly approve of such excesses? Teresa acted as though she had within her, in her innermost depths, a nest of vipers, all of them privy to feelings so secret that if they should ever be exposed to public view, they would forever transform the surface of humanity.

Eulália had no wish whatsoever to learn whether Teresa de Ávila, in a moment of weakness, ever went so far as to stroke her skin, in a brief caress, while bathing or dressing. Or for that matter whether, driven by the passion with which she surrounded ecstasy, she in fact yearned to forget human forms and the desire that impelled them.

At the sight of Eulália's face all alight, its radiance seemingly a boon within, Madruga realized that he had never visited the far end of the courtyard of that heart. He was reconciled, however, to never seeking entry to it. He too had avoided baring his heart to her or to his fellows. Never favoring them with the fullness of his emotions. To all appearances given to grandiloquent gestures, when in fact he was simply a hunter hidden in the bushes, ready to wield sharp-honed weapons against those who trespassed upon his honor or his interests.

On pursuing such thoughts, Madruga felt absolved of the burden of guilt. Distracted for a time from the harsh constraint of human anxiety. Coming back to it, however, when the world weighed heavily upon him. Above all the fact that he was now past his eightieth birthday.

As always, the family gathered round the dinner table on Sundays. A confusion of voices that bothered Madruga and Venâncio, a longtime friend. Venâncio never missed a Sunday lunch. Coming to the house on foot, at a slower pace nowadays, but still not allowing them to come fetch him by car from the distant working-class district where he lived. With old age, both Venâncio's gestures and his turns of phrase had become stiff and awkward. The two men had grown more and more alike over the years. Hence the two of them scarcely looked at each other at table, both wanting to avoid seeing their reflection in the other. Everything about Venâncio betrayed his modest circumstances, in glaring contrast to the ornate trappings that surrounded Madruga.

By nature a restless sort, Madruga wandered here and there about the house. Finally dragging Venâncio out to the veranda. From there he pointed to the sea.

"The sea is my memory, Venâncio. I've always thrown my memories into the Atlantic. Especially the ones I'm ashamed of today. But you don't care about our sea anymore. Your one concern is politics. Discussing Marx's manifesto of 1848 is much more to your liking than talking about Atlantic currents. Well, I'm here to tell you that even without Marx we'd have come up with his theories. But where would we be if European man hadn't ever gone past Gibraltar, confronted the Atlantic, and gotten the better of it? Only the ocean is capable both of robbing us of our extraordinary vision of reality and of restoring it."

Venâncio didn't answer. He chose instead to turn away and go back to where he had been sitting. Obliging Madruga to follow him. Spoiling his illusion of being able to share with him a sea that meant nothing to him now. Once they had sat down in the living room again, Venâncio declared, with visible annoyance:

"Fortunately for you, at your age, you still hold to a good many things as certain truths. For me, transcendence has lost all meaning. The only belief I have left is that earth is my one last resting place."

Madruga stopped listening and directed his attention elsewhere. That way, both of them would be able to get through the afternoon. Venâncio in silence, still not reconciled to Madruga's acquisitiveness, which he had condemned since they had first set out to conquer America. When Madruga, on the point of losing his soul, had refused to listen to his protests. Trying in turn to poison Venâncio with false blandishments and discreet bribery. Whereas Venâncio, faced with the threat of Madruga's biting off his consciousness and swallowing it whole if he ever relaxed his vigilance, fended him off with the harshest of gestures.

Venâncio always chose the plainest armchair in the living room. He thereby hid his feelings, while at the same time his poverty affronted Madruga. For nothing could offend Madruga as much as Venâncio's inability to handle money.

Venâncio saved his blue suit for Sundays. He brushed it carefully in the morning before putting it on. It had faded slightly and the collar was beginning to fray. On arriving in Leblon in the morning Venâncio would halt directly in front of Madruga. Just for a moment, yet long enough for him to note the insignificant details that were the sum and substance of his entire existence. At such times, Madruga's face went white. He almost snarled, and had a sudden urge to attack Venâncio bodily. In protest against a maneuver that was obviously meant as an insult.

In the face of this habitual confrontation, Eulália would hasten to patch it up between them, to make the dinner a peaceful one. She had the power to head off the imbroglio that threatened to enmesh the two of them.

After Venâncio had left, Eulália would calm her husband down.

"Aren't you the one who has always said that Venâncio has more talent for dreaming than we do? Who in our family, may I ask, has the same ability? Dreaming is a mark of distinction, Madruga. It's like knowing how to build a perfect cage or boat, so that it looks like a Moorish palace."

And she added:

"What's more, I have the feeling that Venâncio abandoned Brazil a long time ago. And I don't even know where he is exactly. Maybe he needs your help."

On this February morning, Eulália took from her wardrobe chest a new, discreetly tailored dress. One she had had made for the Pentecost holidays. From a length of cloth that Antônia had given her as a present. The daughter always on the lookout for high-quality imported silks. The farther the material had traveled, the more taken she was with it. Antônia could judge the quality of Oriental silks out of the corner of her eye, according to criteria ordinarily applied only to human skin. As she smoothed the fabric, her lingering touch noted the suppleness of the fibers, a surface exactly like a young, perfumed skin bearing traces neither of caresses nor of rough handling.

The bath was exactly the right temperature, intended to preserve her energies. Under the shower, Eulália's strength, surprisingly, returned. Had she perhaps mistaken the date, the hour of her death not having yet arrived?

Seated in front of the mirror, Eulália put up her hair with hairpins out of the drawer of the commode. She did so without the aid of Odete, who had insisted, as usual, on helping her. The maidservant stood watching, not understanding.

On gazing into the mirror, whose reflection Eulália usually avoided, the thought occurred to her that it was a pitiless object. At that moment it was beaming back the face of an old woman. Someone a stranger to her. That face of hers had surely journeyed far, and she had not always accompanied it.

Odete insisted on applying foundation makeup. Eulália agreed to a few light touches of the sponge, and a bit of rouge to accentuate her cheekbones. Why not allow herself this frivolity if there was nothing the least sinful about it? Simple gestures of everyday life, time-honored because common to all mortals.

And besides, she had no intention, at that moment, of changing a single habit. Or of giving up any of her functions that the family had grown accustomed to. Life repeated itself without vainglorious parading, dissonances, sudden breaks. Even tragedy sometimes slowly trickled away along the paths of comedy and sobs.

Eulália had learned from her father, Dom Miguel, to immerse herself gently in grief, as one bathes in the tepid waters of a river and is grazed, with the lightest touch imaginable, by the fish and the mosses that rise to the surface, attracted by the light of the sun. The earth was only a little stream in summer, a mere passing appearance. She herself being just one of the many inhabitants peopling the landscape. And always of merely relative importance. Precisely because few seeds survived, most of them succumbing to the cycle of the seasons. And what was more, being present in a dining room adorned with silver place settings, candelabra, simply meant being one more guest at table among the millions enjoying the same frugal repast.

For Eulália, that was a peak moment. And yet a feeling of loss constricted her chest, till she could scarcely breathe, very nearly succumbing even before death could claim its rights. Perhaps it would become necessary to disengage herself as rapidly as possible from the voices and the bodies round about her, everything being relative in the face of so dramatic a plot.

Eulália prayed for a farewell that would be the equivalent of the tea ceremony as dusk fell, life brought to her, steaming hot, on a tray. The day thereby giving every sign of going on, with its vapors and scent of herbs, even if she failed to fulfill her obligation to live.

The premonition of death had come over her suddenly. At first, she took the burning in her chest to be the summer heat of the month of February. She had had a cough the evening before, which did not go away despite the syrup brought by Odete, who threatened to call the doctor. In the stifling atmosphere, the hours took on a different, slow dimension. But as darkness fell, on her way to the living room, where Madruga was sitting reading in his armchair, Eulália's sight was blurred by a play of shadows moving before her, and for a few moments she was unable to make out what was inside the house.

She forced herself to overcome this unusual situation by concentrating on Madruga, a familiar silhouette. Her vision immediately cleared. She could see Madruga, a stranger to events, leafing more or less anxiously through the pages of the newspaper, for he was practically ripping them to shreds. Perhaps trying in this way to set the heart and stomach of life, which was consuming the two of them, to pulsating.

Eulália averted her eyes. Avoiding looking straight at her husband, through whose forehead there seemed to be circulating a message decreeing that she fulfill an inescapable fate. One against which she rebelled. Why should Madruga be obliged, once more, to determine her fate, to transmit premonitory signs to her? Especially now that old age had smoothed his rough edges and he no longer reacted as he once had. Only his eagle eye, blazing now and then with anger, revealed a desire to strike the family dead. And at such times a look of rare pleasure could be seen on his face. The same face in which Eulália read at last the message that only she could decipher.

Eulália, however, hit upon a simple defense. It was not easy to admit that death was that close, announced by way of the face of Madruga, that stranger to everything. Despite the noticeable tiredness that she had been aware of in the last two years. She made a noise in the living room to attract her husband's attention.

"What's the matter, Eulália? You look as if you'd seen a ghost!" Madruga said as the darkness softly fell. Worried about his wife standing there looking at him as though awaiting his pronouncement.

Madruga's words sounded hollow to her. When there were words that seemed to come to him at a gallop, amid a cloud of dust. And with such power they could mean the opposite of what they said. It was her father, moreover, who had warned her of this, as the two of them sat beneath the trellis resting after lunch. Dom Miguel's slender fingers poised on his cane. They were enjoying the Galician summer and Eulália had not yet met Madruga.

"Be careful, Eulália. Never trust words. They affirm as often as they deny. And it's our vanity that's to blame. We want at all costs to be poets, when in fact we're cripples, mortal, and arrogant."

Because of this disturbing lesson, Eulália ceased to associate the intangible, belonging to God's orbit, with the perceptible, belonging to the human realm. In her opinion, it was necessary to go directly to God. Rejecting, meanwhile, the vicious backward kick of violence, whose continual practice was proof that the power of the word was unavailing.

For lack, however, of resources to oppose Madruga's reality, from which God was far removed, Eulália took to praying, with fervent stubbornness. And in liturgical prayers in particular she gave free rein to various feelings. Even though a great many of them immediately vanished, despite her intense effort to retain them.

Nothing, however, brought to the door of her house the clear, sharp face of reality. The sort of reality that comforted and distracted Madruga. Hence Eulália, feeling contrite, suspected reality of lacking a sense of reality.

Installed by Madruga and Dom Miguel in the very center of the house, with the windows caulked against drafts, everything snug and cozy, she had had life half explained to her by the two of them. Not that this sort of certainty displeased her. And besides, certain excesses would have offended the face of God.

She refused to argue with Madruga about human events. She had her own technique for interpreting them. What was more, she had no opinions to offer. And from an early age she had sensed the uselessness of competing with natural voices, such as thunder and storms. Madruga was one of those voices.

Madruga looked at her with candid brow. Even so his forehead warned her of death. Eulália thought of telling him of this odd phenomenon. She very nearly said to him, I'm sorry, but I must leave you before the day that you foresaw. She said nothing, however. She had suddenly perceived that it would not be all that painful to leave him. Or the family.

The grandchildren were already prowling round the house, just waiting to devour the memories naïvely collected during the years in America. It didn't matter. For some time now objects had been nothing but a bother to her. And besides, burning photographs, documents, letters was something that survivors were bound to do one day or another, she thought with a certain heartache.

Eulália moved away toward the window, to have a look at the garden. There were trees in it older than she. The fact that feelings cannot be handed down consoled her. Moreover, someone had once revealed to her in secret that feelings are born and die shut up in the same shell, rarely venturing out to brave the sun. But who? Who had crystallized so well a knowledge that is attained only on the eve of a battle without quarter?

Since her marriage, Eulália had avoided trying to clear up misunderstandings. So that they would settle themselves. What would be the use at this point of sharing the end of the affair with Madruga? He would be white-hot with rage, forbidding her to die. Just as she was beginning to feel pleasure at coming to a decision of this magnitude all by herself.

On getting up later that morning, after tea, Eulália refused to go to Mass, though she dressed as though to go out. This upset Odete, who hovered about her with such concern that Eulália was touched. But not even Odete could keep her from fulfilling her destiny.

She was certain that Odete would sooner or later accept her decision. In all those years she had never surprised in her gaze the least hint of rancor or the sort of unpardonable feeling that drifts across eyes bloodshot with rage.

Odete too had aged. And consulting her memory, Eulália tried her best to recall a moment when Odete had earned her ample praise. To her shame, she could not remember one. Could that be the reason why Odete sometimes abandoned the house in spirit, going off to some place or other, and long lingering there before returning? When, once back from this imaginary outing, her retina betrayed that she had visited the manger of wretchedness, had hammered on its door? On her return her thirst was cruel. She would then fall upon the clay water jar and drink in great gulps. With the water dribbling down her chin, to Eulália's embarrassment for her.

Odete's appearance nonetheless was proof that she was of noble stock. Her body assuming aspects that took her back to Africa. Odete thus retracing, via the paths of ancestral memory, the same trajectory ordained by the notables of her tribe, who from inside stinking slave ships had known Brazil and captivity.

Eulália kept her silk dress on for an hour. Then she agreed to don the nightgown that Odete brought her. It was also Odete who tucked her in bed, adjusting the pillows for her. And also brought her mineral water, biscuits, and tea, certain thus that she had banished her pain.

Odete swiftly cleared off the night table, a fine piece of marquetry, covered with Eulália's many medicines for her permanently delicate health. Not remembering their names, Odete knew them by their labels.

Eulália felt slightly dizzy, as though she were in the hold of a boat anchored in the Bay of Guanabara. Beneath the watchful eye of the country alongside whose territory she too had moored so many years ago. She settled herself beneath the sheets, in such a way as to assure Odete and the other members of the family, who would soon begin coming to visit her, that she had no intention of ever rising from her bed again.

Odete had difficulty understanding her intentions. She had not been explicit enough. Despite the fact that her breathing, slower now, spoke for itself. What could she say to make them believe in her plans? Even though she would not forgo delicate attentions, and longed for a demise that would spare her vomiting and death rattles. So as not to gasp for breath with her mouth yawning open, drooling, giving her the appearance of senility.

"My hour has come, Odete. God has always spoken to me in whispers. So that I would be the only one to hear," she said with a faint smile.

Pretending to wipe away the sweat of her brow, Odete stroked her forehead. At other times too she had taken pleasure in her mistress's body, the intimacy imposed by successive illnesses. Each of them accentuating Eulália's fragility. As meanwhile Odete refused to believe that Eulália, under a doctor's care, could possibly die. And take her own life with her, imbedded like a precious stone in the breast of that woman, now lying in the antique double bed.

Madruga refused to believe the news. Certain that Eulália would soon be on her feet. Vexed at his wife, however, he sent for the doctor and the entire family. Once these steps had been taken, he recovered a certain vigor.

The doctor noted the extreme weakness of Eulália's heart. She would have to be hospitalized. Eulália refused. Mistress of her own life, she was free to choose where she would die. Admitting no impediments.

The doctor left the room. "In view of the circumstances, I will not be responsible for Dona Eulália," he said. Above all because the patient's will was more inclined toward death than toward life.

"Are you suggesting that my wife is determined to die?" Madruga raised his voice.

Being long familiar with Madruga and his terrible temper, the doctor sidestepped the question. "I am merely suggesting hospital facilities. I am not indulging in metaphysical speculations."

"In a word, doctor, is she going to die or not?" Madruga could scarcely conceal his anxiety.

"She is in an extremely delicate state. Her cardiac problems have long been growing more severe. As for death, Senhor Madruga, I have nothing to say in the matter."

"Well, you ought to have, doctor. Death is our number one enemy, and if we aren't sufficiently acquainted with it, how are we going to face up to it?"

Madruga hurriedly returned to Eulália's room. His wife had once again allied herself with her god so as to mock him, excluding him from her esoteric pacts. Visibly irritated, he seized her hand. Eulália's cold fingers clutched his in an unexpectedly strong grip. Madruga was suddenly terrified. He sensed the presence in the room of the old woman with a scythe in her hand, ready to fling it at someone's chest, in her habitual passionate eagerness to reap lives.

Struggling against the sinister presence, Madruga, in torment, held Eulália's extremities tightly in his grasp, wanting to restore the flow of blood, and to protect himself as well. He then observed that Eulália, aware of his effort, had averted her gaze, wishing to be alone.

"I don't want you to die, Eulália. I don't want you to, do you hear?" He lost control of himself, his voice sticking in his throat.

Eulália beamed back at him the smile with which she had rewarded him for more than fifty years. The smile he had seen fade with the years and the wrinkles in her face. Her beauty of the old days was gone. She now bared a shiny, pernicious set of dentures, the enemy of the memory he had always had of her, since Sobreira.

And so, besides death, I must confront your false teeth, a smile doubtless stolen from some dead person? And where has your smile gone? Confess, Eulália, so I can go look for it! Where, finally, to meet this woman who, in all truth, died many years ago, without our realizing, she and I? Had their stubborn clinging to one last deceptive scrap of life been worth it? When in fact existence had already abandoned them, leaving them nothing but pieces glued to cracked walls covered with mold? Surely he too had died, without one son, the most pious of all, advising him of the disastrous event. The vile, base act of which he had been the protagonist.

Bewildered, Madruga buried his face in his hands, murmured words of protest. Let his wife hear them and repent. Eulália asked him to speak louder. Life as it fled was so diverting that Madruga's words sounded faint, inaudible.

"You betrayed me, Eulália. You knew I was dead years ago and you didn't have the courage to tell me," he said.

Eulália raised her right hand, touched his arm, as rigid as usual. How many times she had been aware of that body prepared to attack at the least sign of human tenseness.

"I can answer only for my death, Madruga," she said in hesitant syllables, forcing him to bend down to hear her. "If we were together in life, we shall be separated in death."

Tobias was the first child to arrive. Miguel, Bento, and Antônia filed into the room immediately after him. The grandchildren too, obeying the order of succession. Eulália watched them. They repeated familiar words and gestures. Afraid that her death would drag them all off together. Eulália noted Breta's presence. Breta was on her guard against intense emotions. Eulália was sorrier for Madruga than for her. She had always handed this granddaughter over to her husband. Thus allowing Madruga to indulge in all sorts of caprices with Breta. She sensed that between grandfather and granddaughter there existed a demanding, competitive bond. Each wresting from the other what was felt to be missing.

Ignoring the presence of Tobias, who was eyeing them closely, Madruga importuned her once again. His words filtered through his son.

"Don't leave us, Eulália. Don't forget our agreement. To see me to my grave. To be my widow, to weep for me, and not for you," Madruga said, not noticing Eulália's delicate smile of disbelief in an agreement never signed.

Tobias seized him by the arm. His father's despotic authority cast shadows over the house, a mark of disrespect for the dying. Perhaps Madruga wanted to contend with Eulália for the honors of death. As he looked at his father, he squeezed his arm.

Madruga did not react. His son's gesture was a judgment. And it brought up to date the battles joined between them years before. They eyed each other, then, like two strangers. Both of them slashed away with imperceptible, razor-thin blades, so that Eulália wouldn't notice.

"Leave Mother alone. She deserves to die without the burden of our presence. What she put up with from us in life, without complaining, is quite enough," Tobias said, in a conciliatory tone of voice now.

Tobias had put on weight. He had unseemly rolls of fat around his belly. He could easily be taken for a prosperous banker. Madruga thought of his son as a leech clinging to his body. In exchange for this daily plasma, Madruga plunged into Tobias's universe, always with the expectation of a confrontation. Both fought their duels with words that did not kill. Words that were waterproofed and echoless.

Madruga imagined the linked series of Tobias's gestures on the day he was buried. In the funeral chapel, his son would go up to the casket several times, for the one purpose of straightening the knot in his tie. Certain that this was a detail of fundamental concern to his father. It occurred to Madruga to wonder who might be present at his deathwatch to witness such an act which, however unobtrusive, could perhaps explain life. Must every son necessarily decree his father's end, in his eagerness to succeed him? Becoming the enemy who loved himself and by whom he was madly loved?

Madruga left the room, anxious to see the sea from the veranda. The smell of the salt air permeated the garden. The astringent smell of fish and seaweed. Breta came out, throwing windows wide open. Still impressed by what she had seen in the bedroom. Her grandfather, gnashing his teeth, condemning Eulália to live at whatever cost. This forcefulness expressing his grief at the loss of his wife, or because he would be losing, from that moment on, the principal witness of his life?

Breta felt herself reflected in her grandfather. She too fighting against a loneliness from which she would no longer be able to wrest cries of triumph and chunks of power. Madruga's loneliness seeming to her to be a slice of raw meat, sliding down his gullet at any hour of the day. At breakfast or in the dark of the night, amid the howling of wolves.

Madruga was struck by his granddaughter's pallor. "Are you all right, Breta? I'm the one who's losing my companion, not you," he finally said, worried about what might be going on in Breta's mind. There were times when she pitilessly dissected him.

Breta kept her thoughts to herself. Madruga's power extended to the whole family. He was a wise and obstinate patriarch. He received all of them in his cavern, there to be guarded by his watchful eye, enjoying the fire of his hearth. Who but he gathered meat from the trees, the rocks, the water, grilling it to provide food for them?

Madruga adamantly removed the blindfold from his granddaughter's eyes, resentful of probable feelings damaging to his image. After all, he had sacrificed himself for the family. He had done everything in the name of an affection engraved upon his breast, for which he had not hesitated to mutilate certain dreams, in the belief that life was a pitched battle wherein he made it his duty to unfurl the banner of the victors.

"Eulália banished us from her dreams and from her prayers. There is no longer room in her for us. Only for her disastrous decision," Madruga said.

Though a breath of fresh air had entered the room through the open windows, Madruga felt that human love at that moment was making his body ache all over. Perhaps he would feel better in the morning. Now, however, he appealed to his wife in secret. Are you listening to me, Eulália? Or would she choose to lend an ear to Tobias, who in the future would be left the care of only the fraudulent parts of his father's biography?

The house had been transformed since Eulália's illness. All of them behaving without ceremony. Madruga settled himself in his armchair. Still thinking about Eulália. Come on, Eulália, tell me, who's going to end up with my story? And what's going to happen to the dreams you value so highly? Does there exist a single mortal who possesses the authority to collect the stories of the dead buried in the shade of trees without memory?

"Here, grandfather. This will do you good." Breta handed him the cup of coffee.

Both were readying themselves for the prolonged vigil. Madruga sipped the sugarless, bitter coffee. Fruit still on the tree, before roasting. Night threatened to fall slowly, to be intransmissible. The streetlamps had gone on. The city had no reason to know that Madruga and Breta were keeping vigil for a lady prepared to die with remarkable decorum. Clutching the cross to her bosom.

The last drops of coffee were cold. Better that way. Everything suddenly seemed more serene. Except that all at once Breta's face perturbed him. So much younger than his. No one accepted the unsteady rhythms of his reality the way she did. Teasing him into calling upon all manner of memories. As a matter of fact, no prospect seemed to him more pleasing than to have Breta beside him through the long night.

The story of Breta, and of this family, began at my birth, in Sobreira. A village that dreamed of earning from Pontevedra a promotion in the administrative sphere. Perhaps becoming a county someday?

My mother gave birth to me in the house belonging to Grandfather Xan, where she and Ceferino had lived since their marriage. Xan himself named me, perhaps in return for the privilege of being the first to hold me in his arms, almost the moment I emerged from Urcesina's womb. Though my mother protested, unwilling for her father-in-law to snatch her firstborn from her, his body filthy with dirt.

The house, made all of stone, had two stories. The lower one, whose entrance gave directly onto the road, provided a shelter for the cows and sheep, especially in winter, when they very seldom went outside. Hence the animals' smell and heat, creeping up the walls, were practically table companions as we ate beef stew on feast days. A state of affairs that in no way troubled those who lived on the floor above. For besides constituting our worldly wealth, the cows were solemn creatures, with full udders.

Grandfather often ordered me to come out into the yard. From there he would point ecstatically to the mountains holding Sobreira submerged in the green valley, surrounding it on every side. The Romans, the Visigoths, the Celts, and other peoples had come across them and invaded our blood, becoming mere constituent parts of us. I promptly agreed, admitting that they did indeed form an insuperable cordillera. Only if I

so conceded would Grandfather Xan go back into the house for his afternoon nap.

The river, a modest stream that ran through Sobreira, could be seen
from the bedroom window. An insignificant river, doubtless, compared to
Brazilian ones, vast expanses of navigable waters. We nonetheless dived to
the bottom of it, especially on summer days, when the sun was reluctant
to leave us.

Sometimes I drove a fish pole with a baited hook into the riverbank,
just at the bend, certain of catching a trout or two. Skinny, ugly creatures
at the mercy of cold currents, they never reached the same size as their
sisters in the Pyrenees.

Then, after crossing the bridge, I would run along the steep bank on
the other side. Just so I could lust after the legs of the women kneeling
along the flattest stretch of the river, washing clothes. Amid gossip and
laughter, their bars of soap would slip out of their hands. They would
hurriedly bend over, baring their opulent thighs. I could feel my body then,
stiff and taut, telling me that as yet I had not known a woman. And there
they were, lush and succulent, furiously beating the clothes on the rocks.

But how could this universe, bounded by chronological limits and
accidents of terrain that are beginning to escape me, have any possible
meaning for Breta? It all sounds remote; it doesn't seem to be my story.
Nonetheless Breta has always been interested in hearing me tell about
things. Even when she was little. An interest I've repaid by recounting
scattered episodes. As though anonymous voices were speaking through
me. In particular those oldsters who came to Sobreira before me.

She followed my trail, convinced that in order to please her, Grandfather would make use of misleading signs, and certain obstacles as well,
whenever he spoke of Brazil and Sobreira. At such times her face would
light up. What if she were to turn out to be the first writer in the family?

"The problem, Breta, is that it's not every man who manages to
wring emotions from words. And it's only essential words that are truly
moving."

Seeing my granddaughter's face fall, I added: "There are people who
don't care and let their entire life go by without uttering a single important
sentence. But that's a misfortune that won't come your way. Always remember my Grandfather Xan."

Breta always approaches me with ceremony. Sometimes she announces her arrival beforehand, thus giving me time to choose what suit
or sport shirt I'll wear. I'm like a fiancé before the wedding, doing his best
to keep from falling under the sway of sad songs of love foredoomed.

I sit down in the living room and look at my watch. Breta has never
been late. She comes to me and kisses my hand. A gesture that strikes no
chords of happiness. As night falls, especially when all by myself, I dis-

cover that Breta is not my joy. Nor I hers. What could bring joy to two hearts that roar with rage when they find themselves excluded from a living room? Is ambition at once an impure blood and a bearer of glad tidings in our breasts?

We drink tea from delicate porcelain, and I entertain the illusion that I am nourishing her existence. I open my pores to allow memory to invade me with its noisome water. Breta is fortunate that this is so.

"Don't worry, Breta. I still have a few remains of Sobreira to give you. You're afraid I'll die before you've extracted everything you need from me. And that it will be your secret in the future. My one regret is that I lack Grandfather Xan's talent."

Returning from the river late in the afternoon, I came upon Ceferino. Father's gestures were ponderous because of his stoutness, which always reminded me of an oak tree. At table, however, he grew lighter. Taking on more carefree, roguish airs. And this despite Urcesina, whose face continued to bear signs of bitterness, striking one blow after another, scowling in disapproval of her husband's indiscretions. All she wanted was to spoil his fun. For the pleasure of bringing him to heel, with no protest from Father.

Grandfather Xan bent his head over his plate. So they wouldn't see his shame, his displeasure at his son's failure to react to his wife's forwardness.

"Listen, Ceferino, isn't it time you were taking the cows up-country?" Xan said, attracting his attention.

Vexed by his father's rebuke, Ceferino went up into the mountains, whence he returned satisfied. Cows, apparently, were better company for him than men. Enjoying up there a solitude he shared with no one. Thus having no one to witness his behavior amid the pines and the cows. Or to bear witness to his thoughts, which trickled away down the streamlets watering the harsh Galician countryside.

When faced with exhausting tasks, Ceferino gave proof of a stubborn will. Unfailingly finishing whatever work was assigned him. Though never inspired to seek practical solutions. And easily frightened when confronted with certain questions. But facing them with a ready smile nonetheless, making me believe that essentially all was right with the world. For even though there were those who wanted to better it, it was still necessary to earn one's bread with the sweat of one's brow.

This resignation brought out a tenderness in my father that I wanted to be free of. I never loved my father with the natural affection I take to exist in the heart of certain men, sipped slowly like a fortified wine. Perhaps because he was not, like Xan, given to profound explanations and the pursuit of chimeras. And this gave me the measure of his fear.

He sensed my feelings and forgave me. And forswearing his bear's strength, he clumsily stroked my hair. With visible disbelief in words. He was simply a peasant who bet that there would be sunshine and rainy days, on which the tilling of the earth depended for its proper balance. Setting in motion a sort of wisdom which, bonded to the man's gums, his heart, his bowels, created an indestructible crust, as a defense. Life hard at work. Growing older without help from his son. But did he really need me?

Father's only worldly goods were the house and its foundations, yet to be inherited from Xan. And, following Galician tradition, this meager fortune would belong to the son who took the best care of his parents to the end. They were such small quarters that the plow, a pair of cows, and two people barely fitted inside them at the same time. Not that money meant nothing to Ceferino. His eyes gleamed as he spread out on the table the coins that had come from the sale of smoked hams, calves, and other produce. After expenses were covered, the profit was shared between him and Xan. Very stealthily, Ceferino hid what was left over for him underneath the mattress. Certain that no one in the house knew his secret.

Urcesina didn't worry about the coins. She was sure her husband wasn't free to spend them. Not even to make a dream come true. Without Urcesina's permission, he didn't buy so much as a new suit for the feast days of the patron saint of Sobreira. Urcesina meanwhile breaking her back working so that more coins would end up under the mattress.

Ceferino quietly watched the seasons come and go. Not complaining when the weather was bad. Urcesina ranted and raged for him. She scolded the children, made the meals, and decided which pig to sacrifice in winter.

People in Sobreira had the habit in those days of speaking of America as a fountain that could cure ills and exorcise demons. A debate that sometimes began with their morning coffee, drunk amid the cold and the fog drifting in through the cracks around the windows and the door, and ended after breakfast. Each member of the family inventing an image of America that struck his fancy. Which for me turned out to be an inevitable summons. As though outside of America there remained only exile.

When there was a stranger in the house, I would seat myself beside him. Searching for signs in him that he had visited that continent. It was difficult, however, to distinguish a person who had been there from those who had never left Galicia.

"Have you been to America, sir? It must be paradise, isn't that so?" I would hastily blurt out before Urcesina banished me from the room.

Urcesina was always on her guard. She was bristling as she brought a cordial.

"You don't know what you're saying, my boy. America is full of Indians and blacks. Not to mention the Portuguese with their mania for invading other people's lands. They tried their best to cross the Minho and take Galicia. But since they couldn't, they went off to plunder Brazil. And there they are, those Indians and blacks, just waiting to devour our men, salting them to taste. Life in America is like a bed of nettles. It hurts you, makes you itch, and doesn't let you sleep. And to top it all off they don't have any spring there. The heat melts everyone's brains, dissolves the will to work. It's hell itself all year round."

Grumbling the while, Mother went on peeling potatoes with a sharp knife. She managed to pare off a transparent peel. Pleased with her prowess, she returned to the attack.

"And why the devil do you need America? Aren't things good enough for you here? Why don't you settle in Vigo and make your living as a carpenter? It's Christ's profession."

"If I don't go to America, mother, what other future do I have left? Vigo isn't going to settle the question of my life. What business do I have going there? I want more, mother. I want to live Grandfather Xan's stories," I said boldly.

But seeing Mother's puzzled face, I immediately changed my mind.

"I'd rather stay in Sobreira. Where else can I be as happy?" I tried to lower my voice, to make Mother forget. I feared reprisals, too watchful an eye.

I was determined, however, to prove that Mother's predictions about Brazil were wrong. On arriving in America, exhausting all my resources, driving sharp bargains to keep body and soul together. If I was going to be required to keep a coffin studded with nails at the foot of my bed in order to stay in Brazil, I would do so.

Dona Aquilina had the right idea about America. And that's why she lived on the hillside leading up to the church of Sobreira. From there she could see all of us and not be seen by anybody. Unjustly accused of being a witch, of working with herbs and spirits.

"It's better to lose the world all in one go, rather than a drop at a time. And besides, my boy, what would you do with those cows and those miserable plots of land? They're not worth one peseta. You're lucky that that's how things are. Because it's poverty that makes a person fight tooth and nail for money and a full larder. What wretch can resist the sight of hams and sausages hanging from the ceiling? Choice fare like that is well worth selling your soul to the devil for, just for the right to lick 'em and bite into 'em," Aquilina said in the churchyard after Mass, to anyone who might be listening.

Sobreira, as one, repeated that life had taught Aquilina to be a penny pincher and pigheaded. She looked like a bird with a hooked bill and no wings. Always dressed in black, with a shawl wrapped tightly round her, restricting her movements. Carrying her crook in her right hand.

Grandfather Xan constantly warned me against that cackling crow. By all manner of means I must keep away from that coarse-minded woman who confused America with pork innards. Garlic with gallnuts. Therefore lacking the instinct for grandeur and dreaming.

Oblivious of Grandfather Xan's warnings, I would go to her house hoping she'd come out. Slamming the door after her, Aquilina would begin scratching in the dirt like a hen. Searching for coins, chestnuts, branches, greens. She practically stole from the neighbors. Fruit and ears of corn hanging down over walls disappearing into her basket and the sack on her back. All to be consumed by her old stomach, her flock, her hearth, and her fear. She had the look of one sentenced to death, awaiting her doom.

"Sobreira condemns me, but I condemned it first," she muttered spitefully. "You're the only one I wish good luck. The rest can go to hell."

Trembling with fear, I tried to escape her evil spell. Aquilina's old age struck me as a dramatic stage in a process of disintegration wherein there had been no reciprocal construction of a wall beneath which she might take shelter in the expectation of a dignified death. She gave me her blessing, however, in answer to my fears. Her dirty, peeling hands made me sick to my stomach.

Aquilina was the first woman to speak to me of America with the knowledge of someone who has planted her feet in America and gotten them scalded. By way of intriguing wrinkles round her eyes she revealed which were the good points of the continent and which the bad. And she hinted at the existence there of so much treachery that I almost threw up, given my love for America on the one hand and the flu that was raging that winter on the other.

Her hoarse voice nearly leaping out of her throat, she nonetheless emphatically stated that the universe was worthless, the one exception being the new continent. Spared black plagues, crusades, and the roots of Christianity. Where there were only bare-naked pagans with their privates showing.

The more Aquilina plunged to the depths of delirium, the more emphatic her pronouncements became. To the point that she swore that certain fountains in America gave forth not water but pus, simply to conceal the diamonds amid the pebbles. Fortune thus favoring those brave souls who felt no aversion toward life.

After her discourse, I questioned her. Seeking improbabilities and absurdities that might be favorable signs of my future. My body was eager to set forth. It had increased in stature that year. The one thing that kept me in Sobreira was Grandfather's gift for storytelling. The legends he recounted held me spellbound. Even though I was preparing to venture into other magic realms, damp and disastrous, where, to the sound of drums, a man risked becoming as bloated as a drowned victim of shipwreck were he to let his guard down for one moment.

I did not confess to Father that I was about to depart. Nor to Urcesina. I did not tell them that for many long years I would cease to see their furrowed faces with the taste of salt. The first faces to speak to me, with the authority born of affection, of the poignant desire that I should survive them. It had never seemed to them a vain act to feed me porridge, to fatten me, since their one thought was their need for me to bury them with the dignity that their last coin of all would afford them. Was it for this that they had brought me into the world and mated?

Once I had left for America, I would have to think of them as dead. Causing them to endure greater suffering than my own. The loneliness of a person left behind is a remedy swallowed with despair and misery. This truth made me ache all over, but how much pain could a thirteen-year-old boy accumulate! With adventure ahead, a more powerful spur than the pain about to be inflicted on another!

It was cold on the mountain heights. I built a brushwood fire. Keeping watch on the little flock of sheep that I had brought up there to pasture. Those creatures were sacred beings. With a life reaching back in time that I did not have. Though diligently seeking to satisfy their hunger, they knew how to move amid the stones and the rough vegetation in gentle ways. Whenever I imitated them, I hurt myself amid the thorny gorse bushes. I was not possessed of that harmony granted by nature to those creatures enjoying from close at hand her intimate flowering.

I began, that afternoon, the long farewell. From the top of the Pé de Mua, I was not able to make out the house. At that hour, Mother was cooking the evening meal. The iron pot receiving pieces of pork, vegetables, potatoes, turnips. The repetition of a habit going back centuries in the village.

Seated at table, anticipating the pleasure the meal would bring, Father made a mental inventory of his few worldly possessions. The better to deal with the future. Ceferino and Urcesina were the beings who had given birth to me amid heedless, forthright, frank gestures. At a far remove from courtly love, the whisper and rustle of silk. That race of Galicians, lying at the foot of the mountains, made love as an expiation of a primal fault perhaps taught them by a Church which, beneath the aegis of sin, had distracted them with legends and bitter duties. They dared not spit into genitals an energy meant only for the earth! So they refused to believe in a love that abandoned them once satiated.

I came down the mountainside with the animals. When almost in sight of the house, I felt I had killed Ceferino, Urcesina, and Xan, whose disconsolate hearts sought to stand in the way of my destiny. There began in me the slow process of dissolving a solid womb formed by language, affection, legends, and food. Only in that way would I be able to swell the sails of my ship. What else had crystallized in my Galician soul? In the end, of what use would the Galician treasures proclaimed by Grandfather Xan be in the fight against the reality of America?

"What's wrong with your eyes, my boy? A bit of dust in them?"

Mother was surprised at my red eyes. But she immediately forgot the fact as she went about her work. Her one concern being to put hot food on the table.

"Hurry up and eat your soup before it gets cold," giving me a look of reproof that she herself could not have justified.

I warmed myself by the fire. The smell of grease permeated the house, relieving the pain in my breast. Urcesina had no reason to suspect that I was killing her. And that the hours spent on the mountain had given me the strength to smite her with dramatic boldness, in order to free myself from the duties imposed by her shadow. On no account would I leave for America with doubts in my heart and circles under my eyes. It was necessary to be alive, awake, shrewd, a bird of prey. Keeping Ceferino, Urcesina, Xan at a great distance from me, warmed by their memories. They could not affect the fateful dream of anchoring my galleons in that sad and sun-drenched America.

I planned my escape in meticulous detail and with the greatest circumspection. Getting my family used to gestures that left no mark or echo. I was careful not to allow my eyes to betray me. All I had left to do now was to find someone to finance my boat passage. Grandfather Xan had refused. He hoarded his coins in the strongbox and wasn't about to invest them in his grandson's ruin. He wanted me at his side listening to his stories, burying him with the emotion he'd dreamed of.

I looked about me in dismay. There was no one who would get me out of Galicia. Suddenly I thought of Uncle Justo, Grandfather's brother. A cantankerous, inhospitable man, who acknowledged his neighbors' greetings with a curt nod of his head. Not wanting a soul to set foot in the house. Hiding the cooking pots when neighbors came in sight.

I knocked nervously at his door. He came to answer, grim and scowling. Practically driving me away. "What is it you want, at this hour?"

He scolded me for having come at that particular time. As he saw it, I ought to be in the fields or up in the mountains, working. Through the slit in the door, opened just a crack, I saw a bleak setting. He lived there all by himself. He had never wanted to marry. He used to say that there wasn't a woman alive who'd do for him.

"The minute you take a wife you lose her. She either cheats on you or ignores you."

And to back his claim that he was better off without such creatures, Justo worked with true grit. His tough body never gave in to pain or to affection.

He finally let me in. Leaving me standing there just inside the door.

"Well, speak up."

"I have to have America, uncle. I need money for the passage."

Justo stood there in silence. It was as though he hadn't heard. I spoke of Brazil, once more, as a country I'd been to, the reason why everything was so familiar to me. That country beyond the sea.

"No, not the sea," he hastily corrected me. "The sea won't do for us Galicians. Only the ocean. Preferably the Atlantic, our neighbor."

Uncle had no reason to be worried about the loan, to be paid back with whatever interest and profit he decided on. I knew how to talk about money. Long before, I had glimpsed coins circling through human hands. The greed with which fingers clutched the coins to keep them from falling. The radiant gleam of the metal illuminating one and all. In the tavern, for example, eyes automatically converged on the bright coins displayed above the counter. My own father gripped them with a strength he doubtless lacked when he held my mother in his arms. Worse than epidemic, money had become entangled with the soul of man. And Uncle was not immune to it. Moreover, he always affirmed that at the sight of gold his will to resist human intercourse, that irksome and bastard contact with his fellows, had been appreciably strengthened.

He was not surprised at the request. With no change of expression, he did his best to extract confidences, to drag up what was at the bottom of the well. Who knows whether I didn't pledge him my very soul, over and above the debt to be repaid?

"So you have to have America, do you?"

And for a few moments a cruel expression came over his face. Perhaps I had injured his feelings, just because of the money. Or could it have been because at my age he had demanded his right to America, and no one had helped him? On the contrary, they had forced him to mix his dream with cow dung, their way of trying to teach him never to lose himself in daydreams again. Thus becoming a sour, unsociable old man, with no one to bear witness for him, abominating demonstrations of human feeling? Had I appealed to the wrong man, knocked on the most resentful door in all Sobreira?

I did my best to tell him my dream, even at the risk of aggravating the situation. But I could do nothing now to halt the process set in motion. I simply admitted that, as long as I lived, America would be the one land I wanted. Hence I was obliged to leave straightway. Despite Grandfather Xan's trying to seduce me with his stories, to pin me down in Galicia.

"It isn't that I was born in the wrong place, uncle. It's just that my destiny is to set out for one land trailing the memory of another behind me. Without Galicia, which I'm about to leave behind, America would fall to my lot without my appreciating it, without the passion I'm possessed by. Can't you see, sir, that I even have a fever?"

Justo took a wineglass from the shelf, dusted it off with a napkin, held it up to the light to examine its transparency. Only then did he pour the wine.

"This is to warm that impassioned soul of yours even more," he said dryly as he offered it to me.

For the first time I felt America close. Uncle's hard heart was melting through the workings of generosity. Even if he had offered me water, his gesture had the weight of an embrace.

"I know that many come back failures, with their heads hanging. But I promise to come back with my head held high. Have faith in me, uncle. And besides, if I don't have a go at it, how are you going to know that I was defeated, that America robbed me of pieces of my body?"

Justo looked deep into my eyes. He invaded my body in order to judge, with the aid of the wine, what sort of blood ran in my veins.

"And how does a thirteen-year-old boy dare contract a debt in the name of nothing but a dream?"

Uncle spoke of dreaming with the naturalness of a farmhand gathering in hay for cows. Enjoying a familiarity with a chimera that I had not supposed him capable of.

To the point of making dreaming an ever-present object in his stable, amid his cows. The only females, incidentally, in his life. He stroked their rumps with a strange torpor, which I noted to my surprise on an unexpected visit. On realizing that he'd been caught in the act, Justo was angry, banishing me from the pen, claiming the animals couldn't abide strangers. Especially inexperienced ones, who hadn't yet assimilated certain rules.

"Uncle, I need to go to America. If I stay, I'll die. And you'd be helping to kill me, sir."

Justo observed his nephew taking at one and the same time his sword and his illusion in hand. Confronted with the difficulty of explaining to him an America traced by the testimony of the unsuccessful. Those men who arrived in Galicia with stony smiles on their faces. None of them knowing exactly how to describe the feelings that had left their ugly mark on the return voyage.

"Anyone who comes back gives up what he left behind, my boy. So you don't know, then, that America is a colossal, tragic dream?"

"And who told you it was a dream, uncle?"

Had Breta been there, in that year of grace 1913, she would have perceived that I foretold her birth at that moment, linking her lot to mine. Beginning with the moves I made. With my finger raised in warning, frowning, I was all set to overtake Uncle, to get ahead of events.

"It's not a dream. What I say here will come about."

Justo would have to understand that this reality of his nephew's was tangential to dreaming, went beyond the level of illusion. The one thing he wanted was to go in search of his future, which awaited him on the other side of the Atlantic.

Uncle marshaled arguments to oppose me. Perhaps he was right. The pitilessness of America was proverbial. It spared no one. But staying home beneath a roof festooned with spider webs had as strong a taste as death.

"I'm off, uncle, even if you stay behind."

Justo insisted again that I give up my plan. In the end there were few who succeeded. The majority turned into human wrecks, beings without a country. Did I have any idea of the stuff that failure was made of? Pity the poor wretch who dreams, he's fated to be defeated! Defeat is the sister of the dream. Those who finally came back to Galicia crept down the streets, apologizing for their empty hands and their trunks with nothing of value inside. Wearing the same old suit, and their eyes fixed on the ground. The return of these people marked the onset of tragedy in the house of their birth. All at once the roof began to cave in, and there was no way then to work up the strength and round up the money to prevent the leaks from flooding the floor.

"Is there anything sadder than a house with rain pouring in, its windows broken, the paint peeling? The worst of it is that these immigrants can't even weep. Pride keeps them from shedding tears. For those who left, the one remaining consolation is to live out their exile in their own land."

Justo paused, but did not permit interruptions. He sipped the last few drops of wine still left in the glass.

"A person wins the right to return to Galicia only when his body actually sags with the weight of coins and victory."

He spoke without a letup. I never saw him so vehement. He wanted, with all possible force, to keep his nephew from leaving, to keep Breta from being born. Me from building a sun-drenched house in the country called Brazil. I countered his arguments immediately, swearing to carry out the necessary rites.

"Should I fail, uncle, I shall come back to Galicia and remain at your side. I accept the burdens owed the defeated. I will see to the work in the fields, care for the herd, and open the windows to air your house. And at the hour of your death, I shall help you close your eyes. I swear, uncle."

He hesitated. He thought it more convenient for a neighbor to see him to his grave. It was a simple matter to dig a hole in the ground and throw him in. He could do without ceremonies. Afterward they could sack his house. I persisted nonetheless, suborning him with proposals painful to both of us.

Justo was silent for some time. He got up and went over to the stove to make black coffee. He was inclined to generosity that evening. He waited for me to appreciate the quality of the coffee. Only then did he draw closer to me.

"Why do the two of us come from such a tragic race, my boy?"

I felt for the first time that he was deeply moved. Affection is a sword in the breast, I was learning. And likewise the absence of affection was the equivalent of a Toledo blade thrust into the heart, giving life's movement its quietus.

After coffee, another glass of wine. Constrained by his own generosity.

"I don't want you to bury me at the cost of your defeat," and with a gesture he bade me leave. He had things to do.

"Are you going to help me, uncle?"

He practically pushed me to the door, from where I looked at him anxiously. My life depended so much on the answer that I was in a fury at his share of gold, his loneliness, the lack of pity, the cruel words. Miserable, miserly, my murderer. Killer of dreams and of human lives.

Justo stretched out his arm till it touched my shadow. Then he nodded as he slammed the door in my face.

The road grew dark as I made my way down it. But once in the yard of our house, I quickly pulled myself together. A few minutes later I asked Father why Uncle Justo, unlike other men in Galicia, had never had a go at America.

His mind occupied with his own tasks, Father paid no attention to his son's inability to find his bearings. Or had we foundered in falsehood and indifference? I repeated the question. He was whetting on the emery wheel the big heavy knife he used to shave thin slices from smoked ham. A task he performed with gusto. He stopped for a few seconds, as though taken aback.

"Who told you he never did?"

"So Uncle Justo's been to America then?" I could not conceal my astonishment.

"Many long years ago."

And without offering any further details, Father went to his room, coming out with the jacket he always wore when he was going up on the mountain to spend the night with the cows. Just as he was about to leave the house, however, one particular or another came back to him, for he turned to me and added that even before leaving for America, Justo was always regarded as a peculiar sort. So much so that the family never understood him. That was everyone's opinion at least, including Xan, ordinarily so indulgent.

That night, under the covers, I thought about Uncle. All alone in his bed, he too was feeling the rigor of that cold night. We were both surely thinking about America, which he had visited in the past, and I was soon to come to know. Each foreseeing the consequences of that journey. I was dreaming of proclaiming America's name and scattering its gold to the four winds like a sweet perfume. While Justo was prophesying my return to Galicia with holes in my pockets, thorns bruising my heart, after my brush with the American continent. Thereby repeating his humiliating trajectory. Not daring for that reason to embrace his neighbor, to share a meal with him at the common table.

The mattress creaked as I tossed and turned. My ice-cold feet plaguing me. The voluptuous pleasure of dreaming failing this time to warm my joints as it once had. It grew colder still as I lay there awake. And all of a sudden there seemed to appear before me a shadow that barked like a dog. Despite my fear, I said to it, bristling with rage: We'll see which of us wins!

 Tobias was the last son to be born. Madruga was no longer thinking of having a bigger family. And even Eulália was startled at her body's eagerness to reproduce itself.

"I want it to be a boy. Another Brazilian to figure out this country," Madruga said on hearing the news. Anxious to move the lives of his offspring like pieces of an imaginary chessboard.

Tobias grew up in the shadow of his siblings. They stroked his head but then immediately forgot about him. Drawn to Esperança, the sister who created tensions and wove fantasies. Tobias rebelling against the fact that he was a late arrival in a family that had already divided up its affections and areas of influence among the other members.

His son's failure to measure up, giving in to uncontrollable impulses merely to attract attention, met with Madruga's constant disapproval. The two of them angrier each time they locked horns. Till one night Tobias fled the house out the back door, with the deliberate intention of provoking his father.

Madruga waited for the clock on the wall to strike midnight. Whereupon he left him to his fate and retired to his room. Tobias waited till dawn to steal back into the house. Immediately locking himself in his room, regretting at this point his adolescent adventure. His heart pounding, he was afraid his father would take a pruning hook to his future acts, visiting punishments on him that would humiliate him.

At lunch, Madruga said nothing. To the relief of Tobias, who concluded that the episode was over and done with. A week later, his father waved in his face a key ring with two shining metal keys, one to the doors of the house and the other to the garden gate.

The immediate effect of his father's gesture was to wound Tobias to the quick. He interpreted his gesture in the most literal sense. An explicit warning that beneath his father's yoke his acts of rebellion were useless. Madruga was handing the keys over to him merely to prove to him that his freedom depended on his father's will.

"He wants to make me his slave," he complained to Venâncio, lacking the courage to have it out with Madruga face to face.

In the end, unable to tolerate this unbearable situation, Tobias left the key ring on the dresser, in full view, to prove to his father that he deliberately forbore to use the keys left at his disposal.

Madruga flew into a rage, demanding explanations. How dare he defy his will?

"What good are these keys to me, father, when what I need is my freedom? To move about my country with no restrictions. Just as you, sir, left Galicia without explaining your reasons even to your family."

Tobias was claiming the right to learn about life even if that involved misguided acts and words. Therefore needing to leave the house even in the dark of night, with no fixed hour for his return or any definite itinerary. With no feeling of indebtedness toward someone already in possession of the treasure, and thus able to use it to clip his wings.

Madruga was unmoved. Tobias felt bogged down in words that found no echo in his father. He thought it prudent to propose a quiet reconciliation. Reminding his father that he himself was the one who had fostered his sons' sense of adventure. Spurring them on by the dream of wealth, of territorial expansion, to conquer Brazil. Hadn't he always told them that Brazil was a fish with golden scales hugging the very bottom of the sea? And that they must go after it, not allow it to escape their fine-meshed nets? For whoever caught that fish would have landed Brazil for all time to come!

Madruga did not identify with Tobias. After Tobias's birth, his heart was touched by the babe lying in its cradle. But then he immediately left the room, yielding his place to Venâncio. He sometimes suspected that on handing Tobias over to Venâncio for baptism, he had handed over his fatherhood as well.

"You're mistaken, Tobias. When I ran away from home, I won that freedom with the sweat of my brow. I washed my bread down with sweat. As though it were water. So don't take it into your head that I'm going to hand you a freedom you haven't fought for."

They came to grips with each other on the slightest pretext. It was useless for Eulália or Venâncio to intervene. And even after Tobias was a married man, the look in his eye provoked his father, testing as it did whether he was still under the tutelage of that fierce bull, whose horns were polished on the family each and every day.

Madruga and Tobias would not allow their wounds to be dressed after their violent encounters. They saw to it that disharmony ruled between them. Faced with the two contenders, Breta did not know which one to side with. She wondered, however, what sort of family this was. Stubbornly programming the life of its members, expecting thereby to justify Madruga's crossing of the Atlantic, decades before.

"Father's a tyrant. For all I know, he wants to take my place even in bed. When he screws, do you suppose it's in the name of this glorious family?" Tobias said to Breta.

Since '68, Tobias had put himself at risk to defend a number of political prisoners. Lacking the money to hire a lawyer with a reputation, mothers sought him out in his modest offices on the Rua Primeiro de Março. Tobias barely knew his clients, having only a photograph or a vague description of them. Most of them not even allowed visitors. Shut up in filthy cells, in a lamentable state. It was even suspected that many of them had died without their families being able to claim the body.

Tobias pitied them. And in certain cases, once they had been found guilty, he ended up paying the court costs on seeing the weeping mothers, their dresses in tatters from having sat so long in the antechambers waiting for news. Begging him, fingers intertwined in supplication, to relieve the suffering inflicted on their sons.

"Our sons are being murdered, Doctor Tobias, and nobody cares. As though no one believed our stories. Is there no longer any justice in Brazil?"

Tobias nourished their hopes, convinced that he could return their sons to them within a reasonable time. Free them from hell, through the rule of law and order, reestablished at last. The women smiled faintly, begging him to act quickly. They were afraid that, in the daily round of torture, the brutes would hasten the death of their sons.

"One of them died only yesterday. Just a youngster still. He didn't even have a beard. And he died all alone, without a soul to hold his hands. They could hear him moaning even in the upper tiers."

The women had set up a system whereby, besides exchanging politenesses and worries, they took turns at the gates of the barracks, as soon as the presence of their sons there had been confirmed. And as the days went by, their sense of smell grew so keen that, despite the intervening distance, they could describe the smell of human flesh sacrificed at that moment.

When they visited him, Tobias kept the windows closed, with dark curtains filtering the light. The clear light of day always irritated him. And there amid the darkness, as those women came before him demanding signs of life, he was protected.

He soon felt the weight of failure gnawing at his bowels. Holing up in bars till dark, he found himself unable to understand the country that he had inherited thanks to his immigrant father. Having lost faith now in any collective effort, through which they might all regenerate the tissues of a history which, in its course, had succeeded in destroying essential values. Thus making it difficult for the Brazilian people to discover at what precise moment of its social constitution the divorce between the dream of a growing nation and the practice of reality had taken place. A divergence doubtless so dramatic that it had plunged society into a daily round of life so wretched and apathetic that the effects of this break, which had led to a loss of ethical ties, were still being felt today, on every level of society. Hence millions of sad eyes and downcast souls on Brazilian street corners everywhere, despite the tambourines and the African drums.

"Our institutional freedoms have always been a farce," he said to his godfather. "Beginning with the judicial system, a cripple that can't stand up to strong regimes. And so we all turn into tyrants. Of the same breed as Getúlio, Médici, and others. We offer coffee to visitors the moment they arrive on our doorstep, whip in hand. We've done nothing but waste a patrimony that some people call a nation, others a country or a fatherland. Brazil lies to itself at every turn. And there is no elite worse than ours. It condemns the weak and the poor to extermination or to exile. The exile of silence and social nonparticipation. Of debarment from their human rights."

Tobias's financial obligations were more of a burden each month. And when he had no other way to meet them, he went to Madruga in desperation. Getting back at Tobias for the money he spent defending terrorists, Amália kept running up more household bills. He then picked fights with her so as not to have to sleep with her. Amália applauded the state of belligerence that had finally set in between them, after reconciliation proved impossible. But every time their arguments threatened to end in violence, one of them, followed immediately by the other, would run into the living room, a region declared neutral territory by both, where they never fought, and often occupied by the little girls, whose eyes Tobias and Amália veiled to blind them to reality.

Lacking the courage to ask Madruga for further resources, Tobias resorted to banks to solve his problems. Forgetting how easy it was to get more credit. How obliging the manager was about explaining this or that little detail. To the point that he became irritated, hesitating then to sign the promissory notes on the desk. But his obligations were so pressing that he overcame his own scruples. Haunted above all by descriptions of the scenes that took place in underground prison cells covered with mold, urine, and blood, ridding himself of his anxiety by offering money to the mothers who still came to his office, despite his poor professional record.

Informed of his brother's promissory notes that were past due, Bento did not turn a hair in front of his banker friends. Grateful for the word passed on to him, he assured them that Tobias's way of doing business had his father's approval. Though he regretted that the debt had not been discharged on time, owing to Tobias's artistic nature. He asked them to see to it that the episode was not repeated, and therefore to let him know before another promissory note fell due. He summoned Tobias to his office immediately. When he paid no attention, Bento insisted. This time Tobias hung up on him, demanding that he be left in peace. His brother should stick to the sordid questions he was continually involved in, many of them subsidized by the people's money.

Miguel resolved to intervene. "I'm not obliged to listen to you, Miguel. You're a brother who's never mattered to me. What's more, all you're interested in is money and sex."

"Let's not argue, Tobias. Let's please try to understand each other. I don't even know why I still come to those damned Sunday dinners. It must be for the pleasure of seeing the old man sitting at the head of the table, like the absolute master of the universe and of our souls."

"And where else would we be likely to meet?" Tobias said testily. "In the cemetery, the day Madruga's buried? Or the day his will is opened?" And he walked out of his office without saying good-bye.

Madruga called him that same sunny afternoon. Offering him a lemonade, a sign that they would be talking without the influence of alcohol. He motioned to him to sit in his own chair, but Tobias refused. As they exchanged politenesses, Luís Filho arrived unannounced. To Madruga's annoyance, since he'd arranged things so as to be alone with his son.

Luís Filho sat down, giving every sign of staying. Madruga did not feel at ease with his son-in-law. He was always aware that his marriage to Antônia had come about through a transaction in which the son-in-law had cautiously weighed the benefits forthcoming from that union. At the time, under pressure from Antônia, Madruga had allowed him to reap excessive profits. On the eve of the wedding, however, he had voiced to Venâncio his scorn for his son-in-law, a penis bought for its weight in gold. With the great advantage of being accompanied by a pure bloodline and matchless professional competence.

Luís Filho pretended not to notice his father-in-law's uneasiness. And to conceal his embarrassment, Madruga steered the conversation round to pleasant, pointless subjects.

"But was this why you summoned me, sir? Didn't you say it was urgent?" Tobias rudely broke in.

Tobias considered that he had the right to attack his neighbor, claiming not to be afraid of any loss he might suffer as a consequence of so doing. Such an attitude ensuring a certain offhandedness on his part. Thus challenged, Madruga turned beet red. Very nearly training his guns on him, disregarding any possible acts of retaliation. Tobias was not sensitive enough to respect Madruga's constraint toward Luís Filho. Madruga forced himself, nonetheless, to control his gestures and his emotions.

He began by emphasizing the care and concern that Bento and Miguel had shown for the family. And for Tobias in particular, in direct confrontation with the present government, in the exercise of his profession as an attorney-at-law. At precisely the time when the military regime had suspended civil rights. Thereby exposing society to arbitrary rule and certain citizens to torture. With no prospect for the moment of the voiding of the sentences passed on terrorists, subversives, and mere militants. The majority condemned in absentia, with no formal charges being brought and no public trial.

"Many of your clients are still alive and breathing, but in point of fact they're legally dead. They've suffered civil death. It's as though they were living under suspended sentence. And so, Tobias, as long as this military system lasts, they're going to rot in jail. But don't fool yourself, the military aren't going to be in any hurry to declare an amnesty. They have no intention of extending their vote of confidence to civil society. So I fear that only death will free your clients. As they leave their cells in a coffin or a burlap bag. These are cruel times, Tobias, but on the other hand, look at how prosperous they are. People have never bought household appliances, clothing and accessories, trinkets and baubles in such quantities as now. They're no different from Indians. And that's why the middle class doesn't believe that torture and prison cells exist."

Tobias averted his face from his father, regretting that he'd come. The usual conversation. It never varied. They simply grew older with each visit. He could not contain his impatience. His eyelids began to blink uncontrollably.

"Your description of Brazil is realistic, father; it corresponds to the truth. Yet my duty is to go on. The duty, moreover, of all of us, cowards and weaklings though we are. But what you're deploring, sir, is not what you see as my devotion to lost causes, but rather the fact that at each and every moment I give proof of an irresistible vocation for defeat. For you, everything I do ends in failure. I agree. I don't know why, but I've always associated myself with losers. I'm more drawn to them than I am to winners. Despite the rejoicing in victory and the collective hysteria they arouse, there's something sad and ridiculous about them. Perhaps because triumph is so short-lived and the winner so soon enveloped in the shroud of contempt and oblivion. I've never been on the side of those who profit from living. Hence I've doomed myself to failure before the fact. Remember, father, that despite your fortune, I belong to the legion of losers."

Madruga helped himself to a glass of whisky, without ice, thereby violating his own rules. Returning to his seat, he moderated the tone of the debate. Luís Filho was about to hold forth. His elegant, dignified gestures worthy of a cardinal were in keeping with the dark suits he invariably wore.

"In the beginning I thought that Tobias would pursue a career in politics. In view particularly of his university days, when he was deeply involved with the old National Student Union. I was disappointed when this did not come about. Every family possessed of a solid economic structure has need of a politician who carries weight. To lobby in the halls of Congress, on congressional committees or in our courts of law, as the case might be. But perhaps you're still in time, Tobias. I see, for instance, in the defense of political prisoners, those who are really representative, the solid beginnings of a future campaign. Putting Tobias in a position to lead the opposition, taking up popular causes, defending civil rights, unfurling in a word a banner leading to the Chamber, or even to the Senate. I am certain that in the future those prisoners will be of great value when election time comes round. They will leave their cells with the halo of martyrs. As will those who return from exile."

Luís Filho discoursed with elegance. In no hurry to finish. And speaking to no one in particular. As he concluded, he accepted the coffee brought in delicate porcelain.

"After that speech, Luís Filho, I better appreciate how well you discharge your duties to Father. No impresario in his right mind can do without your services. I only wonder why you yourself didn't choose to become a senator of the Republic rather than Madruga's son-in-law."

Luís Filho was unruffled. But before he could reply, Madruga spoke up in a stern tone of voice.

"I will not allow anyone to be insulted beneath my roof. I must therefore ask you to leave this room. Or else I myself will leave."

"I merely thanked Luís Filho for his advice. It's too bad his recommendations have come too late. They no longer apply to me. The National Student Union and I have ceased to exist politically. I've kept quiet because I had nothing to say. And the Union because it was forced to. It's now gone underground. And the same thing can be said of Brazil today. The whole kit and kaboodle underground. And now that I've seen your spirit of prophecy at work, I'm certain I'll have nephews with a brilliant future. Who knows? Maybe you'll provide us with a bishop we're badly in need of."

"Did you take me for a father unmindful of his duties?" Luís Filho said complacently.

Madruga eyed the two men, both born in Brazil. Whereas he had come from the rough mountains of Sobreira, peopled with sheep, goats, cows, animals of extraordinary antiquity. Wondering whether that origin separated him from them. Since at that moment he experienced a confused rush of feeling toward them, something between scorn and indifference. He felt cheated, far advanced in years. A white-bearded billygoat, obliged to climb still farther up the narrow paths of the cordillera, from whose summit he would contemplate the vast sweep of the horizon. Once again, he had best control his urge to lash out against Tobias and his son-in-law.

"I summoned you to propose a permanent expansion of your practice, and the setting-up of a complete staff, with assistants experienced in all the various branches of the law, including political prisoners. I have an agreement with Luís Filho now. But should this suggestion not interest you, I insist that you join us, to take care of the legal end of things. It is inadmissible not to be able to count on your professional experience. There is a place waiting for you on the board of directors. It's time you took over your inheritance."

Tobias listened intently. He was wearing a khaki jacket and mismatched pants. He chose to pace up and down the living room, his hands in his pants pockets. His hair recently cut as short as an army cadet's. Until the week before it had straggled down his neck.

Absorbed in trying to estimate how many more years he would have to put up with his father's tyranny, Tobias did not answer immediately. He did not feel in debt to him in any way, save for the fact of having been born through his intermediary. A tie becoming more and more irksome to him. Once he'd pulled himself together, Tobias returned to his seat.

"Ever since I left law school, you and my brothers have been writing out prescriptions for my destiny, in incomprehensible scrawls, indicating the sort of remedy that's going to save my life, even against my will. It would seem in fact that I exist for you only when I follow those orders. Each time I've obeyed, you've declared my life to be legitimate. It's always been that way. It's as though I were a little child still and you were leading me about by a halter, showing me the path to success. Isn't it success that you're offering me, sir? Aren't you trying to bribe me with success? But haven't you learned even yet that that kind of success is an insult to me? And that it's not in my plans to lose what soul I have left? To measure up to your sons Miguel and Bento?"

Oblivious of Luís Filho, Madruga made no effort to contain himself.

"In that case, before signing your name to that high-flown, self-denying little discourse, start paying your own bills. Or have you forgotten that freedom is quoted on the stock exchange and requires putting up margin? I've had enough of your vomiting up your fake independence in my face, while at the same time making me feel guilty for helping you. When it takes my endorsement, my money for everything. I finance your battles, your drinking, your women, your comfort, even your ideology. What right have you to send me your debts to pay, as though you were my wife and not a grown son?"

Tobias turned pale, appeared to fall into a faint. Madruga for his part felt a pain in his chest, realizing immediately that he had tried to kill his son with deadly words having a delayed effect. Both of them bent on murder, for their mutual convenience. Deeply ashamed of himself, Madruga covered his face, enveloped in a shroud that kept him from giving a helping hand to Tobias, defeated once again by him.

Tobias couldn't get a word out. Never had his father struck back at him so directly, hurling at him expressions blackened with hate. Were the two of them in the act of cursing each other so violently that death was their one remaining consolation?

Madruga slowly bared his face, looking for his son. Luís Filho was there before him, impassive still, immune to human passions. Tobias's shame was visible. He had been cruelly humiliated in front of this arrogant and predatory son-in-law. Bought, moreover, by him. A man who had cost him a pretty penny, just waiting for his fortune to fall into his hands. And who remained cool and collected in the face of family quarrels. As though he endorsed discord in order to ensure his rule. Antônia and he dreamed of holding the controlling stock in the companies. They applauded the dead bodies strewn about on the floor. So as to dissemble, however, Luís Filho had now assumed an air of disbelief. Had Madruga accumulated all that money, over those long years, merely to include his son-in-law among the heirs?

Luís Filho went over to Tobias. Apparently at one with the loser, yet wanting to touch him nonetheless. Without Tobias suspecting. Cowering in the dark, the son was experiencing a cruel, disembodied panic.

Madruga could bear his silence no longer. "Speak, Tobias," he begged.

Pained and vulnerable, Tobias's face traced a straight line to Madruga, aimed directly at his father's heart. Throughout the uncomfortable examination, the son doing his best to free himself from his father's vigilance, oppressive since his childhood. To the point that Tobias sometimes could scarcely breathe when his father demanded his presence in the living room. He loved and hated his father with equal intensity. A plait of painful, alternating feelings, not a single hair of which ever let go so as to relax the tensions.

Madruga for his part was deeply disturbed by the oscillations of that affection. From his son there would be forthcoming now a friendly gesture, now a blow that instantly severed several joints of his fingers.

It also affected him to go through his son's exuberant phases. When this happened, he immediately banished him. Only to repent the next moment. Unable to rid himself, however, of the opinion that Tobias and Venâncio, swashbucklers both, were flourishing a partially moth-eaten flag. The two of them betting on the dubious glory of this pennon, though each lacked what it took to venture forth in its defense.

It had been Madruga's suggestion, seconded by Eulália, that Venâncio baptize his son. During the ceremony, round the baptismal font, Eulália was touched at the thought that by virtue of that act Madruga and Venâncio would be symbolically repeating their first Atlantic voyage, when, still in search of the continent called America, there had arisen that affection between them which promised to follow them to their graves.

Despite this new tie, Venâncio refused Madruga's offer of a helping hand. Altogether detached from material possessions and trivial everyday occurrences, maintaining that there existed other realities beyond that espoused by Madruga.

"Be that as it may, let me help you, Venâncio. The years go by quickly here. And in no time you'll have grown old without making good in America. Perhaps you don't want to work altogether on your own, in which case I'll set up a little business for you."

In the early years, Venâncio smiled at this sort of proposal. Before his face took on shadows and wrinkles, which never went away. Madruga forgetful of the fact that Venâncio had not come to America to make his fortune. America was only a dream copied from other men who had gone on the same journey before him. Even though in Spain Venâncio had never asked those who had left America, who surely survived thanks only to memories and lies, what their reasons had been for crossing the Atlantic in the past. A crossing known to be perilous, since once the journey was undertaken, there hovered over them the threat of losing their souls and their original passion, both theirs from birth, and thus held to be gifts of the gods, who kept them company from the cradle.

Venâncio was opposed to the thesis that only the myth of gold, or rather, the nuggets of disgrace and corruption, had served as the initial impulse inducing the Portuguese and the Spanish to set forth in search of great discoveries. On the contrary, behind their ambition was a latent dream, black and full of syphilis, which had invaded their blood and from which death in America would free them. The incomparable fortune of feeling that continent pulsate in their hands. Dante himself had dreamed of this America, without a name as yet, by virtue of the extraordinary intuition that had impelled him to proclaim the existence of other lands that lay far beyond Gibraltar. Even though the only horizon he knew was the Mediterranean, within which he undoubtedly felt confined. And if this was so, why would Venâncio, a prisoner of the twentieth century, scorn to follow in the footsteps of Cervantes, Dante, Camões, who had never forborne to brave the fierce currents of the imagination?

"You'll never understand my contempt for money, Madruga. Don't forget that I belong to the race of dreamers. And if I chose America, it's because here I would be able to master the disquieting sorcerer's art of tracing the outlines of my personal map. Knowing the while that in the end the traces devour the solid lines of the dream, leaving nothing of this imaginary cartography. Not even memory."

Forgetting the legends that Grandfather Xan used to tell him, the equivalent somehow of Venâncio's map, Madruga flung harsh words in Venâncio's face. A court jester, who couldn't even count on the king's deigning to listen to him. No buffoon or jester moved him as much, however. He feared that in the future Venâncio would take to begging in the suburbs, on the train tracks of the Central and Leopoldina lines. Right alongside the disinherited. He vowed then, in secret, to protect him, as long as he lived. He would lack for nothing.

Venâncio spent hours investigating the streets of the downtown district. With his eyes in the service of the secret life of a city in general dirty and sordid. At times he was overtaken by dark anxieties, when he swore he would go off into the backlands. Amid the cactus and the mythical stink of the goats of the Northeast, he would bring into clearer focus the destiny outlined by his map.

"Where should I go next, Madruga? Is the interior of Brazil really to be found on the open prairie lands scaling away from drought? In the humiliated soul of its people?"

Before Madruga could render an opinion, Venâncio announced that the people, plunged into an absolute state of poverty and ignorance, would, in the end and against their will, arrive at a pact with the powerful, choosing them as a model and a target to aim at.

Ever since Sobreira, Madruga had intuited that reality simultaneously killed and fostered life. The adjustment to such a process obliging each and every one to make every moment live. Life not being a sheet of carbon paper enabling words impressed on it to be readily reproduced on other pages of the notebook. They had to be written all over again each day, thus firmly establishing existence as a practice.

Madruga himself, in the name of victory, preferred to forget once and for all the humiliations suffered in Brazil. Leaving Tobias unmoved nonetheless. The son questioned the merit of winners, whose triumph consisted of flaunting a suit of English cashmere, on the wrong side of which, however, the crude basting and the backstitches leapt to the eye.

"You were the last son to be born, Tobias. Why do you refuse my heritage, my traditions, my words?" Madruga asked pleadingly, in front of Luís Filho.

Tobias did not reply. Indifferent to his father's show of emotion. Regretfully, Madruga withdrew. He would once upon a time have slapped his face, making him pay for his transgression. He chose, rather, to go out onto the veranda, to distract himself a bit. Whence he was summoned by Breta, who had just arrived. She immediately felt the tension. She supposed that their differences had once again concerned Brazil, a controversial subject that kept them constantly keyed up.

Breta did not join in the argument. Appreciating the play of contrasts, she did not defend her ideas with the same ardor as Tobias or Miguel. She never missed a chance, however, to criticize Brasília. A fief surrounded by insurmountable walls, which, on becoming a seat of power, deepened social dissensions, sanctioned corruption and the intolerable privileges of a state bureaucracy.

"It's the city itself that's just waiting for a chance to establish a dictatorship. After the coup, the military approved the plans drawn up for Brasília, its rigidly segregated architecture, so as to form an irresponsible, insensitive, corrupt elite. With a thoroughgoing contempt for the rule of institutions. This dictatorship is the opposite of Vargas's. Vargas's was at least run by civilians. Civil society managed to humanize the system thanks to the class rings and diplomas of its bachelors-of-law. Beginning with Getúlio himself. And it was humanized above all by the fact that it was based in Rio de Janeiro, a city with vices, virtues, cabarets, with Lapa, Mangue, secret sewers. Brasília is impermeable to the stench of the people. It has a perfect layout for defense. They took special care to build drawbridges and moats everywhere. Nobody is going to be able to reach its heart, beating all by itself up there on the plateau. For them alone, the only ones to enjoy the use of this heart irrigated by power and privilege. This heart devours everything else, except the military and the technocrats, who take turns ruling."

All enthused, Tobias forgot about his row with his father. He now used Breta, with her more incisive arguments, as a shield.

"Meanwhile, we have thirty million pariahs. Practically on death row. They're merely hypothetical figures for Brasília, and cynically doctored ones at that," Tobias said, his face flushing.

Breta appeared to be speaking for the exclusive benefit of Luís Filho, who was all ears.

"The errors that have followed one upon the other since the military coup represent a serious drain on our independence. And it will involve an almost impossible social cost to redeem them. Who is going to answer one day for those who died in the name of this supposed development? For those who were deliberately sacrificed? Whether through starvation, ostracism, torture? Costa e Silva, Médici, Geisel, Figueiredo? Who else will appear in the witness box of history? Perhaps Luís Filho can answer that question for us."

"History tends to be just, Breta. Or rather, indulgent," Luís Filho said in an even tone of voice.

"History will not always be kind, Luís Filho. It's going to depend on who writes it someday. I have faith that in the future the son of an illiterate will again speak to us about all this. That's the only way we'll ever know the truth."

The afternoon dragged on for all of them. Luís Filho poured himself another drink, slyly imposing his presence. He enveloped Breta in a friendly smile. She answered with subtle probes. Such as asking him for further details concerning the luxuriant genealogical tree that had borne him. Having apparently familiarized herself with the stories concerning the São Paulo side of Luís Filho's family, with its many close connections to the Minas branch. A circumstance on which Luís Filho prided himself, the ring with the family seal never leaving his finger.

He noted her cleverness. The clear distinction that Breta made between the family from which he came, with its coat of arms and verbal eructations, and the one founded by Madruga, at the cost of his life's blood and money. He returned her ironies, with a courteous bow each time, throwing Breta off-balance for a few seconds. But then, at the top of her form again, she flung more darts at him, ready to slip through any breaches he might leave open. So that the news of the skirmish would reach Antônia.

Breta wanted to draw her aunt out again. To protest against the insinuations that Luís Filho had been the target of. As she had done recently.

"I'll have you know that Luís Filho is far better than my brothers. And not because of his noble origins," and she drew herself up proudly, flaunting at the same time the ring with the family seal that had been handed down to her by her sister-in-law.

"Better in what way? Because of his money, his talent, or his prowess in bed?" Breta retorted.

Antônia went to Eulália to complain. Her mother calmed her down. Breta had inherited Madruga's insolence. Both of them failed to take into account the effects of certain words. Active and overbearing as they were, who could nonetheless deny their generous streak?

As Luís Filho and Breta crossed swords, Tobias sat down next to his father. In the course of their conversation, he offhandedly mentioned his wife. He accused Amália of having the instincts of a hunter. Nothing satisfying her appetite, by nature voracious and rapacious. And because she knew he was Madruga's son, she constantly set him a high standard to live up to. He was the first to admit that his marriage had been a mistake. He'd seen on their wedding night how greedy Amália was. And not because his wife's body had confronted him with a hunger that in the beginning might even have given him pleasure. The wholeheartedness of these confessions sent a sudden chill through Tobias.

"It was you, sir, who practically ordered us to marry. Perhaps because Amália was a rich heiress," he burst out, as though deliberately intending to offend his father.

Madruga had always been irked by the vainglorious airs of Amália's father, and was therefore constantly at sixes and sevens with that elderly Italian, who had landed in America with poverty in his very soul. Madruga accused him of staying on in Brazil without the least appreciation of what the country was all about. When America's original aim and real end were to oppose the European structures left behind. Something that Madruga had realized immediately, thus making his love for that territory all the more intense. A land all the more exciting the more it came to resemble human thighs seething with desire in the act of love. Everything in Brazil was outsized, nature producing trees over two hundred feet tall. And a country that could tap into so tumultuous a force of nature was destined by fate to be a giant. To rise above its sordid and lazy rulers. Sprung for the most part from the middle class, a parasite on the body politic and willing to sell out to foreigners since colonial days. Without question unworthy representatives of the people's powers of imagination.

"It isn't only a da Vinci who makes a country," I once said to Fornari, the Italian. "A nation is built above all with the eyes, the bone-tiredness, the dreams, the illusion, and the death of those who toil day after day, thereby preparing themselves to admire da Vinci, Cervantes, and Machado de Assis."

Because of her marital difficulties with Tobias, Amália visited Madruga less and less often. In her stead she sent his granddaughters, superbly dressed featherbrains. In contrast to the slovenly appearance of Tobias, permanently in need of a shave. The stubble serving to conceal his anxiety. One could rarely glimpse even a fleeting smile on Tobias's face.

Though sympathizing with their father, the girls did not spare him their criticism. Or hide how ashamed they were of him, because of his shabby cubbyhole of an office, with ancient, battered furniture. Not to mention the penniless clients, waiting resignedly in the anteroom. What they wanted was a father like Uncle Bento and Uncle Miguel, who frequented the Jockey Club at lunchtime, and expensive restaurants.

Madruga tried to reconcile them with their father. He never humiliated Tobias in front of Fornari's granddaughters. In order to make it up to them, and help them forget their father's misfortunes, he offered them splendid presents. Asking them at the same time to respect Tobias's temperament, with a peculiar charm all its own. Not to mention his extreme dignity, accepting nothing from his own father so as not to be indebted to him for his career.

"But what kind of a career can he have, if nobody sees it, grandfather?" one of them said, doubtless rehearsed by Amália.

Miguel was the first to find out that Amália was being seen with a lover in public places. After learning more of the particulars from Bento, he alerted Madruga as to what had been going on. The latter condemned his daughter-in-law and the apathy of his son, who undoubtedly knew of this turn of events. A family's ruin began with the first cracks spied in a wall. He demanded that Tobias put an end to such a situation.

"My wife doesn't belong to me, father. She's anybody's who wants her," he said indifferently.

"This cynicism is unforgivable, Tobias. I won't tolerate such scandal. A son cuckolded in public. There's only one way to repair the damage. You must separate immediately."

Offended by his father, Tobias disappeared for two weeks. Madruga being informed that his son was making the rounds of the Lapa bars. Unable to bear this affront, he aired his complaints to Eulália.

"And on top of everything else he's a shitty lawyer," he said irritatedly, carelessly using language he'd always avoided in his wife's presence.

"Just because the boy defends thankless causes?" she said, reprimanding him directly for his bad manners.

Madruga shut himself up in his study, not wanting to see any of his other sons. On Monday, he summoned Tobias. His son came at his bidding. He arrived clean-shaven, in a new suit, almost unrecognizable.

"What is it you want this time, father?" he said before he even sat down.

Madruga came straight to the point. "Apparently you've never given a thought to Amália. Do you at least sleep with your wife?"

Tobias was obliged to admit that they'd been occupying separate rooms for some time. Without his regretting the loss. The noises the woman made were unbearable. As was seeing her body through her transparent nightgowns. He hadn't left the house because he had nowhere to store his books. Many of them presents from Venâncio. Besides being moved by the sight of the garden, there before him, when he opened the shutters of the bedroom window at break of day.

"And besides, father, the house is mine. It was your wedding present," he said emphatically.

"I'm giving you exactly a week to leave that damned house. Leave the walls, the roof, the furniture, whatever, to Amália and the girls. I want you out of there."

Tobias disobeyed. He seemed to be anchored to the house. Despite not courting Amália's favors in the right way. As a matter of fact, the marriage had gone on the rocks in the first months. A breath of life still left in it only when he felt drawn to the warmth of Amália's bed. Caught in the beginning in the toils of her body, which he described as a serpent, he made straight for her breasts, gluing himself to them so tightly that Amália begged him to restrain himself a bit, for the way he sucked them hurt her, scarcely giving her a moment's peace.

Very early on, Tobias condemned the woman's heart, an arid zone that could be irrigated only by an abundant rain of splendid gifts. Her ambition, smoldering in damp, half-closed eyes, corrupted everyone.

"Amália is unfeeling. She needed to suffer and go off by herself to weep in secret," he confided to Venâncio when he stopped loving her.

And to aggravate the situation, Tobias took to staying out night after night. Ending up in Barbosa's mother's bed, where the shadow of Barbosa, a political prisoner, haunted them, demanding his freedom. Sensing that presence, the two of them clung to each other in such distress that at times Tobias was unable to get his member inside the woman so as to attain a pleasure together that, for a few moments, would have put to flight the anxiety that gripped them even in bed.

At such times, the woman comforted him with gentle caresses, secure in the knowledge that love in their day and age was difficult. For her especially, enjoying orgasm would have been the same as a slap in the face of the son cuffed daily by the myrmidons of the dictatorship. And the more she consoled him, the tighter the bonds of impotence became.

"We'll free your son too someday. I swear to bend my every effort to this end, till justice is done."

With a long embrace, the woman paid his fee, never mentioned, in advance.

"Worse still than Barbosa is the shadow of Médici and his accomplices among us. I'm never going to be able to screw in my whole life."

He lit one cigarette after the other. Submerged in the dishonesty of defending lives deliberately sacrificed. The dishonesty of living any sort of love doomed from the start to go down the drain. The dishonesty of not admitting the break with his father. Refusing only in appearance aid from him which in fact would have represented his moral emancipation, only to end up accepting Madruga's monthly remittance that demeaned him so. What had become of his pride if everyone attacked him without provoking any reaction on his part?

Tobias studied Breta, her splendid mimetism, her body undergoing changes in response to the threats that hung over her head. He hadn't yet seen her, he supposed, in her adult phase. Breta got along well enough with Madruga and Miguel, showing everyone else few kindnesses, keeping her life and her heart a closed book to them. At times she was willing to take up the gauntlet and argue, fearlessly. At other times, she would side-step a debate. But her reaction to purely personal attacks was always un-predictable.

As he stroked her hands, a gesture Breta appreciated, Tobias was quite simply trying to invade her privacy. To find out how she calmed her passion down and played around with her feelings just for the fun of it.

In the presence of Luís Filho, Antônia, and Bento, Breta closed her eyes, causing them to disappear. Till the conversation took another turn. In a simple, natural way, she fed her own mystery, without ever forgetting to bar the door to her soul and to her apartment. Her life sealed off from the curious. To the point of taking her guests to public places to pay back invitations, in order to keep her house to herself. It was suspected that Breta, shut up in her own quarters, chose, with exaltation, those whom she would favor. But with what gestures did they strip themselves bare before her?

The vision of Breta in amorous agony in bed disturbed Tobias. He pondered the subject for the first time. He tried to banish the thought. But more questions occurred to him. Who entered the body of that woman, to dominate it or to understand it through tenderness? Who freed her of the sweat born of passion, drying her skin with avid lips?

Something in Breta reproduced Madruga's spirit and his transgres-sions. Without following her grandfather's biography step by step. But there had been forged between them a chain with countless links, one tending to exclude the family. When Breta came into the living room, Madruga brimmed over with a strange energy. And seeing his father over-come by the magic of that presence, Tobias was envious of Breta. Asking himself, then, seized with anxiety, what kind of hopeless failure am I, if I'm unable to fascinate even that old Galician?

America too was a bone of contention between Madruga and Tobias. Father and son inspecting the American continent with a magnifying glass clouded by pride and intransigence. Both laying claim to an America that was their exclusive possession, despite their knowing that it had been sliced up centuries ago by foreign invasions, by the creation of captaincies for life, at the service of a limited number of family lines.

Incapable, the two of them alike, of describing America with a cleverness at the service of the conspiracy of devils threatening to bury these lands, leaving them forever bankrupt of all hope. Tobias's America wavered, however, between a debased sovereignty, the practice of self-deluding dreams, and the existence of sacred temples. With its vast plains, mountain ranges, and dense jungles, the solitary figure of America dangled like a hanged man from a rope. This oscillating movement, possessed of supreme freedom from the limitations of space, having thus far enabled America to escape the grasp of those bent on her irreversible historical rape.

Madruga had gone through countless versions of America by this time. Never forming a clear picture of it to place on his bedside table. Instantly rejecting Tobias's tortuous, resentful vision, which betrayed America's destiny. For how could the inhabitants of this continent, among whom he included himself, come up with any precise definition of a land that clung with equal ardor to gold, magic, legends, putrefaction, massacres, sun, maritime rituals? Not to mention its being a continent fervently oriented toward the sea. An America therefore proclaiming, for those with ears to hear, its status as the favorite daughter of the Atlantic and the Pacific. The latter, as it happened, an ocean that had neglected to bathe the shores of Brazil.

Madruga and Tobias loved each other by way of their adversary relation, brought into clearer focus amid heated debates. And amalgamated perhaps by money. But was money Tobias's prime motive for visiting his father's house? Or were these visits connected with Madruga's intelligence, pouring out a steady stream of threatening archaic signals aimed at his son, who had always lacked the imagination to follow his intricate maneuvers? Tobias's dream in this case could be summed up as a simple lack of imagination. The supreme misfortune of not conceiving of the universe outside of the dimensions of reality, of being, thus, of an almost vegetable nature, comfortably imbedded in the earth. A modest raiser of bulbs, when there were stars to worship.

Madruga felt tempted to take his son apart with a crystal gaze. To disassemble that body, spread the parts out on the floor, and after having done so, conceive a new Tobias. In the same way that he had erected buildings, simply following the model for masonry construction. Tobias rebelled against this talent of his, holding forth on the crudity of his soul. A sort of flesh that shed black blood. So that in the end his father would meet up with a mind imprisoned in a rented room without furniture, with peeling walls. With the power to strike Madruga dead with disgust, thus wreaking its vengeance on paternal reality, which in its turn was doing its best to crush Tobias with its Napoleonic splendor.

Amália finally sought a divorce. It no longer pleased her to attract critical notice. She was afraid her brothers-in-law would catch her in restaurants, with an escort. But she demanded that Tobias turn the house over to her with a written deed of conveyance. In addition to other property. The battle not being joined out of mere mercenary motives. Fornari's money allowed her to do without Madruga's. Her dignity demanded full proof, however, of the failure of the marriage, in which she judged she had played no part. It was necessary, moreover, to look after her daughters' interests.

"And where did I fail?" Tobias blurted out.

"Do I need to tell you again?" she insinuated maliciously.

Tobias grabbed a precious Chinese vase, a favorite of Amália's, and sent it crashing to the floor. Amália said nothing. At Madruga's, she demanded explanations.

"That macho son of yours is irresponsible," she said in a louder voice.

Madruga contained himself out of consideration for his granddaughters. It was a story he had nothing to do with, having neither added to it nor subtracted from it. On hearing the news from Amália, old Fornari had called him on the phone, stammering in a heavy Neapolitan accent. Madruga lost patience. He accused him of playing a part in a mediocre melodrama, rehearsed all too often, the leading characters of which were unfortunately their children. He was only too familiar with the scenes and the intermissions of the past. His job, in all truth, had been to father Tobias, and as for the rest, they had fornicated with absolute autonomy. That marriage had also taken public root in the church of A Candelária, with every seat filled. There was no reason to straighten out twisted lives that had come to no good end.

He sent a generous check to Tobias, to make the necessary arrangements. Permitting him to forgo his visits in the weeks to come. Eulália urged him to reconsider his position.

"It's only death that merits consideration," he said, sinking into the armchair in the living room, near the window.

Miguel and Bento interceded on Tobias's behalf. At her husband's prompting, Antônia sided with her father. Tobias, an incompetent and an ingrate, must be punished.

You're another idiot, Antônia. God is good enough to lift your front feet for you, Madruga thought, remembering the Portuguese proverb. And he smiled at that wisdom born of the steep, rough mountainsides of the upper Minho. He decided to take his son back.

"What can I do for you, son?"

Tobias asked to take a rest in the room he'd had as a bachelor. To renew acquaintances with the objects of his youth. The room had been left untouched, exactly as before. A rest that threatened never to end would do him good.

"I don't have a house, father," he confessed with a hard look in his eye.

Madruga sensed that his son was out for vengeance. Fencing with a delicate foil, against adversaries invisible for the moment. Lacking the courage to spare innocents, having yet to learn by heart the enemies' names and their wicked deeds.

"We've never exchanged confidences, father. We haven't traded a single secret," and he turned his back on him, heading for the stairs, thus sparing Madruga the necessity of replying.

Madruga's soul had been closed since birth. The gods of Sobreira, free in the air, invaded his body despite him. He himself did not want to give them shelter. Yet he feared them, because they had always demanded human sacrifices, since the timeless beginnings of Galician civilization. To which fact they no doubt owed the stories that seemed most obviously to be of divine origin, as did their incantatory aspects. What right did his son have to demand that he share his secrets with him? By the mere fact of his having injected a few drops of semen in Eulália's womb, would other prerogatives above and beyond those announced in his will fall to Tobias? Even Eulália had received modest, measured words from him. With the exception of those born long ago of passion, whose voracious verbal appetite the body misappropriates. And who takes responsibility for the authorship of the enthusiastic outpourings that come gushing forth when sex leads us to madness?

At the sight of his face in the mirror, Madruga asked himself searching questions about a life that always came to him by way of unfinished chapters, difficult to read. And which naturally obliged him to participate in a network of mysteries, where it was the law to strew pieces of oneself all about the field, so that this scattered patrimony would never regroup, coming one day to constitute the definitive human portrait. Each man becoming responsible, then, for the confused image one has of him, when no element combines. Man being responsible still for the establishment of safeguards that hem in his soul and inevitably condemn him to loneliness. All this owing, who knows, to a millennial instinct that zealously sees to the preservation of human complexity. Judging, doubtless, that it is only through this complexity that man is assured of his individual existence and his vocation for freedom.

Madruga had coffee brought to him so as to rid himself of the dryness in his mouth. Certain that death would call his life into question by way of the written records first of all, awesome documents, among them his body. It calmed him to think that Breta would zealously guard his belongings. The one who would inherit the papers, letters, books, portraits.

He categorically forbade his family all access to his personal mementos. No one was to touch or lightly finger his memories. Breta was responsible for separating the material, burning what she thought best. Not feeling obliged to file away what deserved to be dumped in the trash. A man's life ends with him. Only artists prolong their existence indefinitely. When it is a question of works of potentially surpassing quality.

Madruga had no illusions. After his death, he would die each time his friends died. And yet again, when his grandchildren no longer uttered his name. And if the last voice to invoke him fell silent. His memory would persist as long as Breta lived. While Tobias, held prisoner by his bitterness, cursed his father's name each day.

Odete brought her the jewel box, as she had asked. Outside of Eulália, Odete was the only one to tell the story of each jewel. Eulália's breathing grew steadier. It did not appear to be that of someone about to die. Her eyes were bright now. She asked everyone to leave her alone with Odete. Especially at this hour when she would be dividing her last possessions.

They had lived together for almost fifty years now. In the beginning, Odete had become part of the household like an object picked up at a fair. Without Eulália's paying any particular attention to her. In that day and age, the sight of blacks in the city, skin drenched with sweat, gleaming like satin, still came as a surprise. Their eyes usually bulging, from worms and from terror at the abuse they had suffered.

Back then, Odete wore her kinky hair in braids, in boundless fidelity to the ruling custom in the days of slavery. As though oblivious of the abolitionist movement. Those braids choked the life out of her hair and her feelings. And since they scarcely knew each other, Odete mumbled when she spoke to her, looking at her with sidelong glances. After finishing her assigned tasks, she withdrew to her room, never emerging from it.

Years later, Eulália began to demand more of her time and care, merely to have her company. Eulália, a gentle creature by nature, ran the household to please Madruga. And as Odete sensed the distress of that stranger so indifferent toward everyday tasks, so concerned about not being late for church each morning, she gradually took over the running of the household in her stead. Discreetly, giving orders as though it were really the mistress of the house issuing them. Eulália perceived in turn that when she had Odete close at hand, the house became much less of a burden, thus enabling her to concentrate on her own soul. As though Odete had rubbed ointments on her body, relieving her sufferings. When it came to satisfying her little whims, that black stranger was even better than Madruga, ever hustling and bustling to amass a fortune.

She began to give Odete her own dresses, which hung loosely on her. And though Odete tried to put on weight, her body never matched her mistress's more ample proportions, with a secret sensuality that would have frightened Eulália, had she been aware of this. With its prominent cheekbones, Eulália's face did not deny its Celtic origins. Its ethnic traits disavowed only by her noticeably slanted eyes, which turned her into a Eurasian rather than a legitimate Galician.

Her husband laughingly insinuated that in the past Dom Miguel's family must surely have been sinful fornicators to have ended up with such an exotic-looking daughter. With traces in her face that one followed without knowing where they led. To China perhaps? Eulália's brothers had the same absent, distant air about them, all of them having drifted off to the Orient or beyond the Atlantic, with an evident scorn for the confines of the Mediterranean.

Even in the beginning, the smell emanating from Odete's armpits forced Madruga to leave the table when she was close to him. Because this disturbed him, he wanted to get rid of her. But Eulália promised to take care of the matter. Two weeks later she mustered her courage. With her cheeks on fire, she finally suggested to Odete that she should freshen her body more frequently, since in the tropics, as everyone said, everything called for redoubled efforts. This exaggeration being an integral part of American vitality. The variety of human odors and fruit blending together.

Odete said nothing. She disappeared for the entire afternoon. And did not come to the table to help serve dinner. Eulália respected her unexpected grief. The next morning, Odete's eyes were swollen.

"What's the matter, Odete? Did I hurt your feelings?" and she regretted having caused her irreparable damage. She recognized that the human soul was sensitive, brimming over, ever following stony paths. With each sentiment an unexpected pain, in no way making one's human tasks easier. Moreover, she was a stranger in this country, despite her first Brazilian sons. Many of the habits and customs of that people slipped through her fingers, yet she did not go in search of them. The degree of passion of those people almost made her pant for breath. Those bodies gave off a primitive sensuality, somehow perceptible even when they lay motionless beneath the shade of a tree. And they had a sense of time that affected their most intimate substratum. Sitting for hours in a row just outside the doors, nothing kept them from becoming part of a reality that in practice freed them of the obligation of engaging in historic undertakings. Since it made no difference what they did, or failed to do, to all intents and purposes they embodied the history of Brazil.

Eulália noted the indifference with which Odete, for instance, tore the days off the calendar hanging on the kitchen wall. A gesture hinting at a singular pact with time. The days not coinciding exactly with the Gregorian calendar.

Through Odete, Eulália saw blacks as gentle and dramatically obedient. Madruga hastened to justify their apparent submissiveness. Slavery had so deeply wounded their souls that, for decades to come, they would be forced to subject themselves passively to the dominating, racist impulses of the white man.

Though Madruga expressed his feelings discreetly, as if keeping chapters of his own life to himself, he doubtless nourished deep feelings of human solidarity with that race, in his eyes an especially beautiful one. Many times, his heart moved, he thought: They arrived in Brazil before me, even though they did so against their will. And they were princes in their forests, till the day they were robbed of their scepters and turned into slaves.

On certain summer nights in Rio, Madruga dreamed of Africa, one of the burning-hot wombs of the country called Brazil. Years later, Breta came to him, urging on him the belief that if it had not been for the African presence among us, we would be incurable despots and a bloodthirsty people. And we would not have at our disposal words that enhanced new feelings. If we owed to the Portuguese our robust idiom, which had never formed isolated cysts imbedded in the national territory, it was to the Africans that we owed the softness that had seeped into all the strata of the language, thereby teaching us verbal intonations welling up directly from the soul.

"Answer me, Odete. Did I hurt you all that deeply?" Eulália said.

Odete did not reply. She would rather have felt the overseer's whip than mention the humiliation suffered. Eulália thought it prudent not to press her further. She respected her sense of modesty toward her own body. Her condition as a black might well have brought its share of personal troubles. Without examining the conflicts in depth, she suggested that Odete visit her family that afternoon.

In the first years, Odete was close-mouthed. Unwilling to describe to her the faces of the family whose features she had inherited. Eulália suspected that she did not do so because she found their ugliness repellent, since in her eyes her race lacked all trace of beauty.

Odete returned from her days off every other week with a downcast air. Whereupon Eulália immediately handed her the vitamins she herself always took. Since her health was subject to ups and downs, Eulália frequently went knocking on doctors' doors. With Madruga resigned to having a wife in surpassingly delicate health, demanding his constant attention.

"Don't worry, Eulália. I'm working for the two of us," he said in moments of affection.

Like a bull that never slept, Madruga was possessed of unflagging energy. For him, the world was merely the meadow round the house, and he need only gather in and chew the damp grass so close to his jaws. From six in the morning till midnight, they saw him rushing about. And confronted with the wear and tear of certain parts of his body, he himself made the repairs, with every confidence in its driving force. And despite everything, not forgetting the hours set aside for reading.

"I don't want to be accused of being an ignoramus." Eulália always smiled at the sight of that warrior, on his own in Brazil from the age of thirteen. And whose path through life was not the same as that of men who had found the banquet table laid before them, ready and waiting, as his own sons had. How many times Madruga had lined his shoes with newspaper to keep the water from seeping in through the holes in the soles on rainy days. He had arrived in Brazil with no more than a handful of coins, lent him by Uncle Justo. And without the Portuguese language in his mouth and heart. Only an iron will had fed his wild, indomitable spirit. Capable thus of shifting easily from kindly courtesy to an impenetrable posture, that of an enemy almost.

When angry, Madruga complained about everything. He railed against the house, the children, the food. Especially against the future, which was taking its time about favoring him. He demanded proofs of abundance from life, and endless quantities of food on the table.

With her jewels spread out on the bed, Eulália hesitated as to how to divide them. She called her husband into the room. Madruga crept along the walls, with Breta tagging after. Old age, always so deeply feared, had finally overtaken him.

"What is it, Eulália?" pretending to be unconcerned, offering her no signs of crediting her decision to die before the week was out.

"I've decided that it is your duty, as my husband, to help me distribute these jewels."

Madruga bridled. His wife was proposing that he agree to an apportionment whereby he tacitly acceded to her fervent desire to die in the next few days. He wanted to shout: Am I your executioner, Eulália? Am I the one who's forcing you to die? Beneath his granddaughter's gaze, he contained himself. Breta stroked her grandmother's delicate fingers.

"You and Odete decide. You've been together for all these years, just as the two of us have been together for a whole lifetime," Madruga said, excusing himself from participating in such a ceremony. Meanwhile thinking with remorse, Apportionments are invidious. He was the first one, however, to have created the necessity for them, since his one reason for accumulating a fortune was to dispose of it in the future. Nonetheless he was not elated when he caught his heirs being prodigal with his money, as if by so doing they were casting him out of life all the sooner. He could do without the painful freedom granted by old age to draw up his last will and testament as best suited him. After all, why should anyone worry about those executioners who come after us? All of them ready and waiting to devour his inheritance, his bones, his memory, that accumulation whereby he had naïvely thought that he would eventually touch their hearts. When in fact they were dogging his footsteps as he went to his death, eager to reward him with worms and that final destiny that cannot be refused. He kissed his wife on the forehead and hurried off.

Odete spread the jewels out on the linen sheets. At the sight of the pieces stored away until that moment, Eulália was suddenly certain that her pleasure in wearing them and Madruga's in acquiring them had definitely come to an end. And thanks solely to Odete, the jewels were being resurrected. The two women admiring them, as if through them, and at a single glance, they would be able to take in their entire lives. Unable now to escape the truth clinging to these jewels, the powerful witnesses of a story fortuitously buried, about to be reconstructed now by Eulália and Odete.

"What pain I feel seeing them, Odete!"

With nervous gestures, Odete gathered them up in a pile to return them to the box. Quickly, to spare Eulália any uneasiness.

"Don't do that, Odete. I need to conquer this fear." And after a long pause, she added: "I'm ashamed of being rich in the hour of my death."

There were tears in her eyes. Perhaps because she remembered Madruga's recent confession once he'd finished drawing up his will.

"From this moment on, Eulália, they'll begin to hate me. Even though they aren't aware of how strong this latent feeling is, slowly insinuating itself, day by day. Despite the fortune I'm leaving them, I've been unfair to my children. That damned division of my estate that I decided on was wrong."

Madruga had always veered toward the dramatic side of existence. In his case certain rituals of possible Celtic origin, in which the most sinister legends came to the fore, were fulfilled more regally. Lying in bed now, the Japanese-paper transparency of her fingers more striking then ever, Eulália decided that he had done the right thing. And besides, a person who is still alive is always right. Wasn't that why men defended their ideas from convulsions that might ruffle the least little surface of their reality?

"Ah, Odete, what a twisted, overwrought world we live in."

There came back to her the memory of a young, intensely handsome Madruga. Predisposed to fly into a rage for the shakiest of reasons, and yet, impelled by this same vortex, he had managed to expand in America, and had never ceased to love her. At this memory, Eulália searched for the gold bracelet, her wedding present. Then, pointing to it:

"It's yours, Odete," she said in a firm voice.

Odete drew back, almost offended at Eulália's suggestion. Her pallor and her agonized gaze signing that she would die in her place.

"It has always belonged to you, Odete," she said simply.

The first time Odete saw the bracelet, she looked at it with a covetousness born of an inexplicable part of her body, not under the rule of her will. Eulália surprised the desire in her eyes and feared at the beginning that such a look might rob her of her fortune. Until she understood that Odete's covetousness was not aimed at stripping her of her possessions. Odete coveted in the same way as someone who wants something but does not know if she has any right to it. From that moment on, she felt such affection for Odete that she swore to herself to give her the valuable in the hour of her death.

Sometimes Eulália wondered whether Odete had not been rewarded with an anonymous, untraceable life simply to keep her always at her side, wiping the sweat from her brow until the end. Thus transformed into her shadow, which, on turning her head, she never failed to see. Even in the refuge of the summer house, when she fled from everyone. Leaving her only at the hour when Madruga burst into the room. And Odete had copied the very timbre of her voice, marked by a foreign accent she never lost.

On a certain morning, when Odete was polishing these same pieces of jewelry with unusual care, Breta began watching her. Unable to resist remarking that Odete looked as though she were burnishing with emery the body of an imaginary lover.

Odete pretended not to be listening. She easily removed herself from realities foreign to her mistress's. But Eulália, close at hand, heard the remark and was offended. With a gesture, she interrupted Odete, who promptly obeyed her.

"Let us leave off this task, Odete. It's use that brings jewels to life. Happily, we have no reasons now for making them more beautiful than they are," she said, for Breta's ears.

Odete sometimes asked her to tell more about certain aspects of these pieces of jewelry. Eulália hesitated. How to be scrupulous about details concerning an episode dating back, for example, to February 1940 and still respect its spirit unconditionally? How to be faithful to a memory that constantly failed her? Or preserve stories that time, of its own accord, undertook to sacrifice or to leave behind for good? The stories, when she told them now, seemed vague and imprecise to her. Because today's ears no longer displayed the same patience when confronted with those endless tales, which by their very nature lent themselves to any number of versions. Even within the bosom of the family, only Miguel and Breta proved to be excellent listeners.

Moreover, as life flowed through her, it left marks on her whose meaning it was beyond her capacity to judge. Above all because life was subterranean, so that publicly proclaiming its deeds was not enough to turn them into reliable material truths. Still and all, her marriage to Madruga seemed to her, invariably and in all respects, an absolutely concrete fact, from which she did not flee even in the midst of her prayers.

She had been united with Madruga in the church of Sobreira, back in 1923, after the two of them had gone up the hillside, crossed the porch, walked the length of the nave, and reached the altar, with the simple altar-piece above it. Under the auspices of Dom Miguel, whose sober gaze surveyed the ceremony as though he were not part of it. For him too life went by without his ever enjoying the feeling that if he chose he could retouch it.

From that day forward, Eulália was convinced that she had fought harder for the marriage than Madruga. Her husband staking everything on the battle outside, in the streets he had come from, without giving due value to what he had left behind, within the walls of the house. For Madruga life at home would have been a prison. Whereas for Eulália it had been more than enough to divide her time between her husband and the church. This latter a sort of house wherein she dreamed extravagantly.

Madruga offered her the bracelet on their wedding night, in a little hotel in Vigo, near the pier. Through the window there came the strong smell of the fish being auctioned in a nearby shed. From the room they could see ships weighing anchor bound for heaven knew where. And also the faint outlines of the estuary of Pontevedra, the lights of the distant houses. For the very first time they found themselves alone in a room with the door closed. They had not exchanged many words without the presence of Dom Miguel, the brothers, the uncles.

The following morning they would board the ship for Brazil. A difficult voyage for Eulália, whose soul was overcome with fear and misgivings. Allowing herself to be dragged along only because of her husband's faith of a crusader. For him, who had crossed the Atlantic before, it would be one more confirmation of the dream embarked upon ten years before, under conditions of great hardship.

A cocky young man and a chatterbox, Madruga talked of America as a person speaks of his own house and of everyday objects. She had never seen his soul being eaten away by fear and therefore cowering in some dark corner of the room. Of what stuff was this man made, recovering immediately from tragedy, letting nothing get the better of him? Could he be all that insensitive to reality, or did his surpassing strength immunize him against possible capitulations?

Madruga carefully opened the little velvet box, seeking to create an air of expectancy on that wedding night. Not hiding his anxiety in the face of the first delicate object he had ever acquired through his own efforts. Eulália waited patiently. She said nothing. He finally brought the box to her to let her see the bracelet, in delicate goldwork, immediately extolling, unable to contain himself, the merits of the piece, which had come from France.

"It's a present that will unite us for life," and he handed her the bracelet.

He did not try, however, to snap the catch and the safety chain shut around her wrist of a princess. So that Eulália would learn to free herself of it all by herself. The way she would have to deal with the first obstacles that America inevitably placed in the way of the arriving hordes.

Eulália stroked the bracelet with well-manicured hands. She had given them a special treatment on the eve of the wedding, convinced that in the future she would not have much time for little vanities. Up until the wedding, Dom Miguel had shielded his daughter even from the sun's rays, which he did not allow to burn her.

"My daughters are pure gold. I want them to be gentle and kind, like the life I have destined them for," Dom Miguel used to say.

Lost at times in daydreams, he imagined himself still rich, sustained by the illustrious surname on his coat of arms, that of a noble family fallen on bad days, nailed to the façade of the house. Its splendor, however, had slowly faded without his noticing.

The two of them became self-conscious as they confronted the double bed, in full view before them. They would lie down in it, in exact imitation of their ancestors. Their children being born in it one after the other in accordance with a biological fate that had nothing to do with feelings, as if this were a love without choice. If Breta had been on the scene, she would have announced that Madruga and Eulália, like all their mortal kind, had been bewitched by historical contingencies. Because, prior to any act of freedom, human economic destiny prevailed. Eulália rebelled against her granddaughter. What could she know of her grandmother's destiny? And what did Breta know of human life, if she had inherited a story with a looser plot, one that included a means of flight that Eulália had lacked from the day of her birth in Sobreira?

"Ah, Odete, I'm dying. It's just a matter of hours now."

Odete rubbed her hands in open combat with death. She refused to accept losing her, even with the guarantee of being able to stay on in the house after Eulália's death. Her future was assured. But what was the use of leaning on Madruga with little crumbs of Eulália in her heart? And was there anything that Eulália had not given a thought to in her behalf? Her happiness, since being happy was not something for her mistress to resolve.

Madruga embarked for Galicia with the express intention of marrying. Though he loved Brazil, he had to have a Spanish wife. Thereby making it unnecessary to explain, to anyone, the dramatic origin of Galician legends. Urcesina and Ceferino had long been pressing him to return. We're getting old and we won't have you at hand when it comes time to bury us, they said in their letters.

Madruga wrote back, returning their affection, but reproaching them nonetheless: if on the other hand I die in Brazil, I run the risk of being buried like a pauper should Venâncio and González fail to offer me Christian burial, with a gravestone and all. Faced with the threat that if Madruga were to die in Brazil he would remain there forever, Ceferino and Urcesina had dissolved in floods of tears.

"But what kind of a son is this, abandoning Sobreira in the name of money?" Ceferino said, in a rare confrontation with Urcesina, who recognized America as being the destiny of the Galician male.

Now and again, Justo consoled them. He had grown more ill-tempered with age, but took pride in the money Madruga had sent him to pay his debt in full, before his fourth year in Brazil was out.

"Here's a man who honors his debts," he announced to everyone in the tavern, so the news would get around in Sobreira and environs.

Ceferino let his friends stand him to a glass of wine because of what Justo had said. And this homage striking him as insufficient, Justo wrote to his nephew: I know now that you will never fail. Madruga felt his strength renewed. His uncle's painful lack of success in America had given him the means to judge when a thoroughbred is ready, willing, and able to cross the finish line at full gallop.

Madruga arrived in Sobreira with his trunks stuffed full of presents. The family hauled them into the house, celebrating the return of the prodigal son, brought back to life at last. After setting the presents out all over the parlor and the bedrooms, Madruga took a bath in the wooden tub, shaved, and readied himself for the festive dinner.

At table, Urcesina pointed to the meat and vegetable stew set out on the big platters that came down out of the cupboard only on feast days. Ceferino immediately broke the loaf of corn bread so as to allow his son to appreciate, along with the ruby-red wine, the civilized refinements of Sobreira. It was a well-known fact that the ovens of the village produced the best bread in the region. His father had close-cropped hair, the better to disguise the fact that it was graying. Visibly upset, he spoke of neighbors, of names retained in Madruga's memory. Some had died without his knowing it. The letters of those years did not correspond to the truth. They had left endless blank spaces.

After dinner, Madruga went for a walk around the little village square. The news of his arrival had gotten around, and everyone wanted to welcome him back. The American who had come home, attracted by the possibility of marrying a girl from Sobreira. Near the old oak tree by the prefecture, he saw Eulália, returning home from church, grave-faced and in a hurry, after long prayers. As she walked past Madruga, who immediately drew himself up proudly, she felt the man's eyes stare at her body with a power exactly like her father's when he severely reprimanded her. An intensity rarely met with in Sobreira, where people's eyes seemed to her to be dull, almost lifeless.

"I'm Madruga, Ceferino's son and Xan's grandson. Do you by any chance remember me?" he said straight out, as he removed his hat. For a moment, Eulália gazed into his blue eyes. But she did not utter one word in reply, walking away immediately.

Back home once again, talking with his mother, Madruga brought up the subject of this rebuff that had wounded him to the quick.

"And old Dom Miguel, is he still as full of his own importance as ever?" he said resentfully.

"Don't create problems for us, son. Whoever you choose, let it be a cause for rejoicing for all of us," Urcesina ordered.

That night, even though the bedsheets were scented with Myrurgia lavender water, a token of his mother's affection, Madruga was unable to sleep. He thought with distress of Dom Miguel's daughter. Finally he decided, in annoyance, It'll be Eulália or I'll go back empty-handed. I'll marry a Brazilian girl, take the time to teach her Grandfather Xan's stories.

As for Eulália, she scarcely touched her supper. She pushed the food on her plate about with an unusual lack of interest. The glowing look on his daughter's face obliged Dom Miguel to question her closely.

"What's the matter, Eulália?"

Already informed at this point that Madruga, just arrived from Brazil, had dared to address a certain number of words to his daughter. Enough for the news to have begun to circulate in the tavern, as the men of the village sipped the good wine of Ribeira, that Dom Miguel's daughter had for a certainty been the one chosen by Madruga to be his wife. A very cheeky young man who dragged America about with him, slung over his shoulders as though it were a glistening flying fish to be exhibited at fairs.

Though her father pressed her for answers, Eulália said nothing. In the face of this unexpected rebellion, Dom Miguel decided he must act quickly. "If you pay the least attention to him again, we'll lock you in the house. And you won't be allowed to go to church."

Her father's threat obliged Eulália to join forces with Madruga. And to fight a family, from which she came, consisting solely of eccentrics, beginning with her father. Obsessed, all of them, with tracing the family history, rooted in Galicia long before Castilian rule, through written records and a few vague stories. On whose heraldic trajectory there weighed the shadow and the stain of an ancestor who, out of ambition, had served none other than the conquerors Isabella and Ferdinand. Whose court, moreover, seethed in those years with intricate intrigues bespeaking the importance of New Christians, an illegitimate force predominant in the kingdom, and on the American continent, recently discovered by Columbus.

"After this adventure of our family in Madrid, we went back for good to Galicia, which, moreover, we would never have left had it not been for the temptation undergone by that forefather of ours, may God keep him in a good place. Bearing this cruel example in mind, daughter, I pray you never lead us to perdition. Do not throw away a patrimony that has been ours for centuries," Dom Miguel explained to Eulália on her fifteenth birthday.

After coming to know Madruga, Eulália was of a mind to defy her father. To tell him in no uncertain terms, Isn't America more important, father, than coats of arms and your obsessive preoccupation with heraldry? She decided, however, to give in, confident of her fate. Following that afternoon in the little square, she dreamed each day of Madruga. That man's blue eyes, serving her as a compass, pointed toward Brazil. She was eager to learn what Brazil was like, that place that everyone said swallowed up the best sons of Galicia. So completely that they never came back again except to die, in painful silence. Might not her father have been taken in by the European dream when he stated that from the mixture of black, white, and native races, perpetrated in Brazil with boundless frenzy, idiots and fanatics were inevitably born?

Through the glass of the closed window, she spied Madruga in the distance, signaling to her to follow him. She finally allowed her cousin to drag her to the square, thereby disobeying her father's orders. She found Madruga there, ready to confess all to her.

"You'll come to America with me, won't you?"

"Is that where you live? Is that where you're going to die?" she said.

Madruga did not lie to her. He had cast anchor once and for all in Rio de Janeiro, like a ship being eaten away by rust, but ready nonetheless to be shipwrecked on a welcoming shore. No other land in the world offered him more opportunities to face adventure and bend it to his will.

"My sons are going to be Brazilians, Eulália. As for my bones, they too are going to be taken in by that land and drenched by Brazilian storms. Galicia has lost me forever."

He readily admitted that as yet he did not have a fortune to offer her. Perhaps it was his good fortune to be possessed of passion, that of trusting absolutely in the future. He was the future. He alone. Reason enough to challenge the new continent from his window as he sipped hot coffee in the morning. In a triumphant voice he would say: We'll see, O Brazil, which of the two of us is stronger! Having roared out these words, he would drench his shirt and his body with sweat till he was exhausted. So as to have gained possession at the end of the day of yet another gold coin to add to his collection. He polished them with a flannel cloth, hoping thereby to make them multiply. Despite the temptation of gold, which was precisely the temptation of the American dream, he admitted the existence of other dreams, lying underneath the gold-bearing seams. Nor had he stopped reading. Only a trained intelligence could penetrate men and see through human wiles. Making him better able to fight with friends and enemies. To tell sheep from serpents.

"Bet on me, Eulália. I swear I'll win, whereas all of you here have died long since. You live off the memories of pictures on the walls, of parchments, of coats of arms, of families with no survivors."

Up until then Eulália had awakened in the mornings certain of repeating the ritual gestures of the day before. No nervous tension disturbed the daily routine written down beforehand in a document conserved by virtue of the guardianship of time. At home, her attention devoted to delicate tasks, her gaze resting on some distant point, everything seemed familiar to her. And the same gaze also shifted to the altar of the church, where the colored lithograph of Christ dripped blood and emitted a mystery that attracted her far above and beyond any other human event. Madruga was the first powerful sign the earth had offered her as proof that she too, like other mortals, had an obligation to serve reality. For reality had insuperable laws.

On Palm Sunday, coinciding with the second week after Madruga's arrival in Sobreira, he sent her a box of marrons glacés, ordered in Pontevedra. In the form of a heart with a red cloth cover, the top was decorated with a bunch of tiny pinecones, perhaps gathered on the slopes of Finisterre. The expensive present was his way of crossing swords with Dom Miguel. The package arrived without any written message. Since nobody else in Sobreira would do such a thing. A stranger feted wherever he went in the village. By everybody but Dom Miguel.

Eulália hastened to set the box in a prominent place on the dining room buffet, in plain sight of her father. By so doing denying herself the pleasure of touching it again. Dom Miguel's eyes followed his daughter's gestures, but he pretended not to see this box that had come from alien hands and invaded his privacy without his express permission, representing a formal insult. He began a circumnavigation of the room, pacing round and round the table, so as to prevent his daughter from approaching the present, thus making certain that the candy would sit there spoiling in full view of everyone.

On the following Sunday, Madruga headed for the church. Eulália would no doubt appreciate his gesture of setting foot in enemy territory, ruled exclusively by the clergy, where pharisees and hypocrites gathered together. And all this just to see her from close up.

From his earliest years, owing to the influence of Grandfather Xan, Madruga had fought the clergy. Above all else the incense wafted along the nave and into the nostrils of the faithful, by means of which the men in cassocks bled credulous creatures of worldly goods, will, and imagination. And by dint of prayers in Latin, they kept pruning life away as though it were rotten fruit. Using the word *sin* to designate natural manifestations, out of an absolute contempt for the human condition.

In the aisle set apart for women, Eulália's eyes met his and immediately looked away. She was afraid to turn round to look at him a second time, after this first glance. On her knees, head contritely bowed in prayer, she suddenly confused Christ and Madruga. Both with flashing blue eyes. For in the Galician version the Nazarene was not dark-skinned, Semitic, or Andalusian. But Aryan, rather, with blond hair and a fair complexion, like many men in Sobreira.

Eulália had not worn the bracelet for years. The gold, tarnished now, reminded Odete of the days when the two of them used to while away the time remembering things connected with each piece of jewelry. Both quick to correct each other when the one caught the other in a factual error. Thus obliging Eulália to warn her about mistakes owed to forgetfulness.

"Didn't I tell you that memory is an ingrate? Whatever is once experienced is buried forever," Eulália said, this reflection being a favorite of hers.

Odete shrank from any reminiscence that might hurt Eulália. As a counterbalance she would evoke a situation regarded as a happy one. She especially liked trotting out the scene in which Eulália, in a long dove-gray dress, managed to smile into the mirror at the very thought that Dom Miguel, buried in Sobreira, would no doubt be present in spirit at the ceremony that would be taking place that afternoon, her son Miguel's wedding.

Odete's kindness touched her deeply. She was in the habit of repaying her by wearing about the house some piece of jewelry she was particularly fond of, if only for ten minutes. Long enough to draw forth from Odete a relieved expression as she hurriedly rid herself of the jewel, a weight on her heart. She was aware that Odete copied her life even though she lacked the means to reproduce it. Thus it was she who provided Odete's constricted imagination with bits of life. An imagination surely stifled by the long years of bondage endured by her grandmother, whose anguish Odete had yet to free herself of. Though she transmitted to her mistress, in abundance, the warmth of Africa, a land centered in her bosom.

Again and again, Eulália pondered whether she had not stolen Odete's life merely to enrich herself in these hours. As though sensing that her mistress was suffering from an obscure complaint associated with her black shadow and her kinky hair, Odete, grateful for her compunction, brought her the clear, pale laurel tea reserved for these occasions.

During Mass, Madruga perceived that Eulália had become as inaccessible as the holy patroness on the altar, wreathed in flowers. He decided then to confront his adversary. He left the church without waiting for Mass to let out, thus foregoing the possibility of seeing Eulália. Hat in hand, his suit carefully brushed, he headed for Dom Miguel's house, which had the most imposing façade in the village. Near the tavern, he was stopped by Amâncio, a friend of Ceferino's.

"Where are you going looking so upset and anxious, if I may ask?"

Madruga blushed, embarrassed that his feelings were so evident. He decided it would be prudent to confide in Amâncio.

"I don't know what to do to marry Eulália. Time is going by very quickly and I'll be an old man before long. What's more, I have to go back to America. I haven't made it yet."

Amâncio didn't give him any encouragement. He knew Dom Miguel's family well, the deep-rooted Galician traditions of that breed, which banished all intruders from its genealogy. And which, despite the progressive impoverishment of the house, would not accept him. They dragged the antiquity of their walls and of their blood along after them as an appanage.

"And what do you have to offer them besides poverty? Not to mention your burying yourself in an America that never tires of killing our best sons, ever since she took a liking to the taste of the blood of the first navigators. And when she finally decides to return them to us, these men come back badly wounded, humiliated, useless."

"And what do you have to say about the winners?" Madruga broke in.

"They're ingrates. They still haven't come back to us. We don't even know what they look like. They've forgotten us. It's only when they turn up someday with money and a satisfied look on their faces that we'll come to love that place called Brazil."

Madruga's respect for Amâncio was long-standing. He had learned to hunt and fish with him, the two of them spending whole days together up in the mountains. So he tried to patiently explain to him about Brazil, that country with a perfect physical configuration and possessed of an expansive and luxuriant soul. And possible to conquer only at great cost. But what other country had such splendid sun?

"Even the Mediterranean can't equal Brazilian sun. And according to what they say in those parts, not even the sun of the Aegean casts it in the shade. And the earth there is so incredibly rich that when it's sown it flowers three times a year."

Filled with enthusiasm, Madruga grew expansive. Above all else because Brazil, unlike Galicia, did not cripple its sons in order to provide them food.

"It would appear that it's not shit but gold you people in Brazil are swimming in," Amâncio said testily.

"Come on, Amâncio, don't forget that Europe envies America. It's never forgiven itself for having discovered a continent only to lose it in later years. To a European, memories of the great conquests aren't enough, and neither is the American silver that fills the cathedrals and museums over here," Madruga burst out, on edge.

Amâncio was fond of Madruga too. A spirited, restless animal, even as a little boy. He had personally thrown him into the river at the most tender age, certain that Madruga would bob back up to the surface, safe and sound. He saw before him now, for the first time, a face ruled by feelings that escaped definition. Had he always had this harsh face, without his ever being aware of it before? It seemed to place him in a gallery of men who in every period enjoy power, doing so because they have been capable of burying pity and commiseration. The suspicion that Madruga was a tyrant made him feel uneasy. In any event, he had the sort of face that needed only a helmet to interest Dom Miguel.

He remembered him as a boy, herding cattle with a firm hand. He would come to meet him with a smile on his lips, baring all his teeth, eager to give him the apple he'd pulled out of his pocket. Already polished on his shirt sleeve to a gleaming red. Happy to deprive himself of something in return for his friendship. Amâncio would take a first bite of it in front of him, to show that the feeling was mutual. A boy different from all the others. In his hands an animal was never lost. The truth of the matter was that he was the one who never got lost. And so his flight to America, with no letters or other signs of life from him, did not worry Amâncio. He only felt sorry for Xan, Ceferino, and Urcesina, unable in the beginning to accept their loss. They'd lost him long before, of course, without their having noticed.

"I always thought we wouldn't have you here with us for very long. That's how it is with a born adventurer who wants out of the land of his birth. As though he spurned the shelter of family walls. Unfortunately, this Galician earth has a terrible gift for driving its men away. And yet it's those expatriates who best define this country. Maybe it's necessary to suffer some sort of exile to really feel our dreary, drizzly *morriña,*" Amâncio said.

Madruga explained himself once again. Amâncio shouldn't get the idea that his life in Brazil was a bed of roses. It so happened that he constantly came up against painful obstacles. He was up and about by four in the morning and was up at night till all hours. He didn't even take Sundays off. A man faithful to a dream, in a word, despite all his troubles.

"Even so, it's only a dream, isn't that so, Amâncio?"

Earning a living in a foreign country was the equivalent in the beginning of undergoing a series of painful amputations. Losing one's soul and one's language at the same time. He was at a loss for words to describe the discovery that his world, a known world up until then, was totally at odds with everything he was now coming to know. What this meant, first and foremost, was stumbling over the most trivial words, seeing the possible effect of them escape his grasp, even though he had used them correctly. Aggravated by the fact that his condition as an immigrant made him an object of general mistrust. As though his body, fresh off the boat, might be a carrier of spells fatal to the Brazilian born in comfort in that land. So he always had to fight twice as hard to earn his freedom, to win the confidence of the legitimate lords and masters of the land, to simulate sufficient familiarity with the Portuguese language to mesh speech and sentiment smoothly, even when overtaken by a storm of emotion. And finally, he needed, ideally, to tone and tune his brain and his muscles to the same pitch.

"Ever since Cabral, Brazil has been made by us, and our sons, whether born on the right or the wrong side of the blanket. I too will try to father offspring in that land. I'm in a hurry to start a Brazilian family. To see through to the end, step by step, a battle I began years ago, when I fled from Sobreira."

Madruga knocked determinedly on Dom Miguel's door, but he was unable to answer. Madruga hurriedly wrote the following note, in the shadow of the trellis: "I am very sorry, Dom Miguel, but I can't wait. The winds are in my favor, so I must tell you that I am firmly convinced that your daughter Eulália is also part of my American dream."

In less than five minutes, Dom Miguel appeared, dressed as though to go out. He nodded curtly, though he did not put out his hand. But before the nobleman could make a move in his own territory, Madruga stole a march on him, walking over and sitting down at the table where Dom Miguel presided over family repasts.

"I would like to ask your advice, Dom Miguel. How should I go about marrying your daughter Eulália?" he said, skipping any other preliminaries.

Dom Miguel drew up a chair and sat down beside him. Sensible no doubt to the young man's courage, he was willing for the first time to parley. Perhaps because life had long exasperated him with its shabby gestures, food always the same, cold caresses, the prospect in a word of living the future as a burden. This young Madruga, however, like a navigator about to set out from Seville with his sails unfurled, flung his future on the table, in the form of a banquet. A feast surely invisible to those who did not know how to embroider lush fruits and vegetables on white linen tablecloths. And had the future not been, in the remote past, in the archaeology of Dom Miguel's soul, a great fiesta for the ancestral house from which he had come? But where would the future of his children find shelter now, after his death?

He was doubtless the last defender of the family traditions. Beneath the yoke of Galician history, he had labored under the illusion that this history would one day reproduce, on a major scale, the memory of his own lineage. But now there was no one left in his flock to take on the responsibility of preserving the priceless patrimony. His own children, impelled by other interests, were manifesting a reality quite different from his own. Only Eulália understood him, because she had inherited his melancholy. The same eyes turned heavenward, thus reconciling spirit and matter, the latter in the form of legends.

Dom Miguel sat with his head in his hands. At times he seemed frail and weary, his pride of the old days now gone. Some ineffable sentiment had divested him of the adornments he so greatly prized. Madruga had taken him by surprise, finding him temporarily dislodged from a domain where in time past he had reigned unchallenged, through rules prescribed by his knowledge and inflexibility. There was, therefore, not a moment to be lost. Taking advantage of his enemy's weakness, Madruga attacked with his arsenal of weapons and dreams. He immediately proclaimed Eulália's love for him. This certainty having been borne in upon him by the way in which she comported herself in the town square or in the church. Her behavior, however, never betraying her father's cause, since he had forbidden her to speak to him. Nor ever giving proof of a lack of trust in Dom Miguel by having hidden her affection for him. It was shyness alone that had struck Eulália dumb.

Madruga was well aware that the surname he bore was a humble one. In his house coats of arms and parchments were wanting. But he had other escutcheons, symbolically affixed, if anyone cared to have a look at them, to the reality of that country called Brazil. Might it not be time for Dom Miguel to admire his intelligence and tenacity?

"Far be it from me to offend you, Dom Miguel, but no man of your house is more competent than I."

His head held high, Madruga promised to adorn the portal of that proud house with olive branches, to bring it worldly goods and wealth. Everything, in short, constituting an incomparable future.

In the first months Eulália would find the round of daily life in America strange. But how to demonstrate one's solidarity with that long-suffering, lacerated continent save through perplexity and bedazzlement?

"I swear to bring Eulália back to Sobreira decked in silks and jewels. Or whatever you please." He paused and went on. "Moreover, Dom Miguel, there is a death sentence hanging over Galicia. And its people merely postpone this execution from day to day. God has long since forgotten this land. Despite obstinate and brave men like yourself."

Urcesina learned, through a quick visit from Amâncio, that the fate of her son, now visiting Dom Miguel's house, was being decided at that moment. To distract herself, she tidied the kitchen, purposely causing a great stir all through the house. Madruga arrived, but she did not question him. He explained that despite Dom Miguel's long silences, there was still hope. That gentleman, the most elegant in the county, had promised to call him the moment he had an answer, the fruit, naturally, of long meditation. Reason enough, moreover, not even to consider strolling about Sobreira in the meantime. No one would see him in the town square, much less in the tavern, till the following week. Beyond the fact that Madruga's proposal occupied his days, he felt bone-weary. Dom Miguel exacted from him, however, the promise that he would leave Eulália in peace during this period. A sort of truce declared between enemies studying the clauses of an agreement that is to govern their future relations. Kept, however, from speaking with Eulália or so much as looking at her, even if the two of them saw that they were the only ones out strolling round the square at siesta time.

Urcesina backed Dom Miguel. A great lord and, as such, respected. No word or deed of this well-born gentleman ever came as an unpleasant surprise to her. She held him in the highest esteem. Even in his youth, despite being a most handsome young man, he never took advantage of any girl in Sobreira or thereabouts, all of them held spellbound by his charms and his prestige.

"Over and above these many virtues, we also owe him our past. If it weren't for Dom Miguel, son, we would know very little about our history and where we came from. And still less about the workings of our Galician soul, which after all is said and done has always terrified us. The one thing he's ever done is explain why we're stubborn and dour by nature, with a tendency to burst into tears or into song when least expected."

Urcesina was preparing his dinner, with calm, deliberate gestures: Madruga was no doubt famished. As she fried peppers in oil, she begged him to be patient. Dom Miguel would summon him soon.

"When Dom Miguel admits he's ill, it means he fears death is just around the corner and he needs to clean out his drawers, to put his papers in order."

"But he didn't say anything about being ill, mother. He simply said he was tired."

"Around here it's the same thing. Dom Miguel has no illusions. When death calls, there won't be a hale and hearty man standing guard at the door. He's like a boat without a helmsman to read maps and feel storms gathering."

Odete gently stroked Eulália's cold hands, making her see that the bracelet belonged to her children. Eulália disagreed. But she had no time for useless explanations now. And besides, nobody deserved the bracelet as much as Odete. Always trailing along after her to pick up the fearful, blood-red pieces of the story that she kept letting fall to the floor. Though she couldn't say how much Odete knew about her life, since she herself had difficulty pinning down the exact localities of a marriage lost in some hidden compartment of her memory. Though Madruga boasted of reinforcing certain memories, in his eagerness to perpetuate them. Conspiring hind-side-to against an imminent death.

"We'll be immortal," he said good-humoredly one scorching hot afternoon. And wanting concrete proofs of existence, he casually pointed to the bracelet his wife happened to be wearing.

"I beat Dom Miguel. But if he'd beaten me, how could I have faithfully fulfilled my destiny? And come back to Brazil empty-handed, without you?"

Urcesina was confident that Madruga would eventually get round Dom Miguel. Sitting by the hearth, with the logs burning, they nervously awaited a neighbor's knock on the door, coming to tell them the good news. Ceferino was sorry that Grandfather Xan was no longer alive to entertain them with his stories.

"It's a good thing Grandfather Xan's no longer with us. He'd end up robbing us of reality someday with his endless stories," Urcesina said crossly. Allowing them no distractions when Madruga's destiny was at stake.

Amâncio stole in. The stink of his stogy immediately filled the room as he puffed away. Ignoring the fact that Urcesina was fanning the smoke away with the dish towel. He gave a hearty, easygoing laugh. Warming his hands by the fire now.

"How come I don't deserve a brandy?" Amâncio said.

"You only get one in return for the news we're waiting for," Ceferino said.

"Well, bring me the brandy then."

On tenterhooks, Madruga poured him a glass. Amâncio savored the brandy appreciatively, between slow swallows. Reaching the middle of the glass, warmed in his rough hands, he said they ought to trust that there would be a happy ending. Because the news was going the rounds that Madruga had come out the winner in his fight against Dom Miguel. After all, the young American bore on the left side of his face, the heart side, an irresistible sign of fate.

"Didn't you notice?" Amâncio interrupted, certain of the details that guaranteed Madruga's good fortune and success. "If Madruga's destiny is at stake, so is ours. His victory serves to confirm that even though life is difficult, it may undergo a sudden radical change."

"Whatever does all that mean?" Madruga said impatiently.

"Merely that you've won. And do you know why? Dom Miguel has just returned to the tavern, after a long absence. And when he came in, he leaned against the counter, smiling at everyone. And he politely invited us all to have a glass of wine, on him. And as we raised our glasses, he allowed us to drink to the happiness of his house. And what else could that happiness be but Eulália's coming marriage?"

This time even Urcesina helped herself to brandy, as did Ceferino. They clinked glasses contritely and drank a toast. Forgetting to invite their son to join them. Madruga perceived that his prolonged absence from the house and from Sobreira had robbed him of the ability to interpret the signs of reality of his own people. He smiled at his mother, finally yielding to those superstitions, for his happiness depended on them. His thoughts already practically turning to the trip to Brazil, in the company of Eulália.

Madruga's voice, in the room in the boardinghouse in Vigo, rang out once more in solemn tones. "This bracelet must go wherever we go, Eulália, to the very end. Right next to your skin, just as in the past it was close to my heart."

Madruga's voice wavered between gentleness and a syncopated harshness. From that night on they would be inseparable. It would fall to death, that highborn mortal foe, to separate them. Better, however, if he went first. He suspected that Eulália might be tested by pain and win.

Continually self-preoccupied, Madruga forgot to look after his wife and things about the house. Or was it that, knowing it to be an irremediable part of his destiny, he detached himself from his home, from his children, thus giving existence a temporary, fleeting quality? In obedience to the world's command, passed on to him by way of nervous tremors?

Odete clasped the bracelet tightly in her hands for a few minutes. Then, in order to free herself of the warmth of it, she slipped it into her bosom. Embarrassed by the intimate gesture, she lowered her eyes, not daring to look directly at her mistress.

"Why, Dona Eulália?" she murmured almost inaudibly.

"So that you may feel, close to you, the emotion of an affection that goes far back in time," Eulália answered, visibly tired.

Odete brought her water. She wiped Eulália's forehead with a handkerchief. And discreetly listened to her breathing. She was panting almost imperceptibly. There were no signs that she would die any time soon.

When I was a little girl, Grandfather surprised me with presents and unexpected proposals.

"Shall we go to Petrópolis to see the Emperor? Pedro II is expecting us for tea."

He was out to charm me, by whatever means, so I'd pay attention to him. And forget Miguel, and Grandmother's allurements in the beginning. Sitting beside me, self-absorbed, he reeled off strange names, and events I had never had any part in. Teaching me to respect the flow of his storytelling. Without words dragging him under, robbing him of breath. We had an agreement between us that the moment Madruga lost himself in conjectures, I would interrupt him.

Some of the episodes, fragmented and disjointed, undoubtedly did not reflect his own story. Though Madruga didn't seem to be bothered by that fact. Since he had learned from Grandfather Xan that only a teller of tales able to fertilize and broadcast collective stories had merit.

His aim was to instill in me the cult of invention, long present in his family. Even before Xan. This being a Galician custom, whereby this people made mock of the calendar, so as to keep reality from vanishing. In this way a Monday, any Monday, full of adventures could be kept tucked away in a pocket, alongside a stem-winder. Though there was always the risk of forgetting one or another of these stories. But forgetting was part of the universal patrimony.

"People can only forget if they invent things in a hurry, so that nothing will be missing. At least that's what Grandfather Xan used to say. He was certain of it. After all, isn't life a starvation diet?" Madruga said.

In the late afternoon, in his study, on the veranda, or on walks to the downtown center, Madruga would take his granddaughter by the hand to show her the city. In the Bar Luís, formerly the Bar Adolfo, where we were taking time out to rest, he admitted that even though I hadn't inherited his blue eyes, I had come by his appetite and his dream.

"But what is that dream you're always talking about, grandfather? You make it sound like a piece of chocolate cake."

This always started him off on his supposed adventures. Ocean voyages occupying his innermost heart. Whereupon the Atlantic took on a magic air, on account of the many symbols he fell back on in the telling. He spoke of lost islands, of the thrill of finding himself face to face with stars, and of a supposed anchor, pitted with rust and illusions, that he and Venâncio, on first arriving in Brazil, decided to cast in secret to the bottom, just offshore.

As far as I could see, he made no mention at all of crossings with Eulália. Both of them always in a hurry to get to Sobreira, in time for all the joys of spring. He spoke, rather, of that crossing that brought him to Rio de Janeiro, at the beginning of the century. All the others being compacted in just this one, dramatic and intense. When aboard the English ship the crew heaped insults on him in an incomprehensible tongue. Madruga never forgiving them for the deliberate humiliation visited upon third-class passengers, one of whom was himself.

"The Atlantic is an unforgiving ocean, Breta. It reveals its true nature just once. After that passage, on later voyages, it's as though we'd died that first time. All it does is swallow up our dreams."

Madruga always wanted to make America his home. Even though Ceferino accused that continent of sowing discord in Galicia. There being families that sent their good-for-nothing sons to America, as punishment. Whereas others, faced with the threat that their offspring might flee to Brazil, chained their youngsters in their cellars. Deaf to their sons' cries that America was the living lung of imagination, the only way out for Galicians, in debt as they were to Castile.

From the moment that Justo guaranteed his passage, Madruga searched through the wardrobe chest every day, trying to decide what clothes to take with him. There wasn't much choice. Ceferino's money covered only essentials. And so, finding nothing but threadbare garments, his jacket in particular, with leather elbow patches, the first thing Madruga asked of his mother was to patch the seat of his trousers.

Urcesina had never given signs of patience or cleverness with needle and thread. "Is that a proper task for a peasant woman, child? It seems more like work for an old woman waiting for death. And death is no fancy embroideress. A woman who darns perhaps? Patching as best she can till there's nothing left to mend in a man's life, and nothing to be done then but take him off to the depths of hell!"

Madruga avoided his mother in the days preceding the journey. Busy working in the fields and fattening the pigs, she didn't notice that her son was behaving like a thief, robbing her of objects and illusions. Uncle Justo and Madruga, however, went ahead in secret, according to plan. Fearful nonetheless that sharp-witted Urcesina would discover what they were up to.

Madruga had forbidden his uncle to give away his secret by revealing the now-imminent adventure. There was less than a week to go. And Madruga did not know how to guard against possible obstacles. If for instance Grandfather Xan begged him, with tears in his eyes, to remain in Sobreira till death came his way. Or Urcesina advised her son to wait three years before braving the diabolical hunger of America, where he did not have a single friend to call on for help.

Madruga's uncle went along with the suggestion that he board the boat in secret. The look of a criminal, as with the first outcasts to disembark in Brazil, would work to his advantage. His heart becoming hardened more quickly with such an investiture, enabling him to devote himself entirely to sacking and pillaging. Though America was also, according to common belief, a continent of indescribable enchantment. Nature gleaming in splendor everywhere.

"Have they told you of America's charms?" Justo said to him absently, peeling a pear.

In the last weeks, on his way to visit his uncle, Madruga looked carefully to his right and to his left before knocking hurriedly on the door. Sitting around the table, fortified by the chicory coffee, they went into all the particulars of the journey. His uncle would accompany him to Pontevedra. Where they would arrive very early, in time to take the first train for Vigo.

"Here's the ticket. I've fulfilled my part of the bargain. Now you must fulfill yours," and he showed him the envelope that would open the doors of America to him.

And he looked at Madruga. Very tall for his age, a bright gleam in his eyes, bold, nothing seeming alien to him. He suddenly feared his nephew's precocious ambition.

"I smell the stench of Brazil," and he angrily waved the ticket in his face. "From now on, if you're out to win, you're condemned to oblivion. We no longer exist for you."

Madruga was moved. He wanted to embrace his uncle, to beg his pardon for forcing him to repeat acts and gestures that reminded him of his own failure. He stared at the ticket on the table, and once again bet on the future, in the form of a well-laden table, a splendid house with the chimney smoking, and the joy of a family. He therefore avoided comments that would betray his knowledge of his uncle's past in Brazil. Justo must suspect nothing.

"Come here on Monday. Don't worry about the money for the initial expenses. I've decided to make you further indebted to me. So you won't lack money for your first meals in Brazil. This way I enslave you and fight your excessive pride. Bear in mind that the gods are implacable in the face of happiness." His uncle smiled, relaxing for the first time.

Madruga headed for the Pé de Mua, his favorite mountain, one last time. He wanted to retain the country air in his nostrils and in his heart. In those days just before leaving Sobreira his memory had grown keener. And he felt a mounting fear of meeting sudden death in Brazil, buried by hands heedless of any need to mark his name on his gravestone.

He looked at the cows on the mountainside, baptized with the same names for decade after decade. Brindle, Bess, Buttercup, Star, Big Babe. They had a patience that he had always lacked. Whereas he rebelled against a plodding life, these animals did not know how to express their feelings. Though they were spared, on the other hand, the thorny path of imagination.

Madruga loved those cows. He did everything but lick their teats. He suddenly felt himself to be the heir of a herdsman who had preceded him in that same place. And who, in his eagerness to pay homage to animals, had begun a sentence but then found himself lacking the time to end it. Because his attention was diverted by a sheep that had strayed from the flock. But in that case, what had happened to that sentence left unfinished? Whose lot was it to reclaim this sort of anonymous inheritance?

The north wind of that Thursday lashed Madruga's face as he bent over to bind himself more closely to the cows, the goats, the sheep, the trees, through a feeling about to dissolve into the future, when other interests would beckon him.

Madruga's appetite at table grew ravenous in his last week in Sobreira.

"What's the matter, son? Isn't what we've given you so far enough?" Ceferino said in alarm.

Intimidated for a few moments, Madruga finally smiled. He blamed his mother, who outdid herself in the kitchen, valiantly toiling away despite the time spent laboring in the fields. How to restrain himself when a stew fit for the gods was set before them? He stuffed himself on the corn bread, always stored in the oven, so that its taste would linger with him indefinitely. And follow him to the cheap boardinghouse where he would reside in Brazil. Alive on his taste buds, especially when his daily routine seemed to have a scowl on its face.

He even thought to ask Grandfather Xan what reasons forced a man to abandon his village, at the cost of losing his soul. And why Galicians supposed that life on the other side of the hemisphere would be any easier, immediately transforming adversities into advantages.

Lying on the grass, breathing in its smell, Madruga slowly searched the firmament, beneath the wind's sharp insistence. At his feet lay the Galician countryside, but his own desire was to reach Brazil, whose inhabitants reproduced themselves by means of incessant copulation so as to compensate for the butchery that went on there. They took jealous care to ensure that life would go on after them, despite acts of savagery.

Madruga knew little about Brazil. Except that after the fall of the Monarchy, a popular-type republic had taken over. Not one king and queen having been left them under this regime. Contrary to what Madruga was used to in Spain. Hence not being in a position to judge of the benefits of such political changes. And what difference it represented to the people to depose a monarch, with a purple mantle and an intangible crown, and put in his place another tyrant without a noble title.

Madruga did not even know, there in Sobreira, that Brazil was already four hundred years old, counting from the time of the discovery. And that among its firmly established customs, the strictest was that of repressing any public demonstration, although an exception was made, under false libertarian pretenses, in the case of popular complaints whose sole origin was dripping genitals exhausted from fornicating. Collective orgasm thus constituting the single public act compatible with its precarious legal institutions. Thereby explaining why the tormenting stimulus to fuck to exhaustion had spread to town squares and open fields. Till the day when this great fuck would become confused with the exercise of political power, and substitute once and for all for parliamentary rule. The Church itself lending its backing to this madness, since it too fornicated. The dissolute clergy supplied the country with countless bastards.

Madruga not being able to foresee, while still in Galicia, that Washington Luís, Getúlio, Dutra, Juscelino, Jânio, Jango, were preparing to appear on the national scene. At once defensible and indefensible. Unable also to foresee the formation of their family, an eight-legged octopus sweeping the surface of the earth clean. Or even to foresee his granddaughter's ambition, her eagerness to gather together and tie in a neat bundle the stories sprung from a popular source, personified by Grandfather Xan.

The Galician sky, with tattered blue clouds, offered itself to Madruga's contemplation. That same sky had witnessed the pilgrimages to Santiago de Compostela. When, beneath its immense vault, the pious, the wicked, the gullible, murderers flocked to Galicia. After getting past the toll collectors, who, under the aegis of faith, had invented a system of money, good nowhere else, thus impoverishing the pilgrims eager to reach Compostela. Not to mention others who sold poisoned water to the pilgrims, with the intention of following after them, expecting that the poison would gradually take effect. Thus giving them the chance to rob them without useless bloodshed.

The subject sent Xan into a fury. As though it were a recent phenomenon. Taking the pilgrims' lives was grave enough, but what was worse still was preventing them from fulfilling the promise made, in their countries of origin, to pray one day before the bones of St. James.

Those prayers to St. James the Apostle were, after all, inevitably commingled with those once offered to the Druids. There being little difference between them. Together they formed a ritual practice that had been handed down from indissolubly intertwined Christian and pagan currents. So that it was difficult to know where one began and the other might end. The legends of both cultures fusing, despite the god that had presided over them. Moreover, the authorities noted very early on that one troublesome legend could not be stamped out without forging another to replace it. Hence the survival of pagan legends even today, though recast in a Christian mold.

Under the influence of Grandfather Xan, Madruga paid close attention to Galician legends. He was afraid that, through carelessness on his part, some of them might be lost. When all of them together formed such a vast repertory that even Xan couldn't keep track of them. Perhaps for this reason Madruga asked his grandfather, on this last week, to pick up the pace of his storytelling, so as to enable him to store up a greater number of plots.

Xan did not readily yield to his grandson's impatience. But in the end he gave in. Except that at times, forgetting the function of a bard, he railed against Castilians, accusing them of despoiling Galicia. A point of view also embraced by Dom Miguel. Both convinced that Isabella, Ferdinand, and company, in addition to depriving them of their autonomy, had robbed them of their language and their heritage of myths. And many of these Castilian legends, dragged in the dust to Madrid, across the dry, desolate plains which nature had given them as their just deserts, were now passed off as a product of the imagination of Castilians.

"They made away with precisely those stories that we invented to put us to sleep and make living in human society bearable," Xan said to his grandson.

Xan was referring to those legends so much a part of the Galician spirit that the characteristic facial type of the people of Pontevedra, thanks to the same stories having been repeated for ages, could easily be identified on the street.

"Woe to us without those legends!" And seeing that Madruga wasn't paying attention, he cried out vehemently:

"Bring our legends back, O my grandson! Bring them back to the home fires burning!"

I too pressed Madruga to tell me the legends he chanced to recall. He resisted, however. As though he felt he had no right to them. Or as though not one of them remained in his memory. The subject did not appear to leave him indifferent, however, for he still gave signs of irritation at the vaingloriousness of Castile, which had misappropriated and paraded as its own the most powerful forces of imagination in Spain.

"This gift we have for telling stories is owed to the fact that we're Celts, Breta. It's our greatest heritage. But besides that, what's left of a people shorn of its wealth of imagination? That must be why the first act of dictatorships is to forbid imagination. Nothing is more stifling than to see ourselves kept from inventing."

Still there on the fresh grass of the Pé de Mua, Madruga pleaded, beneath the watchful eyes of the gods, to return one day from America, bearing to Sobreira, along with gold, the lost legends. As a recompense for Grandfather Xan, who had frittered his life away searching for the legends stolen by the Castilians.

At the sight of the clouds forming, his soul burned. To his vast annoyance, America had first been dreamed of by Castilians. Except that they had launched out in that direction impelled by the urge to plunder. Indifferent to the cultures that they would decimate in this pilgrimage of blood and expansion. Coming by the privilege, along with the Portuguese, of baptizing the trees, the accidents of the terrain, and even the feelings that were to arise for the first time there in America.

Madruga suddenly sensed that America, offended by so many outrages, would never pardon its aggressors. Thus predisposing itself to prevent explorers of any era from being rewarded by the simultaneous conquest of gold and legends. Thus denying them, for all time to come, a double fortune.

He stole back into the house. And at the hour set by Justo, he rose from his bed. He had not slept a single minute, fearing he wouldn't wake up in time. He had hidden his sack of belongings in the cornloft the night before. And to keep from making noise that might awaken his mother, a light sleeper, he had unbarred and unbolted the door before going off to bed.

Once outside the house, he quickened his pace across the beaten earth. He arrived at his uncle's house all on edge. Justo locked the door behind him and headed for the mountains. He did not say one word to him during the journey. It was some fifteen kilometers from Sobreira to Pontevedra. The two of them knew any number of shortcuts, however.

Walking in front with a firm step, Justo did not offer to take the sack now weighing heavily on Madruga's shoulders. They arrived at dawn at the Pontevedra station. The train whistle sounded to Madruga like a strange attack on his heart, forcing him to realize that there was no way back.

Contrary to his expectations, his uncle began to make it difficult for him to leave. Still frowning, saying not a word, he kept puffing at his cigarette, rolled with the aid of his Cordovan pocket knife. Perhaps thinking back on the journey that he himself had undertaken years before, and he had always tried to forget, a memory now mercilessly recalled to his mind by Madruga.

With the jerks and jolts of the train and the landscape gliding past, his uncle relaxed. He offered him bread and a piece of sausage. In Vigo, as they left the train, they nearly lost each other in the crowd, made up largely of women with baskets of sardines and vegetables on their heads, heading for the markets. Those solid bodies balanced the heavy weight with enviable ease.

In an amiable mood now, Justo insisted on taking the Rua do Príncipe, lined with the elegant shops of Vigo. So that his nephew would not arrive in Brazil without at least an acquaintance with a fine Spanish city.

When they had almost reached the pier, at the end of the Cajal, a steeply sloping street which began at the Puerto del Sol, his uncle halted.

"I'm staying here, son. The rest is yours to conquer. The boat leaves sometime after noon. Keep your eyes and ears open. Good luck."

He handed him the little leather pouch, stitched together the evening before, with the necessary coins and papers. Madruga prepared to give him the traditional farewell embrace. Justo noted his gesture, but immediately cut it short. Merely holding out his hand, which Madruga shook firmly.

This was the first time Madruga had set foot in Vigo. The narrow world in which he lived had thus far not permitted him to step through other gates. He did not lose heart, however. And gazing at the buildings round him to screw up his courage, he kept his mind on the thought that at long last it was as though he had already left. America now awaited him.

As he waited to embark, he sat down next to a pile of cargo about to be loaded into the English boat. Thinking only of the pouch and the money inside his shirt, next to his chest. For brief moments, he was aware of the defenselessness of being himself the one god he could call upon if danger threatened. He slowly chewed the bread stolen from Urcesina's oven, and controlled his urge to urinate. He preferred to stay in full view of everyone.

And as the first passengers went aboard, Madruga hung back to study their gestures, making sure that he could imitate them. With head held high, he got past the authorities, worried still that they might detain him for some unknown reason. In those years, however, no one paid any attention to those who went into voluntary exile. Spain rejected its sons without a second thought.

A sailor pointed to the passageway leading to third class. In reality a stifling hold, with a few scant portholes here and there along the sections separated by partitions where the passengers, allotted places by sex and family, huddled one atop the other. This assignment of separate places forcing certain couples to divide between them, with anxious gestures, clothes they had brought with them in the same suitcase.

The ship announced its departure with three long whistles. Madruga hurried to the quarterdeck, now that the pier was being slowly left behind. He needed to part from his homeland with his eyes fixed on the landscape outlined by the mountains and the low buildings in the distance. Above all to breathe in the penetrating smell of salt air, of fish, both in the water and in the frying pans of the houses along the edge of the estuary. Galicia doubtless had a face like his own when he looked at himself in the mirror.

Clinging to the rail, with his sack of clothing on the deck between his feet, Madruga fingered once more the money on his chest. He had not yet deposited his belongings in the hold for fear that his modest possessions might be stolen. At this moment especially, as he was beginning to leave the land behind. He pulled his cap down tight over his head to keep the wind from blowing it off.

The city grew smaller as the ship drew away. In just a little while now there would not be a single image left, of the many reconstituted by Madruga between rapid blinks of his eyes. Playing the game of holding onto the landscape and then immediately letting go of it. Suddenly, he seemed short of breath. And he took himself back to the warm shelter of the house. Urcesina, with a serious expression on her face, bringing tea to her son snugly tucked between the sheets. At this memory, Madruga felt completely alone. With a leaden heart dying on the rooftop of an abandoned house. He had no one to turn to, to seek help from. Simply subject to an oscillating force, contrary to what he had imagined. He rubbed his hands over his face, so that the wind would blow away any bad omen. He must confront the tasks of the journey as though life had the property of saving the forsaken, those who had only themselves to depend on.

Someone tugged at the sleeve of his jacket. Madruga saw a slight, swarthy lad, with intense dark brown eyes, looking at him questioningly through a discreet blur of tears. Madruga was not afraid of strangers, much less this one. He returned his look.

"Why aren't you weeping too?" the lad said.

Madruga was disconcerted. Why the devil did this creature want him to shed tears he would not permit himself? He was on his way to America at last. A continent with the implacable habit of sacrificing, right there on the dock in Rio de Janeiro, half the immigrants who disembarked, knapsacks on their backs, as an offering to its gods. Not to mention Indians who lived on the flesh of whites, and whites thirsting for black blood. A cruel dragnet extending its appetites to Levantines and converted Jews. He decided not to answer.

"How can you leave your own land without at least shedding tears?" he said insistently.

He was decidedly not a Galician. He looked like a gypsy, one of the band that sometimes descended on Sobreira, like birds of prey. From whom everyone fled, because of their reputation as contemptible thieves. They stole not only children, but even chickens and clothes hanging out to dry. Wretched deeds, in short, that dishonored a people.

"Cry, it'll do you good," the youngster said, with a smile this time.

Madruga had a frog in his throat. He wanted to prove to him that he had been brought up not to cry. He wasn't like him, someone to whom tears came easily, not at all embarrassed at allowing himself to be seen in such a state.

"Where do you hail from?" Madruga said, dissembling.

The youngster didn't answer. He now pretended to ignore him.

This contrariness irritated Madruga. He controlled himself.

"What province are you from?"

"The only thing that matters is my name. It's Venâncio."

Judging by his physical type he came from the south. One of those raggle-taggle Andalusians, without a home, a name, a family. But if he had been born in Seville, or its environs, why hadn't he shipped out for America from there? They had the Guadalquivir for that, a river with stories that Spain was proud of.

The look in Venâncio's eyes was accentuated by the dark circles around them. Madruga felt sorry for him. The frail frame of this youngster would soon be dashed to pieces in the famous Brazilian storms. America was waiting, jaws gaping open, to devour him. No region in Brazil, north or south, east or west, would forgive the sensitivity that was already only too evident in Venâncio. Above him there hovered, almost visible, an uncertain dream, without roots, of an alien nature, wherever Venâncio might land. Including the village where he was born or his mother's own bed. Even in Spain, Venâncio would be insistently pressed to come over to the side of reality. A painful lot for that lad, since America took its vengeance on dreamers, giving them a taste of poisonous nettles, of the sort that make a person's legs and esophagus swell till they burst.

Venâncio moved closer to Madruga. Both seemed to belong to a family united by strong feelings. Madruga allowed Venâncio's body to lean on his arm. And after this gesture they no longer spoke. Nor did they look at each other, having memorized their respective faces. At which point

Madruga began quietly to weep, as he lost sight of Vigo. Indifferent to Venâncio's presence, he wiped his tears away with the sleeve of his jacket. Certain of returning one day with his chest thrust out, his head held high, and many coins jingling in his pocket.

"I swear I shall return," he murmured, trusting that Venâncio had heard him.

𝒯he boardinghouse, near the Praça Mauá, reeked of oil and fried garlic. A smell that reminded Madruga of Sobreira. Immediately after disembarking, he and Venâncio took a room in the pension of Senhor Manuel, who kept an eye on the goings and comings of his guests, and the dining room as well, from out on the sidewalk. Sitting in his cane chair, strategically located outside the front door. Wearing pajamas, no matter what the hour of day.

"My name is Madruga. And this is my friend Venâncio. We've come to make good in America," he said, by way of introduction.

In the mornings, taking advantage of the fact that the lodgers were still dazed with sleep, Manuel gave them strict instructions for cleaning their own rooms and the common rooms downstairs. Concerning himself with keeping an orderly house as well, making it known that any miscreant under his roof would get short shrift. His muscles, tough as steel from his days as a stevedore, before his retirement, were more than strong enough to throw them out into the street.

The room, bare of all adornment, was located at the very end of the dark hall. When it came time for bed at night, Madruga would lie there thinking. His heart was touched to realize that there in that bed he was free to sleep and dream of Brazil, now that he had knocked on its doors. His clothes, hanging from nails on the wall, served to decorate the place. Even the heat of the city raised his spirits. And the stifling room had the advantage of driving him out of the pension in the first hours after daylight. Straight to the Praça Mauá, which no doubt far surpassed the tumult of the city of Paris. From there, he would go wandering about the immediate neighborhood on foot, then head for the Avenida Beira-Mar, lured by the waters of the Bay of Guanabara. Venâncio would come tagging along at his heels, complaining about the rapid pace he set. With a beret pulled down over one eye, the two of them attracted more than one curious stare.

Aboard the English boat, a Spanish barber, eager to try his luck in Bahia, had furnished Madruga with addresses of people from the old country established in Rio who might employ him. That was how he came to knock on the door of González, a truculent Galician, the expressionless white of whose eyes was striking, in the hope of working in his hotel. Promising him, at the same time, to see to it that the rooms were kept clean, to take over the reception desk, to do the shopping, and if necessary, since he was handy with tools, repair the damages to the building, which appeared to be badly neglected.

His cockiness impressed González. In addition to behaving like a man, Madruga talked in a steady stream, splicing one fact to another, without losing sight of the essential objective.

"What part of Galicia are you from?" González wanted to know.

"I was born in Sobreira, County of Cotobad, Province of Pontevedra. The saying has it that Corunna lives it up, Santiago prays, Orense eats, and we Pontevedrans work like slaves."

"In that case the job is yours. But if you don't do it right, I'll fire you in a week." González's habit of chewing on a bit of toothpick between his teeth made it hard for him to speak.

With his letter of recommendation in his pocket, Venâncio headed for the butcher shop, where they immediately put him to work behind the counter and unloading the supply truck. During his rest periods, he hurried over to visit Madruga in the hotel. Both insisting on keeping the other company. They even hit on the idea of sharing the same room again and dividing it up between them. On being consulted, González had no objection.

In less than three weeks, Venâncio lost all interest in the butcher shop. He was not only clumsy with the butcher knife as he hacked away at the slabs of dried meat but constantly made mistakes when he weighed things, always in the customer's favor, and this irritated the boss. As if this weren't enough, his frail physique prompted mocking remarks from the very customers he favored. Irked at this, he began to loiter about the Passeio Público when sent out to make deliveries in the neighborhood. Despite constant warnings from his boss, who finally fired him.

Aware of what had happened, Madruga was worried. He immediately urged González to hire Venâncio's services. González finally agreeing, on condition that Madruga would answer for his friend, who did not strike him as being equally trustworthy.

In the beginning, Venâncio diligently did anything he was asked to do, receiving as his reward Madruga's satisfied smile. But as the months passed, preoccupied by his own prospects of getting ahead, Madruga neglected to keep track of how Venâncio was getting on. Making it a point to criticize, to González's face, the outsize dimensions of the rooms, each one large enough for an entire family, thus cutting down appreciably the profits of the hotel. What was needed, therefore, was to divide the rooms in such a way as to quadruple the number of guests. He personally accepted responsibility for carrying out the new plan, using wooden partitions which, in addition to lowering the costs, would make for a more efficient layout of the electrical wiring. Demanding along with this proposal a salary commensurate with the scope of the undertaking.

Proud of such a progressive-minded plan, Madruga expected ample praise from González. To his stunned surprise, his boss turned down a construction project which, in addition to being costly, aimed at packing a faithful clientele, his only livelihood in that stifling-hot country, together like sardines in a can.

"Nobody's going to sacrifice your customers, Senhor González. And besides, anybody who needs that much space can go to the Passeio Público or take a boat over to Niterói. From Cantareira he'll have the view of the whole Bay of Guanabara all to himself. But as far as these rooms are concerned, people ought to pay for the comfort they offer."

"Listen here, my boy, don't tell me how to run this hotel. I've been in charge here for more than fifteen years, and I haven't died of hunger yet," González said, taking personal offense.

Turning a deaf ear to González's objections, Madruga pressed his point.

"On the other hand, you haven't gotten rich, even after more than twenty years in America." He stepped closer to González, his hands resting on his hips, standing tall and straight with his legs apart.

"Lady Luck didn't give me a helping hand, that's all. What's a person to do when she's not on our side?" González said mournfully, his pride as a property owner forgotten.

"It's time to change your luck. Let's begin by doing the rooms over. With that for a start, we'll come out on top." And in his enthusiasm, Madruga's gestures became less tense, more amiable. "When all is said and done, Senhor González, sleeping doesn't take long. All that's needed is a bed, a clean sheet, a handy wardrobe chest, a bedside table, and a chamber pot. Otherwise guests soon turn into lodgers. Is that what you want? Some of them even have alcohol stoves in their rooms for making coffee, soup, fried eggs. And shelves full of groceries, in plain sight. It's only one step from there to being owners of this hotel, with rights in perpetuity."

González finally allowed himself to be tempted. In the end the youngster's firm voice, correcting him countless times, proved his recommendations right. And his work produced more results than two men put together. He had no fixed time for sleeping or waking. Madruga was right. He had long offered his guests too much comfort and received no thanks for it.

Madruga nosed about the square in search of wood, carefully comparing the prices of lumberyards and salesmen. And also buying at auction, for next to nothing, a lot of used cedar, without a sign of termites or deterioration. In sufficient quantity to partition off the rooms, and build several dormitories from the scraps as well, at the very back of the court-yard, now heaped full of trash.

Pilar, González's wife, applauded his initiative. Thanks to Madruga's effort and vision, the modest hotel, cramped for space, would one day have forty-four rooms, rather than the twenty it had now. As for getting rid of the old guests in the place, a touchy subject that González didn't want to deal with, Madruga undertook to explain the new administrative policy of the house to them. The hotel management, concerned with the problem of providing the city of Rio de Janeiro with a greater number of vacancies, which it lacked for the moment, had decided to subject the building to radical reforms, which unfortunately left no place for them. Hence the establishment, though it had not reached the Downtown Hotel category, would do its best to offer future guests comfort, a decent appearance, cleanliness, and easy access to Cinelândia, thanks to its splendid location. From there, on the Rua do Lavradio, Lapa and the adjoining districts were close at hand. All this at attractive prices.

Once work on the project was completed, without consulting González, Madruga had business cards printed with the names GONZÁLEZ & MADRUGA in large type. In small letters, the card offered, in addition to the usual hotel services, the assistance of a business agent and an accountant, both available to visitors from the interior coming to the capital to talk business but lacking technical resources and urban contacts. The hotel charged a percentage for such services, which also included following up on administrative and legal procedures, even after the guests' return to their hometowns.

Venâncio took charge of distributing the cards in the Leopoldina and Central stations. Especially to passengers from Minas and São Paulo, climbing off the night train exhausted and dazzled by the city lights. A task that Venâncio never felt comfortable doing, even after receiving practical demonstrations from Madruga, on the spot in Leopoldina, swooping down on the passengers with the cards and his persuasive cries.

Unlike Madruga's aggressive technique, Venâncio's way of going about things, once he was alone, was to hand the cards out to the passengers almost without looking them in the eye, the latter's thoughts still occupied with their baggage and the new life ahead of them. Madruga checked up on his work, however, by questioning him closely. His diligence leading him to such extremes as asking Venâncio, back in the hotel, to identify which guests had been corralled in that way.

González went about the streets in a new suit, his teeth yellowed from smoke, so that his neighbors would notice his sudden prosperity. Proud that the occupancy rate of the hotel did not fall off even on weekends. And that the rooms, despite the turnover, were still clean and well kept up. González's happiness lasted till his discovery of the cards, whose existence he would have continued to be unaware of had it not been for a guest who dropped his. On taking a look at it, González felt betrayed, in the strictest sense of the word. He was of a mind to fire Madruga immediately.

"And to think that I received you like a son! I even took you home for lunch once! You ate at my own table!"

His wrath was translated into shouts that reached the upper floor. Accompanied by wild gesticulations that Madruga did his best to calm down.

"Is it a misrepresentation? Am I not in fact your partner? Who gives you ideas, who works like a slave, and who fills your hotel every night? The one thing that needs to be done is to have this partnership recorded in the public registry, with notarized signatures and all the rest. But if you're still not satisfied, I'll be on my way. I don't want anything in return. Somebody's sure to take me on. The owner of the Hotel Central has asked me already, in fact, but I didn't accept out of loyalty to this house."

It wasn't in González's plans to lose Madruga. Faced with this threat that he would make his escape, he was suddenly panic-stricken. His eyes bulged. He looked like a gluttonous toad on the edge of a marsh, ready to burst from its excesses.

González now begged him to calm down, forgetting how overwrought he himself was. He insisted that they have a talk together in the bar on the corner. A cup of coffee would steady their nerves. Standing at the counter, they avoided the delicate subject. Still piqued with each other, they walked back to the hotel like two strangers. They sat down stiffly in the lobby in the high-backed chairs. Madruga awaited González's decision in silence. González finally confessed that despite his having had the wool pulled over his eyes, he still considered him a son. The firstborn son he had never had. This being so, with the right to continue in the business, though with certain definite understandings between them. There being one just and simple demand he wouldn't back down on. That Madruga remove his own name from the printed card immediately. Thereupon, pleased at his indulgence, he looked at Madruga.

Madruga crossed his legs, a gesture learned from the bank manager with whom he sometimes conversed. "I'm very sorry, Senhor González, but I am unable to comply with your request. Even if I wanted to. What would people say of me and you? Simply that you have a partner, sir, who's a liar, a schemer, a perfect fraud."

"Stop right there, Madruga. What partner are you talking about? I've never had a single partner in all my life!" González lost his temper once more, in contrast to Madruga's cool composure as he watched him.

"In that case, we have nothing further to discuss. I'd better leave. Perhaps it's best. For one door that's shut, there's always another one that opens. I'm certain that Grandfather Xan, if he were here, would use the very same words." And Madruga headed for the door.

González hurriedly stopped him, pointing to the chair. The negotiations must proceed.

"It's no use arguing, Senhor González. I'll only stay on at the hotel in
return for a partnership and a share of the profits," Madruga said circumspectly.

González appeared to be debating with himself. He was in fact thinking about his wife Pilar. Ever since he'd known Madruga, she had been
dreaming of marrying him to her youngest daughter. And she never tired
of extolling the newfound prosperity of her husband, in days past a modest
businessman who was a poor provider. After Madruga, however, the situation had been changed. They might lose him somehow, Pilar kept saying.
Urging her husband to watch out for enemies eager to lure young Madruga away with better offers. She would never forgive him if out of negligence he allowed a disastrous bloodletting to take place. Pilar was unable
to tolerate the mean and paltry life of days gone by; she had unpleasant
memories of that time. She even refused to go back to the row house in
São Cristóvão, the scene of privations that had been heartbreaking for her,
which she had every intention of fleeing.

At the mere thought of confronting his wife, González felt a cold
shiver. The threat was grave; poverty was prowling round the house again.
The look in Madruga's eyes, moreover, offered him just five minutes to
decide.

"Very well, Madruga, you'll be my joint partner. And I hope I won't
come to regret having helped you, the way a man helps no one but a son."

Madruga became even more enterprising. In two years, he decided
that they would buy a building on the Rua Álvaro Alvim. Though in a
precarious state, it was located in Cinelândia, a promising area, where
movie houses and theaters were beginning to move in. González resisted
the idea. He was afraid of losing everything he owned in such a venture,
of taking on debts that would bankrupt them. A person had to know, after
all, exactly how much of a chance to take. And learn that prosperity is born
first and foremost of prudence and good sense.

"Since when does Brazil call for good sense? If you don't want to run
risks, that's fine with me, González. I'll get another partner. If it was a
question of settling down, I'd have stayed in Sobreira, milking cows. If I
don't take risks, I'll never make a fortune," Madruga said peremptorily.

Madruga's daring impelled him to resort to banks, to open new lines
of credit, to seek loans from men from the old country who practiced usury
on a small scale. Even going so far as to buy the building and oust all the
tenants once more. Beginning immediately, with the help of three workmen, to brace the walls, reinforcing those that could still stand on their
own, taking care to replace those that leaked. On each floor, he added a
large bathroom. And keeping in mind that it was going to be a hotel, he

installed in the rooms, in addition to a washbasin, a bidet, French-style, with a screen around it, to ensure the privacy of anyone using it.

Seeing the bidets, unpacked from their crates in front of the workmen, González blushed. And in a voice that everyone could hear, he swore that that indecent merchandise wasn't meant for them; the truckers must have made a mistake in the address. Despite the invoice, González insisted that they be returned at once. Summoned to solve the problem, Madruga smiled at González's embarrassment. In order not to make him lose face, he didn't go into details.

"Those pieces are ours, González. They're to go in the new rooms."

González didn't like the idea. "Are you thinking of turning this hotel into a maison de rendezvous?"

"That's not a bad idea." Whereupon Madruga returned to work.

Without his realizing, González's power of decision was being whittled away with each month that went by. And when it dawned on him, much later, that he was no longer being consulted, he felt humiliated. At home, in bed especially, he avoided his wife's eyes and body. And Pilar was so happy at seeing her husband get ahead that she failed to notice his anxiety, or his neglect. González decided it was best to do nothing. Taking into account his wife, his daughters, and life as well, which in the last years had come to reward him with a comfort he had never known before, and a source of great pleasure. So much so that he entered Portuguese restaurants with the studied air of a comendador, his watch conspicuously draped across his waistcoat, immediately ordering a codfish stew and wine to go with it. Everything about him expanding, even the pain he felt.

"That young Madruga is a treasure to us. It was God who sent him to us. We ought to join our hands in prayer and give thanks. You must be very sensible about this, González. Not go about the streets laughing out loud for no good reason, or rail against fate, speaking of Madruga, who's hard to get along with, as we well know. We'll be rich very soon, as long as we continue to hang on to the tail of that Galician from Sobreira for all we're worth," Pilar said to him at home on Christmas Eve, having just seen Madruga to the door, and feeling the effects of too much wine and too many chestnuts.

Obsessed by work, Madruga sometimes eyed Venâncio as though he were a stranger. And in the room at night, he was too tired to talk to him. The strong feelings of the early days were slowly fading between them. Madruga trapped by the demon of money. He almost didn't sleep in his stubborn determination to save, to pay off debts, and reinvest. Venâncio was irked at seeing him subject to mercenary impulses. His soul not casting a single shadow beneath which to take shelter in moments of reflection.

"When do you dream nowadays, Madruga?" Venâncio said dejectedly.

Madruga was not annoyed. He watched Venâncio meticulously peeling the orange as he addressed these remarks to him. Venâncio did not offend him, because he in fact thought of himself as a dreamer, though absorbed in endless labor.

"Isn't that the way I'll fulfill my destiny?"

To restore his damaged authority, González began to find fault with Venâncio, whom he treated with obvious contempt.

"A Spanish tramp. It's plain to see he's not from Galicia. Good-for-nothings like that aren't born of our soil."

Madruga protested. He would not allow people to talk about Venâncio in front of him. He was part of his affective territory.

"The knife that strikes him wounds me as well, and don't you forget it," he spoke up angrily.

González followed him about everywhere, under the illusion that he could sit in for him on business deals whose outcome Madruga had already foreseen. But no matter how hard he tried, Madruga could not bring himself to respect that lumpish clodhopper, who had made it across the Atlantic yet had failed to acquire a taste for adventure. His body, which expanded daily under the pressure of wine, beer, and fat, had not retained one gram of the magic salt that the waters of the Atlantic scattered in sprays all during the crossing.

Avid devourers of newspapers, Madruga and Venâncio manifested a passionate interest in Brazilian politics, a subject on which they almost never agreed. In these arguments, Venâncio antagonized Madruga by pretending to ignore him just as he was about to speak up about some burning issue. In these skirmishes each of them stubbornly making the most of their conflicting personality traits. Venâncio's thorny soul reminded Madruga of the gorse bushes of Galicia, with their delicate yellow flowers streaked with green.

Madruga was spellbound by figures in the limelight, those close to the orbit of power. He remembered the faces of senators and deputies of the Republic, seen in photographs or, in person, in the Rua do Ouvidor and in the Confeitaria Colombo. And in the effort to familiarize himself with Brazil, so that nothing would be foreign to him in the future, he refused to speak Castilian or Galician, even with Venâncio or people from the old country. Though his Portuguese very soon improved, he lacked the time to master the grammar, the subtleties of the language. The country as a whole assailed his respiratory passages. An overpowering presence, which he confronted with equal excess. He slept less and less, exhilarated by the feeling of having ingested a strange mixture of palm oil, olive oil, babassu, vinegar, weeds, and heaven only knew how many unidentifiable substances. A cruel vortex which he did not renounce, but which little by little stained his clothes and his soul.

Joining battle with Madruga's manifest pride, Venâncio pruned the excesses. "How can you proclaim your love for this land if you've never known it? Even today, you still haven't visited the Passeio Público, if only to see the agoutis, who are freer than we are."

Madruga played dumb. "I leave the Passeio Público to you. I don't need to visit it to know what it's like. All I need is for you to tell me about it and describe it. Isn't that the same thing? What's more, this country circulates through my veins. As though I'd been born in the very center of this tumult, of this mixture of races, of the coins tinkling in the cash registers."

In less than four years, Madruga had paid off the debt he owed his Uncle Justo. Ceferino wrote him in the meantime, insinuating that his progress had made him forget the family. As usually happens with certain thankless, hardhearted children. His father's criticism stemming principally from the fact that Madruga sent them very little money. A legitimate complaint, certainly, but one that Madruga was unable to satisfy. He had decided not to spend his resources in that phase. Concentrating on getting rich quickly, he was not able to suffer hardships for his parents' sake. Ceferino and Urcesina had the means, after all, to get along by themselves. If life had been hard for them thus far, let them sacrifice themselves a little more. He promised to redeem himself altogether very shortly.

"I don't know why those people in Sobreira ask for so much," he said to Venâncio. "Seeing as how they don't lack for potatoes, turnips, corn bread, and pork."

Madruga was careful about appearances. Even though he had only two suits, he kept them spic-and-span so as to look prosperous. And because he wanted to widen his circle of acquaintances, he regularly sent off postcards from Rio de Janeiro with greetings to faithful guests of the hotels. For the most part coffee planters and cattle breeders, owners of businesses, or professional politicians on the way up. Apologizing for his awkward Portuguese and his lack of the flowers of rhetoric.

On a certain morning, he turned up in his office in the Cinelândia hotel, smoking an impressive cigar. He had often lingered about outside the Tabacaria Londres, trying to work up his courage to become a client. The first time he walked up to the counter, he hid his embarrassment by simply pointing to the various brands on display in their elegant multi-colored boxes.

Facing it out with the clerk, he finally proudly squeezed a Romeo y Julieta between his fingers, admiring its gold ring for a long time. Venâncio noted the pleasure Madruga took in sporting such an expensive habit. Not realizing that Madruga bought just one havana a day, intending to make it last all afternoon. He lit it with all the deliberate care of the connoisseur, so that the puffs of smoke exhaled in the air in front of the well-dressed customer would symbolize his conquest of America. After two or three puffs, Madruga left the room, immediately putting out the cigar without damaging the tip. And he went back to this same havana, stowed in a drawer, only when another customer turned up. In which case he went into his office, returning with his morning cigar lighted.

When he discovered them, Venâncio's unyielding nature disapproved of such tricks. But being unable to tolerate judging his friend without openly confronting him with his shortcoming, he approached him edgily.

"You're going to end up losing your soul any day now, Madruga."

"It's a hell of a soul if it can do itself damage that easily! A soul's not something that takes a tumble, Venâncio, and then gets taken care of with disinfectant and adhesive tape," Madruga said, dashing about as usual. Nothing being able to convince him to cut down on his activities.

Once past the humiliating phase, González again consulted Madruga when in doubt. The two of them had finally ended up splitting the profits and the company down the middle. Madruga had promptly settled the negative balance on the books having to do with the hotel on Lavradio. Madruga now proudly passing himself off as the sole owner, as meanwhile his business acumen brought in financial profits on an ever-increasing scale. He had a thick growth of beard now, and had taken on Ceferino's stature, without his father's drooping shoulders. Vain about his way with women.

Venâncio was of two minds about the changes in Madruga. He wavered between applauding his friend and restraining him. Wondering uneasily whether Madruga's willful and impulsive nature wasn't the one that was better adjusted to Brazil. Quite unlike his own, melancholy and reasonable, always shaking off the dust of Brazilian history. The victory of this hypothesis proving to him that he had followed the wrong course. It would have been better to have landed on the shores of the Pacific. Peru perhaps? And if the facts had told him that he would feel just as out of place and alien wherever he might go? With this certainty would he at least be free of envy? Of the tortuous feeling that takes the form of a spider with a thousand legs, entangling a person's soul with its shining strands, luring him into a trap where he might encounter Madruga's face?

Madruga's active nature kept him from examining the consequences of his own acts. Everything about him went beyond the simple rhetoric of success. Categorized as a modest little streamlet feeding into a great current that had met with failure for centuries, Madruga rebelled against this fate. Prepared to break by force a spell that bound him to misery. And his instinct for survival was always so legitimate that Grandfather Xan's stories, brimming over with tears and poverty, roused him to violent protest. To the point of demanding another ending from his grandfather, quite contrary to the narrator's intentions.

"If you don't change the way the story ends, grandfather, we'll be lost. We'd be better off dying here and now."

"And what kind of a story is it you want, my boy? One contrary to legend?" Xan asked, offended by such cheekiness.

Madruga offered him a pharmacopoeia of principles guaranteed to work. Because legends ought to be strengthened by the tonic effect of hope and belief.

"Pity anyone who does away with the heroine or the hero, grandfather."

In Brazil, Madruga woke each morning all wound up to get ahead in life. Whereas Venâncio observed the world through a sour sweat, fleeing like the plague all affectionate caresses and loving acts. It had not been by chance that, disregarding Madruga's warnings, he had first stepped onto Brazilian soil with his left foot. In his eagerness to forgo pomp and circumstance. Yet destiny had drawn him to Madruga on the deck of the English ship. Why? Without Madruga would he perhaps be doomed to wash dishes, to sweep floors, sleeping in some squalid cubbyhole?

Madruga did not care one way or the other about Venâncio's daily trips to the Biblioteca Nacional during business hours. To González, however, he told a number of different lies to justify his absence. Being careful to provide Venâncio with a safety net for use in an emergency.

Venâncio roamed hither and yon, never at home with the concrete world. With the same look in his eyes that Madruga later surprised in Eulália's. And that awakened fear in him, as though this sort of dream blotted out the whole of immediate reality and caused dangerous collisions. He felt a deeper respect for Venâncio. A feeling close to what he had felt for Bento, their only son to have been born in Galicia. An unexpected link with home.

When Eulália announced that she was pregnant, Madruga decided to make the trip to Galicia, certain that he would be fulfilling a promise. Or obeying the call of Xan, now dead and gone, who had never forgiven him his absence in the hour of his death. Xan had dreamed of having his grandson at his side, holding his hand as he told him, between fits of coughing and sighs, his last story, doubtless not a long one, before entering the kingdom of shadow and of fallen heroes.

"This son will be a Galician, Eulália. I owe a debt to Galicia. I promised Grandfather Xan to give Galicia back at least one of its lost legends. And only with this birth will I pay that debt. Isn't it true that a man too is a legend?"

Eulália sensed shadows in her husband's heart. But she did not ask him a single question. The same veil that shielded them from others' faces also lay between them. Eulália thus plunging precipitously into a region darkened by the spirit of God, where she was free to trespass, without fear of erring. What, after all, was hers to hide that God did not already know? Existence as she saw it was marked by obscure truths, and faced by dint of lies and contradictory versions. Nonetheless, she never condemned falsehood, a pressing human need.

Venâncio paled on hearing of the journey. Though Madruga promised to return immediately after his son's birth, leaving him as surety their rock-solid ties of friendship.

Dom Miguel, dressed in his best suit, received Eulália at the portal to the Sobreira estate. His gestures under rigorous control so that his emotions would not risk harming his daughter in her condition, about to give birth to his grandchild in the coming months. He did not know how to act with Miguel and Esperança, still babes in arms. He noted, in a daze, his family line expanding in a country noted for the smell of fruit and palpitating human sweat.

Madruga had been as good as his word. His wife was wearing silk and discreet jewels. And, spared household tasks, her hands were of a surpassing delicacy. Madruga kept in the background so as to give his father-in-law a chance to appreciate the family brought from America. Only after night had fallen, once Eulália had retired with the children, did Madruga agree to share Dom Miguel's repose. The two of them side by side appreciating brandy, with no barriers between them.

"I've kept my word, Dom Miguel. And I still have no fear of America."

Face to face with his father-in-law, doleful and grave, he felt no inclination to take revenge. The marriage with Eulália had erased his resentments. Dom Miguel's opposition had corresponded to the interests of his class. Why should that austere gentleman have had faith in Madruga's ability as a builder of dreams? If dreaming was only a house without a roof, without walls, still invisible for those who lacked shelter and disbelieved.

At times Madruga gave evidence of a taste for liquidating his enemies with a look and promissory notes. Keeping the spoils. In an attempt, however, to absolve himself of certain acts, he tried to forget them, thereby freeing himself of dark burdens.

"I wouldn't like to drag the dead around behind me, Eulália. They weigh more than any gravestone," he said, indirectly referring to a long list of adversaries.

"Aren't you simply burying them?" Eulália said distractedly.

In Sobreira, Madruga was moved once again by trivial details. Deeply affected, however, by the absence of Grandfather Xan, to whom he would have liked to recount Brazilian stories. Above all because, after having so closely interwoven the stories of the two countries, he could no longer tell them apart.

Free meanwhile from the burden of work, his heart began to pound, from the first night on. Legends suddenly glimmering everywhere, like fireflies. Or wandering stars. Everything crying out to be recounted. The legends and the stories of Xan and Dom Miguel. He took to getting up early then, in his eagerness to take dawn in Sobreira by surprise.

He stole out of bed without a sound, not wanting to disturb Eulália.

And wherever he went, he was accompanied by the certainty that the child was developing just as it should within the woman, despite his concern. That was how it had been with Miguel and Esperança. Once born, they had naturally become part of his life. Without his reflecting deeply on that arrival in the world. Now, however, strolling among the trees of the estate, he thought about the Brazilian children. They were the house he was building in America. Hence he was not at all certain of the reasons that had led him to make the child still in Eulália's belly a Galician, undoubtedly disturbing the family equilibrium. As though in the past he had acted unscrupulously, and there thus remained in his consciousness traces of an act that gnawed at him and hurled him toward Sobreira, in search of a possible redemption—by way of the labors of his wife's womb.

The fact was that he was there in an attempt to be reconciled with Galicia, from whose spirit and tradition he had abdicated, proud and belligerent. Feeling himself for the first time shifting like quicksand now, linked to dark zones, from which there mounted to the surface memories, episodes, emotions that would weaken him in his future dealings with the things of America, should light not be shed on them in time. America did not pardon such incoherent fantasies when they did not embody it in concrete form. Or when that continent ceased to be the definite moving force behind any dream-policy.

Dom Miguel sensed his son-in-law's distress. Inexperienced in matters of the soul, Madruga was unable to dissemble. This being, however, a subject to which Dom Miguel had devoted his entire lifetime. Hence he thought of speaking to him, but Madruga's pale face forbade entry into areas that were his exclusive property, where he must be left to himself.

During that week, Madruga went up into the mountains with the express intention of reconstructing the moments preceding his departure from Galicia at the age of thirteen. He wanted to recover his natural ties to the basic elements of the country. He sensed that his old obsession with America had obstructed delicate channels of existence, had damaged areas corresponding to words and feelings that he was now lacking.

At the top of Pé de Mua, surrounded by mysteriously carved stones, Madruga had collected scattered impressions. And like a stranger, he had explored the resources that the earth might have to offer him through previous arrangement. As nearby a tiny rivulet of water, almost without the strength to go on, trickled past.

On these afternoons the hours went by slowly. Moreover, ever since his arrival in Sobreira, Madruga had fallen into the habit of marking off time by means of Eulália's belly. Expanding with each passing day through a creative process from which he had been dramatically banished. Stroking nonetheless that territory of his wife's, full of stretch marks and white patches now, with cautious gestures new to him.

Touched by this concern, Eulália for her part was not at all perturbed

by the proximity that the child taking shape imposed upon her. She too
had her refuge. In the afternoons she headed for the Romanesque church
of Sobreira. In the empty nave, sounds were amplified, her sighs attaining
an unsuspected dimension. She enjoyed the tranquillity of this medieval
vault, feeling no remorse at having left her children with the servants.
Provided heart and soul with the elements that her legitimate house on
earth offered her. She had only to sit down on the wooden bench to feel
herself surrounded by God, by her own soul, by the child in her belly, by
the presence, in a word, of a reality wholly inclined to accumulate examples. Life thus doing permanent battle with anyone striving to drain
it dry.

Never had the reality of Sobreira seemed to her so ancient and so
everlasting as in that year. With reworkings and defects centuries old. A
land antagonistic to progress, hence forgotten by one and all. Obliged to
conserve its soil with the respect owed its natural limits. The same respect,
moreover, that was due Galicia's past. So sensitive to pain when it was
mistreated. When it was faced with those who wanted to make factories
spring up, there where there had always existed the solemn majesty of the
open countryside, with its bitter memories and endless empty spaces. Forgetting that reality was also where human feelings lay hidden.

In summer, however, there was the illusion of the new in Sobreira.
The very houses, with their stone façades, were washed clean of mud
when it rained. Everything was renewed; the age-old universe of the region regained its charm. No wind bowing the corn crop. Eulália was
moved by the modesty of that rural life, capable of making bread, working
the earth, bringing forth children, and seeing its dead buried in potter's
field.

There in Sobreira, she sometimes thought of her house in Rio de
Janeiro. Planned and built by Madruga, with his growing family in mind.
He boasted of its two bathrooms on the upper floor, such as no other house
in the neighborhood had. To Eulália, however, that house in Tijuca, or any
other, seemed a mere stopping-off place. Even Sobreira was becoming
simply a way station, loved because of Dom Miguel. Her natural state was
that of a traveler. Mistress of a manor invisible to the naked eye, she had
no idea what region it was located in. Her being concentrated only on
collecting the original enigmas of faith.

Yet the body of her husband in bed, when he came to make love, was
not strange to her. Many times she rejoiced to see Madruga's passion burst
into a shower of sparks inside her. And though reaping the enjoyment of
those ardent sentiments, she was afraid to imitate them.

After the birth of Miguel and Esperança, she discovered that giving
birth had not brought her the intensity she had hoped for. Perhaps because
other intense emotions also occupied her. Moreover, if Madruga had not
suddenly appeared in the public square of Sobreira that afternoon, she

would have entered the convent, against Dom Miguel's will. She had always felt the attraction of lengthy circumambulations of the cloister, breathing in the flowers, as the beads of the rosary slipped through her fingers, the trifling details of everyday life forgotten.

She never confessed to her husband that she had dreamed of the life of a nun. Madruga would be indignant. He would not condone her intention of belonging to an institution as profit-minded and authoritarian as the Church, whose laws, on the individual and collective planes, continually deprived human society of the right to choose its own advent.

Madruga's blasphemies forced Eulália to turn her face away toward the garden. And pretending that her mind was elsewhere, she gave him a few moments to recover his composure.

"Who is that stranger visiting Sobreira in this sun? And not even a hat to protect himself!" she said.

Following these naked displays of feeling, Madruga would hurriedly leave the room, returning in a calmer mood with some little present in his hands. Without apologizing, when the Church had been the subject at issue.

Madruga received, by post, the Brazilian newspapers sent by Venâncio. As he undid the packets, Madruga perceived in each knot of the twine another of Venâncio's bitter laments at his absence. But he could not help him. He too was living through a difficult moment, isolated from everyone. Even from Eulália.

Urcesina could not forgive him for wandering about in the mountains. Almost not coming to visit her, even in the late afternoon. His mother was extremely critical of him. Quite the lord and master now, putting on high and mighty airs that only suited Dom Miguel. The neighbors had come round soon enough to tell her that Madruga, like a professor from the University of Santiago, was spending hours on end meditating alongside the cattle.

"The world is lost," Urcesina said to her neighbor. "Even those who live in America have lost their sense of reality."

Urcesina demanded his immediate presence. On the pretext that he needed to go straightway to the specialist in Pontevedra, because there was something inside him that risked getting out of order. And a person's nerves, above all, were not to be trifled with. She offered to accompany him in secret, so the fact wouldn't leak out. But if he refused to see the doctor, he ought to go to Mondariz, to take the waters.

His feelings hurt by his mother's remarks, Madruga suggested that she concentrate on her housework and leave him in peace. For the first time in his life he devoted his time to repairing the roof drains of a house located square in the center of his chest.

Alone with Ceferino, Urcesina bewailed the fact that her son was becoming a stranger to her. And just when he had every reason to be happy. Instead, he took perverse pleasure in scratching that confounded chest he'd spoken of, so that he'd get wounds there and blisters filled with pus. Not to mention the way he neglected his wife! Going up to the mountains with the cows following after. What would people say about a man who made a public show of his afflictions instead of hymning the praises of American gold?

Ceferino turned on her, insensitive as usual to the pain of others. There she stood, her heart as rough as her hands from all that drudgery in the kitchen.

"For the first time Madruga comes to us humbly and you criticize him, woman. Can't you see that his outings up in the mountains do him nothing but good? Doesn't a man have the right to think, whether or not it means a sacrifice to him? Even Christ needed forty days up there on the mountaintop to think about the world."

"And just look what happened to him. No, I don't want Madruga to forget about reality and turn into a philosopher on us now. Let him go on paying more attention to business than to matters of the heart. As far as I can see, the heart is a poor ruler of life. And what's more, it's never been the mainstay of a family," Urcesina said to her husband crossly.

One morning Madruga came in with a big hug for his mother. And to prove to Urcesina that she had her son back, he consented to have lunch with her. On condition that she make him a potato-and-pepper omelette. Urcesina trembled with emotion as she tossed the omelette out of the frying pan onto the plate, and out of the plate into the frying pan, her hands becoming slightly stained with the beaten eggs in the course of this operation. An act born of her skill and local customs. But what would become of them, Galicians that they were, when they lost the little knacks with the savor of salt that seasoned their existence?

"Whenever you're hungry, son, come see me. In Dom Miguel's house there's too much talk of dignity and tradition, and never any about food. They don't eat their fill there the way we do at our house. What's more, aristocrats are so fussy about their food they leave the table hungry," she said, regretting now having misjudged her son. Though Madruga's blue eyes troubled her, since she could no longer catch a glimpse of herself in them as she once had.

"What a shame you weren't here for Grandfather Xan's funeral. You missed out on the finest story of all the ones he ever told in his life."

"Maybe you'll tell it to me someday," Madruga said offhandedly.

"I'm not a master storyteller like Grandfather Xan. It was a gift God gave him on account of the gold coins he never had. It was to compensate him, don't you think?"

The baby was expected in October. Autumn was a season with a sad beauty. And as the date drew near, Madruga went off by himself. Recognizing Eulália's rights, however, to erect a paling of thorns around herself to control her own impulses. She too had a harsh and distant soul. Again and again Madruga had stretched his hands out to her without her reciprocating the gesture.

On returning from one of his visits to the mountains, Madruga learned of the birth of his son. In the parlor, Dom Miguel was weeping disconsolately, sensing his own death. Births in general were a presage of the imminent departure of the oldest. In a daze, Madruga did not know where to turn. Whether to Eulália, with the baby in her arms, to Urcesina, measuring the child's size, or to Dom Miguel, who had refused to entertain those present with his stories, despite his son-in-law's urging.

"One story at least, Dom Miguel, in honor of the boy, who's going to be called Bento. Tell us again about Priscillian."

Seeing his son, Madruga was present, for the space of just a few seconds, at his own arrival in the world. As though he saw Urcesina holding him roughly in her arms as she offered him her breasts. But a certain gesture of Eulália's and the smell of the recent delivery, which still hung in the air, blotted out the fantasy.

He felt he was there for no other reason than to ask little Bento to let him take back the permission granted him, before his birth, to change the course of his life, once he was back in Brazil. On seeing his son already come into the world, however, and possessed of a physical form unlike his own, Madruga realized the absurdity of having attempted to reconstruct, at whatever prompting, his own existence.

Eulália was not the only one, then, to bleed between the thighs after the delivery. He too was bleeding, and lowing like a cow. He was an idiot and a liar. He had not come to Galicia to be weighed in the balance, since the results might be prejudicial to him. He had never contemplated dislocating his bones in exchange for a spiritual revelation. He was a mere starving brute, clinging to trees, to living beings, addicted to the rapture of the body, the one instrument in fact capable of confounding acts and words, and of tearing off pieces of life above and beyond necessities. All that was left him was the courage to applaud excesses, thanks to which he was about to cross the Atlantic once again, with a wife and three children.

Despite Dom Miguel's lamentations, Bento's birth had the merit of restoring Madruga and reestablishing his ties with Galicia. And it offered him the chance to relive for brief moments the mystery of his own birth.

"Those were difficult months, father. But I learned once and for all that I shall never rule myself with faultless symmetry. That's Venâncio's role. I'm venturesome and bursting with energy, so the time has come to go back to America. That's where the great chaos is," he said, as Ceferino looked at him in silence, as though he hadn't understood one word.

Life would soon separate them. Several years more would go by without seeing Urcesina, Ceferino, Dom Miguel, friends. They were indispensable stages on life's way. Though the separation gnawed at all their hearts.

Madruga invited his mother, Ceferino, and Dom Miguel to accompany them to Vigo. They stayed in the same hotel from whose window Eulália and he had contemplated the Pontevedra estuary, after their wedding. In the morning, they even went for a walk down the Rua do Príncipe. Madruga remembered Uncle Justo. Immediately after lunch, they went down to the pier.

Candid and gentle, Eulália was rocking little Bento to sleep under the covers. The whistling of the north wind foretold cold. Like a bird dog, Urcesina tracked her grandchildren, wrinkling her nose at Madruga's impatience to get aboard. He could not bear lingering farewells, words uttered in tragic tones. Irritated by a family that ate pieces of his body, he feared he would give way to anger, and as always immediately regret having done so.

Urcesina cut her son short. "Let's begin the good-byes. Before they kill us all. Nobody here is young enough to say farewell twice."

She embraced Madruga, Eulália, kissed the grandchildren. Ceferino did likewise. Dom Miguel stood apart from the others. Suddenly he doffed his hat, bowing to his daughter.

"Dona Urcesina is right. I prefer to keep my distance, as though we were not even saying good-bye. As though the boat, instead of heading out into the waters of the Atlantic, would arrive in Sobreira before us, as we go back by train," he said half under his breath. And in the face of Eulália's impulse to go to him, Dom Miguel stopped her with a gesture, immediately thereafter turning his back on her.

From the deck, they watched the boat pull away. In a certain way Madruga was repeating the gestures of his first voyage. On the pier, Urcesina insisted on standing rooted to the spot, deaf to Ceferino's pleas to come away and start back home with him. Dom Miguel's shadow had long since disappeared. Madruga suggested they go below to their cabin.

During dinner that night, the captain stopped by their table to welcome them aboard. The wine seemed to Madruga to have turned. But he thought it best not to complain. On the third day out, beneath a starry sky, Bento developed a fever that the doctor could not bring down. And that kept going up every hour, to Eulália's and Madruga's despair. Having finally diagnosed it as croup, the doctor hurriedly made an incision in his throat, soaking the sheet in blood.

His body in shock, Bento gasped feebly for breath. At his son's side, Madruga implored the doctor to save him, at whatever cost. Eulália had withdrawn from the painful scene. Taking the offering of prayers upon herself, she allied herself with God in the fight for her son's life. Beseeching him to spare Bento's life and take hers in its stead. But as her eyes beheld Miguel and Esperança, still tiny children, she could foresee their helplessness. Was it permissible to offer herself and leave them orphans?

Eulália handed the children over to a nurse. They should not be witnesses to Bento's death. Once this step had been taken, he died in exactly five hours. The doctor had assured them that he would live another day. His prediction had been wrong. Death had been in a hurry.

Clinging, in tears, to his son's body, Madruga pleaded with him to live. "Come on, my son, a little more courage, come back to life. Come on, life is waiting for you, Bento. Or are you afraid?"

His son's body was growing cold. Madruga had not given a thought to Eulália at his side, on her knees, motionless, her eyes fixed on the figure of Christ she was holding in her hands. They finally separated Madruga by force from Bento. A son who had been fashioned with care, so like Madruga. The same blue eyes.

The nurse took Bento's christening robe from the chest to dress him in. His mind distracted at first, Madruga reacted immediately, drawing the woman aside as he muttered something. In rapid jerks and tugs, he removed from the bottom of the trunk the jacket he'd taken to America on his first voyage, when still a youngster. That garment, from which he had never been parted, old and faded now, somehow symbolized his destiny. Pointing to the jacket, he ordered the nurse to wrap his son in it. Bound up in the jacket with the threadbare collar: that was how his son should be dressed to go to the bottom of the sea.

Seeing his son bundled up in the garment, he felt as though he were the one about to be buried. The idea of his own death did not pain him greatly, occupied as he was with the loss of his son. Suddenly his lips parted in a smile of fury at the thought that he now belonged definitely to Brazil. He decided, then, to accompany the ship's officers up to the deck, from which they would cast his son into the Atlantic.

"I always suspected they'd bury me in these waters one day," Madruga murmured, paying no attention to the silent presence of the officer who was following the ritual of burial at sea.

His hands trembled as he heard the thud of his son's body on the surface of the waters, before being carried off by the waves in a dizzying whirl. Before that the captain read a passage of the Bible aloud to them. At the end, the crew present saluted Madruga and did not speak of the subject again during the voyage.

Venâncio came down to the Praça Mauá to welcome them. During Madruga's absence he had taken care of the house as though it were his own. Having slept for several nights in the couple's bed, from which he arose exhausted and regretting having spent the night there. On the pier, he had difficulty identifying them. It was some time before they appeared, perhaps because of the children and their voluminous baggage. Till finally Eulália came slowly down the gangplank of the ship. He perceived in that face a shadow threatening to spread all through her body. And in her arms there remained the trace of a gesture meant once for a bundle that for months she had held close to her breast. She did not know what to do with her hands.

Venâncio drew back from the thin, threatening tentacles that Eulália held out to him from halfway down the gangplank. She immediately cried out for help. Venáncio stepped forward and hurriedly grasped Eulália's arm, assisting her down the last few steps. She let herself be guided without demur. On setting foot on firm ground, however, she straightened, free once more. As Madruga let go of Esperança and Miguel to embrace Venâncio. The friend sacrificing his own heart so they would not hear it unburdening itself.

During dinner, they scarcely spoke to each other. Though Madruga praised the food. When the coffee came, his spirits revived, once Eulália had retired with a quick good-night. He then began to list the projects with which he was about to occupy himself, none of which made any concession to his state of exhaustion on arriving. He seemed obsessed by the desire to see his house again, to take stock of his possessions. Despite his fatigue he gave evidence of a certain nervous excitement. He was tempted to open the door and get back to work that very minute. According to what he said, there was no time to be lost. There was a great deal to be done in that country. Brazil had always given proof of its love for him. Freeing him from recent illusions, back there in Galicia.

It was time to dig into Brazilian soil again, in search of treasures. He had always been certain he would find them.

In recent years, Madruga used to like to tell me how Grandfather Xan had promised him his first trip to Cebreiro as soon as he reached the age of twelve. He'd done so because he was the firstborn of the grandchildren and the most outstanding pupil in the school. He had easily mastered his first reader and arithmetic, and above all Spanish history. This latter interwoven, so his teacher, Gravio, said, with Franks, Celts, Visigoths, Levantines, Phoenicians. All of them peoples who had resolved to sow the dust of discord and fabrication over the entire peninsula.

In the classroom, Gravio avoided looking at his pupils, maintaining that he was not at all interested in youngsters whose adolescent features the work of time would soon transform. The boys acquiring coarse features and the beginnings of a beard. And the girls protrusions and a veiled look in their eyes.

In retaliation, Madruga plied Gravio with endless questions, till finally he yanked the schoolmaster out of the dense and impenetrable terrain into which he had plunged in order to protect himself from the torpor of everyday routine. Gravio cast a cold eye on Madruga, reproving him for his cheekiness, but the boy bravely met his gaze. This fact meriting from the schoolmaster the assignment of a desk where Madruga was to sit from that time forward, for Gravio did not want to find any other pupil there when he looked in that direction.

Despite his irregular class attendance, Madruga read, till far into the night, the books lent him by the schoolmaster, who dreamed of having him as a conversational partner someday. Gravio lived with his wife in back of the school, in a house belonging to the municipality, for which he paid no rent. And because the authorities had forgotten him in Sobreira, the idea of removing him from there never having occurred to a single official, he simply accepted, as a matter of course, gifts in the form of milk, potatoes, bacon, and whatever else would eke out his meager salary.

One night in the tavern, in his cups, Gravio outdid himself extolling Madruga, leading Ceferino to believe that Gravio's praise of his son was aimed at getting him to pay for the schoolmaster's wine. Ceferino pretended not to have heard, thus avoiding uttering words he might have occasion to regret in the future. Gravio was so insistent, however, that Ceferino was finally persuaded of Madruga's aptitudes. And because the wine had also comforted his soul, Ceferino agreed to pay for the glasses of Ribeiro that Gravio consumed on Fridays.

Contrary to his habits, Ceferino arrived home in a boisterous mood. And still amazed at what he had learned of his son's achievement, he passed the good news on to Urcesina. Cautiously retouching his account, however, so as not to prejudice an opinion bound to mean a great deal in Madruga's life. Urcesina served Ceferino's soup with a scowl on her face, chewing over a vague uneasiness that was proving difficult to express. As her husband bit into a pear from the garden, she finally spoke out against an intelligence that had begun very early on to be a drain on their pocketbook.

"Since when are we obliged to pay for an intelligence that came our way through the grace of God? If we owed a debt, God is the one we ought to have sent a barrel of wine to. Not to that Gravio fellow, who's well enough paid already with potatoes and chickens for soup."

Regretfully, Ceferino conceded that Urcesina was right. In all truth, they were not in debt to that man so eager to seduce them with quotations in Latin. God was the only one responsible for the talents given Madruga. The matter, then, was not within his competence or Urcesina's.

In the tavern, he was uneasy as Gravio drank his fill of the wine he'd promised to pay for that Friday night. Around the schoolmaster's lips were signs of a sensual pleasure long buried, now coming freely to the surface.

Ceferino foresaw disaster, but found himself unable to budge. He simply stood and watched the schoolmaster's face pale when he was presented with the bill. Incomprehensible whispers from Gravio, even pleas for mercy, perhaps, reached his ears. Ceferino nonetheless refused to come to his aid. And his studied indifference kept other habitués in turn from siding with the schoolmaster. The whole thing had turned into a private matter. Finally, with unexpected hauteur, Gravio dug down into his pocket and pulled out the last coins in it.

In bed, Ceferino felt like crushing his wife, from whose heaving breast there came one snore after the other. He lay awake, tossing and turning between the sheets, haunted by the figure of the schoolmaster with his threadbare olive-colored jacket, which he shed only on Sundays. Giving evidence of poverty on every hand, in sad contrast to a rich personal culture absolutely useless in Sobreira.

In the morning, feeling remorse at his own avarice, and at having given in to his wife, Ceferino sent Gravio a hen that he fed once again as it left his house. In his eagerness to have the creature show off its fine craw, bulging with the grains of corn it had just swallowed.

The misunderstanding was finally ended through the delivery to Ceferino of a poem by Rosalía de Castro, which Gravio had personally copied out in Gothic script. In the last few months, to his teacher's displeasure, Madruga had fallen into the habit of not reading the books that he kept sending him, claiming he didn't have the time. The reason being that he had recently begun to spend long hours in the carpenter's shop of Sobreira, training as an apprentice, with the intention of having a respectable occupation in the future.

Through Grandfather Xan's influence, Madruga had begun pestering the oldsters again, worse than ever, trying to get them to tell him, while they still had their teeth and their memory, stories they knew, usually ones having to do only with Galicia. He immediately gave signs of impatience, however, when one of the old men forgot the ending of a story that had gotten a good way along in the telling.

"If you don't tell me now, just give up. It's the last time you'll have me to listen to your stories."

Madruga's impatience was appealing, however. Especially since he was Xan's grandchild. A master of the insuperable art of telling popular stories, Xan had only to open his mouth, with a straw-paper cigarette invariably dangling from it, for a solemn silence to ensue. So it seemed odd that with such a splendid narrator at hand, Madruga found it necessary to extort from neighbors stories he had more than enough of at home.

Xan interwove facts and legends in colorful, lively language. And whenever he needed to graft new elements onto the story, he opened parentheses, though without losing the thread of the plot by so doing. Confronted with his audience's eagerness to learn how the whole story ended, he nonetheless never speeded up the telling. He condemned in no uncertain terms anyone who put pressure on him to make the story shorter.

"If a story takes a year before it's told, it would be a crime to lop off its beauty and imagination. If a person has no ear for them, he can go live in hell. Or begin living without them."

Xan listened to his colleagues with interest, thus repaying them for willingly hearing him out. And when one of them got all mixed up in the middle of his story, without hitting on a way to go ahead, he never blamed him, understanding human shortcomings very well.

What he did instead was first ask their permission, and once it had been readily granted by all, he would then take up the person's plot as though it had been his own from the beginning, immediately filling it in with a wealth of surprising details, which would turn out to be relevant only at the very end of the story. This feat sometimes winning him wild applause.

These legends delighted Madruga. Legends for centuries essential to Galicia's sense of nationhood. And, quite rightly, a required subject in school. Yet no one brought them to life the way Xan did. His voice, roughened by too much alcohol and tobacco, took on a very effective whispering register, especially when he was trying to hold his grandson spellbound. To this end Xan equipped himself with wine or brandy, and the makings for rolling cigarettes. At such times he barely moved, trying his best to spare energies inevitably consumed in the course of the endless telling.

"There is no set time limit for this story, for instance. It's one meant for patient listeners," Xan said, thus short-circuiting his grandson's restless impulses.

There at his grandfather's side, ready to offer him proofs of his esteem, Madruga would willingly endure hunger and cold. In the face of his grandson's probable sacrifice, Xan realized the power of a story of which he was not even the protagonist, and whose beginning he had not witnessed. And yet a story which, by its very nature, full of mixups, signs and portents, twists and turns, and questions obscure even to its tellers, made his grandson's eyes sparkle.

And using words as though they were the pendulum of a clock swinging back and forth, Xan obliged him to believe that many of those legends, preserved thanks only to the memory of the old men, formed an integral part now of the cultural legacy of Castile. So that today, to the misfortune of the Galician people, their authorship was attributed to Castilians, down on the central plain.

"They're legends the Castilians stole from us. But they shouldn't get the idea in their heads that we've forgotten this pillage. Every morning, when I eat my bread-and-milk soup, the very first thing I do is call a curse down upon them. Who knows? Maybe someday someone will bring those legends back to Galicia."

The conflict between Gravio and Xan grew more intense in the last three years. From the day that the two of them decided to do battle for Madruga's imagination. To the point that they no longer hid their injured feelings in public. When one of them came into the tavern, the other left. Gravio was perspicacious enough to foresee his own defeat in the offing, shortly before Madruga's trip to Cebreiro in Xan's company. After the event, he began to hint that Xan's words, being oral in nature, were unfortunately doomed to be forgotten, for lack of someone to write them down. The effort of that wise peasant thus being of no avail.

Such innuendo affronted Madruga, who threatened to abandon the classroom. After all, books did not have the right to cross swords with a man like Xan, who quite to the contrary prompted one and all to stroke the spines of textbooks as though they were veritable jewels. To comfort Xan, undoubtedly offended, Madruga inveighed heavily against country life, always thankless, with its fixed date to begin work in the fields and the outcome of the harvest never foreseeable.

Xan took pride in the fact that a member of his family had such spirit, without thereby losing his sensibility.

"This grandson of mine has the temperament of a wolf. And the claws too. This, moreover, will save him."

Madruga had recently learned that even though men cultivated certain gestures and words in private, in the hard give-and-take of daily life delicate emotions were taboo among them. Hence, as a man country born, he would be obliged to learn to pan reality like a gold prospector in order not to become mired in it.

The road to Cebreiro was rocky, more like a goat path. Since the medieval pilgrimages it had been the gateway to Galicia for those who came by way of Asturias. A cruel, legendary gateway, however, for the pilgrims who took this route so as to come to know its sanctuary, the hostel, the age-old Celtic thatched huts, and the forbidding setting viewed from the mountains. This inhospitable region, beset by punishing cold and wind, moved the errant heart of one who halted there, anxious to forget the hardships of the journey and time slipping away.

After Cebreiro, however, the pilgrims gained their second wind. Convinced now that they would reach Santiago de Compostela, from the beginning the reason for their journey. Where the pilgrims, some from as far away as Poland, would offer the rites before the saint and fulfill the promises made before setting out to cross Europe on foot.

A dramatic people, that, which had devastated Europe in the Middle Ages with its decision to move about without fear. Eager to be off, at a sign which the elect in particular recognized. Whereupon they vanquished mountains and rivers, proceeding from points that came to form the throbbing heart of Europe: Vézelay, Le Puy, Arles, Paris. Nothing stopped them. Until they passed beyond Somport and Roncevaux, the last frontiers before entering Spain, borne on the pitiless winds of the Pyrenees.

There they were in sandals, cord about the waist, sack on the back, scallop shell on the breast, body beset with fever. Because bad water had made them fall sick, or because faith, in the ardor of the adventure, had simply set them afire. It was worth much more to them to know the world than to know the saint himself, installed there in Santiago de Compostela, almost at Finisterre, the edge of the European continent.

And whenever the pilgrims met along the traditional routes, they resorted to Latin, the language common to all, for greetings and exchange of information. They might be in Spanish territory, yet they did not know the languages of Castile and Aragon. Despite these difficult conditions, however, they yearned only to kneel at the feet of the unfortunate saint who, from among the many coasts of Europe, with the entire Mediterranean at his disposal, with its tepid waters, beautiful bays, beaches of fine sand, crystal cities, had taken it into his head to cast his own skeleton up on the shores of Galicia, near Iria Flavia, under the protection of Queen Lupa, the renowned Celtic matron. The saint having thus clearly sought out the Atlantic, the same waters which bathe the coast of Brazil. A littoral so vast that it can never be taken in at a single glance. Not even with the aid of field glasses, a spyglass, a telescope. A country which, because it is American, can only be glimpsed through the power of the imagination, that perfume which so soon evaporates.

On the veranda in Leblon, Madruga and I bowed before the weight of Xan's legends, which sometimes came within our reach. Though I lacked the courage to confess to Grandfather that the Serra da Mantiqueira, in the light of the midday sun, caused me the same confusion as the Cebreiro of his childhood. Because, facing that range of mountains, I believed I saw the crucial history of Brazilian colonization pass in review. Even managing to hear the moans and shouts of the bandeirantes, of the smugglers, of the New Christians, of the tax collectors, advancing westward in lumbering wagons and on the backs of animals. A humanity ready to serve as the foundation for the formation of a limping people.

And above Mantiqueira, especially, there hovered the eternal clouds of Minas. A Minas that had always subsidized tragedy in order to lend greater substance to its own history. Thus capable of banishing poets, certain of finding others with equal talent to take their place. In accordance with the Brazilian spirit which, arms in hand, has always exterminated prophets with rare prodigality. On the pretext that they belong to an accursed race with no shame, which publicly exposes its burning genitals as it wrests pleasing words, keen sounds from the Portuguese tongue. With such instruments bringing to the surface precisely those expressions which had hitherto reposed in limbo. For all this and more besides deserving of oblivion, the worst form of exile. But to hell with all of them. After all, who asked those mad artists to describe a country whose very existence is doubtful?

Perhaps Madruga deliberately confuses memories of Cebreiro with others that came his way in any number of cities. Merely to prove that no other city allowed him as bold a dream. Or turned into a thirst for passion and adventure, to be lived with the courage of a master. Or gave him a key as a gift, to be smoothed with a file in the mornings, so as to bring him luck. And learn by means of it that bouts of confusion are an intrinsic part of any journey, which once begun ends without warning.

Madruga's features were still hard as stone, despite his advanced age. Now that he rarely smiled. And he did not even smile when asking me, unceremoniously, to assume for a few minutes the role of Xan, and thus speak to him of Cebreiro.

Grandfather had doubtless gone too far by asking that of me, failing to take into consideration my probable puzzlement. I pretended, however, not to have heard. Nor did I point out to him, by way of protest, that thanks to him I had sprouted on the American continent like a wild cactus, and therefore necessarily understood Cebreiro only in terms of the light it might shed on Brazil. After all, what the devil did I have to do with Madruga's Celtic origins, with the blood-red wine, the blazing cheeks, the mountains full of wolves and the gorse of Galicia? It was to him, in the end, that I owed my damned imagination, I thought apprehensively.

Madruga did not admit defeat. He promptly returned to the subject that invariably aroused his fervor.

"Medieval pilgrimages doubtless served to fertilize the Galician people, to enrich the stories of Xan and Dom Miguel. But they ended up poisoning us. Who can forget an era of greatness, Breta?"

Madruga's soul was stained by that mythical visit. Present within him as he crossed the Atlantic, after running away from home with the aid of Uncle Justo. So much so that, all alone on deck, free of Venâncio, he thought of Xan. He had lacked the courage to confess to his grandfather that he was off to America the following morning. The return from there taking twenty years sometimes.

On the eve of his journey, still in Sobreira, he stared at Xan during supper. His grandfather was preparing his straw-paper cigarette with rare pleasure. Madruga knew how much Xan loved him and the stories he inspired. With a love that never failed him. And the uncertainty of this sentiment swelled his chest with pain.

His mind on the straw-paper cigarette and words, his eternal temptation, Xan's suspicions were not aroused by Madruga's nervous gestures. On going off to his room, he bade his grandfather farewell with a casual wave of his hand, burying him at that moment. Certain that he would not keep the promise made him to sit at his bedside to carpet his way as he went to meet death. The death already close to his grandfather, since his words were no longer uttered with the firmness of the old days, despite his precious memory and his collection of flowery figures of speech.

On deck, tormented by the whistle of the sirens, Madruga decided to kill his family with the firmness of pilgrims forsaking their homes with no assurance of returning. Santiago de Compostela was comparable to America. In every century there was a land to dream of. To chase down. Even if it was not to honor the dead, who are always the first to demand passions and adventures of those who are still alive.

Grandfather Xan always endeavored to prove to those Galician country folk that, despite their being buried in Sobreira, there at the end of the world, they deserved to live. And so he told them endless stories. To Madruga especially, pointing to his clever interlocutor to single him out.

Xan and Madruga left Sobreira on foot. Cebreiro would be Madruga's first long journey. They traveled by daylight, stopping at night to sleep in the open air. To orient himself, Xan searched the stars and the wind. Or dropped by the taverns. In certain villages they were supplied with bread, sausage, bacon, as a proof of hospitality. Very close to Cebreiro, they rested in the shade of an oak tree. Xan explained that, once they arrived in that territory, they would be invading the heart of Galicia. And, consequently, making it bleed, if they wanted for something.

Moved, Madruga did not suspect that in a very near future he would come to desire the heart of Brazil. A heart that had begun to bleed more than four hundred years before. And would continue to lose blood and substance, through his handiwork and that of his descendants.

At the foot of the mountain of Cebreiro, Xan lost heart for a few moments. He leaned unsteadily on his staff. Everything was failing him, except for the recording of the details indispensable to the historic moment. Madruga took him by the arm and helped him up the mountainside. Till at last they looked down on the landscape from the summit. Before them a complex whole of disturbing beauty could be seen. Nothing must be forgotten in the future. The trees, the breeze, the age-old stones, and the feelings vested in things. Endeavoring to hide their emotions, Xan and Madruga turned their backs to each other. Xan was proud of his grandson, at once fearless and sensitive. Though it would be difficult now to teach him to live this ambiguity. He drew closer to Madruga in order to form a solid alliance. At that moment the two of them were the only ones to crystallize the history of Galicia.

They drank from the spring without fear of dying. Those waters were no longer poisonous, as they had once been. Xan showed his grandson the scallop shell of Santiago, with which pilgrims had helped themselves to water when Galicia was the spiritual center of Europe. Xan expressed himself with such conviction that both of them looked round for the ghosts of the Poles, Czechs, French who never got farther than Cebreiro, remaining there for good.

"We are living all those memories. Even the lowliest Galician peasant. Once the so-called French way fell into disuse, we were never again the same. Our happiness is melancholy, steeped in tears. Don't you see the deep sadness, the *morriña?* When all is said and done, what is it we feel such nostalgia, so many *saudades,* for? It can only be for lost grandeur. A country is soon impoverished when it is robbed of its stories. Or when its children neglect to tell or to invent others in their place. Has it ever occurred to you that there was a time when all of Europe dreamed of us? And that, in yet another time, Castilians, Andalusians, and people from Extremadura composed their works in Galician?"

Xan searched for a shelter for the night, out of the wind. Having brought blankets and other equipment with them, they ought to save the few coins they had. They hunkered down there and ate their sardines and corn bread, cut by Madruga with his grandfather's hunting knife. Madruga was careful not to down the food in the same swallow as the legends. So that they'd enter his body by different channels. Xan reprimanded him. It was necessary to share the bread, the fish, the ham, with the myths, for they deserved to stuff themselves.

"And why not? After all, myths are hungry too. What's more, they never have enough till they've had too much," he said, smiling.

The grandfather applauded the difficulties imposed upon the travelers. One could get to Cebreiro only by way of sacrifices. In winter, for example, the pass was covered with snow and the countryside became niggardly, implacable. But when one spent the night there, in the very epicenter of the shadows and the winds, there was nothing to compare with such a challenge. Not to speak of the fact that the thatched huts there today shed light on how the Celts had lived as they impregnated Galicia with legends. In those days man was everywhere, his body and his imagination his only resources.

"There were fewer laws, my boy. And each man drew up his own code of honor. And so, on meeting up in camp with another man with a like code, they journeyed along together, as accomplices. In this way, countries and groups gradually formed alliances. The same with languages and stories. The stories I always tell in bits and pieces."

In the middle of the night, Xan awakened Madruga, offered him his hand. The two of them were numbed with cold, and the grandson could feel his stiff anklebones. Down below, in the valley, one or two lights could be made out. Xan's heart was touched by his grandson's sudden starts of fear. But Madruga did not have the right to be caught unawares by events. Beginning when Madruga was a little boy, Xan had been preparing him for these intense days. Despite this long apprenticeship, Xan feared that his grandson would overlook the meaning of the pilgrimages to Santiago.

"They were wanderers, men of faith. Death didn't matter to them, once they felt in their mouths, along with piquant foods, the sharp bite of freedom."

Xan's breath reached him with the smell of sardines and oil. Madruga drew closer. He had many doubts during that long night. He wanted to talk to him of the bones of the Apostle, buried in the crypt of the cathedral. To bring up the matter of the lies that cunningly prowl on the edges of legends. The more they were embroidered on, the farther the thread of invention was stretched. But could this fact be morally correct? Mightn't those old Galicians, including Grandfather Xan, be misappropriating reality, staking too much on legends?

Xan expected the question. He had brought his grandson to Cebreiro for that very reason. He was summoning him to the truth; they must not leave there with a false peace in their hearts.

"Speak up, Madruga, don't be afraid you'll hurt my feelings," Xan urged.

Madruga suffered there before Xan. Suddenly he noted in him a soul sufficiently chastened by the age-old duty of telling endless stories. His face showing little knots like the bark of an oak tree. He longed to embrace him, foreseeing a separation soon to come.

"I just wanted to tell you that I learned to dream from you, sir. I will owe my dreams to no one else."

Madruga abruptly let go of Xan's hand, entrusting himself to his own fate now. And turning his back on him, he prepared to sleep.

Madruga has always ruled over the house and the family. At the age of eighty, he retires, after the long battle. They are eighty years of yearning to die. Keeping a close eye on him, death is planning his funeral. And when the time comes, I shall weep for Grandfather, thus anticipating my own death. I never stop watching him, heiress of his solid origins that I am. Divided between three, four women, each suffering the pain of contradiction and of intense affection.

Odete sometimes opens the door for me. Certain that she holds sway over my coming and going. We confine ourselves, however, to discreet, polite formulas. Exchanges barely capable of overcoming an embarrassing social situation. Hence I don't know how to judge Odete's importance. Whether, at her funeral, I shall reveal a sudden respect for her. Do we perhaps count on death to purify feelings kept in that trigger-sprung trap wherein birds and human griefs struggle to free themselves?

Odete has aged in recent years, but her eyes have grown no softer. The fire in them flares up when she merely looks at Eulália. Grandmother begs her to stay with her all the time. They separate only at mealtime and bedtime. Her assigned task in the house is to prove that Eulália is alive and, consequently, Eulália does not excuse her from any of her duties. The one justifies the existence of the other.

Odete came to the house long before I was born. In fact, just after Eulália gave birth to Miguel. Nonetheless Odete does not look after Eulália's grandchildren, nor do they seek her out. They sense that that woman, as black and stiff as a broom handle, has no room in her heart for anyone but Eulália. Madruga, for his part, approved of that devotion that banished him from Eulália's intimate company. When she was with that native, he regarded his wife as being safe from harm. Then too, in his effort to make good in America, an expression he still uses today, his aim has always been to offer Eulália the well-being that he was unable to assure her on their arrival in Brazil as newlyweds, when they spied Venâncio alongside the gangplank, in the scalding-hot sun of the Praça Mauá.

In her first house, Eulália tried her best to learn how to cope with objects, the vegetables and fruits of Brazil. Pricking up her ears, therefore, to pick up the alien sounds coming from her neighbors. She gave proof of her goodwill as she went about making a home, consisting among other things of a table, chairs, and prints of Don Quixote hanging on the wall. Through the knight, she commemorated her people's unsurpassable talent for dreaming.

Aware of the necessity for saving, Eulália helped set aside money that went immediately into the bank. Despite her very best efforts, she was inept at running a household. Above all because she kept thinking of Sobreira. Of the stories recounted by Dom Miguel, with whom she maintained a steady correspondence, in an effort to keep their many plots going, though it was only through gestures and a wide range of vocal resources that they took on their full meaning and flavor. Many a time Eulália went to the kitchen to get dinner started just as she spied Madruga walking in the door, starved and sweaty after a day's work.

At such moments, Madruga would catch Eulália eyeing the kitchen ceiling stained with grease spatters, fixed on a center across which there moved landscapes and scenes visible only to her. An overly abstract world to Madruga. But when Eulália offered him coffee that was too sweet or heavily salted food, he appreciated the effort that had gone into each gesture. All of them originating in a woman whose entire body bore marks of elegance. Capable, therefore, of choosing certain words with a caution that did not stem from a fear of using them, but from the certainty of how needlessly hurtful and treacherous those same words could be. His love for Eulália had undergone changes over the years. Never ceasing, however, to be a love that shielded him from his own folly. It continued to exist in strictest secrecy, outside the narrow confines of the house. He would not allow Eulália to suffer. Her fragile health, and her tendency to daydream, were already quite enough for her to contend with. And above all, he had deprived her of Sobreira, beneath whose blue sky she had been born, where her father had charmed her with the existence of princesses, barons, a clergy at times cunning political schemers, at times soulless oppressors, and endless legends. What else he had deprived her of Madruga never dared ask.

Grandfather was convinced that certain truths that reside in the heart are incommunicable. Any dart launched from that dark, tough recess ended up wounding the breast in which it lodged.

"We are liars from birth, Breta. And condemned by fate to truths that we ourselves do not understand. As though out truths came from scrap iron, from a junk heap. And so we're inhabitants of a ship graveyard, coated with melancholy and rust. The only ones who escape this corrosion are artists. Perhaps because they partially illuminate our tunnels, without fear of encountering debris, monsters, and strange forms without a name, which Eulália calls a soul. I believe that only the possibility of experiencing tragedy would redeem us, Breta. Because tragedy brings truth drenched with blood to light. But who has the courage to pay this price for truth?"

Odete was moving about the house with gestures stolen from Eulália. Developing within these confines a mimicry of which she was proud. She very rarely left the house, and would never give up of her own free will these sheltering walls that isolated her from the world. Eulália, however, urged her to visit her family, to submit to the rule of the little society in the working-class suburb in which she lived.

On Odete's days off, Eulália presented her with a bag of food and clothes for the family. They ought not to go without the necessities. Her family consisting of her mother, an aunt, and her niece, the daughter of an only sister crushed to death beneath the wheels of a Leopoldina train. This niece not being able to contribute to the household expenses, all her wages as a worker in a textile industry going for cosmetics, clothes, and lunches. Not to mention the weekly visit to a beauty parlor, where she had her hair, as kinky as Odete's, straightened.

Eulália often felt sorry for Odete's niece, unresigned to her condition as a black. On these occasions, she manifested visible surprise that no one in this family had visited Odete's after her many years in the house. She knew them by name and through Odete's descriptions. But even though Odete reluctantly revealed certain details, she withheld others from her so as not to submit her past life to her judgment. In the face of such secret feelings, Eulália resigned herself to the empty spaces surrounding the figure of Odete.

Madruga criticized her for complaining. "And what difference would it make to have a more intimate knowledge of them, if they're exactly as Odete described them?" he said testily.

On perceiving that he had hurt his wife, who averted her eyes at such times, Madruga hastily apologized. Insisting, however, on the uselessness of inviting them to the house.

"And where would they have lunch, Eulália? If we take them to the living room, or the veranda, we embarrass them and us at the same time. They'll end up in the pantry, where Odete eats even today."

Tobias, present at the discussion, reproached his father. He accused him of having betrayed his own origins.

Madruga was furious. "You and Breta lie more than I do. You only fight for the changes that don't take away any of your privileges. You're both colonizers and exploiters. The only thing you don't exploit is the individual who lives in misery. Venâncio, for example, is the only innocent one of all of us. He still hasn't noticed that his pension is doing its best to kill him before his own death. What's more, it's a second death, crueler than the first one."

With a discreet gesture, Eulália hinted that he should lower his voice. Odete mustn't hear him or have her feelings hurt.

"So you think, then, that Odete doesn't know that she's a sort of servant in this house, without a future and without the right to choose? It's a disgrace to be black and poor in this country!"

Odete seemed oblivious of her condition. Perhaps because of her unusual status, whereby she spent long hours in the intimacy of the master bedroom. Although she was obliged to return to the kitchen at mealtimes. Where she ate hurriedly, eager to be close to Eulália once more, keeping her company till after dinner.

They parted at night, Odete yielding her place to Madruga, who never complained of the situation established years before. In her ample quarters, the former sewing room, Odete watched the hours go by. She was the first to awaken, expecting to find Eulália waiting for her coffee. In recent years, they were in the habit of attending Mass together each day. With such occupations, Odete's spirit, at least in appearance, shielded itself from any sort of examination. Permanently on guard against anyone who might try to open her eyes to a social reality that favored a few, and led the majority into exile. Undoubtedly her dreams, boxed up inside Eulália's, were responsible for her apathy.

Odete would not have worried about what would happen to her family during a visit to the house. Especially since the kitchen seemed to her a grand place, where tasty dishes were made. They might well be served on chinaware and with cutlery ordinarily used at table. She never found fault with the contrasts between the common rooms and the pantry. On the contrary, she identified with Madruga's fortune, the fruit of insane work, grubbing for money on the streets from the age of thirteen. After vowing to transform his America into a seedbed of works that would produce goods and illusions.

In the bosom of the family, with Eulália, Madruga masked the cruel and bloody face of reality. Avoiding doing business at home. Though for the children the dining room table was frequently an extension of his office. They sat around it for hours. All of them especially concerned now about Jango Goulart's activities in the office of president. It was clear to them that the President threatened to alter the essence of his own regime. Prompting strikes, as meanwhile he formed ties with union groups and labor sectors on the left, already working openly. With popular leaders such as Brizola and Arraes in the forefront of these movements. The country on the verge of social and economic destabilization.

Moreover, as a consequence of this grave crisis, the sailors began to demolish the basic principles of military hierarchy, turning the rigid order of the naval barracks upside down. The presidency of the Republic serving, however, as a stage for the promotion of a social model to be implanted in the country, and oriented toward the left. A new Cuba on the continent, this time affecting a country as important as Brazil. The beginning, finally, of anarchy, spawning insecurity and unrest.

"We'll soon have a dictatorship. Either of the left or of the right. You can tell by the stench. It's the same stench as always. It hasn't changed," Madruga said.

Tobias's vision of things was the opposite of his father's. The process under way aimed only at the independence of the country and the dismantling of the authoritarian social model, which tended to reproduce itself without limit. And invariably, to sanction repressive principles, unfortunately deep-seated in all social classes at this juncture. And against this de facto situation Arraes and Brizola were rising up in arms.

"Even the Brazilian slave was educated to be overbearing and despotic. Since birth we've been placed at odds with the most elementary democratic principles. Nobody's escaped the false cunt and the dominating prick. And this on an endless scale."

Madruga nervously suggested that his son change sides and join Brizola, who was preaching to the nation and enrolling disciples. But Tobias ought at least to be certain of the choice made. He, personally, would be against lawlessness and the creation of chaos.

"Chaos engenders nothing but despotism, Tobias," Madruga said.

"Rather chaos than dictatorship and systematic opposition to progress, father. A well-behaved country refuses to accept the emancipating rules of imagination. There is only one kingdom to serve, that of insubordination and the imaginary. Any military or even liberal ruler ought, therefore, to be banished. On the other hand, we should consecrate and anoint those who are at once statesmen and poets. It is not possible to live with social justice unless there is also a clear poetic mission for reality. King

Dom Diniz is an excellent example of what I am saying. And I repeat once more: outside of the establishment of poetic rules with which to mark off the world, perdition and public scorn lie in store for us," Tobias said, all upset, leaving the room without hearing his father out.

Madruga allowed Eulália to console him. He unburdened himself with her. "These children of ours are tied to us by affection and money. If we offer them only affection we'll lose them, Eulália."

In recent years, on other days than Sundays, Venâncio paid them brief visits. Sometimes he sat down in the living room only long enough to have a cup of coffee. And in order that they would note how harried he was by time, an ever-conspicuous consumer, he then took his leave immediately.

"You'd think you had ants in your pants," Madruga complained.

It pleased Venâncio to resist Grandfather's plea to stay. "I only happened to drop by to find out how you were. Since you're fine, I can go back home." And he accepted the offer of another cup of coffee, thus avoiding Madruga's eye.

"Well now, Venâncio, if a person just happens to come by, he's heading somewhere else. Where are you going, may I ask, after these fifteen minutes?" Madruga asked insistently, turning a deaf ear to Venâncio's explanations that over the years his own house had come to be his favorite nesting place.

That disparaging remark struck Madruga as being intolerable. Before Venâncio could get to his feet, he had a snack brought, so as to make him his prisoner. He refused to accept the idea that it was Venâncio's privilege to decide out of sheer caprice which days were visiting days. Venâncio might drag him out to the edge of the city just to take his temperature.

"Whatever did we do to you, Venâncio, to make you want to clear out of this living room without so much as a by-your-leave?" he said, feeling let down.

When Venâncio smiled, discreetly as always, his teeth, tiny ones as a matter of fact, scarcely showed. The same smile with which he disembarked in Rio de Janeiro, determined to step onto Brazilian soil with his left foot first. Thus refusing to share Madruga's superstitions. The weight of the legends and the fantasies of his Spanish village which he had abandoned forever, the moment the ship pulled out from Vigo, were quite enough for him.

"I left Spain like someone who shatters a legend into a thousand pieces because he's lost all confidence in it," Venâncio confessed to me one afternoon, just before Grandfather came to join us in the living room. I was not able to ask him for more details. Venâncio immediately gave the impression of regretting having shared a confidence.

Venâncio's reserve was touching. But as soon as Eulália had come to America, he brought her wildflowers on Sundays. Eulália had the pitcher filled with water all ready. She received the flowers and smelled them in an age-old ritual. By coincidence, these flowers, on the sideboard, always faded very slowly.

He, however, was reluctant to accept her presents. The guava paste from Campos in particular, in a red tin decorated with a leaf pattern. Expecting his visit, Eulália went to buy it herself, worried that there might not be any in the kitchen pantry. It was Venâncio's favorite sweet, which Eulália offered him, foreseeing that he would refuse in the beginning merely to oblige her to plead with him. As though there were a permanent agreement between them that Eulália would never take his no for an answer. After this ceremony, Venâncio would clasp the tin to his chest, as though it were a book, holding it there till all of a sudden he would rise to his feet, making as though to leave.

On certain dates, Christmas for example, she tried to embrace him, despite the fact that Venâncio reacted as though he had been painfully bitten. Thus warning her not to insist the next time. She forgot, however, in her eagerness to offer him proof of her respect and that of Madruga, the friend in whose company Venâncio had stepped onto American soil with practically the same foot, the same old shoes, the same visible hole in the sole.

Venâncio was becoming the other half of Madruga, a half full of shy reserve, fearful of embracing Eulália, as though by virtue of that exchange of heat his joints would ache. Inflamed by Grandmother's feverish fingers.

Madruga accompanied him to the door. Though they were at odds with each other, their uneasiness clearly visible. Each with a different gait, Madruga ever resolute, Venâncio now hesitant, watching out for the roots that he could tell existed beneath his shoes. And because of the mismatched pace, Madruga arrived at the door first. Pleased at having accentuated the difference between them.

As they made their way along, Madruga insisted that Venâncio allow the chauffeur to drive him to Quintino. Venâncio's voice, never very resonant, became almost inaudible when he was forced to refuse. On the pretext that he ought to walk. At his age his legs risked turning stiff. Hinting thereby that Madruga had lost the use of his own members by choosing to have a car take him everywhere, like an invalid.

Madruga could see Venâncio's itinerary in his mind's eye. First the bus, then the train. Listening in both to the popular gossip going the rounds.

"They're my sort, Madruga," Venâncio said proudly.

These words had the effect of irritating Madruga. They struck him as being petty innuendos, Venâncio sinking a dart in his chest, fighting against a fortune that, in his words again, occupied a solid place in his heart. In this state of mind, they bade each other good-bye. Madruga about to take refuge in his office.

Once reconciled with Venâncio, Madruga stood in the doorway

watching him till he was out of sight. Moved at noting how his footsteps were growing wearier by the day. He remembered then the heroic times that both of them had been caught up in.

Thus moved, he wanted to run and catch up with him. Just to say to him: What is it you're accusing me of, Venâncio, if I too had a dream? Or is it a dream, this nightmare that's pinned you to the ground, like an octopus with a thousand tentacles, never allowing life to embrace you?

Venâncio troubled Grandfather's conscience. And so, trying to banish him from his mind, Madruga dissuaded his children from following the paths of failure and disillusionment. Not allowing certain acts and details to prejudice their future.

Eulália sensed from a distance the constraint between the two of them. She then discreetly offered herself as intercessor. Whereupon Madruga, one afternoon, abruptly sheared her of that pretension.

"It's no use, Eulália. The problem is that Venâncio wasn't born in Galicia. That's the difference between us. He's a stranger to me at times," he said, anxious to free himself of a friendship that suddenly weighed heavily upon him. A painful burden perhaps.

Grandfather's spiteful pride shocked Eulália. Disillusioned, she sat down out on the veranda, pretending not to see me.

"Which one is going to bury the other first?" And feeling herself under close scrutiny, she averted her face. In effect dismissing my testimony.

"What difference does it make, grandma? One of them must endure the pain of the other's absence."

She appeared to be moved. She sincerely believed that all affection stemmed from a natural impulse to save a person who was foundering.

There were odd bits and pieces concerning Madruga and Venâncio that I did not know how to use. I did not want, however, either to tarnish or to embellish their respective biographies. They themselves were the first to lash out at each other. Simply to establish contrary positions. Two opposite poles of light. The two of them, nonetheless, forming a mosaic that could be better appreciated at a distance. When the disturbing play of colors would work in favor of both. Seen from up close, however, the overall picture was affected by the visible imperfections in the individual chipped stones.

Together with Madruga, I saw that my appraisal was limited and therefore faulty. And that I was incapable of sharing with my neighbor an immovable point of view.

"Do you know what the fundamental defect of reality is, grandfather? It's that it keeps us from seeing reality."

Madruga smiled. His granddaughter too was certain that stories deriving from intimate human contact were products distilled from falsehood and ambiguity. There thus being no way to reconcile Madruga's and Venâncio's interests. Even though they had been born in Spain in the same year. The same sun burning their chests when they took cattle up to the mountain on a certain occasion. Their sex throbbing in their trousers at the same time. Their penises swollen by the sick passion for life when they dreamed of the neighbor girl's vagina. A life now escaping them each day. As they rebelled against this larceny as though endless years of life still lay ahead of them, and hearts eternally aflame. And the pleasure, vague and ill-defined, of awakening in the morning, voracious, rapacious brigands.

Odete repaid Grandmother's attentions with rare diligence. Not allowing her name to be uttered a second time once an order had been given. In truth, she anticipated her mistress's desires. All her pride centered on Eulália's universe.

She remained for hours at a time in Eulália's room, sitting on the carpet alongside the bed or on the chair. The two of them spoke in whispers. In that retreat, as peaceful as a garden, their affection expanded. As though there would be no end to her time for staying in the room, from which she would be systematically banished once Madruga appeared, at about ten o'clock, even though a word for Eulália was just then hovering on her lips.

At Madruga's entrance, Odete rose immediately to her feet. And without so much as a glance, the one took the place of the other. She transferring to Madruga the responsibilities for Eulália. Turning the bed over to Madruga to occupy.

Madruga gave no signs of impatience with Odete. Both kept up an impeccable show of politeness. Odete's one repository for her troubles was Eulália. And it was not easy to filter out her emotions. It was necessary to look deep within her thin face to see it succumb to emotion. To all appearances, Odete was bursting with pride over her niece. Applauding her rebellion against fate, which had caused her to be born black, condemned to esthetic exile. Her niece therefore throwing money hand over fist buying cosmetics. With the illusion that she was thereby concealing her ethnic background. Perhaps dreaming as well of the covetousness of the white man. Being the object of a desire that would free her from social slavery. On this hunting expedition the niece depriving herself of nothing, perfumes, marcelled hair, dresses in the latest style, waggling her hips and buttocks, both located in zones on the very edge of lust. A lust that, once glimpsed by the white hunter, might impel him to uproot the niece from the hillsides of the *favela* so as to savor her for a time. Freeing her at last of the five-gallon tin of water atop her head, and of the functions of her own uterus, working away up there like a machine in need of oil.

Eulália finally gave Odete a house as a present. Odete insisted on depositing the deed to the building in Eulália's strongbox, along with the jewels. So as to confer on the house the same importance as the stories surrounding each of Eulália's jewels. And in order to please Eulália, she told her how her mother, in the face of the dream of her own house come true, had cried so hard during the move that she was hours late arriving at her new home with its gleaming modern kitchen and bathroom.

Despite the comfort of the new house and her love for her family, Odete came back exhausted from her days off. The bitterness in her face took from two to three days to disappear. Her state was such that Eulália wanted to suggest to her no more than a monthly visit, so as to spare her from being so inexplicably upset. Lacking the courage, however, she confined herself to treating her like a woman who had escaped enemies, in whose flesh the marks of bondage were still visible.

On one occasion Odete did not return. Nothing being known of her in the days that followed. Eulália slept badly. Worried about Odete, who had never behaved in this way. In fact, she had accustomed them to perfection. Madruga made up his mind to send an employee to Odete's house, a suggestion that Eulália vehemently rejected. How could a stranger be sent to track Odete down, just to see if she'd died! It was the family who ought to take on this task. Should there be no volunteer, she was ready and willing to face the difficult test herself. Madruga hurriedly delegated the mission to me, however. Confident of the steps his granddaughter would take.

Odete's house, in Inhaúma, was not far from the hill where she had always lived. She herself had chosen the house on a paved street. All painted white, with a small front yard. All well cared for, reflecting Odete's taste.

I checked the number again, so as not to knock on the wrong door. It embarrassed me to be there, about to see Odete, from whom I had never gathered evidence of friendship. Suddenly, however, far from this enduring indifference wounding me, I felt a strange admiration for the poor black woman, in whom I discerned, for the first time, a strong streak of independence. Resolutely choosing whom to love. The opposite of me, who accepted false affections, displeasing caresses, friendly exchanges with enemies, acts in short that tore away living pieces of my heart.

"Are you looking for someone, senhora?" a man said.

I mentioned Odete's name and he pointed to the whitewashed house. I went through the yard and knocked on the door. With the shutters closed, nothing could be seen through the slits. I heard feet shuffling to the door. The key screaked, resisting. Finally Odete's frightened face appeared. She blinked her eyes repeatedly to correct her distorted vision, refusing to believe what she saw.

"What are you doing here?" Her voice trembled.

We looked at each other for a long time. She inside the house, I with one foot in the door.

"May I come in?"

Odete didn't budge. But on perceiving that she would not be able to drive me away, she let me into the house. In the living room, in darkness, the television set lighted my way to the sofa, from where the table and four chairs could be seen. Accustomed now to the darkness, I admired several landscapes on the wall. There was not a trace of a human presence in the room. Undoubtedly the mother, intimidated by strangers, had gone off to the bedroom. Odete, however, insisted on keeping the room dark, so that life in the outside world would not disturb her.

Settling on the sofa, I prepared to talk, to get to know a member of the family. Odete sat down farther away, her eyes fixed on the china cupboard. The two of us all alone, she on the defensive. Immersed in a silence so disturbing that I hastened to deposit the money on the table.

"It's for medicine and the doctor. If you need more, Odete, you have only to speak up. You know how fond Grandmother is of you. She won't allow you to lack for anything."

Odete didn't budge, sheltered beneath an inaccessible pride. The silence, however, appeared to make her uneasy. She moved over to the chair closest to the sofa. Even so, there was still a profound distance between us. And it seemed to me that I suddenly glimpsed Odete's Brazil, torrential and incomprehensible, well on the other side. With a miserable face, forlorn and obedient. Capable nonetheless of reproducing itself for the purpose of rendering service to those who, from the other shore of the river, contemplated everything and lost sight of nothing.

Confronting that statue of salt, I saw myself reluctantly returning Odete to the slave quarter, from which her family had come in the past. I too now beat her black skin, made her life a martyrdom each day. As though it gave me pleasure to lie each morning, simply to avoid plunging into the dark hiding places of my soul and probe the privileges of my class. I was sitting there feigning a kindly indulgence that offended Odete and myself.

Nor do I know what temptation I succumbed to. Because Odete's feeling of constraint was not enough to satisfy me. Aware of the prerogatives of my class, and aware that life belonged to us, I forged resolutely ahead.

"Where is your mother? And your aunt? May I meet them?" I said, not hiding my curiosity. Did I at least feel pain when I plunged the knife into her chest? After all, were these not my people, though their misery was not mine?

Odete went out into the hall, not returning to the living room for some time. She was naturally draping the mother and the aunt in protective coverings. Or perhaps tricking them out to look their best, anxious to bring about a meeting of our respective houses, which the two of us represented.

She came back to the living room, bringing a tray with coffee. The first sign of hospitality. Or was she bribing me to forget my request? The cups, presents from Grandmother, were spotless. I sampled her coffee with pleasure. She had absorbed certain refinements from Eulália. I returned the cup to the tray, in the hopes of a final spectacle. Odete owed me a ritual whose performance had now become inevitable.

I noted her even more pronounced pallor. "Do you want me to call the doctor? To go to the pharmacy?" I hastily asked, filled with concern.

Odete looked at the Swiss mountains hanging on the wall. That European landscape in Inhaúma and Odete's visible distress upset me. I did not know how to remedy the situation. I felt it would be a discourtesy now to leave in haste or forsake her family. Or was Odete feeling ill at ease because she was ashamed of her mother and aunt? Did she so thoroughly despise her wretched African origin? Or did she suspect that I would reject her black Brazilian family, wanting them to be fair and beautiful and possessed of the unquestionable gift of speech?

My tongue sat heavily in my mouth along with the taste of coffee. And the silence made us feel ill-disposed toward each other. Who could help us? We heard a faint knock at the door. Odete looked intently at the clock on the wall, pretending not to hear. More knocks followed. Finally Odete opened the door and a plump lady entered, bearing a steaming tureen. With a self-assured gesture, she set it down on the table, immediately grabbing the tablecloth and place settings off the shelf.

"Hurry, Odete, before the soup gets cold," she said. Only then did she notice me there on the sofa. "I beg your pardon, I didn't know Odete had a visitor." She paused. Then decided to go on. "We here are very fond of Odete. We never leave her by herself. What's more, we take care of her as though she were one of the family."

Odete let the woman leave, forgetting to thank her or accompany her to the door. I averted my eyes, so as not to surprise Odete's look of grief. The entire family suddenly dead, wiped out by the plague.

"Go on, Odete, help yourself before it gets cold. I'm on my way." I made a move to leave, using the soup as a pretext.

With a gesture, she motioned me back to the sofa. "Stay, Breta. Please."

Her eyes bulging, she stretched out her right arm asking for help. I went to her and she flung herself on the floor, her arms about my body, auscultating my belly with her head. Her sobs resounded all through me as she was buffeted by my ragged breathing. Slowly, I fingered her kinky hair, so soft and delicate that I was deeply moved. As though I had journeyed through Africa with her. There Africa was, resting firmly in the middle of my belly. The Africa that had borne us and cradled us, and that we were ashamed of. But who were we after all, an arrogant, mongrel people, to suppose we had the right to choose a land, to mark off areas of exile, and settle masters and slaves in them?

At that moment, it was all too much for me. I experienced toward

Odete a feeling as powerful as the one that assailed me when the thought came to me that I had Brazil in my hands, my body, my own genitals. It seemed to me then, in those hours of emotion, that Brazil palpated me with exaggeratedly minute precision, not scrupling to penetrate even the intimate parts of my body, going up inside my vagina, where it turned round and round, exhausting itself, till finally it left me alone. Incapable, however, despite its enormous territory, of containing all of me. Me or anyone else. But could that be true? Or would Odete, the fucked and desperate Brazilian woman, in fact be able to point out to us the hard roads to our origin, thus becoming the only one to reestablish the ties of a society and of a language that threatened to give way beneath the weight of so many contradictory and confused feelings?

"Stay on my belly, Odete," I said finally, deeply moved.

The woman's weeping spread through the house. She kept shedding words, teeth, saliva, mucus, amid her story. Dramatically begun on the third day after birth, when they left her at the door of the orphanage. The one who bore her did not have the courage to throw her on the trash heap or down the privy. But though they did not want her in the house, she fought for her life. And so she grew up an orphan, among strangers.

"In the beginning, they called me Ana. At the age of ten, the directress found this odd. Whoever heard of a little Creole girl answering to the name of Mary's mother? So then they began to call me Odete, the name of the cook who lived there many years, till she ran off with the stonemason hired, as it happened, for the job of raising the height of the wall over which several girls had managed to make their escape in recent years."

When Odete was thirteen, two spinster sisters took her to live with them. In return for services rendered, they saw to it that she kept her virtue. So that her body would be more untouchable than theirs. At the same time they were stingy, rigorously measuring out every spoonful of sugar. Till, unable to bear such hardships, she looked around for another house. And yet another after that, till Eulália took her in, and offered her the first affection in her life. In the form of a warmth that, on mounting to her temples, made them pound.

"And why didn't you ever tell us, Odete?"

She had considered it. But when she took a liking to the house, the desire came over her to do everything possible to strengthen the affection that Eulália was beginning to bestow upon her. She feared that her ignoble birth, her orphanhood, would offend the delicate sensibilities of Eulália, so beloved of Dom Miguel, there in far-off Sobreira. And so she had invented a family for herself, and by so doing automatically come to believe in it. The mother and the aunt immediately turned into the model of a dream. To the point that the imaginary niece disgusted her, at times, with her shameless frivolity.

The sister's sham funeral caused her to shed tears as she went into mourning for her. But the worst thing of all was going out to the *favela* every two weeks. In the beginning, she would lock herself up in the hovel, especially rented for the purpose, as she waited for Sunday to end at last. No day made her happier than Monday. She would run down the hill before arriving back at the house, and then on the train she would be overcome by an emotion experienced only in those moments. One that left her, on the other hand, with a pallor that worried Eulália, who kept giving her remedies, as though sensing intuitively that life, for secret reasons, had wounded Odete more deeply than she could bear.

I forced Odete, on her knees there before me, to rise to her feet. She resisted, amid humble pleas.

"For the love of God, do you swear that Dona Eulália will never know? And less still Senhor Madruga? Nobody, only you. Swear, Breta!"

I recalled Odete's departures on Saturdays. Eulália hurriedly handing her the bagful of presents. Both obeying a ritual that went back many years. And that would one day be interrupted when Odete decided to announce the mother's death. For this was a pain she was not about to deprive herself of. Eager to bury the mother with pomp and ceremony. Shortly thereafter, she would lose the aunt, far along in years. Then the niece would get married, going to live in Pirenópolis, Goiás.

Finally, Odete rose to her feet. I came one step toward her, and took her in my arms. I embraced her as if I were embracing the miserable Brazilians who pass through me without my paying them any attention.

"Yes, I promise, Odete. Nobody will know. To all intents and purposes, I had coffee with your mother, your aunt, your niece. I embraced your worthy family."

And I ran away as fast as my legs would carry me.

He never lost the habit. At five in the morning, Venâncio was always up. And this had been so ever since he had arrived in America, as he still continued to call Brazil. He made fresh filtered coffee, heated the milk, and sitting at the kitchen table, dunked his buttered bread in the hot liquid, as though he had no teeth. He gave up this habit temporarily only in Eulália's presence.

In the early morning quiet, seemingly the only person alive, it was as though time, for him, would never run out. He would sit at the table for hours on end, now that he had retired and had no obligations to fulfill. Only to wake up, look at the sun, and go back to sleep when it was dark.

In all truth, Venâncio's mind was only too inclined to wander. Even in the early days when they lived together, Madruga often pointed this out to him, on coming upon him sitting in front of the stove, stewing his thoughts, unwilling to plunk his feet on the floor and get moving.

The little house, in the stifling working-class suburb, had a yard at the back, with fruit trees whose branches reached to the neighbor's wall. Behind the kitchen, near the cistern, the cement covering the area had begun to crack from the pressure of an expanding mango tree. The very spot where Venâncio spent his mornings reading, sitting in the chaise longue, a present from Eulália. He went out less and less. He did the household shopping himself, however. And for a modest sum the woman next door provided his lunch.

From the veranda of the house, in the mornings, Venâncio could hear the news vendor sliding back the iron grille of his kiosk, a familiar sound that automatically sent him down to get the papers. And then he would sit reviewing the ongoing life of the country and the world, with an expression on his face conveying no sign of outward interest or worry. Nothing was of any concern to him now. And he seldom looked at his watch. He learned what hour of the day it was by way of subtle attunements to reality. Through the sound of the factory whistle as the workday began, or through his next-door neighbor, shouting from the doorway to let his wife know he was home for lunch. Venâncio knew then that it was noon. But the train whistle, not far off, disconcerted him. It scorned schedules and the ugly, undernourished people jammed into its cars. Whom he looked at with unlimited patience when he went to Madruga's house. A less faithful visitor now, despite Madruga's protests.

He had almost no callers. Now and again a neighbor would knock on his door to ask to borrow a box of matches. Or a child would come for the ball that had landed next to the hundred-year-old mango tree. His few friends had begun to die off. The ones who were left acted as though they were dead. Having renounced their own lives, they mentioned the names of grandchildren misled by familial virtues. And finding them always by themselves, lonely and dejected, Venâncio avoided them.

Eulália was the only one to talk to him of Spain. Through her he was certain that Spain was still alive, attached to the map of the world by a thin steel thread, visible only if he made a special effort. Beset by doubts, he would consult her. Whereupon Eulália, proud of conferring existence upon the far-off homeland, would artfully depict it in vivid colors, to the point that she was moved and interested by this country that had just been born thanks to her diligence and skill.

Venâncio's retirement severely restricted his budget. Hence all the fruit, cheese, and sweets forthcoming from Madruga, despite his protests. Venâncio, however, had learned to anticipate certain facts. At the sign of any weakness in his organism, he went off to the clinic of the Spanish

Benefit Society. So as to spare the neighbors nasty surprises. He felt uneasy at the thought of bothering them in the middle of the night sometime, because of the stench his body might give off. He was cheered by the hope that the news vendor on the corner would notice if he failed to come by for his papers for two days in a row.

At a distance, he loved postmen, so often the bearers of bad news. He had always seen them flying through the streets, borne on wings. Carrying on their backs a weight distributed over the whole of humanity. As they conveyed the illusion that the countries of the Orient and invincible beloved faces in fact existed. And to this the letters were witness.

At the hour when the postman came by, Venâncio interrupted his reading. He went out onto the veranda to greet him with a slight nod of his head. No public servant knew his name. Since there was no one nowadays who would write him even one letter, the postman did not knock on his door. He remembered, however, the days when there were people who wrote to him. At once saddened and elated, he received and sent back word of developments involving the two continents separated by the Atlantic.

On Wednesdays, Madruga's chauffeur came round to get news of him. Till Tobias forced Venâncio to let a telephone be installed, which would allow them to get in touch with him immediately. This fact proving especially reassuring to Madruga, Venâncio's deliberate isolation being not at all to his liking.

Venâncio's visits fulfilled the agreement made in the first years in America. The two friends acted as though they lived in adjoining houses, thus dispensing with formalities and the performance of a daunting ritual. Now and again, giving proof of an intimacy which nonetheless left no room for any sort of abuse, Venâncio would go to Leblon, yet after the usual politenesses, stay no more than fifteen minutes. The attitude of a neighbor, who has only to cross the street to knock at another's door.

Madruga shied away from sounding out the reasons for this behavior. He forced himself to find it only natural that Venâncio, arriving from the suburbs, should stay at the house just long enough to say hello to them. Finally, in latter years, they scarcely spoke to each other. Had it not been for the presence of Eulália, they would have skipped the polite phrases indispensable for proper social interchange. The rare words uttered did not suffice to threaten the silence now permanent between them. But when exactly had they ceased to speak to each other? And what had they said to each other in the past, and what was an entire life worth, now that it was about to unite them forever?

In the days when Venâncio frequented the Lyrico, it gave him pleasure to approach Madruga, just so he could be quizzed. And still beneath the spell of the dream that Eulália always set him to dreaming on Sundays, he tried to share with her such information as would interest her. Which in truth was intended, rather, for Madruga, who plied him with questions.

"What about Fleta, is he already past his prime?" he said anxiously. Madruga fearing that the tenor had come merely to offer Brazilians what Spain no longer wanted to receive from him.

Even in his bachelor days, Madruga rarely accompanied him to the Lyrico. He preferred to spend his money in the cabarets in the Lapa district. Certain of finding the Brazilian soul there, stripped of affectations and exaggerated politenesses, intent only on opening the floodgates of instinct. As he himself would allow his body to explode with pleasure.

Madruga's tales about his nocturnal exploits made Venâncio practically gasp for breath, vicariously sharing his friend's intense sexual pleasure. Both thus suddenly bursting into loud nervous laughter, contained only by the knock on the wall of a neighbor bothered by the noise in the middle of the night.

"The body is an unbroken filly, Venâncio. So it has to be tamed. If I don't take steps, there won't be a lasso that can corral it. And alas, the soul also bolts, with disastrous consequences. I'll end up possessing an imagination worse than yours."

Both avoided confidences that might wound their respective sensibilities. Between them were areas of dissension ready to erupt should they throw caution to the winds. They therefore cultivated a discreet reserve immediately extended to Eulália following Madruga's marriage.

Madruga saw the 1930 coup coming. The political crisis that would seek solutions through new onslaughts on the Constitution. And this because he had armed himself with information supplied by recent friends, all of them rising rapidly in the world. Silveira being the comet to whose tail Madruga clung with special pride. A gaucho from Alegrete, Silveira was forging a brilliant political career. No one had foreseen his arrival on the scene. Perhaps he would one day occupy the presidency of the Republic, an honor hitherto never conferred upon a gaucho of pure stock such as he.

Ablaze with enthusiasm, Silveira guaranteed him, in the middle of a stein of draft beer in the Bar Adolfo, in the Rua da Carioca, that the movement then in gestation, carrying in its belly the profound dissatisfaction of the country over the events taking place, would explode by 1930. That year was the outside date. Pressed by Madruga for details supporting these prophecies, Silveira laughed, expecting to be urged on by his listener. Knowing this weakness, Madruga mentioned his talent, his bird-dog flair, that allowed him to catch a scent underneath a door, till Silveira added that Brazil would no longer put up with the affront of Washington Luís and company, who, in flagrant disregard of the agreement between Minas and São Paulo, whereby this time it was Minas's turn to have its presidential choice favored, had put up Júlio Prestes as a candidate, thereby flying in the face of a power previously shared and sanctioned by the political classes in whose hands the decision in fact lay. And besides that, Júlio

Prestes had to his detriment the stigma of elegance, wealth, and good looks.

Following his daily trip to the Passeio Público and the Biblioteca Nacional, Venâncio went to Madruga, seeking information. The latter suspected that very shortly a number of Brazilian states would rebel. Some of this news had been hard to come by. To do so Madruga had made it a habit to wander about Cinelândia and the Hotel Central, dropping by the Bar Simpatia, where he would strike up a conversation with strangers and acquaintances alike.

Because of his status as an immigrant, Madruga had recently made his way into a sphere where information having to do with the power structure circulated quickly, spreading the dung of an invariably distorted truth. To all appearances, Venâncio applauded the advance of the opposition. Excited by the possibility that social privileges would be abolished. Above all that the country would soon undergo a dramatic political mobilization, paving the way for a break with current models and practices. In his opinion deserving to be condemned, according to the facts concerning Brazil that he had collected thus far.

Madruga, however, was against such prognostications. These many changes would be bound to affect the life of immigrants, a people with no legal recourse, no forum to appeal to, in case of necessity or emergency. A corrupt and resentful internal revenue agent was quite enough to make their lives hell. Or a police official, entering their names on the list of immigrants to be ordered out of the country with no right of appeal.

He had not forgotten the iniquities perpetrated by the planters of the state of São Paulo against Italian immigrants. Arriving in the country with the illusion that they would make a fortune, the hapless Italians had become victims of an implacable system, a concerted plan to reduce them almost to the condition of slaves, as a substitute for black labor. Moreover, they lived like servants at the hands of the coffee growers. This being the case, how could Venâncio talk to him about social changes that would somehow benefit them! Them or the people! That argument was surely limited to those in power.

"Anybody who speaks of the people runs the risk of being lynched, Venâncio. I advise you to watch what you say in the cafés. Don't forget that we're immigrants, who carry that idiotic Type 19 card. Subject to expulsion at the drop of a hat. Our protests worth nothing." The words came out through clenched teeth in Madruga's impatience with Venâncio's naïveté. A fool who allowed himself to be led into a trap time and again.

Madruga's admonitions did not prevent Venâncio from cultivating a new passion, the movies. Above all the mysterious silhouette of Greta Garbo, whose expression on the screen devastated him. He now divided his money between the Lyrico and tickets to the movies. The faces projected on the screen in front of him brought discreet tears to his eyes. An invention, that, meant to make a person daydream all the more. Just what Brazil needed.

He insisted that Madruga go with him to hear Chaliapin, performing in person. Madruga refused to accompany him. Beneath the calm that reigned at the moment, something was about to happen. Silveira, a member of the Chamber of Deputies, again hinted to him that Rio Grande, Minas, and Paraíba were already up in arms. How to appreciate the great Chaliapin in such circumstances!

He felt nervous, threatened. And during that very week his fourth child was born. Altogether different from Venâncio, whose responsibilities were limited to himself, since he had decided to shun marriage. For him too Brazil was a utopia, an argument he used whenever he wanted to avoid committing himself.

"What do you mean, a utopia?" Madruga asked, good-humoredly, enjoying roast kid with chicory salad. "Can the two of us be talking about the same utopia?"

In this unstable period, Venâncio almost never left him. Ready to help him if need be. In the face of the threat of a civil war, it was necessary to take steps, seek refuge, save the family. Both thought it prudent for Venâncio to sleep at the house during this time. Eulália immediately found a place for him where he'd be comfortable, near the children.

The country was living through difficult moments. The severe aftershocks of the crash of the New York stock market reached them with a thundering roar. Though suicide was not as frequent in São Paulo as in New York, where a number of people had leaped from skyscrapers at the same time, countless families had been ruined. Madruga prospered, however, despite the economic crisis. He had recently bought a row of tenements, intending to erect a three-story building on the site. And because he had confidence in Brazil, he was contemplating setting up a factory. His dream and his future were pointing in the direction of industry.

Venâncio had become Madruga's agent for accounts received and receivable and enjoyed his absolute confidence. The reason being that Venâncio refused to accept a partnership or a share in the profits. Having no wish to assume major responsibilities.

"I'm your employee. And that's enough for me. You can throw me out on the street whenever you like. We'll never quarrel over money," Venâncio repeated any number of times.

The partnership with González was limited to the initial businesses. González did not participate in the other rapidly expanding undertakings. Madruga had perceived that Brazil, still immersed in the rural world, was badly in need of the opening of new areas of production. The simultaneous creation and turnover of capital. Hence with no need to remain dependent on a single investment, subject to the risk of being buried by the evolution of time. He was working as he never had before, enjoying the family very little. With the exception of Sundays, when he shut himself up in the study, after dinner, to be among his books, papers, and bottles with colored labels. His ambition was to have a costly wine cellar, with choice vintages.

Although he suffered restrictions because of his status as an immigrant, he had observed that the Brazilian bourgeoisie, almost the whole of it of Portuguese background, preferred to do business with Iberians, taking them also as a model of industriousness and honesty, to the disadvantage of the poor native, a mixture of white, black, and indigenous. It being an advantage in the end to be a white immigrant, with blue eyes to boot.

His confidence thus bolstered, Madruga nonetheless proceeded cautiously, never revealing his intentions. He got on closer terms with them, to listen to them, learn their methods, their double-dealing ways. Above all he mastered the art of the tactical retreat, counterattacking only from a position of strength. The clever men of that country were noted for their habit of letting a conversation go on for hours without a concrete proposal ever clearly taking shape. In Brazil, it was not recommended to go straight to the heart of the matter. It was necessary first to prevaricate, to camouflage, to set up false coordinates. Styles of discourse imbedded in action. Anyone who violated these norms was liable to lose his reputation as a negotiator. Besides giving proof of discourtesy. A mode of being at which Madruga rapidly became an expert, like Galicians, also consummate defenders of crooked lines, thereby exhibiting unusual political staying power.

Between beers or coconut milk shakes in the Bar Simpatia, Madruga pinned down his deals little by little. Especially when he gave in to the pleasure Brazilians took in talking about women, always in minute detail, to the point of creating in their conversational partner an excessive, lascivious salivation. Whores merited special mention by one and all. French ones in particular, even though they were in fact Poles, were regarded as great courtesans. Consummate practitioners of fellatio, they employed techniques regarded as daring in that dissolute and moralistic society.

In this area of publicly advertised sex, Madruga took offense, though not out of a lack of appreciation of ample hips, which made his heart go off like a firecracker at every street corner. He simply was averse to verbalizing, in front of strangers, the sexual pleasure he experienced in bed, between four walls. Or making up lustful laudatory speeches in honor of a woman's behind, whore or not. He had a reserve learned at home, back in Sobreira.

With Venâncio, he behaved differently. Though without ever letting himself go altogether. He never called bullocks by name, as he himself put it. Talking to himself, or to his partner in bed, he used scatological terms, which better defined certain parts of a woman's body, and by so doing further aroused his desire. In the bar later on, in his eagerness to overcome his inhibition, he had recourse to alcohol, whereupon there would come to him words that excited them all, but that he immediately tried his best not to utter again.

He decided to explore a new way of behaving. Leading his table companions to believe that he was a debaucher of women. Doing so by means of discreet but constant hints as to conquests superior in number to what his sex could expect. The words slipped unctuously out of his mouth, on the verge of a transcendent revelation, when suddenly they were cut off, on the pretext of maintaining the honor of a lady intact. The use of this technique soon achieved the desired effect, whereupon Madruga came to enjoy the reputation of being a man of discretion and a real macho.

Venâncio had nothing but scorn for these sexual tourneys that faithfully reflected a picture of general decadence. Moreover, as an employee of Madruga's, he felt he ought not to frequent the same places as he. Thereby displeasing Madruga, who demanded his presence. Venâncio excelled, however, at accentuating their differences. If they happened to be sitting together at a table, he would immediately leave when an acquaintance of Madruga's joined them. Especially now that Madruga's prosperity could be foreseen. A rise in the world feared by Venâncio, moreover, since it bore within it a poison that might prove deadly to all.

On the other hand, Venâncio found himself incapable of guiding Madruga. What sort of life to recommend to a man like him, whose impulses induced his own body to convey to him pleasures, a lush existence, and ever-heavier doses of power? Since outside of these elements, nothing else would have justified his existence.

Venâncio felt at home in the reading rooms of the Biblioteca Nacional. On the eve of a revolution, he read with delight the tales of travelers who had visited Brazil in the middle years of the seventeenth century. Having identified with them, he too felt himself leaping astride mules, climbing peaks, heading along the trails to Minas Gerais. To these travelers the world owed the revelation of a strange people, buried in the tropics, speaking a Portuguese suffering from a visible transmutation, already straying far away from Lusitanian patterns. But why proclaim them a strange people? Weren't the living in general exotic, even though life far outstripped them with its extreme and singular reality?

As Venâncio advanced in human understanding, an anxiety overcame him that drove him out into the streets. This failed, however, to calm him. All alone and lonely, he would stumble toward the Bar Adolfo, expecting that Madruga would be coming along. He had only to think of him, and almost without fail he turned up. He would arrive eventually, with an insatiable appetite. He would eat the potato salad, the rye bread, the cold cuts, washed down with long swigs of dark beer, as though he'd not eaten any lunch. Only then would they talk.

In truth, a near-monologue. Madruga spoke aloud so as to hear himself talk. Scarcely listening to Venâncio, equally eager to exchange confidences. Madruga's roundabout discourse breaking off only in the face of some unexpected difficulty encountered with this or that episode of the history of Brazil. He asked Venâncio to unblock his sensibility, since he wanted it to be fine-tuned, ready to master the Brazilian character.

"What with all those visits to the Biblioteca Nacional, you have an obligation to master Brazilian life. Isn't that what books are for?"

Asked to speak of a country he had learned about from books, though he hesitated to include the passion of its inhabitants within the knowledge thus gained, Venâncio took pride in showing off a store of information regarded as useful by Madruga, a brother to him. Besides, what other family did he have outside of Madruga's? He had always encountered difficulties in establishing relationships, in getting past the initial contact, in general superficial and uncertain, when words between men glide glibly over the tongue without sacrifice and, consequently, without responsibility.

He could foresee the danger of words in the game of friendship. The risk of using them without keeping the other person's interest in mind. He had a tendency to say only what came close to the other person's truth. And, as a consequence, very close to pain and hurt. This being so, by what right upset someone who offered him only neutrality, in return for being treated in the same way? Moreover, didn't this eagerness of his to tell the truth betray a horror of his fellow man, whom he approached only in order to wound, to mark his presence with fire?

He had positively not been born for friendship. His clumsy gestures did not mesh with the physical harmony that he detected in certain beings whose elegance tempted him to become reconciled with the human race. To that end seeking the inward signs that corresponded to beauty, and thus occasioned it. His feelings sometimes pulsed in powerful beats. He could hear them leaping out of his chest. On seeing a stranger on the street, he felt affection for him. A loneliness immediately devoured him, though he rebelled against it. To combat it, he did his best to set a bridge in place between himself and the world.

At breakfast or lunch, he addressed a few polite words to the waiters in Madruga's hotel, where he was still living, wanting desperately to say to them, Here I am, trying to be your friend. He did the same with bill collectors and suppliers. And the results disappointed him, though they did not suffice to explain the reasons for this failure.

In the Bar Adolfo, speaking of the family, Madruga praised Eulália to the skies. And as he went on hymning her virtues, more and more deeply moved, Venâncio paled. Frowning in severe disapproval of Madruga's amorous infidelities, making no secret of his state of mind.

Made the target of veiled criticism, Madruga vented his irritation on the waiters at the slightest pretext. A man of headstrong temperament, he nonetheless embraced them as he left, visibly filled with compunction.

Giving them tips in excess of the amount stipulated. Hence Madruga's arrival at the bar always caused a great stir. Everyone knew him. With his imposing physique, his shoulders erect, a cigar between his fingers, his head soaring above possible obstacles, Madruga made his way among the tables looking for a horizon that could be expanded beyond the walls.

Venâncio passed unperceived by the crowd. His medium stature supported a very small, bony body, making him resemble an Andalusian gypsy with dark eyes. His timidity was stubbornly fought by Madruga, determined to extirpate from him a vice incompatible with America. Seeing that this continent, tough and alluring, winner and loser at the same time, demanded of its inhabitants calamity, lofty pride, the courage to make claim to a life which, despite being enigmatic, would overflow with abundance, like heated milk boiling over the pan. An image that Madruga was pleased to parade. Especially since milk would soon be dripping from Eulália's breasts directly into the mouth of their son, about to arrive any day. The fourth child, moreover, of Brazilian issue. All born from the belly of Eulália, who, despite her frail health, calmly came through pregnancy without complications. Prepared to give life to the child native to her womb, a womb where Madruga had never been. He had merely passed close by in agonizing movements, aided by a virile member eager to love Eulália with the same fervor as in the first years.

The coup finally came. Returning the Old Republic to the steamer trunk of history. Everyone spoke of new times. An insurrection that surprised Madruga after all those years, as Getúlio Vargas, the major beneficiary of the movement, began to attack labor questions for the first time. And this amid the repressions that followed. A subject, moreover, that assumed gigantic proportions all through the national territory, making the wily gaucho an even more popular figure. The people, in search of charisma, adhering to causes put forward in a soft, persuasive voice, and a gaucho accent. Not hesitating to proclaim, in a mestizo chorus, as future conflicts loomed, "Give us . . . Give us . . ."

"When you come right down to it, Venâncio, what can they give us or grant us? Nobody is going to give us anything, unless we take it upon ourselves to go grab our rights with our own hands," Madruga said impatiently.

In the first moments of the rebellion, he feared that under the pressure of political events there would be street riots against foreigners.

"It's always easier to attack the gringo, the Turk, the Galician, the Portuguese than to confront the powerful. The political mob, for example."

"Calm down, Madruga. We seem to have reversed roles. You're defending my ideas without giving me time to defend them myself," Venâncio exclaimed in surprise at this agitation.

"You're wrong, Venâncio. I'm only defending my money and my right to make a fortune. Brazil's where I chose to live and die. I think I deserve to live here in peace."

He kept mulling over his plan to set up a little industry that would make his future a sure thing. He was anxious to manufacture a permanent consumer product, one not affected by fluctuations in demand.

"Clothing, for example. Can people go naked? Of course not. Ever since man abandoned his cave and learned to wear clothes, he's done nothing but change his wardrobe. Inventing styles every year. But you have to be careful nowadays. I'd never manufacture canes. Even if they're all the rage. They're elegant as well, they lend dignity, especially to somebody who has none. But I ask you, Venâncio, are they indispensable? Just let one of those dandies here in the city, or in Paris, or London, decide that a cane is something for an old man, or a victim of an accident, and you know what the result will be. So canes are out. And hats are risky too. Take those highfalutin' young chicks ankling up and down the Rua Gonçalves Dias, all of them wearing hats, ready and willing to sell their souls to the devil, just to go buy hats from Madame Douvizi, who's not even French, despite the name. She's probably a nice girl from the old country, straight off the farm. Nobody dares go into the center of town without a hat. It's like going naked or going down on the social ladder. And then there are the men, real fops, at the Porta da Colombo, chewing on toothpicks along with their yen for the women parading past. They're wearing hats too. It's a symbol of elegance and distinction. And here we are, we runaways from Spanish villages, imitating them. Even so, I don't envy that Remanzoni fellow, from São Paulo, for all his money and his success from hat manufacturing. One of these days a torpedo's going to fall on his head, one of the ones from the '14 war."

Madruga long pondered the problem of how there could be an object of industrial manufacture that would be, in its innermost nature, not only permanent but the equivalent of a work of art, adaptable to every day and age to come, hence capable of being held in as great esteem as books, as oil paintings, as the legends of Grandfather Xan. As Venâncio understood it, these were the anxious concerns that guided his choice. Worries that Venâncio could do nothing about, however. Merely prick up his ears at Madruga's long sentences, which, once begun, never spent themselves amid the draft beer and the appetizers.

In that week the gauchos arrived in Rio de Janeiro, ready to stand behind their promises. Mounted on horseback, in balloon trousers, with colored bandannas round their necks, they alighted directly in front of the Obelisk, close by the Palácio do Monroe. And they immediately tied their reins to the monument symbolizing the city, thereby designating it a symbol of their victory as well. Venâncio witnessed the spectacle as a passive observer. Resenting an arrogance that rode roughshod over the sentiments of a collectivity deeply affected by the invasion. These men came from the South, a region unknown to him, all set to stick the pointed snouts of their conquerors' boots farther inside the country.

In truth, it was difficult to predict who would be the winners and who the injured victims. The directions in which politics was heading seemed confused to him. Fortune certainly would not favor the nation's forsaken. Would Brazil grow amid the crisis? The crisis operating as the propellant of inevitable social changes? Perhaps Madruga was right to suggest to him that they remain on the sidelines of political events. Up until then, no responsible segment of the country had come out in defense of immigrants. Or recognized their legal existence. To attain this they would first have to father Brazilian offspring. Through paternal power, certain rights would be rendered them as their due. Only a son assured the conquest of the national language and access to reality. The definitive appropriation of the country.

"You're right, Madruga. The powers that be won't yield one inch of Brazil unless we take it. This damned revolution isn't ours, nor does it belong to this miserable people, living in wretched tenements, in slums, and going about in wooden clogs," Venâncio said in a low, choked voice.

"What did you expect, Venâncio? Have you ever seen anyone improve his lot by way of a fake revolution?"

Madruga ordered a cognac and immediately lighted his havana, wedged between his fingers as though a part of him. He now consumed cigars without fear of bankrupting himself. He slowly dipped the end of the havana in the cognac, and raised it to his lips. A sensation of pleasure that almost transfigured him.

Venâncio read all the city papers, especially *O Paiz*. Eager to supply Madruga with news that he might not yet have come across. Only to note forlornly that Madruga was better at gathering information than he was. On the other hand, he left Madruga trailing far behind when it came to reading books and seeing performances at the Lyrico.

Fascinated by Greta Garbo's face, Venâncio haunted the movie houses. Confronted by a lingering close-up on the screen, far beyond his expectations, he would heave a sigh, submerged in profound emotion. And smitten with shame by such a sentiment, he did not share it with Madruga. Madruga would have made fun of him. Not letting the chance go by to accuse him of living his life in search of the inaccessible.

"The earth is what's beneath our feet, Venâncio. Where we find ourselves is right here. Or have you forgotten that we were born amid excrement, urine, and blood? And who knows whether it's not best that way?" and his face projected a shadow of doubt and nostalgia.

Both were careful to restrict their disagreements to areas under control. They never permitted themselves an argument in front of strangers that would make them appear to be disloyal opponents. The walls would not come tumbling down about them owing to the impact of a deadly outburst of emotion. When Madruga lost control, he immediately went in search of Venâncio, as though nothing had happened. Certain his friend wouldn't complain. Hence neither of the two noticing the abyss being hollowed out between them, its existence and enlargement nonetheless constituting the basis of a friendship safe from fundamental friction and definite ruptures.

A disconcerting emotional tie. Suggesting to Venâncio the thought of relating it to the history of Brazil itself. On making his way through the Brazilian past, Venâncio had not detected, in the course of the primordial events, a single dramatic element that might have served to establish a firm and definitive breach in the evolution of history, thereby presenting the people with an opportunity to break away, irreversibly, from previous structures. There remaining no other way out for them except to plunge headlong into a regime which might enable a new society to be constructed.

After sixteen years in Brazil, Venâncio's life was going on as it always had. Poor still, he would end his days in poverty. He suspected that his fate had been determined on the English ship that had brought them to Brazil. He kept wondering if his lot would have been different if he had taken another ship instead. But since he chose precisely that English boat, everything that his destiny held in store for him naturally flowed via the estuary of Madruga.

He then pondered the question as to whether his life had been the work of fate or had deliberately passed him by altogether, just so that time would vanish before him and hence no ties be formed that called for celebrations and concrete proofs between him and life. His greatest adventure being limited to the area of the heart. Where everything prospered, in an absurd way. With him burning away his desire in unknown genitals, or weeping at the sight of the puckers that unexpectedly appeared in the crystalline face of Greta Garbo. Hence invariably bearing inexpressive witness. But wasn't life equally inexpressive?

For that Sunday dinner, Eulália provided an ample repast. Without Venâncio's overeating on that account. Though it gave him pleasure to see Madruga appreciating the roast suckling pig. Madruga acted like a guest, all the honors of the house naturally centering on him. Between forkfuls, he made gestures indicating that he was about to speak.

"I've finally discovered an indispensable object for Brazilian society, in terms of consumption. For us in particular, living as we do in this torrid city," and Madruga went back to chewing the tender flesh of an animal sacrificed on the altar of gluttony and greed.

Eulália asked them not to talk about business matters at the table. They always ended up souring the meal or making it tasteless.

Madruga laughed. "Well then, what'll we talk about, Eulália?"

Venâncio hastened to defend her. He proposed that they divert themselves by pleasant discourse about Galicia, a subject familiar to Madruga
and Eulália.

"Galicia is too far away, Venâncio. I can't reach it with my hands. This
plate of food is worth more than the distant homeland." Madruga lowered
his head so they wouldn't see his face. His voice sounded upset. And the
silence that followed made them think that he had abandoned them.
Headed for some remote corner devoid of pasturelands and animals with
full udders. Having no reasons left now to celebrate life. Hence allowing
no one to come along on the journey.

Eulália had grown accustomed to such behavior. It came and went
with equal ease. She nonetheless regarded this oscillation of Madruga's as
being determined by natural law, against which she never rebelled. Eulália
too traveled, leaving him behind. She never invited him along. When her
spirit, free of concrete tasks, wandered in strange lands, with not a single
reference at hand so as to be able to tell herself, after her return, where she
had been, what she had finally done. Because she came back relaxed, possessed of wings with which to exercise the natural right to fly.

Her husband in turn did not interrupt her flight, or ask her awkward
questions, during her absence. Madruga wasn't the sort who decides that a
love object is lost on seeing it far in the distance, in a place out of reach of
hand or thought. Eulália was grateful to him for this freedom. She repaid
her husband by letting go of him, a kite in the air, whereupon he took off.
And Madruga returned home only because he in fact wanted to. Had he
decided to stay away forever, Eulália would surely have wept. Never a fit
of convulsive, desperate, rebellious weeping. She held back her tears and
held on to him, knowing that Madruga decided his own destiny. And perhaps she was part of his mystique, of his fate.

Madruga was convinced that reality, for immigrants like him, ran on
narrow-gauge rails, it being their duty nonetheless to enter the fray with
rare courage, in the effort to become integrated with the country. They
ought not, then, to misinterpret favorable symptoms, or feed on false
hopes.

"We've been in Brazil almost twenty years now, and nobody's even
realized that we exist. It'll be up to us to take on a concrete dimension. But
we'll only come to have real power in our hands through the children and
the fortune we've accumulated. Otherwise we'll be underdogs forever.
There's nothing worse than an immigrant who hasn't made it."

The subject got him all excited. He went on and on about the future,
unfailingly connecting it with possessions and prestige. His ambition
proving unlimited. Aware, nonetheless, that the exercise of power began
with the running of his own household. Since power, regardless of what
form it assumed, made it necessary to maintain a mystique that presumably was a vehicle for legends and even realities.

"In such cases, reality is what matters least. Reality is real only to the person who constructs it. Above all to the principal actor, who is not limited to remaining in the wings watching, amid romantic sighs. Unfortunately, reality becomes abstract and remote to those who don't make it. They can't do anything to change the course of events."

Venâncio rejected this heartless argument, which swept losers from the face of the earth, when obviously they constituted the majority of the population.

"What's to be done with them, Madruga? Does it seem right to you to throw them all into the Bay of Guanabara?" Venâncio controlled his voice out of respect for Eulália's presence.

"Don't take offense, Venâncio. They're not aware of their own state. What's more, I myself belong to this group. Ever since I arrived in Brazil, I've been shot at every day with a short-barreled rifle. Loaded with bird shot, luckily. All of us in this room are losers, till proof to the contrary. To all intents and purposes, we count for nothing in the eyes of the Brazil that rules and condemns. That's why the census statistics are deceptive and inhuman. They make us believe that there are a great many of us, and that we therefore constitute a preponderant work force when it comes time for decisions to be made. But since when has a single Brazilian authority, tax official, policeman, schoolmaster, the whole damned lot of them, ever asked our opinion about anything?"

Venâncio was not taken in by Madruga. His aim was simply to adhere to the point of view of the winners, at the earliest possible moment, becoming their most uncompromising defender. Because he realized that winners never give up the privilege of narrating even the most modest stories, of whatever house, in the first person.

"And what if we, the losers and the failures, were all of a sudden to refuse to live, simply to deprive the winners of a chance to tell our stories?"

Venâncio smiled, full of enthusiasm for a project which would permit them to punish despots and the powerful as they deserved. One which, among other things, was meant to leave them alone in the assembly hall, with no one to serve them. Thus deprived of the audience before whom they dangled enticing words to feed the people's fantasies. Thereby giving them no chance to practice creating dreams and fantasies of their own.

"What would happen if we refused to shine imported boots, to polish the silverware, to serve at table with consummate elegance? And what if, moreover, we shut ourselves up inside our houses for a long period, so that they'd see that their stories are not of the slightest importance? And that once they no longer had a single captive listener, they would automatically cease to exercise power?"

Venâncio's verbal flights of fancy, though sporadic, held Eulália spellbound. She felt herself transported into the presence of Dom Miguel, in

Sobreira, from whom she always garnered precious information. This spell was soon broken by the sounds in the room, bringing her back home. To Venâncio's words, which she did not regard as having political weight. Grateful, nonetheless, Eulália offered him more coffee. Serving him his favorite cordial, in hopes of stimulating his excogitations.

Madruga got up from the table. Irritated by a utopia that at the same time turned against Venâncio and strengthened his enemies, ever on the alert for maneuvers that might threaten social customs established many thousands of years before. It was of no use to know that it was those who worked behind counters, in factories, those who tilled the soil and sowed it who made the world go round. While the magnates, the political class, the Church, legal institutions, continued to believe that it was their responsibility to determine how many rotations per second the earth needed to make, and society along with it, in order to suit their convenience and correspond to the inexorable nature of their financial and political investments.

"No one wants to lose his share of power, no matter how limited. And man is fated to command, to give orders. Even though I may try to get out of it, I rule, willy-nilly, over Eulália, Eulália rules over the children, the children rule each other, and they in turn submit to my command. In this unbroken chain the other is assured of the illusion of ruling, even though he is obliged to obey. And by way of this stratagem, there is continuous command. Even I, who occupy a modest station, am forced to rule over certain persons. And these same persons, in turn, do not forbear to rule over that many more. Whether in the work environment or within the home. How can this authoritarian succession be broken?"

"You forgot to mention who has command over you. Or doesn't anybody rule you, Madruga?" Venâncio said, upset by the turn the conversation had taken, seconded by a tense Eulália, prepared to separate them. She was wearing blue, and in the dim light of the room as twilight fell her face had paled.

Madruga laughed. The memory of the suckling pig still lingered on his palate. Enjoying his cognac and cigar, never once setting them down.

"A world of people. Beginning with the bankers, who may well cut off my head. But as long as I keep this head on my shoulders, I'll work with it the better to serve them."

He poured himself another cognac, beneath Eulália's reproving gaze. He paid no attention to her warning. It was Sunday and he was under his own roof.

He went on with what he was saying, as though Venâncio hadn't interrupted him. "Let's not fool ourselves about America. This is a cannibalistic continent. It has the habit of eating men and burying them in its memory. Nothing remains of them. Beneath its pleasant appearance, Brazil itself is an authoritarian country. Everything here is an imposture. But since I have faith in this false amenity, I've learned to deal with it. I'm certain that Brazil and I will understand each other in the end. By that I don't mean to say that this land is any the less mine because I wasn't born in it. I may not have been born in Brazil, but I've decided to die here. My mortal remains will end up in the São João Batista Cemetery, preferably under a mango tree."

Far from being moved by the final part of this speech delivered with a note of languor, owing perhaps to the heavy meal and the cognac, Venâncio made a wry face, not hiding his discomfort. And he refused Eulália's coffee.

"I'm about to catch you out again, Madruga. You forgot to list me among your belongings that you do with as you please."

Eulália paled in the face of the imminent conflict. She stirred restlessly in her chair, looking at her husband pleadingly, practically begging him to see that apologies were in order for this affront to a friend. Madruga saw Eulália get up from her chair, threatening to leave the room unless the words spoken were disavowed.

She offered him a few minutes to repair the damage. Madruga unbuttoned his waistcoat, which he always wore at home. He took out his watch, a Patek, that he was very proud of, and looked closely at the hours, fascinated by the minute hand, obedient now to his wife's stern rule.

He in fact did not know how to proceed to correct a legitimate, impeccable statement, words which corresponded to the truth. Since he gave orders to Venâncio, and ruled over his time, over the service that it was his duty to render him, and over his salary. What to say to rectify a situation accepted by Venâncio himself?

Eulália was still looking at her husband. A few minutes and the time would be up. Madruga was aware of this. He did his best to restrain Eulália and Venâncio.

"Please, Venâncio, let's not be dramatic," a phrase he resorted to whenever he did not know what to say or do.

Thus gaining time, he began searching about for more clever resources. He stared at Venâncio, feeling out the delicate situation.

Venâncio remained absolutely silent. Refusing to help him. As he searched within to discover whether he had come to America with the aim of gaining a soul or losing it. Deeply distressed, he joined his hands, using them to reinforce his body, collapsing to its knees at that moment. Perhaps Madruga had indeed contrived to gain his soul by tucking it away alongside the coins in his pocket. Or did Madruga's soul attract other souls to itself with the intention of using them up or squandering them whenever it suited his purposes? Above all when his own soul threatened to give out?

Madruga was quite capable of believing that human wisdom also lay in accumulating others' souls. A peculiar sort of stock, doubtless, and every one of them disposable. In accordance with this theory, it being only right for him to lord it over his neighbors, to possess many women, abundant offspring, countless houses, slaves too, so as to keep reality well oiled, everything in perfect order. So that his existence, of finite duration after all, would not find itself threatened as night fell and he plunged into sleep.

Venâncio made a move to leave. In alarm, Madruga went over to him and cautiously touched his arm.

"Mark my words, Venâncio. My situation is as precarious as yours. Perhaps I have a few pennies and a few more houses than you. As for the rest, I'm still a stranger in this land, under permanent suspicion. My one dream is to conquer Brazil. A dream superior to the ones that Grandfather Xan taught me. And why won't I hold Brazil in my arms one day, as I've wanted to since I was a youngster? Will this privilege be denied me? My punishment in that case being to await the coming of a grandchild, on whom I shall depend in order to conquer Brazil in my old age and acquire all the rights of citizenship?"

Madruga was moved. He spoke in a rush of words, convinced now that Venâncio would give him his hand as a sign of good faith. He searched his face for the desired answer. Venâncio's stubbornness nonetheless impressed him. Especially on seeing him head for the front door. Eulália followed him as though they were about to leave together.

Standing at the door, he buttoned up his coat, which Eulália had helped him into.

"And you, Madruga, are you still dreaming?" Venâncio's voice found a neutral tone that protected his feelings, not leaving them bared.

Madruga controlled himself in the face of this irony. He did not want to lose Venâncio. He was part of the story to be told in the future by his family.

"I still dream sometimes. But my dreams are intermingled with blood and spit. America has been hard for me. How many years is it now that I've been working like a slave? As though I had to buy my letter of manumission. But if you stay with me the rest of the evening, I'll tell you about my next dream." Madruga hesitated to go on. His pride would not let him take another step. Finally he gave in.

"Please stay."

Venâncio turned the handle of the door that opened onto the little garden in front of the house. He did not wait for Eulália to open the door for him, as was his habit. Before leaving, however, he suddenly felt indebted. He had an obligation to meet.

"I'll be at my desk early tomorrow morning to receive your orders."

I chose Breta to go with me to Spain. She was ten years old, with a gaze precociously corrupted by reality.

"Breta will come with me on account of her future," I explained, on being confronted by the jealousy of the other grandchildren.

I wanted to see Galicia again through Breta's first glimpse of that wild, green land. And so, beginning on the boat, as we left Rio de Janeiro, we did not lose sight of each other for a moment. Till Eulália finally separated us, taking her granddaughter far away.

On deck, I could foresee the emotions that Breta would undergo. When she would give names to Galician objects and encounter the feelings of that land, long since rusted by time.

After disembarking in Vigo, we were taken by car to Sobreira. To the house of Dom Miguel, who was no longer alive to receive Eulália's granddaughter. We crossed the courtyard of the house at exactly noon. The church bell rang, celebrating our arrival.

The house was still in absolutely impeccable condition. I never allowed that property to deteriorate, even during the time in America. Had anything fallen to ruin it would have buried the dreams of Eulália and the departed Dom Miguel. Both heirs of a world whose rules had denied me entry in the past. And even though I had not had a rightful share in the customs and habits of this universe, I always recognized that those people had told the official story of Galicia. Whereas it had fallen to my family's lot to live in the shadow of that heritage. Dependent upon their gestures, their authority, even the smoke that came out of their chimney. And seeing as how they were lofty lords and ladies and exemplary models, my ancestors did not hesitate to serve them with the joy of simple peasants.

Perhaps for this reason I decided, when just a youngster still, to contest these heraldic memories. By staking my claim to an America that had sprung from a feverish, chaotic legend, which could not be recounted. I had convinced myself that once this golden America was mine, people such as Dom Miguel would open their living rooms and bedrooms to me. That way I'd get to sleep with their women in their beds with imposing canopies.

In Brazil, I sometimes found it necessary to act like a Vandal. As when I bought Luís Filho and gave him to my daughter Antônia as a present. He had to give up his valuable surname in view of the price paid. And at the engagement dinner, I made it a point to inform him that the legends of my village were older than the ones making the rounds today in his family, which goes back four hundred years. He simply buried his face in his plate.

I did not tell Breta, however, that I had brought her to Sobreira because, in a manner of speaking, I had suffered the humiliation of winning. The dramatic humiliation of someone who, from the age of thirteen, felt with his fingertips each day the defeat that prowled round about his bed.

Eulália's brother and sister-in-law had come from Madrid to receive us. They personally opened the doors of the house for us so that we could see that everything was exactly as though Dom Miguel were still alive.

It was cold and the rain had flooded the roads. Winter stubbornly lingered on, even though by the calendar it was spring. The north wind howled in the distance. I feared I was disappointing Breta, offering her signs of a hostile nature. When I had predicted only charms and a beautiful countryside. It was necessary that Breta not reject my origin. Or discover Sobreira with indifference. I would not forgive her any heedlessness toward her own roots.

From the moment that Breta had come to us in Leblon, she had heard us speak of Galicia as an abstraction. By way of the scantiest of stories, intermingled with those of other countries. In a word, her soul had begun in a young America, having within it as yet no feeling of heritage. Thus far, she would have found it difficult to believe concretely in other worlds, outside of Brazil.

Breta gravely inspected, at one and the same time, the furniture and the persons belonging to the house. After that she immediately began boldly ferreting about the neighboring houses, the little village square, the cemetery, and the church. And after that, marching across the cornfields, which still bore the traces of the last harvest. A new world was being born for her, and Breta instinctively made herself part of this act of creation.

Quite unlike Brazil, Galicia was an old land. With a people surrounded by stones and beings. The stones strewn about everywhere. They could even be found in the Galician soul. A person needed only to go up the mountainside to discover vestiges of Roman fortifications and of Druid altars, where human sacrifices had been performed. Proof, moreover, that those peoples had left memories and sperm behind there.

Breta began to sense that Galicia, where she had only just arrived, obtained energy from its own enigma, fed upon its dark and indecipherable side. And did so with the aid of a vegetation at once poetic and rugged. Except that while the stones of Argos engendered tragedy and desolation, Galicia commingled grief and song in exaltation. In order, perhaps, to merit reality itself.

Breta grew and grew in those months. As though her skin were being peeled away with a scalpel in the process of coming to know. And pressed by the need for food and adventures, she abandoned for the time being gestures and words brought with her from Brazil. So as to incorporate into the unconscious and the sheepfolds of fantasy everything she was lacking. Little by little another culture was being built within her, rich and indissoluble, capable of making her sensitive to two worlds. Divided only by the waters of the Atlantic Ocean.

I pressed Breta to take wine at meals. She tried it, wary and mistrustful. I watched as her lips took on a purple tinge, and her heart, doubtless, a warm glow. On seeing these effects, I talked to her about what drinking meant. Drinking was an art, but one that demanded caution and devotion. Whenever she practiced it, she should make certain first what mood she was in. Only with a tranquil soul could wine have the desired effect. Beginning to speak in exactly the right words.

"Did you know that wine speaks?"

I explained to her, however, that if she felt thorns stabbing her, no matter where, she should shun wine. It could turn into a deadly enemy. Contrary to the natural destiny of drink, which was to communicate an appreciation of life, never to destroy it or make it more difficult.

Breta also acquired a strong taste for local food and local sayings. She encouraged us to talk. But then at the first chance she would obey the call of the wild. And go clambering up the mountainside, her body's weight supported by thick wooden clogs heavily studded with nails to keep her feet from slipping on the rocks. And at her waist, in a leather pouch, she carried with her fruit, corn bread, and smoked ham. She was so attuned to the life of the village now that it was as though she had been born there. Nothing seeming foreign to her.

She came back from these solitary outings with her eyes contaminated by a strange light. In the face of this evidence, I asked myself whether this was the right dream for my granddaughter. So that she would not come to be a product of mine, of Venâncio's and Eulália's.

But how to guess what her anxieties were? I easily confused my granddaughter with Brazil, making her the bridge to be crossed whenever I went to the heart of the country. She embodied, each day, the love I felt for that land I had chosen to die in.

Eulália also went out. Prudent as always, with a straw hat to shade her from the sun. Straight to the church. Her faith had been born in that soil permeated with religion. Eulália seemed happy seeing me occupied with Breta. And thus with no time to attack the clergy and give rise to misunderstandings between us.

Breta asked me for nothing. Except the freedom to move about, to come home at a late hour. I was the one responsible for providing her with money and presents. And so she abandoned us for hours at a time, drawn to the countryside beyond the gate. She had made friends through her personal merits. Speaking Gallego with a naturalness that put me to shame. How could a language be mastered by affection alone, without the intermediary of study and serious practice?

We had only to go to Madrid for Breta to become impatient. Coming with us under protest. By what right had I deprived her of Sobreira, where there was so much to do? And which she already loved. She was so insistent that we returned by the first night train.

As though intuitively aware that we were returning, Adélia and Nemésio were waiting for Breta at the entrance to the house. Eager to make the mountains, the meadows, the neighboring villages their very own territory. Geography was wherever their legs took them. Their green years, devoted to activities that excluded me from their epicenter.

At dinnertime, I could contain myself no longer. I asked my granddaughter for a detailed account of her adventures. Breta blushed, finding it difficult to explain her feelings. The words came tumbling out, one atop the other, trying to embrace everything.

Eulália was critical of my greed. "If you offered Breta freedom, don't ask her for explanations. Don't impoverish her life," she said in a heartfelt tone of voice.

I had contradictory impulses. While Breta was little by little becoming integrated with the country, I felt myself driven out of it. When what I in fact wanted was for Breta to be a living part of Galicia. I was eager to hand down to her a patrimony in the form of Grandfather Xan's legends. So that in this way my granddaughter would refuse to believe in a mean and paltry reality and stretch out her hands to wrest legends from the trees, from the chamber pot of oldsters, from the animal pen, where the cows secrete an age-old wisdom. Or else from the Roman ruins that contemplated us with their immortal silence.

I soon perceived, half envious and half touched, that Breta's imagination, once freed, reached its peak in Sobreira. My envy owing to my having been long ago barred from a reality that accepted only the company of magi, of the purified, of the storytellers of history, like Grandfather Xan.

Even today, sitting in this living room in Leblon, Breta and I feel the presence of those stories, just as they happened. And they come to us as fraternal phantoms, incapable of doing us harm. How often she visits me with the sole aim of remembering, through my face, some bit of history erased for the moment from her memory. I ask myself, then, if she is capable of rigorously isolating the emotions of that magic year, when life swelled her veins and caused to circulate through them a current of tales which now flow freely in her heart.

In Sobreira one night, Breta awakened me by pounding on the door. Eulália feared the worst. A cable bringing news of sudden illness in Brazil. On opening the door, I found Breta, trembling, wanting to speak to me.

And in the front room, coming straight to the point, she mentioned Adélia. She reminded me of her visit after dinner that night. When Eulália had insisted that Adélia have dessert. Though she turned down even the cordial she was so fond of. Interested only in getting Breta to go off with her. On the pretext of having exciting things to tell her.

The two of them finally left the house. This was a frequent occurrence. For those three friends were in the habit of rehearsing the story of humanity with exceptional brio. In a torrent of words, stealing them out of each other's mouths. With everyone's willing consent.

"As soon as we were out in the courtyard, grandfather, I saw that Adélia was all upset," Breta said.

Breta could see the fear in her eyes in the light of the lantern enveloping them in its halo, near the entrance to the cowpen.

"I kept asking her so many questions she finally confessed that they'd met the billy goat."

As it happened, Adélia and Breta had decided that day after lunch to go for a stroll down by the riverside. They delighted in going for a dip in the stream in summer, when the current would take them as far as the bend by the mill, from which point they could swim back upstream. Whiling away half the afternoon in this way.

In between dips, however, they had long talks together. And whenever there was something Breta didn't know about Sobreira, she would ask Adélia and Nemésio. Both would then pass what they'd learned in the cradle on to her.

There was, moreover, a clear difference of opinion between Nemésio and Adélia as to who had the right to be her number one servant. Though both complained of Breta's inordinate ambition in wanting to add all the local magic spells to her store of knowledge. Fearing that she might use these spells against them in the future. Or even dispense with their services altogether.

Nemésio in particular suffered heartache because of that friendship, soon to end. Not only would Breta return to America, whereupon the enchantment would be broken, but he in turn, being about to enter a state secondary school, was getting ready to go live in Madrid at the end of the summer. This future privilege, however, did not free him of his obligation to help out in his father's tavern.

When it came time for him to work his shift, Nemésio would head for the tavern with Breta and Adélia as a solemn escort. Their parting taking on a dramatic cast. As though they would never see each other again. And the two girls would not take their leave until they were absolutely certain that Nemésio would not come back to the door to wave good-bye to them one last time.

Breta was attached to the two of them. No longer able to imagine life without them, her heart shrank when she was taken to Madrid. Far from the friends who drew her to the center of the earth.

Nemésio was not free to accompany them on their afternoon outing.

They compensated for his absence by exchanging confidences. And sitting there on the riverbank, they could see, on the other side, the far end of Senhor Saavedra's property, the whole of it surrounded by water and by impenetrable walls.

For a long time the three friends had been pondering what sort of world must exist in those domains to justify so many precautions. A house that could be seen from the walls and also through the front portal, opening onto the road to Senra. And through the back gate, which gave directly on the river, though it was accessible only by boat or by swimming across the stream.

The idea of invading this impregnable domain at last came that afternoon from Breta. Adélia was opposed, fearing the consequences. She did her best to curb Breta's enthusiasm. She was not unaware of Saavedra's enmity toward the inhabitants of Sobreira. A sentiment widely known to be so bitter that people wondered what they had done to deserve it. And why, in such a case, he had chosen to end his days in Sobreira.

In the tavern, owned by Fermín, Nemésio's father, Senhor Saavedra never sat down at the common table to share a meal with the others. Nor did he drink or play cards with them. Born and educated in Madrid, from the beginning he emphatically proclaimed himself a Madrileño and, as such, a member of a superior class.

At the very most, he accorded them a nod of his head. The few times he spoke, he voiced nothing but contempt for Galicia. Despite having entrusted everything he had to the Bank of Galicia. As was proved by the bank statements that were periodically sent to him through the mail, which, as it happened, was delivered at the tavern.

The source of his supposed fortune was not known. Inasmuch as he never mentioned the past, save to hint that his noble origin exempted him from having to live cheek by jowl with the common herd. It was suspected that the only family he had left was his wife. She being, incidentally, nothing but skin and bones, a creature with feverish eyes who very rarely appeared outside the walls of the house. Except for a yearly journey, from which she returned altogether dejected, more stoop-shouldered than ever, with not the least sign of happiness on her face. Gossip had it that her womb had never brought forth a child. For the precise reason that no son of theirs ever showed his face there in Sobreira, not even to claim, in advance, a share in the inheritance.

Breta tried to convince Adélia that they should no longer forgo the doubtless fascinating discoveries to be made inside the walls. And even though Nemésio wasn't there, they couldn't put off the raid any longer.

"And if you don't go with me now, Adélia, swear that you'll relinquish all claim to Senhor Saavedra's gardens forever. Because if I find out someday, there in Brazil, that you came to know this house without me, I'll never forgive that act of betrayal," Breta said, her eyes ablaze, clutching her arm.

Adélia was all on edge. Egged on by Breta, she was afraid to pass up an adventure associated with the river she so clearly loved. And there were also reasons to suppose that extraordinary events took place behind those walls. Beginning with the trees in the gardens, from which there were gathered, according to commonly held belief, fruits unknown in the region. Not to mention certain herbs which grew there, possessed of the virtue of transforming beings into creatures the precise opposite of the original model. And above all, people suspected that the perverse Madrileño kept in a private jail a bunch of prisoners who were prepared to relate, to anyone who overcame the obstacles of the river, the story of their cruel captor. Prisoners with features so sinister that they prompted Saavedra to keep them under the strictest surveillance. A single declaration of this sort would have been sufficient cause for his expulsion from Galicia.

In the end Adélia took up Breta's challenge. She immediately removed her shoes and plunged into the water. Considering herself more likely to carry out the operation successfully. With quick strokes, she got a firm grip on the doorframe, trying to lean against the door, till by kicking her legs she reached the handle. With her feet now resting on the sill, her body stretched full length, by making a leap she was able to catch hold of the top of the gate. The impetus of this acrobatic leap bringing the rest of her body along. Thus enabling her to swing her legs nimbly over the door and jump inside.

Together again, they excitedly explored the gardens. As far as they knew, anything might happen. But as they went on, there was, to all appearances, nothing to explain the prohibitions. On the contrary, they had not seen a setting so lacking in magic for a long time. Disappointed, Breta raised her voice in protest, though Adélia calmed her down. And as she stood there cursing out the old crank, they heard a loud stamping of feet directly behind them. Their attention attracted by the sound, they turned their heads. A billy goat, of magnificent bearing, straight out of a storybook, with regally intertwined horns like the branches of a tree, was heading straight for them. Running faster and faster, he bore down on them. His fury so visible that they had only just time to scramble up the nearest peach tree.

From its top, they watched the animal butting against the trunk, without this violence damaging his luxuriant horns. But because of these thrusts, everything round about began to tremble. So that Breta and Adélia would be in danger if they stayed up in the tree any longer.

They very nearly shouted for help. What kept them from doing so was the certainty that Saavedra would be the first to deliver them over to the horns of the animal. And just as they were about to fall, the animal finally gave signs of tiring. The panting tongue he was sticking out was bright red and grainy. His eyes betraying the desire to lick them with raging voracity.

Adélia decided to goad him further, so as to wear him out completely. And so with one accord the two of them began to throw peaches and leaves at him, made faces at him, jeered and hooted so that the animal would take notice of the insults. The billy goat soon responded by butting repeatedly with his horns. Till finally he withdrew to marshal his strength again. But he was no longer the haughty animal of a few moments before. Adélia noted his dispirited air, his head hanging. It was time to act. She signaled to Breta and they quickly threw themselves to the ground. And in a headlong dash, they plunged, floundering, into the waters of the river.

"Go on, Adélia, tell what happened with that blessed billy goat," Breta said, all upset, in the courtyard.

In their hasty flight, they were unable to close the gate behind them. Thereby leaving the animal within sight of the mirror of water which he had never before seen from so close up, and which immediately fascinated him. And whose reflections, miraculously, sent him back his own image. When, therefore, impelled by the irresistible archaic instinct to touch himself and the other animal reflected in the waters, which he took to be his brother, he threw himself into the river.

At first his body struggled on the surface of the water, overcome by the euphoria of being freed at one and the same time from captivity and from the burden of its own weight. Immediately, however, his body, of noble stature, began pulling him toward the bottom of the river, from which he quickly emerged to take another breath. Until his resources were exhausted and he was found dead, all opulence lost, at the bend of the river just before the mill. This fate of remaining forever in Sobreira, near his master, owing to the fact that his horns had become caught in the branches of the mulberry tree bending over the river.

The news of the accident spread immediately, arriving at the tavern at the very hour when, by coincidence, Saavedra was drinking at his table all by himself. Adélia's father, present that night, was later able to relate, at home, with the family gathered round the table, what exactly had happened.

Saavedra was not at all perturbed. Utterly contemptuous of a spiteful and false piece of news. A prize animal such as that would never abandon his gardens, where it had always been happy, so as to know Sobreira from the outside, since it had nothing to offer it. A land completely surrounded by thorns and forbiddingly steep slopes. And Saavedra was still holding forth in this vein, to everyone's astonishment, when the messenger informed him that the billy goat in question had a single white spot on its skin, right next to its testicles.

Saavedra blanched, leaning his elbows on the table. Something had touched his heart of hearts. Surely that particularity was not unknown to him. Consequently, he took another tack altogether. And began lighting into everybody, shouting at the top of his lungs, accusing them of spiriting away his billy goat named Menelaus. Giving him every right to call them murderers.

He then denounced the conspiracy afoot against him. In which they were all involved. There was not a single innocent in the village. That nefarious crime being owed, doubtless, to his being Castilian, and from Madrid to boot, and his not wanting to have anything to do with people of their sort. But things would not go on that way. He intended to wreak his vengeance on Sobreira. Unreconciled to the loss of an animal that had no equal in all of Galicia. With the further aggravating circumstance of having a chestful of medals won in contests in the capital.

"Menelaus was the crowning pride of his breed," Saavedra emphasized before leaving them.

Alone in the tavern, everyone now feared the consequences of the accident. Above all the arrival of the police, as Saavedra had promised, searching for the criminal. Adélia's father, the sort who was easily frightened, immediately began to lament the sad fate of Sobreira, which had caused them to fall victim to such a momentous episode.

"Didn't you notice, grandfather, that after saying good-bye to Adélia in the courtyard, I went to my room without even asking for the family's blessing? For fear you'd suspect, just looking at my face."

Lying in bed, Breta did not know what to do next. She had at least taken the trouble to swear Adélia to strict silence. Forbidding her to confide even in her sisters, for she and Adélia were in serious trouble. The two of them had killed a mythological animal that looked as though it had come from a cave whose decorated interiors had chosen it as a subject for its paintings.

"What are we going to do, grandfather? What if someone saw us and tells Senhor Saavedra and the police that we killed his animal?"

My granddaughter touched my heart. I stroked her hair. She should sleep, forgetting the episode. And assure Adélia the next morning that Grandfather Madruga too had passed through Saavedra's gardens. And thus had seen the furious beast from close up, had identified its original traces of Greek Antiquity. A being lacking only a flute perhaps.

"Sleep, Breta, I promise to solve this case."

Breta's distress evaporated. She smiled happily, eager to visit enchanted gardens again, wherever they might be. Exactly the way I wanted her to be, free, lighthearted, treading the Galician ground without bitterness or resentment, her only task being to accumulate memories that would be her rear guard in the future.

Alone in the living room, warmed by Breta's happiness, I too felt young and immortal. Capable of felling Saavedra's animal, since life forced me to do so. Repeating, through this sacrifice, a spectacle from which our ancestors had not fled. In a way, on confronting the billy goat, Breta had recovered the spirit that must have presided over the hunt amid endless forests. Thereby reproducing the age-old gestures, almost lost, of those bloodthirsty hunters. In Saavedra's gardens, without realizing it, she had fought in imagination buffaloes, bison, reptiles.

Restricted up until then to the domestic sphere, Breta was now beginning to conquer the earth. Because the house was not her home. Her home was everywhere. Hence confronting the billy goat had helped her to grow, to placate her fears of nature, to accept the enemies that proliferate, by preference, amid garden flowers.

The moment had come to wage war on Saavedra. And through him fight against the central power, headquartered in Madrid, that had deprived us of autonomy. And robbed us of our imagination in the bargain. Even going so far as to sign their names to our stories.

And the episode made me remember how joyfully Venâncio and I had followed, from Brazil, the nationalist fervor that swept through Galicia in 1924. The daily papers and the news reports described the festivities in honor of Saint James the Apostle that took place in Compostela. At the same time that the first Day of the Galician Language was celebrated. The poet Eládio Rodrigues had just won a literary prize with his poem "Oracións Campesiñas," whose refrain proclaimed: *The whole countryside is a prayer.*

The festivities in turn were the occasion for the organizing of a bagpipe contest which, initially, did not attract the attention of the press. The students, however, immediately intuited how well the bagpipe represented the Galician soul, being played in general by groups of peasants bent upon extolling the rocks and the gorse of their distant villages.

Gathered together in the square, they awaited the performances. At the very first bagpipe chords, sounding throughout the adjoining neighborhoods, the people left their houses, taking to the streets, the windows, in great excitement. All assuming, in public, a civic emotion long forbidden. Clinging, in unison, to memories which, having surfaced now, seemed to restore their dignity. Moreover, thanks to the magic effect of the indigenous music of the bagpipe, they were able to recall, amid their tears, those nameless men and women who had abandoned Galicia, wandering all about the world now. And this because Madrid, in addition to the restrictive measures that were little by little undermining their souls, denied them a means of survival.

But when Avelino Cachafeiro, of the group from Soutelo dos Montes, laid his hand to the bagpipe to give it life and breath, no one had the slightest doubt. At that precise instant another legend had been born. A legend that the people would legitimate, as long as it uttered his name and heard his music. And whose appearance coincided with the birth of Esperança, my first daughter, in Rio de Janeiro. Whom I gazed upon in the cradle, thinking of the women of the family, all of them of strong character. Urcesina being a typical example.

That year 1924 seemed favored by grace. Although the libertarian sentiments of Galicia did not reach us until long afterward. Amid magazines in tatters, cans of oil, barrels of wine, smoked sausages being offloaded from ships from Spain and Portugal tied up alongside the Praça Mauá.

Venâncio and I arrived at the dock early in the morning, eager for the ship to be unloaded. Several hours later, the sun at the zenith, the crowd dense, with damp armpits. No one gave up. We stood there sniffing the Iberian smells that had been brought in the hold and on the deck of the boat.

There were always acquaintances. So we asked them for news of the group from Soutelo dos Montes. Of those bagpipers who had succeeded in eloquently discoursing, in the name of the Galician people. Speaking to this people of its genesis buried through successive dominations. The same bagpipe with which the Scots gave breath to their furious nostalgia.

I had, then, the marks of that year in my heart. Relived now with the episode of the billy goat, which touched the core of my pride. And in that long sleepless night after Breta left me, I reviewed the legends of Galicia. All born of a natural intimacy with certain sacred entities. Many of them having abandoned us without our bidding.

In those mountains, from earliest childhood, we felt angry. There was no other light save that shed by the lamp of memory. By men like Xan and Dom Miguel. I had brought Breta to Sobreira for that very reason, in my eagerness to transmit a heritage to her. And taking her to the very heart of my country could also be a sign that I was beginning to understand the anticipated meaning of my death.

Saavedra goaded me into retaliating. I was going to fight him not only to shield Breta from her first murder. But also in defense of my native land. I went back to bed but couldn't get to sleep. Feeling cold, I moved closer to Eulália's burning heat.

By morning, however, I had come up with a plan. And I went by car to Pontevedra. From the office of my cousin Muiños, I made several calls to Madrid. The necessary steps gradually took shape, each linked to the next in such a way as to achieve the objectives. And, back in Sobreira once again, I smiled at Breta at dinnertime.

"It won't take more than a few days to settle the matter. It'll be a surprise, Breta. But don't say a word to anybody."

Breta sensed that she shouldn't ask questions. Her bright eyes foresaw events. On Saturday morning, a loud noise was heard in the living room, coming from the courtyard, near the vegetable garden. Attracted by the noise, we leaned out of the window. Before us was a billy goat of rare majesty, which upon arriving had immediately begun to crop the grass with the strictest parsimony.

His coat was splendid, his beard impeccably trimmed, his horns reminiscent of an exotic Catalonian cathedral, so numerous were their volutes and intricate intertwinings. Busy chewing, the animal nonetheless watched the house closely, eyeing it sternly, as though he were already a long-standing member of the family.

Nothing around him bothered him. And his reaction to the chorus of joking and flattering remarks rained down upon him was one of grave composure.

The news of this arrival swiftly spread. A long line of visitors soon forming and filing past him. He stood there like the governor laureate in person.

"And what is this animal doing here? Can Madruga have given up on Brazil and be thinking of settling permanently in Sobreira?" the visitors commented.

To each visitor, all I said was: "As of this date, you gentlemen are going to appreciate how we Galicians take care of those Madrileños."

Fermín was entrusted with the mission. He received precise instructions. There was no reason why it should turn out badly. Nobody better than he for such services. Because of his exemplary spirit of obedience, constantly put to the test, in the eyes of his wife, the neighbors, and the habitués of the tavern.

Fermín chose lunchtime to visit the Madrileño. At this hour on the clock, Saavedra's raging appetite almost made his clenched teeth snap off. Sometimes making it necessary to go to the dentist to have them filed down.

He pounded on the Castilian's door with all his might. He had the animal with him, having dragged it there by the rope around its neck. Fermín's apparel, exceptionally clean, formed a sharp contrast with the billy goat's stink.

Saavedra received Fermín with a snort. His face set, his bad humor giving his skin a greenish tinge. And he was about to forbid him entry into his domains when he spied the imposing presence of the billy goat, a creature in every way superior to the departed Menelaus.

"Speak up, what do you want?" Saavedra muttered, his eyes avoiding Fermín's.

Fermín did not answer. Heading through the door, he was immediately followed by Saavedra. He did not stop till he reached the veranda.

"I came to tell you that the animal is yours for the time being. Don't fail, then, to feed it and give it fresh water. As for the rest, await word from Senhor Madruga, in about five days."

"And who the devil is this Madruga to dare abandon this bastard on my doorstep without any explanation?"

"If you don't want the animal, I'll take it back." Fermín began to drag it toward the door.

"One moment," Saavedra said, his eyes fixed on the animal. Unable to restrain his covetousness. As though he were observing the burning hot thighs of a woman stretched out on the ground, taking the sun.

"Just tell me one thing. Who is this Madruga?" his voice less aggressive now than before.

"For your information, Senhor Madruga is a respectable manufacturer and businessman based in Rio de Janeiro."

And so saying, Fermín untied the cord from aound the billy goat's neck, gave it a gentle pat on its hindquarters, and headed it in the direction of Saavedra's pasture, in a swift accord between man and animal.

Saavedra did nothing to keep the grazing animal from stealing his grass. The billy goat, moreover, appeared to feel so at ease in its new home that it was now making loud noises as it chewed. By contrast to its previous good manners, just after it arrived in Sobreira. This behavior subject to the intense appreciation of the Madrileño, who, absorbed in contemplating it, took no notice of Fermín's departure.

And Saavedra no doubt spent several days in this way, for no more was heard from him, and he did not show up at the tavern. Nor was there any sign of the formal summons he had threatened to have sent to Fermín for having trespassed on his property.

At night the last customers of the tavern, straggling home tipsy on red wine, glued their ears to Saavedra's walls and front portal, in an effort to determine what sort of outrage the animal might be suffering at the hands of the wretched Castilian.

Despite the silence, there were no cries to be heard. The animal appeared to be dead or simply to have fallen into a deep sleep. Thereby thwarting the spirit of intrigue of these men, who went home to bed no better informed than before.

A week later, Fermín knocked at Saavedra's door. This time he was immediately ushered into the living room, decorated with furniture imported from Paris. Among the various pieces one stood out, a large mirror above the console table, draped in sheets, thus keeping the glass from reflecting the face of anyone looking in it.

The room reeked of tobacco. There was not one fragrance of feminine origin. Thus forcing Fermín to conclude that the Madrileño did not allow his wife to frequent this particular sphere. In a few minutes, Saavedra appeared. In the half-shadow of the room, with the curtains closed, Saavedra offered Fermín a finger of brandy, of dubious origin. Seemingly bent on preventing Fermín, with a single word, from taking the animal away with him.

For five minutes it pleased Fermín to play his game. Until he was ready to punish him.

"You must accompany me this instant to the house of Senhor Madruga, from Rio de Janeiro."

Fermín dramatically pushed the glass of brandy away toward the far end of the table, without having tasted it. Thus showing his disdain for vulgar spirits of this sort.

"If this individual wants to see me, let him come to my house," Saavedra said indignantly.

"As you like. In that case, I'll take the sacred billy goat in your place." Fermín laughed, pleased at the shock he'd given him.

Saavedra said nothing. He rose to his feet, smoothed his hair, and with hat and cane, left the house without looking to see whether Fermín was following him. He did not say one word on the way. And demanded that Fermín open the door of Madruga's house to let him in.

In the living room, he found cups of hot coffee waiting on a Portuguese silver tray. Proof, in fact, that the precise moment of his arrival had been determined beforehand. This detail alarmed Saavedra. Without, however, making him any better mannered. For with his usual rudeness he did not even greet the five men present.

"Keep your protest for later, Senhor Saavedra. I advise you to sit down now and have coffee before it gets cold," I said to him curtly. "And allow me to offer you the opportunity to drink a Brazilian coffee, the first one in your Castilian life."

Cornered by so many pairs of eyes, Saavedra deigned to accept the coffee. And before even tasting it, he asked for more sugar. He served himself more than liberally, obviously wanting to spoil the taste of the coffee so as not to feel obliged to judge the quality of it. The cup trembled in his hands. He finally drank it down without one word of appreciation for its Brazilian origin.

I purposely sipped the coffee slowly, praising its virtues to the skies. Seconded, moreover, by everyone. After a long pause, I pointed out to him, without beating about the bush now, that there wasn't a single soul in Sobreira who esteemed him. There were serious complaints against him. Among them, that of having accused them of murdering Menelaus. This being the case, Sobreira, as one, was eager to expel him. In fact, they did not understand the bad luck that had befallen them, that of all the many places in Spain, he had chosen none other than Sobreira as his home. And as if the misfortune of having to put up with him alive were not enough for them to bear, they had learned of his plans to be buried one day in Sobreira. It was necessary, however, that as of now he be apprised of the fact that such a project would constitute a frontal attack on the interests of the village. For which reason no funeral honor would be rendered him. They even intended, when the coffin passed by, to close windows and doors just so as not to see him, even if he was dead. Galicians were indeed rude folk, but never hypocrites.

Saavedra did not hide his impatience. But indifferent to his fate, I went on with my argument. Admitting to him now that, as it happened, a citizen of Sobreira had opened the door, leading the animal to drown itself. An act whose motive was revenge, because of the bitter feelings that Saavedra had aroused in that person. But no one in that room felt that he had the right to criticize anyone who had acted in this way in secret. And this for the reason that they too had wanted to punish him, to make him suffer. This being the case, they assumed, conjointly, responsibility for the murder. Therefore they had sent to Madrid for a billy goat like that one, crowned with medals. Which would soon become his property, as an act of compensation.

Saavedra allowed himself to show his emotion at emerging as the victor of a battle in which his best animal had been sacrificed. Facing him were Galician enemies, mountain people of Celtic origin. And, as such, worshipers of an antique pride. Wanting to force him to believe that they were generous adversaries. When Saavedra knew that, beneath the wax mask, they were concealing a lust for vengeance and dramatic suspense.

Saavedra rubbed his hands together, his eyes staring into space. Suspicious, however, of a situation that offered him, at one and the same time, severe reprimands and the possession of an animal superior to Menelaus. The papers, spread out before him, left no room for doubt as to the impeccable breeding of the animal, a biography dotted with prizes won in the various regions of the country. The animal having made a journey almost like that of Ulysses in the Aegean, returning to Ithaca.

Prudence counseled Saavedra to be cautious. One careless word and they would rob him of the prize. After all, he had never trusted that people, of such heterodox origin. Consisting of assorted sperms, with a predominance of Celtic sperm, this latter verbally oriented, thus explaining why Galicians lost themselves in rhetorical contests, in courts of law as in taverns. Lying and telling the truth indiscriminately, without Saavedra's ever mastering, despite his years among them, the same rhetorical and narrative style.

At certain moments, the present seemed to constrain him. He stared at us, as though assuring us of his hatred. At me more than the other men in the room. Though he no longer rejected the treasure unexpectedly brought to his door. I noted his suffering. And I wanted him to soak a bit longer in this marinade of salt and vinegar. He ought to suffer for at least a few minutes in a briny deep.

We helped ourselves to more coffee. This time Saavedra refused our hospitality. While immersed in his own feelings, he was also investigating our style of corruption.

"That settles the matter, Senhor Saavedra. After this meeting the animal is yours."

I paused briefly. I then perceived that Saavedra was slumped over in his chair and thought he'd fainted. When I hastened to help him, he immediately sat up straight again. He was a forbidding man, and a fighter.

"There's one detail we're missing, however, in order to complete the transaction. A condition for its being your property," I finally ended the sentence.

Saavedra bristled. If we were going to charge him his soul for the deal, he had decided to negotiate.

"First you gentlemen kill Menelaus, and now you want to tame my will," he said dryly.

These words did not prevent him, however, from clutching the papers to his breast. Forgetting to put them back down on the table in front of him. His eyes gleamed with rage and ambition. He was gradually losing his independence, but he hadn't yet forsworn his arrogant gestures.

"In that case, Senhor Saavedra, where is the billy goat? Why didn't you return it immediately? Bring it with you to my house, knowing that I'm its legitimate owner?"

Saavedra's face turned beet red as he sat there motionless in his chair. His body rigid, caught between the horns of his dilemma.

"And the billy goat, Senhor Saavedra, where is it now? Is it still eating grass?" I added ironically.

Saavedra said, stumbling over his words: "Very well, Mister Manufacturer from Rio de Janeiro, what are your conditions?"

"We are asking very little of you, in view of the fact that you owe us material and moral damages. And it will not be difficult for you to comply."

In point of fact, he was the first to proclaim his antipathy toward Sobreira. Refusing to extend a friendly greeting to a single living Galician. And not respecting the dead either, since when he was seen at the crossroad of Olvido, near the school, where the homesick ghosts of Sobreira gathered at night around the big stone cross after vespers, even then Saavedra, deeply troubled by so many mysteries, did not fraternize with one or another of his neighbors, all as terrified as he was.

"From this day forward, Senhor Saavedra, you are to abstain from frequenting the tavern. From setting foot inside, even if you don't have a box of matches in the house to light the hearth fire in winter. Or even if the aroma of a marvelous Ribeira wine reaches your nostrils. Or you hear Fermín shouting for help. This tavern is forbidden you. And woe unto you if you disobey."

Saavedra was frightened. And for the first time signs of humanity were seen in his face. Signs of a certain awestruck admiration even. He had never suspected that Galicians would abandon the lyrical, bucolic territory in which he had seen them mired for four centuries, a period marking our decadence, in order to kill their enemies today, to devour their entrails with unexpected gusto. With no apparent fear of living with the tortured flesh of others or engaging in acts of cannibalism.

Suddenly he discovered for himself the symbol of the pleasure we took in the blood of our enemy. A satisfaction that would again circulate freely among us, once we managed to wipe out a thousand Castilians like him each day.

So as to make him even more overawed, I added: "And you are fortunate that we do not extend the same prohibition to holy places, including the cemetery and the church."

Saavedra tried to recover his wounded dignity. Needing in order to do so only to refuse the animal, spit in our faces, call us a despicable people. But instead he scratched his face and blinked his eyes repeatedly. His long eyelids forming a curtain that veiled his face. As he offered a justification meant to convince himself of the difficult situation he was in. He doubtless told himself that if he were to refuse our proposal, we for our part, impelled by our barbarous origins, would not hesitate to sacrifice him, and his wife, on the stone altar, reviving a Druid ceremony. Or else simply throw him into the river, like Menelaus the billy goat.

He rose to his feet with a certain elegance. Certain of his own dignity, immaculate still. He went immediately to the dining table, on which he deposited the papers, in full view of everyone. He then asked us to point out, on the protocol establishing ownership, where he should sign so as to take possession of the animal. He was in a hurry to leave us.

We proceeded in silence. He signed with a trembling hand and made a move to give me back the pen. At that point he looked at me with fathomless violet-colored eyes. His face, however, looked rusted to me. With the documentation under his arm, he turned his back on us. Leaving the room without bidding anyone good-bye.

That night the tavern was chock-full of tense men, suffocated by smoke and alcohol. There was an expectant din of voices, having to do with the minutes of timepieces being consulted from moment to moment. The hands moved on, close now to the hour at which Saavedra customarily arrived at the tavern with exemplary punctuality, going immediately to the counter, without looking round as he asked for his red wine.

There were five minutes to go. Following his arrival in Sobreira, several years before, Saavedra had never once in his life been held up. Extremely methodical, he was in the habit of drinking three glasses of local red wine, always from the same oak barrel.

At last the wall clock, brought from Fermín's house to help him keep track of the time that night, struck eight on the dot. The smoke, thicker than ever, made it hard for us to breathe; our noses were stopped up. It was hot, but no one protested, eyes fixed on the door. Despite the solemn ticking of the clock, the door still didn't open. The only sound detected in the tavern came from lips sipping wine in sufficient quantity to warm the souls there present.

Fermín's eyes kept wandering from me to the door, invested now with a special historical significance. The future of Sobreira depended on what would happen there in the tavern in the next few minutes. Five of them in fact gone by already. "It's still too soon to celebrate," said Fermín, hanging back as usual.

"On the contrary, we've got two hours to catch up on. This being the case, wine for everybody," I said to those present in a loud voice, breaking the painful silence.

"This round is on me. Enjoy yourselves," I added.

Nobody moved. Not even Fermín, to attend to the order. A crowd unable to believe its ears, just sitting there, all hope lost. I shouted to Fermín, I called upon him in the name of obedience, an ideal he slavishly served. And even so he didn't budge an inch.

"What are you waiting for, man? Is defeat what you're all hoping for? What you really want, then, is for that damned Castilian to come walking in the door on us?"

Fermín came alive, feeling suddenly outraged. The same feeling seemed to come over all the men.

"Take this clock out of here, we don't need it anymore," Fermín bawled, finally convinced that Sobreira had overcome time and defeated the Madrileño.

Mugs and glasses of wine were circulating freely about the tavern. Everyone was drinking with gusto, the wine staining their mustaches, their beards, and their shirts. They had no doubts left in their hearts now. They had beaten Castile.

"We won, Madruga. We've seen the last of him." Fermín tearfully embraced me. A few minutes later, he left the counter and came over to me again.

"I have a question to ask you. Who did kill the animal?" he murmured contritely.

"Who could it have been, if not Saavedra himself? Who else wanted to get us into trouble? To take his revenge on Sobreira, the object of his eternal hatred? Counting on the fact that in the past our ancestors always practiced rites of veneration and human sacrifices. And so quite capable of killing the he-goat. Except that Saavedra forgot that billy goats always merited our devotion. And that we never shed the blood of others wholesale."

Fermín was not persuaded. But before he could go on, I gave him my glass to drink from, as a token of affection.

"Don't worry, Fermín. The one thing that matters in this episode is that we beat the plain of Castile. We acted as if we were the heretic Priscillian and his worshipers. And even so we weren't burned alive."

Fermín drank eagerly and joyfully, returning the empty glass to me. That was, in fact, the one thing I wanted.

All of a sudden, Venâncio began to skip the Sunday dinners, which had been a rigorous ritual for seventeen years. Without explaining his absence or offering apologies. Eulália nonetheless left his plate on the table, in the usual place, till dessert came, whereupon she had it removed. Still hoping that Venâncio would come bursting into the house, with gestures that Eulália had seen ripening down through the years, in time to share a beef stew with them.

Madruga allowed Venâncio just five minutes after the appointed hour to prove to himself that he had cheated them once again. Without saying anything to Eulália. Because he had never wanted to teach her about the pitfalls of everyday life. On the contrary, he always spared her certain petty realities.

On Monday, at the office, he summoned Venâncio. How dare he behave that way, toward Eulália of all people, the distinguished daughter of Dom Miguel?

At the mere mention of the name, Venâncio lost all his composure. Hurriedly offering apologies. For some time now he had been suffering from so many shocks to his nerves that he scarcely knew how to tie them in one bundle. A demanding life, that didn't give him time even to breathe. And as he talked, he seemed greatly agitated. He had lost considerable weight in recent months.

"And don't you have at least one Sunday free to come visit us?" Madruga said reprovingly, on his guard against a possible lie.

On inspecting the hotel to which in principle Venâncio was devoting part of his time, Madruga rarely ran into him. After breakfast, Venâncio went directly to the high seaside wall on the Avenida Beira-Mar, where he calmed his nerves by contemplating the Bay of Guanabara.

"Brazil began at the bottom of these waters. It's false to maintain that its one birthplace was Bahia," he stated to Madruga.

Fascinated by the sight, Venâncio went to extravagant lengths to defend those waters. In whose silt, he would say, lay countless historical memories, the majority of them buried forever. Anxiously echoing the illustrious Portuguese and French names that had happened to cruise past without approaching terra firma.

Facing those waters, he relived his own sea voyage. With which Madruga was associated. Both crossing an ocean in whose abysses lay Iberian caravels, English ones, ships of black and other pagan peoples. A recollection, however, that did not always please Madruga. Wavering, in that period, between the desire to give way to his emotions and the imperative need to make them disappear, to free himself of such a prison. If on the one hand he was still much given to dreaming, owing to the influence of Grandfather Xan, on the other he was afraid to assume a way of life that laid everything else aside, leaving room only for daydreaming. Hence in his eagerness to defend himself, whenever Venâncio tempted him to desert reality he loomed before him in the guise of an enemy. Madruga found it quite enough to have a dreamy wife, who covered the furniture of the house and her feelings with a delicate tulle veil so as to protect them from wear and tear.

In those three years of the Spanish Civil War, Venâncio made every effort to explore Madruga's subordinate feelings, his obvious aim being to undermine his morale. Unconsciously wanting to enroll him in the legion of the defeated, whose symbol had always been Uncle Justo. Madruga answered such moves with impatience, obliging Eulália to intervene.

Venâncio did not always listen to her. Unreconciled to the Republican defeat, he never ceased denouncing the peoples of Europe for having failed to appear on a scene where a people saw itself slowly decimated by force of arms.

"As long as Franco and his accursed followers hack the defeated to pieces, sack houses, and drive the people across the Pyrenees, I am unable to find a moment's rest. And I still deeply regret the fact that I did nothing to help them," and he hid his face so that they would not witness his anguish.

Madruga's consolation was to bring him coffee and cognac. Making him see, however, that it was not a question of defeat. No one in Spain had the moral right to claim a victory founded on piles of ruins and bloodshed.

"Not unless their aim is to exalt death. The one victor. The country reeks of corpses. There are so many dead that they still haven't found the time to bury them all."

Venâncio continued to pour his heart out against the Nationalists. They were the ones who had interrupted the dream of building the great Spanish Republic! And, in his acute phases, his hatred was focused on the Guardia Civil in particular, an institution invented to wipe out weaklings and poets. He was referring, naturally, to the death of García Lorca, whom he had always followed from a distance. Above all when Lorca visited the city of Buenos Aires, often known as the fifth province of Galicia. He had come close to setting foot in Brazil.

Madruga, for his part, felt aggrieved by the Republic, which had not granted Galicia autonomy. Thus having failed to free their language, their history, their legends.

"And why didn't they emancipate us?"

"They needed time to mend Spain."

From the very beginning of the conflict, Venâncio had taken to looking in on Tobias, just born, in his cradle. He would stay just long enough to leave a note on his godson's pillow each Sunday. Couched in phrases that varied according to the outcome of events on the battlefront. In them was a morbid tone of bitterness and disillusionment.

In the first of the long series, Venâncio pointed out: Tobias, I want you to know that in this month of July a fight is beginning that will shame and humiliate an entire people. But we'll win even so.

He never failed to end the notes with the phrase But we'll win, even so. And after looking down at his godson for a moment, he would leave. As Eulália came to the cradle, hastening to fold them up and tuck them away so that it wouldn't be Madruga who collected them. Later on, she put these notes, in Venâncio's own hand, in Tobias's box.

Eulália, moreover, had five of these boxes, all different. One for each child, to which only she had access. Without Madruga's ever questioning what was in them. Material that in the future would enable the children to tell their stories thanks to the facts stored in them.

Eulália always handled things with the most delicate care. So often bringing home certain odd-shaped leaves off the street, putting them between the pages of her missal. There to dry for a length of time that her peasant instinct decided would leave them physically intact. Only then were they divided up among the boxes.

A year after the war, Madruga decided that Eulália deserved a box in which to preserve her own memory. For a week he searched in the downtown antique shops for a piece worthy of a heart threaded with veins along which he pretended to journey when he held her in his arms. Moved at the thought that she had the surprising gift of absenting herself in spirit from the bed, as if searching for some remote stopping-off place.

In the Rua do Lavradio, he found the bright-red box, painted with *sangue-de-boi*. A vegetable dye extracted from brazilwood. At the sight of the present, Eulália blushed with embarrassment, certain that the box would one day speak for her more loudly than words.

To veil Madruga's criticisms of Venâncio's notes, Eulália maintained, during dinner, that thanks to their friend's expedient, their son would grow up with a horror of war. Without noticing that these words saddened Madruga, vexed at this confirmation of the similarity between Eulália and Venâncio.

The child grew up, not knowing that his bed had become a focal point of dispute. The weekly repository of Venâncio's anxiety. The place to which poignant notes came. It being of no use for Madruga to mutter out of the corner of his mouth. Not reconciled to the fact that his son's cradle was being overburdened by such a cruel reality.

The habit was suddenly interrupted when the end of the war came. And this coincided with Tobias's third birthday. In the face of this event, the note was laconic. I hope, godson, that in the future you will see the victory that today was denied me, wherefore my heart bleeds. And I with it.

It raised Venâncio's spirits to think that there now existed a pilgrim Spain, made up of the vanquished. Of those creatures who, in their flight, had either taken to the Pyrenees or boarded the few ships still tied up along the Spanish coasts. Without time to look back on a land fertilized with blood. Especially since the victors were beginning to wipe out the surviving Republicans and supposed sympathizers.

Spain, which so excited Venâncio's passions, had come to exist outside of the country itself. Daily swelled by the best men. Even though they were wretched men, wandering about the African deserts, roaming through French villages. Or else through generous and bitter Mexico, which understood so well the despair of exile. Men ready to offer their hosts, in return for bread and shelter, the substance of their tragedies.

Venâncio cited numbers, figures. When they were all accounted for, how many Spaniards were encamped throughout the length and breadth of America? The same America that now welcomed the cruel monsters of the past with a sentiment from which it had, to all appearances, rooted out all trace of rancor. One more reason for Spain to lose its lungs, its tongue, its brains.

Reflecting on this subject, Venâncio sought supporting facts in the past, the better to understand the present exodus. Undoubtedly this pilgrim Spain had put forth roots as far back as the era of the Conquest. A pilgrimage that in those days was undertaken in the name of faith, of syphilis, of expropriation, of plunder, of adventure, of dreams become bloody and fantastic realities. Within a historical framework in which Spain's decisions were ruled by fanaticism. The Conquest thus never able from the beginning to be carried out beneath the aegis of justice and self-sacrifice.

"Once the Spaniards and the Portuguese landed on these beaches and in these quagmires, they lost control over the course of destiny. No destiny could resist the colossal excesses of this continent. And hence everything began to be lived and recounted in a way diametrically opposed to the accounts of the official chroniclers. Those poor scribes who shat with fear at what they saw before their eyes, not understanding one thing. But if you really want to get a little closer to this adventure, to smell the stink of it, take Bernal Díaz, and tell everything so that it's precisely the reverse of what he wrote. Or else take Pero Vaz de Caminha, and imagine what sort of letter the Indians would have written about those Portuguese belching codfish and garlic!"

Madruga listened, criticizing Venâncio's arrogance. His abuse stemming from the fact that Venâncio had accumulated information that he himself did not have. The subject that had given rise to the discussion rubbed him the wrong way.

"And why exclude us immigrants from this dramatic pilgrimage of yours? Don't we deserve to be regarded as pilgrims, simply because we left Spain without making a big fuss about it, without rebelling? If it was misery alone that brought us?"

Venâncio's line of argument struck Madruga as snobbish. Without even noticing, he was erasing immigrants from the picture, for the one reason that they had always trod the boards of a humble stage, usually hidden away behind shop counters and in factories. With no achievements to boast of, no high-sounding names.

"We're as good as they are, Venâncio. To all intents and purposes we're pilgrims too. I'm part of that discontented and persecuted Spain that you're beginning to glamorize now. And isn't it true that we were expelled, that we were deported, that we were forbidden access to the land, to the profits of production? The only difference is that we were combatants in an undeclared war."

Venâncio disagreed. Immigrants such as they no doubt belonged to a category apart. They acted only on an individual basis, divorced from any sort of political ties. This detail nonetheless marking the difference between them and the others.

"What we need, Venâncio, is a party, ideology. In short, political thought. We're pilgrims without a political cause and without charismatic leaders," Madruga said in a louder voice.

"Don't forget, Madruga, that it was wealth that tempted our souls. Money is what brought us to America. So how can we dispute the label they've pinned on us?"

"You're wrong. Hunger is what brought us here. And hunger will always be a political act, wherever it manifests itself. Unfortunately, Venâncio, you're nothing but a lackey of the intellectuals, simply because you love books. Your admiration for books blinds you to the point that you absolve a class which is not yours and to which you have no entrée. On the other hand, you indirectly condemn the people, who are us. We who have had a declared civil war in the backyards and on the porches of our houses for centuries now. Almost no historian has undertaken to write about our misadventures. Why would they be interested in the battles waged beneath our roofs, in our humiliated hearts? Don't you see that we weren't the ones who started this damned war? That it was those who have always dominated us? And that they end up gaining the upper hand in any explosive political process? How come you protect people of this sort and absolve them from blame? Don't you see that the Francoists, the highest-ranking Republicans, the intellectuals, are all bastards?"

In a hard-pressing counterattack, Madruga demanded that Venâncio produce some sort of evidence that he might have had an adventure in this American territory that would justify his contempt for money and for certain constituted forms of power. It was absolutely necessary that he explain what moral shelter he had found for his dream to keep it so immaculate, even today.

As Madruga was speaking, Venâncio voiced not a single complaint. He passed his hand across his chest, as though trying to extract the barbs sent flying his way by his adversary. His face, however, became more and more contracted, till Venâncio haltingly admitted that not only had he lost material possessions, but his ability to dream had become more and more elusive in the last three years. He was finding himself more and more troubled by transfigured, hence unrecognizable, visions.

He paused briefly, still with the same disillusioned look. He picked up the bottle brought by Madruga, and held it up to the lighted lamp. He was thus able to examine its transparency, to catch sight of any dregs. He poured himself some wine and drank it down in one gulp. Then rested his head on his arms. He appeared to be asleep.

After these arguments, which wounded his pride, Venâncio would lock himself in his hotel room. Caring nothing about his work, reproving glances mattering little to him. And as he ate his meals in the restaurant of the hotel, he remained aloof from everyone. Chewing his food and his rage at the same time. He acted oddly, indifferent even to Madruga's pleas to look after his health.

"Forget the war, Venâncio. Spain has always fed on the flesh of its children. Don't go die for it now that there's no need to," he said hurriedly, busy as usual. Wanting him not to forget, however, that all countries wove the fabric of their collective destiny with the threads of discord and hatred.

But Madruga's advice was of no avail. Even living in Brazil, there was no way to escape the effects of the curse now gnawing away at the fragmented Spanish nation. For this very reason they could not resist the impulse to mourn the dead, even as they downed one beer after another in a bar on the Praça Mauá. Venâncio offering toasts to those who escaped by way of the frontiers and ports.

Venâncio's unhappy face finally exasperated Madruga. "Calm down, man. We haven't lost Spain yet. Anybody who's suffered eight centuries of Saracen domination is in a position to survive any tyrant. How many years do you think Franco's going to live? And even though he dreams of perpetuating himself in power, once he's passed on to eternity nobody's going to make a showpiece modern Cid out of him."

Madruga urged him to change hotels. It might do him good to live in Botafogo. To have a house of his own, with furniture and kitchen utensils. He was old enough, after all, to have a place of his own, away from his fellow workers, who unceremoniously knocked on the door of his room, irritating him always. The proof of this being that Venâncio didn't speak to them for days. Naturally earning the reputation of being eccentric.

But his comrades did not esteem him any the less for all that. They would even come to him asking him for stories that he would sometimes reluctantly agree to tell them. In a low voice in the beginning, lacking energy, but eventually working up to a rhythm that held the hushed audience spellbound, amid the steins of beer and the cigars.

Sometimes Madruga chanced upon him as he performed this function. And far from being appreciative, he was resentful of his friend's recent vocation as a narrator. As though Venâncio were putting into practice everything that he himself had learned from Xan, and in a manner of speaking transmitted to Venâncio during those years. He discreetly forced him to give up this undertaking. After all, what kind of a public was that, listeners as fickle as they come, immediately turning their backs on him, quite prepared to forget his stories?

Learning of this new aspect of Venâncio's personality, Eulália disagreed with her husband. She thought it necessary for Venâncio to explore this facet. Especially since life was simply a journey that took between fifty and eighty years for one to reach the end of the line, the last station of its destiny. This long trip requiring, however, a goodly supply of food and words.

To do battle with Eulália, Madruga suggested to Venâncio that he marry. Marriage not only had the seal of approval of the Church, and of society, but also served as an anchor for the average man. Among other advantages, money would necessarily assume a new meaning for him. He would finally take on the financial responsibilities that followed in the wake of affection and regular hot meals.

After twenty-seven years in Brazil, Venâncio still stubbornly steered clear of going into business and turning fat profits. If he didn't win, he didn't lose either, he always said. Not to mention his violent rejection of the acquisitiveness that any fortune represented. The advent of gold in man's life.

Madruga heaped sarcasm on the use made of these images coined by his friend. The one thing Venâncio hadn't yet gotten around to doing was developing a scatology wherein money was something to wipe one's ass with. And it could well be that he acted as he did in order to protect himself from the attraction it had for him. A spell, moreover, to which the Iberian peninsula had always succumbed. It was well to remember that Spaniards and Portuguese had been brought up to love money. From a very early age they placed their trust in the power, and in the efficacy, of gold.

"It was of this love, moreover, that America was born!" Madruga said jokingly.

And he suggested to Venâncio that he place a gold piece in his mouth and note the taste of it. The refreshing coldness that emanated from the hard surface of the coin. The voluptuous sensation of a shape with the power to buy empires and jewels.

He immediately offered to finance whatever house or apartment Venâncio chose. Or pay his rent for him till he was on his feet.

"Leave Cinelândia, Venâncio. That's no place to live. Only hermits persist in living in those buildings that are completely dark after six at night, as thought they'd died. What a dreary thing a marquee with its neon lights turned off is!"

Venâncio roamed the back streets of the city till he was exhausted. Sometimes he entered the Palácio do Monroe, to attend the sessions of the Chamber of Deputies. From the gallery, he accompanied step by step the agony of an orator of the likes of Roberto Mangabeira, still on the floor of the Chamber, about to mount to the speaker's platform. How many times he had managed to get a good look at him. The man's hands were surely ice-cold, yet every inch of his massive body was throbbing with life. He shook uncontrollably from head to foot. And, finally, he would begin to speak. There immediately came forth the main proposition, an outpouring that nonetheless outlined the objectives perfectly. Always the desperate search for a clarity with which to organize, from beginning to end, words which, overstepping the bounds of natural syntactic order, would be placed in the service of passion and the conscience of a country coming into being.

"Whenever Mangabeira speaks, I sense the drama. He knows very well what's hidden behind each word delivered from the speaker's platform. And that it will depend entirely on him to regulate the flame of his oratory, to keep it alight. Mangabeira is acutely aware of this burden. And he suffers because of a reputation for which he alone is responsible. So when he is on the dais of the Chamber, he is afraid the whole time that the spoken word, and what is behind it, may fail him at the opportune moment. And that he may begin to die, then and there, in the limelight, in full view of everyone."

After hearing different speakers, Venâncio would leave Monroe not knowing what to think. Their impassioned speeches did not seem to him to express the reality he sensed in the streets. But was there any politician capable of expressing this confused and wholly disregarded reality? Or was it in fact only silence and failure that told the story of a people invariably possessed of little feeling for hierarchies and glorious chronologies?

Eulália would offer him tea with sweet biscuits and toast when he paid her a surprise visit in the middle of the week. Anxious to calm him down and keep him from losing even more weight. While at the same time suggesting to him, discreetly, that he not embrace so wholeheartedly emotions originating in voracious and unstable countries, such as Spain and Brazil, resembling leeches. For how could he give house room to so many contradictions, lies, and hypocrisies, without being threatened by illness, the specter of death?

Venâncio would sit very straight in his chair, concealing his frailness. Yet his shoulders sagged beneath the weight of his fatigue. He seemed, at such times, to be carrying Spain on his back, as though it were a leather knapsack. While Brazil, despite its young and falsely lyrical tenor voice, weighed as much as a boulder that he must lift from the ground all by himself.

"One cannot live in intense coexistence with two such deadly countries as Brazil and Spain. You will have to make your peace with one of them within your soul. Otherwise they'll end up killing you," it was Madruga's turn to say.

Venâncio refused to move from the hotel. He was fond of the little bars of Cinelândia. Of getting wind on one street corner or another of what was really happening politically. Of being on the spot as intrigues were born, amid warm straw.

Haunting the Amarelinho Bar, in that decadent, phantasmagorical district, he harbored the illusion that he was counteracting his own reserved, shy temperament. Confronted with strange faces, he regained his ability to dream, to enjoy emotions that he would never have known how to engender by himself. Even though, there too, he felt like an outsider. Setting foot in a country which, in disparate movements, alternately accepted and rejected him. As though in this way he would not be able to forget that Brazil had not been his first manger.

Once the war broke out, Venâncio walked the streets in a state of panic. Fearing that he would suddenly be included under the terms of a law meant to exclude foreigners. Threatening to stigmatize him as a stateless person and, perhaps, as a traitor. Without knowing which way to turn, should Brazil no longer want him. Would he go to a Spain at war, the roar of whose exploding bombs rang continually in his ears?

In these wanderings, his loneliness lay heavily upon him. The absence of a home or even a homeland. And this despite his carping at the notion of a homeland, which was simply an idealistic invention. Merely an area where taboos, repressions, terrors piled up. Vital forces never allowing the citizen to devote himself to the building of his own republic. The homeland then turning into a territory through which to pass fleetingly, in an alcoholic stupor. With geographical and cultural contours drawn only by the managers of public affairs, charged with expelling from that homeland any dissident voice.

On the streetcar taking him to Glória, the sea breeze lashing his face, Venâncio heard the clatter of the streetcar tracks and the tinkling of the coins in the conductor's nimble fingers. Observing the motorman's erect posture. Catching stifling whiffs of his neighbor's armpits. Feeling at one with those ugly, toothless faces, he felt rancor at having had no share in the genesis of that people. How many of them born of rapid, compulsive couplings? Genes sprung from guilt and garbage.

In bar conversations, he had difficulty identifying with past memories of this people. As a general rule going back only as far as the days of slavery. This impediment owing to the lack of grandfathers and fathers to tell about Brazil. He had landed in Brazil, after all, like a migratory bird. And stayed there beneath the shade of a tree with a luxuriant leafy crown, whose branches spread over the whole of Brazilian soil. At the mercy of storms and lightning. Having brought with him, as baggage, his inheritance of stories full of acts of vengeance and arbitrary will. Which enhanced the spell by intimately associating them with fear. Stories, these, whispered in his ear in childhood, by his mother, blowing her garlic breath in his face. Eager at the same time to condemn her neighbors and their predatory ways.

As for Brazilian stories, they had a less dramatic genealogy. Perverse, nonetheless, since it involved captive blacks and whites scratching their balls in front of pilgrims. Shut up in slave quarters, the blacks heard from their elders the tales come directly from Africa. Viewed with scorn by the whites, who sucked on gleaming black nipples. From Portugal, the whites were pleased to spread, beneath the aegis of the Christian, Lusitanian home, phrases dripping with venom, elegance, and power.

As a matter of fact, Madruga could not understand Venâncio. He had no notion of what it meant to live in the very heart of Brazil. Cinelândia becoming, along with Lapa, the sensual, promiscuous redoubt within which there circulated the only subjects powerful enough to transform a mere city into a capital. This truth was so evident that Getúlio Vargas, the official occupant of the Palácio do Catete, sent his spies there to auscultate the mystic body of the nation. And thanks to this practice he managed to delay his downfall, maintaining himself in power for fifteen years.

The very streets, the asphalt, the paving stones from the Praça Mahatma Gandhi to the Rua Senador Dantas exuded not only passions but the vague and confused enigma which normally envelops words in an impenetrable cocoon. From these blood-soaked areas, however, came signals which the backlands, the scrublands, the pampas, all the Brazilian provinces interpreted correctly. The rest of the country, in a way, reproducing Cinelândia. For this very reason, any project aimed at permanently interpreting the national soul, in accordance with a single model, capitulated and collapsed in the face of the confused and tormented imagination ruled by Cinelândia in its frenzy, picking up at the same time vibrations coming from the Palácio do Monroe, with its legislators from the regions hardest hit.

As for the necessity of living by himself, away from the hotel, Venâncio finally gave in to Madruga's arguments. Within a week he chose a little apartment on the Avenida Beira-Mar. From the twelfth floor of the building, facing the bay, all of Brazil lay before him. A view thus rousing, alternately, his sense of delight and his sense of indignation. With the advantage of allowing him to take the elevator downstairs, and tune in again to the clamor of popular voices. To take in, from close at hand, the cathartic, desperate mood of the nameless mass drinking coffee or beer. Knowing himself before the fact to be doomed to oblivion.

Madruga hid Venâncio's state of mind from Eulália. Though Venâncio declared himself satisfied with his new home, Madruga nonetheless had misgivings about the absent look in his eye, his wild, obsessive pronouncements. Coming to fear that there were cracks and seepages in him that could not be seen. Perhaps he had not paid close enough attention to what was happening to Venâncio, failing to notice that, in the course of events, something secret and delicate had wounded him deeply! In the end, the process of modernization sought by Venâncio had in a way impelled him to live on intimate terms with a humanity steeped in exacerbated passion and moral misery. The only thing he'd managed to turn up being a heap of vile and offensive material.

Unlike Venâncio, Madruga guarded against profound self-examination. Tied to money, he had become complacent about a society from which he benefited. Not to mention his disillusionment with the course of history, which had never taken any notice whatsoever of his interests. For that very reason he resisted the attraction of any language that bore promise of substantive reforms. By thus rejecting the use of certain verbal and emotional equipment, Madruga erected a barbed-wire fence around himself as protection. Though still counting on the family, who fed him liberal servings of the normality he craved.

As this was happening to Madruga, Venâncio was slowly hiding himself deeper and deeper in a dense black forest, from which he was to have a hard time emerging. And as if the effects of the end of the civil war were not enough, he suffered at close hand from the dictatorship imposed by Getúlio.

He wandered about the streets with an eye out for Filinto Müller's myrmidons, staked out on every corner and in the bars. Sending to the prison on the Rua Frei Caneca, on the pretext of cleaning up the nation, men such as Graciliano Ramos and Hermes Lima. Whereas nothing was known about Prestes. Whether he was still alive, after horrible mistreatment.

The prisons had turned into temples where exquisite pathologies were practiced. There were rumors that, *intra muros,* the nipples of the wives of Communists were permanently damaged. Berger's own wife, Elise Ewert, had been brutally tortured and raped before her husband's eyes, the luckless man having already been driven half mad. They were thinking of sending her to the Nazi concentration camps. The same fate was in store for Olga Benário, despite her being pregnant. Decisions that were really death sentences, signed Getúlio Vargas.

Madruga tried to bring Venâncio back to reality. Having made his escape, Venâncio turned a deaf ear. He was like a kite fluttering this way and that. Off on a journey into fantasy and anxiety. As though there were no way back. He had simply succumbed to the weight of a history made up entirely of demoniacal labyrinths. A table companion sharing, at a distance, raw and bloody episodes.

Eulália sensed Madruga's tenseness the moment he came into the room. Connecting this fact with Venâncio, she did her best to keep her husband from thinking the worst. After Venâncio's repeated absences from Sunday dinner, Eulália had stopped urging the family to make it a festive meal. She thought it unfair of them to enjoy the pleasure of the dining room now, forgetting all about him. It was a matter of finding out if something had happened to him on that Sunday to make him fail to show up. Since Venâncio would not call them in case of emergency. He dreaded bothering them. He always refused favors and extra comforts.

Suspecting that Madruga was lying to her so as to spare her any unpleasantness, Eulália took a deep breath, demanding the truth. After all, her husband's destiny, in America, also included Venâncio. She herself had met Venâncio on the dock, at the foot of the stairs, on disembarking in Brazil for the first time. Discreet and reserved, holding wildflowers in his hands. The nicest flowers she'd ever received. She tended, moreover, to value such politeness, hence she never forgot the flowers of this meeting. Of this Venâncio who, despite his scrawniness and his forlornness, seemed to her to be a stone shelter illuminated by a little lighted hanging lamp.

Madruga was always protective of Eulália. When he wounded her sensibilities with his violent temperament, he would hasten to apologize, expecting one of her little smiles. In view of these susceptibilities, he had avoided confessing to her that Venâncio, though still among the living, had dug a hole in which to hide himself and his numbed soul. He was afraid that something serious had happened to him.

"Venâncio is ashamed to tell you that he's in love with a widow. She lives in Méier, with two children. It's there on the veranda of her house that he spends his free afternoons. But since Venâncio hasn't allowed their relationship to come to light, the widow isn't able to come with him when he visits friends," Madruga said, suddenly resorting to deliberate falsehood.

But immediately, taking pleasure in what he was saying, he added that Venâncio himself admitted having learned a great deal from this lady. All he needed was to work up his courage to tell her of his affection. Or perhaps to express it.

"I think Venâncio's going to get married at last. In a little while we'll be having more guests for Sunday dinner."

Eulália seemed to attach no importance to the matter. Except that the next day she declared to her husband that in her opinion Venâncio was too young to get married.

"And what about me then, Eulália? I already have five children and I was born in the same year as Venâncio! On the contrary, Venâncio's too old to marry."

His wife's remarks irritated him. In the city, he had already asked Venâncio to tell him what the new apartment was like. He would not describe it in detail, nor did he urge him to come see it. Merely mentioning that he was a neighbor of Manuel Bandeira, the famous poet he had already seen strolling around the block, in dark-framed glasses setting off mischievous twinkling eyes.

Madruga was not displeased, considering that Venâncio had finally decided on a place to live. As proof that he was improving. All he needed now was a woman to warm his bed and his meals. Once those steps had been taken, the somber visions of Spain would fade away, leaving Venâncio again enraptured by the world of the imagination, which he always spoke of as being humanity's finest product.

Venâncio promised him to come by that Sunday. Madruga planned to celebrate the occasion with a special red wine. Informed of the visit, Eulália ordered beef stew. On Saturday, a note from Venâncio curtly informed Madruga that for an unexpected reason he had found it necessary to be out of town. He suggested to him that he dock his salary for the days he'd be gone.

Madruga resented Venâncio's discourtesy. His leaving on holiday without at least bidding him a few brief words of farewell. Despite his hurry, he could very well have come by to give him a friendly hug, and in passing, have asked to borrow a monogrammed sheet, an indispensable item in one's going-away outfit.

In the hotel, he made inquiries as to what had happened. None of the employees could tell him where Venâncio had gone. They had simply seen him leaving in the afternoon, after work, with a furtive look in his eye, which they all recognized. On reaching the front desk, however, he had asked the boy for a frozen apple, which he'd eaten there on the spot. First complaining of the fact that the coldness of the fruit, besides hurting his teeth, wouldn't leave much of a taste in his mouth. The manager, in particular, swore that a blond woman, on permanent night duty on the corner by the hotel, had taken him to Cordeiro, in the interior of the state, where she had been born. It not being possible for Venâncio to resist such insistent solicitations.

"Who is this woman I've never seen around here?" Madruga shouted nervously, suspecting dangerous mischief afoot.

It occurred to him to go to the Biblioteca Nacional, in search of clues. To discover, for example, what books Venâncio had been reading recently. He was informed that the Spaniard, a frequent visitor, had not yet gone any farther back in time than the Brazilian history of recent years, for which he appeared to have a veritable passion. In the last week he had reread in particular the speeches of Bernardo Pereira de Vasconcellos, giving every sign of knowing them by heart.

Somewhat relieved, Madruga began to have his doubts about the woman from Cordeiro. But in order to justify Venâncio's absence to Eulália, he again trotted out the story of the widow. A case threatening each day to become serious. With the aggravating circumstance that she was now giving every evidence of understanding how eager Venâncio's soul was to take wing. Having therefore learned to hang on to him without using force. Making him alight gently on the vacant lot in Méier, on which they intended to build his house.

"Can Venâncio have abandoned us for good?" Eulália said sadly.

Madruga had the impression he was involved in a real potboiler. It would have been better if Venâncio had taken off with the blonde, thus proving the hotel manager right. What was certain was that Venâncio's discretion had never given them the slightest opening through which to glimpse his sex life. He refused to verbalize the nature of his feelings.

Madruga regretted his absence. Venâncio was the only one he counted on to help him when he needed essential facts concerning his own life. On seeing him downcast, Venâncio would enumerate details that put his state of mind in a more favorable light, thanks to a memory placed in his friend's service. Ever on the alert for moments in which his sentiments might attain full expression. And, this being so, Madruga could not face the idea that Venâncio had betrayed him, fleeing into the shadow with the intention of wounding him.

He gave an anxious start on hearing knocks at the door of his study. In his mind's eye he saw a clerk from the Spanish consulate, bringing him official notice of Venâncio's death. Or else the arrival of a letter, with a Spanish postage stamp, in which Venâncio regretted his sudden departure, due to the fact that the Dutch cargo vessel he was leaving on had been obliged to advance its sailing date from Rio, thus giving him no time for the usual farewells. Not mentioning, however, in what part of the country he had taken refuge. Whether the village was near Seville, Cadiz, or Córdoba.

He immediately discarded this hypothesis. He did not think it plausible that Venâncio would return to Franco's Spain, not even to visit the family he had left. Even though the tyrant lived in Madrid, under the protection of the perverse Moorish guard, he detested sharing Spain with him.

Suddenly, Madruga was worried. Had Venâncio perhaps managed to overcome these moral and political obstacles for the one purpose of shutting himself up in the Seville Library and consulting the books that described an America long dreamed of, even before its discovery?

A week later, Venâncio appeared. Looking well, and neatly dressed. With a light tan, typical of the mountains. And in contrast to his long silences, he gave an account of the journey that had provided him with prodigious details of a country that lacked historical records.

Influenced, doubtless, by foreign travelers of the past, Venâncio had tackled the subject of Brazil as seen through a confusing magnifying glass. Its defect being that it enlarged those details that the ordinary Brazilian would have ignored. He emphasized, over and over, that the myth of the earthly paradise had, in fact, arisen in Brazil, owing to its prodigies of nature and its colors so bright they hurt your eyes.

Madruga was amazed at this exuberance. And dumbfounded that, out of sympathy for that unknown civilization, Venâncio should attempt to purge himself, amid a spew of words, of his last remaining European traces. As he kept pointedly consulting the clock, as though expecting a call.

His worries laid to rest by Venâncio's return, Madruga grew impatient at this long account. Whereby Venâncio set about inventing a country in perfect accord with his utopia. Madruga eyed the clock. He was sorry, but he had an engagement, he had to leave. He promised to hear him out at dinner the following Sunday.

On Saturday, Madruga received another note confirming Venâncio's recently acquired love of travel. He had taken off again, without saying where he was going. Pursuing, this time, the idea that he ought to explore the vast coastal regions. So as to steal from the Portuguese discoverers the feeling of disbelief that had assailed them as those great stretches of land loomed before their boats approaching the shore. Standing rigid in the prow, every last man of them, fearful of the consequences of acts that had indirectly expelled them from Europe, hurtling them once and for all into the belly of America. Utterly stupefied, surely, in the face of that enigma with which reality confronted them, even before landing. The Portuguese, of all people, whom Europe had taught to disbelieve in enigmas, having assured them that the supply of mysteries and adventures had run out. And there America was, hairy and barbarous, squarely confronting Europe with its neatly explained soul.

Madruga could no longer contain himself. And he set Venâncio's dubious fate before Eulália. But, to his surprise, she put his mind at rest. A man with Venâncio's soaring spirit would surely come through the most difficult tests with flying colors. Anyone as capable of dreaming as he was, without getting lost in the oneiric universe, would know how to swim back to earth, leaving behind the inevitable temptations.

"It's better for him to go off traveling than to bury himself in a marriage that may not turn out right. And if Venâncio has been eager to go off on trips these days, that means he wants to save himself. What he wants most of all is to forget the Spanish tragedy," Eulália said cheerfully.

Already, in the dying days of the war, Madruga had come to fear a dramatic outcome for Venâncio. Venâncio, however, had survived the sound and fury of the final defeat. Yet Eulália was right. He had gone traveling in order to cure himself permanently.

Despite everything, Madruga's mind was not at rest. He felt guilty. He hadn't paid the attention to him he should have. When Venâncio spoke to him about the war, he found ways to avoid listening to him, as though the Spanish tragedy did not concern him. With a feeling of compunction, he imagined Venâncio's body, at that moment, on the rough concrete of some wretched train station on the Leopoldina line, through which he had chanced to pass in search of affection. Alongside his body, a lighted candle, brought by a stranger, whose flame warded off the darkness of the deserted spot. And, for lack of anyone to reclaim the body, they would bury him in a common grave. Without whispering memories of his native village, of the years spent in America, in his ear. Those years that had robbed him for good of youth and hope. There Venâncio was, dead, with no name and no flowers. And Madruga unable to touch his hands in farewell.

That vision left Madruga deeply distraught. He wanted, then, to be present among Venâncio's belongings, to rest, perhaps, in his apartment. Without further thought, he went immediately to the Avenida Beira-Mar. Insisting that the doorman open Venâncio's door for him, since he was a friend. He urgently needed to retrieve certain documents in his friend's apartment. He was prepared to reward him handsomely.

The doorman tried to interrupt him, but Madruga, in his eagerness to persuade him, wouldn't let him get a word in edgewise. Already taking out his wallet, when a sullen look suddenly came over the man's face.

"That's not necessary. Just go up and knock on his door. He's waiting for you."

"Is he back from his trip already?" Happy that his friend was among the living once again.

"Senhor Venâncio hasn't been away. He doesn't like to go places. As far as I know, he's never even been across the bay to Niterói."

He didn't dare back down in front of the doorman, who accompanied him to the elevator. He needed only to knock on the door now. Venâncio let Madruga in as though he had been waiting for him. Indifferent to the fact that Madruga had caught him in a lie. Politely showing him the apartment, invaded by books and piles of old newspapers. He called his attention to the periscope mounted on a tripod, next to the window, facing the bay. So as to observe the mysterious waters.

"There's not one boat, under any flag, that enters and leaves the bay without my knowing it," he said proudly, with a feverish look in his eye.

He remained for hours at a time at the window, inspecting the foreign ships about to tie up in the city. He mistrusted all of them, naturally. The majority bent on pillage. Intending to take back to their home ports a substantial part of the wealth of Brazil. Colonial practices were thus being revived, even today, in modern dress. The ships and their crews having in their favor the extreme avarice of the ruling classes, who saw their share of the loot appreciably increased thereby. And even the boundless naïveté of the natives, ready to hand themselves over entirely in return for praise and a handful of trinkets.

Above and beyond such information, the periscope offered him the rare opportunity of abandoning the year in which he lived, simply by making use of its lenses. Not to go visit the future, which in fact was of little interest to him. But to land in the first part of the nineteenth century, where apparently certain of the key bases of the country had been established. This was such certain fact that if Eulália, Madruga, and he had arrived there in that precise period of grave political changes, they would have actively participated in the history under way. With the result that he would have taken personal possession of the feeling of belonging to Brazil. And been freed, consequently, of the oppressive burden of coming to terms with two native countries, each at once cruel and ambitious. Both of them impressing, by force, a sensibility upon his living flesh, at the mercy of human harshness.

"What's the use of my being so wealthy as to possess two countries, if the two of them want to divide me, if both make me feel I don't belong anywhere?" Such an unsettling situation making it necessary to adopt contradictory points of view concerning the same question. Time and again not even knowing how to think it through.

He paused. Heedless of the effects he was producing in Madruga. Beginning to hold forth once more, he immediately asked him to forgo questions having to do with the Brazil of a hundred years before. Since each time he came close to a verbal formula more or less coinciding with the world brought into view by the spyglass, he practically lost sight of this Brazil. The confused vision brought him only a handful of blacks, Indians, whites, all lying in a heap together on the ground and around the table. Obsessed with making a country and sex at the same time. Their sole motive, moreover, for repeatedly discussing politics, even as they fucked. And speaking of genitalia as they created legal institutions to rule their social life. These lapses in fact confusing them, since despite this sort of impediment they were striving to conceive a nation.

Lately, the periscope had presented him with a problem. Though he cleaned the lenses with alcohol and flannel, they frequently fogged. Whereupon the instrument, with no apparent explanation, would automatically bring him back to the year 1940. In total disregard for his will, which wished to go on its own way in the nineteenth century.

An incident that immediately became most unsettling. Since he felt torn to pieces, with essential parts of himself frankly at odds among themselves.

"Try the telescope," Venâncio said, keeping it glued to the window, Madruga not daring to disobey. "I suspect it goes backward and forward in time, depending on what sort of person is looking through it. In your case, the glass is going to take you into the future. Which will be a shame, Madruga. I think you lack the tragic inclination to lose yourself in the past."

Venâncio's eyes, little blazing craters, rapidly opened and closed, emitting incomprehensible signs. And from his mouth there trickled a thread of spittle, without his having noticed.

Madruga was frightened, not knowing how to act. As though it were Eulália and Grandfather Xan there. He loved them all. Deeply moved, he folded back the sheet. With extreme care, he slowly wiped the corners of his mouth. Venâncio did not budge, approving his gesture. He looked like a shipwreck victim whose legs, entangled in the seaweed of historical events, were carrying him to the bottom of the sea.

Suddenly Venâncio shuddered from head to foot, freeing himself from the claw next to his face. Madruga leaned back in the armchair, pretending to appreciate the room cluttered with meaningless objects. On the console table were three glass owls.

Venâncio, embarrassed, went over to him. And in a quick gesture touched his friend's hand. Immediately drawing away, without giving him time to reciprocate. He had gotten the better of a heart of marble.

"What's happening, Madruga? What are you feeling?" Venâncio said, reversing the roles. The words chosen as though he were removing them from his throat with tweezers.

Madruga was afraid. He felt himself incapable of saving a friend. Venâncio's loneliness made him the sole passenger of a boat captured by the fogged lenses of his field glass. Without a doubt, Venâncio had capitulated before the advances of the barbarians, among whom he, Madruga, was included. Perhaps the excessive pain had finally destroyed the delicate fabric of Venâncio's imagination, rent now, unbalanced and aimless.

Deeply distressed, Madruga attempted to speak. It was necessary to confront the situation squarely.

"You're not well, Venâncio. You need rest. And a doctor to take care of you. Perhaps it would be best if you went to the Spanish Benefit Society, of which we're members," he said warily.

Madruga's initial tenderness had given way to an assertive tone. Madruga gained strength in moments of decision. His mind felt at ease now.

"Come give me an embrace, Venâncio. Let's seal this meeting."

Venâncio drew back, in defense of his threatened territory.

"I shall not abandon my observation post. That is what the enemies of Brazil would like. And my enemies. For me to stop keeping a close watch on them."

Venâncio's self-absorbed face examined Madruga, accusing him of betrayal. An adversary in the service of foreign interests.

"Please, leave me alone now. I have a lot to think about and a lot to do. I promise to visit all of you next Sunday."

Madruga still wanted to persuade him to come out. But Venâncio confronted him with outthrust chest. Madruga judged it prudent to hold his tongue. Immediately, however, Venâncio's face darkened.

"Can it be that there is no place on earth to calm a wounded man?"

With a gesture, he refused Madruga's aid. He slammed the door in his face, not waiting for Madruga, in the entry hall, to head toward the elevator.

On Sunday, Madruga woke up in a state. He regretted not having canceled the invitation extended to Venâncio. He thereby risked exposing Eulália to the harsh light of the truth of their friend's condition. Eulália, however, bustled happily about the house, followed by Odete. The two of them working out the details of the dinner. And when the doorbell rang, Eulália herself went to answer. In a rush of affection, wanting only to embrace Venâncio, without further ado. But Venâncio, who always dodged those warmest of welcomes, sidestepped her again. On the other hand, he had not forgotten the flowers, immediately arranged by Eulália in the pitcher already filled with water.

They seated themselves politely in the living room. Madruga crossed his legs, preparing to offer his usual welcoming speech. When suddenly Venâncio cut him short by pointing to a book, apparently with neither title nor illustrations, for the moment in his possession. It was a diary, hitherto kept in secret, in which for the last three years he had been recording his personal impressions. And which was now to be handed over to a faithful guardian.

Madruga stirred proudly in his armchair. He interpreted Venâncio's attitude as atonement for the episode in the apartment. By entrusting the diary to him, Venâncio was indirectly proposing a reconciliation. Madruga was happy that this was so. He settled back in his chair then, awaiting events.

"I see no one better than Eulália to take proper care of the diary. First, however, I should like to beg a favor of you," Venâncio said.

"You have only to ask," she replied modestly, without looking at her husband.

"Nobody is to be able to read it except you. You and you alone," and he pretended to ignore Madruga's feelings of perplexity and undoubted hurt at his choice.

Obviously excluded from the inheritance, Madruga contained himself, out of pride. He remained silent, thinking of the next step. He had to act, on pain of being thought a coward or deeply wounded.

"What a surprise, Venâncio! I had no idea you had literary inclinations. Now that I know about the diary, I agree with you. Eulália is the ideal person to keep it. I too would have chosen her. It's a shame I don't have a diary," he said in a thunderous voice, smiling.

Eulália clasped the diary to her breast. Moved by an object filled with memories. She hastened to thank him for his confidence. She intended to read this testimony in the future, in a moment of contemplation. After coming home from Mass.

"Enough of all this polite bowing and scraping. You'd think we were diplomats," Madruga said, with a jovial air. "Let's go on in to the dinner table this minute. That's the place to pay tribute to food, which is still humanity's most valuable daily record. Nothing worse than cold food."

At table Venâncio meticulously separated the food on his plate. A habit he took to when depressed. Meaning that he would leave it almost untouched. Eulália felt bad. She had been counting on the traditional beef stew to make sure he'd eat with a will.

Late in the afternoon, it began to rain, as they were resting in the living room. Madruga yawned, feeling a bit sleepy. He fought his drowsiness by amusing himself with the children, running excitedly around the table now.

"I'm ready to leave. We can go whenever you want." Venâncio suddenly said.

"Go where?"

Venâncio didn't want to say anything in front of Eulália. The woman sensed from his silence that the situation was delicate.

She tried to calm them down. "I don't know where, but I'll go with you too."

Venâncio begged her to stay behind. She had to take care of the children and the house. Where destiny was taking him, she was not able to follow him.

"And where is it you're going, that a friend can't go with you?"

"Only Madruga can take me, Eulália."

"Where to, Venâncio? Don't leave me all on edge," Madruga insisted.

"To the Spanish Benefit Society. That's where I'm going to stay."

Madruga feared the consequences of a decision he himself had suggested. He wanted to back out. Perhaps there was time.

"Calm down, Venâncio, we mustn't act hastily. This is a serious matter."

"It's already been decided, Madruga. And you mustn't feel responsible. I'm going on my own," avoiding his eyes.

Eulália drew closer. "Are you certain you decided all by yourself? It wasn't Madruga who persuaded you?" she questioned him in a harsh voice, one never heard from Eulália.

Venâncio shook his head. He was the master of his own fate. Madruga did not have such powers. He then went over to the children to say good-bye. Tobias was the only one to receive a kiss on the forehead. Then he headed out of the room, with Eulália at his heels.

At the door, Eulália halted. Her arms were crossed over her bosom. Sensing how upset she was, Madruga enfolded her in a close embrace, from which Eulália gently drew away.

Venâncio went on ahead, without bidding Eulália good-bye. On the veranda, however, a few paces farther on, he looked back. He felt in debt to the woman.

"I'm not out of my mind, Eulália. I simply need to adapt myself to the reality made by men such as Madruga."

Resolutely, he went to join Madruga, who had reached the street and was standing waiting for him.

The photograph on the wall, visibly aged, appeared to be possessed of life and movement. From it there leaped out, a bit restless, the seated figures of Madruga and Eulália, and their five children grouped around them: Esperança, Miguel, Bento, Antônia, Tobias. Though I could identify them by name, I felt that they had lied to me down through those years. Up until that time, they had contrived to shelter their secret passions behind their best Sunday clothes. Perhaps deliberately aiming at my unveiling them in the future. They were nonetheless my family, the apparent mark of my blood. All bound together by the feeling of anxiety and perpetuity.

Immured in Grandfather's study, I was awaiting a knock on the door announcing Eulália's death. Grandmother was taking a long time dying, despite her effort to fulfill a desire newly possessed of the lineaments of revelation. Surrounded by Grandfather's books, I was keeping my distance from Eulália, who was awaiting her end like a mere mortal. Oblivious of a family scattered about the house now, having life on their side, and a limitless drive toward human objects.

Madruga had summoned me immediately, after learning that death was tracking his wife. As, angry at this fate, he forbade the members of the family to speak to him without his express permission. Eulália's death, before leaving him heart-stricken, was robbing him of his memory.

At his side, as all of them arrived, I observed the events ruled by Grandmother's lingering death. There was no one who did not make every effort, amid tears and feverish gestures, to inquire into the last moments of that woman who had watered plants and showered affection with profound moderation. There was within her children an anxiety to see her body from up close, to palpate a sickness about to take her so far away that none of her gestures would be reproduced save with the aid of the memory of each one of them. A memory bent in its turn upon effacing mother-images, the reality of which Eulália was a part. Until everything became blurred, as though Eulália had not existed.

Perhaps Eulália's children, who had entered life by way of that aged body, who had successfully negotiated a woman's tunnel of passion in order to be born, wanted only to enter her vagina and, by way of this last journey, come to dominate the mystery of their own genesis.

But what strange properties had that woman developed to keep them forever united? In what way did she join together, with her fingers and her heartstrings, those shards of glass that repelled each other, so as to form a stained-glass window that would reveal to them, despite their imperfections, a story of which they were an indissoluble part? With a pair of shears, doubtless, Eulália had pruned away their excesses of love and hate. She had likewise shorn them of their rancorous words, hiding the scraps inside the wardrobe chest. Who could Eulália have been, for each child to weep for her coming death as though it were his or her own?

Lying in her bed, Eulália emitted discreet gestures and a certain amount of warmth, that of someone who had begun to take her leave. Grateful for the presence of a family eager to respond, there round her bed, to the world's perceptible, tragic appeals. For even when they withdrew, doing battle with the onslaughts of passion, behind this reserve lay a strange intensity. In the depth of those eyes, a white sheet was raised, waving farewell to a boat lost on the horizon, whose specter and form were a legacy from Madruga and Eulália. Both natives of a land stigmatized by the pain of separation and the awareness of death.

Perhaps we were concealing in those hours a disturbing sensitivity, come down to us through ancestors who had approached the abyss of human greed as they drank wine and goat's milk, and stubbornly preserved legends that for centuries stuffed souls full of lies and temptations.

Odete cared for Grandmother with the conviction that she would follow her after the funeral ceremonies. The gestures of that black woman, who had never known the salty taste of another body, appeared to indicate that she would be the one who would seal Eulália's definitive embrace of death. On that night, lashed with particular violence by the southwest wind blowing against the windowpanes of the house, Eulália's breast breathed discreet sighs. Life making itself manifest in her with the force of a mystery that whispered to me how inaccessible Grandmother was.

Madruga's study was maintained as an unbreachable fortress. To which he repaired when out of sorts. In that room Grandfather taught me to identify accumulated objects, shared with me the bottles of cognac long laid away that he was so proud of. And through belongings such as tro-

phies, medals, diplomas, insignia, books, photographs, Madruga's itinerary since his arrival in Brazil could perhaps be reconstructed. How many
times, clad in Grandfather's skin, I looked at Brazil as though I were he.
The Brazil seen through photographs, through newspaper clippings,
through silences that the two of us forged.

I saw Brazil in Madruga's face. And in it, also, traces of Eulália and of
Venâncio. As if the three might at times form a single face, composed of
wrinkles deriving from the trials and tribulations of each of them. That
room, however, housed Madruga's untamed spirit. There thus being no
possibility of visiting it without his automatically subjecting the visitor to
the scenario he judged most appropriate for making that room understand-
able. A sort of foreign province, where he spent hours. And the fact of
having once gone there did not mean that one could return to it casually.
But with the excuse that Eulália was dying, I had invaded the study, so that
my soul could bleed on the carpet under the guardianship of objects that I
had seen gradually fading away since my childhood. I now contemplated
Grandfather's leather armchair, worn out from all the sweat and torments
of his that it had absorbed. The wear and tear of the furniture thus practically paralleling Madruga's aging. The signs alerting me to the fact that
Grandfather had begun to die appeared on every hand. Collecting his
memory was a task that should not be put off.

From when I was just a little girl, Madruga had clung to my very
skin. He never left me, so that I wouldn't leave him. He made up his mind
to prolong his life through me, inhabiting part of my soul as he added
years to it. Reflected in him as though his senile presence would not let go
of me, I had not had the strength to banish him in time. Because, my story
having begun with him, he was still the one who was recounting it. In
obedience to a dramatic instinct for succession, which obliged me to go
into the question of who would take over my soul in the future. Whom
to will it to, so that its owner would take it into his safekeeping at the
appointed hour?

Undoubtedly, the photograph on the wall had aged, despite the gilt
frame. Only the members of the cast portrayed in it had not aged a day
past the instant that the camera had captured them, with the intention of
fixing them in time. The surface, a light sepia in color, appeared to oscil-
late, as though behind each figure there were a reality contrary to that
visible to everyone. As I looked at the photograph, it too questioned my
right to ascribe to it truths unknown to its participants.

There were no contortions, no dramatic expressions on those faces.
Or even a connected story. Before posing for the photographer, they had
been careful to empty their faces of all distress. So as to convey a polished
politeness that would not pain the observer. Their aim was simply to husband a truth, which perhaps had not been shared equally by the members
of the family.

Madruga had decided to banish friends, cousins, and Venâncio from the photograph. For the purposes of that portrait, life was summed up in Eulália and the children. And even though Eulália and the children had pointed out to him that by so doing he was eliminating the others present in the room, Madruga stood his ground.

There Eulália was. Her white skin enhancing her simple costume. She was wearing the bracelet from Madruga and the ring. Despite the still pose, I suddenly noticed a tremor in Eulália that was eventually communicated to the entire family. Except for Madruga, whose pose was irreproachable, in a suit and waistcoat, his pocket watch plainly visible, all of him demanding the eternity of that instant.

Of all of them, Tobias was the youngest. He was not yet eleven, and dressed in short pants. With the same anxious look in his eyes as always, he very nearly moved his head in Madruga's direction, so as to go on with a battle which his father, however, took no notice of. Hence the debris thrown at Madruga by Tobias hit that breastplate of his, and the helmet of his gaze. And since Madruga did not punish him according to his just deserts, a terrible guilt, stemming from this frustrated rebellion, came over him.

Madruga, for his part, never freed him of this feeling. On accepting Tobias's eventual apology, he always made him see the enormity of his fault. Both, however, were unable to tolerate living in a state of truce. Tormented by this supposed peace, they wasted useless gestures on each other.

Eulália protested against this seeming indifference on the part of her husband, whose real nature was hostile. The subject immediately causing his rancor to surface in his face.

"You know why I'm offended."

Eulália could not believe that offenses were meant to be eternal, if life itself did not last forever and would one day run out. Then too, had temperance not been Madruga's reward now that he was older? She immediately gathered that this admonition had had its effects on her husband. But in the face of his insensitive attitude, she quietly withdrew. Emphasizing in this way her sad understanding of the feelings in conflict, which, having nowhere to hide except in the heart, a terrain itself heavily mined by contradictory versions, there instituted discord and passion. Hence the divergences between father and son, within the framework of this reality, might come to an end only with the death of the two of them.

Confronted with such a dilemma, she thought, in almost resigned relief, Well then, let them die and have done with it. Seated in her room, with Odete at her feet.

Tobias's prolonged absences worried Madruga. Not wanting to telephone himself, he sent Bento or Miguel to Tobias's house, in search of news. Face-to-face with her brothers-in-law, Amália lost her patience.

"Who knows what's happened to that man I unfortunately chose to marry?"

Bento brought her back into line immediately, in a stern voice. He had not come to gather disparaging comments and secret grievances. If she and Tobias still insisted on staying in the same house, let them come to an agreement.

Tobias had disappeared, leaving no trace behind, as though he would not be coming back. Madruga spread the map of Brazil out on the table and took a close look at the cities that might arouse his son's interest. As he did so, having phone calls placed to various hotels, at no time did Eulália suppose that her son was hurt or in a morgue somewhere. She had grown accustomed to seeing father and son immersed in the same bubbling pot. In order, however, to contain Madruga's anxiety, she asked Venâncio to come calm him down.

Together, Venâncio and Madruga appeared to banish those present. Except for Eulália, who gauged the degree of their misunderstandings. They greeted each other with distinct coolness, a certain annoyance even. But that gesture nonetheless had deep, almost age-old roots.

Face to face with Venâncio, Madruga announced, in a dramatic tone of voice, that Tobias, gone now for over twenty days, was dead. Venâncio was not impressed. He argued in favor of the resurrection of his godson, soon to come bursting in the door. A man, that one, for whom life was a prey trapped in his hands, he could hear it cracking apart like dry wood creaking at every step. Tobias had surely taken refuge in some nameless corner of Brazil. With the intention of discovering the hidden nature of the country in which it had fallen to his lot to live. Moreover, no other son of Madruga's demonstrated such a heartrending awareness of his land.

"Wherever Tobias turns, that awareness is always with him, and it makes him suffer," Venâncio said gravely.

Madruga was annoyed at Venâncio. Not even at a moment such as this did he respect his grief. There he was, referring to awareness as though it were laundry hung out on a clothesline, which the wind of misery ripped to shreds merely to be able to wave the tatters like little flags.

"Calm down, Madruga. Tobias is alive and will soon be with us."

"In that case, you know where he is, and are keeping his address a secret from me," Madruga shot back.

They fell silent for a long time, Madruga's gaze fixed on Venâncio, who did not avert his eyes for a single instant. Till Madruga was convinced that Venâncio had not betrayed him, and that Tobias, that shameless, unfeeling, irresponsible wretch, was alive, spending these days enjoying intense pleasures, bought with his money, the one reason they hadn't heard a word from him. At the thought that Tobias, free of Amália, of the girls, and of himself, might be off chasing after a woman, he began to laugh, to laugh in such a way that Venâncio, as ever far removed from the magic spells of passion, would be unable to share in his splendid discovery. And hence not steal Tobias from him yet again, and not even perceive the weight of his victory. His exultation was such that he had a Rioja, ruby red and transparent, brought up from the wine cellar. Slowly consumed without wasting words.

Behind Eulália, and next to Tobias, the photograph showed a very young Antônia, without that covetousness today so marked, especially in her eyes. Leaving no further doubts as to her actions, focused each day on laying in crumbs to add to her pile. Only when Antônia has a full knapsack does she go back home, where she divides her booty up into two precise parts. One going into the strongbox, to which she has access with her husband's permission, and the other docilely handed over to Luís Filho. He has always thanked her, in the expectation of owing her further favors the following day.

On awakening with renewed strength, Antônia proclaims her love for Eulália. In the hope that her mother will respond in the form of affectionate embraces and bank checks. Nothing seems to appease her. At times, unable to sleep, she fears that Madruga, influenced by her brothers, will overlook her husband, thus placing her marriage and fortune at risk. Luís Filho is the first to make life a torment for her, being unable to accept the fact that Bento and Miguel take turns as head of the companies, without his being considered for the same position. Yet, urged on by her husband, Antônia arrived at her father's house visibly exhausted, with circles under her eyes that aged her. Immediately declaring herself at war with her father, who was slighting her husband, without the shadow of a doubt the most competent one in the family. And she began to jabber like a carrion crow, in a hoarse voice that was the result of an accident. Madruga was able to put up with her confused cawing for ten or fifteen minutes. During which time he tried to dissuade her, hinting that business matters, by their very nature, have secret rules. Antônia ought never to forget that he had raised his sons to succeed him. From the time they were little, he himself had taken them, still in short pants, to the office, to the factory, construction sites, hotels, and all the rest.

At the beginning of the conversation, he had tried his best not to hurt her. But once Antônia was convinced of her power to refute her father's arguments, supported by a logic faithful only to her husband, she pressed her point.

Madruga could not bear with his daughter a moment longer. "You're lucky I keep him on as director of all my business enterprises!"

After these words, Madruga felt relieved. It pleased him that when Antônia delivered his message to Luís Filho nothing would be lost. Thus making it unnecessary to join issue directly with his son-in-law. A task, incidentally, that invariably fell to Bento. Luís Filho and Bento met in the best restaurants of the city with the one intention of fighting it out. In such surroundings they could be certain they would not raise their voices. They practically whispered like lovers. Having chosen as referees the waiters and the occupants of nearby tables.

At each of these matches, Luís Filho offered as justification of his pretensions the fact that he was the one responsible for safeguarding Antônia's rights. As legitimate an heiress as he. Or had Bento forgotten? Well then, let him be advised that from this day forward, on no account would Antônia and he withdraw from combat, on any ground whatsoever. And should the necessity present itself, their children would succeed them.

In the beginning, Bento pretended to trust to luck, which up to that point had favored him. It being quite possible that everything would change after Madruga's death. When the heirs might conceivably enter into new arrangements that would damage his interests. But as long as the present situation obtained, Bento would remain at the head of the entire operation. Luís Filho had no reason for complaint, however. His fortune at this point far surpassed the one he had had claim to before his marriage with Antônia. His being married to their sister was no reason for ousting Madruga's sons from the board of directors. Despite his competence and his illustrious family name, Luís Filho ought to recognize, by any rigorous accounting, that Madruga's fortune, today, threw more doors open than the weight of his four-hundred-year-old surname.

"I think we're quits with each other, Luís Filho. Everything we owe you has been regally repaid," Bento said, very softly, as though thanking him for services rendered.

"As far as I'm concerned, you may be right. But now Antônia's rightful share has gone by the board."

Sitting exhausted over dessert, they had a saturnine look about them. As though they had eaten raw meat with their fingers. They no longer made their moves with the same elegance as before. They traded veiled, underhanded blows. Bento accused Luís Filho of everything but marrying for money.

During coffee, Luís Filho made marks on the tablecloth, as though for a game of tic-tac-toe. Or as if branding Bento's face with a red-hot iron. Bento knew he was the object of his hatred. He retaliated with words and gestures that would not make them eternal enemies.

"I can't compete with you, Bento. You have an apparently unbeatable advantage. You're Madruga's son. Heir of a fortune he himself made."

"I know what you're hinting at. I can only tell you that even without Father, I too would have made it in my America. And you know very well that that's true. And as for you, what America have you made good in?" The words were muttered between clenched teeth.

"The point, then, is that neither you nor I have managed to prove anything. We're merely high-ranking executives of a business that came into existence thanks only to a humble immigrant," Luís Filho said. His look accusing Bento, however, of not having managed to go beyond his condition as the son of an immigrant who had come off the boat at the Praça Mauá in wooden clogs, his knapsack on his back, his heart pounding.

Bento submitted to this thorough examination. With his chin held high.

"That's why we must put up with each other till the end, Luís Filho. And, for as long as possible, I'll be the one to give the orders. But if this wounds the sensibilities of your illustrious surname, it's only to put you on notice that we're settling accounts with you."

Antônia was at her father's house early the next morning. Bento had offended her deeply, not sparing a single member of her family. Madruga must put an end to her brother's arbitration.

"Otherwise, father, we're going to have a battle over the inventory."

Madruga couldn't bear the idea of the family being separated, atomized, refusing to greet each other on the street and in people's living rooms. Cutting each other dead. Or trading knife thrusts in the dark.

"Leave me alone, Antônia. You can all go to hell. Especially that ambitious husband of yours. Isn't what he's already accumulated over the years enough for him? Or did you come here just to tell me to drop dead?"

Antônia cried for a week. Not neglecting, however, to send her father messages every morning to charm him. And always by way of her children. Luís Filho meanwhile goaded her into weeping and wailing to such a point that it would reach Madruga's ears.

Finally Madruga summoned his daughter, on condition that she not cry. She'd either shut up or he'd kick Luís Filho out of the companies. Faced with such a threat, Luís Filho calmed his wife down. And sent Bento a note suggesting that they have lunch at the Albamar. Where they would enjoy a fish stew and a battle without quarter. Bento accepted the terms with pleasure.

From the study, I hear not a single sound from outside, in the hall. This means that Eulália is still alive as I look at the photograph of Madruga with his children. A photograph that has carefully left out those who, in one way or another, helped to make them an orderly group. Or who were close to them at the time. Venâncio, for example. And the photographer himself. Why did they have no part in a scene that is being recounted by me? Who else with valuable evidence stayed out of the picture, and for that very reason intensified the play of life that passes across the photograph?

At the other edge of the photograph Bento appears, standing. He always did lack his father's handsomeness and Miguel's. Perhaps that was why he was inclined to protect Tobias, who was likewise shorn of such attributes. And who came to talk with him, in a grave tone of voice always, about a reality to which he was condemned for life.

Bento was the opposite of Tobias. He gave vent to words and feelings with extreme caution. Forearming himself against enemies that he spied in every corner. Even in his school days, minor defeats in gym class made him take to his bed. He would run a fever, which did not go down until he was ready to fight again. Eulália thought his temperature was due to tonsilitis. Whereas Madruga forced him out of his bedroom, not wanting a weakling for a son.

Bento grew up determined to outdo his father and Miguel. An undertaking that led him to extremes. He studied much too hard. And got on closer and closer terms with his father, in an attempt to steal his experience. To learn from his father to lie in the face of an opponent.

The title of doctor lent weight to his name. As the son of an immigrant, he needed to apply for posts, open doors, make his father's fortune more solid still. Bento's precise manner of speaking attracted people's notice. He took care to intercalate brief silences among his striking phrases, holding his diaphragm in for a few seconds, his nostrils slightly dilated, disclosing, at the corners of his mouth, a discreet sensuality which would have displeased him had he been aware of it.

His sober appearance, in suits of an impeccable cut, betrayed careful attention to himself before his mirror. Not allowing even his wife to glimpse his vanity. A woman of surpassing discretion, she had been handpicked. The daughter of a member of the Federal Supreme Court, an intimate friend of Juscelino Kubitschek's. Hence able to meet her husband's requirements in his climb up the social ladder.

Through this marriage, Madruga was able to expand his heavy earthworking business. Thanks above all to Brasília, the President's dream. It was also to be the making of many another fortune.

In partnership with Senator Silveira, Madruga did not hesitate to invest heavily in equipment, certain that this would enable him to carry through on winning bids already submitted. Especially since the Court of Audits was acting out a farce staged on the pretext of speeding up the building of the capital and the development of the country. The audits, swiftly approved and never independently verified, increasingly strengthened the executive power, to the detriment of the legislative and judiciary. As the new capital was going up, Bento broadened his fields of authority in official spheres, whose basic oligarchies were not affected by changes in administration.

In a dark suit, his hair neatly trimmed, Bento stood tall and straight for the photograph. He was aware of his own importance for the planned pose. He had studied all the details deemed essential. Taking into account the composition of the group. He wanted his career to be foreseen by dint of no more than a simple examination of the picture. He was certain that the photograph would merit a silver frame and a place of honor on the little table in the reception room. He could not have guessed at that point that Madruga, a prey to Galician superstitions still, thought it prudent to remove that Brazilian flock of his from the gaze of any and every evil eye.

This respect for legends on his father's part was an object of Bento's criticism. He could not manage to identify with those stories so deeply rooted in Madruga's heart. He was proud of his father, certainly, but he had not inherited his myths and his gods. He would not be the right son to succeed him in his love for the Galician language and for Sobreira, two shadows still pursuing his father from the other side of the Atlantic.

Eulália immediately perceived, after their marriage, that Madruga, despite his professing himself to be an unbeliever, had a great fear of the wrath of the gods. Beings, in his view, ready and waiting to make people pay for their lack of respect for them. And his grandfather was so terrified of them that he avowed, on a certain occasion, that happiness had to be kept under lock and key so as not to make it appear excessive in the eyes of the world. These anxieties of Madruga's doubtless stemming from studying Galician nature, from listening to those old men, veritable echo chambers of memory.

In Galicia they not only cultivated the gods, but also took them into their houses, like domestic animals, licking them, stroking them, and forgetting them underneath the table. These entities were part of the family economy, of a natural, ecumenical vision of the universe. And so they shared their food with the gods. They offered them fat rendered from corn-fed pigs weighing four hundred pounds and more. Certain that by so doing they were appeasing the fury roused so readily in those creatures. Galicians were well acquainted with the rancor of the gods as they decided man's fate.

Before Bento was born, Eulália wanted to call him Pedro. A strong name, that of a penitent and a fisherman, and one attuned to the sounds of human tongues. Madruga was firmly opposed:

"If the gods robbed the first Bento of life, we'll replace him with another son. He's going to be called Bento, with the difference that this time he's going to live and prosper."

Sometimes Eulália imagined what the first Bento would be like had he not escaped them through the unexpected gate of death. Perhaps he would have a career in the Church, an old tradition in her family. Even against Madruga's will. She suspected, however, that Brazil, a country of vast forests, of beaches reeking of human and whale oil, of bodies exuding sensuality, was not likely to arouse a priestly vocation. Yet if it were the case that Bento resisted temptations, would he, in the event, seduced by pomp and hierarchy, choose a priesthood oriented toward a Church jealous of its temporal prestige while at the same time divorced from humanity's social goals? Or, committing himself to the humble simplicity of monastic life, would he live in search of the prayer that would at last touch nameless hearts?

The Bento, however, whom they still had with them was caution personified. No symptoms of passion were visible in him. Everything about him smooth, a wall without a single crack, immaculately painted. His words could readily be erased the next morning. He never became involved. His wife probably the only one to get any fun out of sex, which is doubtless a bore for both parties now. Bento becomes terribly excited at the very mention of power, in any form. He therefore applauds decorations, medals, titles, diplomas. He collects them all with gusto.

And to be truthful, he is never unmindful of the vibrations broadcast by social movements. He does not lose sight of the agitation and the anxious hopes of the labor unions, for example. He publicly professes himself, with exaggerated pride, to be an entrepreneur faithfully following Christian principles. Eager to widen his workers' profit margins. Certain slight adjustments in the social scheme of things appear to him to be indispensable. And he preaches this as doctrine to his peers.

On certain occasions, however, long since past now, I sounded his innermost heart, and to my surprise, the answer was a more or less temperate one.

"It's necessary to trim excessive public expenditures and stem this tide of nationalization. Unfortunately, the State is not a good business manager. It doesn't know how to produce profits and manage them," he said with a smile.

A man attuned to the situation, however, he goes along with the military regime, under whose aegis Brazil has seen unprecedented progress, despite the social costs. He takes pleasure in criticizing the government *en famille,* knowing that his agenda in Brasília coincides with that of several ministers. After these meetings, his statements concerning the nation's economy appear in the papers.

He advances steadily. He has a target he's aiming at and is putting on a false front. He acts as though existence, in certain circumstances, were simply a job he's taken on at his family's dictates. When Bento's boredom became plain to see, Madruga's back was up. Taking any sort of affectation or apathy as an attack on his Galician roots, calling for dramatic and pathetic moves. Madruga discovered that the heart harbored secrets of such magnitude that the aggrieved expressions which uncontrollably flooded his face were justified. At such times, confronting a passionless Bento, his forcefulness evaporated.

"What a pitiful thing a creature without passion is. How can you live without it, Bento?"

Bento avoided arguments with his father. Showering him, rather, with paeans of praise. No one had yet surpassed him when it came to entrepreneurial vision. Hence they ought always to consult him. Madruga remained unmoved, however.

"Consider me already dead," he said in a rage.

Madruga recognized that Bento and Miguel had outdone him. And it was better that way. New times called for different men. The changes in the market had driven out old forms of life. Nonetheless, he closely followed developments in the economic area, criticizing State intervention in the private sector, since this did not mean a widening of the domestic market. He felt constrained with Bento, however. Incapable of having a heart-to-heart talk with him. And meanwhile Bento tried not to disappoint him in any way. He surpassed himself in every field, to make sure that Madruga took note of his progress. Despite his credentials, there were barriers between them. Bento took offense when he saw that his father was being excessively stiff and formal. To capture his fancy, he talked to him of Brazil, as though he were Venâncio. The only one able to squeeze every last drop out of the country, as meanwhile his own life slowly drained away.

This sudden interest in Brazil did not carry conviction with Madruga. To test it, he pressed Bento to dive into the past, the nineteenth century in particular, a field in which Venâncio was master. Thereby discounting contemporary Brazil from the very outset, as being beneath his notice, without spiritual grandeur.

"Going back to the past revives us. If necessary, Bento, go to the Celts, from whom we're descended. And if you aren't able to make the trip, you'll be proving you have no imagination," Madruga prodded him.

In the face of Bento's silence, he went on. "Every country is a cunt one penetrates without measuring the depth of the pleasure. All one wants to do is touch bottom, the maximum number of times possible. And Brazil is no exception to this rule."

By way of such images, it was Madruga's intention to offend Bento's false sensibility. And in fact they immediately brought the desired results. There in his father's presence, Bento blushed, immediately looking about for someone to bring him a cup of coffee. He didn't want to be caught unprepared.

When Madruga suddenly announced that he would die soon, Bento lost control for a few seconds, his eyes staring wildly. Unable to believe his ears. He seemed to regard his father as an immortal being.

"Let's change the subject, father," was all he said.

"Well, think it over, Bento. Besides, it won't hurt you to suffer. I am certain of this," Madruga said, already savoring the taste of his own death.

Eulália calmed everyone down. And immediately looked at Miguel, who had inherited Dom Miguel's features. And, consequently, his beauty. He could easily pass for a pedigreed bull. His eyes gleamed with an uncomfortable intensity. And that was what clearly showed in the photograph.

In the portrait, Miguel had chosen a strategic spot, behind Eulália and Madruga and between the two. Easily able to envelop both in a single embrace. Leaning just slightly toward his mother. But as he stood there, head erect, in an attractive pose, it was difficult to know in what stage of passion he found himself in those days. For Eulália's benefit above all, he was acting out a life that was a fiction, so that she would not discover his love affairs. He hoped to deceive her forever.

To please his mother, he one day went so far as to proclaim, shortly before his marriage to Sílvia:

"Between a lie and the truth, I'll stick to the lie, mother."

Eulália exulted with her son, able to follow his reveries. Never noting his almost feverish body, when he came home exacerbated by passion. A passion forgotten when the next one came along.

"Tell whatever story you please, mother, but don't stop," he would beg her, hoping to relieve his tension.

While Bento and Tobias lived in Madruga's orbit, Miguel languished in Eulália's presence. Visiting her every day. In no hurry to leave. At her son's side, Eulália automatically returned to Sobreira. She seemed to hear the voice of Dom Miguel, telling her of traditions so imbued with creative imagination that they came to haunt not only her heart but her very bowels. In her father's house, dreaming flowed out through the window slits. Transcending human limits by all possible means.

There with his mother, Miguel forgot about business and women. It was easy for him to feel himself to be a shepherd, a farmhand. Or his own grandfather, whose features he had inherited. And a certain vocation for understanding life as a sort of institution, from which one collected more or less valuable pieces each day, in exchange for others of a like category. A risky game of repositioning that never gave us any indication of how good a given move had been.

Proudly, Miguel embarked on one or another of Eulália's narratives. Since time out of mind, both had been relating a story destined never to end, being the basis of the affection uniting them. Madruga saw them on the veranda, or strolling in the garden, without ever interfering. And counting on the respectful acquiescence of his father, Miguel devoted himself intensely to Eulália. The one woman to tell him that on earth there existed not only gold, but the mining of dreams. A dream that Miguel felt he was betraying at every moment.

On discovering in her son a trace of sadness, Eulália proved to him that it might be a gift well worth its cost. And that he ought not to rid himself of it. In her eyes, it was never morbid to suffer if new doors of perception were opened thereby.

"Stories can be a heavy burden. Because the more they teach us to dream, the more onerous it is to live," Eulália said, lost once more in reveries.

He smiled there before his mother. The fervor she demonstrated in church, wanting to reach her God through the mediation of prayer alone, surely corresponded to his transports in bed. There he was, wandering about the streets chasing after a body to appease a desire that had never found an anchor-hold. A desire present on earth, and incarnated in the body of another.

Miguel would arrive in Leblon, going directly to Eulália. Kissing her hands with extreme delicacy. He was in the habit of bringing her discreet gifts, to prove that his love for his mother demanded modest forms of expression. Only his heart spoke. The same heart that sometimes confused him in the middle of a long negotiation. Thereby making him an interlocutor subject to embarrassments of a personal order. Immediately establishing him as someone who would be a conciliatory element, cooling down the adversary and himself. Whereas Bento, jealous of victory, rarely gave an inch.

On the eve of certain decisions, Bento avoided his brother, so as not to undergo pressure. Sensing his stubbornness, Miguel would ask his mother to summon him. Bento came obediently, though mistrustfully. Never open and spontaneous with Eulália. And when she looked at him with a gaze different from that reserved for Miguel, Bento felt slighted. His mother, however, in the face of his constraint, spoke to him of Sobreira, asking in passing if he was up to date on his soul.

"I ask because life is so ephemeral, Bento. Just yesterday your father and I arrived in America. And before long, in just a few years, we'll be leaving it forever, without the right to ask for a postponement."

Made uneasy by the subject, Bento begged her not to speak of death, when they hadn't even had time to get to know each other.

"Ah, my son, how wrong you are. We've been given all the time in the world, which you and I haven't learned to put to good use."

Bento was overcome with emotion. He wanted to hold her close. How many years it had been that he had not felt her body next to his. He found himself unable to move. Till he repeated to himself, I'm Miguel, I'm Miguel. Only then did he rise to his feet and kiss his mother on the forehead. A bitter taste immediately came to his lips. The sensation that he had stolen a kiss. And that only in the role of Miguel could he caress that woman who dwelt among them as though she had already taken her leave of them.

Eulália slowly sipped her tea. Discreetly passing in review details familiar to her son. Far from being overcome with emotion now and dipping his biscuit in his coffee, thus reviving a childish habit, Bento wriggled in his chair, indifferent to a language with symbols common to the two of them. He was not taken in by his mother's words, used for the particular purpose of holding him spellbound. The same words he had heard her share with strangers.

Bento left, depressed by the visit. At the office, apropos of a trivial incident, he attacked Miguel. He was suddenly envious of the love his brother was able to awaken. Miguel said nothing. He sensed that Eulália was responsible for the surprising lack of control on the part of Bento, who had arrived utterly dispirited by the visit. And he thought of his mother with a heavy heart. Did she not have the power, then, to save one of her sons? Or was she unable to save them because her mission on earth was to redeem herself? Miguel hastily abandoned this line of reasoning. He could not bear to imagine Eulália concerned with herself alone, leaving behind for her sons only those scraps that she did not manage to take with her when she went to meet her God.

He telephoned Eulália. He would not be able to visit her that afternoon, or on the afternoons that followed. He had to go to São Paulo, among other things. As soon as he could, he would come and give her a warm embrace. Eulália, sensing her son's hurt, shut herself up in her room with Odete.

Madruga knocked on the door. "Isn't Miguel coming to hear from his mother's lips the portents of his salvation?" he said to his wife with a smile, hoping to brighten her doleful countenance. Eulália answered him with a faint smile. And Madruga left her, burdened with doubts. When all was said and done, for whom was she suffering? For him, for life, for Miguel, who was the living image of Dom Miguel, now dead and gone?

After any sort of misunderstanding with his mother, Miguel was very late coming home. In a fever of anxiety, he made love with an unknown woman, making her do things he deeply regretted later. As dawn was about to break, back home once again, he chose to stretch out on the sofa in the study, so as not to awaken Sílvia. And after two hours' rest, he was up again, thinking about the house, life, which the sun was slowly melting away, detail by detail. In summer, he had his morning coffee served him on the deck, from which he could see the twin peaks of the Dois Irmãos. The entire city encircled by mountains. Perhaps like those that surrounded Sobreira, the village that he had known as a child, that he no longer remembered. He was reluctant to return to Galicia. Afraid of undergoing an emotion whose source was his mother. Suddenly, in desolation, he thought of what would happen when she died. Tears came to his eyes. Then he straightened, remembering recent resentments. When all was said and done, with whom was he doing battle? To what point was he responsible for Bento's dishonesty? And who would answer for his own deceit? Eulália's sons were still and all his brothers. But did the figures of brothers, father, mother in fact exist in the twilight emptiness of a memory slowly fading away as life begins to approach its end? On his return home, his mother received him like someone who had never left. They immediately resumed the interrupted conversation, with no mutual harm done. And his mother, giving proof of her goodwill, telephoned to Bento in front of him, demanding his presence. Exultant, Miguel kissed her forehead repeatedly. Delighted once again to be enjoying the pastries that Eulália offered her son as part of the pleasure he found in her company.

In the photograph, almost demanding to be left until last, there Esperança was. Between Bento and Miguel, and hence behind Madruga. Seated in a low-backed chair, with his face fixed on the photographer, Madruga had no way of keeping an eye on Esperança, who, there in his rear guard, had inherited his face, his gestures. She had even stolen his blue eyes from him. A genetic theft that at times made him feel uneasy.

Esperança smiled faintly. Her proud bearing, even in the portrait, seemed to be resisting fulfilling her father's demands. Madruga's orders were firm ones, even though he lined his words with soft down so that his daughter would follow them as though she herself had issued them. Out of concern for a daughter whose frailty lay quite precisely in her heart. Esperança already preparing to love that which as yet had no name, but which might suddenly lodge in her body. A feverish, intense body, which succumbed at times to sudden outpourings when something excited her. Also because everything affected her breath, exhaled in rapid rhythmic pulses through her nostrils. In an effort to bring back the life in her.

In front of her father, Esperança claimed to be not only a native of the Iberian peninsula, but of Africa as well. And thus belonging to a restive Brazil, which had transmitted unfathomable secrets to her consciousness and her sensibility.

Madruga refused to accept this analogy. Fearful that Esperança would trust primarily in the force of instinct, which he saw as very strongly established in Brazilian bodies. Esperança perceived that her father, on restricting her freedom, was being ruled by the mistrust she inspired in him. He felt, in a certain way, liable to social condemnation should she give in to life. But every time she stifled certain very powerful impulses, everything in her rebelled against such an absurdity.

Before the age of eighteen, Esperança understood the historical nature of the circumstance of having been born a woman, and to cap the climax, born in that family. Such a fact automatically robbed her of half of her attainments. Having only a second half left with which to live, one, incidentally, not amounting to much.

She immediately protested. Offended by the accusation, Madruga flew into a rage. Why did his daughter want from him more love than he had already given her? He had never done anything but anticipate his children's desires, providing them with gifts that he himself had never had. Not permitting Esperança to explain the exact tenor of her protest.

For days, Madruga merely greeted her in passing. Feeling that her father had wronged her, Esperança repaid him with equal coldness. Esperança's attitude made Madruga see his daughter's helplessness in the face of his male children. He perceived that he too had condemned her to the apathy of domestic life for the sole reason that she had been born a woman. On the other hand, he could not repair an error that was not his alone. Whatever he might do for Esperança, the outside world would immediately undo. Therefore she must be kept under close surveillance, within family patterns.

Esperança resented a fate that kept her from coming to grips with masculine society at decisive moments, and that at the same time had made her so vulnerable to the feelings and the claims of her body. And aware of this pendulous movement, which shaped her personality, Esperança anticipated her defeat. As though she lacked the proper conditions, above all because she was a woman, to do battle on the only terrain that in fact would have been worthy of her courage.

Slowly, without her even realizing it, she was leaning toward the world of feelings, which required space and intensity in order to expand. A vocation that promised to be dangerous, because it pitted her against her father and her brothers, who wanted to condemn her to submissive, blameless, caustically conjugal love.

Madruga sensed her precocious impulses. And mounted guard so that she would not go beyond the territory that by convention was hers to set foot upon. Though he could not prevent her from edging toward feelings and emotions that kindled fires, none of this must touch her honor. That being so, on seeing that she was confused, he was patient. Above all when Esperança tried to follow in Miguel's footsteps, since he enjoyed different freedoms. At such times, Madruga spoke to her gently, fearing to fleece her alive. At the same time avoiding her confidences. He did not want to be able, from the beating of her heart laid bare, to see her naked and exposed.

In view of Madruga's efforts to cool her ardor, Esperança hardened her heart. Doing almost nothing to explain to him. She had long since confided only in herself. She had even taken to talking to herself in front of the mirror, without witnesses. Thus scattering about the room words that no one could put together and make any usual sense of. And use them to invade her dense universe.

Esperança's dress, in the portrait, had been bought in Paris. She had decided to wear it for the first time for the occasion. Hoping it would make her look beautiful. For a long time now Madruga had been giving his children presents without worrying overmuch about economizing as he had in the early days. The dress was sky blue, with discreet trimmings, and it went well with her clear, bright eyes. Esperança looked herself over in the mirror and foresaw that her father would perhaps reprove her for her vanity.

Madruga escorted Esperança into the living room. She had the air of a princess, walking with a firm step, ready to receive her due. He looked at the dress and regretted offering her presents that made her appear even more beautiful. Each carefully avoided the other's eye. For that very reason Madruga, distressed, sat down in the chair that the photographer pointed to. Wondering if there was anyone in the world who could discipline Esperança without impairing her beauty and breaking her spirit. Those portions allotted his daughter fattened by entire pieces of a restless heart.

There in the midst of her brothers and sisters, Esperança forgot her father's indifference. Venâncio, urged to stay for dinner, refused Madruga's invitation. Madruga insisted, inviting him at the same time to pose with them for the other picture. Since he would not be including him in this portrait, one that today has visibly aged. From the beginning, moreover, even before summoning the photographer to the house, his thought had been to hang the photograph on the wall of his study, far from strangers' eyes. Certain that the photograph would take on added importance with time, at least as long as all of them were alive. Through it he would have preserved the memory of his family. Only in that way would he prove to his grandchildren what Eulália, he, Esperança, Miguel, Bento, Antônia, and Tobias had been like in that magic instant.

Ever since Getúlio had declared war on the Axis, Venâncio had been expressing the desire to return to Europe, on condition that he would find it free and democratic.

"As long as there is a single dictatorship, I won't set foot there."

"What kind of an illusion is that, Venâncio? If that's so, what are you doing in Brazil, with Vargas's dictatorship?" Madruga said incredulously.

Dumped off in Italy, Brazilian troops soon learned to say *buon giorno, buona sera,* and *grazie.* They ate American rations as they trained with war matériel that was just as American. And under the command of General Mascarenhas, they marched up the hills and marched down again. Heedless, in the euphoria of the first attacks, of Nazi grenades and machine guns situated in privileged positions. The strategists, however, insisted that they fight on, despite casualties. Thus, with a helping hand from death, many soldiers got rid of boots that pinched.

In those months, Rio awoke to chaos. The battle joined in Italy, the first war of an international nature, dragged the country at one and the same time from provincialism, from the clutches of the political police, and from Filinto Müller's goon squads. Mobilized for defense, civilians wore gas masks, in frantic drills, as society ladies took charge of patrolling the streets on blackout days, when the city was plunged into darkness.

Venâncio walked through every district in the city, taking a close look at the effects of the civilian campaigns. Sometimes helping to collect scrap, everything that would help Brazil destroy its enemies. Putting his recent stay in the sanatorium behind him, he had traded one war for another. Certain of emerging the victor this time.

On Sundays, he spread the map of Europe out on the table, between the fruit bowl and the empty coffee cups, and gave Madruga and Eulália a detailed account of the troop movements on the various battlefronts. A war being waged this time by battle-hardened peoples, given to fighting since their earliest days.

"Those peoples fought the Romans, the barbarians, they survived plagues, the Inquisition, with daily massacres becoming the general rule among them. Nobody knows where and when they learned to fight. The Germans, for instance, have been fighting since the cave era."

European history, examined by Venâncio in minute detail, made Madruga forget his economic worries. He was particularly cheered by Hannibal's crossing of the Alps with his elephants, a feat belonging to the realm of fantasy. He asked for particulars.

"That's nothing, Madruga. There have even been warriors who crossed abysses on nothing but a rope, though by doing so they didn't claim the right to enter history." All excited, Venâncio didn't let him get a word in edgewise.

Madruga immediately realized intuitively that war tended to make people rich or reduce them to poverty overnight. Hence requiring a new way of doing business. He was ready, however, to meet the challenge. Especially since he could see that Venâncio had taken up his old habits again. With the advantage of having another war to keep him occupied. Without the frustration that the Spanish Civil War had caused him. Madruga had finally stopped urging Venâncio to participate in his expanding businesses. He had learned to select partners in robust financial health. And to keep associates such as González in limbo. His aim, from now on, was to be the major shareholder in himself.

Free of his disease, Venâncio for his part no longer pretended to go off on trips. If he felt an impulse, rare these days, to make up lies, he told them naturally and spontaneously, quite certain that Madruga, to all appearances at least, respected his dreaming and had no major objections.

The beads of the chaplet slipped through Eulália's fingers one by one, her intention the Brazilians at the mercy of the rigors of the Italian winter. And as if they were not enough for her, she made endless vows to the saints, above all for Cláudio, a member of the Brazilian Expeditionary Force and the son of Dona Maria.

Dona Maria came to Leblon, with the bundle of laundry on her head, twice a week. She always insisted on going over the entire laundry list yet again with Odete, so as to leave no room for error, in view of the difficulty she had reading and writing. The pencil hung from her hand like a hoe, the one with which she had tilled the land in Portugal, before going off to Brazil. It was her eager hope that these exercises would enable her to master the written word, of which she stood in such great need.

For a long time now Eulália had not taken part in household activities. To please Madruga, who always insisted on sparing her such responsibilities, in fulfillment of the promise made to Dom Miguel. The war, however, drew Eulália to the service area of the house, to listen to Dona Maria.

Amid smiles, Maria boasted of the son called up to save the country in danger. Cláudio of all people, the frailest of the children with which God had blessed her marriage. An unpredictable son, from the time he was just a babe in arms, on up to the day he'd come bursting into the backyard, all excited, showing her his enlistment papers. Heedless of the work she was doing, the sweat running down her face as she ironed her customers' clothes with her charcoal-heated iron.

"I'm off to Italy, mother. Brazil needs me."

Maria held the iron suspended in midair, her cheeks almost as burning hot as the iron. "What kind of a story is that, child? Don't trifle with your mother, you devil!" she shouted, indifferent to Cláudio's happiness, his one thought now the voyage across the Atlantic.

That night, Viriato sobbed right along with her. The two of them rebelling against their lot, they barred the windows and the door, as though they were in mourning. The news, however, of Cláudio's enlistment brought their neighbors in Botafogo running. They soon invaded the entire house, not respecting the privacy of the bedrooms or even of the toilet, at the far end of the backyard. All exultant at the destiny that had alighted like a dove on the roof of that humble tenement. As the spellbinding voice of Getúlio, on the radio, called upon the Brazilian people, including therein the immigrants received with open arms in this miraculous land, to drive Fascists and murderers out of Europe. Having already forgotten his sympathy for the Axis, shared, moreover, with half of his cabinet. In a calm, deliberate voice, Vargas went on, calling forth continued bursts of applause. Till Viriato and Maria, bowing to the evidence, also began to pride themselves on having been visited by so generous a fate.

The proud recruit reported for duty with the best-pressed uniform in the regiment. Maria smoothed the olive-green cloth with the iron as though she were stroking her son's arm. She had never taken such great pains. With extreme care, she prepared the starch to be applied to the uniform. And in the morning, as Cláudio was about to leave for the barracks, he found his boots already polished, without a single speck of dust. Maria's strength was indomitable. And to spur his wife on, Viriato told her of the long streamers hung along their block of row houses, with lofty watchwords: BOTAFOGO HAS A HERO / HAIL CLÁUDIO, OUR SOLDIER BOY / THE OLD MAN KNOWS WHAT HE'S DOING / FOR GOD AND FOR COUNTRY.

Via shortwave, Churchill and Roosevelt spoke in defense of democracy and victory. Words that despite the static, and despite the English, an unknown tongue, were immediately recognized by Brazilian listeners. Both words, uttered by the two great leaders, coming to them with a dressing of saliva and novelty, becoming part of their own vocabulary, then and there. The voices came roaring out of people's radios, the volume indicating the degree of patriotism of families and their loyalty to the Allies. A fact in one's favor in an era of rumors of espionage and sabotage.

Although Getúlio Vargas accepted the honors stemming from the feverish state of war, he forbade in practice any democratic incursion into his territory. Ironically, while Brazil, on the international plane, aligned itself with nations that were fighting Nazism, at home the political police were controlling the words *democracy* and *communism*, rigorously banished from newspapers and from national life. The accord established between the censors and the press began to break down, however, due to breaches occasioned by the war itself. Venâncio kept vigil alongside the radio. Studying English the better to follow the BBC broadcasts. And Filinto's police, which on so many occasions had used radio as the medium for ideological propaganda and instant popular indoctrination, had no way to silence the sets in use.

Venâncio's information was passed, through Eulália, to the laundress, with the exception of those items deemed to be upsetting. And through letters from her son, Dona Maria often knew of developments before Leblon did. Cláudio brimmed over with enthusiasm, especially in speaking of his zealous care of his uniform, still brand-new, and his boots, polished daily. The minute handwriting described Naples, on the shore of the Mediterranean, with its bay that reminded him of Rio de Janeiro. The landing there had set off a great celebration. Nobody had stayed inside in the houses. Amid applause and kisses, people tossed flowers at them as though they were Yanks. Rome, the capital of the country, was exactly like the ruins shown in Hollywood films. Especially the Colosseum, where the Christians, with radiant smiles, allowed themselves to be slaughtered for the entertainment of the Romans. Even so, he missed going to the movies on Sunday, listening to soccer games on the radio after dinner. And his arguments with his father, trying to prove to him once and for all that the Basques were unbeatable.

"They'll soon be back, Dona Maria. Apparently Getúlio agreed to send troops only because he knew the war was already won," and Eulália clasped the laundress's heavy hand, resting on the table, with her almost transparent fingers.

She encouraged Dona Maria to talk about Portugal, separated from

Galicia through the work of the Minho. A river, incidentally, that a person could swim across by stroking hard. Even as a little girl, Eulália had loved rivers. The Minho always made her feel sad because a strange trick of destiny had fated it to bathe two countries at once.

Venâncio, however, came to her rescue. He comforted her with the example of the Solimões, the river which, after traversing part of the national territory, had never earned, in return for services rendered, the right to arrive at the Atlantic with the same name that had honored it all during its course. Just as it was about to empty into the ocean, and thus become greater still, they suddenly rebaptized it the Amazon.

"The Minho is lucky to keep the same name from its headwaters to the estuary. Through a miracle history spared it such a cruel fate," Venâncio said.

Venâncio's happy historical acts of providence enriched Eulália's imagination. While she was grateful, it was her belief that even though science probed the intimate depths of rivers, such streams emptied into their own mystery.

"The Sobreira River, for example, is born and dies in a modest way. Yet it never failed to provide us with trout. Do you remember, Madruga, how we bathed in it in summer?" Eulália said.

Whenever left out of the conversation, Venâncio withdrew within himself, his feelings hurt. At such times, Sobreira, where he had never set foot, seemed to him remote and hostile. Eulália, however, did not notice his boredom, the heavy silence. Occupied, now, in recalling the time that she and Madruga had visited Santa Tecla, on one of their trips to Galicia. When they had spied, as they climbed to the top of the mountain, the remains of Celtic ruins to the left and to the right of the road. There the two of them were, treading the very ground where many of the Galician legends had been born. Those legends for which Dom Miguel had fought in the belief that, however remote, they still nourished the heart of the land of Galicia.

From the top of Santa Tecla, the two of them could see the Minho emptying into the Atlantic. Before their eyes the love rite of waters was being celebrated. The contractions of the Atlantic forming a buttress against the penetration of the waters of the Minho. These latter making their solemn departure from the Iberian peninsula, whose lands they had irrigated and fecundated. The confrontation of these waters exciting Madruga, even as it constricted Eulália's spirit.

Maria's accounts of her youth in the Vale dos Lafões seemed to interest Eulália. And so the laundress, vying for her attention, boldly launched into a narrative, strung together in a most peculiar way, in flagrant disregard for any sort of chronological order. With events thus taking place, alternately and simultaneously, in Portugal and in Botafogo.

Because of this circumstantial magic, surely, the people in Maria's story were linked together in such a confused way that Eulália, on seeing them so lost, strayed, and straggling, had no idea how to put them in their proper places in the stories just heard. And also because the natures of these characters defied all logic.

And all these ambiguities entered the picture not only because of Maria's narrative vagaries, but also because of Eulália's inability to bring order out of chaos. With, to make matters worse, Eulália's refusal, in her usual polite, modest way, to correct the laundress or press her for details that were missing so as to complete the hopelessly jumbled mural.

Perhaps the extenuating circumstance was the fact that Eulália was not profoundly interested in the occupants of Maria's universe. Lending her an ear only as a function of her intense desire to return to Portugal, if only for a few moments, by way of the confusion of voices and the imagination of the Portuguese woman.

Thanks to Maria, the precious view of the Minho was instantaneously projected before her. That mirror of water in which the obscure history of two countries was pitilessly reflected.

"My Viriato, who even has the name of a hero, is a better storyteller. If you'd care to hear them, Dona Eulália, come have coffee at our house. We'd be so pleased if you did."

Then she amended the invitation. The visit had best be put off till Cláudio came back, covered with medals, happy to be home. On that day they would kill suckling pigs, turkeys, chickens. A feast such as never seen in the row house on the Rua Mena Barreto. The neighbors had promised to lend a helping hand with the turkey, the rice with chicken, the mayonnaise, the cake, not to mention contributing their joyous, boisterous hearts.

Fortunately, there in their row house, they had noisy neighbors, whose racket easily penetrated the adjoining walls. Another plus being that all of them tuned in together to the serial on Radio Nacional. The volume of the sets turned up all the way whenever inexplicable pains rent the hearts of Ismênia Santos and Paulo Gracindo, living the parts of characters whom reality insisted on treating badly. The whole block suffered in unison, right along with those creatures thought of as practically blood relations.

The peace of the neighborhood was broken, however, by Maria's unexpected laments. "Oh, my Cláudio, what you must be suffering in this war, covered as you are with mud and lice!"

Her unprecedented behavior being owed to just one thing, Cláudio's failure, in his most recent letters, to refer, with the same pride as before, to the spotlessness of his uniforms and to his boots regularly polished each night. He merely hinted, with a certain haste and offhandedness, that his chest and the chests of his comrades were weighed down, as a consequence of their victories, with so many medals that they could hardly drag them up the hills with them. Making him more homesick than ever for his mother's porridge. And his heart leaping at the memory of the green turf of the Botafogo soccer field, where the mad, labyrinthine performances of Heleno de Freitas were staged. Always preceded by the barking of Biriba, the club mascot, led on a leash by Carlito Rocha.

"This son of ours is hiding the truth from us," Maria said, weeping and wailing for the third day in a row.

"What truth are you talking about, woman?"

Viriato severely reproached a woman without faith, whose lack of trust deserved to be condemned by the whole block and the whole neighborhood. Couldn't she see, in her stubborn blindness, that the moment her son set foot in Brazil, he'd be offered a job in the Federal Savings Bank, the dream of many a university graduate with a law degree? And that once he'd become independent, Cláudio could take care of the two of them in their old age? Not to mention other gifts that the Brazilian government had in store for veterans of the Expeditionary Force, as befitted their heroic deeds?

On Sundays, as he awaited the Porto cod sprinkled with oil and fried garlic, accompanied by a jugful of sharp red wine that Maria was going to serve him, Viriato had plenty of time to dream of Cláudio's destiny.

It moved him to imagine that his son's heroism, now being put to the test on Italian soil, was comparable to that of the legendary navigators, in general products of the school of Sagres, sniffing in the very wind an Atlantic with no beginning and no end. From the tip of Cape Saint Vincent, those wise, rough-hewn Portuguese began to think of crossing those waters, of tucking them away in their knapsacks like gold nuggets. And all because the dream of the Indies spurred them on. At no time did they fear winds, storms, sirens, monsters. On the contrary, confident that the trade winds were a safe route, they sailed before them till they had circled America. Stubbornly going the whole way round a sea route initially laid out by imagination.

So why wouldn't he think that his son Cláudio too was a modern pioneer? Except that he had gone in the opposite direction. Impelled by the urgent need to save Europe, he had not had time to touch down in Portugal and thank that country, the most daring in the world, for having arrived first in Brazil, before other cruel gringos. Gringos who would surely not have coupled with creatures already there on the land, thereby keeping Brazil from being a people descended from an incalculable mixture of races. He doubtless trusted that that Luso-Brazilian, his son, would now be committed to a stubborn defense of the offended soil of Portugal and Brazil.

On his one day off, Viriato tuned in the Radio Nacional program featuring Dona Teteca and her pupils Manduca, Colonel Fagundes, and Seu Ferramenta. His mind at rest, being certain that he in no way personified the figure of Seu Ferramenta, a symbol of the stupidity which older people in the immigrant community were taxed with. Thus never feeling at all offended by the nickname "tailless donkey" that a pushcart such as his own went by. To which he owed his thanks for his well-laden table. And above all for its having been the one work tool that Brazil had offered him among the many others he had never come by in those years.

His possible frustrations were immediately relieved when he thought of all the people who depended on his efforts to get their moving jobs done. People who had turned out not to be strong enough to haul on their own bent backs their colonial chests, their imitation Chippendale furniture, their broken-down chairs, all junk left sitting in the street.

Luckily there were moves every day. While some people left the place where they lived to better themselves, others were evicted for nonpayment. Those who had the worst time of it were the ones who received, from bachelor uncles, as an inheritance, battered pots and pans, old clothes smelling of mothballs, nondescript furniture, and piles of magazines that nobody read anymore. And on top of it all the obligation to pay for their funeral and clear out whatever else was left in the place, so as to make way for the new tenants.

"That uncle of mine was a miser, Seu Viriato. He no doubt had a bit of money. Only nobody knows where he kept it or who hid it for him. All that ingrate left me was a few knickknacks and some old paper. And by that I don't mean paper that's negotiable on the stock market!"

Viriato was embarrassed by those bitter feelings being paraded before him. To change the subject, he hurriedly asked the heir where he should deliver the modest legacy.

"Well, that old heap of trash ought to have ended up in the dump. But I don't have even that right to take my revenge that way, seeing that hauling it that far would cost me a fortune. So just throw everything in the nearest vacant lot."

Of these moves marked by misfortune, certain things served Viriato as vivid reminders. On observing on Sundays those objects without an owner and without a history, he was consoled by the certain knowledge that he had no fortune to leave behind, thus sparing his offspring any arguments. On the other hand, he obliged them to set aside a bit of money among them, to be used to bury him and Maria. A fact of which they were already aware, hence having no reason to complain about where the money would be going. Maria and he had gone to great expense to bring them up, to feed them. Even now, when they came home, they were welcomed with lavish dinners, with plenty of wine and beer to go with them. To be able to provide all this, Maria helped him by doing washing and ironing far into the night.

His friends from the old country criticized him for the excesses at table that kept him from being able to accumulate any savings. And thus never managing to buy the tavern he'd dreamed of on the outskirts of the city. He hastily rallied to the defense of an inheritance consisting of nothing but the memories of these feasts.

"You'll leave your son a house. And you'll be remembered only because of that house. They may even light a candle for you on Mondays, the day of souls. Maria and I will be remembered only for the lavish dinners we gave. It's our sole family estate."

Viriato drank his ice-cold Malzbier in long swallows. His swollen paunch obliged him to wear suspenders to keep his pants from falling down. Pointing, however, to his belly, he said with pride:

"I owe my build to beer well chilled."

In the taverns, he received warm embraces. "And how's our soldier who's fighting overseas, Viriato? When are we going to capture Monte Castello?"

Leaning on the counter, Viriato quoted passages from his son's letter, enthusiastically adding news items he'd heard on the radio and other information he'd invented. He had noticed how docilely everyone accepted phrases delivered with a professorial air.

"I'm turning into a specialist in war matters. And it's no wonder. Cláudio is finally at the top of the mountain, with his rifle slung across his shoulder. And whenever he has time to spare, he tells us military secrets."

With the heat as an excuse, Viriato downed one glass after another. Referring, then, to General Mascarenhas in extremely familiar terms. Zenóbio had personally promised Cláudio to act as godfather of his first child.

"So you can rest assured that once the war is over, General Mascarenhas will come to our house to have codfish stew."

Maria allowed herself to be won over by Viriato. Hence smiling once again and telling Eulália stories. Urged on by the lady from Spain, she embroidered the facts with names of neighbors she barely knew. Not scrupling to tell slight untruths, since by means of them she was more likely to touch Eulália's heart. Moreover, she believed in the power of lies, which soon turned into truth. It pleased her to flesh out any reality that struck her as scant and shabby.

Her aim was to amuse Eulália, by nature distracted, for a few minutes at least. Being compensated for this by kind attentions she had never before merited. Only now, thanks to her son in the Expeditionary Force, was she promoted to the center of interest.

Paying close attention to any sort of popular unrest, Getúlio launched a whole handful of clever measures. And, as always, the sound of his voice, broadcast by radio, become a more and more transcendent medium, held the population spellbound. Through the microphone, making use of slow, deliberate phrases, Getúlio injected one and all with the courage and the fortitude to enable them to face up at one and the same time to war and to rationing. In the last analysis, Brazil had more than sufficient reason to rejoice in a future that throbbed in their hands like a quivering bird, once the people were able to palpate the demands of that future and, having done so, give themselves over to contemplation of it.

In response to such stimulants, the Civil Defense groups went through the neighborhoods collecting donations contributed out of patriotism. In a certain way repeating the collection made in São Paulo, around '32, when the State rose up in arms against Getúlio, thus initiating a fratricidal war. There being no one, back in those days, who did not donate gold rings, representing marriages of more than thirty years, as well as other jewelry, for the purchase of arms and supplies.

In that phase, Venâncio was opposed to the President, though he was in favor of the war. And above all of Brazil's effort to ally itself with the democratic forces confronting an ideology that threatened to spread throughout Europe. To distract himself, he pasted articles that met with his approval in albums stacked up alongside his bed.

"Once the Allies have won, Fatty won't be able to hold out. He'll fall flat on his belly with his cigar in his mouth," he said, calm and untroubled.

Madruga didn't believe that the nation's institutions were in peril. In the end Getúlio, by proclaiming labor laws, a juridical measure that took into account the basic needs of the worker, had at the same time managed to act in favor of capital. In the face of rising social unrest, he had extended to the people benefits they had never before enjoyed. Thereby profiting from an incalculable popular prestige to discharge effectively his role as absolute arbiter between capital and the urban labor force. Without putting undue pressure, however, on employers, who, slowly, absorbed the regulations and the laws already proclaimed, by means of which he succeeded in maintaining public order. Then, while Getúlio granted workers the equivalent of their rights, at the same time he did not let the opportunity go by to demand their rigorous abstention from public and trade union activities, which might stand in the way of the wielding of his dictatorial power.

As Venâncio set forth Getúlio's situation, Madruga ironically defended his policy of short-circuiting class struggle. In his opinion, the one thing he could rightfully be criticized for was his pronouncements regarding the regime of exceptional powers that had been instituted, whereby the President had decreed censorship, the suspension of civil rights, indiscriminate imprisonments, and torture.

Venâncio countered this argument. "Getúlio's despotism, in a way, is the equivalent of Franco's. The two of them employ similar methods. Why spare Getúlio? Are his populist language, his paternalistic attitudes, and even the Collor laws sufficient reason for us to absolve him? If so, Madruga, we must extend the same tolerance to the usurpers of today and tomorrow."

Madruga's defense was centered on the construction of the National

Steel works, in Volta Redonda. It must be conceded that Getúlio, by putting an end to the corrupt and oppressive English presence in Brazil, with which we had been embroiled for decades thanks to endless debts, had achieved a notable victory. Even though Getúlio had found himself obliged to replace the country's former economic dependence on the English with dependence on the Americans, in return for the right to found National Steel.

A real masterstroke pulled off against the giant of the North, which, from the beginning, was violently opposed to such a project, its aim being to condemn us to the eternal consumption of its own steel. Only when the gringos perceived that Getúlio was slyly approaching the level of German technology, represented by Krupp, thereby threatening them with the loss of their economic hegemony on the continent, did they give in to his request for a loan, thus allowing Brazil to seek self-sufficiency in the basic sector.

"Even if Getúlio has the long-suffering people on his side, the world won't be the same after the war. The consequences of a victory that his political strategy never foresaw are going to be thrust down his throat. The Allied victory is going to defeat him right here, inside Brazil itself," Venâncio said.

Cláudio's latest letters no longer hid his homesickness, which Viriato promptly attributed to the way his mother had always spoiled him. That was why Cláudio was now beginning to dream of clean sheets at home and his mother's good cooking.

"Nobody in Botafogo has cleaner sheets than ours," Viriato said, swiftly smoothing the wrinkles from the face of a worried Maria.

She no longer hid her tension, not even in Eulália's presence. But not wanting to deprive Eulália of the habit of listening to her stories, she continued to recount them, though visibly blundering. Seeing to it, however, that she eliminated nearly all the known characters, reducing them to a maximum of three.

At each instant, her stubborn heart told her that her son's suffering exceeded the tribulations peculiar to wartime. Cláudio threatened not to be the same after the conflict. Maria didn't exactly fear losing him. The son to whom she had given birth was indestructible. Life had taught her that poverty did not necessarily being death with it. On the contrary, in fact, the sons of God, marked by vicissitudes, were more resistant to life's challenges. Hence reproducing themselves more than the rich. No one would ever manage to wipe the poor from the face of the earth.

As for Eulália, at the thought that she had Miguel safe at home, though old enough to be drafted, she offered the laundress unexpected presents to even the balance. Madruga sensed her fear and prepared to talk her out of it. Under no condition would he allow his son to be placed on any damned draftee list. He would have him removed from it at whatever price. Miguel was not going to die in that war, and then be buried in a cold grave, without Eulália and himself close at hand to mourn him. As a precaution, he spoke with friends. From Deputy Silveira to Colonel Cardoso, his tenant in Tijuca, to whose apartment he always sent someone to paint, without charging him any tax or extra fee. The two men assured him that he had nothing to fear. Before Miguel was called up, a substantial proportion of young men would have been decimated.

On Sundays, holding Tobias close, Venâncio spoke to him of the war, beneath Madruga's reproving gaze. Venâncio's godson heard his stories with a shrinking heart, not moving. Till he began, shortly before the end of the war, to wake up screaming at night, terrifying the whole house, not calming down even when Eulália or Madruga appeared on the scene. Sobbing, Tobias proclaimed his desire to join the Brazilian soldiers dying in Italy. In his dreams, he saw them with their faces buried in the mud, as jeeps with loud exhaust pipes passed close by without even picking up the corpses.

"Cláudio died, mother, he's never going to come back!"

With his mother's arms around him, clutching him to her bosom, Tobias caught the odor of her coming through her nightgown. Deeply distressed, he tried his best to breathe in the life of the woman within arm's reach. Which made it even harder for him to breathe, consequently intensifying his fear of not arriving in time to save the soldiers of the Expeditionary Force, depending on his help alone so as not to suffocate to death along a trail somewhere in Italy.

Madruga blamed Venâncio for being mad enough to glorify war in the hearing of a youngster as nervous as Tobias. Not to mention the fact that Venâncio's triumphalist vision, prefaced by sermons preaching social revolution in the name of a brilliant future, struck him as being logically inconsistent. Above all he resented the growing friendship between Venâncio and Tobias, an intimacy that cut him off from his son. To the point that he lacked the power to erase the wavering doubts that surfaced in the boy's eyes.

Calming her son, Eulália forced him to sleep. Rather than distracting him with stories, she chose to pray aloud at his side. She had no means at her disposal to comfort Tobias. Or to promise him that this would be the last war to disgrace humanity. Holding him close, she stroked the hair of her youngest son, a child who had been a surprise, at a time when she had not expected that her body would reproduce again.

And thus little by little he calmed down. The same thing occurring on the following nights. Until he slept normally again, for good. But the war was a heavy burden on everyone's heart. Even though the armistice was only a few days away. Dona Maria, on the other hand, was happy once again. She and Viriato ruffled the drums in their row house in Botafogo. While they hadn't made good in America by following the classic patterns, they now had at their disposal a living treasure, in the person of Cláudio. In a few days veterans would receive a fat pension, and even be in a position to own a house of their own through the payment of a token sum.

Maria's dream of a house of her own would soon come true. Even if it was in a working district, at the sacrifice of her clientele, all located in the southern part of the city. Viriato was already refusing to leave Botafogo, to bury himself alive in some neighborhood where he had no friends and not a single son of his had been born. That old and ugly row house they had lived in had at least been his love nest down through the years, he repeated aloud. Between those walls, he had fathered children, eaten many a fine codfish stew, and drunk wine from good stock. A number of bottles having been presented to him by Madruga, in gratitude for the happiness that the laundress had passed on to his wife. Even though Eulália hadn't breathed a word to him, Madruga had noticed how much she appreciated that smiling Portuguese woman.

When he sought to discover the source of the happiness plainly impressed upon Eulália's face, he would question Odete: "Who has been here?"

Odete would show him the laundry list written by Maria's rough hand. Enough of an identification for him to hasten to provide Seu Viriato with a supply of wine.

Once the armistice was declared, the country was in a fever during that month of June. Eulália agreed to hold a reception for the soldiers who would be disembarking at the Praça Mauá. A friend who was a wholesale merchant had offered them a vast office on the Rua do Acre, on the corner of the Avenida Rio Branco, from which to watch the parade of the Brazilian Expeditionary Force, the famous FEB.

Madruga provided beer, soft drinks, ice cream, and sandwiches. In the Confeitaria Colombo, he ordered a three-layer cake, decorated with green and yellow sugar flowers, forming a circle around the centerpiece, a marzipan soldier. As well as the sort of salty appetizers the family liked. The evening before, he had the office decorated with flowers, colored balloons, and Brazilian and Spanish flags. And, to touch Eulália's heart, he secretly removed from the wardrobe chest the silk bedspread they had had ever since they were married, so as to hang it in the window, as the balconies of the Iberian peninsula were traditionally adorned on feast days or for processions.

At Madruga's urging, Eulália provided new clothes for the children and Odete. "Brazil is going to receive her heroes. It's as though we were about to be reborn, in the hour of their setting foot on this earth."

The crowd stretched all the way from the Obelisk, through Cinelândia and the entire downtown district, to the Praça Mauá. Their proud faces, drenched with sweat in the bright sun beating down, were hidden behind little paper flags. Waved by the populace, which, seen from a distance,

formed a multicolored sea. In a few hours the parade would begin marching up Rio Branco. And already it had become difficult to walk along the
streets. Venâncio elbowed his way through the multitude. He had not felt
so at ease for a long time. He had promised Madruga that he would watch
the parade from the office that Madruga had been lent. And that night he
would accompany them to the Rua Mena Barreto, for Cláudio's victory
celebration.

True to her word, Dona Maria had disappeared in the last week. So
as to work out, with the neighbors, all the details of the party honoring the
only hero of that block in Botafogo. Advised beforehand, Odete did not
complain about the accumulation of dirty laundry. She too tuned in, with
heartfelt emotion, to Getúlio's voice on the radio. She considered the President a saint, no matter what Rome might think. She had enthroned him
without asking Eulália's advice in the matter.

In repeated announcements, in firm tones, various speakers, above all
the Esso Reporter, encouraged the populace to move about the city, as in
between they played the hymn "However many the lands I roam, God
grant that before I die, I may first come home. . . ."

It was barely light when the taverns opened their doors. No Brazilian
heart could remain unmoved by the carnival that was spontaneously taking
shape. Even Venâncio forgot Getúlio's disturbing words on the occasion of
his anniversary: "Today for the first time, I am a man who does not know
what to do, who is faced with a dilemma. I do not know whether it is my
duty to hurl in their faces this government that they think is a very good
thing. Or whether I ought to hold on for a year or two, and hand the
country over to my successor. Now that we have won the war, I want to
win the peace." Having declared as well: "I feel I am leaving a trail of
gunpowder behind me."

These words, attributed to Getúlio, immediately went the rounds of
the Palácio do Monroe and Cinelândia, amid intense excitement, gaining
momentum thanks to any number of different versions. The reason behind
them probably being a Getúlio stung by the Miners' Manifesto, and by the
unremitting groundswell of protest against the dictatorship, of demands
for an immediate return to democratic privileges. Above all because it was
suspected that Getúlio was stealthily plotting some sort of legal maneuver
to legitimize his power. On the pretext that only his sense of duty was
prompting him to ask for an extension of his time in office, was obliging
him to tie himself down in the Palácio do Catete for a while longer. Which,
moreover, his moral principles did not allow him to leave, on pain of abandoning the country to political helplessness, a perilous orphanhood.

Standing before his mirror, Venâncio was shaving, overcome with indignation. Dictators had a refined instinct for moving the people, for making it feel itself to be the orphan of mythical specters which, in fact, it was
every dictator's ambition to incarnate. To that end always counting on the

anxious loneliness of a country. Especially when it was a poor and lost one, with no one to turn to so as to save it.

"Can it be that our countries don't want to grow up? Can they forbid us indefinitely to choose our own destiny?"

Venâncio was mistrustful of Getúlio's overtures to labor. His moves seemed to be part of an international plan, which allowed the employer to better the life of the worker, in return for consolidating the more and more devastating presence of foreign capital in Brazilian society. Which even made sense. Since it stimulated the consumption of imported products and, eventually, those produced domestically under the aegis of foreign groups. With, as a consequence, the creation of new habits aimed at strengthening an economically weak market. And all this taking place as the already debased national consciousness was further exploited and corrupted. The country again invaded by men such as Thomas Sindley, who, in the past, had landed on these shores with the one intention of robbing it of its wealth. In view of all this, could Brazil be a land of miserable scoundrels? Foreigners and Brazilians alike? Can it be that we're all scoundrels by trade, living the dream of bettering human life? Presuming that miserable scoundrels drive a country to progress, despite their immoral acts?

From the window of the office, little flags could be seen, waving in a single, feverish gesture at the announcement of the landing of the troops, whose ship, the *General Meigs,* had already tied up at the pier. In the vanguard, heading the parade, came generals Mascarenhas and Zenóbio da Costa, moving slowly along in army jeeps. Thanks to the popular delirium, Getúlio would be able to capitalize on the victory of the Expeditionary Force as a triumph of his leadership as head of the government. In these moments there was no opposition to counter the climate of euphoria reigning throughout the national territory. The conspirators would be forced to retreat for a time. Even though the conspiracy, already well under way, had come to be less and less of an underground one, to the point that the plotters were now launching broadsides. Vargas's enemies now extending from the Alterosas to the Paraíba. Even José Américo, a former cabinet minister of the dictatorship, had become a powerful spokesman of the burgeoning movement.

"Long live Getúlio, long live our boys!" Madruga shouted. With his arms about Eulália, he offered a toast to victory. Overcome with inexplicable emotion in the face of human deeds of valor. He felt himself to be part of Hannibal's army crossing the Alps with its elephants, a frontline soldier. When it came down to it he loved this country he had chosen to die in. And his status as an immigrant gave him solid advantages. Providing he never wasted time pondering the meaning of Brazil in his life.

During the parade he eyed Eulália and the five children. The well-laden table and the comfort he had earned. The truth was that he would not have resigned himself to poverty. He had fought against defeat every minute, paying an unbearable price at times. Without having anyone to turn to when he felt himself to be on the brink of failure, gambling everything. Hence he'd kept a tight grip on every detail, like a shipwreck victim. And as he for his part fought to breathe in the sweet smell of victory, Venâncio, with an alarming pride, unfurled the banner of defeat.

Madruga even reached the point of asking himself whether he might not have shifted his personal burden of dreams onto Venâncio. Simply to rid himself of the fetid vapors that emanate from dreams and keep good luck from knocking at the door. Having thereby so overburdened Venâncio with empty illusions as to make him incapable of reconciling himself to reality.

At times, unable to sleep, he felt an urge to awaken Eulália in the middle of the night, simply to ask her where in the world his soul was. Or whether he'd lost it forever. He restrained himself, however, hoping he still was in possession of it, even though he did not have it at hand. It had no doubt found refuge with Eulália, who was entrusted as well with praying in his name, for his dead, and for Galician legends.

Suddenly, in the middle of the march of the soldiers acclaimed by the multitude, Tobias began to cry, clinging to his mother's skirts. Madruga hurried over, trying to pull him away from Eulália.

"What's the matter, son?"

Sidestepping his father's welcoming arms, Tobias looked at him in fury. A look that Madruga had seen before. And to his surprise, Tobias left his mother and planted himself squarely in front of him.

"Where are the soldiers who died in Italy, father? They didn't come back, did they?"

Madruga quickly brought him some guaraná juice with ice, in a paper cup. Tobias refused it, bursting into a fit of dry sobs. Madruga was annoyed at the boy, bent on spoiling that historic celebration. Impatiently, he made a move to hand him over to his mother. But then, suddenly repenting, he picked him up, going over to the window.

"Look for yourself, Tobias. Can't you see that they're all here? Look how smartly they're marching. There's not a one who didn't come home, son."

Tobias did not appear to be persuaded. He swiftly fled from his father's arms to Venâncio. "Isn't it true, godfather, that lots of soldiers didn't get off the boat? Did they die way far away over there?"

Venâncio looked questioningly at Madruga, who frowned, demanding that he give the boy a forthright reply. As a look from Eulália pleaded for mercy, for him to spare her son at that moment. She did not want him destroyed by the barbs of reality. Venâncio enfolded the little boy in his arms. He loved him like a son, his affection brimming over within him.

"Don't worry, Tobias, everything is all right. Brazil wouldn't leave a single Brazilian behind in Italy," and fondly caressing his godson, he pointed out to him the live ones marching with resolute step amid the applause of the crowd.

"Do you think that if one soldier were missing there'd be a carnival like this?"

Reassured by his godfather, the little boy leaned against Bento, who got him to wave his little flag. Whereupon Tobias began shouting Long live Brazil and Getúlio. From the end of the table, Venâncio sat watching them all. Madruga came over to him, insisting that he have some food. All he would eat was a piece of the cake just cut by Odete.

At the end of the afternoon, tired though they were, they headed for the party for Cláudio. Eulália embraced Maria, who looked radiant, free of all her fears now. The Rua Mena Barreto was decorated, from one end to the other, with ribbons, flags, and sprigs of greenery tied to the lampposts and the trees, bringing Palm Sunday to mind. Traffic had been routed round the street and a passage cordoned off, leading from the Rua Soro-caba to the row houses. The whole street had thus been invaded by pedes-trians and invited guests. Beer was being drawn from kegs placed at the common entrance to the row of houses, its ice-cold coils of foam fascinat-ing the children. Everyone had chipped in to pay for the celebration. And the big long table, set up along the inside corridor of the building, was laden with various roasts, potato salad, baked rice, cake and cookies.

Cláudio did not show up for some time. Resting inside the house, before being shown off to the community again. Knowing how curious everyone was about her son, Maria was going round reassuring the visi-tors, in her strong Portuguese accent, that Cláudio had arrived in perfect shape, like someone just back from vacation. They'd never seen him so fat, so resplendent. Obviously, Brazil knew how to treat its sons, and with a beaming smile she bared a gold tooth.

Busy with the beer and the food, Viriato expressed his pleasure at finally meeting Madruga. Madruga, in turn, was eager to see from close up the one soldier of the Expeditionary Force whose trajectory in the war his family had followed since the embarkation for Italy.

"Here he comes, Seu Madruga," Viriato shouted, his undershirt soak-ing wet, sweating all over, even though it was the middle of winter.

Cláudio retreated before the avalanche of embraces. He seemed frightened. Everybody wanting to have a close look at the medals he'd won in such a short space of time. He let himself be dragged off without the least reaction or smile. His expression, however, provoked in Eulália a wave that mounted to her head, completely overwhelming her. As though this sort of fever illuminated the presence at her side of an enemy shadow whispering evil words to her, words she did not want to hear. And that in the end she listened to. These words suggesting to her, then, a truth that, despite its fragile appearance, bound her, even more tightly, to the difficult human condition. Her eyelids felt so heavy that she closed her eyes.

Odete noticed her distress. "What's the matter?"

Eulália searched for the laundress amid the crowd. That sweet, rash fool, so trustful of others, felt herself already the mistress of a house whose key would soon find its way into her hands. Certain that the government, from that moment on, would assume the responsibility of looking after those who had one day dreamed of America, in the distant Vale dos Lafões. And for whom America had done nothing except give them countless offspring, along with the codfish and wine of Sundays warmed by a gentle sun.

As Madruga embraced Cláudio, Eulália watched the youngster. His gaze was distant, absent, focused on no one. In it there was a painful melancholy, scarcely noticeable in the excitement of the celebration. He was allowing himself to be devoured by his neighbors, without really participating in a banquet from which the campaign in Italy had excluded him.

Plunged into a painful anxiety, Eulália had no one with whom to share the total presentiment that Cláudio had been brought back home by a body that no longer belonged to him. As if they had put him aboard the boat, there in Naples, and he had obeyed. He no longer had it in him to get his own way or disobey orders and counterorders. He seemed to be destroyed inside, there being little left of him except a dim silhouette. They had gradually stolen pieces of him without Maria and the neighbors realizing. For his lack of any vice, life had led him to perdition.

Faithful to the Portuguese tradition of lavish hospitality, the laundress pressed one and all to eat and drink their fill. They were not to leave the house till their hearts overflowed with joy. The feasting made it necessary to bring in reinforcements of beer and victuals. And the sound as well of the accordion and the songs that now invaded Botafogo, usually a quiet neighborhood with its trees and its impenetrable walls. In it, mansions dwelt, in apparent peaceful coexistence, side by side with row houses, many of them with furnished rooms to let. At the celebration the fraternization had brought the classes even closer together. The senators and aristocrats of the Rua Dona Mariana, moved by patriotic fervor, had shown up to embrace Dona Maria and Seu Viriato.

As Eulália took her leave, the laundress was deeply touched, her embrace overstepping the limits of mere politeness. "Feel free to drop by here whenever you like, Dona Eulália. This house is humble, but it's yours."

In the shelter of her own home, Eulália's thoughts constantly returned to Maria. Though not knowing how to explain, she was fearful of the aftermath of the celebration. And even more afraid that Maria's candid brow might be furrowed by deep wrinkles in the near future. She consulted Odete each day, asking after the laundress, whose prolonged absence began to worry her. Until she was informed that Maria was wandering from one city hospital to another. The doctors persuaded of the seriousness of Cláudio's mental state, which had worsened considerably in recent weeks.

Until finally he had an attack that left him with dramatic aftereffects, thus obliging the doctors to transfer him to the asylum, where, in the beginning, only his mother would be allowed to see him during visiting hours on Sunday afternoon.

This being the case, Maria dressed in her best on Sunday mornings, expecting to take her son fruit and clean pajamas. Knowing beforehand that, after taking Cláudio by the arm, completely indifferent to her presence, they would take a few turns around the courtyard of the old, ash-gray building. When she left, she would take back home with her, in a sack, the torn and filthy pair of pajamas of the preceding week. And despite foreseeing the fate that would be visited on the pajamas and the shirts, she mended them and washed them with scrupulous professional attention. Not neglecting, for all of that, her other tasks.

And she never again mentioned, to whomever she might meet, either Portugal, the people on the block, or the serials on Radio Nacional. The whole neighborhood had suffered a total eclipse in her affections. She often neglected to prepare Viriato's codfish on Sundays, which he for his part no longer ate with the same pleasure he once had.

At the end of each month, Cláudio's pension not only amounted to less and less because of the lack of cost-of-living adjustments, but the government proved to be unmoved by the pleas of the soldiers for a house of their own. And Getúlio himself, by coincidence, was removed from power on the same day that Cláudio received the electric shock treatment that banished him from human society forever. The two downfalls different in nature, however. As Getúlio headed for exile in São Borja, perhaps to plot his political return, Cláudio found himself judged irredeemably insane.

On Maria's first visit, Eulália enfolded her in a long embrace. On her subsequent visits, Eulália almost never remained at her side. And this for the reason that, in Maria's presence, she immediately entered into conflict with God, emerging from the encounter with her body broken and bowed. Shut up in her room, she had no desire to leave it. And wherever she turned, Maria's empty, glassy stare seemed to pin her within a circle of thorns and desolation.

She began to see her less and less. Though sending her presents and consoling checks as substitutes for herself. More than ever, Tobias's protests, prior to the armistice, echoed loudly within her. Her son's voice was the only one that was an appeal to reason, condemning them for an irrational euphoria. Not even Venâncio, ordinarily an attentive listener, had paid heed to his godson. Pride in the war and victory had gotten the better of them. Like Roman soldiers, they too had entered Rome in triumph, mounted on their chariots. Brazil acclaiming its heroes, only to decimate them forthwith through forgetfulness and administrative carelessness.

On a Wednesday on which Eulália was not feeling well, Maria insisted on seeing her. Odete was reluctant to grant her request. Maria promised that it would be a brief visit. Just long enough to say good-bye.

"And where are you going?" Eulália said, seated opposite her.

They were moving, at last, to an outlying working district, where they ought to have gone to live when they had first arrived in Brazil.

"So the government has given you the house you were promised?" Eulália said joyfully.

Maria avoided answering, toying with the little spoon in her coffee cup. She shrugged. For a moment her eyes blazed with wrath and despair.

"Viriato decided to do as I wanted. It's almost certain that the pension fund will give us this house as a gift. And then too, it will be easier to visit Cláudio out there. We'll be neighbors," Maria said in a harsh voice.

Eulália reached out to hold her hands, but Maria kept them under the table. Between them there was now an insurmountable barrier and the certainty that they would not see each other again. Eulália asked her for her new address, which Odete wrote down in a memo book.

"Don't fail to drop by to visit us, Dona Maria," Eulália said haltingly. "But if it should be some time before you come round, I'll send you Cláudio's present." At the mention of her son's name, Maria's face became even more set. Nothing Eulália could do seemed to soften her heart. She abruptly asked for another coffee. She sipped it slowly, far away from there now. Eulália imagined that the laundress was going over, for one last time, the stories that she had told her between those walls, before tragedy had brought her low.

Suddenly Maria shivered. Perhaps she was seeing herself in Botafogo, dreading having to drag furniture about for the last time, for the move that Viriato would see to making in his own cart, or in a borrowed van. She herself diligently sorting out the objects that she would leave behind in the Botafogo row house, not once looking back.

And Maria was so absorbed in cultivating her secret thoughts that she did not even notice when Eulália went off, on the pretext of going to look for a handkerchief. Not coming back later to say good-bye. Maria nonetheless forbearing to request her presence in the kitchen once more. She simply drank down the coffee and quietly stole away, with Odete following at her heels to the door.

Venâncio's voice was scarcely audible in the first days. In his pajamas, under the sheet, he forced himself to keep the secrets of his anxiety to himself, not sharing them with other witnesses. His body uncared for, fear making his face ugly. Now and again a trickle of saliva dribbled from his mouth.

In an unhurried, deliberate tone of voice, he impressed upon the doctor yet again his wish to have no visitors. They ought not to see him in the state into which he had been plunged after abandoning the orbit of dreams and anxiety into which he had fallen in recent years. Within this invisible capsule, he had feverishly sounded the Brazilian past, the nineteenth century in particular, and the Bay of Guanabara. With the aid of nothing but the German field glasses, which replenished his stock of images each day, and revealed the fact that pirates, smugglers, brigands, swindlers ceaselessly attacked Brazil.

His fellow patients bore on their faces signs of loneliness and agony. Mortally wounded by the certainty that illusion had abandoned them. Their eyes fixed on invisible bridges, they wandered about the ward headed for exile, leaning for support on the bed frames with peeling paint. Terrified that their lives would suddenly be demanded of them.

The doctor was adamant that Venâncio remain in close touch with his friends. As meanwhile Venâncio refused to allow Eulália and Madruga to invade his body, which was precisely where the agony had lodged. On palpating himself, he had the sensation that his muscles were shattering, the shards flying through the air. Later, Madruga would come and put things to rights again, forcing him to settle down in bed, adjusting his pillow and the things on the night table, so he would have room enough after his visits for the gifts he'd received. And even though Venâncio upbraided him for being so overbearing, Madruga, busy tidying up, would pay no attention. Certain that he was contributing to Venâncio's forgetting that carnivorous past that quite evidently had devoured appreciable portions of his body.

Though pain-stricken, Venâncio nonetheless went looking for the tag ends of dreams that had not deserted him. Lying in the narrow bed, the prisoner of another's will, he could still marshal the strength to assure himself of a minimum of integrity. It pleased him to imagine that Madruga, forbidden to enter the ward, would fight for his rights. Refusing to go along with Venâncio, damaging a friendship of nearly thirty years' standing.

And in fact, Madruga turned a deaf ear to medical explanations. He did not consider Venâncio capable of making decisions. If his condition required hospital care, the doctor should be the one to decide for the patient. The doctor regretted forbidding visiting rights. Though he disagreed with Venâncio, he would respect his wishes in the matter, in order to hasten his recovery.

Madruga thought of bringing Eulália, but immediately changed his mind about a move that would corner a defenseless Venâncio, having nowhere in the hospital to take refuge. He wanted to visit him with his full consent. Even if his eyes glared at him accusingly at first. Till friendship, safeguarded by common memories, surfaced once again between them. They would soon regain the words that would artfully take them back to that first Atlantic voyage, the epicenter of their affection.

Madruga sent him a note asking his permission to visit him. He waited for an hour on the wooden bench on whose surface names and dates were inscribed. Seeing how distressed he was, the nurse described to him what it felt like to be a patient confined to a bed, a helpless creature who had everything against him, including his injured dignity.

"Your friend is proud, you know. If he finds it hard to see you, it's because he's fond of you," she said.

Venâncio turned down the request, noting as well his strong disapproval of the vehement tone of the written words it was couched in. In them he saw incontrovertible signs of Madruga's overbearing nature, intent on getting the better of life through acts that meant nothing. Hence his hour to suffer had now come. Had Madruga not put a damper on his reveries, beginning with his visit to his apartment, his dreams would not have turned into nightmares. After all, what right did Madruga have to accuse him of having absorbed a paralyzing poison, simply because the past, through which he was journeying, had become the only time compatible with his spirit, possessing in addition the advantage of shedding light on his disaffection for everyday existence?

Madruga suspected that Venâncio's rejection was aimed at testing his affection.

"If that's the case, he's going to find me here every day."

What was more, it seemed unfair to him that Venâncio should punish him for a fault never specifically identified. By having proposed to him that he substitute medical care for chaos, his one intention had been to discipline him, to enable him to create in the future a nest in which to settle himself, in a state of readiness to absorb the minimum rules of reality.

Every afternoon Madruga went to the Spanish Benefit Society. Dropping by the Confeitaria Colombo first, pointing out to the man who waited on him the fruits, the sweets, and the appetizers meant to cleanse Venâncio's palate for gastronomic delicacies. So that, beginning with his illness, his taste buds would become so sensitized that his eyes would close out of sheer pleasure.

Loaded down with parcels, Madruga had the fond hope that he was making a decisive contribution to Venâncio's cure. And that he would linger on, for all the rest of the day, in Venâncio's memory. Till he went to sleep, immediately after the last injection.

Venâncio chewed on the appetizers with profound indifference, sharing what he didn't eat with his neighbors. And systematically tore up Madruga's notes, after a perfunctory reading. The one person he wrote to was Tobias, his five-year-old godson, in an attempt to justify his absence. Though his writing was shaky owing to the effects of his medication, he nonetheless described in detail the enjoyable country life he was now leading. He was living on an estate surrounded by vast green pastures, and was constantly drawn to the corral, to visit its animals, which looked more like Hindu potentates.

Eulália read the notes aloud, after Sunday dinner. With the table unfailingly set with an empty plate for Venâncio. There in its usual place, should Venâncio unexpectedly turn up. As her children listened attentively, their mother lent her voice lively, moving tones. Searching out in each word Venâncio's absent spirit.

Madruga did not agree with Eulália's interpretation. In his opinion, his wife betrayed his friend's intention. For, concentrating on her role, she involuntarily left gaps in the course of her reading, which, consequently, did violence to Venâncio's original aims. So Madruga asked her for the note and read it again. Persuaded that this time he was interpreting the dense mystery of Venâncio, whose spirit had recently abandoned the nineteenth century, in favor of a reality that at last held sway over that table.

A subtle rivalry between husband and wife could be discerned, sustained by the need of both to transmit to their children the secret sentiments of Venâncio, who was being subjected in those months to a touching and unusual situation.

On walking up the Rua do Riachuelo, in the direction of the Benefit Society, Madruga pondered each afternoon the problem of overcoming Venâncio's resistance. To that end rehearsing words free of emotion, which would not hurt the patient's feelings. His heart pounding, he sought an audience with him. Only to be told, yet again, that Venâncio refused to receive him.

At this point, to hide his embarrassment, Madruga straightened the knot in his tie, averting his face from the nurse. He hurriedly made his way to the third floor, one flight down from Venâncio's ward, where he proceeded to collect from those familiar with the case their respective versions of it. And the explanations of Venâncio's clinical condition were so at variance with each other that at times it seemed to him that they were speaking of a stranger.

The wards, despite being cleaned daily, gave off an ineradicable smell of dead flesh. On meeting patients in pajamas walking up and down the corridors, Madruga felt revulsion, while at the same time he feared that they were out to rob him of his health. The thought then occurred to him that Venâncio, being one of them now, had no doubt taken on the same look, the same odor, the same amorphous gestures. Having succumbed to an illness that, according to the doctor, it depended on the patient himself to overcome. Venâncio being the only one able to shed light on the origin of his complaints.

Madruga began to question his own behavior. Wondering whether he had not been hasty in proposing to Venâncio that he commit himself to an institution, when if the truth were told he had paid scant attention to the evolution of an illness whose progress had been masked by the fact that it had no physical effects. Which nonetheless had undoubtedly brought on a loss of Venâncio's sense of reality in recent years.

A reality, however, that Madruga himself hesitated to define or demarcate. It therefore being difficult for him to have an intimate knowledge of Venâncio's real losses, what exactly it was that had slipped through the hole in his pants pocket. To know whether he had the right to consider him unbalanced, meriting commitment to an institution, merely because he devoted part of his time to sighting, through the German field glasses, a bygone Brazil of a hundred years before. And possessed of such verisimilitude that he had persuaded himself that he had captured its spirit and form.

It was in those days that Madruga, torn between guilt and innocence, became conscious of his own attitude, so prompt to label any reality opposed to his own as unhealthy. Amid such self-questioning, leaning over the low wall along the Avenida Beira-Mar, he contemplated the waves breaking against the rocks. Those were Venâncio's waters.

Gentle and tame, they roared, nonetheless, out by the sea wall, near the Naval Academy. Those waters had been witness to the history of that city. In the distance, almost at Glória, he could see crowded streetcars going by with hangers-on standing on the steps.

Perhaps Venâncio had been right when he had tried to prove to him that he had lost, for good, access to the world of dreams, whose basic requirement was the enjoyment of a perilous, unlimited freedom. Because for Venâncio one had to renounce everyday, petty, mediocre reality if one wanted to gain possession of the formula that would bring on dreaming. Despite its sometimes being an unhappy dream.

Venâncio was fond, at such times, of proclaiming that Brazil had been made up, since its foundation, of dregs of humanity who, the moment they landed their ships here, immediately set out to cut down, with one blow of an ax, trees centuries old, animals, Indians, without the least mercy. There not being among those men a single voice to deplore the predatory spirit being implanted here. Or to oppose a first rough outline of civilization, sustained by cowardice, indifference, and injustice. But could this really be the portrait of Brazil traced by Venâncio? And what would his own portrait be like? Or did he lack the commanding knowledge needed to describe this country? It being up to his children alone to assume the tremendous task of defining the reality in which their father had involved himself so deeply that he lacked the perspective needed for any sort of scrupulous examination?

The doctor again informed Madruga that Venâncio took offense at any show of feeling. Solidarity, in the midst of the present crisis, wounded his pride. With the doctor, he was on his guard. He hinted vaguely at earlier troubles. And he always spoke to him in a rush of words about Spain and Brazil, two countries that in his mind were indissolubly linked. Implying that life had given him a merciless beating. Nothing better symbolizing the precariousness of human existence than our acute need to cling bodily to others, even with no assurance of arriving at any sort of understanding. He was sick and tired of seeing tearful farewells in public places.

Madruga bade the doctor good-bye with the firm intention of seeking a bit of diversion in the streets. The geography of the city was familiar to him. His favorite stamping ground was the area adjacent to the Spanish Benefit Society, where his factory turned out its products, almost next to the Praça da Cruz Vermelha. He remembered Venâncio's smile when he told him for the first time about his plans to go into the cold-storage industry. He had surely not been surprised at Madruga's bold confidence, which he was quite used to. Especially since, for Madruga, the development of the country required initiatives of that sort. And if he didn't go into that line of business, someone else would. One, incidentally, that would fill a need in a city that suffered from the heat practically all year round. People's unbearably hot bodies needing ice-cold liquids in the long summer months. Not to mention the fact that one way of preserving foodstuffs, so apt to rot rapidly when exposed to the rigor of the season, was to store them in refrigerators.

With this idea firmly in mind, Madruga had ordered prototypes from England, which had undergone technical modifications for all of two months, so as to make them better suited to the capabilities of a local work force and the need for low-cost production. There was a nearly captive market that Madruga seized upon, offering the advantages of a credit system, something just beginning in the city. And he announced the existence of his factory in newspapers and publications associated with the Spanish and Portuguese colonies. And after obtaining the addresses of the members of the Chamber of Commerce and professional organizations, he distributed an attractive circular in bars and restaurants.

Despite the threat of a second world war, the economy, far from stagnating in those precarious times, made steady strides thanks to continued investments. And anyone out to grow in size was obliged to head toward industry, which, with its basic multiplicative tendency, turned out profits in the same astounding quantities as it did products. The thing to do above all else was to imitate the tycoons in São Paulo, real robber barons under whose dominion the network of the new Brazilian capitalism spread.

Madruga especially admired the trajectory of Count Matarazzo. Whose thirteen children did not keep him from erecting an empire, sowing everywhere his red brick factories, in the style of traditional English buildings, soon imitated by budding industry in São Paulo. A powerful industrial complex, born of the profits from canned lard, whose total earnings in one year came to outstrip the gross revenue of the state of Minas Gerais and the prefecture of Rio de Janeiro combined.

It was necessary to know how to appraise the historical significance of these data, on which the evolution of Brazilian industry as a whole depended, in order to be able to meet the requisites of a potential buyers' market, already beginning to demand consumer goods. The hour had come to free Brazil once and for all from the implacable cycle of coffee monoculture. Did Venâncio know that that count, an immigrant like themselves, through the prestige of money and talent, had humbled the traditional society of São Paulo? Causing his blood to mingle with that of whomever he chose? Thus enriching the social fabric of the country, growing more complex with every passing day. Yet demanding the existence of a society that could face up to the alterations taking place. Brazil was undergoing dramatic transformations, with power once again changing hands.

The factory had barely been set up and already it was unable to meet commercial and household demands. And orders immediately forthcoming from fishing boats. A success exceeding Madruga's expectations. Failing nonetheless to assuage him. His eyes, at the sight of his ever-increasing fortune, still had a greedy, unsatisfied gleam in them. He wandered about the streets collecting facts and friendships that would not damage his interests. As meanwhile he loved, avidly, other women besides Eulália. Gradually getting rid of his old suits. Ordering tailor-made English cashmere ones, which fit him perfectly.

He mounted a campaign to combat Venâncio's indifference. Still wandering about, as aimless as ever. Spending hours on end each day in the National Library, with nothing but contempt for material wealth.

"How to help you, Venâncio, if you yourself condemn yourself to exile? Are you afraid money in your pocket would write finis to your dreams?"

Eulália cried out to Madruga to stop tormenting Venâncio, once and for all. The reasons that had drawn Venâncio to America were the precise opposite of his own. He had not come from so far away in order to dig holes in the ground each morning, leaving his body full of cuts and blisters, in his search for treasure. Venâncio's one treasure consisted in preserving his right to dream. Although personally she had no idea what it was he dreamed of. Nor was there any reason for her to know. People rarely shared their dreams with their fellows. What was certain was that Venâncio's patrimony was located in the clouds, far from this world. From which he gathered the coins that spoke to his heart. Madruga thus being in no position to take upon himself the role of intepreter of human happiness, nor of critic of Venâncio's woes.

Eulália's words never vexed him. On the contrary, his wife's declarations, soft-spoken and unexpected, moved him. Despite the fact that she could read Venâncio better than she read him, after twenty years of marriage. But whenever he had a problem with Venâncio, he went to Eulália, though lacking the courage to reveal that he had come to get his bearings.

He never came straight to the point. He used Spain as the pretext for their conversation. Whether she'd had news of members of the family in Sobreira. One letter, after all, would be enough to reveal a tragic picture. Madruga slowly puffed on his cigar. Accepting the coffee brought him.

Eulália sensed that he had something on his mind. She was in no hurry either. She too had developed her own resources. He went on talking about subjects having to do with Sobreira until he had forgotten her presence. Whereupon she felt free to explore the present and the past with equal ease. Including Venâncio in this trajectory in such a natural and many-faceted way that it allowed Madruga to accumulate information aimed at orienting him in his confrontation with his friend.

Madruga was convinced that Venâncio's outbreak of illness was due to his poor nourishment, his sleepless nights, his near-exhaustion, his unexpected breakdown in the face of everyday life. To the fact, above all, that Venâncio was struggling with an irreconcilable reality. The doctor himself was of the opinion that some implacable frustration had been gnawing mercilessly at him in recent years, to the point that delirium had become the only way out for him. Although the doctor saw that Venâncio was making progress, he advised his immediate transfer to a sanatorium where a stay for the next three months would find him well on the way to being cured.

Madruga was angry. "You guaranteed that we would soon have him back home. And now you're talking about three months?"

Madruga shouldn't find that surprising. Venâncio's sensitive personality easily lost touch with the reality round about him. Hence his cure called for cautious treatment, which would not completely eradicate dreaming.

"If he has no dreams, this man will perish."

Once Venâncio had been placed in the Botafogo Sanatorium, a long way away from Madruga's businesses, he nonetheless went to visit him, knowing in advance that Venâncio would refuse to see him. In recent days

Madruga had taken to bringing Eulália with him. They would sit down together on the bench beneath the mango tree, contemplating the trees in silence. Eulália enjoyed being in a garden which, counteracting human ambitions, reproduced the peace and quiet of the sanctuaries she visited in the mornings. Not wanting, however, to take Venâncio by surprise, as might happen should he spy them from the window of the ward, she never raised her eyes above the level of the greenery. For Venâncio was aware of that visit that began at five o'clock on the dot and ended fifty minutes later. Hence painfully concentrating all his attention on his book, so as to resist the poignant desire to see them.

Venâncio was not unfamiliar with Madruga's combative instinct. The doctor had only to dismiss him and Madruga would be there in the patio waiting for him. Hurrying over to embrace him, to guide him along the walkways in the garden. Madruga's clever power plays deeply displeased him. He was embarrassed, however, at Eulália's presence in the garden, at no time forcing his door with requests, words, and gifts. He regretted not being able to repay her for the generosity with which she always showered him on Sundays.

In those months, however, he could not allow them to invade his heart. For the first time he felt in control of himself, despite what outward signs might show to the contrary. His freedom came precisely from a strange emotion that stripped him of his sense of shame, hitherto a suit of armor that suffocated his body. And now he didn't even care if he wept in the presence of the doctors, of the nurses, of his fellow patients, if he revealed his weakness to them. However, at the very mention of the names Madruga and Eulália, he stiffened painfully.

The doctor took a liking to the timid man who never mentioned Spain without immediately reinforcing Brazil in his memory. Aware that the Atlantic separated the two countries, yet his painful passion had conjoined them. He liked posting himself alongside his patient, hearing him refer to hidden aspects of reality, amid a power of description that Venâncio was able to call upon in order to place in vivid relief certain terrors of the human soul. Despite these confessions, Venâncio was careful never to share information that might be used against him or Madruga's family in the future. And only when he was feeling desperately lonely did he mention Madruga's name in passing.

The doctor sensed that a touching game existed between the two men, with moves to which he did not have access. Fidelity was an outstanding quality in Madruga, for he had not missed a single afternoon. Anyone who went to the garden, at five o'clock, would see Madruga in the shade of the same mango tree. Sometimes he offered the other patients cigarettes and candy. Keeping his long cigar clamped between his teeth. In the last week he had taken to bringing his wife, a woman whose gestures were delicate and refined. They rarely spoke to each other. From time to time Madruga would lean over toward her in an effort to hear heaven only knew what sounds of her heart.

"What a good friend you have!"

As the doctor traced a generous profile of Madruga, Venâncio's gaze clouded. And wishing to conceal a probable emotion, he buried his head in the pillow.

Venâncio was torn between the desire to leave and to remain in the sanatorium. Madruga had led him to believe, in his last letter, that he had all the time in the world. He shouldn't be in any hurry to decide. Being well off in that house, he should extend his stay there. And he promised him, as a proof of his confidence in his recovery, that they would soon be living unforgettable adventures. Life would smile upon them once again. But he ought to know that Tobias mourned his absence. And Eulália's heart was touched remembering the wildflowers that reached her on Sundays through him.

Venâncio summoned the doctor. "Tell me the truth, doctor. If I wanted to get out of here, am I free to decide?"

The doctor pointed to the door of the ward, recently painted blue, to match the windows, and smiled.

"Tell Madruga I'll see him tomorrow," Venâncio said.

Madruga came by himself. Informed that they would walk in the garden as though they were still on the quarterdeck of that English ship, Madruga was deeply touched. Not knowing what words to use, so as to assure him that they not only wanted him back home for good, but that they would never again risk losing him!

As they came through the entry hall, the excessive brightness of the light hurt Venâncio's eyes. Fatter now, he moved slowly. He had several days' beard. Madruga moderated his gestures so as not to frighten him. Not to send him straight back to the ward that had been his home in the last months. In pajamas and a bathrobe, presents from Eulália, Venâncio looked at Madruga as though he had seen him only the evening before. A light embrace and then they began the slow stroll beneath the leafy trees. Madruga fell silent as Venâncio began to speak, with a sudden burst of eloquence. Describing the daily routine of the sanatorium, the peculiarities of the doctors and his fellow patients in the ward. Finally asking about Eulália and the children. Extending his interest to business matters, Spain, Brazil, and the apartment on the Avenida Beira-Mar.

"And have you seen the poet Manuel Bandeira?" he suddenly asked.

When Madruga, overwhelmed by the flurry of questions, tried to answer him, Venâncio interrupted him.

"Don't explain anything to me, please. If you do, I'll be compelled to discover the truth."

After a pause, Venâncio went on to say, less tense now, that he intended to return to his apartment. He had the keys there with him, in plain sight, on the night table. He would not abandon the place that had taught him how to enjoy a happiness rare among mortals. Compounded of conflict and anxiety, thus obliging him to experience it from a distance, until he had ceased to be the subject of his own happiness. Had he perhaps harbored a resentment of a felicity that had stuck to other people's walls, rather than lodging in his own heart?

He would also consult the German field glasses once more. After the purges of the last months, he had learned to shun demoniacal visions, the thunderous dreams coming from those convex lenses. This time he would not believe in the panorama they offered him. He had only disdain now for an apparatus that had forced him to swallow the misery of a country sacked daily by pirates, smugglers, bureaucrats, all of them possessors of the keys to the ports of that luminous shore. Nor would he concern himself with the destiny of the Bay of Guanabara. Even if this destiny reproduced in miniature the trajectory of Brazil.

"I did not manage to save Brazil and Spain. Both were devoured by their respective wars," Venâncio said.

That instant was irreproducible. Madruga would never recover those confidences that expanded amid the shrubbery, the grass, the trees. A silence would then fall between them, broken only by trivial observations. Both prolonging the conversation on Sundays only at the cost of considerable effort. Each one had now formed a portrait of the other bearing little correspondence to the affection that marked their existence. They were having difficulty placing each other.

In the past, however, it had been different. Ever since they had arrived in Brazil, the one had helped the other. Both knowing themselves to be an object of scorn. The one thing not done to them being quarantining them on one of the islands just off the port, before landing in the city. They had finally become bearers of a Type 19 card, issued to foreigners. That more or less stigmatized them, not allowing them to forget their temporary condition. Thus subject to deportation, to insults, to pejorative nicknames. On the part of the ruling classes above all, who classified groups according to their conception of tradition and ethnic purity.

An elite, incidentally, born of expatriation, of the indiscriminate slaughter of Indians and savages. And whose apparent liberalism disappeared beneath the surface in the face of an irresistible vocation for tyranny, exercised each day. And which spread through the social interstices of the country, fostering the slogan Let us kill, in the name of morality and decency. Openly proclaimed in public places. Reaching even stifling bedrooms with a fetid smell of unwashed genitals. As they shared among themselves domains, medals, and tributes.

Confronted with Venâncio's discourse, in a lyrical tone now, Madruga was embarrassed. To dissemble, he tapped him on his slightly stooped shoulder. His impulse was to take him home that minute. To bring him down to earth again. To allow him to suffer like a mere mortal. Ceasing to pass on to his next-door neighbors the unpleasant things that happened to come his way there at his place.

He had long since wearied of Venâncio's friendship, constantly colliding head-on with his own. Both of them liars, under cover of a tricky language, used every day. Out of the fear they had of losing each other. Which might mean losing a little of themselves?

At a farther remove from the fray, Eulália was in a position to analyze an affect such as that, its constituent element being a proud nature. The two friends bound by the tie of the story that each told about the other. A moral comfort they did not pass up. For Madruga, for example, America took on a clearer configuration, not through the work of his children, but thanks to Venâncio, reminding him of the chance details of the first years in Brazil.

They were treading, however, on shifting ground, subject to volcanic action. And Eulália forbore to warn them of such perils. By not uttering the names which would fatally designate the precarious state of that friendship, she fostered their illusion that nothing could make them forget a past that stood as warranty for their memory, with a brightness without which they would have no idea how to live.

Giving signs of weariness, Venâncio sat down on the same bench, in the shade of the mango tree, on which Madruga always spent his afternoons in the hope of seeing him. On those afternoons, Madruga would break the silence only to ask Eulália whether Venâncio would finally receive them that day. Whereupon Eulália would shake her head, indicating that the answer was no.

Madruga pointed out to Venâncio the trees that had protected him from the sun during those months. Venâncio looked at the mango tree, which was casting on them the same shadow that until the week before had also enveloped Eulália. He immediately raised his eyes in the direction of the building. At what window of the second floor had Eulália intended to surprise him? She being almost certain that he would be there behind the venetian blinds, watching the two of them, being careful to draw his head in at the slightest gesture in his direction from Madruga and Eulália. Because Eulália didn't believe for a moment that he had decided to forgo seeing them for all that time.

Venâncio was now scratching the ground with a piece of dry brushwood. He was distracting himself drawing fine lines, one alongside the other.

"I'll drop by for lunch someday," he said, asking for a place at table, though without fixing a date for the visit. He rose from the bench, stopping Madruga with a gesture from accompanying him to the entrance of the building. Noting Madruga's obedience, he wanted to reward him.

"I'll be here next Wednesday, at three in the afternoon, suitcase in hand. I know you'll be pleased to take me home," and he immediately turned his back on him. He still needed those days in order to reinforce his own freedom.

On Wednesday, he got his blue suit back. He gathered his belongings together himself, packing them in his suitcase and in his knapsack. Madruga saw him coming down the stairs, for Venâncio had dispensed with the elevator. And he hurried to take his luggage from him, after formally greeting him. He then took the first step in the direction of the exit.

Venâncio allowed Madruga to be his guide, breaking trails through the forest. He stopped, however, in the middle of the garden to look at the building. He felt a stranger to himself. He would never be the same after that experience now lodged in his soul. He would always live under the threat of a nervous breakdown, with no one forgiving him such a weakness. Madruga himself would try to see in his words and in his acts the malignant traces of an illness capable of recurring, of reappearing in a variety of guises. These psychic impediments placing him under permanent suspicion.

To Venâncio's surprise, Eulália was waiting at the door. Her light summer dress set off the first streaks of white in her hair. She approached him with measured gestures, simply offering him an armful of wildflowers, still damp with dew. Only after this ritual did Eulália's and Venâncio's faces draw closer together, emotion and the flowers standing in the way of their exchanging embraces.

Clinging to Odete, Tobias was afraid and did not make so much as a move in his godfather's direction. Venâncio took him in his arms, so filled with emotion that his tears baptized Tobias with water and salt for a second time.

Settled in the car now, Venâncio was amazed at the people on the streets. Everything seemed strange to him, with vague forms. Only when Tobias, sitting in his lap, hugged him tightly, did Venâncio accept becoming part of the landscape that the car was swiftly swallowing up.

Breta was not an easy conquest. She eyed me hostilely, holding me responsible for her having been abandoned. I turned my face away and pretended not to see that dark-haired little girl who had parachuted into my house, whose presence too made my body ache.

Though she was wary, she knew for certain we were embittered relatives. I was her grandfather and this was her house. And Miguel had dumped her here, with Eulália taking his side. I had lost that argument. And so I called Breta again and again and yet she took her time about coming, using playthings and plants, which she busied herself moving all about, as an excuse to disobey me. She had come up with the theory that living beings jumped out of plants on moonlit nights. Each flower a mischievous little creature, with beautiful wings. The minute it was bothered by humans, it flew over the wall in search of another dwelling place.

Finally, Breta came when I called. In shorts, sandals, hands covered with dirt, an impertinent air about her. Her gaze searching out my faults, certain that I had them well protected in the foul coffer of my heart. That tiny little girl seemed to be thoroughly acquainted with human infamy. Only rarely did I glimpse the slightest charitable gesture on her part. Never toward her grandfather, a probable enemy. She knew more about me than I did. And so, in an attempt to neutralize her acts of war, I went out into the garden, from which she might well be pleased to expel me.

On being brought to the house by Miguel, she took no interest whatsoever in the vast, luxurious mansion, preferring to hide in her room, redecorated just for her. And when she came down the stairs, condescending to have a look at the other rooms in the house, she assumed a sudden air of insolence, the pose of an heiress. With a relative contempt, even so, for objects in the house, for the family silver. Her hauteur was more intense still with Miguel at her side, doing her bidding, stroking her face, now that he had her all for his own, without impediments. And as soon as Breta and I were alone, she scowled, measuring her strength against mine.

Despite her petulance, I began to give her what I had never given anyone before. With discreet little touches, which Breta did not notice in the beginning. Unwilling, at the time, to recognize her grandfather's generosity. Precisely because silence held us back, made our gestures harsh ones. Everything weighed heavily upon us. But I would go to Breta at the end of a gray day, after hours shut up in my office downtown.

Only in the following months, confronted with a grandfather bled dry by either success or failure, did Breta allow me to catch a glimpse of some of her thoughts. Thus healing me with her child's ointments. There was the promise of understanding each other in the future. She too was inclined toward generosity. As I went on loving her with a solemn love, full of rough edges.

Each time she came to stay, I promised her the same thing. To travel about Brazil, the method for doing so being for her to point on the map to the region she wished to become acquainted with. Delighted at the adventure of cheating the map by means of a blind finger, Breta smiled. She feared, however, that she would inadvertently point to a spot beyond the borders of Brazil.

"In which case we'll have gotten out of Brazil," I said to her in self-satisfaction.

"But I don't want to leave Brazil, grandfather," she said, suddenly dismayed.

I perceived then that I would in fact come to know Brazil only through that granddaughter. Including the way she packed her suitcase. Not forgetting a penknife, a silver cup, a corkscrew, a bottle opener, a thermos bottle for coffee on the road. Though she might stay in luxury hotels, Breta delighted in assuming rustic airs. It was her heartfelt ambition to sleep in deserts, on the shores of rivers, suffer hardships, gnaw on stale bread.

On the eve of a trip, as farewell presents Miguel would give Breta candy, books, articles of clothing he'd bought.

"Are you prepared to know Brazil?"

In answer, she embraced her uncle. Both dumbfounded by the map spread out on the table. Persuaded of the obstacles existing between them and that country.

Slowly, however, Brazil took on transparency. Above all as Breta described the landscape in minute detail. Without sacrificing, at the same time, the pleasure of telling a story. Through such a practice forcing me to learn by heart a country that risked becoming abstract and inaccessible to her as well. And whenever I asked her to clarify an ambiguous episode, Breta rewarded me by inventing another story. Doing so in a questioning tone of voice, like Grandfather Xan's. Thereby forging herself and the country in which she had been born.

"Are you sure that's really how it is, Breta?" I wanted to test her, to make her wriggle a little.

"Of course, grandfather. If it wasn't, how else could Brazil be?" she said with unshakable certainty.

Up until that time, Venâncio had been my interlocutor for historical subjects. Now, however, I preferred to hear the echoes of events through my granddaughter's voice, for Breta was eager to pass on to me the results of recent reading. There was always a moat around her accounts, which could be bridged only by fabrication and invention. She herself taking on the task of filling in the empty places, the hollow spaces, that I became aware of only after she'd papered them over with her daydreams.

As soon as Breta pointed out the livestock in the pasture to me, behind the fence, it seemed to me that the smell and the milk of the animals conveyed to me, with a wealth of details, the life of the first whites who had landed in Brazil. Those fat, sweaty men who had found themselves overcome, amid their ambition and their puzzlement, by the feeling of irreparable loss of a country, left behind there in Europe, to which they might never return. An evocation, this, that awakened in me the suspicion that there had been, from the beginning, something sinister in the adventure of the discovery.

"It must have been difficult, grandfather. Because the cod soon ran out and they started eating fruit, fish, grass. Even flies, can you imagine? Not to speak of fever. That's why they were so attached to gold."

Slowly, my granddaughter filtered out for me sensations that otherwise would have escaped me. She more or less said: From today on, grandfather, I'll be your consciousness. In return for my being its story. And by means of this exchange we went hobbling along. Precisely because the years were slipping away. Breta was leafing out luxuriantly, a solitary warrior who knew all the tricks. Not allowing her uncles and cousins to see which of her weapons she used, depending on circumstances.

And so I was afraid of losing her at a turning point in history. Brazil again reduced to a dictatorship, a military one this time. Seemingly a moderate one, in the beginning. Until it led to open conflicts, in which young people were involved. How to control Breta, proud of her status as a university student, a dissident unwilling to accept the consequences of the coup. Above all because there now existed, from '68 on, indiscriminate imprisonments and despicable torture. Young people forced underground, if they didn't end up dead. There was no constitution to protect them.

Breta began to slip away from me. Without calling on Tobias or Venâncio, probable allies, for help. Along with other students she cried out for justice, in the downtown streets. Demanding an end to the situation. She tried to drag me to the protest demonstration attended by two hundred thousand people.

Worried by the popular reaction, my sons warned me that it threatened the very existence of the ruling classes. Moreover, Breta had taken to spending the night at the houses of fellow dissidents without saying where she was going. She spent very little time at home, always ready with reasons why she had to leave us.

"You don't owe me any explanations, Breta. But don't ignore the fact that these are dangerous times. One careless move, and we won't be able to save you."

Tobias was overjoyed at the signs of popular solidarity. With great hopes of bringing down the dictatorship by a general outcry, by protest demonstrations. The country thus going back to the period preceding the downfall of Jango and taking up where it had left off. Without the threat this time, however, of the military coups, the crazy reversals of rank, that President João Goulart had been unable to avoid. The prime concern should be to see to it that a strong, orderly government came to power, prepared to turn the current economic model upside down.

"And by what right are you calling for another society, if you've done nothing to change the one that's in place now? You're as responsible as I am for this regime that you're now so quick to condemn," I said heatedly to Tobias.

Breta, present at the time, spoke up in a moderate voice, a stranger to events. She was in the habit of donning masks to defend her secrets.

"Talking is also a way of carrying on the struggle, grandfather," alluding to Tobias, from whom she received a grateful look. "Not everybody heads for the public squares or goes underground."

She did not allow herself to become involved in private arguments. Not even under pressure from Miguel, showering her with gifts, offers of trips. Despite my granddaughter's artfulness, I began to detect nervous gestures on her part, a certain feverish look. Something was happening to her.

"What's the matter, Breta?"

"Nothing, grandfather." She drew back a step.

She received one phone call after another. They controlled her life. People who came to the house to see her disappeared immediately, their place taken by others. They were nameless. Breta went to demonstrations, meetings, passed out leaflets. The university in an uproar. Tanks appeared in Cinelândia, on the Avenida Rio Branco, like ash-gray lizards, suddenly emerging from a dense forest, which only the military could control. Were they about to take Breta's life? Now that a student, Edson, had been murdered in the "Dungeon," the grim university dining room?

Eulália calmed me down. To no avail. Breta's heroic faith had infected me with fear. I found myself in an ironic position. Adversary of these young people, whom I wanted to defeat, without sacrificing their blood in the streets and in basement cells. I had no illusions, however. There had never been a single victory that had left sacred human life untouched, that was not preceded by cruel exterminations. Thus, against my will, I was condemning my own granddaughter to death.

But which side was I in fact on if I hurt them? Could I accept responsibility for the massacres perpetrated against the popular classes even before I came to Brazil? Or had the moment finally come for me to make up my mind about Brazil? Unable to perpetuate an ambiguous situation, dependent on my foreigner's identity card?

A decision favorable to the Revolution of '64 might be demanded of me, as a means of acquiring credentials that I had always lacked, even though I had offered proofs that I belonged to that land. But what the hell sort of prestige and credit could this authoritarian regime confer on me, when I so badly lacked them?

Deeply distressed, I sensed the dangers surrounding Breta. I could not bear to lose her. Venâncio accused me of siding with old enemies, seeing as how my origins were eminently popular. And the memory of Grandfather Xan demanded that I acknowledge these same origins every day. So why defend those who put obstacles in the way of my ascent, who demanded of me, every step of the painful way, a blood contribution greater than the one that I was obliged to pay them?

Breta split my conscience down the middle. Whichever way I turned, there were reasons to understand her. And grounds for fighting her as well.

For the first time, she confronted me with breaches that my unbridled ambition had left wide open. And so I grew increasingly anxious. Especially since Costa e Silva was dead now. And the Médici period, marching on in triumph, was instituting repressive measures even more cruel than those of the preceding regime. In short, they would mow Breta down, her imprudence leading her to sleep away from home, using parties, weekends in the mountains, at the beach as an alibi. Coming back pale and transparent. No sand in her camouflaged baggage. Maybe there were big rocks and dry tree branches inside.

How often I noticed her bulging briefcase. It was naturally full of compromising documents, which she thought it safe to carry owing to her elegant appearance, her new car.

She continually asked me for the key to the house in Petrópolis. I never turned her down. Bento protested.

"Why does Breta need the house all that much? And furthermore, she wants it all to herself. She kicks all of us out of there."

I smiled resignedly. We'd best leave her in peace. Wanting nothing to do with executives and old fogies was part of what it meant to be young. I never passed my suspicions on to him. Bento would not forgive his niece's ideological deviations. In any case, that show of suspicion on his part represented a warning.

I began to have sleepless nights. I imagined Breta taken prisoner, her body being badly abused. Not daring to think the worst. I weighed the price of her freedom in my mind. Would money rescue her from torture, from confinement? Saving her soul and her tender skin?

I invited Breta to lunch. Pretending we were tourists visiting Brazil. She was all in favor of this amusing game and we met at the Montecarlo. In the bar, we relaxed over drinks.

As I passed her the fish appetizer, I suddenly spoke my mind. "If they nab you, Breta, I can't do a thing for you."

She kept a firm grip on her glass, with no apparent reaction. She helped herself to the bits of fried codfish. She chewed slowly, giving herself more time.

"It's no use covering up, Breta. I know you're compromised with those leftist groups. Don't go on denying it, please." I eyed her firmly. There was no time to lose. My life was in danger too.

"That's not true, grandfather. I don't get into compromising situations with anybody. I'm all alone, on my own. No dates and no mate for the moment, and no commitments except to my own ideas," she said emphatically. Her revolutionary spirit lent her an air of enchantment. That sort of freedom, though transitory, corresponded to an inexpressible emotion.

"Let me help you now, before you're arrested. I can't bear to imagine you in jail, subject to violence."

That week, I had gone alone to Petrópolis. To search the house, the rooms and the closets. An air of conspiracy seemed to me to permeate the house. Urged to talk, the caretaker mentioned that Breta never came alone. A group accompanied her. Young people with restless habits who changed rooms in the middle of the night.

I went on, treading cautiously. Sharing his distress at the disregard of young people for certain social standards. But he shouldn't be concerned. It was all harmless enough. All they wanted was to have a good time.

"The best thing is to pretend you haven't seen a thing. I beg you to keep the matter an absolute secret. Don't say a word about these visits, not even to my sons. I shall be most grateful to you, Senhor Ferreira."

He was visibly pleased at receiving so generous a check. He then offered me a strong coffee as a sign of his appreciation. He too was confident that life forced rebels to mend their ways, put men's virtues to the test. In the end, they turned into pious churchgoers or stern politicians. He laughed in self-satisfaction at his weighty reflections and pleasure at my trust in him.

"Senhor Ferreira has no proof. He's nothing but a simpleminded moralist," Breta said.

"Be that as it may, from now on I'm not giving you the key to Petrópolis. I'll do everything possible to protect you."

To disarm my suspicions, Breta reviewed the repercussions of the coup in '64, to which she was violently opposed. She was even of the opinion that opposing the dictatorship was part of what defined her existence at that point in time. Yet she couldn't have cared less about what faction I identified myself with. She had had at her disposal for some time now a vast dossier of phrases uttered by her grandfather. A great number of them inspired by Bento, a man who knew the score. An opportunist, perhaps, out to make a killing in political futures.

"Don't worry, grandfather, nothing is going to come between us. Even though politics may be as risky a business as settling an estate."

Without a sign of passion in her voice, she went on at an even pace, step by step. Her eyes nonetheless betrayed her as she examined the members of the family. Reviewing each of their names, as though they were there in person before her. Even so, gentle and forbearing, she spared that scattered flock. Giving me, for example, the benefit of the doubt. This absolution owed to my being a foreigner, hence with limited duties toward the country. The same degree of participation in political affairs not being demanded of me. Though I ought to hold myself equally responsible for the moral bankruptcy that had befallen the nation.

"Brazil is my destiny. At least for the time being," she said sternly, the amiable mood that had reigned previously having dissolved. For that very reason, whichever way she turned, she was called upon to participate. Therefore there was no way for her to determine the limits of her future activity, what course to follow.

I held her hand tightly in mine for a second. Just long enough to ask her to leave the country. Till she was forgotten. They were probably tailing her at that moment, her name visible on a priority list. And those men at the next table might be jotting down the details we were allowing to escape, carried away by our emotions.

My face easily gave me away, with its inopportune intensity. As for Breta, she was discreet. Using her head. And her steadfast heart was a striking contrast to her mother's effusiveness. Incapable, had she been there, of disguising her feelings, fear and rashness. Esperança's involvement was always total. Had there been a single crucial episode in the face of which my daughter had emerged unscathed?

Having my daughter unexpectedly brought to mind at lunch annoyed me. Her mere memory planted a thorn in my flesh. And at the thought of her, I am on my guard. I must bury all trace of her. Unable even to remember her childhood. The impetuous gesture with which, in the middle of the street, she flung herself into my arms. By smell alone, Esperança seemed to sense that I was approaching the house. On seeing her bearing down on me like a bull, the only thing left to do was to put my arms around her. Only then was she mollified, tender almost. She slowly laid down her shields, her helmet, her sword, kept hidden in her room. As she held my hand tightly, there was in her gesture a commiseration for her exhausted father, who sold his soul each day for bread and gold.

Breta sensed that some memory had made off with me. And that Esperança was perhaps responsible for the theft. She always saw me return from these places with a hurt expression. As I began looking at her anxiously, trying to determine to what point my granddaughter reflected the will and the whims of Esperança. A trap for me.

"What's the matter, grandfather? Can Esperança have come between us again?"

She was challenging me by pronouncing that name in my presence. I asked the waiter for more coffee, overindulging in caffeine. The coffee came, piping hot and fragrant. I avoided looking at my granddaughter, poised for vengeance, just because I had tried to write finis to her revolutionary project. Breta felt safe at last from shipwreck. She was not part of the inventory of the sea's estate, consisting of seaweed, fish, algae, wrecks of handsome two-masters. Forgetting the soft smile that foreshadows tragedy.

"Nothing serious, Breta. A ghost that came visiting. They're always among us. Grandfather Xan is here at this table too, you know. Seeing us, without being seen. Looking at us, criticizing our affluence, our neat, expensive clothes. Not missing the chance, however, to linger over a glass of good wine. But I don't criticize his presence. I even think that people gather round a table to give the dead the opportunity of celebrating life in some way. Besides, Breta, since when have you been afraid of the dead?

Haven't you been learning to live side by side with them ever since you were a child, back in Sobreira?" This last spoken in a deliberately light tone of voice.

Breta's smile demolished my defenses. And to charm me even more, she went on telling me stories. And as she poured the warm milk into my mouth, the rich cream that trickled through her lips enticed me to live. Through her, Brazil was again being passed on to me bit by bit. With these shards in her possession she was making a mosaic in which I saw myself among the men and animals shown on the wall. A vision that nonetheless troubled me.

"Don't worry, grandfather. I'll always be nearby," she said, coming to my aid.

I pondered my legacy. The ambiguous inheritance meant for my granddaughter. Against my will, I had handed on to her the uneasy burden of living with the spiritual patterns of two countries.

Breta, however, unlike Tobias, always refused to plunge headlong into chaos. In her there was not the demoralizing dualism of being on intimate terms with two homelands at the same time, one in the heart and the other in reality. Obliged therefore to turn the two of them into antagonists, impossible to reconcile. Yet she was well aware that America, indivisible and magical, served her as a privileged lookout point for judging Europe. A judgment at once severe and charitable. Hence she was prepared to wrest from Europe the wealth that she perhaps lacked. And to protect Brazil's possessions, which the gringos wanted to extort from it. Meanwhile surrendering her body to the most intimate reflexes of the language of her country. As though the silences and the pauses that this same language offered the people in order to defend themselves from foreign aggressors spoke through her.

She set up a game of tic-tac-toe on the tablecloth, using toothpicks. Not forgetting to make a point of denying her involvement in political movements. That being a project not pursued for lack of courage. She lied elegantly, however. Lying, after all, is a crucible that consumes what deserves to disappear.

She undid the game, but immediately began it again. The previous subject erased from her mind. This time voicing the dream of one day catching the language of her country in a state of total unawareness. That is to say, in some way coming by a certain magical expression whereby she would contrive to journey through the cracks and crevices and the archaeology of words. And by means of this mysterious poetic transit, reach the exact moment of the foundation of Brazil. That is to say, the first years in which the Portuguese language, brought here by ship, settled on the Bahia shore and simply began gasping for breath and speaking. Being no longer on the Tagus. But in Porto Seguro and in the Bay of Todos os Santos.

Yet it would be possible for her, by setting out on this journey to the past, to net from each era the intimate moans of the men of the Colony, of the Empire, of the Republics. So that her speech as a voyager, on her return from this long circumnavigation, would reproduce those words, fundamental to our development, which no one at the time had regarded as of the slightest importance. Yet words associated with the most intangible and most powerful feelings of that new creature, the Brazilian. Words, these, that having reached us, announced the existence of a people who, from the sixteenth century on, suffered visible anguish at being just barely at the beginning of their history.

In precisely those years in which, beginning to feel Brazilian, they lacked the various instruments of language with which to denounce Portuguese oppression, and likewise to express the fervent impulses of their sensuality. And while they declared themselves to be Portuguese, they were already Brazilians. Hence, in their eagerness to express a desire of genuinely national origin, coming out with a harsh grunt that eventually damaged the interests of the country still in the process of formation.

Breta's voice, in defense of this strange journey through her own people, reverberated, strident, tortured. Not her own, but an echo. The original, which I knew well, she had lent to Brazil. Her youth taking on an unexpected epic, restorative meaning. Capable of rehabilitating the homeland all by itself. Never again finding herself all alone in this task. The people would soon join the students. So that no other human would ever crawl, humiliated, over Brazilian soil, clutching at snakes, lizards, turds and grass.

Breta's country, as we ate and drank, stood proudly erect. A country that Venâncio had talked of without my understanding. Now, however, following in the footsteps of my granddaughter, orienting myself slowly, prompted to think about new realities. For a long time now ambition had impelled me to reflect, to become involved with an obviously complex universe. Knowing, therefore, that behind capital and power there was a network connecting, in an inextricable tangle, gold, passion, cleverness, perseverance, envy, strategy, contemptible feelings.

"Ever since we've arrived here, Breta, we've done nothing but speak of human passion, on the pretext of discussing politics, Brazil, and our dead. We're both acting as if passion were austere and aristocratic. When it is merely a poison capable of acting against logic, rationality, any human filigree. So that, under its effects, we gulp down our words like swine. Excusing ourselves on the grounds that we're the possessors of fine pearls. And in the name of passion as well, or whatever name it goes by for the moment, we murder, we torture. Everything is within our reach. We're even poets and excellent instrumentalists. Tell me, Breta, does anyone play the violin better than we do? On the other hand, I ask myself, what would be the use of living, loving, thinking, without the certainty of this passion within us?"

Breta was moved, though she asked me no questions. She was tactful enough not to consider my words a subject for discussion. There her grandfather was, doing his best to wrest her from the talons of the passions, manifesting themselves in ideological guise. I lacked the ability, however, to measure Breta's dream. To what point would she press her own demands?

"Any dream is always different when we begin to dream with our eyes open, Breta," I insisted. "So that the boundaries of reality will be marked off without major illusions."

We were now the last ones in the restaurant. As the afternoon went by, our voices grew fainter.

"All I ask is that you call on me, if need be."

Breta gave a devil-may-care laugh. "How tragic you are, grandfather! It must be your Iberian origins. Wasn't the conquest of America enough to calm down that imagination that runs riot in all of you?"

"And what about you people over here, who are always wanting to burn ships, exactly like Cortez in Mexico? So your enemies won't get away, and you won't either. You know something, Breta? We're just a couple of country yokels who should have gone on the stage."

Back home again, I went into action. I stored away a goodly sum in cruzeiros and dollars in the strongbox. I got a new passport. Asking Breta to do the same, on the pretext of accompanying me to Europe for a few days. I took Miguel into my confidence. He drew up an escape plan, in case there was a crackdown. He headed for Ijuí, where he had friends who were coffee planters. He there arranged, in minute detail, the means whereby Breta could be gotten across the border at any moment, without risk. On his return, shut up in the study, we ran through the plan till we had it down pat. Miguel's anxious desire to protect Breta was visible. And without her knowing, he had his niece followed by several men he could rely on.

Late in the afternoon, Breta arrived in Leblon looking dejected. "I'm going to split the scene, grandfather. I just came to say good-bye. Maybe you could advance me some money."

I telephoned Miguel. "It's zero hour. Come right away."

In half an hour, he was there, bringing a suitcase with what Breta would need. She didn't understand.

"Where are you taking me?"

Miguel skipped the explanations. They didn't have a minute to lose. It would have to be now or they'd nab her.

"Good heavens! What'll happen to the others?" She was shivering.

They had disbanded of course. The instructions were to scatter immediately after the fall of the first members of the cell. There was no way of saving them.

Breta agreed. After trying her best to convince us that they would have a hard time getting as far as her. She was less involved than the others. Hence able to stay in Rio. Simply disappearing for a few weeks.

Seeing our determination, Breta was surprised at the steps taken. And that, right that minute, there was a chartered plane ready to take off for Ijuí, with her and Miguel bound for a plantation close to the border. Where they would stay just long enough to locate the man already hired to take her, in his jeep, to the other side, to foreign parts. From there they would go on alone, without Miguel, who would go, by plane again, to wait for her to cross the border. It wasn't worth the risk to make the trip across together. Once in Bolivia, the two of them would fly to La Paz. Where they would register in the same hotel, as man and wife. And that same night, depending on the connections, Breta would catch a plane to New York. Alone again. As for Miguel, he would fly, by regular airline, to Buenos Aires, to make it look like a legitimate business trip. Bento had been told of Miguel's sudden departure, in case of unexpected hangups. Sílvia would met him at the Hotel Plaza, that weekend.

Miguel returned five days later. Breta had received instructions to telephone his secretary, using another name. Just to confirm that she was off for Madrid, obeying Miguel's instructions to the letter. On seeing me in Madrid, waiting for her at Barajas airport, she was at a loss for words. She was surprised that I had left Eulália home all by herself.

"And why wouldn't I come, dear granddaughter?"

She gave me a prolonged embrace. I had never felt her to be that moved before. Then she regained her composure. "And what do the papers say?"

"About your people, nothing. Miguel is making discreet inquires. He wants to find out exactly how badly you're compromised. If your name is on the wanted list. But we can't afford to be careless. You'd best stay away a while longer."

Breta was resigned. All she had to do was to choose her place of exile herself.

"And have you already decided?"

"Not yet. But if I really had a choice, I'd go to Brazil. Like you, grandfather, disembarking fifty years ago at the Praça Mauá. Me being young Madruga, and you in the role of Venâncio. And we'd begin all over again, as if nothing had yet happened. Before my birth, then, before that damned coup that drove me out of the country."

With Breta, I kept learning every minute. She was doubtless the Brazil I chose when I was thirteen, foreseeing her birth. That granddaughter who was coming back to Spain clinging to my dreams. Yet at the same time a messenger warning me that death had caught my scent long ago. And hadn't lost sight of me. And what did it matter, if I still had the strength left to love Breta in that Madrid tricked out in such bright colors?

The name of that granddaughter came from my heart. I once confessed to my children, still adolescents, that someone in the family, in the future, would again be called Breta, in honor of Britanny, one of the last Celtic regions. Esperança noted the name down on a piece of paper so as not to forget. That being the reason, perhaps, for Breta's being the one to inherit my dream and my books. Even though she was now forbidden to return to her homeland, whereas I was free to go back. I who would do anything I could to save her. When I can do nothing except stay with her in Madrid. Foreseeing that each separation between us will hurt me more than the one before.

"What you're proposing to me is a journey through time, but with you in charge. Just so as to see me arriving in Brazil scared to death. With my knapsack on my back, going directly to the boardinghouse with the smell of garlic. And what if by so doing my fate took another turn? Would I still marry Eulália? Would you have been born in an enemy family? Would I be in Spain now, at my granddaughter's side, with her propounding a riddle like that to me?"

In Retiro Park, Breta asked for news of home. I refused to telephone Miguel. There was good reason to be careful. Back at the hotel, a letter from Miguel informed me that it had been impossible to close the contract as intended. Those business partners were an unknown quantity. We would have to wait for a few weeks, put them to the test.

Breta appreciated the roast suckling pig brought to the table. The glistening fat making its browned skin shine. Despite the letter from Miguel received that afternoon, she appeared to be happy to be in the Sobrino del Botín. Perhaps seated at the same table at which Hemingway had sat huddled, drunk on wine, his lips smeared with grease, forgetting to wipe them with his napkin.

"If Castile were famous for nothing else, it would enter history just because of its roast meats. Nobody is better at roasting than these Castilians. Moreover, wasn't that what they did to the Indians in America?" I said to be agreeable to Breta, who I sensed was tense now.

The letter had disappointed her. She had had hopes that Miguel would miraculously save her and her generation. With just one sign from him, they would be back in Brazil.

"If those armchair generals wanted to, they could remain in power indefinitely," she said with a marked feeling of frustration, as she soaked up the sauce on her plate with a piece of bread.

"Don't forget that for the time being they're not alone. They can count on the support of the middle class."

Breta shrugged. She had nothing but scorn for a class that in its desperate scramble up the social ladder served several masters at the same time.

"But it's precisely middle-class kids who join guerrilla groups and go in for terrorism. A naïve attitude, moreover, since they'll be wiped out immediately. If the lot of you think you're going to mobilize students and the people by way of heroic examples, you're very much mistaken. The people have no idea what's going on. And the students are scared to death. Not to mention the fact that fathers are keeping a close eye on every move their kids make. They're teaching them the manual of cowardice," I said, my back up at last, clearly indicating my position.

Breta was needled. She stopped eating her dessert so as to give me her full attention.

"I know it's a one-sided battle, grandfather, and that only brings out all the more clearly the inhumanity of this dictatorship. As for our naïveté, it was necessary. Someone has to render this sort of service. But remember too that several revolutions have been born of this sort of naïveté. The Russian Revolution, for example. And now the one in Cuba, there in the Caribbean, under the very noses of the Americans."

"Except that those revolutions had men like Lenin and Fidel Castro. And they could count on unqualified popular support."

"Listen, grandfather, we could have produced our Fidel if they hadn't killed us off so soon."

"You lacked patience and determination. Why didn't you make the Amazon the Brazilian Sierra Maestra? Why didn't you rouse the people first, before launching this urban guerrilla warfare of yours? Your problem is that you always blame the military, forgetting that Brazilian society as a whole must be held accountable for its mistakes and its eternal collusion with the State. Everybody is a public servant or has personal interests at stake. Beginning with you university students, who enjoy advantages from the cradle on. It seems to me the hour has come to offer moral satisfaction to the poor of Brazil. To make a public *mea culpa*."

I felt very tired. I regretted having started the argument. I was afraid I was wounding Breta at this inopportune moment. She seemed undaunted, however. I hadn't made her give an inch.

"You're arguing like a rightist. Your view of society is class-determined. So you always side against those who were history's losers. Whether out of submissiveness, lack of opportunity, bone-tiredness, poverty, or rebelliousness."

"That's not true, Breta. I came from a village. I arrived in Brazil at thirteen, with poverty in my pocket," I replied, my feelings hurt.

"That's not the point, grandfather. The point is that you're looking for perfect conditions before you'll fight. And you think that because of the faults and the petty-mindedness of the class that we belong to we lack the moral qualities to change society. If that were so, then only the man who's poor and wretched would have the de facto right to wage revolution. Only he could demand the reformation of society, of which he's the principal victim. Listen, grandfather, if we were to wait for the revolutionary war cry of the man who's poor and wretched, nothing would happen.

Because the man who's wretched is wretched. And for that very reason he lacks the strength, the organization, the language to begin to fight. His fate would be immediate extermination. The man who's wretched is counting on precisely those people who are contributing to his degradation, since they all belong to the privileged classes."

Her heavy counterattack took the form of abrupt, rapid-fire phrases. When she'd finished, she raised her glass and swirled the blood-red wine around the rim. Taking pleasure in not spilling a single drop on the white tablecloth.

"We'd best finish our dessert, grandfather. Will you offer me a cognac to top it off?" Breta's way of ending the discussion. Thanking me immediately thereafter for the delicious meal. Good manners being her way of getting the better of her adversaries.

In the morning, when I went to her room looking for her, she had already gone out. Having thoughtfully left a note in the mailbox at the concierge's desk downstairs. She was off to the Prado yet again. And she added: "I'll have Hieronymus Bosch for company. He who defined Brazil better than anyone else has. By taking me to his 'Garden of Delights,' a scene filled with fire and blood, damnation and horror. What cries are those I heard? I'll be back at one on the dot. I'm sure you'll take me to another absolutely unforgettable place."

Together again, we exchanged trivial comments, like the ordinary run of tourists. Amid necessary excesses. No one was keeping tabs on us. At no time did Breta criticize my indulgences at table. Perhaps she didn't really care whether I died, when so many young Brazilians were having their breasts and their anuses ripped by medieval tongs. ˙

Breta's casualness did not keep her from putting certain ideas before me in crystal-clear terms. She wanted them to be visible to me. So that in the future I would not go to Tobias and Venâncio in search of explanations that it was up to her to furnish. Just as I had shown her how I had invaded a foreign country, practically at the beginning of the century, so as to ease her birth on a continent groaning beneath the weight of myths and legends, so it was her firm intention to play a role in my conversion. To smooth the way for me.

I avoided arguments. Beholding my granddaughter was more vital than defending ideas. Ideas no longer moved my heart. Though people did. Especially in the face of the fact that in a few years I would be dying. Though I still allowed myself to plunge joyously into the molten lead of passions and anxieties. And made use of glowing words, constantly calling upon the memory of Grandfather Xan. Above all I sensed the number of hours stolen from me each day. A waste I had no way of cutting down on. One more reason not to lose Breta.

In the hotel lobby, hours later, I came across her, thoroughly dejected, a pitiless look in her eye.

"I've made up my mind. I'm going to Paris."

Everything she needed should be sent on to her from Brazil. In Paris, she would finish her studies, getting herself a master's degree. She would make wise use of the time she was forced to be away.

"And will you come to see me, grandfather?"

"You have only to call me, Breta."

Paris appeared to be the right choice. Until we were past the dangers. Only then would she return home, restless as ever. The bearer of a maturity, in her eyes, in her body, that I would not have been a party to. Not having been able to check up on her, with affection and suspicion as my weapons. As I had done years before, when Breta would come into the living room, taking me by surprise as I read or dozed with my eyes closed.

At such times, she never interrupted me. She waited till I had floated back to the surface, like a bit of bark tossed into the sea. We acted like strangers. Until our eyes met, Breta and I either talked or we didn't. A matter of indifference to us. Determined not to complain about the silence that we had eloquently staged in the living room.

I took her to Barajas airport to see her off. We preferred to separate in Spain, a lone brother. And that she be the first to leave. Perhaps we would see each other again only in foreign territory. Breta's eyes stared into space. She doubtless thought that by losing her grandfather at that moment she was also losing Brazil, her language, her family, vague loves, faith. Leaving what? Rage, resentment, cheerfulness?

"This was your first defeat, Breta. But it's no reason to lose faith, to quit for good. Someday you'll cross the Atlantic and win Brazil back. No uniform can keep you from returning."

Breta hurried out to the tarmac. When she turned around one last time, I noted the swift shudder of her body. And lofty pride, always present in her, had given way to the humble pose of one who had been dramatically betrayed, and was discovering, at that very instant, the black, unforgettable face of betrayal.

I never thanked Miguel for the aid he had provided during the events connected with the year '68. Every time I tried to, he silenced me with a gesture. And when I happened to mention the years of exile in Europe, his pleading gaze buried the distant past. Thereby dissuading me from settling a debt that he himself had no desire to collect.

He would quickly change the subject. Preferably by leading the conversation around to the work I was doing. He asked me one question after another. Even though Grandfather, seated at his side, recommended discretion. They were well aware that that granddaughter, by nature rebellious and with little liking for family life, refused to answer questions pertaining to her work or to her own life.

They both smiled, trying to make me relax, to lower my instinctive guard. Miguel plied me with more questions, in apparent disregard of Madruga. But in truth he went ahead only at his father's subtle prompting. Madruga's face with a look on it that seemed to assure him of unlimited protection that afternoon.

Miguel studiously avoided run-ins with his father. When a storm threatened, he retreated in the expectation that Madruga would hold back any painful blow intended for his son. It disturbed him that Madruga's voice could suddenly take on a stiletto-like metallic accent. Meant as a warning that they should not provoke him. For he could be hard on his children. Not forgiving them affronts that he nonetheless regarded as quite natural if they came from strangers. Uncompromising, however, with his children. Maintaining that they had no hold on his heart by right of capture. And so he punished the challenger with a prolonged silence. And when he accepted the kiss on the cheek from the rebel, his clenched jaws were a sign of unmistakable displeasure.

Reconciliation was a matter arranged by him alone. Through a communiqué that determined the day and the hour for this ceremony. All the children accepted such rules docilely, except Tobias. Convinced that Madruga, on the appointed day, would distribute regal presents and the peace so deeply yearned for.

In the face of this conciliatory father, Miguel automatically took on a more youthful appearance. Through overcoming the fear arising from the possibility that Madruga might pass away while in that state of belligerence, without their having had a minute at least to grant each other forgiveness.

Madruga could undoubtedly be charming. At such moments, he wove his magic spells with precious silver thread, thereby making himself appreciated by his family. Especially by Eulália, whose lighthouse beacon could sense the onset of one of his outbursts, sometimes erupting in the midst of fond caresses. Miguel's dexterity, inherited from his mother, made it easier for him, however, to advance boldly toward this grim Madruga. Taking advantage, in order to do so, of his unwary areas, of his sensitive blue eyes dazzled by the overbright morning light, of Madruga's soul thrown wide open at last.

With his face free of the furrows of passion for a few moments, Miguel laughed heartily. He was standing up to his father. Everything favored him that day. He was also counting on my friendship, compounded of affection and shortcomings.

"Is it really the task of mortals to take on creation? Literary creation, artistic creation, for example?" Questions put in a show of transparent humor.

He was as imposing as Madruga. His body stood out in a crowd. I always imagined his chest covered with a great deal of hair that stood on end at the least sign of emotion. Thus readying himself for love at the sound of certain words and a vague, dull look. But was it really true that Miguel's lust had the same splendid range as his speech? Was this lust the imaginary creation of his sex? Words and sex organ forming a single whole aimed at exciting everyone?

"Only pygmies create, uncle. Because they're madly eager to grow. They're not satisfied with their stature. So they resort to creation. As revenge or an affront. But then too, what else do they have to do besides loving, working, and dying?"

Miguel enjoyed a solid reputation as a lover. Able to consume a passion in three days. Each passion corresponding to a batch of bread. Appreciated only when it was hot. He was proud of having an appetite for women at any hour of the day. For dessert or with his morning coffee.

When alone together, just the two of us, he would give me detailed accounts of some of his love affairs. He could sense that I was curious about his voracious body. I gave him time enough to stuff it full of lies. The exchange of these feelings threatening our friendship, however. We quarreled over everything and nothing. Especially when Miguel described passion as though it were his own creation.

Irritated with all these exploits, I tried my best to insult him. "You're like a bitch in heat. Or a tomcat caught fast in the vagina of a yowling tabby. Tell me, what's your favorite animal?"

"I'm a man," he said, laughing still.

"In that case, do your mistresses fuck like a man or like a woman? Do they ride you like Valkyries? Did you ever notice? Or are you too busy making your semen rival the tidal wave of the Amazon?"

Miguel was hurt. He didn't want to be accused of crudely devouring another person's body. Driven by the appetite of a cannibal.

"What do you know about my passions or my savage acts? You keep preaching an orderly passion that, in fact, can be reconciled only with art. Not with life."

"What kind of art are you talking about, Miguel? Since when is there such a thing as an art without torment and without disorder?" I broke in.

"I know that art is born of chaos. But you'll admit that art forces the artist to manage his resources, thereby imposing on him an internal order. Isn't that true?"

I lowered my voice, attracted by his line of argument. "Of course. Otherwise it would become a schizophrenic art, cut off from the real world. But the same thing happens in life. There's an internal economy that rules our acts. If that weren't so, we'd go mad."

He took over again, speaking in fury. Without fear of leaving himself wide open. "The passion I'm talking about is different. It's purely carnal, it doesn't involve mind, soul, feelings. It is born of the dark zones and replenishes itself from out of this darkness. This sort of passion attacks like a virus. Nobody knows where it comes from or how it takes effect. It can sometimes be deadly. It's an ugly passion, outside of the act of passion. Only those who belong to this sect or religion can accept its excesses. And it is so dramatic and necessary that it dispenses with language. Quite literally, passion does not express itself, except through disorder. The typical convulsion of starving bodies. Moreover, since when is there symmetry and logical sequence in sex? No, don't look at me that way, Breta!"

"The one thing you haven't said is that you feel like a wolf. The wolves that long ago used to attack the peasants of Sobreira in winter. They howled with hunger up in the mountains. Does that condition satisfy you?"

"As you like, Breta. I can also be a vulture or a reptile. A reptile's better though. It crawls along the ground and looks like a giant phallus. I feel I'm a shameless animal, ruled by the laws of my carnal state. Are you satisfied? It's better if that's how it is. It's the only way to free us of Christianity, of the notion of sin. Of a hypocritical ethics, that teaches us mercy as we murder our neighbor. In bed, in stained sheets, there are no idealizations possible. There are only bitches, and males sniffing after them."

"There's still the hunter. The hunter who guts and plucks his prey."

"You're mistaken, Breta. This type of passion never acknowledges guilt. It is free. So it stinks and it slashes. And is slashed. Everything I do is ultimately reducible to an age-old desire, that comes to me by way of strange scents and inexplicable lacks. And it transcends culture itself. My human state itself. Who knows if that isn't the story of my origin? Doesn't it preserve my dignity, in a pure state? Who can take my movements away from me as I fuck to exhaustion? Who can inhibit a passion that cannot explain itself and has no need of words?"

"Your apologia is exciting. But it's nothing more than an exercise in anthropophagy. Instead of going to bed, you sit down at the table to carve meat, chew, and vomit. In that order," I interrupted again.

"Don't get the idea that these purely sexual passions are for weaklings. On the contrary, they can only be lived by the strong, who survive the instantaneous earthquake of this ecstasy."

"I admire your courage, Miguel. But I mistrust your passion. It uses the other without regard for the consequences. It is dictatorial and intolerant. It swallows up the body of the other, completely indifferent to the damage it does, to the pain it causes. Or the feelings it awakens. And what happens when you inspire love or a dream, however trivial it may be?"

"Love is forbidden in this game."

"By whom? Who can forbid it? Doesn't it fail to burst into flame only because you're trying so hard not to choke as you devour the woman? Madly anxious to vomit her up quickly, after screwing a couple of times. Till the flesh of this woman repels you. And all this so that love will never happen to you. The only feeling that pardons genital exhaustion."

"I don't hope to love, I've already told you. What's more, I don't desire to love. The choice is mine. It's as serious a one as choosing to love," Miguel said.

"In reality, all you want is to lose the spark of desire as quickly as possible. So that boredom and a lack of pity come to be the only ways left you to relate to each woman. If you'll pardon the joke, uncle, what you really want is not to be able to get it up. However incredible it may seem to you, the goal you set yourself is impotence. Until the time comes to launch another well-aimed attack. Isn't that the best way to hunt? So as not to die of hunger? So as to have your sport?"

Miguel felt uneasy treading ground mined by suspicion. Was I a troublesome ally or was I only trying to unmask him? To hand him over to implacable judges? Was I fighting in the name of feminine solidarity or out of a frustration kept secret from him?

"Don't talk to me that way, Breta. Don't you see that despite everything it's a painful process? Always radiant at its zenith and always sad and lonely in its twilight. In between, it leaves an emptiness like death. Or what one imagines death to be."

Miguel did not want to lose me as an audience. Even though I accused him of chasing women so as to be able to feel a body that with age was eluding him. He never admitted that what he really loved was his own cock. Accusing him of nursing a secret desire being pointless. A Narcissus who began the banquet with his own genitals.

"What you're trying to do is make your feelings evaporate rapidly. So you won't run the risk of coming to love someone. What are you afraid of, uncle? Doesn't it pain you to have faceless, nameless women in your bed? To be the eternal possessor of an anonymous sex organ?"

I suddenly felt useless. These confessions lacked historical value. We were both consuming a narrative from which we were withholding basic elements. Duped by lies and hollow mockeries. We were mere incompetents when it came to total confessions. Just because we sensed that there was a collective story ruling our lives. Determining where we were heading. In that case, in the face of this banishment from life, wasn't it legitimate to divert ourselves with the fever of sex?

"I shouldn't have confided in you," Miguel said, with unfriendly gestures.

"If you don't confess to me, who else will you talk to about your females? To Grandmother, in exchange for Dom Miguel's stories?"

Before making his escape, he said emphatically: "You won't be seeing me for a long time, Breta."

The next day, in Leblon, he pretended not to see me. Even though Madruga and Eulália were present in the room. My grandparents surprised at the recent falling-out. Especially since Miguel had been protecting me since childhood.

Eulália began to act in such a way as to force Miguel to offer me a few polite attentions. At the same time forcing me to reciprocate. He obeyed his mother, hurriedly returning to his armchair, without looking at me. To make me feel guilty.

After the sweetened coffee, I finally took up Miguel's tacit challenge. Ready to wound him. Normally given to proud display of the mark of victory on his body, he needed to be racked by doubts as to his impeccable trajectory. And didn't he always lie to me, didn't he assure me that the urgent nature of his passion was more innocent than mine? Did it not have an essential attribute that I was never able to show to those who loved me intimately? Both absorbed in the game, we saw the afternoon slip away. No one had yet resigned.

The next morning, the secretary phoned me. Miguel kept me waiting on the line so as to hurt his niece's feelings. Finally, his voice asked, in an impersonal way, for time to think about our fight. The glass had cracked almost imperceptibly.

"Why must I give you time to think about our friendship, if that means I must accept it in whatever guise it shows itself? Thereby losing the right to criticize you!"

A heavy silence on the other end. I foresaw the ruin of our relationship. He merely commented that, by dint of my métier as a writer, I had turned into an arrogant word slinger. I had dictionaries and vocabulary in my favor.

"You're only an apprentice of life," he said sullenly.

"And what else can I be, in the face of such a master alchemist of pleasure?" I decided to let him have five minutes more, in return for satisfactory explanations.

Till finally he said: "Okay, Breta, you win. We'll make up, provided that it's temporary."

At my side now, in the bar, he embraced me gently. It had been stupid of both of us. "Luckily we'll have more fights."

Once we were all back home again, Eulália drew Miguel, the most talented one in the family, toward her, to sit at her side. The two of them would divert themselves, trading dreams. Under the watchful eye of Odete, who didn't mind losing Eulália to Miguel. Certain of getting her back again, once her son had left.

"Wherever you go, Breta, I'll be your main character. Even against your will," Miguel said, aiming now at needling Madruga.

Almost always, Madruga acted in my favor. Trying to extract information from Miguel that I would find useful. How often he mentioned his son's adolescence, so as to make Miguel furious. At that moment, the memory of Esperança was a central part of his story. The two siblings bound fast to each other by ties and words that they themselves supplied. From the cradle, Esperança's shadow had pursued him. She would hover, a child still, over Miguel's cradle, till Eulália took them out for their morning walk.

Eulália could hardly hold the two little children in her arms at the same time. She always needed to rid herself of one of those burdens so as not to collapse, exhausted, on the ground, defeated. Both forever fighting for her bosom, without her being able to decide in favor of one or the other. Till they were both bested by Bento, a beautiful, delicate child from the day he was born. Then proving incapable of withstanding the Atlantic crossing and life itself, choosing to leave them forever. Madruga, in return, began to take his memory and his photograph along with him wherever he went. Eventually writing, on the back of the picture: He died, yet he still lives in my memory, and I shall always miss him.

In a certain way, these words warned his children of a feeling that never allowed itself to be replaced. Whenever a child of his died, what that child left behind could never be given over to any other. And he fiercely refused to probe his losses. To the point that Venâncio reproached him for his inability to weep. As though, by having lent Eulália the courage to withstand the loss of Bento, in the days on board that followed, he had kept his soul from unburdening itself.

"Madruga is guilty of the sin of pride. He has never set aside so much as an hour a day for mourning. And it was by cutting himself off so completely from our mortal lot that he's succeeded in making himself a fortune," Venâncio said resentfully.

This did not correspond to the truth. Madruga did weep sometimes. Especially in his youth, on reading letters from his mother. Urcesina wrote him often in winter, from November on, when the earth was resting, and her hands as well. She took pleasure, however, in wielding a pen, though she had never before been called upon to be a scribe. But in her concern to save paper, she crowded the words together, in so small a hand that it was difficult to read. Forcing Madruga to decipher his mother's enigma, a task that did not discourage him. Till at last he understood the text and memorized it. Whereupon a fit of weeping would come over him that made him stronger. As though the emotion had trimmed off all his excess fat, ridding him of human flabbiness.

Before Madruga was twenty, another letter arrived from his mother. Its explicit intention being to celebrate his most recent success, commented upon by everyone in Sobreira. It was said that González, a prosperous businessman in Rio de Janeiro, couldn't even draw breath without him. Calling on him for everything but the choice of suit in which to present himself at the meetings organized by the Spanish Benefit Society, of which he had become a distinguished member. Despite this, whenever he praised Madruga to the skies, González immediately made it a point to mention his extreme youth. Like a sort of obstacle to his succeeding him in the business. A formula he'd hit upon to find fault with him yet keep him hard at work.

Unable to resign himself to González's disesteem, Madruga looked for ways to exact his gratitude. That man, twice his age, whom he even admired, ought not to resort to underhanded subterfuges to detract from his merits. Thoroughly annoyed, he began to show his displeasure openly. Barely greeting him, turning down his dinner invitations.

At home, Pilar listened to all her husband's complaints. But contrary to González's expectations, she turned on him, both in bed and at table.

"If that boy hadn't knocked on our door, I don't know what would have become of us! We'd still be living in that miserable little hotel for transients, that gave us hardly room enough to turn around in, let alone time to think of the future. And what a black future!" she reprimanded him severely.

Put on his guard, González hastened to mend his careless ways. Presenting Madruga with a box of havanas. And with satisfaction, he watched him tear the wrapper from this choice product, which his youth would soon teach him to appreciate.

Madruga noted González's inquiring gaze and allowed himself to be corrupted. Their peace made, González tucked his fingers in his waistcoat, all smiles. His intention was to so enslave Madruga that he would never escape. Madruga's undertakings, bold and successful, would constitute a threat to González if he were not included in them.

Prodded by Pilar, he urged Madruga to drop by the house more often, with a view to landing him as a husband for his youngest daughter. Despite these lavish dinners, however, Madruga and the daughter didn't catch on to the couple's hints. They sat there together, laughing with exasperating innocence. Their bodies indifferent to any sort of overture. Nothing. Nothing kindled their desire. No rapture corroding the limits of immediate reality.

"There goes our fortune, man!" the wife wailed.

Madruga rejected the hint that he marry the girl by cutting his stay at the dinner table short. He would leave immediately after coffee, on the pretext that work the following morning would fatten their respective bank accounts. These last words were uttered in such a way as to strike the couple with all the blinding force of a contradictory illusion, leaving them heartbroken. If on the one hand they wanted him to stay on, thereby making it easier to bring about the marriage they'd set their hopes on, on the other hand they urged him to leave, so as to set the stage for the dazzling spectacle of their rise in the world.

Madruga's heart demanded to be let loose, like an unbroken colt eager to kick up its heels. And to choose a wife without taking the advantages and the future into account. With money in his pocket, he would be free to love. The right woman or the wrong one.

"Perhaps love lies in the freedom to choose and be chosen. Even though this illusion is only a dramatic turn of fate that's practically useless," my grandfather said one afternoon.

During the week Madruga kept the letter from his mother tucked away in the pocket of his trousers, not daring to open it. He merely ran his fingers lightly over the envelope, taking pleasure in the feel of it. Not that he feared news that would come as a crushing blow, capable of felling him from afar. He had long since looked upon himself as fated to mourn his dead without bidding them farewell at the edge of the grave. In the end he had chosen the bitter destiny of separation, when he had decided in favor of America. But in his reluctance to open the letter, he was obeying inexplicable instructions from his soul.

On Sunday morning, lying in bed, he made up his mind to read the letter from his mother. The longest of all her missives. The paper still bore the typical scent of the trees round about the house. He trembled at the sight of the leaves folded by his mother's own hand. She herself carefully placing them inside the envelope in such a way that they would cross the ocean safely. This thoughtful gesture nonetheless not depriving his mother of the right to pass on to her son a word of warning concerning the temptations of this world. Urcesina would never forgive him if he met defeat through the work of chance or thoughtlessness. Certainly not Madruga, a son who had come forth from her womb with the look of a victor. All he was lacking was a chariot and Rome.

After reading the letter, he sought out Venâncio. He too read Urcesina's words with the strange feeling that she was capable of hurting him. Unlike Venâncio, that woman thought of America as a trunk full of gold coins, and the dream of it, petty and persistent, was worth more in her eyes than the grandest utopias.

"I'm writing you this to congratulate you on being the owner of the new Hotel Cebreiro. God grant that this firm, that goes by the name of González and Madruga there in the capital, may long endure, that a star may guide it, illuminating it forever! In conversation, in Pontevedra, someone who knew that you already have a business was absolutely amazed, seeing how young you are, just nineteen. And seeing as how that man has sons in Rio de Janeiro and Bahia, much older, who are still underlings!

Work hard, then, my son, keep your courage up, and don't ever for a moment look down upon your house. Don't try to outdo or think of outdoing your partner. The greatest respect is still necessary, friendship being of short duration without it. After that, my son, and above all, it is necessary to be very careful about the money you lay out, and even more careful to lay money aside, since you won't get anywhere without savings and you won't be able to see and embrace your father and your mother, who so long for that happy day. So then, my son, our happiness depends upon your work, good management, and heavy savings! Senhor Caldelas is now in Sobreira, mind you, cutting a fine figure. He's been going about Orense, Corunna, Pontevedra, buying anything he pleases and all of it the very best, and why? Because he worked hard, made careful calculations, saved even more, and having come by a tidy fortune through his work and the way he handled money, he is now enjoying it and is still a very young man. My son will do the same!

Senhor Caldelas, just now back from Madrid, brought with him our Belmiro, who, as you know, was there in a little grocery store, but we were obliged to get him out of there, because they made him carry heavy loads (he has calluses on the top of his head, poor thing) and many acquaintances of ours met him on the street, looking a mess. We're going to see if we can find something for him here in Pontevedra, or else Orense. He's quite frail.

It's a law that one must fight for life, and to get a good start, with one's morale in the ascendant, with a fighting spirit, prepared to confront all eventualities, successfully performing great labors, surviving great hardships, enduring privations, etc., it is necessary to be strong, both morally and physically. Tell me how your friend Venâncio is, has he done as you asked and is he happy with his work? If you were severe with him at one time, be gentle now, won't you? Remember me to him, won't you?

Inside of some newspapers that came from there for your Uncle Justo, a letter of yours addressed to Belmiro was found. You'd best not do that again, because your uncle might be fined if the packets were opened, because that's not allowed. Your father is still in Pontevedra, on the work projects he agreed to supervise, and your little sisters went there for the Epiphany holidays. On Sunday (tomorrow), God willing, I'm going with Belmiro, who sends you an embrace. Farewell, my son, pay heed to the advice of your mother, who embraces, kisses, and blesses you."

Urcesina injected her son with hard lessons in reality. Transcendent in her, however, was a feeling of love that only her son could arouse. That woman, with her limited vision of reality, nonetheless passed on to me a gift of expression. Her words, apparently intended for Madruga, came from an archaic source. They had been born in the Spanish countryside, inspirited by Galicia. Consequently, they bore cultural signs that I, her descendant, had no right to dismiss.

I had, however, to learn to apply this advice, the product of such a concrete body of laws and uses, to literary creation. Since this creation, of bastard origin, implied the presumptuous intention of journeying by way of the paths of purity and impeccable selection. And how could this be possible, if its genesis was owed to nothing more than a narrative in the course of which everything gradually degenerated, on the pretext of taking on a final form?

Urcesina, however, had learned to go with her pitcher to the well of turbid waters that served her village, and splash them against the stones so that they would clear. In this way using them with exemplary, age-old wisdom. A fact in the face of which what remained for me to do was to explore the resources at hand that would enable me to understand a woman who had given birth to Madruga amid the privations of her village, of her region, of her country, of her continent.

In a certain way, Urcesina pushed Madruga toward America. A continent overrun by demons and beings specializing in sucking the souls of these young people whom Europe fabricated and sent it as a present. And did so because, despite the tumult of the new lands, there was no one who did not fall under the spell of this alluring America.

Above all the women who, facing the picture of poverty prowling about the house, prepared to banish their sons. As meanwhile the latter yearned to fulfill the ritual of embarking and disembarking, taking passage on the boats which, for centuries, had sailed for those lands. A strange union, that of women and sons, made only of captivating dreams, frustrations, ambivalences, marked above all by such intense ferocity that they could hear the sounds of American jaws sinking teeth with equal pleasure into human flesh and wondrous, lush fruits.

Urcesina would not have the words to explain the reason for America's being the destiny of the Galician man. She was offended, however, by the fact that America, at once young and on its last legs, harbored suspicions of that woman in Sobreira, and thus intended to wreak vengeance on her sons.

Madruga understood his mother. How often he had caught himself making gestures inherited from her, which he squandered on the streets of Rio de Janeiro. This force of fate being responsible for the magic current that circulated between them, with the result that the strident cries of Sobreira resounded in the center of his heart. His mother, in turn, simply reproduced a natural inheritance, which kept a watchful eye on bread, turnips, manure, wine, garlic, blood rites, language. And especially, a memory impossible to reconstruct, even if sequence and order were imposed upon it. Wasn't memory disorder itself rooted in human sentiment?

On tilling the Galician plains, plots of earth that the Celts had taught them to fence about with stones, Urcesina felt for the land the same emotion that had touched Xan's heart and haunted his great-grandfather's. A sentiment dramatically common to all, motivated by poverty and by knowledge. As poverty robbed them of hope, knowledge closed off the frontier of the imaginary, using methods that destroyed the universe of legend. With the risk that Madruga and his people would dissipate their basic sentiments if they cut themselves off from these roots. Unconsciously, however, Madruga always fought to preserve the legacy of Urcesina, Ceferino, and Xan. He wanted to keep them warm in his belly and his memory. Even though it upset him to discover himself suddenly a prey to a strong emotion that stubbornly recognized no nationality.

As a young boy, Madruga had learned to get round his mother's rough temperament. Urcesina and he feeling each other out through the language of things. A language born amid meadow and grove, safeguarded by age-old customs. And mother and son instinctively served, with the strictest fidelity, this archaic, secret, and intangible cosmos.

The mother, despite her air of forlornness, her eyes filled with anxiety for crops that risked freezing before harvest, and despite Ceferino's silent accusations that she had grown old before her time, never failed to bring to her son's life the imprint of poetry. Above all as Madruga played in the animal pen of reality, pinning him to the wall, demanding of him sweat, tears, and money. So that her son would one day return in triumph. A Roman emperor, unmarked by the stigma of death, ever smiling on those who entered Rome transported by the euphoria of the populace.

For years Urcesina dreamed of Madruga landing in Vigo, after ten years' absence. Her son, having claimed his baggage, eager to get to the other side of Puente Sampaio, Pontevedra. Not giving a thought to the lovely estuary being left behind. Nor did he linger in the villages along the road, some of them built into the mountainside. Bent on reaching Sobreira. Where, discreetly, the wind had died down and come to rest in the little square directly in front of the church.

Urcesina would be the first to embrace him. A rough embrace, without tears, meaning thereby that she had had a feeling in her bones, beforehand, of the destiny awaiting her son. Despite his having fled from their house without farewell notes or last words. The fact, however, of his having forgone their blessing and their warm farewells, ceremonies that probably would have weakened his will, did not mean that Madruga disdained his family's ways, the traditions that had ruled for centuries at table, in bed, and in Galician legends.

Miguel seemed grateful to his father for striking out ahead of him and marshaling the scattered elements of his past. At times, however, he rebelled against Madruga, who, instead of telling the story of his own past, called on him for one. But Miguel immediately calmed down. He would first offer general remarks concerning the family. And only then discreetly mention his ties to Esperança. Doing so cautiously, so as not to offend Madruga, who tensed at the mere mention of that name.

From the cradle, Miguel and Esperança traded curses and blows. One of them pulling the hair of the other, certain that the alliance being forged between them would bear fruit. Wherever Miguel went, Esperança was close behind. Up the street and down. All the trees, fences, and walls climbed amid uncompromising competitions to find out for themselves which of them was better. They never did discover the answer.

When they were older, they chose adjoining bedrooms. Thus enabling each of them to put an ear against the common wall to try to make out what the other was doing. After breakfast, if Esperança hadn't come downstairs, Miguel complained. On the other hand, he didn't want his sister to appear in the light of day before him, to have that advantage. When Esperança failed to come down, Eulália consoled an anxious-faced Miguel. He must be patient, for Esperança might well be dreaming of adventures that they soon would be embarking upon.

His mother's argument calmed his anxieties. He was certain now that dreams and nightmares had gotten the better of his sister that morning. She would be coming downstairs with her head hanging, shorn of the courage to confront him. At the mere idea he whistled merrily. A few minutes later, he was on tenterhooks again. He went to Esperança's room, knocking loudly at the door, disregarding the possible presence of Antônia, with whom his sister shared the room. Esperança took her time answering, making him think she'd escaped through the window. Already heading for the Praça Sáenz Peña, where the flowers, in that spring season, were in full bloom. Eager to be present at the birth of the world before he appeared. Before Miguel, with his overbearing attitude, forced on beings and objects an interpretation contrary to hers. Seeking victory.

"It's no use trying to fool me, Esperança. I know you're alive, shut up in that dark room full of spiders and snakes," he shouted from the door.

Esperança's torso appeared in the door, her nightgown peeking open. "What do you want of me now? Aren't you satisfied that we fought all day yesterday?"

Before Esperança's radiant beauty, particularly enhanced early in the morning, Miguel forgot that in the next few minutes they would be embroiled in a fierce quarrel, knowing that there was not room enough in the whole world for the two of them at the same time.

The exciting battle between them developed by way of predictable moves, open and aboveboard. This situation being totally reversed from the moment that Madruga began taking his son to the factory. This paternal act forcing Esperança to react swiftly and violently. So that as a result Miguel feared that in his absence his sister would advance by flanks whose loss would be irrecuperable. It took him some time to realize that his entry into the world of business sealed Esperança's defeat.

The first time Miguel was invited to the factory, Esperança, in despair, shut herself up in the bathroom. Unable to face that new development. For the reason that the adventures experienced up to that point had always been aimed at strengthening the two of them at the same time. Whereas their father's unfair decision, cutting her off from the only reality that would provide her with the opportunity for integrated growth, undoubtedly constituted an irreversible defeat. With a sudden sharp crack, Esperança intuited, in anguish, that it would be Miguel who would garner the fruits of passion, in whatever form it might present itself, before her own body did. And this automatic deprivation of a pleasure by nature surely intense and unbearable left her gasping.

In her white-hot anger, her head against the cold tiles, she invoked unknown gods. Crying out for vengeance, wanting to defeat father and brother. The whole of human society, which had pronounced her a failure before she had even bid for its favors or demonstrated her ability. She did not intend merely to marry, to give birth, to spread her legs, as her partner pleased. Life had everything to offer her. And she to demand of it.

She emerged from the bathroom, trying to hide her distress. She sat down next to her mother at the table with the afternoon snack. A lavishness that, though it reflected Madruga's success, also made all of them his prisoners.

Eulália stroked her daughter's hand with great tenderness, touched by the tense, prominent veins, young as they were. The two of them never broached a subject directly, circling warily about it by way of metaphors. Rejecting any direct encounter between them.

"Would you like a piece of cake? Chocolate nut, made by Odete. She has a fairy's touch."

Eulália did her best to calm her visibly distraught daughter. And in order that there might exist for them in the future words that would enrich their respective memories, the mother confessed how happy it made her to go to church. A house where she always found, independent of its eloquent architecture or its resemblance to a manger, a function far above the human. Hence the pleasure it gave her to pray. Finding that prayer spurred her on in her spiritual quest.

"If God is with me, in the whole of my being, that means that He occupies the entire earth. What else can I dream of save that provocative enigma?"

Esperança knew, through oral tradition, that her family, for at least two hundred years, had devoted itself to the art of distraction, to the gradual effacing of certain apparently practical, but in fact useless, objects. And this tradition had taken such deep root in them, by way of a growing faith, that the present itself, the time now passing, seemed to them to be devoid of rigor, and to be based on a fundamentally defective esthetic.

"And do you know what Father used to say, there in faraway Sobreira? Dom Miguel said that only the past is capable of feeding the belly and the soul out of the same dish."

As the two of them were engaged in diverting discourse concerning this sort of affliction, Miguel arrived home from the factory. Pleased with himself and on his guard, not knowing whether he should go directly to the bathroom to cool off or cross swords with his sister, doubtless eager to make him feel he'd lost. And how would Esperança manage to convince him? If their father hadn't chosen him just on this one day. On the contrary, he had decided that Miguel would follow in his footsteps periodically. And over holidays, full-time. Leaving it to Esperança to take care of the house, to attend to the sick. To be at her father's bedside, when his hour came. As her brothers meanwhile expanded the business, they would have free access to brothels and bars. And doubtless make their entrée with a bold, arrogant air.

When he arrived, Esperança did not spare him. Her gaze proclaimed his perfidy. The fact that he'd won by underhanded means. If he weren't gloating over having tagged after their father, she probably would have forgiven him. So she immediately accused him of being her enemy, then forbade him to speak. An intolerable penalty to Miguel, whose goal was to win in such a way that Esperança would owe him boundless devotion.

All alone in the living room, Miguel was unable to bear it for ten minutes without his sister. Going in search of her, he hinted how boring that day in the factory had been, the opposite of what he had been led to believe in the beginning. The reason being that the only place where it was in fact possible to dream was in the tops of trees. Or when the two of them, the one on the heels of the other, fought over the fascinating hidden corners of a daily round that took them all over the neighborhood, beyond the limits of the walls and the houses.

That lie, contrived with such subtle details, did not convince Esperança. She was touched, however, by Miguel's love, prepared as he was to give up all outward proofs of his pleasure. A sacrifice all the greater when one knew that a large part of a person's pleasure consisted of making use of exuberant words, which would act as a foolproof guarantee of one's real existence, before valuable witnesses. Since there was no one who could do without an audience, whose function it was to lend credibility to the most insignificant fact, making it echo in the dull silence of the night.

Miguel, in particular, felt that his life took on substance through Esperança's testimony. Without his sister, who had already begun to reserve for him a jealousy directed only toward men who were handsome and beloved, Miguel saw any plans for adventure going down the drain. Up until then, he had yet to marshal all his forces for a single feat of daring that risked plunging him into the dark depths of greed. She, on the other hand, sensing imminent personal defeat, precociously made of envy a permanent practice, aimed entirely at Miguel.

Madruga's fortune, even in the beginning, did not favor his sons' wasting their time toadying. Esperança, however, immediately sensed the power of a fortune that she would not help to build. Nonetheless, her father's progress offended her. It restricted her to an area devoid of action. In a terrible rage, she would then square off with Miguel, as Madruga

watched from the sidelines, applauding a dispute soon to end in their assuming their conventional tasks.

When he surprised them at table, not speaking to each other, he
brought up questions that would plunge his children into a heated debate.

"Tell me, why is it you light into each other so often? You're like rams
butting each other."

Esperança immediately dissembled, affecting an exaggerated sense of
responsibility for Miguel.

"It's not true, father. We're on our way to the square this minute. Each
looking after the other."

"And why should I look after you? Just so you'll have the right to
keep a close watch on me?" Miguel's irritation made him forget that they
ought not to reveal, in front of their father, the differences that constantly
gnawed at their feelings. This was a sacred rule. Esperança therefore
waited for him in the yard, her finger upraised. She reprimanded him severely for having gone so far.

"Do you see now why I'm smarter than you are?"

Cowed by his sister's victory, Miguel swore not to fall into another
error. He would not be defeated again. She was disturbed by the intensity
of the looks they exchanged. Sometimes Esperança wondered if she were
seeing herself in her brother's face, by dint of watching it so much. Or if
she simply couldn't stop looking at that adolescent body in dizzyingly
sudden bloom.

Miguel made a move to embrace her. To butter her up, he promised
her picture cards of stars for their albums, which both made richer reposi-
tories of fantasy and desire on Thursdays, the day of their allowance. Esperança smiled, pleased and grateful. Outside of Miguel, who was there
who stirred her up so, giving her combat practice? Would he be the last
rival she would confront on an equal footing? Was she really destined,
then, to engage only in petty domestic squabbles, any serious contention
with men being forbidden her? She immediately felt resentful at depending
on Miguel, the only one to grant her the honorable status of adversary.

A man now, Miguel resembled a bear. I looked at him, there before
me, eager to explore the question of whether, in fact, he had freed himself
of Esperança and of the challenge that she had driven into the very center
of his being. His force at this point, almost magnetic, had come from
whom? From Madruga, from Eulália, from his personal experience? Or
from Esperança? For that very reason, wanting to revive the image of his
sister, he demanded that I be a replica of her. Had I, at some moment,
hurriedly spat out certain words altogether like those that Esperança had
also addressed to him? This dramatic coincidence, on top of others, arousing his anxiety? Leading him to go off chasing women with an already
erect penis. With no idea what he would encounter between those thighs,

the freezing cold of a dungeon or the sweet moistness stemming from desire, both being quite possible. Seeing that life, on offering him such labyrinths, had no reason, necessarily, to satisfy him, to offer him a place of refuge, to give him the means to interpret it. Or even to assure him that passion, perverse and virulent, would free him, once satiated, of the feeling of desolation.

It was Eulália's habit to bring Esperança and Miguel together to talk to them of Sobreira. Preparing her children to dream of distant lands. It was easier in adolescence to accept everything that had the coloration of legend. Seated round her, the children pressed her for details about Sobreira, which they no longer remembered. A little village hemmed in by mountains, in whose valleys and meadows were sown the crops harvested in the last months of summer. The green of the landscape, at times too bright, softening only with the rain, a gentle element of the Galician soul. There was also, in Sobreira, a modest river, prompt to lend its waters to its banks and to the washerwomen. Rising in the mountains, fed by the diverse streamlets that irrigated the meadows along its course.

"And doesn't Sobreira, Mother's land, move you?" Esperança said to Miguel, her heart touched by a corner of the world that even today brought a look of intense nostalgia to Eulália's eyes.

Clinging to Eulália, Miguel believed his mother's body to be the essence of the earth itself. It had borne fruits and exploded in rich harvests, in harmony with the seasons. He loved his mother deeply. And whenever there welled up in his bosom an anguish of strange origin, he instantly sought her help. With a gesture, his mother gathered her rags and tatters together into a single object for him to lean on. Calmed momentarily, Miguel was ready once again to face his schoolmates and the world.

At table, on Sundays, Miguel saw his father and Venâncio, between forkfuls, lamenting the intensity of which they were victims. Suffering the spiritual and physical trials stemming from their permanent connection with the lives of two countries, Spain and Brazil. With the aggravating factor of having one of the two always absent, offering them an occasion for tragic imaginings. Thus reaping intense enjoyment from neither of them. Or ever having of each of them a clear image that was not contaminated beforehand by the memory and the interference of the other. Brazil and Spain, in a permanent duel, contended for the supremacy of memory. Each relying on the greater volume of valiant deeds that would bring victory. Both full of sad memories because they shared virtues, realities, and histories that Venâncio and Madruga could eagerly invoke.

These men, in all truth, spoke of countries as though, above and beyond geographical and historical contingencies, they were discoursing on immortal feelings, those that had always been located at the base of human genesis. And for that reason alone, unwittingly, they immortalized themselves and conferred an equal touch of eternity upon the inhabitants of those countries.

Unlike his pals in the neighborhood and at school, Miguel struggled to fix his limits within a single border, to which he would give a name, identifying it at a distance. He did not want Spain in his house. Nor its vapors to consume his imagination. He was Brazilian, and as such, he was in the process of welding together a solid territory thanks to the use of a language which, despite its having suffered divergency, hatreds, ruptures, hiatuses, had never dissolved. This same language bearing with it Brazilian feelings. Given all these reasons, why did those foreigners want to foist off on him a ruined land, without dream or direction?

In distress, Miguel sought out his mother. In an effort to have her reconcile such antagonistic forces. In her room, Eulália was praying in contrition at her prie-dieu. Approaching her, Miguel perceived her eyes gazing beyond the wall, her distant face. For Eulália it was quite possible to take two countries by the hand and, through this gesture, love them without effort or exclusion.

There, close to his mother, Miguel rejected Madruga's and Venâncio's conflicts even more strongly. Despite the sad look in Eulália's eyes now. Something was troubling her and her son could do nothing to help her. Perhaps he resented Eulália and her god, who occupied her so completely, thus keeping her always far removed from Madruga's daily round, from Venâncio's gradual breakdown, from family quarrels, which already were beginning to distill and exude drop by drop the milk of poisonous plants.

On Miguel's fifteenth birthday, Madruga decided to fight Eulália. To put an end to the spell that his wife had cast upon their son. Before it was too late. In a few years, the son would have plunged into idle daydreams, disengaging himself from paternal reality. Perhaps taking no interest in money or in sex. Swathed in Eulália's mantle as she drew him to her with her soft voice.

He went into action, discreetly. So his wife wouldn't notice that he was slowly disenchanting Miguel. To the point that after a week spent with his son in the factory and at the construction sites, he was well on his way to freeing him to go back to the spell of Eulália's stories. With veiled hints to him that these stories would be of little value when it came to dealing with reality.

Miguel was torn between his father's unlimited offer and his mother's charms. Not being yet able to put all thought of Esperança aside, since she was vying with him for precisely the advantages proposed by Madruga. His father now pressed him to decide one way or the other. Threatening to transfer to Bento the preferments in question.

As a final blow, Madruga urged Miguel to bed a woman. Only he himself could satisfy the desire that was naturally tormenting him. He gave him explicit instructions. The whole thing doubtless made him smile. Miguel obeyed. But on returning home, he avoided Eulália's embrace. Pale, wanting no dinner, he retired to his room.

"What's the matter, Miguel?" his mother said, standing at the locked door.

Miguel refused to explain. She insisted, till Miguel gave in. On condition that she see him only with the light turned off and his head under the pillow. He had a headache. Eulália accepted these rules. She did not intend to hurt someone whom the world had already wounded. Her gestures in her son's direction immediately dissolved, out of shy constraint.

"Don't say a word, son, let me remain at your side."

And she added that she too, in Sobreira, when she was his age, often waked with a start. And not out of fear of the dark, but because she found herself unable, at the end of each day, to add her various pictures of the world to her heart, as though there were a family album in it. Without which, incidentally, God seemed even more intangible to her. Whereupon, contemplating the silhouette of the high mountains of Sobreira, she decided that reality was only an immense portrait that would little by little turn yellow as it passed through the memory of each person.

"God is also a picture portrait, son. A negative, however, that nobody has yet developed or been able to frame," Eulália said, sighing, as though everything suddenly fell short of her expectations.

Covered by the sheet, Miguel pressed his penis against the mattress, wanting to punish himself. Shamed by his mother's presence. And so disconcerted that he was panting slightly. But when Esperança tried to force her way into the room, he drove her off by dint of wild shouts and screams, fearing she would penetrate his secret.

In the morning, leaning on the banister, Esperança awaited him at the bottom of the stairs. He alone had seen her as he set foot on the first step, on the floor above. In the face of his adversary, there below, he tried to flee to his room. A futile move, since Esperança was sure to come following after him, prepared to denounce him. He descended the staircase with elegant aplomb and greeted her. At breakfast, he kept his fists and his mind at the ready.

"It's no use hiding from me, Miguel, I know what happened." Not a single muscle of her face moving.

"What are you talking about?"

Bent on revenge, Esperança headed for the garden. For a few minutes, Miguel was afraid to face her. As usual, his sister's eyes seemed to devour him.

Seated beneath the trees, Esperança made marks on the ground with a twig. Lines tracing the shadows cast by the tree branches. She patiently awaited him.

Miguel advanced boldly to meet her. He would not sidestep this challenge. He might well be Esperança's ideal adversary, but at the same time it was thanks to her that he had learned how to handle his combat weapons.

"Enough of all this mystery. What is it you want, Esperança?"

She busied herself holding one finger apart from the other, her hand spread flat. Finally she turned to him.

"Do you really want to know, Miguel? Can you bear to know?" she questioned him, looking him straight in the eye.

That voice had lost its firm tone. Miguel detected in it the tremor that made it sound scratchy. He had certainly hit home. She had streaks in her skin, at the level of her breasts. His sister was cringing beneath the impact of the darts he had launched at her.

"I do want to know," he said resolutely, unable to retreat now.

Esperança displayed the dramatic feeling of one who has been banished from life. Engraved upon her face was the accusation that she had followed him mentally to the woman's house, pointed out by Madruga, with the intention of listening, from outside the door of the room, to the cries of pleasure and the sounds of the couplings of those two alien bodies locked in each other's arms.

"What are you talking about, Esperança?"

Miguel's voice was nearly inaudible. Almost begging her to remain silent. It embarrassed him to defeat her by means of a right that had come his way without effort, with a boost from Madruga, and with everyone's approval. Whereas Esperança, condemned to exile, could not go with him on adventures that in fact were a sign of the end of their adolescence.

The two of them would never again fight over a ball in the yard or climb trees to see who could better withstand the vertigo of swaying from the frail top branch. The time had come for them to exchange words with caution, keeping them veiled and enigmatic for safety's sake. Robbed forever of spontaneous resources, deriving from rage and joy, coins that had heretofore circulated between them. He would not have that Esperança again. Never again would they leap into the fray with the guilelessness of bygone days, when they started fights not knowing who was going to win. Reality had now transformed him, and he would get the better of her no matter what the circumstances.

"Speak, I beg you," and Miguel tried to fling himself into the past, when they were free, happy, and unconstrained.

"Freedom was easy for you. You didn't even have to fight for it. All you had to do was sleep with your first woman."

Esperança suddenly rose to her feet, turning her back on her brother. Without saying good-bye, she began to walk away. Till the morning breeze seemed to drive her swiftly inside the house, indifferent to Miguel's gestures pleading with her to stay.

Eulália suffered when it came time to move. To leave Tijuca and go live in Leblon, in the house built by Madruga, her husband proud now of strolling in the garden, of organizing his belongings in a space that would hold all his acquisitions, of contemplating the Atlantic from various angles of the house.

She did not want a housewarming party. She could do without a big fuss over a routine event. She resented abandoning the house where her sons had uttered their first words. She could see no reason to celebrate the new walls that said nothing to her heart. The history of the family and its feverish gaze had not yet circulated through them.

The furniture, on being removed from the old house, bared the stains on the walls. Eulália begged to stay there for a little while more, in the company of Odete. She wished to rest in the house that seemed to her to be in ruins, betrayed by the former occupants. Filled with emotion, she wandered through the rooms amid memories that slowly surfaced. She had much to say about each nook and corner, even though nothing else was left now. As if it were a commandment of life to shatter the objects and the beings placed in our charge. But she should not be surprised. She too, when she left there, would be beginning, through an act of slow evolution, to abandon her own human territory. Everything round about her would accentuate the necessity of taking her leave.

Eulália accepted Odete's offer of coffee, kept hot in the thermos. Grateful for her attentions.

"Don't worry, Odete. I'm all right. I only want to see the house where we've lived for so many years."

Unhurriedly, she slid her hand across the grainy surface of the dining room wall. It was warm, for the sun had imparted the heat of a summer day to it. Her strength revived, she sensed that she had been accompanied in her gesture. Suddenly certain that the shade of Dom Miguel, interposed between Odete and her in the late twilight, had not missed a single movement of that farewell.

The two women were there alone. One Spanish and the other Brazilian, of African origin. Both prepared to hear from the visitor any stories he might have to tell. Those old stories, which had come from very far away, nobody knew from where. And ended up in Galicia, in a precarious state. Thereby forcing the Galician people to restore them, as though they were sculptures or a painting. They had immediately set about touching up the colors, filling in the details, so as to recompose a repertory very nearly lost. Encouraged by the fact that the stories had long awaited a transfusion such as that, which would bring the old Galician themes back to life.

Eulália looked at Odete. In her place, she saw Dom Miguel. An imposing figure, wherever he was. Despite his slightly stooped shoulders, standing firmly on his feet, as though remains of buried cities had suddenly sprung up from the depths of the earth.

Eulália often surprised her father in the kitchen garden. He would remain there for hours pointing at the stars. Giving them names he'd invented. On feeling himself being watched by his daughter, he would blush.

"One day you'll do the same thing I'm doing. Because it's a family custom. We've been observing the stars since the fifteenth century. Simply because there is no other way of understanding the earth. But we're not the only ones with this mania. Have you ever noticed how cows, especially those with full udders, have a profound look in their eyes, the look of someone who's left the earth from having gazed at the sky so much?"

And to convince her of a fact that he had no way of proving, Dom Miguel stroked her hair. A gesture that his daughter was not to take as being an intimate one.

As he went about Sobreira, Dom Miguel was never without his cane in his right hand, and a hat as well, which he liked to vary. On the chest of drawers in his room, the eight hats he owned continually rotated. He also appreciated waistcoats, which served him as a protective shield. And dressed in this fashion, he had the air of a country gentleman.

Strange things were said of this cane of Dom Miguel's. The most superstitious even attributed certain powers to it. Perhaps because of the fact that Dom Miguel pressed down hard on its silver knob whenever he was asked perplexing questions. As the veins in his forehead protruded and there immediately came to his lips an unrestrained verbal torrent. Whereupon a great deal of what he said to them ended up remedying certain local ills.

That was precisely why peasants from neighboring villages, such as Bora, Gesteíra, Borela, Carvalledo, sometimes came to Sobreira just to hear him. In the hope that Dom Miguel would guide their footsteps, though the reasons that led them to knock on his door were often trifling.

Informed that a peasant was in a hurry to see him because his cow was dying, Dom Miguel made him wait in the entry hall. Taking his time dressing, as though he were going off to visit Pontevedra. On arriving, he refused to go to the cattle pen despite the man's appeals. Even though he tried to convince him that it was close to his house. Dom Miguel turned everyone down. He did not, in fact, have the gift of saving lives, contrary to what people supposed.

No one was willing to accept such an answer. Dom Miguel would then begin to console them. He cautioned them that the nature of animals led them to their death, after serving men for so many years. There were even animals capable of consoling their owner, of giving him the courage to live without their company. Since they searched men's hearts with their wise eyes, which said everything, even though they did not possess the power of speech. This being the case, he advised the peasants to hurry back to the pen. They would arrive in time to read such messages. And they were moved by the death of a cow gasping and drooling amid the straw that reeked of urine. No one abandoned life as meekly as a cow.

After Eulália's and Madruga's wedding, as his daughter stepped onto the running board of the coach that would take them to Vigo, Dom Miguel embraced her without a single tear.

"We'll see each other again, daughter."

Trusting in her father's word, Eulália departed for America. And then gave birth to two children in the little rented house. And when Madruga decided that the third child would be born in Sobreira, she simply packed the trunks, with mixed feelings of resignation and joy. Certain that Dom Miguel would welcome her with the same affection and the same distant gaze. Eager to show her their room. With this gesture wanting to say to her, You see, you've never left this house, even though you happen to die one day in that America that feeds on the flesh of our children, even as it enriches us with gold and murderous memories.

At times, in letters, Dom Miguel was contradictory. In incisive terms he accused Europe of having laid a curse on America, sending it, since the discovery, ships transporting poisonous cargo and wretched scoundrels. Rarely sending it a dreamer, with poetic gifts. The aim of Europe in so doing was to deprive those lands of all sovereignty. In return, America, bent on revenge, sent them back, in fragile barks, at the mercy of the currents that periodically reached the Iberian peninsula, some of their sons. These reached port here overcome with guilt and despair.

"There is not a single innocent European, daughter. To compensate, America rigged up a furnace into whose flames it is in the habit of throwing all those who cry out for justice. Justice, in fact, never succeeded in anchoring in those modern lands."

Advised by cable, Dom Miguel stood in the door from dawn on, awaiting Eulália, his son-in-law, and his grandchildren. They hadn't notified him of the exact time of their arrival. But when the car, coming from Vigo, came through the gate of the property, he did not hurry out to meet it. He embraced Eulália only when he had her directly before him. And pondered, without comment, her belly several months pregnant. He immediately turned to Madruga, inviting him to make himself at home. He had the run of the house, every last corner of it. He could open all the doors, all the closets. Nothing was forbidden to him. He had become a son, and hence had the right to make demands if something appeared to him to be unsatisfactory. Having delivered his speech, Dom Miguel presided over the first meal with the ceremony that guests of honor always inspired in him.

Hospitality as prodigal as that moved Madruga. Fortunately he had brought him many gifts, among them world-famous Suerdieck cigars, from Bahia. Precisely where Brazil had begun to exist, thanks to Cabral and his modest fleet.

Over coffee, Dom Miguel lighted his cigar to show his appreciation. And with each pull on it he appeared to absorb a restored image of Brazil. Curious to know, sitting there next to Madruga, how that country, with so motley a human contingent, was getting on. When there circulated through it the blood of Indians, Iberians, Moors, blacks, pirating Englishmen and exploring Frenchmen. Would this country succeed in constituting itself as a nation, despite this human ferment, whose origins and passions were lost in the night of time? In such a way as to consolidate, in the future, a Brazil equally carnivorous and refined?

"And how does one survive there, under the constant threat of fever and tropical diseases? Can such sicknesses be the expression of the soul of a people offended by such storms and stress? As was Europe in days past, living at the mercy of the plague? Each time the epidemic made further inroads, it carried off half the population!"

As Madruga furnished details, Dom Miguel applied them to the daily round of Galician life, so as to see how they worked out in practice. Only thus did a picture of Brazil slowly take shape in him.

"The only way of understanding the world is to bring it into the dining room."

Madruga backed a hypothesis that would have aroused objections on the part of Venâncio, had he been present. Venâncio delivered sermons each day on the subject of the erosion of words, for the sole purpose of casting doubt on what was real. Moreover, Venâncio would not agree with everything he had said about Brazil, despite Dom Miguel's enthusiastic applause.

"Don't forget to bring Venâncio next time you come. With him here in Sobreira, we'll surely have Brazil present at the dinner table between courses," Dom Miguel said.

Having decided to retire to the bedroom to sleep, Eulália went to her father to ask his blessing. This would be the first night that she and Madruga had been housed beneath that roof as husband and wife. Madruga walked over to the window, leaving the two of them alone. Dom Miguel offered her his hand to kiss. And murmured, in a low voice so as not to be overheard:

"I promise to make you happy during these months. Galicia must be a bounteous memory for you and a damp one. A permanent rival of Brazil."

And scarcely were these words out of Dom Miguel's mouth when the light in the parlor in Sobreira dimmed perceptibly, till Eulália was no longer able to make out his face. The figure of her father appearing to fade away. He was no longer there. As Odete, rousing Eulália from her reminiscences, suggested that they leave. It was late and it had rained that week.

Eulália obeyed. As she went through the gate, with her eyes closed, the thought came to her that she would never again set foot on that plot of ground, where she had remained for so many years. But how many places on earth must she still lose before coming upon the house of God?

Eulália's modesty charmed Madruga. He therefore agreed that they needn't celebrate the move to a new house. He had already offered sufficient evidence of his prosperity. Above all by building a house such as that one, in which to receive the family and be the recipient of the feelings of that family. Moreover, with the noisy rows and the resentments of the children in mind, he had seen to it that the house had thick walls and private spaces.

As work on the house began, he made Venâncio responsible for keeping an eye on the expenses. A supervision that would not make demands on his time, since the construction was in the hands of an experienced architect, a Portuguese from Vizeu, who had been with his firm for many years. A week later, visibly distressed, Venâncio asked to be relieved of this task. Maintaining that Leblon was a long way away from Cinelândia, which meant making endless journeys back and forth.

On the basis of this fact, Madruga realized how upset Venâncio was at the mere mention of the house, which was going up very quickly. But he said nothing. He feared he might crush Venâncio's delicate soul. He suspected, however, that his attitude had something to do with the possibility that in the future Madruga would adopt habits incompatible with his own.

On the eve of the move to Leblon, Venâncio's anxiety grew even more pronounced. And the look in his eyes, hard and cold, seemed to accuse Madruga of leaving behind, without compunction, a patrimony consisting of walls, friendship, and memory.

Madruga could not bear that accusation. He decided then and there to visit him. In the apartment on the Avenida Beira-Mar, nothing had changed since his first visit. The objects had aged only a little owing to constant use and the sea air. Madruga settled himself in the same armchair as before. Prepared to explain to him the reasons for his visit. Venâncio, however, interrupted him immediately. Unreconciled to the systematic demolition of the mansions in the downtown district, whose splendid façades told the whole story of the city. Hence he was offended, overcome in fact by a dramatic sense of loss in the face of these depredations.

"What will become of us without the old city? Those barbarians are out to make us forget the past, to erase memories of the city. But what will happen after the death of the last men whose retinas still bear the imprint of these demolished buildings? What city will then begin to exist? Or must a city be leveled periodically so that each generation may reconstruct it to suit its taste? And not a trace of it be left? But why such a horror of the past? Can this be typical of a new country? Is it that hard for them to accept other ages? Or does each man aim to found his own petty civilization?"

He was determined to move to one of the working-class suburbs. Far from that unpleasantness. With the advantage of finding cheaper rent on one of the branch lines of the Leopoldina or the Central. There on the outskirts he would recover the spirit banished from Cinelândia.

His critical tone indirectly included Leblon, a residential zone with new buildings, with no tradition. Rather than living in such places, a person was better off going off to Goiás or Mato Grosso. Where the beating of the Brazilian heart could be heard, for it had not gone completely dead, despite the inertia of its upper classes.

"Where, I ask you, can Brazil be found? Is there a single artist capable of reconciling, in a perfect synthesis, the visions and the images we fashion of Brazil? Or does the destiny of a country thwart any sort of unity, tend toward fragmentation? So that each inhabitant acts out his personal version of Brazil. And the spirit of this country, squatting inside Aladdin's lamp for hundreds of years now, never becomes manifest!"

His headaches had returned, though sporadically. He was not afraid now that bad luck would catch him in its fine-meshed net once again. He more readily accepted the fact that man was not endowed with words enabling him to shed light on his emotions. At times he lost weight, his trousers hung loose around his waist, and then he recovered.

"What's the reason for this visit? It's the second one in all these years," he said coldly.

And he handed Madruga some Spanish periodicals, ignoring his uneasiness. They had been brought by a functionary from the Consulate, who often visited the house. He read them with disdain, however. What could a country under the aegis of Franco represent? A dictator who ruled even the most secondary moments of the nation. Not only by means of coins and portraits, but also slogans. A Roman emperor who overlooked nothing, not even human reproduction, by wretched creatures addicted to coitus.

Madruga accepted the filtered coffee made within the hour, served in a cup of fine provenance. The only one that Venâncio possessed. He had bought it at the Bazar Chinês, with the thought in mind that a visitor might come one day and be transported at the sight of such transparent porcelain. Thus giving proof of an appreciation of coffee and of existence. But who can have deserved such attentions? Madruga wondered, intrigued.

Madruga finally mentioned the new house. Ready to receive the furnishings acquired with the end in view of their never becoming an affront to the eye or to family habit. Not at all showy. Thereby proving that Madruga was not about to abandon memories that had settled like dust on the timeworn Tijuca furniture. He would be incapable of sweeping these memories away, to be replaced by habits that risked causing a rupture between his family and Venâncio.

"We'll put the same amount of salt in the food. And the chinaware is practically the same. And nothing in the beef stew on Sundays will change," Madruga said.

Both always resorted to obscure phrases when they found it necessary to express equally obscure sentiments. Thereby avoiding insuperable problems. They agreed that the use of masks was prophylactic. It served to conceal certain adjacent dramas pressing to come to the surface.

Venâncio understood that Madruga was assuring him of entrée into the new salons. There being no reason, however, for him to be startled at the newly acquired pieces of furniture, long lying around at antique dealers'. Bearing nonetheless the seal of their good origin. The majority, for many years, had embellished the coffee plantations of the Paraíba Valley, mansions in Bahia, Pernambuco, Minas. And now they were coming into the hands of those with new fortunes, in a transaction that furthered national culture. Since it recovered abandoned pieces and restored to them the dignity they had been robbed of through the negligence and the ingratitude of the years.

Less tense now, they sipped the cognac appreciatively. At the end of the afternoon, the waters of the bay reflected the light, the Morro da Urca almost invisible in the distance.

Venâncio shattered the equilibrium of that hour. "Despite your promise, we will never again repeat the dinners of bygone days. When we had no money, and more than enough dreams."

Madruga's reaction was unexpected. He raised his glass as a toast to him and emptied it as though he were downing poison.

"If someone is destined to deliver me a mortal blow, may it always be you," he said dramatically.

Madruga was suddenly aware of the taste of blood on his tongue. After this effect, he regretted having made use of a maxim that did not sound as though it were of his own making. He thought it prudent to talk about the house. About the advantages of living in Leblon, with the sea as neighbor. The Atlantic would be there in person. That ocean born even God didn't know where. And that he and Venâncio had loved at first sight, in the weak afternoon sunlight. Immediately afterward they had left behind the estuary of Pontevedra, of gentle and compassionate beauty, an Amazon tree, with spreading branches reaching down farther than the eye could see.

From this house, they would be able to contemplate the object of their passion. A dubious passion, stormy and shy. And one that did not keep them, one time, after piling up on the table of the Bar Adolfo the cardboard coasters of the beers they'd consumed, from dreaming of taking the Atlantic to the visitors' room, as though it were a friend, and entertaining it with sweetmeats, wine, and a long conversation between the three of them. The discussion centering on the legends of which it itself was the subject.

How many times, from this veranda in Leblon, would they be able, in continuous exercises of the imagination, to reach Galicia in rapid strokes, borne only by the trade winds, favorable to navigation. When, face to face with the crucial Galician headlands, seen in tragic geological outline, they would make the grave decision to board the first available ship. In the expectation of spending several years on the back of the wild Atlantic waves, which, as they heaved and retched, would this time take them out of this world. And unlike Sinbad, who led people on with his pipe dreams, Venâncio and Madruga would allow themselves to be seduced by nothing save their desire to tame the sea.

Venâncio didn't go along with this game. Madruga's dreams had been too long coming. It was too late now to waste good time trying to rid themselves of the frustrations piled up in their respective hearts.

"Be careful, Madruga. Tides are dangerous. It's not only bodies of water they affect. They also trouble the spirits of those who build their castles near pounding surf. Just look how odd the people who live in Flamengo, Botafogo, Copacabana, Ipanema, and Leblon are. They don't even seem to be Brazilians," he said gravely.

Madruga was annoyed. Venâncio was nothing but a stubborn tortoise, housed in an unfeeling shell, a thousand years old. And still a master of bizarre dreams, who had always threatened him, and ended up sitting at table with him. While they waited for the slow hours of a dull Shrove Sunday to trickle away.

Speaking now of those years, now of the conflicts that once again were in the offing. Already a shadow darkening the national horizon could be seen. Cast by ambitious men, in an unrelenting fight for power. Madruga not managing, however, to hide his admiration for those men who, plunged into anxiety and despair, never lost sight of the necessity of making decisions, of altering the course of events.

At that moment, Getúlio Vargas and Carlos Lacerda were polarizing the country's attention. They had unleashed a duel which only one of them would survive. Lacerda loosing lightning blows against Vargas, once more the occupant of the Palácio do Catete, by way of his articles in the *Tribuna da Imprensa,* solidly lining up the middle class and certain military sectors in opposition.

The imminent crisis did not prevent Madruga from investing every cent he could get his hands on. The moment a situation worsened, he felt the urge to negotiate, to establish new alliances, to take out loans, to extend himself beyond his limits. He was confident of his ability to manage debt. He felt himself to be a kind of Phoenician trader who, with the gods and luck as his guardian, was anchoring his ships in the very ports of his adversaries.

"There is no such thing as an abyss for Brazil. This country has always grown amid crises. Isn't that true?" he said to Venâncio in Eulália's presence.

If there was an abyss, it was situated in the heart of men. The country withstood bad weather, political swings, many of them dramatic. Since he had landed at the Praça Mauá, at the beginning of the century, he had seen Brazil bedeviled by provincialism, incompetence, and the corruptions of its political classes. The debate always revolving round public debt, domestic and foreign. A miserable, diseased, fucked-up country meanwhile offering itself as a backdrop for the incandescent words. Where the privileges of certain classes brought out all the more clearly the state of gloomy, grotesque carnival revelry of the populace. Everything favoring the transmission of the solutions necessary for the future. The concept of a future becoming an integral part of a mystic body that ruled everyone. In practice transforming itself into an entity whose nature, oriented toward acts of magic, would correspond to the power of imagination and the aspirations of the people.

"Nobody here really perceives what he has failed to gain. Despite his rights."

In the beginning, Madruga was scared. Free and on his own in America, with his body budding exuberantly, the hair of his beard still sprouting, he was obliged to learn everything from scratch. Striking out for himself each day. Temporary defeats ceasing to panic him. And, likewise, social unrest or revolutions. Such movements had no serious permanent effect on the social body. So there was no reason to have an excessive fear of the apparent effects of fate, when public events were so rapidly absorbed and forgotten. As meanwhile the nation's institutions proclaimed that restraint on the part of the people in the face of the facts was the best remedy for combatting an adverse reality.

This time, the scandals denounced by Lacerda's daily appeared to go beyond what the middle class and the press, siding in general with the opposition, would tolerate. Only Wainer's *Última Hora*, a daily dogged by the accusation of being financed by the President's office, defended Getúlio Vargas. The voice, however, of Carlos Lacerda, like a furious, brilliant Catullus, outdid itself in denouncing day after day what in fact existed, belowstairs, in the Palácio do Catete, a sea of mud. As soon as he turned into the herald of the middle class, winning its massive support.

But the Vargas of the second phase, brought back to power following the dictatorship, anointed this time by popular vote, now called forth Venâncio's uncompromising defense. An unqualified supporter of the President's measures, all of them strongly nationalistic, hence flying in the face of solid foreign interests.

At dinners on Sunday, Venâncio swore that the President was immune to this sort of corruption. Merely bent on keeping the country moving forward on its basic trajectory. Lacerda's maneuvers, and those of his party, the National Democratic Union, being merely obstructionist tactics, aimed at deflecting the drift to the left that was beginning to take shape with Vargas.

Vargas's old strategy, in turn, of dividing power among certain figures and then slyly setting one against the other, so unerring during the dictatorship, did not appear to succeed as well under democratic rule. The ranks of his enemies swelling on every hand. At precisely the time that the President, in terms of his weight in the balance of history, was ironically approaching the golden age of his life, he was swallowing, on the last day before the eve of his Golgotha, the sour wine of disillusionment and inevitable abandonment.

Venâncio read all the newspapers. He all but knocked on Getúlio's bedroom door to console him. The President was beginning to become acquainted with utter loneliness. Wasn't that how it had been with Christ? The loneliness of those who are betrayed not by a handful of men, but by all of humanity.

Vargas had his daughter Alzira at his side. But, outside of her, who to trust, who could save him from trials and tribulations? Tancredo, Jango, but who else? A dramatic situation for a man who had spent his life cajoling the people into practicing the cult of personality, to the point that his portrait, from the early days of the New State, was enthroned in schools, public buildings, private offices, bars. Being called by many a man straight out of Plutarch. Now, however, he had once again lost the confidence of the armed forces, the absolute arbiters of power.

In the middle of the month of August, Tobias pressed his father to join Vargas's cause, which Madruga had supported up until 1945. For Tobias, Vargas was the embodiment of an authentic nationalist sentiment, capable of taking definite shape by mobilizing the populace behind it. A movement that had cost lives in the past, it could no longer hold back.

Grown callous over the years, Madruga denounced Vargas's depraved maneuvers. And for the sake of argument, he attacked his dictatorial temperament, to which he had previously been insensitive. In Vargas's biography there were dark, spectral blots that needed to be identified. Very much like those black figures of Goya's, in the Museum of the Prado, possessed of an inhuman, tragic dimension. And therefore in glaring contrast to the green fields of the Brazilian countryside. Moreover, how could Tobias have forgotten that in 1941 Luís Carlos Prestes, one of his heroes, had received an additional thirty-year sentence for complicity in a political assassination, despite being in prison at the exact moment of the crime?

Tobias fiddled nervously with the tuning button of the radio in search of news that would restore his shaken confidence in Vargas's survival. At any moment the forces backing the regime could be thrown off-balance. The civilians and members of the armed forces who still supported Getúlio. There had already been a series of defections among his cohorts. There was public talk of sending him back to São Borja, from which they had trotted him out four years before.

In the old building of the university law school Tobias had joined the Brazilian Labor Party, in defense of the country's legal institutions. A party, embracing Vargas's ideas, that favored the interests of the working class. And opposed the National Democratic Union, the party of the wealthy and established upper class, which had also managed to kindle the political imagination of the middle class in its raging ambition to move upward socially. There thus predominating in the law school two highly vocal and antagonistic currents, with a small majority in favor of the Communists, whose leader, Prestes, was in no way overshadowed by Vargas when it came to charisma.

Tobias and his comrades raged up and down the corridors of the law school and demonstrated in the National Student Union, crying out for the preservation of fragile Brazilian democracy. Now definitely threatened by the founding of the so-called Galeão Republic. A bloodless coup against Vargas staged by air force officers, determined to remove him from power gradually through ongoing investigations of the Rua Tonelero incident, in which Major Rubem Vaz had been assassinated and the journalist Carlos Lacerda wounded. The autonomy which these officers conferred upon themselves in the investigation of facts having exclusively to do with the power of the presidency was clearly tantamount to the setting up of a parallel government.

Influenced by events, Madruga decided that the hour had come to oust Vargas from power.

"The man has always had the soul of a dictator, a caudillo type, from out on the pampas, a political boss along Hispanic lines. Capable of holding the people spellbound with his speeches, though they're never inflammatory. Undoubtedly a political genius, in view of the plots he's contrived. Except that everything's now turning out badly for him. He's living his twilight phase. Even so I admire his loyalty to power. I think he loves power above all else. More than family or any woman," Madruga said, summing up the President's personality.

"That was in the past, father. He was then part of the history of Brazil, which needed a dictator in order to weaken the power structures. It was imperative to remove São Paulo and Minas from the main axis of power. To make the rest of Brazil exist. It's not easy to organize a nation. The fact is that Vargas's fall, right now, will constitute a dramatic nationalist defeat. And it is counter to the interests of Brazilian industry, still in its infancy. But we are organizing ourselves badly, and the forces sold out to foreign interests are ready and waiting to smother us. With his fall, the petroleum-is-ours policy, defended at the cost of bloodshed, goes down the drain. In no time the big paws of foreigners take over this country for good. And put an end to Petrobras."

"So drive the English out and surrender to the Americans. What difference does it make? I'm beginning to think that Brazil's worst enemy isn't those gringos, but its own ruling classes, especially the political class. You have to grant that many Brazilians are real traitors to their country. For people like that the country represents only a check, a numbered bank account in Switzerland. I'm tired of innocents who let themselves be used. Dupes like you," Madruga said.

That son anchored in dreams annoyed him. Perhaps because of that very tendency to daydream he was destined, like Venâncio, to failure. Impervious to the plots being invisibly woven round about him. Out of sight, yet they intensified and altered history. He seemed to allow himself to be attracted by old-fashioned leaders, and though they might now claim to be heading in nationalist directions, they had always allied themselves with the powerful. Vargas, for example, had taken a hard line against nationalists, despite his having pulled a fast one on the Americans in the Volta Redonda National Steel Mill affair. On the other hand, many of his labor laws, inspired by fascism, served to demoralize the working class. Some of his measures, in this area, appreciably delayed the dreamed-of Brazilian revolution.

"Vargas protected capitalism. If it hadn't been for him, the armed forces would be in the streets today putting down the rebellion of the workers," Madruga said.

To Tobias, his father had identified with the winners. Capable of exempting themselves from guilt and judgment, no matter what regime might be in power. Remaining extremely wary in the face of any new social pact being formed, until they had assimilated the rules and the immunities that were beginning to apply. Only then offering their services, cunning, and lack of scruples to the new power elite.

Madruga did not seek radical changes. He was in favor, rather, of adjustments on the classical model, gradually aimed at redistributing income. And also intensifying, in this way, popular consumption and savings. And consequently, causing the country to progress within a market economy.

The growth of his fortune forced him to protect it. He was not about to dole it out publicly, nor subject it to the criteria of an envious bureaucrat who had not made his way in America as he had since the age of thirteen. This being so, he defended a rule of law that would not affect his interests. But he did not shy away from having opinions. And the ones he had were heated ones.

On street corners, people talked of Vargas's imminent downfall. And an immediate takeover by a military junta, expected to act as surety for public morality, as it cleaned out the antechambers of the Palácio do Catete itself, making a judicial inquiry into the so-called basement full of muck.

"They're lies invented to overthrow Getúlio. What weight can that Gregório fellow have in the life of the Republic? Since when can a president be judged in the eyes of history and of his contemporaries by the conduct of a subordinate in that category? This is a crying injustice, an immorality perpetrated by an elite that is out for power, using this as a pretext. Following this line of reasoning, no constituted government would remain standing. Here, in France, in England, or in the United States. These false moral purges are simply ideological purges," Tobias shouted excitedly. Taking the sugar water brought by Odete. At that point he would have drunk even poison.

Miguel resolved to join in the argument. He could not hide his anti-Vargas sentiments. "It'll be fifty years before we know the historical truth about events. If that scum now in power doesn't decide to burn the documents first, reducing the evidence to ashes."

With enormous pleasure, Miguel quoted Afonso Arinos to support his apparently anticonstitutionalist theses. As Bento, shifting the discussion to neutral ground, brought up the subject of the country's advance, despite crises. With no fear of their effect on the economy. The destiny of Brazil was being traced by the pressure of its size and its share of the continent's population.

"What history are you talking about?" Tobias addressed the question to Miguel, paying no attention to Bento's interruption. "Can you be talking of the history that's spattered with shit, with corruption, with perverts, a history that has always existed, even before Getúlio Vargas? Made by Brazilians themselves, eternal vassals of the Portuguese Crown, of the English, the French, and now the Americans?"

Bento forgave Tobias's impoliteness. He was patient with this brother of his. How often he took him to the movies, touched by his glumness, a small boy still, waiting for his godfather to come on Sunday. Not understanding that Venâncio had been hospitalized and no one had any idea when he'd be getting out.

Despite Bento's efforts, strong barriers still remained between them. Owing perhaps to the rigid streak in Bento's nature. From adolescence on he did his best to look older than he really was. When he tried on his first suit with long pants, he asked to be fitted for a vest to go with it. Indifferent to his father's mocking laugh. And thus attired, he made the rounds of the entire household, expecting praise. And when compliments were not forthcoming, he redoubled his efforts to solicit them next day. He wanted the family at his feet, offering him the love due an only son.

In the face, however, of the weary gestures of his parents, obliged to divide their attention among so many children, Bento rebelled against the tide of a reality flowing in a direction contrary to his interests. Arrogantly squaring his shoulders to meet it head-on.

At table, till Miguel's marriage, he fought with him for a place of honor. And when he was assigned a seat squeezed in between Tobias and Antônia, he chewed his food with a bored doggedness that did not escape Madruga's notice.

On a certain morning, while still in high school, Bento skipped class, without telling his family. Dressed in his uniform, he headed downtown. His hair neatly combed, his briefcase under his arm. At the factory gate, he thought of turning back. Reflecting, however, on his future, he greeted his father's secretary, and went directly on into the office.

"What are you doing here at this hour, young man?" Madruga was surprised.

He took off his jacket, hung it up on the hook on the wall, and paying no attention to Madruga, went to the file cabinet and began organizing the index cards. This procedure impressed his father, who repeated his question.

"From today on, I'll always come here. I'm as much your son as Miguel is. And I want to learn from you, sir."

Madruga eyed his son with grave uneasiness, since in a certain way he was a stranger he scarcely knew. Undoubtedly ambitious, prepared to rise rapidly in the world. Judging him in this light, Madruga temporized.

"You came because you wanted to. I didn't summon you before because it wasn't time yet. But now that you've gotten a head start on yourself, I'll demand more of you than of Miguel. Do you accept?"

That solemnity had only themselves as observers. The only ones responsible, therefore, for the basic terms of the association founded at that moment.

"You have only to give me your orders, father."

Miguel noted Bento's competitive spirit without being disturbed by it. His one concern the intense feelings that Eulália and Esperança aroused in him. While Bento had great difficulty finding an outlet for his emotions, Miguel awakened them readily in others, favored by his ready laugh and heartfelt warmth of expression.

Bento sometimes looked for protection to Antônia, the only one in the family to see his charms. But immediately his sister's nervous anxiety irritated him and he would send her packing. Antônia would lapse into prolonged silences. Not speaking to him for days on end. To Bento's relief, free once more of any need to express his emotions.

Left to herself, Antônia would seek out Esperança, who, after a quick caress intended to console her, would immediately abandon her. Again rejected, she would hide in one of the remote corners of the house, set aside by Eulália for this purpose. Instead of going to her own hiding place, the one designated by her mother, she would insist on remaining in the area of the piano, Tobias's property.

Tobias, however, lacking all interest in such possessions, would hurriedly bring her a pillow to spare her from having to lie on the hard floor. And seeing her looking dejected, he would sit down beside her. Telling her fragments of the stories which, in fact, belonged to Miguel.

Antônia's gratitude was fleeting. She immediately forgot about him, someone younger than she. Without Tobias's noting his sister's sudden indifference. Whereupon he diverted himself by acting as though he were on a speaker's platform facing an audience, obliged to demonstrate to it his talents as a distinguished orator. In the service of the poor, the weak, against the rich, the powerful, the arrogant.

Tobias's plans concerning his future always seemed vague to his father. He therefore demanded more concrete explanations from him. And that he understand the meaning of a vocation, how to attain results.

"If you've nothing to sell, you're going to spend your life buying. Forever depending on someone who has something to offer and sets the rules of the game. You must arm yourself, before they knock you down, Tobias. Remember that enemies never go about disarmed. And I don't want any son of mine to dream without having at least the means to dream."

In his father's presence, he lost all ability to express himself. When in fact he wanted Madruga to be aware of what was going on inside his chest, where everything was compressed, his pinched vertebras inducing an excitement that soon vanished.

"It would appear that you want to be a lawyer. Very well, but you must be a brilliant one. Whatever you do, you must be first-rate. That's why I want to give all of you the education I never had. Allowing you to lack for nothing."

Tobias rebelled against him in silence. By what right did that arrogant blue-eyed creature, smelling of cigar smoke, demand of him a perfection that his mother had assured him was not to be found among mortals? As sole lord and master of his life, he alone would decide what steps to take. Perhaps he would consult Venâncio, whom he loved. Thereby annoying Madruga even more.

How many times he had surprised the two men, in the living room, amid an uneasy silence. Or saying things to each other that they were certain would be hurtful. But Tobias had only to enter the room for Venâncio to make his peace with his friend. Madruga, who had not seen Tobias watching them from behind the door, was constantly amazed at this sudden about-face.

Instead of being grateful to Venâncio for such thoughtful concern, Madruga would look the other way in embarrassment. Convinced that Venâncio, by acting in such ways, was trying to steal his son from him.

Gradually becoming the only hero in Tobias's overheated imagination, which absorbed human deeds by way of a system of optics colored by immense expectations. This taking place as he, meantime, overburdened by work, had neglected to fill in the nooks and crannies of such a fantasy.

Feeling left out of the picture, Madruga would avenge himself by banishing his son from the room, ordering him out into the garden or the yard. With hanging head, Tobias would make for Wolf Hill, his retreat underneath the piano. In tears, he called his father a tyrant, who ruled over the house with no respect for others' feelings. But unable to bear being all by himself there, he would go off in search of sympathy from Antônia, the constant victim of these failures to understand.

Instead of siding with him, his sister, in a testy tone of voice, laid the blame for the mistreatment they'd subjected him to squarely on him, as if in fact he had deserved it.

It took some time for Tobias to understand the meaning of these words.

"Let's play, Antônia," he persisted.

"Can't you see I'm busy?" she shouted.

The Leblon house, though imposing, offered him no protection against the disturbances that overtook the city. The insecurity of those passing by in the streets was palpable. They all began to suspect that Getúlio Vargas had become the lone protagonist of a story that had nothing to do with the people now, being instead a tale spun by himself alone, amid great suffering. And spurred on by the newspapers and the radio, Madruga's children entered and left the house as though these days had been declared a national holiday.

In the old law school building, near the Praça da República, Tobias met with a group, led by a faculty committee, prepared to join the military troops who eventually would take to the streets in defense of constitutional order. In session since early morning, they had received news that the generals, in successive meetings in barracks, had decided that the one way left them to solve the crisis was to depose Vargas. General Zenóbio himself was rumored to have assured the President of his inability to control the armed forces by any means short of outright combat, bloodshed, which the top ministers, and the President himself, wished at all costs to avoid.

The meeting of the Cabinet on August 2, presided over by Vargas, had been very tense. It had been decided that the President would take a leave of absence from office, until the investigatory commission named the guilty parties. The aim being to relieve the President of suspicion of having played a part in the attack on the Rua Tonelero or of having been involved with Gregório and his hired assassins. José Américo having cried out at this juncture, in ringingly dramatic tones: Now that we've saved the country, let's save Getúlio's life!

Among those present, along with Alzira Vargas, the most notable was

Oswaldo Aranha. Tobias had long since succumbed to the fascination of this romantic figure who, beginning with the Revolution of '30, had astutely cultivated his own myth. A many-sided man, hero of his time, United Nations statesman, and also, according to whispered rumors, a seducer of beautiful women, to whom he was in the habit of sending gallant compliments and flowers.

Born in the South, he and Vargas had gone north in 1920, finally settling in Rio de Janeiro, the center of the country, where decisions were made, applying from there the rules of power, despite dissensions that arose later.

In the historic meeting at the Palácio do Catete, Aranha proclaimed himself ready to die at Getúlio's side, with, however, weapon in hand. It would be a death made to order for entering the pages of history. That was the least he could do, in view of the access of passion that the Republic inspired in him, and the keeping of its commandments. He was not a man to accept a humiliation visited upon Getúlio without feeling himself equally offended.

Madruga feared that Tobias would become even more involved in the student movement, infiltrated at this point by the Communist Party, always active and vigilant. He again begged him to be more careful, since despite the existence of democratic institutions and the dismantling of the secret police, the latter had not destroyed their files, nor had they completely given up using the methods introduced through the power of Filinto Müller. The police arbitrarily used violent means, from head bashing to tear gas, to break up demonstrations judged to be embarrassing to the regime.

Bento hurried out to Leblon from the city. The news had finally been confirmed that the armed forces had decided on a coup, having already halfway convinced certain initially recalcitrant sectors to go along with them. At that anxious moment, nobody had any idea where Tobias was. He had promised to come for dinner, and everyone was worried when he failed to show up.

Bento calmed the family. That brother, practically a beardless youth still, would not dare confront the police in a pitched battle. Even though the *Tribuna da Imprensa,* in one extra edition after another, practically incited the people to take to the streets, clearly demonstrating their disapproval of the old caudillo.

Alerted by the radio broadcasts, Venâncio arrived in time for dinner. Immediately asking after Tobias, a known adversary of those who were preparing to betray President Vargas.

"It was Getúlio who betrayed the country," Madruga countered.

"Since when is one man all alone strong enough to betray a country, Madruga? It's always a whole class that betrays a nation," Venâncio said dejectedly.

Shortly before midnight, Tobias arrived, beneath a barrage of re-criminations from his father. How could he have gone out, scaring them the way he had, on a night like this! On the eve of a coup or a revolution, bursting into the meeting rooms of the Student Union and the law school, discussing political theories and practices, dreaming the while of a rifle.

"A rifle is for a soldier. They were born with a bayonet. And they don't hesitate to run anybody who disputes their power clean through," Madruga said in a calmer voice. It was a good idea to remind him that the Vila Militar, on full alert, was just awaiting orders to start the tanks rolling down the working-class district toward Catete.

"The people won't stand for this insult to their institutions," Tobias said.

"And why not?" Miguel said, taking the lead. "Who has ever had more contempt for the Constitution than Vargas? What's more, the poor Brazilian Constitution is a patchwork quilt that's had rape committed on it a thousand times."

Bento suggested that Odete lay in a stock of food. He himself had brought important documents home. To safeguard them against possible looting in the city. And Madruga, who had once feared Tobias's fits of passionate enthusiasm, observed that he had come back home, that evening, before midnight. Drawn by the warmth of table and bed, though he had proclaimed his readiness to defend Getúlio's honor.

He preferred to keep his mouth shut, not to reprimand him publicly. At times he wondered whether his son's lack of direction stemmed from the fact that in his childhood he had not had the dream of one day conquering America. Since he had been born in it, amid wealth, without ever having to make the effort of crossing the Atlantic and getting the better of it. Hence having no other choice except to invent an America for himself or else succumb to the America forged by men such as Getúlio. Men of supreme ambition who, once seated in power, always ended up corrupting the ideals of the same young people who struggled to keep them on that august chair.

His son was growing weaker under false mentors. In the unfounded belief that Brazil could be saved. Thus being taken in by a process of collective deception, which even São Paulo was unable to escape. On the contrary, even though an eminently progressive-minded state, thanks to its economic and cultural wealth, São Paulo had signed on in the vanguard of populist, politically degenerate myths. This being the case, what could be expected of the rest of the country?

Miguel wandered restlessly about the house. The next few hours would affect the life of every citizen. A decisive moment. If the Old Man were thrown out of Catete, what would prevent the masses from choosing to take to the streets, immediately giving themselves over to protests, acts of depredation? And doing so without prudent leadership capable of checking such excesses, so as to bring about a real and profound change in political habits.

On the other hand, with Vargas continuing in the office of president, there was the risk of his turning into a figurehead, with the boot of the military behind his every act. After the civilian dictatorship of the Old Man, from '37 to '45, the military dictatorship had followed. But what would happen if Getúlio himself, assailed once again by the supreme temptation of power, were to decree, from his pulpit, a bloody battle? States against states. How many would be sacrificed in this conflict, including Tobias, who would easily fall prey to a collective immolation? Being constantly under the sway of a chaotic and disordered system of ideas.

Miguel noted Venâncio's tension. He very nearly stopped speaking. Getúlio's crisis freed him of the necessity of communicating. Now and again he would nervously put his hands over his eyes. Fleeing the vision in which his godson, weapons in hand, seemed to be confronting Franco, on the other side of the stockade. And all of a sudden, through a series of unexpected acts, seeing himself elevated to the category of hero. A sort of contemporary Cid. Utterly determined to withstand the siege of the Nationalists, giving them not a moment's respite in any of the months of the three fateful years of the war. Till they were routed. Or better still, till Tobias, thanks to strange plans, made his way across the Pyrenees, in total defeat, humiliated, barefoot, but with his honor intact.

Miguel noted Venâncio's flushed face, the emotion that went far beyond the limits of his frail body. To relieve his distress, he had water and coffee brought him. Feeling pity for that man pledged as chattel to a dream. In the face of Venâncio's loneliness, sustaining himself on a passion of an almost abstract order, Miguel convinced himself, with a certain shame, that for him no passion had as fiery a nature as that trapped by the sorcery of the flesh. Ever since he had discovered the body of another, and explored its warm and humid territory, at each act of this sort it seemed to him he experienced a pleasure that had the defect of never being sated, even after having reached its end. And that impelled him to give himself over to a new cycle of caresses, not overlooking areas with fine hair, as he plunged to the very bottom of the woman, driven by a desire unable to extricate itself from his partner's most intimate hiding places. His sex having nowhere to tarry save in the vagina of that stranger. From which he felt himself torn away at the memory of his father's authority, shouting at him to get to work, for there were grave decisions to be made.

At times, after making love, he was suddenly haunted by the vision of Eulália, pale and transparent. At such moments, he anxiously worked himself free of the woman's body, locking himself in the bathroom. As he scrubbed himself hard. In open rebellion against his mother, who, having had so many children, had chosen him as the only one to hear her stories, peopled with nonexistent characters. And wasn't it true that those protagonists, lacking the necessary conditions for existing, had merely served to invent a repertory of lies and contradictions? Preserved thanks to the vigor of the oral tradition, so that men would not lose the habit of telling stories at the gloomy hour when twilight falls?

They were all still asleep when Odete halted before Eulália's door. She was reluctant to knock at so early an hour. But she could not keep her sorrow to herself any longer.

"What's the matter?" Madruga opened the door, startled by Odete's pallor as she stood there on the verge of fainting.

"The President has killed himself, Senhor Madruga. Getúlio is dead."

Once this alarm was sounded, the house took on an unexpected animation. All the children came, even the married ones. The smell of strong coffee wafted through the rooms and hallways. Glued to the radio, they listened to the news thundering out at top volume. Unable to believe that Getúlio had resorted to such a drastic step.

That night, Venâncio had slept at Leblon. Sitting at the breakfast table, he found the news hard to believe. He was eating cornstarch gruel, which of late relieved his stomach pains, with his eyes staring sadly into space, and not saying a word. He seemed to be at a wake for a relative. Only Tobias's weeping interrupted, now and again, the silence of this room, where everyone was lost in thought.

His son's lack of decorum vexed Madruga. He did his best to get round the situation. Perhaps Getúlio had had no other way out.

"Unfortunately we shall never know his personal motives."

Tobias took no notice of his father. He forced himself at that moment to experience inside his own skin the loneliness lived by Getúlio before pulling the trigger of the revolver held against his chest, a shot that had hit the mark squarely. The President overcome by a feeling like unto that of the gods who arrogantly weigh human destiny. At what minute, however, of this long dawn, did Getúlio decide to kill himself as the country slept, not suspecting the historic instability that awaited it at daybreak, the tragedy being plotted so that Brazil, finally, might know a new dimension of reality? A reality for which, in fact, Brazil had not been prepared, though it had been indispensable to its entering its maturity. At what minute, then, of an interminable dawn, in which he would have had more than enough time to review all the history of Brazil, from the discovery to that twenty-fourth day of August 1954, the day of his own passing, did Getúlio Vargas, President of the Republic of Brazil, decide that it was better to die than to live shorn of definitive honor and glory?

Antônia burst into the room. Anxious to pass the word on to them that the people who lived in Praia do Pinto, a slum near there, were threatening to lynch a woman holed up in the clinic of the Fundação Leão XIII, which had been built in the very center of the little local square to aid the slum dwellers.

Miguel and Tobias hurried up the Rua Cupertino Durão in the direction of the slum. They could already see the crowd that had suddenly appeared, as if by miracle, throwing stones at the windowpanes, amid the ruins of the citadel. Blending into the landscape, as though they were part of it, men, women, and children were forcing the door of the main entry, stoutly protected from the inside. Where a barricade had been erected capable of holding off the enraged populace.

The conflict had a simple origin. The owner of the pharmacy on the Rua Ataulfo de Paiva, who had long been a volunteer welfare worker in the clinic of the slum, had made certain remarks unfavorable to Getúlio. A prey to the contradictory sentiments that Getúlio aroused in the masses, ranging from hatred to fanaticism, she too had been unable to resist unburdening herself of her bitterness, and had applauded the suicide of the Old Man. Saying that he had done the right thing to kill himself. Because of his disservices to the country, he did not deserve to live.

Such words spread like a trail of gunpowder from one wretched hovel to another. The people living in them immediately taking offense, having decided that the intruder, in addition to wounding their feelings, their mourning barely begun, was trying to yank their dead man, whom the mystery of death was beginning to hallow, out of his own coffin and defame him in a public place.

The ring around the clinic was closed in minutes, giving the woman no time to escape from the building. There then followed an attack of screaming, cursing. On every hand the cry for justice. The immediate need to avenge the death of the President.

In the face of that spectacle, at once frightening and fascinating, Tobias was filled with rejoicing. He was certain that the Brazilian revolution would yet be born, on a day now very close at hand, of just such an orgy of rage and humiliation. He had not managed to hide his feelings, because Miguel, intuiting what he was dreaming of, immediately reproached him for his diabolical line of reasoning.

"Such spectacles fill me with shame. They don't even know the names of the victims. When this madness happens, no one is safe from the blood orgy. Not even its instigators. In the hour of collective violence, justice disappears, giving way to summary deaths, without public trial. Is this what you want, Tobias? You, a law student? Instead of justice, do you want the triumph of barbarism? Tell me, Tobias, how to distinguish the innocent man from the torturer, the corrupt man from a mere victim of private vendettas? Have you already forgotten the Spanish Civil War? Because of a simple dispute over water to irrigate the fields, people ended up facing a firing squad!"

The doors did not hold up for long. The woman would soon be stoned to death, like a modern Saint Stephen.

Tobias was in despair over the situation. Having repented of his previous joy, he said beseechingly to Miguel: "What can we do, Miguel?"

Miguel ran to the house on the corner, knocking on the door. No one answered, all of them panic-stricken. Miguel kept hammering on it furiously, till a woman appeared at a second-story window.

"Call the police this minute, before they murder her," he said in a firm voice.

He went on his rounds, summoning other neighbors. And the door was just about to give way when the truck with a detachment of some thirty soldiers, rifles in hand, bayonets fixed, finally appeared. Quickly forcing their way through the crowd, they ordered the woman to open the door. In a question of minutes the pharmacist was taken out amid jeers and insults. The soldiers held her upright, her face livid, trembling with the cold. Miguel looked at her terror-stricken eyes, which had glimpsed death.

The crowd dispersed. Some people in the barrelhouse, between guffaws, drained their glasses of raw rum, their ice-cold beers, the conflict already forgotten. However, amid the rum, the tears, the rebellion, the frustration, there had begun the enthronement of what was about to become the memory of Getúlio Vargas.

His corpse had scarcely had time to grow cold before people began speaking of him as an intimate participant in history. They would all weave together endless stories about him, attributing lies to him at one moment, truths the next. Everything, moreover, made to fit the trajectory of the myth. Till the people, again set off by the spark of dreaming, rage, and humiliation, began searching for a new idol to keep it company.

Back home, Tobias collapsed, ash gray, in the armchair. Unable to move. Eulália revived him with port wine. She herself still suffering from the shock of the suicide. Filled with pity for an old man who had resorted to death by his own hand when this same death was about to pluck him from the branch in nature's own way. She disapproved of suicide, not because of religious scruple but because she did not believe that life appoints special demons and sirens to attend us for the sole purpose of making us surrender. After all, it was so easy to give in to delirium and the sense of tragedy, ever with us since we had left the caves.

Tobias suddenly grew worse. Eulália discovered that he had a fever. She ordered him to bed. After giving him aspirin and lemon juice, she tucked the quilt in snugly around him. Miguel insisted on visiting him. On seeing him lying in the fetal position, he couldn't resist making fun of his brother.

"From the look of things, you didn't make it through your first revolution. Even though I told you that revolutions always sacrifice their heroes," he said, laughing.

Tobias hid his face in the pillow. He pretended not to hear Miguel's sarcasm. After that, his father came to see him. Tobias did not object to his visit. On the contrary, he docilely accepted Madruga's rare gesture of stroking his forehead, pretending to be checking whether he was still feverish. And when his father left the bedroom, without a word, Tobias curled up, his body aching all over. It seemed to him, then, that human existence asserted itself through distressingly indecipherable messages.

*T*he children were born and it was easy to love them. A feeling that dawned without effort or reflection. Urcesina and Ceferino had taught me a way of family life which I was to follow with exemplary fidelity.

Eulália's love for the children, on the other hand, had more ample resources. Nothing hindered its intense flow. The swollen breasts that fed her newborn.

One time, on the street, at the memory of Eulália's breasts, I decided to have lunch at home. I wanted to catch her unawares just as she unbuttoned her blouse and modestly took her breast out, white and tangible. I stole up the stairs without a sound. So Eulália wouldn't guess that I'd come home.

From the door, standing ajar, I contemplated my wife with the child at her breast. Without moving, so as to spare her son, who was sucking her nipple, the slightest disturbance. There reproducing itself in Eulália the essential animal act of nursing offspring.

Ever since I was a little boy, I had bowed to the laws of nature. In Sobreira, everything was natural. Even the animals copulating within sight of everyone. The impulsive swollen organ of the bull forcing its way into the body of the cow, with no particular discernment. Or how all the animals, in general, dilated the circle of their anus, spilling out, with ineffable pleasure, the endless superfluities of their bowels, which would serve as fertilizer for the land gutted by man and his plow. Nothing went to waste in country life, ruled by instinctive knowledge.

That son, suspended from Eulália's bosom, was noisily going about his work. With his insatiable little lips, he was demanding nourishment from that woman. A precarious life, completely dependent upon Eulália's decision to keep him alive with her palpitating breasts.

It excited me to think that I too, driven by passion, had sucked those breasts. My son was simply imitating me. Though I had enjoyed the advantage of having arrived first in that zone, whose protuberances, for some reason, always reminded me of the lonely peaks of Sobreira. How many times, moreover, lying next to Eulália's body, I had dreamed of Sobreira! The woman's genitals then becoming a dream conductor, it was possible to journey by way of them, as Sinbad sailed the seas. And wasn't it true too that one made love with the aim of abandoning a worn-out earth, in search of another, remote and unattainable?

Caught unawares on the edge of the bed, Eulália quickly covered her bosom. With the same linen handkerchief, a present from her father, thoughtfully kept within reach next to the bed. That handkerchief had protected the six heads to which she had given birth, as she offered them milk. Only the death of little Bento had interrupted her nursing and this natural gesture.

Eulália's gaze reproved me for my presence in the house at that hour. What right did I have to surprise her in an act that included only herself and her son, thereby banishing strangers, those who were not part of that mystery?

Meanwhile, she did not say a single hurtful word. What was more, she never took advantage of my feelings. To keep me prisoner, tied to her by the bond of emotion. That woman, born in a village, though the daughter of the illustrious gentleman Dom Miguel, helped me to be free, to solve my own problems. Lost in thought, she contemplated her son, down whose face a trickle of milk was running.

After putting the child back in his cradle, she circumspectly withdrew to her own universe. Eulália was always grave and serious. Even when, at night, she walked about the bedroom in her nightdress. When I could already see in my mind's eye the secret zones, concealed by the cloth. At certain times, so self-absorbed that she forgot me. Me and my desire. What, in fact, was that woman's territory? Did she marry me out of indifference, another man serving her equally well?

On a certain occasion, Eulália hinted that if she had not seen me in the square, on that long-ago afternoon in Sobreira as she came out of church, if she had not intuited that I was there looking for the helpmeet that Galicia had to offer me, her fate would have been different. Not confessing, however, that perhaps she would have consumed the rest of her days praying, instead of distending her belly with surprising sensuality and expelling, forthwith, those six little heads by way of a tunnel through which they had painfully made their way, in search of the certainty of life on the outside.

They are all my children. Born of certain encounters that were intense and others that were casual, which Eulália and I continued in the marriage bed. That bed which is gradually being abandoned in old age, with its bored disinterest in familiar flesh, after we have hurriedly said good night to each other.

The room is large and has gay curtains. Even so, I see ashes scattered round our bodies. What we still have left are affectionate gestures. I stroke her hair, I kiss her brow, I embrace her, at once urgently and shyly. She leans her head on my shoulder and then frees herself. We are quick about it, in the lighted room. We can no longer count on the protection of the dark, with the light turned off, and on the fervor of passion. Everything was more wanton then, ready to explode. With what shamelessness the loved object was coveted!

Tobias accuses me of being merciless. Forgetting that I have long since plunged headlong into ambition and the golden horn of plenty. What else could he expect of me? Would he have wanted me to be submissive, a slave of family luxury? My son's brow has precocious furrows. Some of those marks I made with a penknife. From almost the very first he wanted to caress me and punish me at the same time. I finally showed him the way out of the house so that he would come to know the mysteries of life, on the outside, beginning the moment he walked through the door.

I am now old and short-tempered. My soul as shriveled as a dried currant. Even so I don't take anything lying down. I learned to protest once I became certain that life was only a brief flash of lightning. And I was quite certain. The proof of that is my body, which can't perform anymore. I feel my genital organ, which gave me a fullness of being in the past, and I note that it has shrunk over the years. A sad spectacle, from which I do not avert my eyes. I slowly soap my body, smelling of perfume all over. This member, once a friend and burning with passion, just barely responds, it has a slight erection, it wanly remembers bygone feats of prowess and grows cold. Is this the sign of death?

On every hand I witness manifestations of this enemy who bears a scythe, a hammer, pincers, an instrument of torture. Does death need that many devices merely to strike us down? Doesn't life take it upon itself to destroy us first, thus sparing death the burden of carrying out an ignoble task?

Eulália was smiling, as though expecting this visitor. A strange creature, this woman of my life! But hadn't those other women been strangers too, the ones who granted me pleasure, happiness, fond hopes, sentiments originating, almost all of them, in my sperm, my heart, my dreaming? My dreaming above all, which kept its distance, just out of our reach, laughing, never materializing?

Contrary to my plans, they flung Breta on my doorstep. She came to me as a little girl, when life was giving out on me. I could scarcely breathe. My granddaughter helped me to overcome the agony. From the beginning, I saw the defiance in her eyes. I clung to her then so as to make Esperança's knife thrust in my breast more bearable.

Today, it's different. Life more or less dismissed me. In a moment of serious withdrawal, Breta arrives. She stays on with me. With her sitting close beside me, we sometimes spend the whole afternoon in silence. Her presence touches my heart. Breta brings life back to me once again, and I call to mind timeworn scenes that return now with another dimension. I raise my eyes, I try to say certain words to her, some of them as thin as gruel. What do words say, after all, in the fervor of pain and happiness?

Breta fights against any sort of surrender. She refuses to allow me to inventory possessions or indiscriminately bequeath memories, buildings, factories, stocks, bank accounts to enemies and friends alike.

"Very well, Breta, now that you've raised my morale, tell me what I'm to take with me in the hour of my death." We both smile.

Breta knocks on the door of the house expecting that this will be her last visit. That all of a sudden I will no longer be there to receive her. And that she'll find herself obliged to pile me into the family vault, along with the other dead. Knowing how much I've suffered because I wasn't able to save little Bento from the waters of the Atlantic. The same ocean that set me to dreaming and allowed the spirit of adventure to take my beloved son from me with one sharp blow.

Because of all this, Breta visits me every day. And when she goes off on a trip, she writes long letters. Like the ones she sent me from her exile in Paris. On edge and all by herself, Breta, in those days, voiced her nonconformity. Though she was not the only Brazilian to roam from one embassy to another, one country to another, seeking refuge. All of them having left Brazil with marks of violence on their bodies and minds. Breta too had left in very low spirits. Her dejection, glimpsed in her letters, hinted at the dense shadow that weighed heavily upon her from the moment another day dawned.

In the beginning, her letters arrived in odd, roundabout ways, in her concern to hide from the censors the words welling up from a wounded and disappointed heart. I reread them till far into the night, all by myself in the study.

"The city is beautiful, grandfather. Autumn imparts its gentle melancholy to the trees. So I'm deeply moved. Because beauty is constraining, and my heart begins to pound. There's a dog in my heart, wailing in the backyards of little Brazilian villages, on moonlit nights. What pity I have for those tiny towns, seen at a distance now. All of them dispirited, disconsolate, with nothing to look forward to but growing old and wasting away!

Am I perhaps a cat cautiously creeping across roofs covered with tiles made by Brazilian hands in my country's factories? Those hands I understand above all others? I who am searching for love! But whom to love, grandfather? If love, in its eagerness to offer an exhaustive description of the body of another, in the end requires the use of the luminous intensity of my own language. Isn't it true that if we don't whisper that language, treacherous and tricky at times, lust may simply cheat us? Does having everything suddenly deprive us of reaching full ripeness?

Forgive me such trivia, grandfather. Which I may regret someday. In the end we inevitably box ourselves in with ashen, almost wintry signs. Determined to speak by halves, for that too is a language.

I remember, this minute, my first visit to Paris. You, grandmother, and I, when I was still a little girl. I showed my resentment at having left Sobreira that week. Life in Galicia had come to be more intense thanks to the adventures shared with Adélia and Nemésio. Even today I have no idea which of them I loved more intensely. I was scarcely aware of Paris, caught up as I was in the memory of rugged rocks, hills, animals. In Sobreira I had been making a sovereign journey that took me into the heart of ancestors and myths, unconsciously bringing to light the origin of the Portuguese language.

There, along with the sheep's milk, the corn bread, the peppers fried in oil, I had my genesis within reach of my hand, throbbing like a bird. Peopled with hostile, unruly, aggrieved forebears, who nonetheless spread the legend of the search for the Holy Grail throughout Europe. One of the Galician stories stolen to enrich the international repertory. Or was it the legend of Amadís?

I remember that Grandmother was wearing blue that morning. The breeze lightly lifted the hem of her skirt. Grandmother was embarrassed because people had seen her legs. As for you, you merely smiled. Perhaps it pleased you to have your wife's body bared for public appraisal. Or did you prefer to keep her for yourself and devour her in private?

Here I go again with my irreverence, grandfather. But if I don't look you straight in your bright blue eyes sparkling with energy, which confer on the world what you judge to be lacking, how can I prove I'm your granddaughter? Your exiled granddaughter! But am I really in exile or was I brought to Paris only through the imprudence of being young? Hence deserving of vile extermination?

We had awakened early. The light filtered through the window revived our enthusiasm. We immediately sipped the delicious coffee. Amused by the jelly, made from blackberries gathered in the Alps, sprinkled with a bit of sugar by the hand of a peasant from Savoy, a sad and disconsolate land.

Near the Arc de Triomphe, the city suddenly seemed to us to be outside of time. Grandmother went off somewhere without telling us. She was a long time coming back. The only thing left for us to do was revolve round our own precarious axes so as not to lose all count of the number of avenues. And not forget a single one of them. Eulália returned with her face beaming.

'Is everything all right?' you asked, thereby giving her the few moments absolutely necessary for her to veil the emotion her face was announcing against her will.

Eulália spoke of the dead. She had halted before the nameless tombs, trying to sketch in the details of modest biographies. Those dead that the abstract memory of the people and the visits of statesmen were celebrating by bringing flowers.

I think Grandmother said: 'What I mean is, in the past those dead breathed in the smell of stables, of fields, of smoking-hot platters!'

Could I be imagining things, grandfather? I know that enigmatic Eulália so little. Always kind and gentle, she forgos brusque gestures. However, after hugging and kissing me a number of times, she left me with the exhausting feeling that I'd taken a train trip, a plane trip, and gone nowhere. Have I no idea how she reacts to intimate contact, so close to her armpits? Did she willingly permit pieces of her body to be torn away, thus offering proofs that passion intoxicates and injures humanity?

Don't get the idea she has hurt my feelings. The problem centers on her mystic vocation, which makes her deaf to all my claims on her attention. While the reality within me is suffocating, Eulália finds sustenance in a faith that allows us to forgo following her example. So she believes, in our name. And fashions God after our dream. Can she really expect that this will remove the excesses of human passion?

Please don't let Eulália read this letter. I don't want to hurt her needlessly. If she's decided to bet on faith, a faultless product of her god, I respectfully bow to her blinding credulity. Who can say whether, one day, if I contemplate it with exactly the same faith, I may not find that passion leads to the text? This text becoming the field where the dead and memories are buried. The specific locale of the battles and the stories that must be told. By wielding the scalpel of criticism, memory, and every sort of insolent affection. See you soon, grandfather. Your granddaughter, Breta."

Breta changed addresses constantly. Confronting the city with her suitcase and the modest belongings on her back. She chose neighborhoods where life spewed forth disturbingly. All the apartments without a telephone. Thus making it difficult for us to reach her immediately.

Hence coming to learn of our deaths with a delay that would spare her the task of burying us. Whereas I demanded that her tears coincide with ours. So that exile would not keep her from closely following our story. Above all the story of this country that I had loved since Galicia. Not suspecting, then, that Brazil would drive from its door someone of my blood. Forcing Breta to cross the Atlantic in the opposite direction, returning to Europe with her soul in mourning.

"Can it be that not even Breta's exile makes you see that a sort of civil war is taking place in Brazil today? Through the sole fault of this military dictatorship?" Venâncio said bitterly.

"Don't put it so dramatically, man. You've struggled with history books for so long you've lost the ability to judge present facts. You're inventing a war where there's nothing more than a conflict. The only thing you've forgotten is to mail Breta a hero's medal."

Venâncio didn't press the point. Eulália, however, joined us.

"Why don't you go see Breta? Take one of the children with you. And from Paris you can go to Sobreira."

"It's too soon still, Eulália."

I would not visit my granddaughter without her permission. On the other hand, I went too far in my letters, trying to play on her heartstrings. Who could tell? She might ask me to come.

"If money is in short supply there in that damned country, Breta, note down figures, amounts, and let me know how much you'd need in order to have a comfortable place to stay, with a telephone in your room, preferably on your bedside table. That way we'll be able to reach you around daybreak, when you're sure to be home."

I sent Breta one check after another, whereupon she accused me of overdoing it. She immediately sensed that Grandfather was suborning her through generosity. Or trying to rule her life so as to tie her down in the street and apartment that suited him.

Confronted with Breta's stubborn silence, I sent her a cable: Respect your unbending desire not to know day hour my burial stop receiving such news one week late matter of no importance stop love stop Madruga.

In her answering letter, Breta did not mention the cable. She simply sent on her new address and the telephone number. She made it clear, however, that she still wanted no visitors.

Breta's days followed one upon the other unmarked by dramatic events. Her daily routine was cautious and unobtrusive. She attended classes at the university regularly, the discipline of studying doing her good. She had friends now, though she did not reveal their names. Names compromised the individuals designated and the one who named them.

She slowly tested the ground beneath her feet in this French territory. Most of all she liked cooking at home. The use of various seasonings in food served to pique her imagination. Each day she noted the difference between the present restrictions and the comforts of home. But she appreciated the absolute anonymity. No one watching her on the street, one face among many. Having no one to turn to for help.

Breta's polite letters irritated Miguel. He expressed his dissatisfaction in the crudest terms: And love, Breta, isn't it burning down the walls of that sacred China?

She vehemently denied him the right to decide her life. Her mysteries became sacred only as a function of the quality with which they were invested. A privilege inherent in everyone. She too recognized that she was tied to human stakes by means of any number of different ropes. A circus could even be set up on top of her, with a vast ring. Because of all the foregoing, she begged her uncle not to clip her wings. She did not want to take shelter in the shadow of what seemed fundamental to her. Being careful, nonetheless, not to lose herself in excessive abstractions, volatile states that she had seen her grandmother resort to. And precisely because of the poetic vision she had of the universe, she demanded of herself daily doses of reality. A realism close to being deceptive and despotic.

Walking along the street, in winter, Breta warmed her hands against the bread just out of the oven. Retracing the probable trajectory of that wheat, so as to bring about in it a transcendence superior to the act of chewing. Household tasks, in turn, were of great value. Through them she situated herself in human society. When her hands were busy she did not feel subject to the physical weakness that comes from having nothing but books to struggle with.

She never mentioned a probable affair of the heart born in Paris and strengthened in solitude and abandonment. Nor did I ask her questions that would plunge us into discord. Miguel was piqued at her because there were so many private memories between them. And because he in particular had privileged antennas for sensing another person's passion, even in a latent state. Was it not true that he himself was leading, at every moment, a most disorderly life? Able, therefore, to tell us who Breta was, her body white and intense, demanding the right to be modern as a way of rejecting archaic passion, which ravages the sacred space of its desire. Who could know, then, how would we know with whom she is making mutual confession: I love you, I desire you, I lust for you. Before whom does she tremble and shiver with fever in a garret reminding us of Puccini's Bohème?

Waiting for Breta's letters, hoping for an invitation to come. Breta rejected all appeals from Brazil. No longer asking questions as to when it would be safe for her to return. Exile was ceasing to be a barb raking her chest each morning. She felt herself to be, like her grandfather, an immigrant. Unlike her fellow exiles, who had not had an immigrant in the family back home to look to as an example. Hence not having been brought up in a way that would prepare them to lose, in one fell swoop, Brazil, the language, the feelings, the landscape, to divest themselves of intangible goods. They had always been Brazilians through and through, the native-born of a country without a tradition of expelling its patriots. A country whose nature, vast and bounteous, spared them the bitter taste and the humiliation of having to scrounge a plate of food beyond their homeland's borders. Never bearing on their foreheads the mark of the immigrant.

At the end of her second year in Paris, Breta wanted to rest in Sobreira. Our meeting must take place, above all, with the rugged Galician mountains as a backdrop.

In Madrid, she embraced me with heartfelt emotion. Observing with one quick glance the havoc wrought upon my body. The obvious aging that she had not followed closely in those two years.

In the Prado, Bosch's painting again aroused her apprehensions. It pointed to Brazil, nonexistent at the time for the painter, as the central theme of the demoniacal contortions of its figures. Creatures crying out the contradictory human condition, amid bared viscera and unbridled lust. At a far remove from her country, it nonetheless was the point of departure of her sharpened perceptions of it. As meanwhile I did not scruple to steal from her the wisdom that dwelt in her instinctively. Simply by right of birth and through her having devoted herself to the chinks and crevices of language, from her first hours as a babe at her mother's breast.

"The spoken word is also the virus of language. It sometimes brings on fever and swelling," she said with satisfaction.

Sitting opposite the Plaza Mayor, we drank a transparent claret. Breta kindly offered answers to questions that I did not dare put into words.

"And how was your birthday, grandfather? How did you feel, that close to the square marked seventy?"

"Old and forlorn," I smiled.

"And how is Venâncio?"

"We meet every Sunday. And every Sunday he takes Tobias farther away from me."

"What did you expect? Tobias loves Venâncio, because he can't forgive you for his owing you a life that you ask him to pay for every single day. Why are you so demanding with him, grandfather?"

"Are you accusing me of squeezing the life out of those who love me?"

The lighting effects of the afternoon sun radiated across the square. That splendid setting which for centuries has served as a place for the crowd to love and to betray, with equal intensity. Through it were passing, and had passed, a people who had raised a glass to the most shameful sentiments, amid which a transcendent passion nonetheless arose. With this lesson before me, even Breta could not goad me into fighting. Moreover, there was now rising, through my anklebones, through my joints, a magic energy that Sobreira was beaming my way from afar.

"It's simple, grandfather. Venâncio is a radical. For him, the winner, in principle, is a killer of dreams and feelings. And so, bearing a stigma like that, this same winner sacrifices almost anything, as suits his purposes. Venâncio, however, doesn't accept a cut-and-dried situation. He's chosen to take his vengeance. How? Well, by constantly opposing the winner's advances. And to do so, always wearing the sad, dingy mask of defeat. That way, he becomes a burden on the conscience of the person he wants to get even with. Moreover, grandfather, Venâncio managed to show Tobias the fascinating attraction of his game, based on pathological pride alone. And so he displays the arrogant hauteur of those who withdraw into themselves out of total contempt for the human banquet. I ask you: isn't that quite a temptation? How could you beat him at his game?"

We were to stay five days in Madrid. To see certain landscapes once again, and in particular to breathe in the spirit of Teresa of Ávila. Surrounded by walls, Ávila, undaunted, offered us the earthly domain of Saint Teresa.

As we entered the city, Breta leaned on my arm. I felt the comfort of that presence. And in an effort to draw closer to Teresa's circle of fire, she began to describe the anxieties of her generation.

"But what generation is it you're speaking of?" I interrupted Breta, in a vehement tone of voice. "To judge from the way you're talking, your generation has only one face. Your face, the face of your class, the face of Rio de Janeiro. Better yet, of Ipanema."

Breta gave a conciliatory smile. Not intending, however, to be indulgent. She explained that, though she indeed belonged to a privileged minority, she was nonetheless still capable of acting outside the limits of her social class.

"If we formed a single face, grandfather, we'd be a defeated generation before we even began to fight."

"Beware, Breta, beware of the arrogant pride of being young."

The portrait of Teresa of Ávila, dimly lit, within a heavy frame, did not allow one to examine her features closely. I was reminded of Eulália, which forced me to ponder the question of whether Teresa's love for God had dispensed with human mediation. And whether Teresa, in the exercise of charismatic leadership, had given God such proofs of her love that she had made little effort to attract men's attention so as to be able to count on them to testify to her glory, a phenomenon in and of itself impossible to resist given the rules of her time.

Breta was all excited. She immediately imagined what the first meeting between Teresa and the austere Philip II, the master of the West, had been like. A Philip tormented at that point by the certainty that the active forces of the Mediterranean were beginning to weaken Spain. And consequently, driving his kingdom toward the Atlantic. Their only way out being to take the perilous course leading to the new lands.

Once Teresa was admitted to the king's presence, he bade the future saint be seated. His eyes undoubtedly beamed forth a cold flame, intended to defeat her. Teresa cloaked the battle about to be joined beneath a broad smile. One who spoke with God, as she did, could boldly confront any human majesty. In the end, that king too was destined to die. Was he not shortly to breathe his last in the Escorial, the palace that his own death, already taking on substance within him, yearned to frequent? So that Philip would thus approach his future death throes with limited resources?

And that in fact was how it was, as though Teresa had foreseen everything at that meeting. Philip headed for the palace, melancholy and dispirited. Doubtless fearful of becoming attached to the outsized dimensions of a room that he had ordered built with the intention of there awaiting death.

It had the form of an open gallery, overlooking the great inner courtyard. And from it there could be seen, from any angle, the royal chapel, for his use alone, on a landing below.

Lying down finally in his bed, Philip, thanks to the aforementioned architectonic design, and provided that he kept his head propped up with high pillows, was able to follow the celebration of the Mass as he lay dying. An office into which he had introduced, by dint of his power and the force of his austere imagination, certain new rituals.

During the frugal repast, Breta pursued the task of merging the present and the past, through Teresa and Philip. Now and again resembling Venâncio, after the war had ended. Except that she dragged the runaway Teresa from one end of the world to the other.

"All you have to do now is transplant iron-willed Teresa and her seductive charms to Ipanema. Except that you forgot to give us an account of the dialogue between Teresa and Philip II."

"What could I have told you? We have never learned exactly what they said to each other so that the one would not be awed by the glory of the other. But it would appear that when they separated they were reconciled," Breta said.

In the night train to Vigo, we awoke at four in the morning. Waiting for the train, nervously making its way along the razor-edged rails, to invade Galicia with its mournful whistle.

"Wake up, grandfather. We're about to enter Galician territory. The passage is so imperceptible we may not even notice," she said anxiously.

Our faces glued to the window, we heard the train puffing. The silence accentuating the night sounds. Inside the car, we too were shaking all over.

"We've arrived, grandfather! We've set foot in Galicia. I'm sure of it. Anyone born right now in this car would be Galician, just as you are," she exclaimed, her voice filled with emotion.

Our faces pressed to the glass, we could almost lick the drops of mist that the windowpane drank in. The fog cut off our view of the outside world. It was hard to tell where we were. But I had the feeling that Breta knew exactly. Out there was Galicia. The mystery of its legends, of its sentiments, of its language penetrated the train, to give us fair warning.

"I can sense Brazil too with my eyes closed, grandfather. By the odor, perhaps, which is unmistakable. How to forget the smell of the dung of a cow from São Lourenço! Wherever I might be, I could identify the green of our countryside. A thatched hut, with a solitary wisp of smoke coming from it. What sort of feeling is this, grandfather, at once so wonderful and so wanton?" Breta veiled her face, to hide herself from view.

Breta, however, knew how to take advantage of the freedom to love two lands, without thereby living the life of someone labeled an expatriate. A resentful creature, for whom the world is eternally divided into two halves.

From the dining car, now that it was light, we finally saw the landscape. The coffee revived us. Breta went through her usual ritual of observing the nearby tables, looking for the face that would move her.
Sensitive to a human presence, she was intimately aware of the power of
the fleeting encounter, the exchange of lightning-quick glances, capable of
poisoning her memory.

She was wearing jeans and a white blouse. Her hair close-cropped,
free and shining. Her hands exactly like Esperança's. I always avoided
looking at them.

Her thoughts seemed to be elsewhere now. Had she suddenly gone
back to Brazil or Paris? Perhaps returning to some room or other where
recently she had been intimately acquainted with a delicate fabric that
answered to the name of felicity. When there had then taken place a rupture that had made her eager to shatter even the objects on her night table,
the same objects that had witnessed the holocaust of her desire.

"Breta," I said, my feelings hurt. She paid no attention. Jealous of
those intense sentiments, I thought, Why has she summoned me to Europe, if only to banish me from her company?

The train slowed down so as to make its solemn entry into the station.
The Vigo platform thereupon immediately overrun by passengers and luggage. Breta took me by the hand, communicating her youth to me. She
was the one who made the decisions. She did not want to stay even one
night in the city. And so it was that we hurriedly made our way from one
side of Pontevedra to the other, like fugitives. Heading for Sobreira, where
we would be greeted by a clean house, a lighted fire, everything ready and
waiting to welcome us.

"This time, grandfather, I want to have Dom Miguel's room. May I?"

She summoned up with pleasure the phantom whom Eulália thought
of as a living being. Capable, like none other, of anticipating the thoughts
and acts that would please Eulália. One time, Dom Miguel went so far as
to guarantee her that as long as his daughter was in Sobreira on a visit,
there would not be a single wake in the house.

"I won't die while you're my guest. I swear to be immortal, my
daughter," he said, his mind at ease. After all, it would be impolite of him
to oblige her to go into mourning amid the festivities to celebrate her
presence in the house.

With firm faith in these words, Eulália moved calmly about the house.
Certain that death would not prowl about outside her window in those
months in Galicia. And she had only to arrive on a visit for her father, with
a simple gesture, to renew his vows automatically. Thus observing certain
ceremonies between them from which everyone else was banished, including me.

I never took offense. I never belonged, in fact, to those walls. I was
duty-bound not to forget, despite my present affluence, that I had come

from Xan's house, so unlike that one, beginning with its modest façade, the opposite of Dom Miguel's, a prosperous one with a certain romantic air.

When a guest of Dom Miguel's, I constantly went off to visit Xan's old house. I would lock myself in there, after banishing the caretaker from the room. I would remain for hours at the foot of the fireplace. Recalling in silence the stories of the clever and resourceful Xan. And as I inspected hiding places full of memories, I felt I was bidding them farewell another time.

This retreat, however, had the merit of renewing my strength. Even Eulália acknowledged that I came back a new man. And wanting to prove that she had not forgotten things confided to her in the past, she would repeat on these occasions:

"And is your secret still intact, Madruga?"

I nodded. She smiled back, showing no sign of displeasure at not being a party to this very secret.

Very early in the morning, Breta knocked on the door of my room. To have breakfast with me. At the table, I noted that she had shed her Parisian air. She wanted to look like a peasant. She would pay the mountains a visit. Full of energy, she planned to follow the goat trails, sidling past the gorse bushes.

"Good luck, Breta. May Galicia always deal gently with you."

She was late coming back. Just in time to have lunch together. Afterward, I asked her to accompany me. It was a pressing matter now. Death was coming on the sly and Breta needed to be my memory.

"Where are we going, grandfather?"

"To Xan's house, where I was born."

"Do you really want me to go with you?" She was feeling me out. She was afraid I would lose my nerve at the last minute. And would banish her from those domains.

"Yes, this time, I do. The hour has come for you to know my Galician anchor. Time has long since corroded it. Except that it's corroded not with saltpeter but with dust."

Xan's old room looked timeworn and far away to me. But still familiar. After all, I had gone out into the world from these walls. Yet the words of Urcesina, Ceferino, Xan, and Teodora echoed still in hidden nooks and crannies. I could almost hear the murmur of their voices. The odor that came from the pots on the stove, as Urcesina threw essences and products of the soil into them.

Sitting around the oak table, cracked now and full of irregular bumps and creases, Breta and I were in no hurry. Haste led nowhere. No gesture of my granddaughter's made me feel in debt to her. Imbedded permanently in that scene, Breta bore a certain likeness to an old woman with whom I had shared the experience of discovering America for the first time, more than fifty years before.

The chair at the end of the table was Grandfather Xan's. It was never fought over. And, to his left, sat Ceferino. My father's helpless gaze, often not knowing where to alight, would finally end up fixing itself on the ceiling. Expecting, no doubt, that Urcesina would scold him. And when this in fact happened, it was as though Ceferino could breathe freely again. Immediately devoting himself to small tasks about the house, which were now being miraculously brought back to life by Breta's presence here with me. Memory making the dead flow again like a mighty river.

"I felt no fear on the eve of my escape to America. I kept asking myself, during that week, what abandoning a country and a family might mean. Overbearing pride had always blinded me. That's why Venâncio, even today, accuses me of provoking my enemies for the sheer pleasure of it. But when all is said and done, what enemies do I have outside of the enmities lodged within my breast? Except that Urcesina never suspected that my departure from Sobreira would be founded on falsehood, deceit, underhandedness. And if she had her doubts, she preferred to keep them to herself. She thought that in that way I would one day come back tougher and stronger, thanks to my lies. However, at the dinner table on the very night that I took flight, Urcesina stared at me intently several times. Without reprimands or chastisements. Perhaps because she knew that the destiny of Galicians was to become expatriates, even with no guarantee of returning home. And that I would go simply because thousands had gone before me. What was more, Uncle Justo's defeat, in Brazil, did not necessarily mean that the sign of surrender haunted our house. Destiny, for example, had defeated Ceferino, without his even needing to leave home. Moreover, through harsh gestures my mother constantly made him pay for his rejection of life. And on top of that, there had been a succession of dreams and plans regarding America that miscarried. Yet even so my mother would not give me a single penny so that I could survive in that inhospitable America. This land that admits us first as enemies, forgives us for the affront of our visit only in the hour of our burial. But could my mother in fact have failed to perceive that she would lose me the next day, that ten years would go by before she saw me again? Or did she sense that letters would have to suffice in order to deaden the pain of my absence?"

Breta listened attentively to me. With an anxious look in her eyes. Afraid she might suddenly interrupt the flow of my confessions.

"At dinner, Urcesina offhandedly passed me a generous chunk of corn bread. I always liked to crumble bread in my soup to make it more substantial. This typical peasant combination managed to fill my belly. Could she have given me a bigger piece that night just because the ritual of farewells had already begun? I for my part lacking the wisdom to understand the generosity and encouragement that my mother, drawing back the curtain before my eyes, disclosed to me by her simple gesture?"

Breta headed for the kitchen. With a sure hand she poured coffee beans into the mill. The teeth of the machine ground away, releasing an intense fragrance. She moved naturally about the house. The coffee was immediately sipped with appreciation. I noticed her impatience with my account. She doubtless wanted me to be carried away with emotion, to loosen my tongue, disclosing material she needed in order to understand my story. A story automatically impoverished when told by me and my contemporaries. But wasn't it possible that Breta was a member of that sect that listens to everything, observes everything, reorganizes everything, with the intention of preserving and restoring reality by way of the written word?

Urcesina and Ceferino never drew up a will indicating who would inherit the house after their deaths. In this way they kept their hold over their children, waiting to see who would come into that little inheritance, till the end of their days. When it came time to divide the estate, I was able to arrange to purchase the house immediately. I thus bought its ghosts, its furniture, and its memories. A house that had been unoccupied for all those years. Only the neighbor, given the job of keeping it clean, ever came to see it. As for me, I kept it just as it had been before. I never allowed changes to be made to modernize it, with freezing-cold bathrooms defacing its tradition. Or a tiled kitchen, from which the odor and the traces of food made by Urcesina would be eliminated forever. The house taking on, on the other hand, a look of prosperity that it had never had during the time we lived there. It had always been the house of a Galician peasant like Ceferino, Xan, or Xan's father or grandfather, whom no one ever spoke of. A succession of ungrateful creatures who had neglected to bequeath us their story. They had spread themselves over the earth like manure.

Breta made herself comfortable next to the hearth. She pulled the chair over carefully, not wanting to scratch the wood floor that time, however, had taken on the job of wearing away. I appreciated her treading those boards demeaned by neglect and human absence. This was my beloved granddaughter, who gave me a bitter conscience so as to enable me still to grow in my old age. But what had I brought her as my contribution?

"Ten years later, I returned to Sobreira. Urcesina was waiting for me on the doorstep. She clasped me in a rigid, inhospitable embrace, befitting the spirit of the land. And she immediately began examining me, attempting to discover where I had failed, despite my air of a winner. She immediately sensed her son's vanity. Had I forgotten that even though Urcesina and Ceferino were poor, in Sobreira they were sovereign rulers? There, in that place, both enjoyed the fruits of their own culture, within the house and without. In that domain Castile had not beaten us. They had refused to yield in any way, shape, or form to the trend toward modernism, which had now reached Galicia through the influence of Madrid. In all those years, they still ate corn bread, bacon from royally fattened pigs, went on with their archaic labor of tilling the soil. She very nearly confessed that they hadn't yet been robbed of happiness and the right to kiss the person who invaded their dreams, whenever, at the cornhusking bee in the farmyard, a bright red ear suddenly turned up, a cause for celebration and a minute's rest.

Urcesina was pitiless. Almost the moment I arrived, she reintroduced me straightway to the local habits. The very first morning, she dragged me out of bed at a very early hour. Even if I had come to visit them from so far away, I must go by Sobreira time now. Surely there were things I must do. She couldn't believe that I had crossed the Atlantic, coming the opposite way this time, just to rest in Sobreira. I still hadn't made good in Brazil. And the truth of that was quite evident, for I rarely sent them any financial help. This being the case, I should be off to the fields, the village square, and the church. And begin making the prize catches I intended to take back to America with me.

Urcesina eyed her son anxiously, to discover what sort of man America had made of him.

"Now that you've been to America, we won't put up with a single downcast look from you. Don't make us remember the defeated of Sobreira. They're ugly, and cringe when they look at you. They remind me of oxen with crushed testicles."

My mother was given to contradiction. She received her son with affection, while at the same time she drove him from the house. Not wanting him between four walls, looking at her. She had raised her sons only to lose them.

Moreover, on the Christmas before this first trip, a neighbor delivered to me, in Rio, a photograph of Urcesina, taken in Pontevedra. My mother assured me straightway, in the accompanying letter, that there was no other copy of that photo. She purposely wanted me to be the only one of her children to have that expression of her in his possession. An expression inspired by her American son, for it was he that Urcesina thought of during the sitting at the photographer's, for which she readied herself with unusual care.

She arrived in Pontevedra at daybreak, bringing with her in a knapsack her new dress, made of a length of material that had been a present from her son. She did not want her husband to come with her. Once in the studio, she retired behind the screen. She first removed the dust of the journey, washed her face, combed her hair. After changing clothes, she did not forget the mantilla that she kept for feast days. Putting it round her shoulders, she combed her hair again. Having decided this time to pull her hair severely back, catching it up in a tortoiseshell comb, so as to set off her hooked nose, a family feature. In this way her son would see in the portrait words never noted in a letter.

At the sight of the photograph, I tried to make out what Urcesina's intentions had been in sending me a present so contrary to her nature. What was she hinting at, above and beyond confronting her son with domestic culture, represented there by the woman?

The photograph was a fair-sized one, deserving to be framed. Days later, I hung it on the wall of the hotel room where I was living. Urcesina's eyes, watching me from the photograph, still gleamed, with a brightness enhanced by the slight sepia tint of the paper. But what exactly was she trying to tell her son? What message did the woman have to pass on?

During that week he asked her one question after another, in the hope of finding his bearings. Was his mother hinting that the moment had come to get married? And that he shouldn't choose a Brazilian woman? Who was there who in his heart did not have Celtic roots? It thus seemed to him to be impossible to solve the riddle of Urcesina's dream. There was only one way of knowing, to go personally to Sobreira, to look deep into her sharp eagle eyes.

"I know very well that this house is going to fall into ruins immediately once I'm dead, Breta. Who except me looks after its shades and memories? At the same time I suspect that this will be one of my last trips to Sobreira. How many years do I have left to live, I wonder?"

Breta stared at me as though asking to borrow my eyes to appreciate the house. I took her by the arm then, over to the charred fireplace. A fireplace made of stones fitted together without symmetry, with visible chinks between the places where they touched.

"I brought you here today, Breta, to learn what has always been behind my story. What has made this story pulse, take on life."

Filled with emotion, I turned her head toward the inside of the fireplace. A recess that could be entered by bending forward. With our heads colliding, I pointed to a tiny splinter of wood stuck in a chink between two stones.

"Do you see that splinter?"

Just before dawn of the day I planned to make my escape, I was suddenly beset by the feeling that I was in the process of depriving my house of essential goods, doing so merely to follow a predatory instinct, with not a care for the honor of those who dwelt therein. I saw myself, then, overtaken by fear, challenging a monster breathing fire through its nostrils, which admitted into its domain only those men selected through the enduring of dramatic hardships. An uneven battle, when all I had in my favor was my tender age and faith. A faith that might well be exhausted in a week in America.

I hurriedly arose, not having slept a single minute. I had my knapsack with my belongings all ready. Without a sound, hugging the walls, I reached the hearth. Kneeling there, I began to sharpen the end of a little stick of wood with my penknife, a present from Grandfather Xan. Finally choosing where to thrust the splinter between two stones so that it couldn't be seen.

By that act, I signed a pact. As long as the wood withstood storms, hidden in that place chosen by me to be the heart of Sobreira, my heart too would keep beating regularly in America. Even if undergoing the impact of the passion that Brazil might demand of it for having defied its borders.

The splinter penetrated deep within the crack, there being nothing left outside but a minute head, nearly invisible. At the time, I asked the gods never to pluck it from there. That would mean my defeat. The sliver of wood, withstanding time, would serve as proof that I was still alive. And bearing the stigma of victory.

On making my escape from the house, feeling my way along in the darkness, I took this secret with me. Never shared with anyone. Not even to Eulália and Venâncio did I admit that the splinter was the symbol of my life. The key of long survival in America. One of the reasons for my afternoon visits to Xan's house, to make sure that the bit of wood was still there where I had placed it, almost sixty years before.

"When I don't find it here anymore, Breta, it will be the sign of death and failure. I know what I'm saying. That's why I think about the neighbor who comes to clean the house. He doesn't know he's dealing with chance. Or that his acts or his carelessness are part of my destiny. And that's the way it must be. It wouldn't make sense to warn him of the need to keep away from the fireplace. Not to touch it for any reason whatsoever. You're the only one now who knows of this episode. Do what you like with the knowledge. All I ask of you is that if you should come to Sobreira in the future, as soon as you have a premonition that my end is near, look for this splinter. To see if it's still in the place it is now."

Breta cherished the symbols that she had inherited from Brazil and Spain. Her blood and her imagination were indelibly impregnated by the two countries. And so, there before the hearth, she did not fear the consequences of the shared secret. On the contrary, she wanted to have a closer look at the splinter. She very nearly pulled it out, hastening my fate. Writing finis to my story.

"From today on, grandfather, I promise to watch over it. Even after your death. Though I may not inherit this enigma of yours, I can understand it better now that I know about this chip of wood," she said, deeply moved.

Returning to our chairs near the hearth, we feared that the splinter, for some mysterious reason, might suddenly work its way loose from the stones, falling at our feet. A battle between the elements of good and evil was taking place before our eyes. But we were confident we would emerge as victors. The bit of wood, consequently, not falling from where it had been buried for so many years. Buried in my heart, now beating wildly there next to Breta, the anxious heir of my secret and my human empire.

Ｔhe festivities in celebration of Tobias's birth ceased with the outbreak of the Spanish Civil War. The family immediately forgetting to pay him homage. Venâncio therefore compensating for this negligence by an excess of zeal. On Sundays, leaning over the cradle, he would repeat to his godson, in the form of a litany, expressions that no one listened to closely. Thus they drifted aimlessly in the air, till Eulália dragged Venâncio away to dinner.

From the beginning of the conflict, he wrote to his godson on Saturday nights. A note in which he set down, after patient meditation, the events having to do with the war. And though this weekly habit displeased Madruga, Venâncio sent these notes, carefully folded, flying into the cradle, not remembering that he might frighten the baby, beginning to grow.

Eulália swiftly recovered the notes. And without even reading them, she put them away in Tobias's box, foreseeing their future usefulness. As though there were a tacit agreement between Venâncio and herself to proceed in this way, in view of the disorder that the war had lodged in the hearts of all the Spaniards in the city.

Despite Madruga's insistence that he felt equal affection for all his children, Bento felt neglected at home and at school. Especially after Tobias was born. Whereupon he fell, from that time on, into the habit of anxiously smoothing his hair, as though it were disheveled, even though Madruga constantly called his attention to this tic.

Madruga had only to approach him for Bento to be overcome at times by a feeling of vertigo. To conceal his discomposure, Bento would hold himself as stiff and straight as a soldier at attention. Pruning gestures of his that might be considered excessive. He nonetheless resented the fact that he lacked both Miguel's charm and Esperança's beauty.

The presence, moreover, of that brother and sister irked him. And so, doing his best to get the inside track with Madruga, he invariably ended up choosing the wrong moment to work his way into his father's affections. Usually when Madruga's attention was absorbed in reading his newspaper. Losing all self-control, Bento would touch him on the shoulder. A touch that would make Madruga put the newspaper aside, just long enough to banish him, in no uncertain terms, from the room. Paying no attention whatsoever to his son's look of dismay.

Bento would hurriedly apologize. But Madruga, having gone back to his newspaper, was no longer listening. And Bento would go off, just as Esperança sometimes came running in, all out of breath, her face beaming. The racket attracting Madruga's attention. Prepared instantly to intercept the intruder. Especially since his face was still set, as a remembrance of Bento's passage, in an irritated grimace.

On perceiving Esperança, Madruga invited her to stay. His daughter, however, volatile by nature, almost always refused his invitations. She had other adventures awaiting her. Hurrying off, leaving Madruga alone. Without either of them noticing Bento hiding behind the door.

Bento finally caught on that he would do better to tag after Miguel and Esperança. In the hope of picking up from them a way of behaving applauded by Madruga. As he drew closer, however, to his brother and sister, they would summarily drive him out of their territory, as though sensing that Bento was about to rob them of a share of their power.

Bento took refuge then on the veranda of the house in Tijuca. At night, in summer, the lighted lamp attracted dozens of insects which immolated themselves before the intense light. Irritated by the buzzing of the insects whose wings dropped down from the lamp onto the place where he was sitting, Bento would climb up onto the chair, holding out a pan of water to the joyous flying creatures. Blindly, obediently, the insects would fall into the water, thus reducing to nothing the circle formed around the light.

After decimating half of that species, Bento would sit down, relieved, in the wicker chair. Only to perceive, immediately, the vanity of his efforts, since a new swarm, equally noisy and delicate of wing, had arrived to take the place of the insects that were dead.

Antônia came to comfort him. He did not want her company. Unless she kept quiet. He took pleasure in subjecting his sister to the same punishment that he had suffered at his father's hand.

It was already getting late when Eulália, with a voice and gestures that sounded impersonal to him, would suggest that he get some rest. He would obey listlessly. Whereas the presence of Madruga on the veranda, where his father came to finish his cigar, galvanized him. He would begin to listen to him with grave interest. Although Madruga, at times, betrayed his lack of discipline in dealing with certain subjects, making it difficult for him to understand. He intuited, then, his feelings hurt, that his father acted in that way in order to keep him from offering comments. Since his stories, though unfolded in full view of everyone, were of his authorship alone.

"When will we go to Sobreira, father?" he asked, to please him.

Madruga contemplated him with a smile, but as his father looked straight back at him, he felt himself to be before a stranger.

"I often wonder whether I've ever really managed to leave Sobreira."

This unexpected confidence of his father's, the very first to exist between them, provoked a happy state in Bento. With a lightness of heart rare in him, he moved toward him. So impetuously that Madruga drew back. The brief enchantment between them being broken immediately. Forcing Madruga to return to reality. A reality represented by the house, this son, the buzzing of the insects darting in the cruel summer, amid a heat so intense they could scarcely breathe.

"It will be hard to take all the children at once. And besides, I wouldn't want to leave the house empty. To give the impression that we won't ever be coming back to Brazil," he said evasively.

This sentence distressed Bento. He immediately suspected Madruga's intentions, that he already had the name of a child in mind for the next trip. Perhaps he was thinking of taking Esperança, who enjoyed the right to new adventures. Or Miguel, so that his son could confirm at first hand, there in Sobreira, the truth of the stories and legends recounted by Eulália.

Unresigned to the fact that his father might be favoring Miguel, he was eager to wrest the name of his future traveling companion from him. For lack of courage, however, he brought up another subject, hoping that his father, in the course of the conversation, would go back to the one left hanging in the air. To his disappointment, Madruga, with a visible expression of relief, went on to other subjects, nimbly putting an end to his son's fleeting hopes.

Bento had, however, the advantage of having his energies restored by a night's sleep. Ready to sally forth to wage other battles that eventually would win Madruga over. To that end, he eagerly downed his breakfast, calling for fruit and lots of milk. He was strengthening all his flanks. In the long run Madruga would be obliged to forget his preference for Miguel and Esperança. On getting up from the table, Bento foresaw victory in the hours to come. Until he discovered once again that he had been defeated.

On Sundays, in those years, on striking a balance of his progress in several areas, he was distressed to see how little there was on the credit side. Reacting rapidly, however, he discounted his own predictions. He might well be exaggerating, in his own disfavor. Thus failing to perceive how much Madruga loved him.

His father's voice, firm and commanding, shattered his dreams. A voice never broken by an inflection that sounded loving to him. As Madruga opened his blue eyes wide, his way of keeping his son in line. Bento resisted this examination by adopting the posture and appearance of someone older. So as to be respected more readily. In the shops, he chose somber, dark-colored suits. And he had restricted his youthful movements, as though his years weighed heavily upon him.

Except that he could not manage to overcome his scorn for Venâncio. Doing his best always to avoid his kindly embrace. Resentful of his father's friendship for a derelict, who frequented Madruga's table despite the fact that he condemned his methods of conquest. And whose rebellious gaze never ceased to criticize his growing prosperity.

Bento sounded Eulália out as to the origin of these Sunday visits. His mother did not notice his animosity. She took pleasure in explaining to him that America had become possible for Madruga only because of the fact that he'd come with Venâncio, both brought here on the same English ship.

Bento was not convinced. His mother seemed naïve and inconsistent to him. After all, countless batches of immigrants had arrived in Brazil in a steady stream at the turn of the century. The majority coming from the Iberian and Italian peninsulas. All of them, incidentally, piled one atop the other in filthy boats, reeking of vomit and the smell of the sea. In that one space, roaming the waves, they traded impressions, dreams, and fears. These ephemeral friendships, inspired by misery, were not to prove eternally useful, however. Or even to last for very long. As soon as they disembarked, each one went his own way. They forgot their brothers in misfortune, whose fate would henceforth be ruled by chance. And therefore there was no justification for Madruga's and Venâncio's acting as they had to this very day because of a chance meeting that had bound them to each other at the beginning of the voyage. Nor for Madruga's now obliging his children to put up with Venâncio's monotonous voice endlessly repeating stories about their past, as though he were trying to revive the whole of it through the magic of his boredom and his nonconformism.

Bento was opposed to Venâncio's revolutionary fervor and his fanatical invocation of the memory of the dead. Whereas Venâncio prided himself on preaching as doctrine the discord that he and his characters maintained with reality. Bento was of a mind to flush any and all defeatist calculations from the nooks and crannies of his memory.

"I have to win, mother. I have to win," he said all of a sudden, immediately fleeing so as not to see the effect of his words.

He was always the first in his class. These qualifications accompanying him to the national law school, where he never once skipped class. Equally diligent when it came to getting to know classmates, remembering their names, he would not forget a single one of those faces. In that old building he had found his alma mater, whom he intended to ask for precious favors throughout his career.

He was counting on joining his father in business someday. But when he tried to advance the date for going to the factory, Madruga vetoed his plan. He would only allow him to come on Saturdays and holidays. Because he must invest his time in studying. Since he demanded of his sons strict intellectual accountability.

At noon, at the end of classes, Bento descended the staircase of the building, heading for the Praça da República, on the other side of the street. Amid the trees, he felt at ease. Seated on the bench, he watched the pensioners and the children. Less tense, far from heated discussions, he examined the age-old shapes of the trees, whose roots exploded on the surface, forming strange anatomies. Those trees had been planted long before his father arrived in America. The bearers, thus, of a noble antiquity in Brazil.

The squirrels in the square passed swiftly before him. Their little turned-up snouts reminded him of Antônia's nose. The memory of his sister, however, immediately grew dim and blurred, overcome as he now was by sudden fervor. As the certainty came to him that he needed urgently to sketch in rough outline a reality that would favor him, in whose service he would place himself, strictly and deliberately. And with no time to lose. Taking no further account of the effect on reality of a life in which personal choice played no role. What mattered to him most, at that moment, was a clear distinction between his individual fate and sordid collective reality, peopled with slaves and losers.

Despite the confused picture of which he found himself a part, he felt strong. Determined to fight, to avoid gordian knots, impenetrable labyrinths. He had in his favor his belonging by origin to a family of indefatigable hunters. From whom he had inherited the drive, the instinct to fight, the flair. An arsenal to be used against enemies. Even if incarnated in Miguel and Esperança. Both of them hindering his access to his father.

The leaves, sensitive to the autumn breeze refreshing the park, were falling. Bento gathered them up so as to appreciate the veins imprinted upon them, the handiwork of embroideresses. Far, however, from finding peace in an act in itself crystalline, incapable of engendering consequences, Bento was suddenly uneasy, ready to clap his jaws together to snap up what would allay his appetite. He must learn quickly to strip the meat from the bones of his prey, though in such a way that they would not notice the dexterity with which he could strip any animal of its flesh. A technique to be perfected with practice and the passage of the years. With economical gestures and the employment of clever tactics.

In the quiet of the garden, Bento imagined a chessboard on which white and black pieces moved, ladies and gentlemen intermingled, obeying his instincts as a player. He began the hypothetical game by choosing white, which offered a better defense of his interests. Once the game had gone beyond the opening moves, he perceived that the enemies, without names or faces, were stubbornly deploying all across the board, paying as close attention to their moves as he was.

He hastened to reinforce the defense of his territory, trying out successive simulated attacks. In a solid position to win now, being able to anticipate moves and then carry them through without a hitch. Many of them, incidentally, inspired by a certain degree of treachery.

Confronted with the idea that it was necessary to wound his adversary, Bento recoiled in shame. But his scruples immediately vanished. He was no longer a child. He was now in his first year of law. Which put him in a position to understand that in certain circumstances it was necessary to resort to subterfuges that hypocrites considered foul play. If, in fact, he really wanted to move with self-assurance in certain salons and inner offices.

Leaving the public square, Bento made his way to the corner bar. Leaning against the counter, he ordered a ham sandwich on French bread and a glass of guaraná with ice. And even though Eulália urged him to eat lunch when he stayed on in the city in the afternoon, Bento took pleasure in observing a certain discipline and continence, mastering his appetite. Sometimes he pretended to himself that he was a poor student who must nonetheless conquer America. Like a latter-day Madruga, fighting bravely for a reality that would grant him the special privileges he dreamed of. In the name of which he would sacrifice his youth, his easy laughter. And get around the pressing need for sex, which he explored with melancholy shyness and careless indifference.

Going to his father's factory on a normal business day was an adventure for him. His father's welcome was unpredictable. Arriving there, he would head directly for his father's office, sweeping past the secretary without a word. After knocking on the door he would go in, locking it after him. Thus making certain that not one hostile word of his father's would pass through the walls. He couldn't bear the thought that the office clerks would fail to see that he was Madruga's favorite son.

When Madruga went too far, a swift hug was his way of offering Bento his apologies. Without the least sign, however, of genuine remorse. Madruga was most reluctant to admit his own failings. This weakness of his encouraging Bento to confront him, just to arouse in his father a sense of guilt that in the end would accrue in his favor.

Suspecting that this was his son's tactic, Madruga would dive into the paperwork on his desk, after complaining of Bento's presence at the factory without invitation. Bento would retreat to one corner of the room, giving anyone who might come in the impression that he was there to relieve his father of his workload.

From there, he would begin watching his father with an appraising eye. Madruga was growing older with the same cool daring that had fascinated Bento since he'd been a little boy. A man who scarcely slept and was rarely found at home. Giving evidence of a vitality that Bento saw as the equal of that of cowboy heroes in the movies. Or of the mysterious bulls whose photographs decorated the wall of the room.

His ambition in fact was to succeed this man. Thus, inevitably, he wished his father were dead. But the very thought that he might become his murderer made Bento tremble. Fearing that he might kill him someday merely through the intensity of his gaze or of his desire. Badly shaken, he went to the water cooler, poured himself a glass, draining it in one gulp. He looked at his father again, making mental calculations. And decided that Madruga was a fitting illustration of his own story. Without his father, his victories in the future would be worth nothing to him.

Even his father's aggressiveness was capable of moving him. After all, it represented Madruga's way of relating to him. The one thing he couldn't bear was the thought of not pleasing him, of not making an impression on him. His ambition could be summed up in the image of Madruga, in years to come, visiting his future office each day, in the late afternoon, in an effort to curry favor with his son.

Sometimes, absorbed in his work, Madruga didn't even raise his head to greet Bento. Saying to him, however, hours later:

"You still here? May I ask what you've been thinking about all this time?"

Bento prepared himself for these difficult moments by trying out lines that could be used to good effect. He practically prayed for his father to be in a bad mood, so as to show off his wit and his way with words.

Certain phrases seemed to please Madruga. For he not only smiled at him but took him to the corner bar as well. Once there, Madruga immediately relaxed. Happy to be in working-class surroundings again, to breathe in the smell of the street and of people. Through this anonymous intimacy he discovered himself to be part of humanity, feeling the head-on impact of emotions.

He offered to stand Bento to whatever he liked.

"Even a cachaça. It's time you had a snort of raw rum," he said happily.

For a few moments, Bento felt himself to be the center of Madruga's universe. Embarrassed, even, by all the attention. In a few minutes, Madruga turned his back, forgetting all about his son. Attracted by his neighbors, whom he would never see again, but with whom he quickly made friends.

Amid the loud convivial laughter, Bento tried to join in the conversation by voicing an opinion that would mark his adult, worldly-wise presence. But when he failed to come up with a single persuasive phrase, the result was ostracism.

Other phrases of his, however, addressed to Madruga at the end of the business day, reflected his inability to deal with words. Steadily worsening as his father's disapproving gaze banished him from his arrogant heart.

"Is this what you've wasted the entire afternoon on, Bento? Do me the favor of going straight home this minute. Your mother must be worried," was Madruga's harsh comment.

The mention of his mother was naturally aimed at humiliating him.

Making him regress to the status of a little kid in short pants, sent back to his mama's lap, where he would be given milk and gentle reprimands.

At the dinner table, Bento distinguished himself from the rest of the family. Whereas the others, through Madruga's influence, were addicted to fancy, heavy dishes, he chose his food with the most scrupulous care, as though everything were harmful to his health. Very much like Eulália, on a diet most of the time. Bento chewed very slowly so as not to give in to the temptation of developing a gourmet taste for food. He wanted to be thin, ascetic, and wear glasses. A man of circumspection, in a word.

Fortunately for him, his eyesight weakened even before he entered law school. Thus making it necessary for him to wear glasses, a nuisance he never complained of. He even rejoiced at the fact. Not removing them at any time during the entire day.

Especially when he began his studies under Santiago Dantas. A teacher for whom he felt an irresistible fascination, never once taking his eyes off him from the moment he entered the law school building. Possessed of a deliberate, solemn voice, a face permanently framed in glasses with dark mountings, an enormous head, a prominent bald spot, this fat man displayed a rare skill in dealing with human causes. Comparable only to his famed knowledge of jurisprudence, which extended to all the disciplines of the law, and his humanist erudition. And even though he held a chair in civil law, he plunged with equal mastery into the intricacies of Roman law.

Bento, however, gazed upon the Master with mingled fervor and mistrust. Sensing that they would soon lose him. Dantas being unable to subject himself to the limits of a university professorship any longer, he would soon yield to the temptation to take the highest power of the Republic by storm. To accomplish which he would make use of shrewd and subtle resources, capable of opening perilous breaches in a jurist known to be adamantly neutral. Sacrificing his destiny as a jurist to remain at the focal point of decisions in this inevitable completion of the trajectory to Power, that moist, perverse mistress who in practice never forgives her lovers the least error they make when visiting the rare fungi of her body.

When Santiago Dantas began to speak, from his chair, his shoulders bowed, his eyes slightly dilated, perhaps because of the thickness of the lenses of his bifocals, Bento surrendered to the act of seduction taking place, the consequence not only of Dantas's notable expertise in the field but also of his incomparable verbal mastery. At any stage in a class, or even in public lectures, his pronouncements went beyond rhetorical frontiers, beyond the simple act of juxtaposing words, making of them an expression possessed of collective scope and effect.

Bento understood, through him, that nothing in the human universe remained rigorously faithful to the mere appearance of reality. The interpretation of reality could be justified only if one were certain that such an approach took into account its absurd and infinite complexity.

Bento immediately envied him his intellectual maturity, attained at such an early age. And also his manner, that of a feline, despite the limpid transparency he brought to his concepts. Revealing himself to be precociously capable of organizing political strategies embracing great numbers of men and countries, as though he were totally absorbed in a game of love, the pieces for which he himself had carved. Which thus allowed him complete dominion over them. So as to prevent any contender from challenging a primacy born of the very fact of his having personally fabricated and conceived each one of these pieces.

Sensing his admiration, Santiago Dantas received him courteously once the class had ended. He allowed Bento the opportunity to offer discreet comments on *Don Quixote*, his well-known passion, on which, moreover, he had written a long essay. Bento chanced to refer to his Spanish origin, to his own father, who from his earliest years as a young man had been eager to cast off his ties to Spain so as to become a part of a Brazil of which Santiago, from an old Brazilian family, was the legitimate representative.

Months later, the professor surprised him by asking him if he would have preferred being born into a family settled in Brazil for centuries, hence one having participated in the war against Paraguay. As was, obviously, his own personal case.

Though flattered by the Master's interest, Bento was troubled. Was the professor trying to measure the degree of his fantasy and frustration in the face of his recent Brazilian past, or was he ashamed of his own ancestors, who far from having made Brazil a strong and independent nation, had, with rare boldness, made every effort to weaken its institutions? Always by way of continuous, shameful acts of historic abuse, of the corrupt undermining of the economy, of the systematic isolation of the people from political and social decisions.

Between Santiago Dantas and Brazil a secret covenant had undoubtedly been established, to which no one had access. By means of which he planned to regenerate the country, though initially through a dubious ideology, along fascist lines. This alone explaining his past as an Integralista, an adherent of a doctrine whose chief mentor was Plínio Salgado.

A political fact that involved other great names of his generation, from which he dissociated himself, subsequently following a path that led him to the labor movement. Immediately absorbing political theories which favored the working classes.

Perhaps the question asked of Bento anticipated, in a veiled, obscure way, Dantas's admission that he was about to undergo a change so radical that it would affect his life from then on. And, therefore, suffer at the same time a mysterious consubstantiation which, as a consequence, would launch him on a career dependent on popular support, joining forces with Jango when the latter assumed the presidency. From this platform, Santiago would acknowledge an even greater obligation to fulfill the needs of the people. From there, plunging with unusual energy into the political race, in an attempt, in a word, to pay off, in a short time, the debts accumulated by the members of his class. An oligarchy responsible for moral, political, social promissory notes, signed in the name of the people and against its interests, which they never took the trouble to redeem.

Bento knew nothing of the secret laws governing the world of the power elite. He had never set foot in it, and therefore had no idea whether it was best to bare his heart or to offer evasive replies, thus avoiding the creation of awkward ties between them. Furthermore, why would the modest entries in a biography of recent date in Brazil, just now taking shape, be of interest to this master?

Bento drew himself up to his full height, suddenly humiliated at not offering him an impressive portfolio of negotiable holdings on the social stock market.

"My father chose the right time to come to Brazil. If he had come before, he would have deprived me of the pleasure of hearing you. Thanks to him, I've learned the virtues that allow me to admire you, Professor Dantas. And regret that you will soon be leaving the faculty in order to enter politics. As for your question, sir, I find it stimulating to be a newcomer in a new country. Moreover, we're sure to have other wars with Paraguay, which will permit recent families to garner medals and honors."

Dantas was straightforward with him. He merely recommended caution, sensing, doubtless, that this was a young man in a hurry. He would have to learn to take the bit between his teeth himself, often amid pain and disillusion. Thus curbing those impulses that tend to make us bolt, heading straight for irreversible defeats.

The counsel was wise. But would he have offered it to himself, or followed it? Had he in fact been able to carpet life over in his swift ascent toward power? Did his rapid blows, always dead-accurate despite the swiftness with which they were dealt, stem from a reflection that had long lain in wait in his exceptional brain?

There so close to him, Bento was overcome with emotion, the sweat running down his shirt. Under the spell of a personality that was to mark him forever. To the point that on attending his funeral, years later, with tears in his eyes, he insisted that his sons accompany him to the cemetery.

"Brazil is losing one of its most illustrious men today." And he added distractedly: "Not to mention the fact that he was in the war with Paraguay. From which he returned with his chest full of medals. We all have reasons to lament his loss."

Miguel paid no attention to Bento's war cries. His hands full with Esperança, a warrior who bore invisible arms, ready to fling herself upon him, throwing him to the ground, from which Miguel would rise to his feet in the expectation of overthrowing her the following day. Both refused to allow Bento to interfere. Forbidding him to side with one or the other of them. The tactics they employed must not be revealed to that brother for his appreciation. Only they were capable of respecting the sadness that devastated the face of the vanquished warrior. Whether Esperança's or Miguel's. The victor therefore held out a hand to the one on the ground, helping the loser to bear the loss. They thus lived on the seesaw of triumph and defeat. With, sometimes, Esperança at the top, legs bared, her dress flying up at the mercy of the forceful thrusts. As Miguel, in humiliation, ran to his mother's room, interrupting Eulália, at the moment occupied in persuading Odete to send for a doctor, because of her pallor.

Odete refused; she was not suffering from an illness. God had given her perfect health, a reason, moreover, to be grateful to him. Eulália disagreed. God did not always err in offering us precarious health with which to live the life that He lent us. Certain morbid conditions following a disease even served as a preventive measure, to put a stop to the torment of our vanity and arrogance. And wasn't it true that we were on earth only in passing, in the role of debtors to the one who had granted us life in order to live it in His name, in this way bearing witness to His existence, without which we would not even have been created?

Odete contritely awaited the moment when Eulália would speak of God. Which was sometimes a long time coming. Eulália reserved Him for moments of distress or gratitude. Being of the opinion that one ought not to use his holy name in vain. Many a time, therefore, she prayed without admitting that she was praying. A discretion that served as a model for not fabricating externally a god capable of being captured and described through the use of banal eulogies.

Despite the pains in her spinal column, Odete did not complain. But her pallor served as proof that something was happening to her. And though Odete invariably refused any sort of treatment, it in fact pleased her that Eulália should suffer on her account. Becoming for her mistress someone belonging to her family. And the better to accept a commiseration she did not have the strength to do without, Odete would half close her eyes, in a somewhat lugubrious way.

As the two of them were idly talking all round the subject together, Esperança knocked on the door of her mother's room, in violent distress. Wanting her permission to leave the house. Confronted with her adolescent daughter, Eulália hesitated to use an authority that she had never sought. She did not see how to control the fury of this daughter who, all of a sudden, was interrogating her as though Eulália were her adversary. As a general rule, the mother, after an initial stubbornness, would eventually give in. Thus making Esperança see that her freedom depended on an imperfect and uncertain will. Thereby earning her daughter's unlimited mistrust. Though she must also have known how much her mother suffered when she set courses for her life.

Noting this weakness on the part of her mother, who was repelled by any form of power, Esperança would then make other insistent requests, knowing full well that she would cause Eulália to suffer should she do anything contrary to her mother's will. At the same time she took great satisfaction in committing sly misdeeds subject to punishment. A pleasure that, in and of itself, was more gratifying than permission obtained from her mother in due and proper form.

Esperança thought out beforehand, in minute detail, any rebellious act. Without sharing such plans with Miguel. But Miguel dogged her footsteps, knowing his sister was out to defy Eulália. He would end up involving himself in the same mischief, without regarding himself as being subject to the same error. The mere fact of being a male would free him, in the end, of blame. Since he already enjoyed certain privileges which exempted him from consulting his mother.

On being confronted with this sort of maneuver, Esperança forbade him to follow her. To reap advantages, even if only indirect ones, from her act of disobedience. Through which she had recently set in motion a universe, by nature impenetrable, which pitilessly banished him.

"And what can you do that I can't?" Miguel said.

Esperança dashed up and down the streets merely to exhaust her brother. Endlessly circling the Praça Sáenz Peña, following a different plan each time. He imagined himself to be in a labyrinth with an itinerary that only she had mastered, the keys to which, secret in nature, could well swallow her brother up forever.

"You're naïve, Esperança. Are you going to spend your whole life inventing paths that don't exist? Just to test me? Knowing beforehand that I end up discovering where you're hiding?" Miguel said on finding her.

Esperança gave a gleeful laugh, agreeing with her brother. She had her good humor back, and her bosom pal as well. Who could tell? In the future, grown old, they might meet in that same place, with the aim of going back over life once again.

All Esperança yearned for was an existence as full of adventure as it was detailed. This latter item indispensable, so as to make it impossible for her to hurry along any narrative and doom it to failure before the fact, were she to reduce drastically the volume of information and the intensity of the emotions.

On one of these excursions, Madruga came across Esperança in the square. It was already dark and there were only a few people about. At the sight of her father, she paled, not knowing what to do with her hands. She was still trying to pretend she hadn't seen him. Madruga halted, imperturbable.

"What are you doing here all by yourself, Esperança? Is this any hour to be running about the streets, as though you had neither house nor home?"

Hidden behind the tree, Miguel sensed the danger. His father would not forgive Esperança for leaving the house, at the mercy of strangers. There was no time to lose. With loud cries, he approached on the run, as though he hadn't seen his father. Making helpless gestures in Esperança's direction, overcome with despair.

"I went back the same way again, all for nothing. I didn't find the money. I think it's lost. We'd better go back home and confess to Mother."

Madruga grabbed him by the arm, not noticing Esperança's confusion, she too having been taken completely by surprise.

"And you too, what are you doing here? What money are you talking about?"

"Father! Imagine you here! Mother wanted medicine for Odete, but I lost the money. Could you possibly advance us what it's going to cost?"

With his hair cropped very short, dressed in long pants, Miguel was about to go into the army. Madruga wanted his son in uniform, so as to broaden his claim to citizenship. Even though Miguel asked him, timidly, to be exempted from this service, which would interfere with his studies.

"It's out of the question. My son must serve in the army. Be a Brazilian through and through. I don't see how this can defer your plans for your life," Madruga protested.

Pleas on the part of Eulália or Venâncio, who knew of Madruga's influence in certain political and military circles, were of no avail. Madruga was convinced of the importance of possessing, among other documents, a card attesting one's membership in the reserves. These little victories reinforced the presence of his family in Brazil. They constituted a social safeguard.

"You'll be a man who treads in buskins," Madruga said, pleased with himself.

Delighted with turns of phrase rarely used in everyday speech, he often went to dictionaries so as to be able to trot such expressions out when the right moment came along, and did so to felicitous effect. He encouraged his sons to practice enlarging their vocabulary.

"The only thing is that you read less, father, than Godfather does, so you know less than he does," Tobias said boldly, immediately seeking his mother's protection.

"That doesn't mean I know less about life than Venâncio, my boy," Madruga said testily.

Determined to prove how wrong Tobias was, he obliged him to remain at his side as he read a book, which happened to be one recommended by Venâncio. In the beginning, Tobias paid attention. Later on, growing drowsy, his eyes gradually began to close, in full view of his father, so that the latter, taking pity on him, would free him from the armchair where he held him prisoner.

Eulália waited for the living room clock to strike. When it chimed nine times, she drew Tobias out of the chair.

"You're going to say your prayers now and go to sleep."

In order not to affront Madruga, and at the same time lend her son courage, she led him over to him to ask for his blessing.

Prudently, deliberately steering clear of Eulália's maneuvers, Madruga extended his hand with exaggerated politeness, endeavoring to prolong the punishment, from which he had not yet freed Tobias. He wanted him, above all, to be remorseful. But the kiss that Tobias deposited on his father's skin, with tight-shut lips, was cold and dry.

Madruga felt, all of a sudden, that the family was abandoning him. A phenomenon not restricted to him alone. Perhaps man's fate was to beget and feed a distant family, without expecting anything in return. Despite the fact that he made everything round him flourish. That sort of devotion finally stifled his heart. His life shut up within the confines of obedience to the call of duty and ambition.

On Sunday, Venâncio presented Tobias with a set of tin soldiers and artillery pieces. After dinner, Madruga offered to try the toys out with his son.

"We're going to divide up the pieces. We'll see which one gets the blue soldiers and the red ones. Then we'll choose which part of the terrain each of us is to occupy. At that point we begin the battle," Madruga said enthusiastically.

Tobias got the red soldiers. He laid them out on the floor with nothing like his father's dexterity. Meanwhile they went about setting the scene in which the battle would take place. Tobias's major contribution was to knead together various bits of paper and soft bread crumbs. With this material, he pretended to create hills, hollows, and tents, dispersing his soldiers among them beneath his father's watchful eye, carefully appraising the deployment of the modest band. Madruga, in turn, found boxes of matches, candles, to be horses, trees. And he also stretched a length of thick twine between the two battalions, representing a river. He baptized the river Sobreira, whereupon Tobias protested.

"Well then, what's it supposed to be called?"

"The Amazon."

"Very well. In that case the hill is going to be called Sobreira."

"I agree. And what's the name of its commander?" Tobias said.

"The Duke of Caxias."

A river separated them. In order to cross it, it was necessary to breast the current, strong and treacherous. Hence it would not be easy for the soldiers to advance in that direction. They would have to go scouting around for a plank. Tobias was annoyed at his father, who confronted him with practically insuperable obstacles.

"And how will we fight if there's always this river between us?" he cried in exasperation.

To perk up his son's morale, Madruga changed strategy.

"We're going to pit the soft inside of the bread against the soldiers. That way it'll be easier to wipe them out."

Tobias flew into a rage: "I accept, but then you're going to have to be the enemy. Only how am I going to destroy you with nothing but soft bread?"

This belligerence pleased Madruga, who rewarded his son with a smile.

"We're going to have many a battle to fight in life, son. Save that energy for later."

After five minutes' combat, a number of soldiers were still on their feet. Madruga stopped the game. Tobias beginning, all by himself, to move the little soldiers, each reduced to insignificance now, from one place to another. Not overlooking a single one in either of the two groups. He felt himself to be a commander with the rare authority to issue orders to two opposing armies. Each the enemy of the other, separated only by the muddy waters of the Amazon.

Bento had watched from the beginning the military maneuvers being carried out by Tobias and his father. Madruga moving the soldiers cautiously, not wanting to lose them. His face visibly falling when the first soldier hit the dust. Without Tobias's noticing how upset his father was, being overly sensitive to any sort of loss. Meanwhile advancing hesitantly, slowly, allowing Madruga to recover in swift counterattacks. Following which his father was visibly vexed by the mutual damages inflicted. Yet never ceasing to praise his son's fighting spirit. To this end having recourse to words that wounded Bento's pride. Eager to take Tobias's place and earn praise long due him.

When Madruga retired from the game, Bento, unable to contain himself, shouted at his father, in a choked voice, close to tears:

"Don't give up the fight, father. Wipe out all the soldiers first. You mustn't spare those deserters and born losers."

Madruga shrugged, as though to say that this sort of victory counted for very little to him. Bento withdrew to the corner of the living room, all by himself. Eulália, however, understood the meaning of this scene. The visible hurt in her son's face.

She had long suspected that Bento's bookishness, his racing round and round the courtyard, his cold manner with members of the family and strangers stemmed, doubtless, from an emptiness in his heart. Never suspecting, however, that Bento was keenly aware of a vacuum to be filled with power, wealth, and Madruga's openly proclaimed admiration. Only a solid victory would relieve this hollow feeling.

Even when confronted with humble acts, Bento assumed a grandiloquence which sounded affected. And because she could detect in him no signs of appreciation of life, Eulália hopefully awaited a time when her son would unexpectedly burst into peals of expansive laughter. Which almost never happened. Making her feel, then, that he might suffer a sudden emotional collapse. She began to hint, discreetly, that he ought to observe a certain moderation. Bento took offense at what he regarded as his mother's invasion of his privacy. But on realizing that in fact she did not constitute a danger, he hurriedly brushed her aside. Claiming he didn't have time to rest. He had the world to conquer. This last uttered with his teeth bared, like a boar. Merely to upset her.

Eulália withdrew to her room, closing the door. Fearing that her son's voracity, which she sensed was growing, would harm the family. She forced herself to contemplate what sort of world Bento had in mind to make him flaunt such an expansionist project and display such absolute conviction. She remembered that on pressing his lips firmly together after having shown his teeth, he had done nothing to hide a tense, unhappy physiognomy, that of an enemy ready to ravage concrete and florescent aspects of the world.

To break off such reflections, Eulália began to pray. She had already said half the prayer, when she decided to cut it short. Leaving the pric dieu, she made her way to the living room. In a firm voice she asked Bento to accompany her to the veranda on that damp, rainy afternoon.

Bento noted that his mother had just emerged from the world of prayer. Startled, he mentioned tasks away from home that urgently needed doing. His mother was well acquainted with the path of falsehood. It began in the slightly clouded eyes of her son. So she took his hand, like a woman who had learned how to relax another's body.

Bento immediately went rigid. He could not bear his mother's warmth, invading his body without his being able to expel it. Eulália nonetheless went on stroking him. A caress that began at the fingertips, proceeding to her son's wrist. It was there that the life that had one day been sheltered in her womb began. Sitting on the veranda now with Bento, their hands touching, she analyzed his face. Of what elements, hers and Madruga's, Bento's face was formed, she could not say. She did not remember a single uncle, a grandfather, who had injected her son with family traits. For a few moments that face seemed to her to be an inaugural one, the first of that lineage invented by Madruga and herself.

She wanted to communicate her impressions to Bento. She feared, however, that her son would see in those words a narrowing down of his origins. Inaccurate words, in truth, since Bento had been born solely of her womb. A womb that had swelled six times, so as to push children out between her legs. And if God had willed that one of them, named Bento, should die on the Atlantic, in this fate were reasons she was far from understanding.

She decided to lift Bento's spirits, to make him feel happy at being her son.

"Madruga is a man of courage. When we lost little Bento, there in the middle of the ocean, in the place where they say that Atlantis once was, near the Canaries, which may well have been, according to Venâncio, the most fascinating country of all those invented by men, I did not see Madruga weep. I do know, though, that he locked himself in the cabin for two hours, obliging me to walk up and down the deck in tears, with Miguel and Esperança, just babies still. He would not eat a thing, though I insisted. As if fasting would do him good. Even during little Bento's funeral he did not shed a single tear. He took part in the ceremony, along with the captain and the other officers, to all appearances one of them. His heart hurt terribly, though, as if they had pierced it with a dagger. It was he who saw the little body wrapped in his jacket disappear in the waters, hurriedly spat so far away that they did not see it a second time. In the face of the hunger of those waters, Madruga straightened to his full height, immediately thanking the captain for the words of farewell addressed to his son. Since he himself had not been able to say the right words. Madruga confessed that the thought came to him, There you go, my beloved son, but know that I am going with you. Don't feel lonely, little son, because I will be keeping you company in days to come. As will your mother and your little brother and sister Miguel and Esperança. As you float on the waves, we are here above them. And it was then, on this passage, that Madruga swore to himself that his next male child would also be named Bento. He was not afraid of death or of the warning that had come to him with that loss. Do you know what Madruga said, Bento?"

Bento could not bear to have his hand held in his mother's lap for one moment longer. With a gesture, he freed himself from her, rising to his feet, facing Eulália, in a visible show of self-possession. Since he had been a small child he had heard tell of this little Bento, who had died on the way back from Spain. All the more dramatic in that Madruga and Eulália had made a special trip to Galicia so that their son would be born amid the same stones that had welcomed Madruga into the world. Without his parents ever explaining to him, however, why they had chosen that son to be the only one born there. With that end in view, Madruga having interrupted his work, leaving his business affairs in the hands of partners and friends. Counting, naturally, on the active collaboration of hardworking Venâncio. Everyone agreeing that Bento should be born in Spain, as though they respected the supposed debt that Madruga must settle with his country. Without Madruga's ever once taking into account the fact that he was depriving Brazil of that little citizen, whose nationality would obviously conflict with that of the other members of the family.

Bento never knew how greatly that loss affected Madruga. They all knew that he had not hesitated, however, to baptize the other son with the same name. As proof, doubtless, that he had not forgotten him. And this being so, had he been born only because of Madruga's insistence that Eulália give him a son who would erase from his memory the moments of pain following the death of little Bento? A baby boy barely three months old. And what was more, healthy, strong, life beaming from his blue eyes exactly like his father's. Madruga promptly offering him a disturbing love, which Miguel and Esperança had not inspired in him. Perhaps owing to the fact that, on contemplating little Bento, he managed to contemplate himself. Born, like him, in Sobreira, where Madruga felt the earth for the first time, ate its potatoes, climbed its mountains, was amazed at the intense summer days, when the green of Galicia shone brightly amid the blunt thorns of the gorse bushes.

Nor did Bento know whether, on receiving that name at the baptismal font, thereby fulfilling Madruga's will, he awakened in his father's heart a joy equaling that felt for the first Bento. Or could he have been named Bento not so as to be offered Madruga's equal love, but rather with Madruga's firm resolve to challenge destiny, which had deprived him of a son to whom he had intended to pass on the legends heard from Xan's lips? And only after taking his vengeance upon life in this way had Madruga freed himself to feel for the second Bento a dull, diffident, halfhearted sentiment. And immediately designate Miguel as his heir. Because his brother had the same surprised smile as the first Bento, when still in the cradle.

"Do you know what Madruga said, my son?" Eulália repeated, noting his distraction. And as Bento did not answer, she drew him closer. He yielded to her gesture only so as not to interrupt his mother's confessions. Eulália suddenly decided to return to her room for her evening prayers.

In Bento's distraught face there dawned a gentle look, a new meekness. For the first time Eulália noted that Bento, free of anxiety, with his hair falling over his brow, had a rustic beauty, as though goat's milk were streaming down from his forehead to his chin, so that frolicking shepherdesses could all lick their share. She discovered in him features that went back to the Galician past, everything leading her to believe now that Bento's face, beyond a doubt, had a provenance capable of being firmly traced.

Beneath his mother's scrutiny, Bento felt that that gaze wanted to embrace him and even pour out over him a loving sympathy whose existence, until that moment, he had not had the slightest hint of in any human being. Moved to contrition at this discovery, he was suddenly disconcerted. But, carried away by emotion, he slowly slid his hand back into Eulália's lap, where it had lain before, a memory pleasant at last to recall.

As Bento drew closer, Eulália followed the movement whereby her son would return to her the hand that his embarrassment, a few moments before, had robbed her of. And without the least hesitation, foreseeing what was about to happen, she reached out, grasping it firmly, to assure him of the naturalness of that gesture which the two of them, in the future, were time and again to repeat anew.

"Do you know what Madruga said, Bento? Well, he said, in a solemn, clearly audible voice, as though he were swearing an oath before an altar or a judge, not wanting to have me as his only witness, but himself as well: The next Bento, my son and Eulália's, and he can only be from her, since I do not want sons from any other woman, will be brave and worthy of our heritage. And this still not being enough, Madruga said again, just a little while before you were born: Bento will succeed me, as I succeeded Ceferino and Urcesina."

On hearing the final words, Bento trembled in his mother's hands. Was it true, then, that even before he was born, his father had fought for his life and made his succession certain? Had he then celebrated his birth, as though he were just beginning a family?

Eulália tightened her grip. In her eagerness to feed the emotions that were now circulating through Bento's blood vessels, dilating his veins, racking his nerves, making him stretch out his long sharp fingers inside that hand, as in a shell.

Invaded by his mother in a rare moment of intensity, Bento looked the other way, so as to escape her scrutiny. He now regretted having offered her an intimacy that was a heavy burden. As a consequence, he made his entire body go rigid. He did not want her to share his emotions. Eulália perceived the sudden transformation. And intuiting that she would risk losing him if she did not anticipate a certain gesture, she quickly let him have his hand back. And rose to her feet, quite evidently in a great hurry to leave the room.

"I need to begin my prayers now. Before night falls. We'll see each other at dinner, son. If, that is, I come downstairs for my soup."

With these words, Eulália vanished. Leaving Bento all by himself, as usual. An isolation that in a certain way he defended. Even though he complained of Madruga's abandoning him, as was the case now, after amusing himself with Tobias.

On that Sunday, particularly, it seemed to him that his father and mother, by common accord, had decided to deliver him over to the loneliness of the living room, at this moment in darkness. Where he began to move about dejectedly among the little lead soldiers, in blue and red uniforms, strewn about, one atop the other, all over the floor.

Madruga woke up in a panic in the middle of the night, his pajamas soaking wet with perspiration. With the strange sensation of having visitors, despite the hour.

In the half-shadow, however, he could barely make out details of the modest room in which he lived, in González's hotel. Slowly, he groped about, exploring the mattress. Expecting to discover, all of a sudden, the ghost of Grandfather Xan seated at his side. His grandfather having decided, in his nocturnal prowling, to take shelter beneath his grandson's sheets, in fair exchange for the stories he'd told him.

Terrified, Madruga finally opened his eyes, forcing them to focus on the white wall opposite him. Because of a slit of light coming through the curtain, he seemed to see the figure of his grandfather, restored with excessive exactitude, actually projected on the wall.

Despite his distress and fear, Madruga wanted to talk with Xan, to ask him to stay. But Xan's image on the wall immediately faded, visibly shoved aside by Ceferino and Urcesina, both also wishing to appear to their son. Anxious to converse with Madruga, after so many years, to clear up certain details. Since they'd never had the time, even in Sobreira, to get to know each other.

More nervous than Urcesina, Ceferino was making gestures, trying his best now to draw, on the same wall on which he was projected, their house in Sobreira. And in such detail that he did not forget the trees in the yard, seen from the window of the dining room.

Ceferino kept making signs, fearing that his son couldn't hear him. Since he wanted Madruga to know how important that house was. That place warmed in the winter by the hearth and the stove, where the family kept soul and body together, after a day in the fields.

Ceferino appeared to be exhausted by his efforts. So Urcesina took over his space on the wall. With the same gestures as always, just as Madruga remembered her. There Urcesina was, dishing the food out round the table. She wanted to fill her children up in a hurry so they wouldn't keep shouting in her ear how hungry they were.

That was how it always was. At dinner or supper, Urcesina's eyes would narrow, as a warning that she was about to teach them some hard truths. The children, thoroughly cowed, paid close attention. And she very carefully described the battles in store for her offspring in the future, trying their best to save up money that would go directly into her copper or tin box, there being no bank in Sobreira.

"I don't want any lazy louts in this house. Chew down raw meat even, if you have to. It won't hurt you. There are worms and germs in men's souls too, after all. And what's more, boys, a peasant who neglects his animals and his crops is an unworthy man. Don't forget that we were made to eat dirt and live on the earth's fruits. Anyone who turns his back on it has no right to a plate of hot food."

Urcesina flew into a fury whenever she was told that an animal had gotten lost in the mountains. It was a crime to let a young critter stray, one born right in their very own pen, practically in the marriage bed. It was the same as sacrificing a son on the altar of greed. Or taking upcountry an old, worn-out father and mother, of no more use at all in the fields, intending to leave them on the mountaintop to die.

"Who's the irresponsible murderer this time?"

"There wasn't any murderer, mother. The animal is still alive. It just got lost up on the mountain."

"It's the same thing. Can't you see that in a few hours the damned wolves are going to be feasting on its flesh?" she said, her eyes brimming with tears, foreseeing the tragedy.

With almost professional skill, she would personally help pull a calf out of the cow's uterus, celebrating its coming into the world with a glass of wine, shared with those present. And immediately begin discussing the lineage of the newborn creature, as though speaking of the dynasty of the Prince of Asturias.

"I'm terrified that they'll take our animals far away. Deprive them of our traditions, of the air of our land, of the cold and the north wind. They must never leave Galicia. Even if our men part from us forever."

There before Urcesina and her admonitions, the children sipped their soup with heavy hearts. Knowing that after feeding their bellies, their mother was going to drive them out of the house to work. They must strive to deserve the food earned thanks to her and Ceferino.

Ceferino nonetheless tried to ease his children's anxieties, stroking their hair.

"Next winter's going to be better. Don't worry. Try and play now. You'll get to know Sobreira," he said, on seeing that Urcesina's mind was elsewhere.

Ceferino knew that just as winter came to make life difficult, to make a person's joints stiff, and face washing an unappealing prospect, so winter went, at the first sign of a leaf budding on a bare tree. Though those months left them as a heritage the melancholy memory of the north wind, whose howls made them old before their time, almost taking away the desire to live.

Cheered, however, by the company of Xan, in whose presence Urcesina calmed down, Ceferino gathered his children together.

"This summer, we'll all go to the fair in Caldelas. We'll take the animals to be sold, and cod and sardine sandwiches too. Not forgetting the *pandereta*, to accompany our dances and songs. And I'm going to buy you doughnuts. So you'll be able to have as much fun as you'd like, to the sound of the best bagpipers in Galicia."

The shadows on the wall followed one another in jumpy succession, turning into different characters, fighting now for the right to be remembered by Madruga. In the heat of the battle, Xan appeared, imperious, pacifying the other members of the family. He then took Madruga by the hand and led him out to the yard, over by the garden, where they always used to go on the long summer nights.

He had never hidden his love for his grandson. The only one to hear certain stories directly from his lips. The stories that covered recent episodes, but were also concerned with the past. And all for the pleasure of having Madruga keep him company.

Madruga had no way of verifying the truth of these stories. Since his grandfather, a proponent of narratives steeped in time, refused to assign them any authorship, era, or origin. As he explained, the fascination of these legends lay in the fact that the people themselves kept adding a boundless crust of lies to them. Since, in the eyes of the centuries, the only legends to survive were those that left the people room for a thousand contradictory versions. All of them born in stables, whorehouses, secret hideouts, fairground shows, caves. There thus being no nice, neat, scrupulously exact explanation of their genesis. Seeing as how they were simply a casual discharge of the popular imagination.

"Nobody knows where they came from, my son. Nor how they were slowly and steadily fattened over the years. All we know is that, thanks to this pleasing plumpness, the erudite pedants of Madrid and Salamanca were never able to get at the solid meat of them."

In Xan's hands, the stories were like a porridge thickened with milk. It had to be eaten hot, by the spoonful. And above and beyond these requirements, Xan also felt the urge to create. And so, following rules subject to change, he split certain stories apart in order to insert among the imaginable beings certain inhabitants of neighboring villages. So that all of them could readily be identified in the story being told. It being immediately evident whether the new character was someone who lived in Bora, Puente Sampaio, the island of Arosa, Betanzos, or even Padrón.

Now and again, Xan rebelled against this method, strictly reversing the order of the story, point for point. He then mixed the ingredients in such a way that, feeling totally lost, Madruga was obliged to seek his grandfather's guidance the day after.

When, on the following night, Madruga insisted, Xan, though unusually chary of speech, went back over the whole process from the beginning. Finding it difficult, nonetheless, to conceal the voracious lust for power that marks the great storyteller. He felt himself, however, to be a simple peasant well aware of the fact that, while there was a certain truth in everything he said, that same truth might very well perish in his hands, should he lack the skill to deal properly with the story that was his to tell. Back inside, at table now, Xan went on slicing the bread with a careless hand. Letting crumbs fall all over the floor. As an act of reprisal against Urcesina, bent on ruining her family with her mania for squeezing every penny.

She did not dare to reprove him. Above all because Xan had begun to lose his teeth, his gums shrinking as everyone could see. Making things more difficult when it came time to tell stories. For all he had to do was open his mouth before his hearers for his voice to come lisping out from the gaps between the teeth he still had left.

Each time he lost a tooth, Xan promptly buried it alongside the roots of a sprouting turnip. Turnip greens being a necessary ingredient in Galician soup pots. Asked to explain why he did this, Xan said that only in this way could he render homage to food, to which he owed the inroads of decay in his mouth.

Meanwhile, he found it hard to believe that he had lost more than half his dental arch. Despite having, for some time, sucked on his food rather than chewing it. This left him sitting at table for many long hours, obliging a member of the family to keep him company.

No one else had the patience to stay with him till he'd finished. Above all on account of the noises Grandfather made, stubbornly persisting in speaking as he sucked on his bacon.

Ceferino decided to do something. "Open your mouth, father! I want to get a close look at the damage the years have done you."

Xan was annoyed at his son's impoliteness. He refused to let him examine his mouth.

"I'm not a horse at a fair. I'm not up for sale."

Ceferino couldn't expect him to possess eternal youth, and have perfect teeth, untouched by time, along with it. Another sort of youth was enough for him. The kind that made it possible for him to tell stories without mixing up the endings. Able to count on a memory with a file of names in perfect order.

In fact, Xan prided himself on being the registry office of the village. Able, therefore, to solve knotty problems. Often being sought out to settle doubts as to the possession of a piece of land in dispute. Making it unnecessary to go to the notary in Pontevedra or the land surveyor in Caldelas.

Consulted on certain matters, Xan would frown, as though it pained him to go to the very bottom of his memory. He would also pretend to forget in order to make the person consulting him nervous. He seemed to take a certain pleasure in blasting other people's hopes. Or seeing the other fellow overcome with remorse because he'd suddenly revealed, in stark black and white, a picture in which his sclerosis stood out clearly.

"Don't worry, Xan. It's a matter of little importance," they would say to him.

He would give a loud laugh, followed by a fair shower of saliva. Insisting on offering his neighbor his own handkerchief. For the pleasure of seeing him reluctant to accept a badly wrinkled one.

"I'll die without having forgotten a single one of the words I've learned so far," he used to say.

It seemed likely, then, that Xan, when the time came, would go straight to bed to await death. And perhaps it was better that way. He wouldn't be able to bear the humiliation of forgetting. It no doubt offended his dignity. As though for ignoble reasons he were being subjected to public disgrace.

One night, Xan dragged his grandson to the tavern. "Taste this wine, my boy."

Leaning on the counter, Xan ordered two glasses of the best house wine. When he was served, he picked up the glass, swirling the wine around the rim of it with an unerring technique. Just long enough to stain the side with the violet color of an open vein, typical of Ribeira wine. He sipped a certain amount, enough to fill his mouth. Immediately rinsing his teeth, his palate, his tongue. Scouring his taste buds vigorously with the wine so as to make his palate bristle and release the flavor. Only then did he allow the wine to slide down to his stomach, meanwhile grinning with pleasure.

"It's a lesson, my son, a moral one. Wine strengthens our national pride."

Not satisfied with this demonstration, he looked around at his comrades standing at the counter, eating sardines on corn bread.

"Who wants to have a go at the memory game with me?" he challenged them.

The bets were limited to a round of wine, paid for by the loser. Thereby minimizing the expense. Even so, no one volunteered. Confronted with this silence, and certain that he could count on himself as an opponent, Xan smiled. Without perceiving that they were all tacitly conspiring to spare him a defeat that would cost him his life.

Xan repeated the challenge each Saturday night in the crowded tavern. Leaving it with his chest puffed out, his beret on his head, and not the slightest suspicion in his heart.

"One of these days, I'll also stand you a trip to Cebreiro," he kept saying to Madruga, determined to take him to the sanctuary.

To pay for this trip, moreover, Xan set aside money from each animal he sold. And he had also cut down on his consumption of black tobacco. In the tavern, on Sundays, he never took offense when they offered him a glass of wine in return for entertaining them with his best stories. But when they asked him to tell them again, he protested.

"In that case, you owe me my Friday wine."

These sudden economies of Xan's didn't call for criticism. They all knew where the pennies saved would go. Money that grew older in a locked drawer. With Teodora, his wife, fighting with him over the key to it, without ever getting the better of him. Xan even slept with it. And had the advantage of being a light sleeper, waking at the slightest sound.

Whenever Teodora looked at him with a scowl, he would point to the key fastened to the belt loop of his trousers, emphasizing that, thanks to it, he would have the wherewithal to pay for his own burial and Teodora's. And the trip to Cebreiro.

"There'll be two of us on this pilgrimage. Madruga and I. We'll go on foot, and be in no hurry to get back. With our knapsacks on our backs, like the men in the old days. Our only luxury will be to take another pair of boots with us to replace the ones we'll wear out on the way. You can't pinch pennies when it's a matter of going to a holy place."

In the end, Xan opened his mouth. And Ceferino could count the number of teeth his father had left. He examined him as though he were appraising an antique. In the upper jaw he found five teeth, and in the lower just three, all of them completely useless, since no two of them met.

Xan refused to go to the dentist's. "What can that wretch do for me? When life has been out to get me for a long time now. Can't you see I'm getting ready to die?"

When Ceferino kept insisting, he finally went with him to Pontevedra. To a dentist he knew, who looked after people in the neighboring villages, charging modest prices. With the advantage of having, back in his office, a glass cabinet in full view of the patients with sets of false teeth of different sizes, all ready to be put to use whenever needed.

An efficient dentist, doubtless. Since he pulled eight teeth at once, and also fitted him with a set of teeth that seemed to have been made especially for him. It had belonged, by a coincidence, to a farm laborer that Xan had met in Sobreira, when he came to the wedding of one of Justo's godsons. A man who, incidentally, prided himself on his appearance and his smile. A smile so bright that it seemed to precede him, going on ahead of his own body.

Unfortunately, this man had not been able to pick up the order waiting for him in the dentist's office because death surprised him as he was standing in front of the mirror, getting all spruced up to go to Pontevedra and see what his false teeth looked like.

"Who would ever have thought he'd end up without that smile so soon! Because nobody can smile without teeth, isn't that so?" Xan said, not minding the fact that he now possessed a set of teeth that had not brought his neighbor good luck. The dentist finally let him have them for a price far less than what they were worth. Moreover, trusting fate, Xan thought that even though the other fellow hadn't lived long enough to enjoy that set of chompers, he for his part had all the rest of his days to do so.

For a week, despite the discomfort, he chewed with the denture. At night, however, he contemplated it on the bedside table, trying to establish some link with the contraption. In the beginning, it seemed to him a distant object, performing a function. And as such, of no concern to him. As the days went by, he little by little began to suffer distress, followed by waves of nausea. And then after that an insomnia impossible to overcome. Immediately attributed to the set of teeth. Not to mention the fact that his food was tasteless now, even when oversalted. It no longer gave him the pleasure it once had. Thus deprived all of a sudden of his sense of taste, he began leaving the table thoroughly annoyed at those teeth which, though in his service, acted openly against his interests.

In despair, he lamented his lot. Obliged to carry around a mouthful of teeth that were his enemy. So that, on looking at himself in the mirror, he no longer saw himself, but a stranger. For that couldn't be him, reflected there, someone he'd begun to despise for having bowed to his son's will and the despotism of that accursed dentist in Pontevedra.

The set of teeth became a target of his hatred. A hatred with a tendency to grow. And that gradually robbed him of the joy of living. And so, unable to bear that disagreeable cohabitation any longer, he decided to remove the denture permanently.

"This is the last time this damned thing is going to offend me without my taking revenge. I don't want to be a coward in my old age. My memories of my defeats at Teodora's hand while she was alive are quite enough for me."

He tossed the set of teeth into a glass of alcohol, leaving it in plain sight amid the other objects in the room. And when he saw himself protesting against nature for keeping him from chewing the fibers of certain meats, he hastened to pay the teeth a visit. Remaining there long enough for hatred to rise to his cheeks. Only then did he return, satisfied, to the table, resigned to his lot, with no complaints.

Every month he personally changed the alcohol in the glass, because he wanted it to be transparent. Scrubbing the enemy teeth with a toothbrush, as he remembered the farm laborer whom death had surprised in front of the mirror. The first victim of a set of teeth made up for the express purpose of liquidating the human species. To make a point of his contempt, he dragged visitors to the room, showing them the diabolical invention for which he had had the unhappy idea of sacrificing the equivalent of three smoked hams of the very best quality.

"Try the teeth again, father," Ceferino insisted.

"How do you expect me to deal with an enemy? To give him sanctuary in my mouth, and then in my privates? Never, I'd rather die than wear them."

Patiently, Xan went on mashing his bacon and potato with his fork. Fraying and shredding what resisted him. He had perfected the technique of sucking his food till it dissolved against the roof of his mouth. And when he spoke, he no longer lisped as he had once done. Hardened now, and the only thing left in his mouth, Xan's gums helped him to talk, as though he had teeth.

Touched by his grandfather, absorbed in the act whereby he was defending his very life, Madruga thought he saw him fighting off, with his fork, the Castilians, the Moors, who had reached the harsh Galician coast.

Aware of his grandson's admiring gaze, Xan wove an endless garland of praise to the food that had arrived at their table after the poignant labor of so many hands, in every way like his own. People of his race, firmly resolved to till the earth.

Even when Madruga wanted to leave the table and go up to the mountains, where he felt himself to be the master of the universe, he never got up from his chair before his grandfather. Out of respect for him and in the expectation, ever renewed, that Xan, once his thoughts had stopped wandering, would tell him of the strange travelers who had long ago visited Sobreira. Always loners, with no place to lay their heads, who rejected the bondage of home and death in bed, amid wax tapers, prayers, and tears.

These men, forever dead and gone now, wanted nothing, according to Xan, save a life in the open air, a shepherd's crook in their hand, a leather wineskin, and the rump of a horse or a donkey.

"Life has always been a war of conquest, my son. Except that it's a war that nobody's declared."

And to lend authority to his own words, he cited Galicia as an example. Constantly changing owners, divided between members of the same family and the Church. Whereas the King, watching over them from afar, wore the mantle of eternity on his shoulders. Never needing, at any moment, to eat the dust and the pork of these lands.

As Xan called up this past, so rich it sounded nonexistent, he inevitably spoke of Salvador. Someone he'd kept very much alive in his memory. Hence bringing him to his grandson's mind so vividly that Madruga, following his instructions, could easily reconstruct Salvador, and along with him Pegasus, his inseparable donkey.

Xan felt comforted reliving the adventures of a friend who was everpresent, despite being dead. There then appeared before his eyes the thin, anxious figure of Salvador, his broad forehead with veins that stood out, so great was the anguish with which he approached life. Salvador appeared so clearly that he seemed to float in the soup or the wine that Xan, thereupon, sipped with closed eyes, to smooth the path of dreaming. There were still traces of Salvador everywhere, of that he was certain.

"Now that you know Salvador, my mind is at ease. I've ensured that he'll live fifty years more. As long as you're alive, Salvador will be with us, in this room."

Xan slowly wound his way through endless details. So that Madruga would absorb them. Salvador was not Galician. He had been born near Santa Fé, in Catalonia. A village with many abandoned houses, as though the villagers had taken off en masse. But Salvador, by nature high-strung, found fault with anything and everything. Voicing his desire to take off very shortly for the Christian territories of Spain, since he detested the inheritance received from his father. Consisting of three plots of arable lowland and five of pastureland. All of them far from the road leading to Santa Fé. Hence worth nothing. And of a small house as well, through the roof of which water poured into the rooms when it rained. So that it was better to seek shelter under a leafy tree or in the mouth of a cave. Not to mention, moreover, the tramontana from the Pyrenees, which at every windstorm threatened to blow the roof down and the rest of the house too.

One night, as rain was falling into the room through the cracks, Salvador opened the door, standing there contemplating the landscape. There was little to be seen outside. In low spirits at the time, because in less than three months he had buried both his father and his mother, who had been unable to bear the grief their daughter had brought them by running away from home with a band of gypsies, Salvador went up on the roof and, at the risk of slipping and falling off, began shattering the roof tiles, even those in good condition, with a stonemason's hammer. He pounded away in a white-hot fury, in violent protest against fate and his wretched lot. Till nothing remained of the roof, thus driving himself out of his own house.

No neighbor, alerted by the noise, came to his aid. The rain had penned them up inside enemy walls. On terra firma once again, Salvador, upset by the indifference of the village, swore never again to accept any sort of permanent shelter. The next morning, with a little bundle of clothing, the hammer and the anvil that would enable him to practice the trade of tinker, inherited from his father, he left the house.

He placed his belongings on the back of the old donkey and made his way down the hill. Deliberately leaving the door wide open. So that the wind would lash it, and so that those passing by would see that that house no longer had an owner.

With his soul in torment, he vowed not to return. Even on the verge of death.

"I know where I was born, but I don't know where death lies in wait for me. I will die, then, among strangers, in a land full of thorns, pines, and wind. That wind has always frightened me."

He was barely sixteen, and never again did he find repose. He journeyed all through Spain without consulting a map or following guidebooks. He avoided those places in which he had even once set foot. In this respect, no country seemed to him as ideal as Spain for traveling on foot. And the moment he laid his belongings and the saddle on the ground, he began soldering pans and metals, with extraordinary skill.

He remained in the villages just long enough to repair what the years and much handling had destroyed. When he left, not a single defect remained. So that when he took one last look at the village, from the top of the mountain as he went on his way, he saw, with satisfaction, smoke coming out of the flue, taking it to be a strong indication that the pans were being broken in again on the lighted stove.

He was proud to think that, had it not been for his eagerness to roam the world, those objects would have remained in the attic or the cellar, completely unserviceable, worthless. Thanks to him, they had another chance at life, in return for Salvador's living free, unbridled, traveling a road to nowhere.

In each village, the landscape and the new faces, which he never saw again, were a surprise. For Salvador, everything was soon over and done with. He too vanishing in others' memory. Whereupon, downcast, he would drop by the taverns. No other place offered him so exhaustive an explanation of the secret recesses of the human soul. Over a brimming glass there came pouring out, with intense sincerity, man's glory and his baseness. Thanks to wine, a god that acted on the sly. And whose fumes steeped the brain in intolerable truths. Thereby reaching the forbidden, a terrain where the causes for any and every banishment were redeemed. Were it not for this ruby-red, bloody wine, certain truths, dwellers in the dark cellars of souls, would never know the light.

Whenever invited to dinner at someone's house, Salvador was extremely reserved. Confining himself to saying thank you as each platter was passed to him at table. Installed in the kitchen, from which there poured an asphyxiating cloud of smoke, the women, their bellies glued to the stove, hurried the food along. And as though they had forgotten his presence, these families, feasting on wine and succulent dishes, began, indiscriminately, to address words to each other that wounded, killed, and comforted. He watched, with relish, the human feast. Those people chewing away, moved by ambition, rage, fear of death, all feelings closely related. And who, immediately after impatiently throwing the plates they had scraped clean into the sink or the basin of water, hopped into bed, wanting to sate themselves with sex, because the urge came over them, wet, immediate, with no time to lose. Or they gave themselves over to quarrels, violent brawls, fights over inheritances.

Excluded from family life, Salvador went off to get drunk at the tavern. Several men spewed up bitter words and their food at the same time. And diverted by jokes and japes, crude and fraternal, they watched the hours go by. Late at night, Salvador would leave with them, arm in arm to keep from falling. Bawling Catalan, Castilian, Valencian, Asturian songs, from that oven that was Spain, its songs as varied as its landscapes.

Their singing, tipsy and vulgar, annoyed the neighbors, who drove them from their doors with angry shouts. Telling them to go damn their souls in some other parish. Which, as it happened, turned out to be the house of their next-door neighbor, who, in turn, sent them back to where they'd come from.

Once recovered from his hangover, Salvador would bid them good-bye, taking with him as a memory a certain bitter taste in his mouth, ridding himself of it only after drinking the clear water of the first stream-let. Those transparent waters that came down the mountainside licking the pebbles and his drawn face.

"How did you come to know Salvador, grandfather? Did he arrive in Galicia on foot? Or astride a donkey? Or did he choose to come by train, or in a wagon?"

Xan smiled. Madruga's curiosity was a guarantee that his grandson would be present at the hour of his death. If only on account of his ever-lasting stories, whose ending Xan would change when he sensed that Ma-druga was on the point of guessing how it would all turn out.

As he listened to his grandfather, Madruga was also peeling the bark from a dry branch of the tree with his penknife. Keeping his ears pricked up for the lies and the contradictions that peopled his grandfather's tale, and hence liable to make it a shaky story. Without noticing Ceferino, watching them from a distance.

Now and again, Madruga found fault with Xan, who in turn repri-manded him for his impudence. Until Xan finally admitted, to his grand-son's face, that an error had indeed crept into the story, very nearly ruining it. And, worse still, casting doubt on his role as narrator. Which would have been the end of him.

Every time they had such a spat, Xan always offered, in a roundabout way, to make up.

"Where was I exactly?"

Madruga willingly allowed his grandfather to go on. Ceferino, how-ever, upset by his son's laughter, stalked over to them in a fury.

"Watch it, father. Don't give away too many secrets."

Xan immediately fell silent, not daring to go on while Ceferino was about.

"Ceferino's come just as the story ended. That's enough for today, right?" Xan said to his grandson.

Madruga saw that his father was anxious to hide from him an episode that, quite plainly, he was ashamed of. Urcesina being equally overcome with embarrassment at times, instantly leaving off her whisperings the moment Madruga entered the room.

"What did Grandfather do, mother, for you to feel so ashamed?" he suddenly asked her.

Badly rattled, Urcesina covered and uncovered the pans on the stove, checking to see whether her son had ruined what was cooking. Then she shut her eyes, as though giving him five minutes to disappear from her presence. And stood there like someone listening for a noise. Finally calming down when she heard the door slam, assuring her that Madruga had fled the kitchen.

In the field, helping Ceferino do the plowing, Madruga took advantage of his father's weariness.

"Why is it that Grandfather Xan keeps his best story to himself? Who forbade him to tell it? What's the secret?"

Ceferino sat down on a stone, wiped the sweat from his face with his handkerchief. His callused hands hung at his sides, the lines of fate in the palms of his hands not visible.

"Don't be so curious, my boy. In life, people have to control themselves. Otherwise, they never get to hear the end of the story," and he headed off to the corner of the field, which lay in the shadow of an oak tree. Among the belongings heaped in a pile was a bottle of grape-husk brandy, a present from Portuguese friends on the other side of the Minho. He put it to his lips and treated himself to a few quick sips. Without offering any to his son.

Abashed, Madruga said nothing. Later, up on Wolf Hill, where he'd taken the cows, he decided his father was right. He had abused the privilege of asking for stories that didn't belong to him. On the mountainside, far from home, the cattle made their way past the thorns of the gorse bushes specked with yellow, so as to get at the grass. There, as nowhere else, Madruga awaited a time in the future when some plot of Xan's would fill the gap he felt yawning wider and wider within him with each passing day. On the other hand, he was sure that his grandfather, despite the promise to keep his mouth shut, would slip at some moment on the grease of his own words, telling him at last what lay at the bottom of his mystery.

Only on reaching Sobreira did Salvador perceive that he had taken the wrong road. And this thanks to Justo, who hastened to tell him that Carvalledo, the place he was trying to track down, was fifteen kilometers farther on.

"For the moment, we're still in Sobreira here. Where we're stuck and where we're all going to die," Justo said gloomily.

The news that the tinker had done everything he could to avoid Sobreira made everyone indignant. Not just on account of the usefulness of his services. They were unwilling to forgive the lack of respect the stranger had shown them by judging them inferior to the people who dwelt in Carvalledo, as a general rule full of pride and false cordiality. When Sobreira had a great deal worth seeing. Beginning with Dom Miguel's house, the only one in the district to have on its own façade, in full view, a prominent coat of arms, whose heraldic history, moreover, could be found in the annals of the library of Santiago University.

Xan manifested a desire to make the acquaintance of the stranger who had provoked Sobreira. And who had sown chaos and discord the moment he had set foot there. But he did not need to seek him out because, from the door of the tavern, he could see Salvador approaching. Passing by him without greeting him or removing his beret. He went straight to the counter, after gazing round the room at all the drowsy faces at that late afternoon hour.

He ordered a glass of wine, in a hoarse whisper. That way, they couldn't hear his accent and tell where he was from. And it never occurred to the stranger to apologize for the hubbub he'd caused in the town.

The tavern keeper filled the stranger's glass to the brim, with the intention of making him tremble as he raised the wine to his lips. And, at the very instant he bent down to drink it, the tavern keeper said, to get even with him:

"The wine in this tavern in Sobreira is the best in the entire district and no one can prove the contrary to us."

Taking no notice of the tense atmosphere, Salvador sipped several drops, holding them in his bulging cheek. Then, however, he spat the liquid onto the floor, giving the tavern keeper a hard look.

"If this wine is the best of all, then what they drink in the other villages is vinegar," he said scornfully.

The reaction was disproportionate to the facts. And this because the tavern keeper vaulted over the counter in one leap, displaying an agility that they had not suspected him of possessing. His fists clenched, instantly prepared to stand up to him, as he tried, shouting at the top of his lungs, to turn him out of the tavern. This brave attitude winning him supporters. And even the solidarity of certain indifferent onlookers and of those who had been drinking since early in the day.

Xan felt pleasingly attracted by the cheeky foreigner, his face crisscrossed with precocious wrinkles and furrows and weathered by the sun and wind. With, as an added detail, a pale, wispy mustache that could only be seen from very close up.

"One moment," Xan said, bringing the expulsion to a halt. "Let's see if the stranger knows what he's talking about."

He picked the abandoned glass up off the counter and placed his lips in the exact spot where Salvador had put his, to taste the wine. He wanted to imitate him perfectly, so that in the future it would not be said, as far as this episode was concerned, that Sobreira had acted unjustly. On taking the first sip, Xan scowled, then immediately spat the wine out on the wooden floor of the tavern.

"It must be granted that the stranger is patient and well bred. This wine shames our land. From what bloody barrel was it drawn?" he said in a fury to the frightened tavern keeper.

Counting now on Xan's support, Salvador found himself surrounded by polite questioners. They asked him his name, where he came from, and why, coming from so far away, he had chosen Galicia of all places, a region on the very border of Spain, northwest of Madrid, forgotten by the Castilians, by the Basques, and other peoples, all of them responsible for the formation of a dispersed country, with countless languages, which made mutual understanding extremely difficult.

Salvador's answers, though evasive, trotted out names that they had never heard of. Despite the close attention the stranger paid them, with a keen didactic sense even, it was plain to see that he was worried about the animal tied to the tree next to the entrance to the tavern, in whose shade people standing in the doorway were watching others going past.

"His name is Pegasus, and he's my soul mate," pointing to the donkey, who repaid him for his attention with a grateful look. Indifferent, however, to the others.

"Pegasus is a good name. Too bad he doesn't have wings and can't fly, despite his name. He's earthbound, just as we are," Xan said, eager to show off his store of knowledge. He paused. "And when night falls, where are you going to sleep?"

"On the ground, under the sheltering stars. Who needs a roof on a summer night?"

Xan envied the stranger's lofty pride, disdaining works erected with human hands and skill. He offered him his house nonetheless, with a bed ready and waiting for him. Salvador thanked him, but could not accept. He never left his animal behind. He must not feel rejected just because his master had bettered himself in life, even if only for a night.

"In that case, I'll put the two of you up in the pen, along with the other animals. I'll fix you a bed of clean hay."

For three days, Salvador, setting himself up in front of the town cross, mended the pots and pans of Sobreira. He took time out only to talk with Xan, till far into the night. On the fourth day, he began saying his good-byes. Confessing, however, that he was leaving a true friend behind in Sobreira, which he had confused in the beginning with Carvalledo.

"The first friend I've had since I abandoned my village, near Santa Fé. Up till now I haven't missed my land or anyone's company. When my heart protests against this sort of life, I smother it in my overcoat. Despite these precautions, I suffer from the absence of the tramontana, the wind that blows our way from the Pyrenees. It came to us with a smell of manure, woodlands, and salt air. Because of the waters of the Mediterranean. But once having left Catalonia, I never went back to a single village I'd visited before."

Xan accompanied him for several kilometers. He had taken a great liking to the stranger, and was sorry to be parting from him now. And before seeing him disappear in the direction of the mountains, he presented him with a bottle of brandy.

"I don't want to say good-bye forever. Maybe you'll decide to come back someday, my friend. Besides finding a companion here, you'll have a roof over your head and hot food. And more old pans. That our hunger and the flames of the stove will soon ruin."

A year later, Salvador entered Sobreira. In his harsh face there was no sign that it was nostalgia that had brought him back. On the contrary, he came down the road in a visible ill humor, dragging Pegasus with him at the end of a rope. The animal, however, was decorated as for a feast day. Clean, silky-haired, with countless colored ribbons wound around his neck, setting off his mane. And wildflowers looped down from his ears to his rump, twining round the objects sitting in the saddle, the anvil especially.

As he went toward the tavern, Salvador kept stroking the donkey's head, with a tenderness he was not in the habit of showing in the realm of the human. At the door of the tavern, beneath the same tree, he relieved Pegasus of the weight of the baggage. He sat down on the doorstep, paying no attention to the curious who spoke to him of pots and pans. He remained there waiting for the news of his arrival to reach Xan's house. A few minutes later, Xan came to give him a welcoming embrace. Salvador avoided his open arms, holding tight to the animal.

"I came back only because I still owe you the end of the story of Elcano the seafarer. He took ship in Cadiz, remember? Well, from that point, this is what happened to him: On the third day of the voyage, because of favorable winds and tides, he arrived in Lisbon. The moment he arrived there, the narrow streets of the city drove him out of his mind. The Moorish quarter in particular, with its women in the doorways and the clothes hanging out the windows. As a result of an inexplicable emotion, he began drinking so much that when it came time to take ship again he embarked on the wrong one. Instead of boarding the one that was his, which would take him to Canada, he went aboard one that dropped him off in Brazil. And he remained in that country for quite a while, in a state of shocked surprise the entire time. And since what he saw far surpassed anything he could imagine, he thought it prudent this time not to drink a single drop of alcohol. Reality there was quite enough to intoxicate a person, he perceived. So he stayed sober the whole time, though he had the sensation he'd been drinking all day long. Till finally he got back to Catalonia. On the way to Vich, however, he stopped in Santa Fé, to spend the night and have himself a big meal. And according to what the old men who'd known him used to tell back then, this Elcano talked on and on about those strange lands in America, past all understanding. And that was because that place, peopled with slaves, jungle savages, and back-country whites, had an emperor with a long white beard, who always wore such elegantly tailored suits that Elcano thought he was seeing things again. Except that he hadn't been drinking. Or could it be one last attack of fever? Because it didn't seem possible to him for Brazil to have an emperor who acted as though he were in Europe. Yet he saw him pass in his carriage, with an air so solemn and aristocratic that even the blacks, credulous by nature, turned their faces the other way as he passed, disbelieving what they saw. They were certain that that being was a ghost. Whereas the Portuguese, those very same Portuguese to be found on the other side of the Minho, their eyes eternally fixed on Spain, applauded him in the streets. At first sight, Elcano could hardly tell the Portuguese from white Brazilians who'd been born there. And that was because in every conceivable way, those Brazilians aped the courtiers of that day, giving themselves over to endless corruption. They resembled our Castilians, who have dominated us for centuries, with an insolence that forbids us even the use of our own language."

Xan patiently heard him out. Interrupting him only for a few moments, to take him inside the tavern. Both deserved to wet their whistles with a good wine.

"Don't worry about Pegasus. He's well off here in Sobreira. Nothing's going to happen to him," Xan said.

They drank toasts to a number of things in silence. None of them accompanied by wishes voiced aloud.

"Perhaps you people might teach Galician in the schools? I, for example, speak Castilian. But of what good is it to me, if I have the Catalan language in my heart? I learned this language with my mother's milk. For that reason alone they're trying to condemn me. It's the same with you people. If it weren't for that accursed Castilian, we might all understand each other better: who can say? As far as I know, from what Elcano told me, Brazil manages to speak just one language, despite its size. And that's something to cause us envy. If only because of that one circumstance, it's worth our while to visit that country. But do you know what finally happened to Elcano the navigator? Or rather, the seaman, since he never got past this rating, once he went back to Spain? And came to see us with his face stripped to the bone by the burning sun of the tropics and salt air?"

In the tavern, the conversation between them was endless. As Salvador talked to him of Elcano, of Urraca, and other characters, Xan learned to listen, contrary to his habits. And whenever his turn came to talk, Xan touched on episodes in the history of Galicia. Giving preference, however, to those legends that hovered above Galician rooftops like guardian angels, with wings outspread, ready to confirm the dreams of that people.

Late at night, they were thrown out of the tavern, sodden with wine and stories. They went reeling home to Xan's, where Salvador slept in the animal pen. As they drew near the house, Xan could see, by the light in their bedroom, that Teodora was waiting up for him with eyes wide open.

Teodora had learned at an early hour that the tinker had come on a surprise visit to Sobreira. This meaning that Xan had gone to meet him, though he had not set any definite hour for his return. After supper, Teodora prepared a plate of food for her husband, leaving it on the table. For the time being, she was punishing him by offering him cold food. Then, wrapped in her black shawl, she sat herself down in front of the clock on the wall to catch the minutes in their flight. And, in less than an hour of constant contemplation, her body began to itch all over, even in embarrassing areas. A reaction that invariably occurred in the face of a fact she found intolerable. Following which, in a brief space of time, she would break out in hard lumps in one place or another, on which creams and lotions had no effect. Or even strong violet-colored remedies.

In the bedroom, Xan watched Teodora scratching herself in the bed, entirely preoccupied, despite her busy hands, with blaming him for the new crisis. Xan paid no attention to her. He recommended rest and sugar water.

"It's your nervous system that's the problem, Teodora. What's happening is that you're the victim of your own nerves," he said in a thick voice.

With her husband lying beside her, Teodora could smell his bad breath, a mixture of alcohol and tobacco, further aggravating her state. She found herself incapable, however, of rebelling against that intruder by the name of Salvador who was robbing her of her husband, which was more than life, her rival, had ever stolen from her.

In the days following, the itch not having gone away at all, Teodora found herself surrounded with pomade and children. Xan thus having more than enough time to divert himself with Salvador, until he took off again.

Xan was piqued at Salvador's absence when he failed to stop by Sobreira. Because after his second visit, Salvador would turn up now and again in the course of his travels, to Xan's joy, for he'd been waiting for this return. When Salvador said good-bye each time, he never promised to return. On the contrary, his face bore the sad expression of someone saying good-bye forever. Xan's spirits rose at the thought that Sobreira was the one place on earth that Salvador always returned to.

One day, Salvador came back minus an eye, lost in a brawl in a camp far up in the Sierra Nevada. Persecuted by enemies openly intolerant of his friendship for Pegasus. The animal seemed to sympathize with his master's situation. And to demonstrate their solidarity, he would often rest his head on Salvador's shoulder.

Salvador couldn't get used to the loss of his eye. Obliged now to glimpse the world by halves, his head kept turning round all the time in his eagerness to fill in angles he might be missing.

This catastrophe upset Xan. He therefore thought it prudent for Salvador to give up his nomad life and settle down for good in Sobreira. He ought not to do battle with mountains in the night. Masses of earth, undermined by water in winter, which slid down the slopes, dragging with them trees, boulders, and men. Not to mention the north wind, or whatever other name it might have, malevolently pursuing the men who defied it. And whose sharp whistle affected the nervous system, penetrating to the bone, very nearly destroying a body. On occasion, not giving a person time to wait for redemption, which came with the first signs of spring.

"Down here you have my house, food, and field work, once you've mended all the pots and pans in Sobreira."

Salvador wept tears of emotion with his one remaining eye. And that because the other one, doubtless damaged, was untouched by human emotions. There being an ugly, angry wound in it, which he did not complain of. A single eye was enough for him to be critical of a life that had taken him all over Spain, till there was not one corner of it that was foreign to his feet. His apprenticeship, then, had come from the earth and from the open sky.

Grieving, he spoke to Xan of the gypsies who had abducted his sister to make her a princess.

"There's no doubt about it, Xan. Wherever that sister of mine may be, if she hasn't died, she's the princess of a tribe in tatters, yet worthy of esteem. She must be down in Andalusia. Maybe our paths will cross without our family blood divulging our presence. What good is the voice of the blood if it doesn't speak up at the right times? If that voice doesn't utter words that would tame men, those cannibals with knives in their mouths? Spain, for example, is a swarming anthill of passions and murders. The only superiority this country can boast of is that we do our murdering openly. Thus defying laws and authorities, the first, moreover, to kill. It seems that we enjoy killing and dying in the middle of the night, just before dawn. Or did you think that Galicia was less murderous than the rest of this shattered country? A country with so many languages that everybody thinks he's speaking the wrong one," Salvador said irritatedly.

Not wanting to wound Xan's feelings, and as evidence of his gratitude, Salvador brought him tree branches and leaves gathered at random. So as to give Xan the feeling that he too had traveled. Xan, of all people, who had never left Sobreira.

Xan kept the leaves and dry branches in the wardrobe chest, sensing that he ought to get a move on before the world began to shrink with age. In the end, what did it mean to travel? Merely to leave one's room, shine one's boots, choose a clean shirt, shave, and let oneself be carried along by the jolting of coaches, of trains, the stride of a pair of legs. Or could traveling be receiving Salvador's presents, accompanied by words that translated the meaning of each object for him? Since a mere leaf served the tinker as the memory of an experience he'd had in Tudela.

Certainly Xan matched the stakes of the imaginary that Salvador laid down with the aim of making his eyes gleam. Hence backing his bet with local legends, the major inheritance of that land. Thus taking the considerable risk that with all their storytelling the Galicians had forgotten reality.

Both of them, however, accepted that life and dreams were, apparently, irreconcilable, one trying to exclude the other. Forgetting these technical obstacles, Salvador and Xan dreamed till dawn. The discussion now revolved round a delicate problem. How could they get to know Brazil, described by Elcano, and yet not leave the shores of Spain?

For hours on end, they went about conjuring up a plan that would enable them to travel without the terrible effort of abandoning the country to which they were forever bound.

"We already know it's impossible to leave Spain," Salvador said disconsolately.

"I see only one way," Xan immediately chimed in. "It's to cast a son out into the Atlantic. Making him promise that, on his return, he'll offer us his version of Brazil. If it's really true that everybody there passes himself off as a European. And that they take the measure of their frustrations by way of the tall tales they invent and by their contempt for their own land. That way, we'll have traveled without the discomfort of leaving Sobreira. And dying in a foreign land."

Salvador hurriedly turned his head away. So that Xan would not see his bitterness. It had pained him lately to think that he had no place to die. A bed to stretch out in before closing his eyes. He'd spent his life proclaiming that his triumph consisted in dying beneath the shelter of an old oak tree, keeping the clouds company as they blended with the outlines of the earth. He nonetheless hoped that some kind soul would dig a hole in the ground to throw his body into. Keeping it from being food for predators. He was repelled by the thought that wolves might feast on his remains.

In the end, Teodora carefully avoided complaining about Salvador's visits. Nonetheless, sores appeared at times on her body. Though they soon healed over. She hoped, however, that she would one day manage to be free of the stranger. And Xan be content to retain the pale memory of a passage that did very little to increase his substance.

With this fleeting dream in her breast, Teodora opened her eyes one morning, groping about among the sheets, sure that she would touch Xan's body. She searched about the whole bed, stretching her arm out till it reached the other edge, without finding him. As a rule, she got up first so as to light the fire and make breakfast. And then, once these tasks were finished, going out into the fields. Xan liked to sleep on for a while more. He ate his breakfast by himself, before caring for the animals in the pen under the floor of the house.

"That wretch doesn't even come to bed anymore," Teodora cried, immediately scratching herself.

When the children were called, they came on the run. Some still in their nightclothes, drowsy, not noticing Teodora's despair. Ceferino, an adolescent still, was sent to the animal pen. To see if his father, having drunk too much wine, had decided to sleep in the straw, next to Salvador and Pegasus, the animal that Catalan refused to part from. In the pen, however, there was no trace of the men and the animal. They then realized that some of Xan's clothes were gone from the wardrobe chest. His winter overcoat and his boots in particular.

"Oh, my God, my man's run out on me!"

Teodora went out into the yard, where the neighbors could easily see her, her weeping and screaming rending the air. Wanting to share with one and all her succulent pain, which promised to yield an abundance of juice. Especially since even the consolation of widowhood would be denied her.

"Why didn't God make me a widow before humbling me in this way?" she asked the women who came to comfort her. Many of them in mourning for deaths long past and long forgotten. There was even a case of one mourning dress being worn for several dead people.

The men, gathered together in the tavern, refused to discuss the subject. Till one of them broke the silence.

"Xan had the courage we've always lacked."

And they stayed there drinking, amid the sadness of seeing themselves prisoners of an exhausted soil and of women with a bitter, salty taste.

The episode of his grandfather's escape, hitherto hushed up as though it were a crime, was not revealed to Madruga till he went to class at school. Called upon by Gravio, the schoolmaster, to tell about America, Madruga was all enthusiasm. He spoke of America as a continent of outsized dimensions and without peer. Hence able to stimulate man's imagination, obliging him to sally forth and experience terrible adventures, and commit the worst follies. Always with the certainty that nothing would happen to him, since America could provide a safe haven for any sort of incendiary instinct. Refusing to establish distinctions between base creatures and noble ones. All on an equal footing.

Gravio smiled at Madruga. "I see you've inherited your grandfather's virtues," he said, with a conniving wink.

"Are you referring to a fondness for telling stories?"

"I'm referring to your Grandfather Xan's spirit of adventure."

Alone with the schoolmaster, after the class was ended, Madruga returned to the subject. He had indeed inherited from Xan the desire to travel about the world.

"This desire cannot be condemned. Moreover, it is almost a torture. Xan nonetheless had the courage to leave home for two years, without leaving so much as a note for Dona Teodora."

And thoroughly enjoying going back over an event he presumed was known to Madruga, Gravio went on to add new elements to the story. He was especially impressed by the fact that Xan had left without deigning to explain to a soul where it was that he was going.

A decision that surprised Sobreira. Hence everyone knocked on Teodora's door, hoping that a letter had arrived. From Seville perhaps. One in which he would describe the city as mysterious. Even though he would omit to mention, naturally, the orgies held there amid the delirium of flamenco music and dances.

After a few months' silence, they began to question whether Xan was still alive. For they refused to interpret his silence as proof that he had been carried away by the people and the landscape.

"It was a difficult period, Madruga. Full of suspicions and wild imaginings. All Sobreira grieved at being forgotten by Xan," the schoolmaster said.

Gravio immediately showed that he understood the weight of that inheritance in Madruga's life. It not being easy, doubtless, to have inherited from his grandfather a spirit given to examining reality as though it took the form of a box, inside which we were imprisoned. Hence certain beings, more than others, fought against these walls that threatened to shrink each year. So it seemed logical to him that Madruga would one day follow in his grandfather's footsteps.

"Here in Sobreira, there is no way to grow. Except within oneself. But it's a monotonous journey, and few people book passage for the trip. What's the use of spending one's life with no other company than one's own guts and one's own soul?" Gravio said emphatically, giving Madruga no chance to speak.

Nonetheless, he advised him to stay away from America. It was better to be a pilgrim within Spain, which was capable, in and of itself, of offering him a life equaling Xan's. For, according to what people said, Salvador and Xan, in their eagerness to get to know the country, had never slept under the same roof twice.

Madruga's heart was pounding as he left the school. He found his grandfather on the veranda, smoking before lunch. Xan immediately sensed his grandson's state of shock, brought on only a few moments before by a sentiment new to him. Accompanied by doubts and misgivings. He invited him to sit down beside him.

"What's the matter, son?" and he put his hand on Madruga's shoulder.

"Why didn't Father and Mother ever want me to know?"

"Are you referring to my running off? I flew the coop, it's true, but to my credit I returned to Sobreira two years after playing dead," Xan said, feeling relieved.

It wasn't Salvador who had persuaded Xan to follow him. It was his own decision. Doubtless influenced by the freedom that Salvador's face showed so openly. And that aroused people's envy. A freedom that made his stories exciting and titillating.

After Salvador's last visits, Xan felt himself to be in danger. It seemed hard to live in Sobreira when he had Salvador's example to follow. Timidly, he questioned him concerning the advantages of that life.

"There aren't many, Xan. Except that your chest pounds with fear all the time. I have palpitations all over, and this never ceases to be a sort of pleasure. Have you ever thought what it's like to remember assuming the risks of living in the open, without a roof, a bed, and a woman?"

"Do you mean that if I don't get away, right now, from the comforts of home, the church bell on Sundays with its promise of saving my soul, and my daily visit to the tavern, I'll be doomed forever?" Xan felt confused, wanting an explanation.

Salvador refused to catechize him. He was the one who ought to know his own life. The owner of a body that, naturally, was beginning to suffer the wear and tear of time.

"Did you know, Salvador, that I've never had even one exciting adventure?" and after these words, Xan decided to leave with him.

Salvador's reply was grave. "Despite journeying together, eating the same food, enjoying the same sky above, our lives will never be as one. You alone are answerable for your fate. And never blame me for any of your failures or disillusionments."

In the end, Salvador accepted him as a traveling companion, confident of his stamina and agility. Able to go up and down the mountainsides without fear of dizzy spells. Prepared, like Salvador, to overcome life's everyday difficulties. Refusing to put up with complaints about the cold, the long days' journeys, broken off at times to crunch a hard crust of bread between their teeth.

Salvador strove to be an impeccable guide down to the last detail. Pleased with the apprentice following him on Pegasus' other side, without grumbling or lagging behind. During breaks in the journey, Salvador rewarded Xan with stories illustrating human misery. Always refusing to be reconciled to the status of ward of Castilian imperialism.

"Even when you're sleeping with your wife, beneath your Galician roof, they're with you. Their eyes fixed on your happiness or your misfortune. There's nothing that escapes their notice."

Like Xan, Salvador had a splendid memory. One fed on potatoes and pork fat. Moreover, as far as gastronomy was concerned, Salvador had a talent for detecting the different tastes produced by the regions they traversed on foot. With his eyes closed, he could tell where they were by his sense of smell alone. Extremely sensitive to the odors that followed them long after they'd passed through a village. Only in the mountains did his nostrils clear themselves of the smell of cooking oil, becoming impregnated with the chlorophyll of oak leaves and the aromatic essences of pine and eucalyptus.

For Salvador, these smells held a rich language. He therefore railed against those provinces that had the habit of drowning out the taste of food through the excessive use of saffron.

"Those people think it suffices to tint food yellow for it to be tasty and attractive. They're brutish louts," he said testily.

His stomach had been positively conditioned to swallow those foods of Spain that clashed the most violently with each other. Accumulating in this peculiar way tales that had been born at table and in bed.

Xan appreciated Salvador's style of making his way into a village. Always with his head held high, sober and dignified, seeking food and work. He would then begin pounding the anvil sitting on Pegasus' back with firm, strong strokes of his hammer.

They would head for the tavern first. Salvador would quickly pour himself some wine, going outside immediately so as not to lose sight of the animal. And for politeness's sake, he never failed to offer Pegasus a drink of the wine he was downing with so much pleasure. The animal would answer with a nod of his head. But he wasn't always docile. When Salvador tried to speak in his name, Pegasus balked. No force was strong enough to move his feet off the ground. Unless Salvador went round to his ear to console him with secret words, which erased his mistrustful look. Only then would Pegasus open his eyes, following him obediently.

Salvador refused to tell Xan how old the animal was. He maintained that he was a creature whose wisdom had come down to him directly from antiquity. And therefore able, for millennia now, along with a very small number of others of the same race, to examine human behavior, including his own.

"Perhaps he was born in Argos, where there are as many stones as there are in Galicia," Xan said.

Madruga listened to Xan with exemplary respect. Grateful to have close at hand the hero sought in the stories told by his grandfather. Xan neglecting to name himself the protagonist of the plot. And on learning the story of how his grandfather had made his escape, Madruga attributed everything that went through his head to him. His grandfather now being responsible for his most violent fantasies. He reached the point of imagining him racing across the Pyrenees, closely pursued by the Guardia Civil, who had taken him for a smuggler of cigarettes, gunpowder, and gold. As for Salvador, he had been transformed from a tinker into a pirate. Casually enjoying a long stay on terra firma, having wearied of the sea.

His grandfather interrupted his daydreams to bring him down to earth again.

"Don't forget that I came back. I was afraid to go on. I was never as smart as Salvador, who never abandoned the mountaintops, the life of a wanderer," Xan said, with sadness in his face.

Teodora spent the last late afternoons of the month of August on the veranda, convinced that her husband would return during that cruel summer that dragged on their lungs, scarcely allowing them to breathe. Her eyes riveted on the road down from Wolf Hill, Xan's favorite mountaintop. Her itch less painful now. Except when she broke out in a skin rash from time to time. And though her children insisted that she must give up all hope of Xan's returning, and not just sit there waiting at the window or on the veranda when they needed strong arms for the harvest, Teodora did not abandon her post in those last days of August.

She was sitting there pondering whether she would put on mourning if her man did not return by the end of the month. She was thus offering him his last chance to remain alive in the bosom of his family. If on the last day of August he hadn't turned up, in accordance with the vow she had made, Teodora would immediately proceed to clean out the wardrobe chest, burning the rare photographs of him, throwing out his personal belongings. Above all she couldn't bear the presence inside the chest, among the clothes, of the leaves and withered branches that had been presents from Salvador. That sere nature, with its capricious forms, now bore a certain resemblance to her, as she was when she looked at herself in the mirror, her vigor and luster gone. The natural oil of her body had drained away, just as her youth had long since forsaken her. Happily, her eyes still had the same intense brightness, so much so that her children warned her to be careful of her heart, since something must be happening to her to make the light in her face so striking.

At five in the afternoon, the sky set afire by a pre-twilight vermilion, Teodora spied the shadow of a man whose walk told her that it was Xan coming down the hillside. A man who had done so much to disturb her life just as she reached its autumn. She did not budge, but as he drew nearer she could see how thin he was, the hollows in his cheeks, his deeply furrowed brow. Now, however, the two of them so close they could each reach out and touch the other, Xan seemed to her to have a sad look about him, a bird chained to a hoop. They said nothing at first. Though she heard the drum beating in her breast.

"You're very much mistaken, Teodora. I'm not returning hat in hand. Nor am I coming home repenting of my errors. I am here in Sobreira only because I recognize that the world is too big for me. It's just that I prefer recounting adventures to living them."

And so saying, Xan sat down on the stairs leading to the veranda, which opened onto the living room and the kitchen by way of different doors. At that moment, the smell of stew cooking was coming from the kitchen, with potatoes doubtless floating in it, the smoke mounting toward the victuals hanging from the ceiling, drying them a bit more with each passing day. And taking a deep breath of the fragrances given forth by the house, from which he had so long absented himself, Xan added:

"What a wretched life a peasant leads! I couldn't even devote mine to the adventures I'd dreamed of ever since I was a little boy."

"You've gotten the punishment you deserved, man. You weren't cut out for this world. Outside of Sobreira, of the walls of this house, or the air of our mountains, you're completely lost," Teodora said, keeping him company now, though seated on the step above his.

Xan gazed distractedly at the meadow opposite the house. It was exactly as he had left it. His eye lit especially on the big stone corbeil, in the yard, to the right of the stairway, where they kept the ears of corn. Life beginning all over again for him in the apprehension of these particulars. In short, he would become one with the details causing him to move in accordance with the earth's revolutions. Till he at last accepted his lot.

"If I made a mistake in not going beyond Spain's borders, Ceferino will conquer the world in my place. He'll go to America in my name, and tell me all about it afterward," he said, forcing himself to reap the benefit of Teodora's presence.

"Would you care to bet that he won't go? And that I'll do the impossible to prevent him? I warn you, Xan, that that's how I'll get my revenge," his wife said in a monotone, without the slightest tension in her voice.

"It doesn't matter. If he doesn't go, a grandson will. Somebody who'll be coming along later. It's not possible for God to have such a disappointment in store for me. And you know very well that our race isn't going to die out all that soon."

Upon these words, Xan rose to his feet. He immediately held out his hand to Teodora, helping her to her feet. He politely offered to escort her into the house.

Teodora accepted his aid. She allowed him to hold her hand for a few moments. And as they went up the stairs toward the living room, where they would have coffee together round the table, she murmured, for his ears alone:

"I'll take you back in my bed. But I want you to know that I won't go to your funeral."

"That won't be necessary, Teodora," and he gently stroked her arm. "You'll die before I do."

One night there was a knock on Xan's door. It had rained all week and the winter had covered Sobreira with such a blanket of fog that hardly anyone ventured out onto the roads or even went outside. In the stalls, the animals lowed restlessly. Their heat and that of the human householders intermingling by way of the walls they shared. Teodora was apprehensive, wondering who could be seeking them out at that late hour. Xan tried to distract her. There was no need to be afraid. There were no brigands in that region. His wife was suddenly suspicious. She looked at him intently, probing his sentiments. He withstood her gaze for some time. Then he hurriedly made a move toward the door, troubled by the knocking, which continued.

Teodora felt that he was lying to her. He knew who it was. She begged him not to go. Or else refuse a hospitality that threatened their family life.

Xan held his ground. "Whoever it is, he'll be well received. If he comes as a friend."

If he lights out this time, he'll have abandoned the house forever, Teodora thought. And before her husband opened the door, she withdrew to the bedroom, concentrating her thoughts on the rain, on the widowhood that threatened.

Xan opened the door. The small voice from without touched Xan's heart. He immediately identified Salvador, leaning against the wall, scarcely able to stand on his feet. In the yard, the drenched figure of Pegasus.

"Come right in, friend. I'll take care of you," and, his arms around Salvador, he felt his body, soaking-wet and deformed from ill-treatment. So thin his bones ached. Salvador drew back, not wanting to come inside. If it wouldn't be too much trouble, he would rather sleep in the animal pen, with Pegasus at his side.

Xan dragged him inside bodily, suspecting that something serious had happened. Deeply upset, he asked him how he had reached Sobreira in that state. He bedded Salvador down on the clean straw and straightway brought him coffee, brandy, and a blanket. And for the animal a basin of water, and dry grass from the winter stores. In the light of the gas lamp next to Salvador, he could see that he was having difficulty breathing. And his velvet garments, which he had come to know well in the years just past, were now only mends and patches.

He freed him of his clothes, rubbing his chest with alcohol. Covering him with the blanket, warming his feet with heated bricks wrapped in newspaper. He begged him not to talk, so as to spare his strength. He looked like a defeated warrior. Moved, he took his hands in his. "What has the world done to you, Salvador!"

Silent still, Salvador did not have the strength to furnish him even the briefest account. Or so much as tell him how he had managed to reach Sobreira in that wretched state. He looked at Xan, half fearfully and half affectionately. Then he averted his eyes to look at Pegasus, distractedly munching the grass. A refined animal, always. Showing not a sign of greediness even when famished. As emaciated as his master. Despite his hunger, he went on ruminating as though he had nothing but scorn for human food, for the well-laden tables from which he and his master had always been banished.

Instinctively, Pegasus' jaws stopped working, and he returned Salvador's gaze. There being established between them a communication that wounded Xan. Xan felt all alone. Never in his life had he achieved, with his wife and children, the same intensity that united Salvador to Pegasus. And he steadfastly yearned to duplicate the feeling that surfaced there with enviable transparency.

Salvador and Pegasus conveyed to him the certainty that life almost never endeavored to construct a platform from which one could bend down to anticipate, simultaneously, the existence of the abyss, of foolish mistakes, of fantasy, and of love. And also the feeling of time, dragging on inexorably, trailing in its net two beings such as Salvador and Pegasus. Had life rewarded Salvador with such supreme bliss only because he had dared to fare forth on the paths of the disinherited of this earth? Of those who possessed nothing? Salvador's only belongings were the animal, the anvil, the hammer, a scant handful of objects. The entire universe on Pegasus' back. Ultimately supported by his shepherd's staff, which also served him as a weapon.

Salvador pulled the blanket up, almost covering his face. "I'm nearing the end, Xan. I strayed from my path so as to reach your house in time. I didn't want to die lying stretched out on the ground, without Christian burial. I thought you'd be happy to bury me. And to know that the life of this tinker, forever telling stories, had been drained to the last drop. There ought to be somebody, at any rate, who was certain that Salvador was dead." He appeared to be exhausted after having spoken at such length. He closed his eyes.

"What is all this, Salvador? Some new story? If so, it's a sad one, that threatens never to come to an end! Are you losing your pride as a storyteller?"

Salvador forced a smile. He appreciated Xan's effort to make his life seem worthwhile. He had always shown him respect, fed him, despite the disapproving gaze of Teodora, who wanted to drive him out of the animal pen. Where the two of them used to spend hours talking together, taken by surprise countless times by the new day dawning. Salvador defending dangerous paths: man must not forget his destiny. That was when Xan decided to follow him. He had his knapsack ready in five minutes. Begging Salvador to hurry up, so Teodora wouldn't catch them.

Salvador made him see once again the risks of such a decision. But Xan insisted that he had a debt to repay, one he owed himself. How to demonstrate the authority of a true teller of stories if he himself hadn't lived at least an eighth of them? They had set out immediately, crossing valleys, rivers, towns. They laughed and wept at the same time. Xan learned simplicity by abandoning everything that was simple habit, including wife and children. In less than two years Salvador perceived, despite Xan's proofs of steadfast determination, that he could no longer resist the distant calls of Sobreira, his only home. And so they bade each other a fraternal farewell, Xan reaffirming his vows of eternal friendship. If Salvador needed him, he had only to make his way to Sobreira.

"It will all be over very soon, Xan. I have only a few hours left to die. On this very night," he said with calm resignation.

He looked at Pegasus, who seemed to understand. Salvador had feared that he would not reach Xan's house in time to bid him a solemn farewell. He was still afraid of leaving Pegasus without shelter, exposed to the wickedness of others, especially now that the animal was so old that he was no longer worth anything.

"I ask you only one favor, Xan." He looked at him pleadingly.

Xan blinked his eyes, forcing himself not to weep. "Whatever you like, Salvador. If it calms your soul. Seeing as how brandy hasn't raised your spirits." He was doing his best to relieve the seriousness of the scene.

"Take care of Pegasus till he follows along after me. He's going to suffer from my absence, but if the pain gets too bad, get his ear and tell him one of my stories so he'll be able to bear the loss of me. That's the only way Pegasus will die with dignity."

With a nod of his head, Xan promised to take good care of his legacy. But Salvador was now concentrating on other tasks. On the alert for the whistle of the north wind, perhaps, reminding him of the tramontana, the wind from the Pyrenees. Or for the smell of the Mediterranean, or the sound of the Catalan language, a rapid rattle of syllables that had warmed him since he was a babe at his mother's breast. And perhaps this discreet meditation could provide the finishing touch to one of his stories. The very one whose ending had always dissatisfied him, despite his having added a wealth of detail to it as he went along. In the supreme effort to be faithful to the very nature of that story.

Xan began to ponder what it might mean to Salvador, in that state, to have Xan and Pegasus before him, seeing as how, in a certain way, they were a reflection of something he'd invented. And therefore disappearing in time, the moment he closed his eyes.

Xan picked up the nervous pulsations in Salvador's hand, which clasped his in immediate answer. That caress shaping the memory that each had of the other. In the face of imminent death, Xan thought, old age is ugly and obscene, and every form of decline is an attempt to degrade freedom.

Confronted with Salvador, Xan discovered that death was merely an adversary reeking of onions. And a coward into the bargain, since it breathed new life, each dawn, into the human illusion of eternity.

"Ah, Salvador, how good it was to hear your stories! To come to know with you this country of brigands and gypsies and mad, mentally unbalanced patriots!"

At these words, Salvador seemed to come to life once more. His face lighted up, as though there were passing in review before him those figures that life had given him and that he, in return, had endowed with character and permanence. To this end attributing to them emotions that those beings had not felt, inventing plots that personally he had come nowhere near living. Immediately, however, Salvador lost his radiant vivacity as utter tedium overcame him.

Xan felt that if something happened to Salvador, his life would be impoverished. Not only would he be the poorer, but Sobreira, Galicia, Spain itself as well. There weren't all that many men like him anymore, keeping alive the taste for adventure. They were all slaves of bread and a roof over their heads. Save for Salvador, free unto death. Ever sharp-witted, Salvador had never gone along with plans that would plunge him into conservatism, into a stultifying sense of well-being. He refused to accept an end imposed upon him by fiat.

On concluding his reflections concerning Salvador's rare talent, of which the world had taken no notice, Xan directed his attention once again to his friend. Salvador's eyes were closed, and within his breast an odd quiet reigned. Nothing in Salvador throbbed, not even life.

Xan placed his hand on his friend's heart, took his pulse. From his body there leapt forth an absolute silence. And he thought, then, with serene simplicity, Tomorrow I will bury him where I too will be buried, and as I cover him with earth, I shall tell him once again the age-old story he liked best. The stories I learned with him.

He slowly closed Salvador's eyes, tried to fold his hands on his breast, tying them with his handkerchief. As he got to his feet, he heard for the first time the creaking of his own joints. He too had aged rapidly.

"Don't worry, Pegasus. Tomorrow you will come with me to bury him," and he drew the animal's head to his breast, stroking his mane.

The two of them kept vigil for Salvador, who appeared to be sleeping. Until Xan, overcome with fatigue, fell into a heavy sleep. Only when daylight flooded the animal pen through the narrow cracks in the door did Xan open his eyes. Hunched over from the cold, he rose to his feet slowly and painfully, by a sheer effort of will. He remembered Salvador then. A cold and rigid corpse now, who had kept him company, as though he were his partner in the marriage bed. On groping round him, he felt a warm body at his side, with hair and contours altogether unfamiliar to him. He looked, and saw Pegasus, huddled next to him, not moving. He ran his fingers over him, but the animal, in a deep sleep, did not react. He shook the indolent animal, as hard as he could. Immediately regretting his brusque gesture. That animal had spent years climbing up mountainsides and down. Not to mention the pain he had suffered at the loss of his friend.

Only then did he note that there was not a single breath of life forth-coming from Pegasus' nostrils. His heart seemingly resting between beats. He had died with the most exquisite discretion. With such uncomplaining solidarity that it upset Xan badly. Especially since he would never take another living being every step of the way with him. At best, Teodora would don mourning dress. Performing ablutions and reciting prayers amid tears, domestic tasks, and a series of intrigues. What was more, she had sworn never to be present at his funeral.

Xan contemplated Salvador and Pegasus without fear of death. A natural event, occasioning simple farewells and a quick burial. The digging of a grave, there on the mountainside, in which to lay Salvador and Pega-sus. He would not separate them.

Madruga asked for more details. Salvador's death, as recounted by his grandfather, moved him. He felt tears come to his eyes. A story that Xan had told him again and again, until his departure for America. What was more, a few days before Madruga took ship, Ceferino had offered him his version. The one version missing was Teodora's. She had passed on some years before. A woman whom Xan seemed to have few memories of.

According to Ceferino, Teodora accused her husband, shortly after Salvador had been laid to rest, of having lured her enemy inside the house once more, thereby offending her personal honor, with the one intent of leaving her insecure and vulnerable.

Ceferino insisted on leaving his mother's portrait hanging on the din-ing room wall, thus paying her simple homage. Teodora's face, seemingly impenetrable, had a hooked nose, like an eagle's beak. A nose that no one in the family had inherited.

"Why was it you never wanted to go to America, father?" Madruga asked.

"I never managed to overcome your mother's curse."

His father, visibly distressed, raising his tone of voice. A voice so loud that, coming directly from the wall now, it made Madruga tremble on that Sunday evening in the room in González's hotel.

Regretting having introduced Ceferino, Urcesina, Xan into that nar-row space, Madruga hastened to turn the light on. Immediately emptying the wall of the family figures, which, seen from a distance now, from an American point of view, struck him as ugly, crude, and clumsy. Though he tried his best to understand them. He had descended, after all, from those rude peasants. Each of them constituting a life difficult to understand. And all of them given to clashing violently with each other amid shattered bones and broken hearts.

With the light turned on, Madruga could see stains on the wall. It ought to be painted, a spotless white. But even if it were, would that by some chance afford those characters the ideal field for justifying their lives? What was it they wanted? Merely to fight for possession of his memory?

Was it possible that there was anyone that hungry for the bread crumbs of memory?

He looked at his hands, on that evening too, and pondered his own gestures. Some of them, doubtless, inherited from Xan, Urcesina, long-ago ancestors. Others, however, stemming from contact with the reality of Brazil. He had realized, for example, that on bending his head dejectedly toward his right shoulder, he was simply filching a gesture he'd noted in his Uncle Justo. The same gesture that his uncle, in turn, had swiped from a sheepshearer who had passed through Sobreira. In the days when Sobreira had had great flocks of sheep. At the same time that pine trees had been systematically planted on the mountainsides, thereby driving out the gentle, docile sheep.

Many years later, long since married to Eulália, Madruga would wake in the middle of the night, unable to go back to sleep. He kept himself, nonetheless, from staring at the wall opposite the bed. Because whenever he yielded to this temptation, it seemed to him that he glimpsed shadowy figures. Exactly like those creatures of Sobreira who, though dead now, insistently demanded his attention.

Closing his eyes, Madruga begged them to go away, if perchance they were there. He did not want to see them again. To his way of thinking, he had paid too much attention to them in those years, even though they had no claim on him. In the end, hadn't they all come to know each other altogether too well? What was it they still wanted to drag into the light of day?

Recently, the faint shadow of Esperança had also turned up on the wall, especially on the nights just before Christmas. This perhaps being owed to Madruga's edginess at that time, fearing that Esperança would suddenly appear during the family's holiday supper, holding by the hand the granddaughter whom he did not know. His daughter thereby forcing a reconciliation that to his way of thinking was impossible.

There Esperança was, projected on the wall, as though she had long been spying on her father in order to make him suffer. Madruga closed his eyes so as not to see her. Then opening them, hoping she was no longer there on that wall where the dead of Sobreira were in the habit of strolling past, against his will. As though those same dead, with Xan at their head, had decided to offer the daughter there on the wall the houseroom that her father had denied her, after the break between them.

The figure of Esperança seemed to be laughing at her father. Meanwhile eyeing him vindictively, totally unwilling to believe the paternal truths that she had sided against.

Esperança's derision, in the middle of the night, caused him terrible pain. He turned over in bed, in a vain attempt to defend himself. But he did not succeed in banishing her from the wall. He asked her, then, to go away. Couldn't she see that he could do nothing for her?

Esperança refused to go along with his argument. She looked on him as an enemy. Madruga hunched over in the bed, afraid he'd awaken Eulália. He sensed that Esperança was testing his strength, now that she'd caught him unawares. But she was wrong. It would be no trick at all to whip her. And in a fury at that daughter who lived a long way away from him, God only knew where, he thought bitterly: Call on her enemies, let them eat her liver, and let her forget me.

The shadow did not disappear from the wall. Madruga felt its cold breath. Convinced, however, that it was only a draft coming from underneath the door, he clutched at the blanket. But his daughter kept advancing, as though wanting the whole room to herself. She was trying to occupy his heart again, to make his temples pound.

Madruga could retreat no farther. And, unable to control himself, he gave a loud shout:

"Come on, clear out of here. Leave me in peace forever."

The shout came echoing back without his noticing. Eulália woke up, taking him in her arms now, protecting him.

"What's the matter, Madruga? Shall I call a doctor?" she said apprehensively.

Madruga buried his head in the pillow. He felt ashamed. Eulália smoothed the rumpled hair on his sweating brow. He shook his head. She did not insist. He settled down next to her. And the two of them pretended to sleep as they kept watch over each other.

On receiving custodianship of Venâncio's diary, Eulália thought it prudent not to read it. It seemed improper to her to appropriate her friend's protests. There was no reason to seek the motives that had led him to take up his pen.

Confident of her posture in this matter, she welcomed Venâncio on Sundays, after his discharge from the sanatorium, with the same naturalness as always. Not saying a word about the diary. Till a certain afternoon on which Venâncio, after giving her a present, inquired as to how Eulália safeguarded objects she prized and, also, those that had been given into her care.

Her attention diverted by the present, Eulália did not hit upon the meaning of those words. Not until the following day, going over the conversation again, did she note that Venâncio had undoubtedly been referring to the diary. He had not only been inquiring as to what had happened to it, but also wanted to know whether she had finally read it.

Eulália felt that she had done Venâncio a wrong. Not having given the necessary careful attention to the diary, a substantive part of his soul. She had practically cast it aside altogether, though she had reserved a special place for it in the drawer of the wardrobe. This error must therefore be corrected.

Odete brought her a cup of coffee. Eulália appreciated the gesture, but asked her, contrary to her habits, to leave her by herself. She needed urgently to offer certain prayers, with the intention of asking a special favor of God.

Odete reacted with a gesture not natural to her. Suspecting that her mistress was banishing her from the room without solid motives. Eulália saw in Odete's eyes, at times, the wrath characteristic of a pagan who sees his gods threatened by a single, powerful god, come to dictate rules never questioned.

"Does Mistress prefer that I remain on guard in the hall or shall I lock the door from outside? That way no one will bother her," she said in a louder voice than usual.

Eulália shrugged just a bit impatiently. A gesture interpreted by Odete as permission to keep watch at the door, protecting her from thieves, from intruders, who do not respect moments of privacy.

Left by herself, Eulália opened the drawer. She unhurriedly removed the tissue paper in which the diary was wrapped. In plain sight now and unguarded. But before beginning her reading of it, she firmly vowed to disregard anything that might offend her. Or that might prove to be excessively pleasurable. She made up her mind to read no more than the first few pages. She would not read the diary to the end. And once she had fulfilled this duty, she would again lock the diary in the drawer, where it had been buried for so many years.

She settled herself comfortably in the armchair next to the window, taking advantage of the natural light. She began to leaf through the diary. She found it difficult to concentrate, however. Everything distracted her. The truth was that she liked only stories told aloud. Stories of that sort were creative and credible. And had the added advantage of being accompanied by the human voice. Especially when Dom Miguel told them. There had never been anything comparable to them.

. . .

26 July 18—   . . . elbow to elbow on deck, in the middle of the Bay of Guanabara, we tried to catch a glimpse of the city, of which wondrous tales were told. The surprising fog prevented us from sighting through the spyglass what was hidden beyond the dock. Of a certainty there were creatures roaming about there with rare, colorful adornments, giant legs, outsized members, and huge snaggled teeth that stuck out from having devoured so much raw human flesh.

As we approached, the smell of armpits reached our nostrils. Or were we confusing it with the smell of the sea, with the perfume of ocean swells peopled with seaweed, corpses, rotten fruit, remains of disemboweled animals floating in the waters?

The captain begged us to be patient. In a few hours we would anchor. We were now on the brink of the paradise we had dreamed of. A mere two or three hundred meters from us. Once we plunged down the stairs with desire in our breasts and a dagger between our teeth. Ready to wipe from the face of the earth anyone who opposed our plans for conquest.

We had been thoroughly indoctrinated beginning back in Europe: to reach America required a defiled and bloody heart. Innocence was left behind for good. The country to be visited in that nineteenth century had been peopled by brigands, murderers, degenerates. Dregs that imposed on the natives a culture shaped by the Christian world view, in the name of which they themselves were exempted, a priori, from guilt or judgment.

And it was in precisely that country that we would be disembarking.

2 August 18— In the first few days, I wandered along the Largo do Paço, Direita, Sabão, São Pedro, and Rosário. Madruga had seen to the practical details, while Eulália mended our clothes and decorated the new house.

In the narrow streets, lighted by oil or gas lamps, depending on the locality, I watched the people passing by. I did not have the courage to approach them. They spoke a language with an accent quite the opposite of that heard previously, on the shore of the Tagus. A piquant tongue, with resounding rhythms. One has to waggle one's hips and roll one's eyes to speak it well.

And thanks to this lively and colorful complexion of things, people used the word *buttocks* without blushing. This naturalness being owed to the African presence in the country. Responsible, moreover, for the introduction of this word *bunda* into Brazilian life. A word so magnetic that, at its mere utterance, certain incontinent men made so bold as to rub up against women of the people, in plain sight on public thoroughfares, to the jubilation of others, who witnessed the whole performance.

I confess I was taken aback. I didn't dare imitate them. Though I doubt that, by so doing, they have taken the first step in the direction of a bright and intelligent nation.

10 August 18— Captain Rugendas, a newcomer to Brazil, was interested, at one and the same time, in power and the landscape. Madruga saw the value of following in his footsteps, certain that he would come to master the city in his company.

They went climbing up knolls and hillocks. There were elevations everywhere. Madruga limped, from exhaustion perhaps. That was not the ideal century for Madruga.

Well turned out, his attire impeccable, Madruga stroked his little red beard. With his eyes permanently fixed on the future. Dissatisfied with a city more like a small village, with rural habits. And so, instead of dreaming of Brazil in any precise way, he spent hours thinking of England, on the eve of embarking upon the process of industrialization.

"How can anyone live in a city like this, divided into two groups? One group at the window, watching the others parade by. And the other parading, in its eagerness to be watched," Madruga said in bored tones, complaining of that province.

As for me, everything seemed to me to be bathed in magic. And I paid little attention to the privations of that century in Brazil. I had long since grown weary of Europe, boasting of its old age, using wisdom as its crutch. I preferred that local culture, blazing with energy, under the tutelage of nature and human excess. An inherently uncivilized people, whose easygoing disposition was not affected by the stench coming from the open ditches filled with shit which cut across the public thoroughfare.

I was amused at their heavy suits, worn in flagrant heedlessness of the torrid climate. Thus far no one had made a single change in European apparel in response to the climatic conditions of the country. They disdained the heat or at any rate took no notice of it.

They paid the strictest obedience to what was left of Portuguese patterns of life and government. By so doing they could think of themselves as being in Lisbon or Paris. In fact, they acted as though they were not here at all. Even when the heat mounted through their legs, softening their will and their genitals, soaking their hairy chests and their bulging tits. Only the men violated this European sense of reserve, scratching their privates in public.

Rugendas himself, forgetful of the imperatives of his education, found great satisfaction in scratching his scrotum no matter where he was. I caught a glimpse in his face of his initial astonishment at the discovery of a gesture, heretofore reserved for the bedroom, which, once put to general use, afforded him such pleasure. Gentlemen, moreover, did so much scratching that the noise they made sounded like fingernails scraping the surface of a slate tablet.

But who will condemn them? Nobody here can easily free himself of the appeals of sex. They have just dawned and there's no end in sight yet.

16 August 18— I remember that the captain, before landing, warned us, in grave tones, near the stairs, that that country was opposed to a foreign presence on its soil.

Was it his intention to save us or to frighten us? Down there on the dock, everyone was eager to fete us. I had never seen such friendly natures. I would even say excessively so. They might almost have been welcoming a foreign invasion.

This reception frightened me. Since such unlimited accessibility is surely a danger for any country. I wonder, then, if they can appreciate the taste of their fruits and their souls, both products of the tropics? Do they at least sense that they are part of America, whether they want a new civilization or not? And as such, are they not obliged to copy, faithfully and faultlessly, values which they are unable to live up to? In the end, what is the format of this people's dream? What land and what model are they thinking of using as their point of departure, in order actually to live their delirium and their saga?

1 September 18— The Biblioteca Real of Lisbon, brought to Brazil in the voluminous baggage of Dom João VI, along with faience, olive oil, and cod, is a priceless treasure. Meant, unfortunately, for a mere handful of readers. But undoubtedly appreciated by the rodents that infest the center of Rio de Janeiro.

Apropos of this king, he is the constant target of waggish insinuations. There is much talk of his habit of giving in to prolonged fits of laughter, immediately after partaking of wine and greasy meat at meals. Which made him piss in public, right in his satin breeches. Without making him feel at all humiliated or ashamed, however. It seemed natural to him to have soaked breeches, since the people of his kingdom had thighs sopping wet from lust.

Moreover, the monarch was not in the habit of using the royal chamber pot. In the event, a most handsome French porcelain vessel, inherited from His Royal Majesty, his father, who for many decades poured precious liquid into this same piece.

But what in fact gave Dom João VI the greatest pleasure was to squat down on the floor, urinating on it like an old woman. Perhaps behaving in that fashion out of sheer nostalgia for his native land. Whenever he remembered, with heartfelt emotion, the washerwomen hunched over in this position on the shore of the Tagus, beating sheets on the stones in the river. As they mingled their golden liquid with the pebbles and the river, amid plots and schemes and Portuguese soap.

As for this Library, one must understand the scorn that the Brazilians and the Portuguese have heaped upon it, from the beginning. From certain of them, I caught the words:

"Damn! What is that monstrosity doing here!"

And from others, confronting the fear that books would cut them off from outdoor life, this declaration:

"Ah, if it weren't for the rats and the termites helping us to wipe out this Library, we'd be running the risk of having one of the best libraries in the world! And whatever for?"

Struck by that contradictory inheritance, I hurriedly made my way to the Library. I imagined it going up in flames at the hands of its many enemies. Dona Mariana, its custodian, assured me, however, with a profound look, that an eighth of the royal heap of documents had, in fact, already disappeared down the stomachs of woodworms and rodents.

"Are you certain of that, senhora? Have you reflected on the seriousness of such an accusation?"

"At this rate, in a hundred years, we'll have half this accumulation."

I noticed her relief. And abashed at this discovery, I left the room.

5 October 18—   Since Madruga was so insistent, I accompanied him to Andaraí, on a visit to an imposing colonial-style house. Surrounded by gardens, with slaves in sight everywhere, like swarms of flies. The owners, for their part, moved about almost invisibly, spared any sort of physical effort.

A lavish table had been laid. Coffee, spirits, choice tidbits. What they referred to as a snack. Heaping their plates, forgetful of the fact that dinner would very shortly gather them round the table once again.

According to what these gentlemen said, not troubling to conceal their thoughts, they regarded manual labor as particularly contemptible. They would never allow themselves to use their own hands for any purpose whatsoever. Far better to let fruit rot on the trees than go out to gather it in baskets themselves.

One thing about them was readily noticeable: their laughter came extremely easily. And the men talked continually. Preferably about politics, a subject forbidden women. And once by themselves in the drawing room they entertained each other with risqué stories. They liked to fornicate during breaks in what they regarded as serious discussions. This was a habit that came naturally. And almost always they got their sex outside the marriage bed.

They used snuff regularly. Whiling away their lives in idleness and pretended politeness. What they say means the contrary of what must be read into their every word. Hence they are fond of intrigue. The one way to keep life emptying away down the social drains. They want things to be this way. And by temperament and upbringing, they avoid criticism and backbiting in public. Even in the case of an enemy. Certain acts are saved for the bedroom and vacant lots.

Madruga delighted in being received in their homes. Even though they criticized him later, behind his back. A local way of proving that they haven't forgotten a visitor.

In the middle of the conversation, the brother of the owner of the house made unflattering remarks about the country's culture. Prefacing everything he said with the names London and Paris. And ending up with the words:

"Brazil is for blacks and half-breeds. We're still lacking everything. There's no reason we should waste our time furnishing our era with the wealth that it is in no condition to appreciate."

11 November 18—   I have a lingering memory of hammocks stretched out on tree-shaded verandas. In them are lying the elite of the city, waiting for darkness to fall. They all cultivate leisure with the greatest of pleasure. Habituated as they are to depending on slave labor.

In the house at Andaraí, I observed that everyone gives orders. The owners bawl commands at the servants. And the female housemaids and chambermaids, being close to the central power, delegate lesser tasks to the kitchen slaves. Thus carrying out the process whereby all parties gratify their voluptuous desire to order others about.

5 January 18—   Captain Rugendas awoke all prepared to throw the entire household into turmoil. He had not spent a night aboard ship for some time, though his cabin boy made his bed every morning, as though the captain had slept in it.

He practically lives with us, in the manor house. Large enough for everyone to be alone. And allow us to pay each other visits. He has already told us that his crew, disapproving of his neglect of his duties, is threatening to mutiny. Or desert his ship, anchored in the Bay of Guanabara.

His tone of voice betrayed no concern, however, regarding this state of affairs. Or the fact that the populace has stripped the ship, emptying it of its entire cargo. The goods belong, in fact, to the Royal Company of the Indies, which has spread surreptitiously throughout the world.

Like so many others who have landed here, Rugendas has plunged straight into utopia. One sustained, however, by the tropical landscape and the sun. In his opinion, Brazil was establishing itself as the perfect paradise. One could practically reach down and pick up the gold nuggets, diamonds, lush fruits lying on the ground.

"Is it only gold and silver you want?" I asked Madruga, paying no attention to Rugendas.

Madruga admitted to having recently became associated with powerful Portuguese, long settled here. And who, with an eye on their fortunes and their future, sent their sons, Brazilians, off to study in Coimbra. With express orders not to love Brazil excessively, because of the risks that this sentiment represented.

They were so rich that half of Rio de Janeiro belonged to them. Lacking only the other half now. In pursuit of which they had already set out. An ambition washed down with strong wine and good, bowel-loosening olive oil. Heedless of the fact that, in order to increase the size of their fortunes, it was necessary to impoverish the remainder of the population.

A fact which, though painful, could not be taken into account, otherwise they would not be able to multiply and revitalize their capital.

Out of vanity, Madruga introduced himself as the owner of the galleon anchored in the bay. And on taking these Portuguese aboard for a visit, he handed out handsome pay to Rugendas and his crew so that they would lend him prestige. At times ordering them to lift anchor so as to scour the Brazilian coast for a few hours.

"Any day now I'm going to order Rugendas to set sail for Lisbon with the holds stuffed full of goods. Anyone who wants to place an order for anything from the Rua da Prata need only sign up."

Such astuteness produced admirable fruits. It was soon whispered about the city that Madruga and his group were about to expand so much that, in less than eight months, the country, at the moment in the hands of fifty families, would become the fiefdom of no more than twenty-five. With nothing to fear from the Parliament. This house would always legislate in their favor. If its members chanced to pass a troublesome law, it would soon be consigned to oblivion. They were past masters at portioning out their gratuities to public officials.

"Well, aren't you going to say hello to me, Venâncio?" Madruga said.

"Only when you become the sole owner of Brazil."

25 February 18— The conquest of the Portuguese language is painful for me. It makes me tongue-tied when I speak it. It is treacherous and tyrannical, and knowing it is not enough. Above all I must overcome those rigid, canonical sentiments in which it cloaks itself. This Lusitanian language, like all the others, was organized in such a way as to prevent the people from taking it over and breaking its chains. The lords and masters of language have always feared that the people would come to live on intimate terms with that subjacent layer of language capable of leading it to the apostasy of the imaginary. To freedom.

And what a long time still it is going to take me to understand it! What to do, so as to taste its marinade? To lick up this tongue at last, as though it were the choicest delicacy.

I was following along behind the National Guard, as it marched down Rossio, when I met Eulália. Coming in the opposite direction, she was discreetly applauding the jaunty lads. Forgetting her distaste for any military cause. But quite evidently she had been unable to resist the love of spectacle that parades always bring with them.

"I was brought up to fear the military. They're the ones who change the face of the earth for the worse."

Eulália was forgetting other threats with equal firepower. Domestic life, for example. Which also obliged Eulália to ignore what was happening in the world. Nothing was more enslaving than a total devotion to pots and pans, the spinning wheel, kitchen utensils, screening off one's view of reality.

"We lack the courage to set the house on fire. To be pitiless toward our trivial belongings," I timidly sounded her out.

I made her see that a folly such as that would bring about a radical change of life. Driving us out of doors, to begin with, to live beneath the inspiration of the open sky. In return, an ever-shifting geography, taking us each night to a different place. Revealing nature's most intimate secrets, to which we heretofore have paid no attention. In the form of gentle streams, waterfalls, rivers, forests, and all the rest. A way of life where the air is free, the opposite of social despotism.

"Despair often has only advantages to offer us. If on the one hand it shows us the way to hell, on the other it forces us out of the repugnant family circle. Loneliness and freedom, both of them born of poverty and this sort of suffering, are by nature revolutionary."

Her attention distracted, Eulália seemed not to have heard me. I pressed my point.

"What's more, Eulália, a country exceeds the narrow limits of the family table. What are well-seasoned food, the appetite of one's table companions, compared to the spirit of adventure?"

"I heard everything you said. And if that's the case, what are you doing here with us? Why haven't you marched off long ago, with your kit bag on your back?"

Whereupon Eulália burst into laughter. My words already forgotten. She felt happy, swept off her feet by a feverish air. I noted the pounding of her pulse as I kissed her trembling hands.

The following day, I watched Madruga closely. He had not perceived certain changes that had been taking place in Eulália. His one attachment being to the politicians who smoothed the way for his business transactions, Madruga behaved like a chameleon. To those who were native-born, espousing an exacerbated nationalism, he proudly proclaimed his love for Brazil. With those in court and business circles, he pretended to be of Portuguese nationality. Claiming that, by matrilineal descent, he belonged to a family from Minho. With ties, through his father's branch, to Spain. And therefore having crossed the Minho so many times that he sometimes forgot exactly which side of the river he was on. So between them, the Olivença episode, that eternal conflict in the Portuguese soul, was best forgotten.

25 April 18— The city is of rare beauty. From the Outeiro da Glória there can be clearly seen great mansions, the Passeio Público, which overlooks the bay, and the Morro do Cão, in the distance. Beneath the watchful eye, on one side, of the monastery of São Bento, whose plainsong reaches the people as they wallow in lust. While the monastery of Santo Antônio is located on the opposite side.

Standing out from everything else, the Bay of Guanabara. Splendid waters, mirroring the entire history of this city. Its waves playfully assault the low sea wall, which lays no claim to being a mighty bastion defending the city.

The seacoast is usually benign. Save when the sea rages. This shoreline has no forbidding geological features, in the form of escarpments, towering rocks, and sea cliffs. Sandy beaches predominate, for the rest and repose of those who give themselves over, body and soul, to sun and inspiration.

Nature here appears in a gentle, even indolent guise. Hence it pacifies the spirit, though beneath the calm of this visible surface, the city accumulates strange effluvia, impulses whose driving force is mystery and latent violence.

But then it suddenly becomes hospitable, its twilight on fire with indescribable colors, moving us and reducing us to silence around six in the evening.

3 May 18— Despite his master's license, Rugendas lays loudest and proudest claim to being an artist. Sketching with strange persistence the country in which we live.

Viewed from close up, his work on paper seems to me to be idyllic, ecstatic, surrounded by delicate shadows. Without anarchic details, awakening critical reflection. A poverty far removed from its classic delineation. What he is doing is doubtless nothing but parlor sociology, prompting polite argument about his drawings.

Out of respect for Rugendas, I have never asked him where he has seen slaves as immaculate and statuesque as these. All framed in scenes of prodigal abundance. I jokingly point out to him that the wealth so prominently displayed in his drawings may arouse the covetous instincts of foreigners.

Rugendas protests. He pleads innocent to the charge. He regards himself as serving the cause of Brazilian history. In time to come, his records will be looked upon as precious documents.

I apologize. Convinced, however, that he is unwittingly revealing a country that is an ideal setting for pillage on a grand scale. And also a peaceable, passive society, easily subjugated.

Perhaps Rugendas is right. And besides, what point is there in persuading him otherwise? The pillage has long since begun. He won't be responsible for stepping up the pace of it. In this regard, the Brazilians and the Portuguese are no more than clumsy figureheads for the French and the English.

Isn't it true that the nation's most precious possessions fall directly into the hands of the English? They have been sacking America, without even using force to do so. They slowly sail into our ports, waving a white flag. And infiltrate the power structure on the pretext of spreading libertarian ideals and awakening nationalist aspirations. The iron hand in the velvet glove. When they lay anchor alongside terra firma, they don't budge till the holds of their ships are filled with the gold, the tin, and the silver of America as ballast for the voyage home. Knowing full well that they will soon be back. The minute they've unloaded their cargoes in England.

7 June 18—   I perceive that we've arrived in Brazil far too late. Anyone who didn't cast anchor here along with Cabral's ships will have little influence on the building of the nation. The idea would be to have an effect on the past. To go back to the knot at the heart of history, where the narrative threads, since the discovery, intertwine and become forever entangled.

The scenes that have unfolded before my eyes are impenetrable. I do not know what path to follow to reach the heart of Brazil. I try, in vain, to reproduce the spirit of those Brazilians who sacrificed their lives in their eagerness to free Brazil from Portugal. I am pleased to discover that this country too has its pantheon of heroes. It was not built by outcasts alone. And that, underneath, there exists a country that is no stranger to ideas, chewing them over in the silence of the night, by candlelight. With the fear that ideas will fall victim to repression and indifference.

I see from the window of the room a nature exploding in an extraordinary flowering. Bearing life and imposing it by force. Why resist its tumult? Why believe that I will be giving in to madness if I enjoy so lavish a nature? Why not marry the cornstalk, the blade of grass, the voluptuous greenery, sex, songs, everything, in a word, to a cultivated soul and a civic consciousness?

Eulália forbears to defend Madruga's merchant soul. Nor does she confront him head-on. As mistress of the house she simply offers hospitality to her husband's guests, his business associates, who constantly turn up here. More and more prosperous as time goes by. When suddenly pressed to speak of changes, they accept only those that offer the country indispensable little retouches and signs of modernity.

"The passivity of the natives works in our favor. As does their ineradicable inferiority complex when confronted with whites and foreigners," the visitor said.

As the talk turns to weightier subjects, Rugendas and I are discreetly banished from the room. They never discuss business in our presence. They doubtless look upon us as adversaries. Or creatures who failed to adopt the proper attitude and seize the right moment where money was concerned. Though they may perhaps regard us as amenable to corruption. Cloaked by the thin mantle of a hypocritical moral code. Might they be right?

29 July 18—   I now suspect that Rugendas's work is not motivated by the artistic ideal. Unbridled ambition is the captain of his soul. His one aim in describing the country is to sell it dirt cheap.

When he sets it down on paper, with undeniable talent, he purposely lends it a serenity and a social harmony that Brazil is far from possessing. Stripping his figures of the feeling of movement and action. In those faces there is no trace of tension or rebellion.

Rugendas is determined to pacify Brazil by force. To make her proud of the way in which slaves are dealt with. Accorded, in his opinion, exemplary treatment. As though pillories, pursuers of runaway slaves, and savage crimes did not exist.

How ardently he defends the cordiality in these parts, which overlooks conflicts and social differences! But he's either a liar or blind. In all truth, he preaches the doctrine of cordiality in the certainty that it will one day prove useful to him. He will then have disciples. Innumerable historians will surely back his view. But is cordiality not a straitjacket, giving men no room to make a revolution, even if motivated by injustice and poverty? Is cordiality not an indubitable synonym of a prudent, ideal spirit that takes up the game of unseemly and unethical conciliations?

Next week I am going to take Rugendas to the Valongo Market. We'll see how he reacts. Or will he confine himself to nailing to his face the typical expression of the mildly offended Christian, capable of forgetting and forgiving everything?

6 August 18—   At night, I take pleasure in walking about the streets. I follow the straggling line of the blocks of row houses, where brothels have usually been set up. Inspecting one by one the faces in the windows, after dinner.

Time crawls. For me and for the others. Slowly burdening us with the listless, apathetic cast of mind of slaves or prisoners. With the one advantage of calming painful anxieties.

A woman invites me into her bed. She informs me of the price and her professional skills, which will make me happy. I go on, driven by a dull, dreary, sensual appetite. America is slowly getting the better of me. It is robbing me of the final portion of an epic I so ardently wished to exemplify someday. I am beginning to be a character without a story and without a book. Without so much as a pamphlet that speaks of me.

I rarely accept the offer of a drink. Brandy doesn't tempt me, thanks to my intolerance for alcohol. It's better that way. Because this country makes me sad. I have very little understanding of it. Who are these Brazilians who speak Portuguese?

This century in which I am now living says nothing to me. It merely points to dramatic privations. And a chronology that succumbs to the monotony of each day, of a week without grandeur. Everything comes to me contaminated by the feeling of living exile. Then where am I?

Should I leave this century or forget it once and for all? I long only to hide from Madruga, Rugendas, Eulália, the nature of my troubles.

8 September 18— We were apprehensively making our way toward the Valongo Market, for our first visit. The market was not in the Rua Direita now. It had been moved from the center of the city, which no longer included the spectacle of slave traffic.

The bell tower of the church of São Francisco da Prainha, surmounted by a cross, followed us wherever we turned. We had dressed with care, so that we would blend in with the crowd of bona fide slave buyers. Rugendas seemed happy. Once again he was about to pin down his Brazilian reality.

The square was a maelstrom of voices and bodies. We finally managed to get a close look at the slaves up for auction, standing like gasping statues. They had arrived in Brazil not long before. Without having been able to appreciate the coast of the new land as the slave ship approached the dock. From the hold, where they were shut up throughout the passage, they merely caught glimpses of water and bits of land through the tiny openings. All of them overcome with an irresistible fear, owing to the hopelessness of their condition. They had not had one free moment during that Atlantic crossing to ascertain what was really happening to them. Or even to discover what land it was that, from the start, robbed them of their freedom, of the soil of Africa, of tribal life, where they had cultivated from time immemorial their myths and totems.

It was common knowledge that the unloading of the ship constituted a degrading spectacle. A number of slaves being dragged off in tears, beneath the lash. Whereas others, dazed, dull-faced, dry-eyed, were swiftly learning, by way of their recent enslavement, marked by misery and ignominy, of the essential theft of their humanity that they would be obliged each moment to endure. Since wherever they set foot, this place of darkness, full of whips and piercing cries, was to become their desolate home.

They arrived in swarms, like flies. With shit on their heels and buttocks covered with sores. And they stank so badly they put to flight the customs authorities, charged with checking the human cargo and herding it from the boat to the warehouses, not far from there. Where the blacks were separated by sex. And, consequently, the scene of family farewells. A different destination for each one, never again to set eyes on each other, once the transaction was completed. But might they have in fact sensed, at this poignant moment, that the spiritual death of their race was beginning?

Odete bade her child farewell with a look burning with fever. There was time enough still for her to stroke her son's head lightly. Life owed her that caress. No tears were to be seen in her eyes, not even when the brutal overseers lathered her body and scrubbed it down. Covering the sores of some of the slaves with salve, to hide them. A gesture never once made out of pity, but out of fear that their damaged merchandise might fetch a lower price.

Odete submitted meekly. As they scrubbed her, they inoculated her with the poison of nostalgia and despair. They washed everything but the women's badly abused genitals. For this, they pointed to a basin full of filthy water with which to rinse the urine and secretions from their blighted pubes, that forest of sticky, stinking hair.

Only after they were cleaned up did Tomas Cachaço appear, belching mightily after the huge lunch he'd eaten. During the morning, he stoked up on cane brandy from his very own private stock. Furnished for him by the local sugar mills, by way of thanks to him. He was always drunk. The better, perhaps, to perform his sordid duties.

With the slaves, he was impatience personified. In no more than five minutes, those pagan Africans were to abjure the belief that they had brought with them, so as to be fit to enter Christian homes. He forbade them to wear amulets about their necks, crosses being excepted. Here in Brazil now, having been sold by whites or by African chieftains, many of them from their own tribe, who had allowed themselves to become a prey to greed, they must immediately forget those gods that haunted their imaginations. And their dances as well, the sounds of which they transmitted through the forests in imitation of a strange language. Brazil needed docile hands, who would murmur the *Ave Maria* in the fields while they labored in the midday sun, as in the pillory when they misbehaved.

Odete found herself lined up amid the blacks in the front row, the first on the list of those to be auctioned off. Tall and thin, of proud bearing, she was surely a Sudanese aristocrat. More elegant than any one of us. Her origin, lost in time, cast ours in the shadow. When we arrived on earth, our families were still eating raw meat, whereas hers, on the Ivory Coast, had refined itself to the point of creating individual gods.

Each one of us eyed Odete for personal reasons. I for my part was attracted by her firm and harmonious behind. I had never before seen such beautiful buttocks. We had recently learned that *bunda,* as a word designating a part of the body, was of African origin and had just begun to take on erotic substance in the Portuguese language. The simple fact of saying the word to oneself being enough to make one salivate. And use, form, and content so suited each other that the word soon gained unusually wide currency. It spread at a gallop through beds, streets, red-light districts, slave quarters. Invading Gamboa, overflowing into the downtown district, the great country houses, confessionals, even the corridors of Parliament. Not sparing even the Emperor.

Odete's bosom, bared there, was delicately curved. And ample as well. Rugendas, Madruga, and I, though slaves of her behind, felt in unison the timeless desire to tickle her clefts with our tongues, to crack her surface gently, to lick her all over.

Since my arrival in Rio, I had never fornicated with a black woman. I do not know if Madruga and Rugendas could say the same. To date I have forborne to experience the intensity of coming to know a race which, having been transported to Brazil, lost a continent of so dense a nature as Africa. And which undoubtedly would have great treasures to offer me.

Standing there before Odete, about to be sold at auction, I weighed my freedom to love her. Whether I could in fact love a black slave. Whether, against my will, my heart might not be subject to those hierarchical criteria which, before the fact, proscribed sentiment. And to compensate, obliging us white masters to feel only wild, irresponsible, predatory desire?

Odete's beauty had made us forget Eulália. She did not seem to matter. Did she perceive the lust in our eyes or a certain bulk in our trousers, there where we had tucked away our genitals? If she noticed, she hid her offense. With firm step she approached Odete, paying no attention to the overseer responsible for that piece of merchandise. And without hesitation, she threw over Odete's shoulders a light shawl that she was carrying despite the heat. A gesture of protection such that it forbade us the sordid desire, the stiff member that demeaned the slave and Eulália herself, each linked in solidarity with the other.

The magnificent gesture impressed everyone; it had the import of a command. The woman must be bought without haggling. Whatever her price. Odete showed she understood that from that moment on she would owe whatever vestige of dignity she still possessed to Eulália. She saw the coins that had bought her body at auction. She drew back in anguish, immediately lowering her head. Eulália took her by the hand. Placing herself between Odete and the world, determined to protect her from the general cupidity. As though guaranteeing her, on going to her house, in this country where Eulália had no idea how long she would be staying, the freedom to nurture the faith that her heart counseled. What would be asked of her in return could be summed up as affection and company. And, as soon as she could, she intended to give her her letter of manumission. The legal document emancipating her. Though, after that, Odete must remain with her for a time. At that moment in history, given her condition as a black, a woman, an African, freedom would be a burden, a useless gift. For blacks it even represented the plunge into absolute degradation.

Odete adjusted the shawl, about to fall from her shoulders. With this simple gesture, she accepted Eulália's kind care. A pact was established between them, as a number of slaves around them fainted and others died, unable to withstand the mistreatment and the melancholy to which Africans are subject. The dead were promptly thrown into wagons and taken to common graves in the cemetery close by, thereby keeping the corpses from infesting the center of the city.

Once home, I analyzed Odete. She appeared to rejoice inwardly at a purchase that in the end was to her advantage. She was not able as yet, however, to use a language common to us in order to express what was happening to her. The sound issuing forth from her mouth inevitably came from a language incomprehensible to us. While from Portuguese she retained curses, degenerate, perverse sounds, everything spoken and murmured amid the worst abuse of her body.

Eulália motioned to her to sit down on the stool pulled up to the kitchen table. Eulália herself sat down close beside her. Looking at Odete, who looked straight back. Eulália tried her best to understand what feelings could be sustaining that woman, come from a jungle to the clearing of civilization.

She insisted on heating her food and was touched to see her eat with her fingers. And even though Odete failed to use the fork and spoon placed there at her disposal, this African seemed to us to be a proud princess.

She chewed her food carefully, lending elegance to her hunger. In contact now, and for the first time, with the taste of a newly encountered food in the country that, from the moment the foul slave ships had landed, had begun to be her country too. Naturally, this notion of belonging equally to Brazil did not come to her until later, after the piercing pains in her heart had subsided. This country owed her a great deal still, until such time as she managed to forget the wounds that had rent her breast, the cause of suffering to which she would have been able to give proper expression only in her own African tongue.

"May I call you Odete?" Eulália said, hurriedly baptizing her. She had to be given a name. A name is the sign of a distinction, of the individuality indispensable to life in human society.

"Because I don't know your African name," Eulália explained.

Suddenly, all of us, even Rugendas, who was sketching her, realized that we were foreigners in Brazil. Our condition precisely the same as Odete's. Slaves too of memories left behind. We formed, there in the kitchen round Odete, a contingent that had bested the storms and conquered the abysses of the Atlantic, with the aim of reaching Brazil and shaping it, of changing its profile, of enriching it with the blood, the culture, and the weakness inherent in all of us.

Though Odete was less tense now because of the presence of Eulália, I vaguely sensed that the mournful look in her eyes subtly revealed the nature of the historic part that the four of us were meant to play in this country's process of evolution. Brazil was all of us. Lost, melancholy souls. Together, we would be the failures and the aspirations of this nation.

. . .

4 October 18— There are back streets and alleyways too narrow for a man and a carriage to pass through. Wherever one walks, one smells the odor of armpits and hot pubes. Bodily hiding places where lice, fleas, dead sperm, and white secretions lodge. Because people fornicate to excess in these zones of the South. According to what I've heard, they do it from the front and the back here. Even though many are deeply troubled by such preferences. And therefore they are intransigent supporters of institutions which proscribe such perversions.

The fact is that all of them have uncommon energy and appetite. Taking great pleasure in fucking after their siesta or at hours regarded as unseemly. With men enjoying the advantage of chasing after their wives and almost anything else in skirts as well. Including intense, roly-poly black women. A storage depot supplying every manner of fantasy. Splendid smiling cunts, with saliva trickling out the corners.

And so, after the groaning board, the sublime slices of codfish, the exasperating roasts, a good fuck awaited them. The way of life befitting gentlemen. Especially since the meager diet of politics and culture induced them to vomit up their luxury. Thereby, to their credit, contributing to the slow pace of the country's progress.

Independence itself, ardently desired by some, did not greatly fatten their pocketbooks. Though it freed them from having to wage further battles to gain it. Since it was now a *fait accompli,* they had an identifiable flag and national anthem. And this, for the moment, satisfied them.

13 November 18— In the gardens of the Passeio Público, confidences take on a certain importance. They immediately form concentric circles, which soon spread throughout the city, evaporating rapidly.

It is a beautiful garden, surrounded on all sides by high walls. The solemn portal at the entrance consists of an iron gate whose intertwined links are surmounted by an escutcheon with the royal arms. Flanking this gate are two stone columns, both the work of skilled Portuguese masons. Of the sort qualified to build cathedrals. And above the parapet of the pillars, marble jars can be seen. And the bust of Phoebus as well, though no one quite knows what he is doing there.

Nature was resplendent, down to the last detail. It is a perfect place for living lessons in botany. Each capable of being illustrated by plants gathered there on the spot. I take enormous pleasure in contemplating them. Even though I do not know their names. Their perfection is quite enough for me. Their names would not add one iota to their beauty. They would, admittedly, serve to refresh my memory, if in the future I were to describe them to a stranger to the place.

During the week, a solemn silence hovers over the park. The words that chance to drift my way slowly lose their foreign character, and I begin to grow accustomed to them. An impressive confusion of voices, no doubt. What myriad feelings must be contained within it!

With what delight Eulália and I enjoy our Thursday afternoons on its terrace, with its incomparable view of the sea. As though savoring a pleasure certain to be brought to an abrupt end. Rumor has it, alas, that soon this area, by orders from the alcaide, will be transformed into a major thoroughfare, in the irresistible drive to modernize the city.

And so nothing will then survive of the moving paintings of Leandro Joaquim housed in the two pavilions at the opposite ends of the garden. Panels, moreover, that faithfully reproduce certain aspects of the city's life. Nor did Leandro Joaquim neglect to depict as well the gold and diamond mines far from the urban center. Nor the sugarcane plantations and their mills, to whose economy it had intimate ties.

Now and again Madruga comes to join us in the Passeio Público. He bursts into peals of laughter on catching us unawares as we breathe in the greenery. And the sea breeze too, with its sweet smell of fish, seaweed, and boats strayed off course and gone to the bottom. Madruga's noisy presence breaks the spell of this place.

His pressing political concerns force him to speak at once of the state of the country. Not noticing our costumes, carefully chosen for this outing. His one interest the news of the day, assuring him of the existence of a country rapidly expanding. On its way to imitating England.

"Don't you agree with me?" he says hurriedly.

I walked on, followed by Eulália, as Madruga trailed along behind. Disappointed by my silence. Till we fell into step together and Madruga forgot where we were. The two of us knowing only that it was a garden and that the last thing we wanted was to leave it.

12 December 18— They all claim to be well-known orators. Oratory is a cherished practice of theirs. In Bahia, for example, there are people developing their skills at public speaking on every corner. From an early age they devote themselves to parliamentary battles and nocturnal skirmishes.

"But what sort of mad rhetoric is it that forces them to talk nonstop, and always at a higher pitch than normal?"

There is no satisfactory explanation. It has a great deal to do with their violent temperament, which suddenly makes itself evident at such times. When it comes to organized protest, however, they calm down. They demand very little. Which is a shame.

9 January 18— And when will the Emperor at last be seen? No one can say. He is so absorbed in his work! He is never indifferent to his reputation as a scholar. A wisdom in the service of Botany.

Meanwhile, in this scholar's country, I searched for a university and didn't find a single one. Even free public education is not widespread. To date they do not print their own books. The people go along with this, however. Convinced that life is really the best teacher. What could a product of Oxford or Heidelberg do for Brazil that Brazil, with its human smelting furnace, could not produce for itself?

14 March 18— Eulália wanted to go out. We kept her company as far as the church of O Carmo. We leapt from the tilbury at a reasonable distance away, intending to take a stroll. To see the latest fashions. Arriving at the church door, we waited for her to finish her prayers.

After some time, she came out, with Odete, properly dressed now. Eulália's face was resolutely abstracted from the reality surrounding her. A total stranger to the history of that city, parading past her without meriting her profound consideration.

She drew back in fright from the impact of the sunlight, after the shadow of the tabernacle. But these moments passed in a flash. As though she were undergoing grievous suffering because of a daily round of life capable of indiscriminately mixing whites, natives, blacks, slaves and masters together, without the slightest pity. With everyone coming out of this mixture degraded. I noted her look of reproof, the loneliness of this woman.

I approached her cautiously, taking advantage of a moment of distraction on the part of Madruga, who had other matters on his mind. Might she have something to tell me? And what was I waiting for?

She thanked me for my concern about rescuing her from the overbright light, from the din of the city. I had little to add to the many words we spoke together, no longer knowing who was responsible for them. In the last analysis, who spoke and who heard? It seemed to her that sentences, high-spirited and allowed to run free, mares in a meadow, did not, in fact, express feelings. And on top of that, reality had a detrimental effect upon her soul. It no doubt intimidated her. The dimensions of what she happened to see round about her exceeded what her hands or the shape of her heart could encompass. And that heart was a special country. Everything there being openly proclaimed, it far surpassed human imagination.

"This country may well jump the track someday and never get moving again," she said evasively, her modesty avoiding venturing along paths that escaped her.

And because she saw that I was downcast, she did her best to make me feel at ease.

"It doesn't matter what we do, Venâncio, our souls are damned before the fact."

She immediately ran off from me. In the direction of the Imperial Palace, knowing beforehand that we would follow her.

. . .

17 April 18— The Bay of Guanabara was very nearly named Santa Luzia. In honor of Ferdinand Magellan, who landed here in the long-gone sixteenth century, on December 13, the very day of this saint, patroness of mariners. A saint who watches at one and the same time over seafarers and people with eye trouble.

In the end, they baptized it Guanabara, a corruption of doubtful origin. A prudent position to take, since the name of the saint could not be indiscriminately associated with rogues, pirates, and agents of corruption who navigate its waters. And who frequently return to the city. Where they are welcomed with applause. As the natives prepare to share their possessions with them in exchange for mirrors, glass beads, and glittering trinkets.

15 May 18— The custom of legalizing discord was introduced into the country beneath the cloak of temporary alliances. Though they may hate each other, they contrive to marry each other, as a way of postponing inopportune misadventures.

As far as I can see, Empire is an inevitable political step. Just as the expulsion of Pedro I, sent back to Portugal against his will, was inevitable. His little son staying behind in his place. Pedro I took the boat with sadness in his eyes and a profound paucity of words. Thereby keeping the people from repeating his phrases.

Yet he enjoyed great popular sympathy. And not only because of Independence, which he proclaimed on the banks of the Ipiranga, in the remote hinterlands of São Paulo. But also because he had sprayed the city with bastards. So many he couldn't count them. All we know is that he popularized semen and contributed to giving local families a boost up the social ladder.

Old José Bonifácio kept his eye on him. Except that he didn't keep track of him at night, hours when the Emperor availed himself of the services of other women. On the other hand, Bonifácio did shape his political thought. To this end intermingling Portuguese doctrine, forged in Lisbon and overseas, with decrees already in force in Minas Gerais. So that from the union between Lisbon and Minas, almost theological in nature, a new political decalogue would come into being, to contravene that of the Northeast, more blustering and gross.

But when questions were raised as to what master plan or doctrine this political thought was based on, a grave silence fell. Nobody daring to define a thought deriving from such a strange marriage. This silence, however, was not simply a sign of discretion. On the contrary, it was a requirement of the political project itself, whose meandering nature prevented its origin from being closely examined. And it likewise made theoretical illustrations set down on paper unnecessary. It consisted basically of secret signals, hidden signs, marches and countermarches. The whole in close alliance with slyness and cunning. Political reality shifting at the breathing of a single word or one wink of the eye. The references serving as a base for any sort of reflection were always insufficient and inexact. Though precious nonetheless. With them vital decisions were made. Even so, in order to express them, they resorted to tangential discourse. Thereby generously offering listener and speaker alike the opportunity to reconsider a move that might be dangerously progressive. No word, therefore, was intended to mean what it said. And each assertion afforded a glimpse of the existence of the reverse and obverse. A game that fascinated the parties involved. With a thousand subtle rules that obtained, absorbed only by those sensitive to the slightest political breeze.

It was said, in the city, that the Lisbon side, possessed of a certain ingrained verbal harshness and a temperament always just about to explode, was unable to hold up under the siege by Minas. Being forced, therefore, to withdraw. Which brought about the fall of successive heads over the years. Who could say why Pedro I's didn't roll?

Bonifácio offered no explanation. And Pedro I, involved in nocturnal carousing on neighbors' rooftops, was always closemouthed.

19 June 18— The Spanish in America were regarded as more cruel colonizers than the Portuguese. Portuguese excesses having been watered down through their fucking, long and lustfully, with native vaginas and anuses. They thus democratized copulation and sensuality, and fostered the appearance of new racial mixtures. Thereby establishing a genteel empire, albeit one brought about by means of brains and genitals wet with terror.

18 July 18— We sometimes nibbled on Surinam cherries after our morning snack. Small, slightly bitter fruits, which stick in my throat. As Madruga counted his coins again. His strongbox was full to bursting.

Suddenly I raised the specter of the dissatisfaction of the popular classes in the face of the general picture of misery confronting them. He smiled complacently. Confident of the course of history. This history rarely jumped the track, damaging his interests. And whenever it did it promptly returned to its original rails.

"This is a peaceable people. It will never demand of us any more than it already has."

I proved to him that he was in error. He could not forget the rebellion that had taken place in that very city of São Sebastião, in the long-ago seventeenth century. The people, in revolt, under suffocating economic pressures, reaching the extreme of deposing the governor, an implacable oligarch.

"If I am not mistaken, this governor was named Salvador Benevides.

He had connections with the famous Correia de Sá branch. A family with enormous power, accustomed to lassoing whatever it took a fancy to and garnering all the benefits and advantages it considered it deserved."

Captain Rugendas pricked up his ears at this story. Scarcely able to believe that that beautiful and untouchable city would ever adopt revolutionary stances capable of overthrowing a governor of the Colony.

"Brazilians aren't any different from other people, Rugendas. You're forgetting that politics and indignation came into this world out of man's hind end, along with his feces. They form a solid block, a single thought."

The motive, to all appearances, had been ignoble. The uprising stemming from the prohibition of the sale and production of cachaça in the city and in sugar mills throughout the country.

"Only blacks were exempted. The only ones allowed sugarcane wine. And this was because alcohol was a source of energy, and recommended for slaves."

Prohibition reduced the political expansion of the region. And in practice, curbing the production and sale of mead, cane brandy, and rum automatically brought on the financial failure of the sugar mills, and of Rio de Janeiro. A violent reaction set in against observing the law. Resistance groups then forming, headed by Dom Luís de Almeida Portugal, an illustrious nobleman. And in the wake of this popular movement, the governor was eventually dismissed from office.

Rugendas began to draw a number of stills, making them spurt forth, in a spiral, a simulacrum of the precious liquid. A conventional drawing, lacking the excitement felt by the conspirators, who, after they had succeeded in driving the governor out, took over the government for a six-month stretch.

"Thanks to cachaça, Rio de Janeiro secured administrative autonomy in the seventeenth century. And put the people in charge. *In vino veritas*."

It was easy to foresee the end of a revolt that had imbued the people with wild euphoria, threatening the Portuguese mother country. The forces of the kingdom were reorganized, with the immediate advance of Portuguese troops. Followed by the recovery of power. Whereupon the authorities caused the rebels to pay for their crimes on the scaffold or in jail. Such penalties not succeeding in erasing from popular memory the remembrance of a rigidly disciplined group that had dared to oppose a repressive government, contrary to the interests of a colony already dreaming of emancipation.

Madruga proved inattentive. He took a sip of passion-fruit juice, freshly squeezed. He turned toward me.

"I admire revolutions. They have a dramatic purport and a cathartic force. Revolution comes about when the body suffers from an infection, from which it must free itself. There's a barbarous bloodletting then and the blood streams down the sewer pipes. Except that after the hurrahs and the hymns in praise of revolution, it's the same men who take over. Almost no new faces. Whereupon they garner power and seize the reins. And the people, once again, are plunged into historical silence."

I ended up having a glass of the passion-fruit juice. I found it warm and sweetish.

4 August 18— At one time it was feared that Brazil would no longer retain her geographical unity and the same linguistic pattern.

Bernardo Pereira de Vasconcellos himself mounted to the speaker's platform, rallying his peers round the nation in crisis. If energetic measures were not taken, the internal convulsions would spread, threatening to tear Brazil apart.

Feijó, the regent, in a dark cassock, sensed the danger. From his office, he drafted articles containing certain loopholes that would preserve the system sanctioned by the Constitution. Among other measures, he created the National Guard. A body of nonprofessional soldiers who, though possessed of a fighting spirit and subject to army life and discipline, would not enjoy unlimited military power.

Hence shorn of the prerogatives accorded traditional armies. Not even having definite access to arms. While at the same time recruitment would be based on a simple appeal to civic conscience. The recruit not losing his status as a civilian, citizen, and voter.

Though the act that created this militia attracted supporters and fierce criticism alike, the truth is that the National Guard reestablished public order. Thus meriting the sympathy of the multitude. Especially since it was a body that included half-breeds, blacks, and aborigines who, by way of the uniform or recruitment, ascended the social ladder. Thereby taking on substance, though without the backing of the law, whose statutes stood in the way of its growth.

I recently supped with certain officers of the militia. Their attitudes, in public, are identical to those of army officers. Filled with *esprit de corps* and pride in their uniforms. And already they speak of power with the careful neutrality of one muddying the trail of the plot in which he knows himself to be necessarily involved. They exchange smiles among themselves, making outsiders of those who do not enjoy equal prestige. And though they admit to being pacifists and mere integrators of national unity, I suspect their appetites and the human heart. Who is ordering their eyes to gleam, their chests puffed out in their eagerness to fit into the uniform of the corps, as though it were a second skin?

They pride themselves on the danger through which the country has passed, with its hegemony badly shaken. Its very language threatened. It must not be forgotten that until 1823 indigenous languages expressed fundamental sentiments and necessities throughout all the national territory. Brazil spoke Tupi and other tribal languages as well, except on the sea-

coast. Thus giving the impression that Portuguese had still not been sufficiently consolidated.

It may perhaps be said that thanks to the Constituent Assembly of
1823, the loosened ties of a beautiful language were finally drawn tight.
The language, in essence Lusitanian, which today is heard in the streets as
in homes. Is it not true that language anticipates the shocking revelations
of a reality in constant evolution?

20 September 18—   In the streets, the influence of Lusitanian education is noticeable. Capistrano, moreover, points out that this education
"is limited to erasing vivacity and spontaneity from the soul of school-
children."

I do not know if I agree. Inasmuch as once they leave school these
pupils move back and forth between orgies and processions quite naturally.
And, as grown men, they wear surplices on holy days, and follow the
procession carrying lighted candles, while hiding their souls and their stiff
members beneath imposing canopies.

I observe that Dom Pedro II did them the thankless favor of acclaiming their circumspection, their reserve, their moderation, as virtues. And
their prudence as well, which here tends to decline into inertia and medi-
ocrity. All these traits being conjoined in public administration. Thereby
barring provocative and lively intelligences from government. Whereupon
they bury themselves in the teaching of Portuguese, Latin, Greek, in the
public school system. Preferably in the Pedro II High School, which recently opened its doors.

The truth is that Dom Pedro II gave no proof of any real appreciation
for culture, as is so loudly proclaimed.

5 October 18—   Eulália came into the living room wearing a white
suit. Having been brought there by Odete, who was following her instructions. The unexpected heat of that afternoon was suffocating us. Eulália
headed for the veranda, hugging the shadow that the mango trees cast onto
the group of straw chairs.

Only then did Eulália look at me, as though about to speak. I noted
the sudden tenseness of her face. Was some secret gnawing at her soul? I
picked up a few fallen leaves at random and offered them to her, as though
they were flowers, without a word. She thanked me. I did not know, however, what the next step would be. Did she want me to explain . . .

.   .   .

Eulália broke off her reading. That's enough, she said to herself. She
was afraid that the other pages might embarrass her. A quick reading
showed that Venâncio had decided to disregard practical reality. Unlike
Madruga, who went to extremes, pretending that his excesses made him
happy.

Eulália put the diary away in the drawer. She would not read it again. She had not been able to identify with the Brazil of the nineteenth century, of which she had no firsthand knowledge. Perhaps the country was precisely as Venâncio had shown it. He had no reason to lie. It was odd, though, that he had devoted so much of his energy to that century. As though he were trying to escape from a period and a country that had brought him great suffering.

America was undoubtedly his passion. In this respect, Madruga and he were two of a kind. That was why Venâncio described it exhaustively in the diary. And always with brushstrokes that varied according to his state of mind. He was quite aware that America escaped him, even as he chased after it.

Eulália smiled faintly. Luckily there was a man such as Venâncio, who nourished the illusion of an America full of parrots, treasure, the confused voices of the new families being formed here in an unbridled eagerness to colonize, to realize dreams and bring about liberal genetic combinations.

She opened the door. There was Odete, wide awake, sitting on a step of the staircase. Waiting to be allowed to come back into the room, from which she felt herself to be temporarily banished.

Eulália summoned her in a gentle voice. She came to her, treading the floorboards with a certain hauteur. Thereby regaining the possession that had been wrested from her so shamefully. First she sat down next to Eulália. Next, however, she chose to tidy the objects on top of the chest of drawers. Immediately thereafter, she left the room. On her return, she brought Eulália a trayful of tea and biscuits. Acting in such a way as to give Eulália time to ponder the question of what she had done in her absence. And also, whether or not it was necessary to reveal to Odete the reasons that had determined the recent separation.

Eulália gradually let down her defenses. The tea did her stomach good. Restoring to it a warmth that it had oddly lost as she read.

"God knows what He meant when He chose me for His daughter," Eulália suddenly said.

Indifferent to Odete's look of surprise, incapable as she was of understanding the meaning of such words, Eulália went on.

"Had I not been so frightened of earthly things, I would have risked engaging in improper acts. Compromising my life by the momentary seductions of this world. So God was right when He brought me to Sobreira, just to hear my father's stories. Up till now the only storyteller who ever used his wiles on me."

Odete's eyes opened wide. Suddenly understanding what Eulália was trying to convey to her, without thereby betraying Venâncio. Odete also knew of the diary in her possession. And that to date it had not been perused by Eulália. Unless she had read it that afternoon. Was it with that end in view, then, that her mistress had wanted to be left by herself?

"Tomorrow is Sunday. The day that Senhor Venâncio comes to dinner here. It's the only day he has a family, isn't that so?" Odete said.

"Nobody has a family every day, Odete. Venâncio will come tomorrow. He's never stopped coming to our house, ever since I arrived in Brazil. Except on the Sundays at the time of the Civil War. Do you remember? And he'll bring me wildflowers, held in his left hand. So as to leave his right one free to greet people. He's a good man, who worries excessively about the world, forgetting himself. He worries about Brazil above all. And you, Odete, do you worry about Brazil?"

Abashed, Odete did not know what to do with her hands. What was there about Brazil that deserved such concern or a firm answer, at that very moment? Should she speak of Getúlio, of Chico Alves? As though it were really possible for people to speak of their country, to say of it the sort of things one says to a person one is fond of?

"I don't know, Dona Eulália. I think so. Except that I don't really know what Brazil is like. It's always hard to understand a person's country. Don't you think so, senhora?"

Venâncio arrived in Leblon wearing a suit and tie, ready for a funeral. Lost in thought in the living room, Madruga did not budge. Tobias hurried to offer his godfather the armchair next to Madruga's. Only then, still prostrate, did Madruga turn his attention to that living shadow, prepared to settle accounts with him. He very nearly told him that the hour feared by both of them had finally come. But he did not dare.

Tobias brought him coffee. Venâncio's hands trembled slightly as he held the cup. Tobias was touched by his father and godfather, the two of them as one in the face of Eulália's imminent death. She had always had the gift of bringing them together, amid heated disputes.

Venâncio was in no hurry. He had come with the intention of staying on till the end. He did not ask after Eulália, however, or make a move to go to her room, to find her repenting in her bed, clinging to one of her favorite saints.

In the half-shadow of the other end of the room, Miguel shuddered now and again, whereupon he immediately made his body go rigid all over, overcome with shame. Breta hesitated between staying where she was, offering him coffee and affection, and maintaining a respectful distance. In the face of Miguel's grief, his reserve keeping him from freely expressing the pain of losing Eulália. After having been singled out, since childhood, as the favorite son of that woman of Spanish birth, who told him endless stories. As she plied him with pastries, transparent and fresh.

The southwest wind, coming directly from Patagonia, blew on Leblon, making the panes of the closed windows shake. Night had not yet fallen.

"Where's Odete?" Venâncio whispered to his godson.

Madruga pricked up his ears. He knew very well what Venâncio's words meant. His timidity not permitting him, even at the hour of death, to ask about Eulália. It was easier for him to inquire as to the whereabouts of Odete, undoubtedly keeping watch over her mistress.

Venâncio's naïve tactic moved Madruga. Venâncio too would soon be lying gasping his last, all alone in his house on the outskirts of the city, with no one to call upon for help. No one would bring soup to his bedside to nourish his stomach and comfort his lonely heart. And all because, submerged in the sin of pride, he had turned a deaf ear to Madruga's plea to live with them in Leblon. Hence being quite capable in the future of lying, if he should fall ill. Anxious to prove to Madruga that he was hale and hearty. Immediately setting out for home, on foot, as though he were without a care in the world. It being of no use for Madruga to insist. Stubborn as ever, Venâncio would stoutly maintain that his pallor and his heavy cold were no more than a touch of the flu, brought on by the damp night air. Hence curable with a cup of orange-leaf tea. Quite unable, however, to confess to the fear of dying all alone. As though he cared nothing for the rest of the world. A man shut up in the little mother-of-pearl box that Eulália had given him as a present.

Madruga suspected that the key to Venâncio was in Eulália's possession. So safely tucked away that no one had ever found it and made use of it. And now, so many years later, everything led him to believe that that key was so rusted that it would no longer unlock Venâncio's hardened heart.

Venâncio's godson answered his question. Odete was with Eulália, as she had been for years. Never leaving her side except for the most urgent reasons. Venâncio seemed to take no notice of him. As though he had known, beforehand, where she might be found. He had only to mount the staircase and enter the room upstairs, whereupon Odete would greet him politely.

Odete had long since forgotten the alliance that had been concluded between them, immediately after Getúlio Vargas's suicide. On the very morning of that death which had turned the entire house topsy-turvy, Tobias and Venâncio had taken refuge in Odete's room as soon as they saw her in tears. They immediately realized that the tragedy had brought them together, for the time being at least. Heartbroken as they listened to the news over Radio Nacional, with bulletins practically every minute. And as Venâncio solemnly seated himself on the bed, Odete and Tobias, on the floor, sat side by side, their elbows leaning on the mattress. Odete appeared to be praying, with hands joined.

The news on the Esso Reporter was disturbing. Odete's sobs grew deeper as the unmistakable voice of Heron Domingues repeated, over and over, passages from the President's farewell letter.

They had never seen Odete in such low spirits. Not even at the death of her sister beneath the wheels of the Central Line train. Even reaching the point of refusing to be comforted by Eulália, who came to pay her a brief visit. Tobias further incited her to revolt by angry protests against American imperialism, which, by its disapproval of the passing of the law concerning the repatriation of profits, had posed a threat to national sovereignty.

Odete kept repeating Getúlio's name in a monotone. She slowly stroked the blue cotton coverlet on her bed, as though she were before his coffin. That man, now dead with a bullet in his chest, had always given her the illusion of having spoken in her name. And, for that very reason, of mounting to platforms and reproducing, before the microphones, words that took her heart by storm, to the point that many times she wept with emotion. Grateful that he had sent forth those signs that only she was able to interpret.

She had never forgotten a summer when they had all been together in São Lourenço. Eulália, herself, and the children, strolling through the Parque das Águas, with Madruga leading the way, in long strides. When they had seen the President approaching, in their direction, having just emerged from paths decorated with blue hydrangeas. A straw hat clapped on his head, a cigar clenched between his teeth. She could almost touch him, see the cavities in his teeth. Vargas was partial to white suits, which made his paunch even more noticeable. He looked to her like a boss politely expressing his thanks for freshly made coffee.

For a few seconds, Vargas looked her straight in the face, wishing to imprint his charisma on her eyes. So that Odete would never forget, thus contracting, from that instant on, the obligation of mourning his future death. And on top of that, he offered her a smile whose like she had only seen in Eulália, as she prayed before an altar crowded with saints.

Odete refused Venâncio's handkerchief. Rather than avoid her pain, she preferred tears that made her look ugly. The President merited her most copious weeping. Hadn't he always been called the father of the poor? And being herself poor, miserable, should she not, then, look upon him as her father?

"Weep no more, Odete. We're going to recite an *Ave Maria* for him," Tobias said, to Venâncio's surprise.

Now, joining hands, the two of them began to pray aloud for Getúlio's soul. Out of the corner of his eye, Tobias kept careful watch on the door. He did not want to be surprised at prayer. He of all people, a militant of the National Student Union, fighting with his comrades for the microphone, for space on the speaker's platform, as they debated the political question, a particularly heated issue in those days. A debate in which he was defeated. Because, at the height of emotion, the necessary words had always failed him. At such moments, his whole body throbbed, his hands trembled, his heart harbored a gale. The microphone seemed to him an enemy he must fight. He was simply incapable of moderating his language, of following a line of reasoning reflecting the political stage in which he suddenly found himself. Feeling lost, he resorted to physical confrontation, filthy language, from a fertile vein. Which later made him ashamed; he felt affronted. These brawls widening already existing divergences, resulting in the creation of other groups that did not permit a common idea to be stitched together between them. Tobias perceived that they were treating him like a child, taking no notice when he intervened.

"Ah, Seu Venâncio, I have two thorns in my heart now, right here," Odete pointed to her chest, just to one side of a medal of Our Lady of Fátima. "The first one was on account of Chico Alves's death. And now Getúlio's death. I don't know which one to weep for most. For the President or the singer we idolized. Though it's two years since he met his death on the highway, it still seems as though it were today."

For the first time, Odete was confiding in Venâncio. This secret-sharing interrupted by the voice of Heron Domingues, the same voice that had brought her, in the past, the news of the automobile accident of which Franciso Alves had been the victim. A voice that brought only despair and grief into her room, decorated with images of saints, Spanish landscapes, and a leather wineskin, a present from González, Madruga's former business partner.

"When Chico Alves sang 'The one who departs has eyes about to drown,' he forgot to mention those who are left behind. What happens to people like us, Seu Venâncio? Aren't we the ones left weeping? I only pray God to take me before Dona Eulália."

For the singer's wake, Tobias accompanied Odete as far as the Assembly, where the body was on public view. With Cinelândia and the Avenida Rio Branco taken over by the crowd, it was no easy task to climb the steps of the building, to enter the line moving forward inside the great hall. Before Francisco Alves's bier, several admirers broke out their own violins, brought from all corners of the city, in homage to the artist who had sung in the name of the people.

Ordinarily reserved, Odete wept on seeing this show of grief. Tobias passed her his handkerchief now and again so she could blow her nose. And at the moment when they finally took the casket out of the Assembly, without her having had a chance to get a close look at the singer's face, Odete felt her body tremble; an unrestrained thrill of emotion ran through the entire crowd. Chico himself, there present, alive among them, could not have helped feeling moved by the spectacle.

Without realizing, she dug her fingernails into Tobias's arm. He did not protest, and slowly they followed the procession on foot, behind the fire truck, to the São João Batista cemetery.

"If the people at Chico Alves's burial almost wrecked the cemetery, what is it going to be like at Getúlio's? Who's going to protect this people? I don't know the first thing about it, Seu Venâncio, but I've a feeling in my bones that that man was murdered."

Venâncio spoke prophetically of other Odetes in the future determined to demystify the redeeming paradise of tears, substituting for it practical actions, of a political nature. As a reaction against the will and the fiery, spellbinding language of politicians of the populist lineage such as Vargas. Any number of them being nothing but mercenaries and murderers. Even Getúlio, despite his having redeemed himself upon his return to power, following his exile in São Borja, had a bloodstained throne in the eyes of history.

Venâncio had decided, without hesitation, to support him in his second administration. Without nourishing any greater hopes. Vargas's truth, or the truth of whoever governs, depended on the suffering of the weak. Therefore they did not scruple, when at the forefront of power, to sacrifice the simpleminded and the gullible, as often as circumstances required. Precisely because the substance of such ambition, on principle, called for the limelight, a stage, glory, at whatever price. It was necessary, therefore, to identify in Vargas his zones of light and others steeped in shadow, contaminated by base and cruel acts.

Venâncio looked at Tobias, clinging to Odete. Enjoying the passion of loss, coursing through his most secret hiding places. At that moment everything he might have said to him became useless. Who was he to strip his godson of his illusion, to rob him of an ardor that at times roils the world's gut, in an instinctive urge to cleanse itself?

Venâncio felt dominated by the dour, sour mood of old age, whose discreet signs were already approaching. He could identify in old age a summons to regress. Capable of attracting man to conservative viewpoints. Perhaps because death had a basically conservative content, what with its tendency to pare away excesses, in whatever form they might present themselves. He remembered, as a case in point, Bernardo Pereira de Vasconcellos, who ended his life as a monarchist reactionary. Despite having shouted to the heavens, in his golden moments of liberalism: "Disastrous government! Abominable government! At once stupid, despotic, and prodigal! Abominable government, here perfectly represented by that accursed trinity: force, will, and money!"

There he was, on the speaker's platform, with his wrinkled face, his body deformed by disease, precociously senile, vehemently inculpating the ministers of War, Justice, and the Treasury, present at that moment, seated in the plenary assembly. A discourse still necessary today, substituting different names and juggling with time, that plotter endlessly conspiring against human honor.

Vargas, however, chose to put a bullet through his chest. Because he trusted in the judgment of history, which would always turn out to be in his favor. Trusting in a gesture meant to seduce history. So canny and effective a gesture, as it happened, that it was destined to create, in the future, serious obstacles to a calm and impartial examination of the way in which he had acquitted himself as a politician.

The cards laid out on the polished table of history were reshuffled. Nonetheless, the deaths of Chico Alves and Getúlio Vargas, both given secret shelter in Odete's heart, became insurpassable in popular memory. Was this not, then, the service lent to history by myth? Taking no account of the deviations and the errors committed?

Tobias went over to Venâncio. He made a move to help him out of the armchair next to Madruga.

"Don't you want to see Mama? She may not be sleeping."

Venâncio paled, unable to make up his mind. Madruga eyed him sternly. A look acknowledging that the friendship between them was drowning in the swamp of feelings insufficiently explained. Both were fated in the end to be covered with ashes, now that the wood of youth had burned down to charcoal. But when, in fact, had the two of them dealt each other a nearly mortal wound? Had Eulália become the dark dividing line, entering them through the rectum or the prostate simply to mark her insuperable presence? That same sweet Eulália who was more at home with the ways of the Church, forever distracted in the face of reality. Hence reality might well dispense with her presence.

Despite Madruga's air of constraint, Venâncio seemed to be asking him to accompany him. As the husband, it was easier for him to visit the room where he had spent so many years. From whose window, so many times, Madruga had seen the grass thrive in the garden, as his prosperity grew. The same room in which he had stroked Eulália's head not long before, on the pretext of seeing how much of a fever she had. Because, having robbed him of youth and ecstasy, the years had also eradicated in him the spontaneous gesture of cuddling up next to his wife's now-withered body and exacting from it the wanton pleasure of long ago.

Madruga's eyes had a metallic gleam and his face a distant look. In no state to aid those who were suffering as he was. And who insisted on living all alone on the outskirts of the city. Venâncio looked straight at Breta, just arrived. She, however, did nothing to help him make up his mind about visiting her grandmother. Her sympathies lying entirely with Madruga, she felt that Venâncio ought to suffer the consequences of the meeting with

Eulália. The moment had come for him to thank the woman, on her death-bed, for the best meals in his whole life. When Eulália had presided at table, so as to keep Venâncio and Madruga from quarreling. The same altercations that had begun aboard ship, on the very first day, as they left the port of Vigo. A journey that had not yet ended. They were continuing to offer their discourses of the deaf, neither permitting the other a single aside, a single word that would change their destinies. Coming more and more to lack all notion of the directions and the intensity of events that they themselves had engendered.

Breta sensed that Venâncio was readying himself to steal essential parts of Eulália, now that she was leaving forever. Her grandfather not having enough time and energy left, however, to recover those same sentiments for himself or allay the suspicions that might take root as Eulália breathed her last.

Breta left the room. As did Madruga. Both agreeing that Venâncio should stroke Eulália's hands, should take a close look at the wrinkles, the yellow blotches on that face. The little tremors that had always been there, unnoticed. Living at last an experience long overdue. For the sake of which, in the meantime, he had endured the loneliness of the little house in a working-class district, in which pride and the lack of affection had always made themselves felt. Not even when Tobias knocked at his door to have dinner with him and spend the night, anxious to forget the family, did Venâncio's spirits lift. Each week the impression was further borne in upon him that he had dreamed in vain. His dreams had been compromised by a pale and petty daily life. Hence his feeling of being the victim of predation, against which he was helpless to rebel. Perhaps, given these circumstances, Eulália's death would endow his memory with the good he lacked. The one irredeemable, nonnegotiable good.

Venâncio knocked tremulously on the door. Behind the walls was a familiar scene. A sick woman, attended by her maidservant, who was moving about in concentric circles. Odete bade him enter. He approached the bed. Her eyes closed, Eulália was still breathing. Venâncio was searching for words that would express affection and confidence that she would recover, once she opened her eyes. Odete did not help him. She merely brought him a chair so that he might sit at the bedside. He armed himself with patience. He had never had the time to be alone with her. As a rule they talked in the presence of third parties. He looked at Eulália again, moved to see her both resting and running away.

In her bed, Eulália still had herself well in hand. Clean and fragrant, her nightgown freshly ironed, not a hair on her head out of place. Odete ruling her mistress's every hour with a stern hand. Ready to found the memory of Eulália with that of her dead, installing her in the pantheon of heroes. To the right of Getúlio Vargas, and to the left of Francisco Alves. Venâncio always suspected that beneath the thin flesh of that black woman lay a highly sensual nature. Inclined toward passions fed with a parched tongue, a fearless body, without apparent emotions. An intensity to which there had been added her feeling for Eulália.

Odete interrupted his reflections by bringing him water. With the glass in his hand, he felt protected. Though at the mercy of a fate hesitating in the balance, Eulália gave no sign of acknowledging his presence. Completely withdrawn into herself, she acted as though it were her desire that Venâncio, in the future, should describe her death, surrounding this event with words indispensable for the description of her emotions. Not omitting from this inventory her most secret recesses.

As he tried to calculate Eulália's age, Venâncio immediately recaptured her face when young, descending the stairs of the boat that brought her to Brazil for the first time. Following Madruga's lead, Eulália made a brave show of courage. It was she, moreover, who held out her hand first to Venâncio. He bowed to her in greeting. There coming over him, at that very instant, the sensation that Eulália and Madruga, just arrived from Spain, through some inexplicable art, were cutting him off from part of his energy.

Eulália immediately looked all round, her eyes sparkling as she appreciated the landscape. It was a Saturday, in June. And the Brazil that she saw at that moment was turning green along the slopes, on the hills, in the gardens, down to the beaches, which could be reached by carriage and streetcar. From every hand came odors so intense that Eulália felt a strange pain grip her body. She rejected such a poison, calling upon her pact with God. She must surely be on her guard. There were signs that life here below the equator, tremulous, nervous, would more than once threaten to soak her thighs and breasts with sudden sweat. All this incompatible, however, with incense and prayers.

Madruga sensed Eulália's fear of the tropics, and put his arms about her.

"Don't worry, Eulália. That's just the way it is. You'll soon get used to it."

Eulália was grateful for this kind attention on the part of her husband, whom she scarcely knew. They were newlyweds, after all. For that very reason accepting the love that marriage brought, amid fears. She for her part a little perplexed on being confronted with the fact of bodies coupling and uncoupling in imperative obedience to impulses sanctioned, despite their nature, by the Church. Having also observed that these impulses outmatched the interests of the soul. Not even trying to find out where they came from. Knowing quite well, perhaps, that they came from everywhere.

In those days, whenever they were alone, Madruga embraced her forthrightly, without hesitation. Determined to subject her to a very natural event. Whereupon Eulália noted that her husband's arms, despite his visible emotion, did not tremble. His body always coming up with the proper responses.

He courteously turned the light out so that they could make love in the dark. Out of respect for her, sensing her fidelity to secret vows. Not reproving her for her sudden shy withdrawals, her hesitant gestures. He understood her discreet way of lovemaking. And was surprised, therefore, when his wife, distractedly, gave him eager kisses. Madruga tried not to say a single word as little by little he penetrated her. Out of fear that such intimacy, so far beyond her every conception of human relations, might offend her. And with thoughtful concern, he confined himself to leading her toward pleasure. Through perseverance and obscure attitudes, which were never to reach the light of day.

In bed, as his wife slept, Madruga enjoyed watching her. He had not a single memory of her as a very young girl. Perhaps because Eulália had always been beneath the shadow of Dom Miguel when she played in the yard. A man so excessively possessive of his daughter that he practically kept her shut up in a magic dungeon. Keeping her inside the house, making her forget, by virtue of stories and succulent fruits gathered in the garden, what the countryside of Sobreira was like.

In the front room, till late at night, as her father talked, Eulália forgot the world that existed on the outside. From the beginning, her instinct inclined her toward words, and thus away from life. Taking great delight in stories about the outstanding figures of Galicia. Her father's most ardent enthusiasm being inspired by Priscillian, the great heretic put to death at the Black Gate of Treves. And also by Diego Gelmírez, responsible for the construction of the cathedral of Santiago, and the austere and astute counselor of Afonso VII.

It was amid such figures as these that Dom Miguel had kindled his Celtic imagination. Never abandoning his sense of commitment to the dense mystery that had surrounded this people since its creation. Despite the decadence that had overtaken them in the middle of the fifteenth century, which he had never been able to bring himself to accept. Therefore asking himself who had set fire in their memory to their achievements in this world and to the folios of their great codices. And at what exact moment the Galicians had lost their sense of history, with the result that they would one day be easily put to flight by the Castilians.

When his children reached adolescence, Dom Miguel took them to Santiago de Compostela. They must appreciate the Pórtico da Glória in his company. Together they would gain the vision that would enable them to dream. Their feelings must be refined through the confrontation with stones carved by perfect craftsmen.

He felt like weeping in the great square in front of the cathedral.

"Standing before this portico, words become immaterial. I feel deaf and dumb. Tell me, Eulália, am I exaggerating? But if this is so, what place do words have in the order of creation?"

Eulália, as always, paid careful heed to her father's instruction. She straightened her dress, tucked in a few locks of her hair ruffled by the wind.

"And what happened to us, father, when they robbed us of our language? Is it painful for us to learn Castilian? Can that be why it's so hard for us to speak it even today?"

Dom Miguel was touched. At times he felt his strength fail. Exhausted from keeping watch over a poor and rainy country. From continually safeguarding its myths, which threatened to desert them in the face of the mistreatment they received. He went about things, however, in such a way that Eulália wouldn't notice.

"Nebrija said that language follows Empire. But that isn't so. He doesn't know what he's talking about. Despite Castilian domination, we still speak Galician today and nobody has yet managed to snuff out our legends, for they're firmly lodged in our very bowels."

Dom Miguel paused. He seemed calmer now.

"How would we ever forget the group of women who followed Priscillian, like faithful guard dogs? That same Priscillian who advocated a boundless fidelity to the intuitive state, to the kingdom of intuition, even though this might be to the detriment of the rational, against rules and against straight lines laid down by a ruler. According to him, it was necessary for us to go back to the most remote past, to strike roots once again. He was not afraid of preaching sermons that went against canon law. And so, for that very reason, those women held firmly to his commandments, understood his words, the fever of his Ember days. Perhaps because they were Celts, Westerners, Spaniards. For all anyone knows, they might even have been priestesses in the past."

He pointed again to the Pórtico da Glória, with its timeless mystic theme. "Look there at the shadow of Master Mateo gliding in and out among the statues. He's always here, day and night. He won't ever abandon the stones on which his men and he carved the history of human passion. And with nothing but a chisel and their own hands."

Eulália lay so still it worried Odete. She bent over to listen to her breathing, slow and regular. Venâncio's thoughts accompanied her as she did so. His mind likewise set at rest by Eulália's serenity. Quite in keeping with her usual discreet reserve. Very much like his own, moreover. Both forever hiding in dark corners, so that no one would see the sudden flash of light in their eyes. The two of them cautiously observing each other. Each knew so little about the other. And almost no one knew Madruga. What was certain was that the three of them broke trails before them, amid thick fog, hoping to surprise a powerful emotion in any one of them.

Odete decided to awaken Eulália at teatime. Venâncio, however, begged with a pleading gesture that she be spared. He would not know what to say to her. What would they talk about? Of bounteous beef stews, of memories of the Civil War? Or of Eulália's suffering at the loss of loved ones? When her grief threatened to bring her to her knees on the floor, yet as she voiced her lament she resisted, like a queen.

In the face of this long-suffering Eulália, he always felt like tearing his heart from his breast and offering it in sacrifice to some being. One without a name, since he was not a believer. But could there be a single creature with no sense whatsoever of the divine? Was the notion of God an offense to human prerogatives? And when such gods were acknowledged, was it merely out of a desire to equal them? What mattered most to man was finding firm footing on a territory undermined by miracles and magic entities. But wasn't it also true that man was inclined, from the beginning, to interpret blasts of wind as an expression of the authoritarianism of a god whom it was necessary to obey in order to be able to wrest the secret of his methods from him?

Ever since he had met Eulália, Venâncio had admired the boldness with which she defended human honor. Thereby preserving the memory of her country, of her language, and of her family. And, reassured by these human possessions, she immediately placed them in the hands of her god. Gentle Eulália thus doing battle against the widespread dissension among men.

To Venâncio, time seemed to be dancing now. Leaping forward one moment, flinging Eulália and himself back to some remote era the next. Seeing Eulália before him once again, standing at his door, waiting to be invited inside. Her serene face nonetheless did not reassure Venâncio. Something was the matter. Feeling abashed at having glimpsed her secret feelings, he ushered Eulália into the living room. He was not expecting her visit. Especially by herself, without Odete.

After offering her a chair, he occupied himself with pointless details. He made her fresh coffee. He brought her ice water. To make the two of them feel comfortable in that modest dwelling.

Eulália scarcely moved. Now and again she wiped away the thin trickle of perspiration on her forehead. Her apparent calm at last giving away to sudden pallor.

"What's troubling you, Eulália? Is it something about the children? About Madruga?"

After a long silence, she gave signs of being willing to talk.

"The trouble lies right here in your house."

"I know. Tobias."

Madruga and Eulália had not seen their son for months. He had never come home. As though he'd died. In the first days, Eulália thought that Tobias, prepared to forget family misunderstandings, had not left for long. She was confident that Venâncio, after calming him, would be able to make him change his mind. Not agree to allow Tobias to stay at his place. Side, that is to say, with her and Madruga.

More of a realist, Madruga had kept her from getting her sleep in recent weeks. He would wake her in the middle of the night to give vent to his despair and rebellion at the situation. Declaring Venâncio an enemy and a usurper.

"What else does he want from me? He's taken my son. My past and my memory are in his hands. Isn't that enough to satisfy him?" His blue eyes sparked with anger.

Eulália calmed her husband, proving to him that the impasse was a great trial to Venâncio. Obliged to take his son in for lack of the means to persuade Tobias to return home after the quarrel with his father.

"It's just a matter of days, Madruga. This very next Sunday we'll be having Venâncio and Tobias for dinner."

She began to pray, hoping for a miracle. And that the loaves and fishes would multiply there where life had dried up. If Christ could do anything, why could He not bring Tobias back, a much less complicated under-taking?

"Don't be simpleminded, Eulália. Come back to earth and help me," Madruga said peevishly.

He noted, however, Eulália's immediate withdrawal within herself. Not only had he wounded her feelings; he had been unjust. He had caused his own wrath to descend upon her, making her responsible for the troubles besetting their household.

He flung himself upon her, overcome with remorse. "Forgive me, Eulália. I'm the only one to blame. I think I fight Tobias tooth and nail just because he antagonizes me so. He wants to get even with me. His whole life is spent demanding feelings of me that I haven't the least idea how to express. Can my own son be my enemy?"

Feeling aggrieved, he drew away from Eulália. "Would he rather be Venâncio's son? One not born of my blood?"

"Never speak such words to me again, Madruga. How dare you offend our son and Venâncio himself?" she raised her voice, silencing him for the first time.

After this heated exchange, she decided to visit Venâncio in the morning, certain that she would not run into Tobias. She too was piqued by her son's absence. The family structure had been seriously altered. It was necessary to put things back in their proper places, to sweep away hurts and bothersome problems. Father and son had gone too far, had deserved punishment. But all that had gone far enough, and they had best forget now. Could human feelings be important enough to rend a neighbor to bits in their name?

"Ah, Venâncio, only God is the perfect refuge for those who flee this strife-torn earth," she said remorsefully.

Eulália had spoken at length. He had heard her out, his heart touched, without interrupting her. They were all alone in the house; no one knew where they were. Dressed in a gray suit, her hair drawn severely back, her features bared, everything about her accentuated her sadness. As she spoke to him of her son's desertion, Venâncio went back over those years in America. An America that each of them denied in the name of reasons founded on perishable principles. She had doubtless allowed herself to be driven by the sensuous, passionate propellers of Madruga's dream. Madruga time and again saying yes and no for her. His burning gaze forcing that destiny upon her. A gaze that had first penetrated her in the little village square of Sobreira. Both hesitating as to what to say. A meeting that had sealed their lives. To the point that Eulália, confronting Dom Miguel, broke in on the stories rehearsed at table, even though it was mealtime, merely to speak to him about Madruga. Whereupon Madruga had sworn to Dom Miguel that, in his own way, he would make some of his stories come true, once he was given Eulália's hand. By taking his wife across the Atlantic, in the wake of its foaming waves, so conducive to daydreams.

Eulália observed Venâncio. Regretting having talked too much. But sensing what he must be thinking, her eyes brightened.

"Perhaps fate is only a dream that ends badly." She smiled faintly. Whereupon she recovered her serenity, as typical of her as silk dresses in pastel colors, and white linen ones, in summer.

Stirred by Eulália, Venâncio drew his chair closer. Taking a path contrary to the one intended. He was always confused in Eulália's presence. Above all by the way in which she showed that she knew where to alight and in which direction to proceed. A self-assurance stemming perhaps from death, of which she spoke with implacable naturalness. As if, being surrounded by divinities, her slightest act was immediately categorized. While at the same time this certainty spurred her on to abandon the earth for a peaceable kingdom compatible with her soul.

He felt like a displaced person in Eulália's presence. A woman who ruled unhesitatingly over her church. Even with her eyes closed, she could describe the draperies of the saints, the details of the endless liturgical ceremonies. Taking great care not to forget to add to each of them what seemed crucial to her in order to immortalize them. To give them a reason for existing.

As for himself, he was incapable of describing the house in which he had buried himself, claiming thereby that he was free. A sort of freedom that had settled over his face in the form of ice, to his great detriment. Separating him in the end from human society. Barring his access to the sources of understanding of a reality that he had thought it possible to dissect by viewing it through his own poverty.

He saw himself as a member of a class jammed into the trains of the

Central and Leopoldina lines, out of whose windows there leapt the distressed and desperate. At home, the shadow of the mango trees and the sound of television turned up to full volume on Sundays were the usual distractions for him and his neighbors. The winning soccer goal echoed in his ears. Life thus proving itself to be without consolation. Looking forward to a better meal on Sundays. Straying members of the family gathered round the table. Now and again there came to him the reek of rotting garbage in the vacant lots. It occurred to no one to clean them up, to drive away the rodents. Along with the stench the wind brought the sound of lying words, chaos, feeding the hope of a closed-in community, without a future.

Tobias sensed his anguish. He bent over backwards, then, to care for his godfather's needs from day to day. He brought him cheese, fruit, fresh vegetables from the market close by. His heart touched, Venâncio appreciated that effort.

Immediately, however, Tobias returned to the subject of politics. Still on his guard against his own class.

"The people don't have an agenda, so they don't remember," he said, in a fit of righteousness. "Therefore they lack the capacity to get down to a list of items that would serve their interests if brought up at a round-table debate. Their one remaining possession is their labor."

Venâncio loved him like a son. The son of Madruga and Eulália. The two fleshes had given him the son he had never had. He went along with this argument, spellbound, measuring Tobias's capacity to resist luxury and comfort. By means of a rhetoric that resembled his own.

"The common destiny has always been decided by the oppressing classes. My father now belongs to them. This means that I too am a beneficiary of this oppression. So what am I to do? Do I take my stand against them and suffer the repudiation of the master class? Or do I make my peace with them, as I await the opportunity to get a good shot at them?"

To Madruga, Venâncio symbolized failure. And now his son was threatening to assume the same role. And why shouldn't his godson share with him the ineffable feeling of defeat? Of a defeat that bore in its most intimate depths the virtues impugned by Madruga. But who, in fact, could judge which were the winners and which the losers?

Looking at himself in the mirror, it seemed to Venâncio that something was missing. A mustache or a son? But didn't he have Tobias? His godson was in the habit of asking him questions. But before he could ask, he forbade him to question him about his love life.

"That's my business. Not yours."

Feeling contrite, Tobias brought him his soup in bed, renewing his energy and his will to live. Or lured him to the kitchen table. Where they talked for hours. Tobias felt safe in that house, as though he had been born there. At peace with his godfather.

"If I could choose, you'd be my father," he said, moved.

Venâncio discouraged this line of thought. Madruga was a generous father and provider. These arguments seemed inconsistent to Tobias.

"There's only one problem. I still want Eulália for a mother. The only solution would have been for Mother to marry you," he said, satisfied with the solution.

"Don't ever say that again, my boy. What a lack of respect!" Venâncio roared, avoiding his godson's gaze.

Tobias had never seen him in that state. Pale, his features swollen, his lips trembling. He left the table and hunched over the kitchen sink. Washing the morning dishes with brusque gestures.

"I apologize. I didn't mean to offend you. Or Mother and Father either." He came over to Venâncio.

Venâncio turned on the faucet. The water gushed out, soaking his shirt. He did nothing to prevent the damage. Tobias noted that his godfather was on the point of tears. A painful situation for both. Not knowing what to do, Tobias ran to the bedroom. Throwing himself on the bed, he hid his head under the pillow. He felt miserable, disloyal to his family. He tossed about on the bed, and finally got up. In the bathroom he tore off his clothes impatiently. As though Madruga had driven him from home again. Beginning a cycle of emotional blunders all over again. He had not only hurt Venâncio, but could not depend on Madruga's affection. Even Eulália, forgetful of human love, could not give him the necessary attention.

He soaped himself furiously. His hand sliding down his belly till it brushed his genitals. Could that be where the fountain of life was, as so often proclaimed? Could that in fact be the source of a pleasure of nature so voracious as to make him forget all the annoyances, all the mistreatment, blot out every last repugnant vestige of memory?

Without further ado, he began to scrub his penis with the foaming lather. And unlike other times, his rage made him patient. There was no need to hurry. Keeping a steady rhythm, up and down, very nearly succumbing to the pleasure. He went on, under control, appreciating the while the dauntless rod, acting independently of him, heroic, with medals pinned to the prepuce. How many medals in all would there be room for on that member? But now he could no longer bear to rein it in. He finally came, his orgasm hitting him like a slap in the face, just as Venâncio knocked at the door.

"Are you all right, Tobias? I need to talk to you."

Venâncio's words came to him as a muffled murmur. He was unable to answer. Leaning against the wall, he slumped to the floor. Not letting go of the small, humiliated member offering him no protection against Venâncio, on the other side of the door. Feeling the sob rising in his throat, he stifled it with his hand, so as not to be heard.

Eulália's breath suddenly came faster. Alarmed, Odete drew closer.

But Eulália, receiving the strength lent her by Odete, opened her eyes. The surrounding world did not seem to her to be a cause for concern. Known and familiar, it included Venâncio. She smiled at him, approving his presence. The same Venâncio who had received her, hat in hand, a concerned look on his face, at the foot of the stairs leading down from the ship, arriving in Brazil. The city was resplendent that morning, beautiful and tropical, amid the din of voices demanding passage. Eulália overcome with astonishment at the blacks, naked to the waist, moving along the dock like gazelles. Venâncio welcomed her most politely. Almost apologizing for not offering her addresses and words that would give her immediate entrée to the reality of this new country.

He promptly spoke his name, slowly and distinctly, to identify himself. Like a total stranger whom she had never heard of. Or might he have taken pains to tell her his surname as a way of hinting to her that, inasmuch as he had not been born in Galicia, she need not show him the special courtesies owed compatriots?

"Here I am, before the gate of the Lord. I'll soon be passing through it," she said in a low voice, from her sickbed.

"It's a gate that lies before all of us, Eulália. But the hour for you to pass through it has not yet come."

And Venâncio began to remonstrate with her. She must take care of herself, so as to return to the church she attended every day. He had sometimes come upon her praying on her knees before the altar. All by herself, her face alight. Not suspecting that he was observing her from behind a pillar so that she would not catch sight of him.

The faith that she displayed at such times moved him. He asked himself whether this sort of belief could be reconciled with the tragedies now unfolding on the human stage. A faith that kept her on her knees for hours at a time. A sacrifice that left calluses on them. As she remained totally absorbed in thoughts that took her far afield. Seemingly no longer living among human creatures. As though she had turned her back on a reality that permitted access only to dark, dimly lighted passages. Could they have lost Eulália because the earth abounded in injustices and ambiguities?

Deep in prayer, she had, happily, never caught sight of him there in the church. Besides not knowing how to justify his presence, he might not have been able to count upon her spirit of charity. Though Eulália had never reproved him, not even when she insisted that he persuade Tobias to return home.

From behind the column, Venâncio envied a woman who, through the mystery of faith, was reviving an age-old Christianity. In Brazil especially, where life embraced itself like a serpent in paradise. After a time, Eulália would sit down on a bench, busying herself putting away her rosary, her missal, folding her mantilla. Little gestures indicating that she was about to leave. Venâncio would run down the street, disappearing round the corner bar, where Eulália's chauffeur was waiting.

Eulália was having difficulty speaking. She thanked him for his visit. The fact that he had come from so far away. But it was a necessary sacrifice, since she had only a few hours left to say her good-byes, which must be brief ones. And she wanted to have him at her side. She had always had him there at difficult moments. Especially when death knocked on their door. At such times, Eulália came to fear that the pain in her chest had settled there to seduce her or to tempt her. To make her lose faith. God, however, had been merciful. He had made her understand why she would remain untouched by the tragedy of losing her children, since Christ himself, on being crucified, had lost all of humanity.

"We don't have much time left, Venâncio." She paused. "Take care of Tobias. But what's the use of my asking that! You are old and will soon follow me. In that case, who will take care of Tobias?"

"We needn't worry, Eulália. Life will take care of Tobias. Life is an enemy that devotes itself entirely to looking after our interests. If that were not so, what business would life have among us?"

Venâncio adopted a light tone. Seeking Odete's complicity in so doing. She, however, refused to share secrets of any sort with him. Hovering about Eulália, safeguarding her reserve. So that Eulália's habits would be respected to the letter, despite her decision to abandon them. Though for the first time she doubted Eulália's word. She could not believe that her mistress would die before her. Her life made sense only from the moment each morning when she headed for Eulália's room, where she remained until night fell.

In the last few years, Odete had taken to accompanying her to church. Confusing in her prayers the beings of voodoo rites and Catholic saints. A religious alliance that did her good. She sensed that in the past she had trod a ground ruled by gods completely opposed to those she was now cultivating. As though she had suffered, in some way, a sort of profanation that had resulted in her forgetting religious rituals, passionate language, certain physical practices. Hence her feeling that her real existence had begun far from Rio de Janeiro. In a land with an unknown name. To which she owed her race and the look of nostalgia in her eyes.

Eulália never forced religious precepts upon her. This thanks to the teachings of Dom Miguel, an ardent defender of Priscillian, who in the fourth century had passed his virulent heretical calling on to Galicia. She learned, then, that man sought God even by way of departures from dogma. Since he necessarily had the freedom to fashion a god in accordance with the love that he inspired in him. It not mattering, then, that this religious scheme lacked solid contours, or was opposed to statuary forms and canonical words.

"You're right, Venâncio. I mustn't worry about my children now. Merely occupy myself with the simple preparations for my death," Eulália laughed happily. Her eyes urging Venâncio to join in her laughter.

He had never learned to laugh. Instead he looked upon her with eyes filled with compassion. Certain that in two or three days only Madruga and he would still be left to tell the last story concerning the three of them. He thought sadly, however, of the vocation of storytelling, ever enveloping itself in a thousand veils. Inflammable fabric in truth, and their souls surrounded in that case by fire.

However, on that far-distant February morning, Eulália had had more courage than he, returning home all by herself. Despite her helplessness, she was demanding of him an act of justice. The return of her son.

There was not a single breath of a breeze at that hour. Taking her fan out of her handbag, Eulália discreetly fanned herself. Venâncio tried to raise a slight draft of cool air from the backyard. Both felt constrained. Perhaps because Eulália knew, after giving vent to feelings spewing forth in a torrent, that the reasons for her visit had been exhausted. She had nothing further to add. The small craters between them would have to be filled in by Venâncio's sensibility.

Eulália made as if to leave. He offered to accompany her to Leblon. She said no. Life was painful to her in those days.

"Once through this door, I shall go on alone."

Venâncio obeyed. He stood in the entrance, his eyes following her till he lost sight of her as she rounded the corner. She was walking slowly, slightly stooped over. Her gaze wandering distractedly over the façades of the neighboring houses.

In less than an hour, Tobias arrived, whistling gaily. With a certain ferocity he began to tear up papers, removed from a number of file folders. He took a certain pleasure in this task. Venâncio cleared his throat, but Tobias paid no attention to him. He shuffled over to his godson, his house slippers flapping. He took him firmly by the shoulders.

"I dreamed that you'd gone home. When I woke up, I was certain that this was a sign that no later than tomorrow you'll be embracing Eulália and Madruga. I'll help you pack your bag if you like," he said hurriedly to hide his distress.

Tobias let go of the papers, as though shocked beyond belief. "Whatever are you saying, godfather?"

"It's very simple. Tomorrow, and not a day later, you're going back home. The party's over. And I'll stay right here, sweeping out the front room, the remains of these months of living together."

Refusing to discuss the matter, he went off to the bedroom. Stretching out on the bed, he pretended to be reading. Tobias came tagging after him.

"Very well, if you don't want me around anymore, I'll go to a rooming house. But I'm not going back to my house."

"Did you hear what you just said? My house. Precisely. That's the only house you have, the only family. Madruga is your only family and I don't want to steal you from him any longer. It's all over, Tobias. Go back home, even if it's with a scowl on your face."

"I don't have to answer to my father."

"Well then, don't say a word. Keep your mouths shut, both of you, at table. It won't make any difference. But get your ass out of here and be quick about it. Your body was something they fabricated, not me. I can't keep it here any longer."

"I don't feel as though Madruga is my father. I'm not going home," Tobias shouted, sitting on the edge of the bed, waiting for help.

"Not even if I ask you to? Pretend I'm a condemned man and that this is my last request. Will you say yes?"

Tobias looked at his godfather. He seemed to be wasting away before his eyes. Tobias felt incapable of turning a deaf ear to his appeal. The following day, they knocked on Madruga's door. Madruga invited them in without effusion. He was hoping to disarm them by this attitude. Venâncio came on in, asking Eulália to leave them by themselves. And take Tobias with her.

Madruga was surprised at Venâncio's authority, giving orders in his house. He said nothing, however. Once they were alone, he manifested his displeasure.

"We have a great deal to talk about, Venâncio. And if need be, we'll stay here all day."

"I have no explanations I need give you, and no apologies to offer. I didn't bring Tobias back in order to enlighten you. If you accept us on those terms, well and good. If not, I think you'll lose Tobias forever. And my friendship as well."

"Is that a threat? Are you trying to gag me? Can't I even speak in my own house?" Madruga said angrily, not weighing his words.

"I'm not responsible for your acts of madness and Tobias's. The only thing I did was to make him welcome in my house. And I'll do the same whenever he needs to be taken in. Tobias is my godson."

"He's much more than that. You love him as though he were your own son," Madruga said resentfully.

"I won't allow you to pin a label on my feelings, Madruga. I'm the only one who can say what I'm feeling. From the day we left Vigo, so many long years ago now, you've done nothing but try to explain what I feel. But I don't want to fight with you. Today is a special day. I'm returning Tobias to you, and at the same time I'm asking you to give me back the right you think you have over me," Venâncio declared categorically.

Madruga felt he'd lost a battle. For the first time Venâncio was allowing his anger to show. He was courageously repudiating a friendship of many years' standing, all on account of an obscure feeling, hovering threateningly over the two of them. He scratched his head to free himself of these instants. Venâncio could not fail him. He rang the little bell, asked the servant to bring a Marqués de Riscal up from the cellar. He wanted to win Venâncio back with good red wine.

He poured the wine for him and stood there for a moment studying the transparency of the liquid before handing him the glass.

"It's always the proper time to drink a fine wine. Even enemies celebrate certain occasions," Madruga said ironically. "Happily, we're not enemies."

Venâncio tasted the wine, accepted the offer of a chair alongside him. He had not slept that night, his eyes glued to the ceiling. From time to time studying Tobias, lost in a deep sleep, almost within reach of his hand. It was his godson's last night in his house. Soon he would be packing his bag, taking with him pajamas, slippers, toothbrush, objects of inestimable value. He had let him go for good, for Eulália's sake alone. A sacrifice that wounded him deeply.

He watched Madruga as he drank his wine. A man at once hostile and affable, capable of giving expression, with complete spontaneity, to contradictory feelings. But what was it that bound them together so painfully? Would death alone be responsible for separating them? Or did there lie before them the gradual fading of an affection that had attained its full perfection when they were young, declining now without there existing in the world any experience capable of renewing the ardor of their friendship, of bringing them the same happiness that had bathed their faces as they strolled together along what in those days had been known as the Avenida Central?

Venâncio suddenly interrupted Madruga as he was drinking his wine. "The time hasn't yet come to seduce me." Whereupon he opened his wallet and handed him a piece of paper.

"What have we here? Another surprise in store for us?" Madruga smiled, not knowing what to expect. On seeing the check, he made a move to tear it in two. Venâncio kept him from doing so.

"If you destroy this check, you'll be tearing our friendship in two. I'll never set foot in this house again."

"But I'm the one who supports my son," Madruga said, flying into a rage.

"In your house, that may well be. In mine, it's a different matter. I'm the one who pays the expenses. Even though we live a modest life there. And the one reason I didn't return the sums paid me every month was that it seemed to me to be grossly impolite and pointless. Given the situation, it would only stir up more trouble. I thought it better simply to put the money aside, knowing I'd return it along with Tobias. What's more, Tobias never knew anything about those checks. I thought he ought to be spared that knowledge. But if you think I acted wrongly, you can tell him the truth."

Madruga probed his friend's heart. Up until then, Venâncio had always coddled him when he lost his temper. But now it was the other way around. Both bore the traces of a rough and ready friendship. What had happened to those moments of tenderness? Perhaps Venâncio knew, better than he himself did, how to provide him with the elements they were both missing. He gave up the fight. He pocketed the check and raised the glass of wine. He thought of a profanity, but didn't have the courage to offer it as a toast.

"I think we deserve this stout red that crossed the Atlantic the way we did. Though many years after," he said, relaxing.

Odete eyed Venâncio insistently. Surely hinting that he should leave. His presence was tiring Eulália. Venâncio had long suspected that Odete was jealous of him. He had always pretended, however, not to notice the forcefulness with which she defended the object of her esteem. Being quite capable of putting arsenic in her enemy's coffee, so as to protect her own feelings, as well as to defend herself from those of the persons who were the object of her hostility.

Venâncio was about to leave Eulália's bedside when she begged him, in a faint voice, to stay a minute more. This might well be the last time they would ever see each other. He went back to his chair, feeling as though he were about to faint. He had a clear presentiment that he was losing her forever. Without having spoken essential words to her. During all those years he had chosen silence as his way of communicating with Eulália. And she, delicate, diaphanous, had respected his decision, thinking that silence to be the wiser course.

Venâncio looked at her lying there in the bed, and was close to tears. The thought came to him that Eulália was not beautiful. She had never been beautiful. But hers was the most sensitive countenance ever to have been composed on the face of the earth. A Galician face? No, it was not a Galician one. Nor was it a Brazilian one. Where, then, had it come from? Merely a face, made up of delicate lines that had become accentuated with age, as the frail Eulália kept a wary eye on veins about to burst, giving her skin a blue-violet tinge.

Venâncio could contain himself no longer. On his feet now, he bent over the woman, quickly kissing her hand. As he straightened up, he had the impression that Eulália, her heart touched, was applauding this gesture awaited for so many years. But who could assure him that this was so?

He slowly drew himself upright. His knee joints ached and his emotion seemed to have made his legs stiffer still.

"I'll be in the living room, Eulália. We'll be seeing each other soon," he whispered, not wanting to attract her attention.

Eulália asked him to lean down. Venâncio obeyed. The woman's voice rang out firmly, without a trace of a tremor.

"I wanted you to know how much I appreciated the times you went to church with me."

Sometimes, just as a joke, Grandfather accused Venâncio of being a gypsy. Perhaps on account of his swarthy skin, his black hair, and his skinniness, which reminded one, especially in his old age, of a rush bending in the wind.

"You might have been born in Andalusia, even though you don't have an accent. If not in Seville, in Córdoba," Madruga said, insisting on associating him with a people whose nomadism had laid the notion of a fatherland to rest.

Venâncio was not offended. Indeed, he even perked up a bit. Pleased to be reminded of a people who, thanks to their instinct for freedom, refused to live for very long under the same roof and on the same plot of ground. Having so decided, they gradually forgot the names of the countries visited, the villages and the families they came across along the way.

Venâncio never confirmed Madruga's suspicions, however. And so they would sit for hours, around the table or in their armchairs, not saying a word. With dark looks in their eyes, absorbed in mutual accusations. Without access to each other's feelings, which had been changing and taking on new form in recent decades. Bound to each other with stout cords, they shared the expectation that they would be spared tragedy as long as they remained together.

Venâncio's repressed nature made it difficult for him to express his feelings. Madruga, from the beginning, had found in far-flung gestures the means to free himself. In the past, Venâncio's mere presence at his side gave him the illusion that, somewhere quite close by, a ship was awaiting them, ready to sail, borne on favorable winds. Toward lands never before visited, of which they had long dreamed. Where, amid treasures and nature in the raw, they would encounter creatures capable of bearing them up and away into delirium, and off on flights of fancy.

With Venâncio, Madruga would be caught up in the dream for a few moments. Since, possibly, Venâncio was the only man to have arrived in Brazil who had gone against the rules that made it mandatory to accumulate goods and resentments. To the point that he had shed, in the name of his principles, the scales of his body, sentimental pleasures, and the symbolic emeralds of legend.

Almost the moment the English ship set out from the estuary of Pontevedra, Madruga had insisted on knowing where Venâncio had come from. Where, that is to say, his new traveling companion had been born. Confronted, however, with Venâncio's silence, and sensing that they were not going to separate all that soon, Madruga began to talk of Ceferino, Xan, and Urcesina.

He had abandoned his family without even waving good-bye. In the certainty that there existed between them an enduring tacit accord capable of forgiving such acts of insubordination. Thanks to which he had found himself with a free soul and the urge to sharpen his fingernails on stone, his aim being the conquest of America. America would not escape his grasp.

Venâncio felt immediately attracted by this chubby, vivacious lad, whose words came tumbling out in a rush, giving him no chance to speak. On deck still, as darkness fell, Madruga again plied him with questions. He needed details with which to construct the biography of his new friend. Venâncio would tell him only his name and surname.

"You can at least tell me where you come from."

Venâncio's Galician was a recent acquisition. Yet he didn't sound like a native Castilian either. Why had he come to Vigo to take ship, if Spain had other gateways to America?

"I had to choose between Vigo, Seville, and Cadiz. What difference does it make?" Venâncio said curtly.

"Don't get the idea that I'm going to let you off that easily. Before this voyage is ended, I'll know where you were born."

Madruga landed in Rio de Janeiro without having found out. Even though both were awakened by their successive bouts of vomiting during the passage, Madruga had not wrung a confession from him on those days. Venâncio resisted as though in possession of an impenetrable secret whose revelation would have endangered his life.

But the sadness in Venâncio's face, from the moment he awoke in the morning, allowed Madruga to see that the youngster's decision to abandon Spain was connected with a great bitterness. He suddenly feared that his new friend might fail in America.

When the boat docked in Rio de Janeiro, Madruga took him by the arm, just in front of the stairway via which they were about to disembark.

"Watch your step, Venâncio. When you step off onto the ground, use your right foot, to bring you luck."

Madruga concentrated on descending the stairs. His mind focused on not getting off on the wrong foot. He went first, and now there was just one step left. His heart beat faster. He stopped for a second, just long enough to raise his right leg and lean it firmly on the ground. Relieved, he turned his attention to Venâncio, who was coming along behind him.

"Don't forget what I told you to do," he said to him again.

Having reached the last step, Venâncio stared at him defiantly. And patently ignoring his advice, stepped squarely out onto Brazilian soil with his left foot. Thus opting, before Madruga's eyes, for a grim and gritty America.

"Why did you do that, Venâncio?" Madruga shouted fearfully, immediately pushed ahead by those following after, as impatient as he to be free of the yoke of the voyage.

Amid the confusion of reclaiming luggage, Venâncio muttered: "It's not important. If I don't like it here, I'll go to the interior or to the Amazon jungle."

Madruga pretended not to have heard him. He did not intend to begin life in America by eating humble pie. Venâncio had a right to proclaim himself a loser before the fact. As for himself, he had reserves in his heart. Wherever he went, Xan's words came along with him.

He promised not to ask Venâncio any more questions. It wasn't really a matter of fundamental importance to find out what miserable village he had come from. What was certain was that he had been born in a poor house, the parents dividing the children up among the few rooms in the house. Till the day they found themselves obliged to empty the table of two or three children who were a drain on the family pocketbook. So that the soup at the bottom of the pot would be more nourishing for those still left. And Venâncio was the first to be driven from home and fireside. The father chose him for unfathomable reasons. Because they could no longer bear the sad, penetrating look in his eyes? Or was it owing to the mere fact that he was the most intelligent person in the entire village, and thus capable of working his way free of the bonds of poverty?

Madruga noted his acute intelligence from the very first moment. Alert to everything happening round about him, Venâncio was also deeply attached to books and newspapers, ever eager for knowledge. Giving proof of a memory that marshaled facts with a great wealth of detail, of which Madruga became the beneficiary.

"I'll be your memory, Madruga. If you forget something, you have only to consult me," Venâncio said, in an uncommonly gleeful tone of voice.

The first years in America went by quickly. Both apparently forgetting that Spain had banished them, being unable to provide them with food unless it sacrificed other hungry mouths. Madruga did not resent being an immigrant. Everything served to spur him on. Even the letters he received, plaintive ones in the beginning. His mother complaining of the way they'd been abandoned. But at the first signs of Madruga's prosperity, Urcesina's letters took on a livelier note. Even reaching the point of joyous excitement, seconded by her husband: ". . . and when you come back someday, son, Ceferino and I will welcome you as befits a winner."

Unlike Urcesina, Xan wrote to make it clear to him that this was the first and last letter of his that he would be receiving. He confessed, clearly and unequivocally, that he had spent his life in the exclusive and intimate company of legends and stories that readily evaporated. Hence he now found himself in total disagreement with these words set down on paper. Words that, by their arrogant and static nature, collided head on with words that were merely spoken. And wasn't speaking the only thing he knew how to do? And wasn't it through this unique resource that he had transmitted to his grandson a rich and fertile Galicia, with which to confront America and enrich the country called Brazil?

That letter, in a visible tone of farewell, sent Madruga into despair. He was unwilling to allow his grandfather to take his leave of him without telling him other stories, in writing. Even though they risked taking on, in letters, an interpretation contrary to Xan's will. For wasn't it a known fact that books, though coinciding now and again with reality, clashed with it as a general rule?

He insisted his grandfather write to him, if only five lines. To just those few lines, he would know how to add flour, water, and eggs. Madruga exhausting himself trying to make Xan understand that, even after his death, he would always keep his memory alive.

For page after countless page, Madruga buttered up his grandfather and awaited his reply. A few weeks later, Ceferino thanked Madruga, in Xan's name, for his interest. But, as Xan had promised, the correspondence between them was definitely ended. The grandfather not meaning thereby to keep Madruga from sending news of himself. He would be very happy to have word of his grandson. Whom he had loved more than all the others and who, nonetheless, had bowed down before America, without so much as consulting him.

"And who wrote to Venâncio at the time, grandfather?" I asked Madruga.

Grandfather hesitated for a few moments. "I can speak only of my own letters. They were affectionate and friendly. Only Grandfather Xan, true to his word, did not write me again. I heard from him through Father and Mother. And also through the memory, ever fresh, that I kept of him. Could Grandfather have acted as he did so as to draw me to his rocking chair and make me listen to stories he purposely never ended?" Madruga commented, amid sighs and a show of emotion.

"And Venâncio's letters?" I persisted.

The letters for Venâncio, for unknown reasons, came to him in the months of May and December. Never before or after those months. And during each period he received just four letters. A clear hint that his family consisted of four members who could read and write. Possibly two elderly ones, since in a few years' time they fell silent. The letters being reduced to just two. This reduction coincided, incidentally, with strong bitterness on Venâncio's part.

Madruga was concerned at the time about Venâncio's depression. And on the pretext of saving him from a dramatic bout of melancholy, Madruga set out to chase down the mailman in an attempt to discover where the letters had come from and the names of the senders. But the mailman, sensing his curiosity, smiled discreetly and would never hand Venâncio's letters over to him. Madruga had to be content, then, to follow their scent from a distance, like a bird dog.

"What's the matter, Venâncio?" he kept asking insistently. "Has something serious happened in your village? Has somebody died? Do you need money? You can count on me to help you."

Though grateful, Venâncio said nothing. The fact was that from the very first, he had always trembled with emotion at the sight of the May and December letters. But on seeing that he was being watched by Madruga, he immediately withdrew into himself. And giving immediate proof that the letters meant little to him, he made no move to open them and did not even ask permission to go to his room.

With slow gestures, Venâncio tucked them into his trousers pocket, and for the rest of the day he not only disappeared from Madruga's sight but came up to their room at a late hour. Suggesting to Madruga that they go to supper late, since he wouldn't be sleepy before midnight.

Madruga looked at him mistrustfully. He saw how a single letter could swallow up a person's heart, make him weep, put an end to his most precious dreams. And he began to believe, as far as Venâncio's specific case was concerned, that he was a victim of pride and for that reason alone he would open and read the letter in the coming week.

Whenever he got the chance, González would come out with some sarcastic remark about Venâncio's emotional problems. Proving himself insensitive to his fate, forever waiting for the May and December letters with his heart in his mouth. Had it been up to González, he would have fired him long before. He considered him to be not only incompetent, but an ingrate as well. He had never said one word of thanks to him for having assured him of a room and employment from the moment he arrived in America.

Now and again, González would turn to Madruga, occupied with figures and plans, asking his attention for a minute. The matter to be dealt with was of extreme importance.

Madruga answered curtly. "If it's to talk about Venâncio, you're wasting your time. I'm very busy, making money for the two of us."

The young man's harsh, gruff voice immediately put an end to the conversation. And with a gesture he banished him from the office. Far from being irritated by this impoliteness, González was fascinated by Madruga's boldness, his constant willingness to lock horns with him. To all appearances, González meekly backed down. But at home, alone with his wife, they both thanked God for the young Galician's talent.

"Woe unto us had it not been for that youngster. It was the Lord who sent us that golden head," Pilar was fond of saying.

"Now all we have to do is keep him in the firm," González would answer.

Not hiding his desire to see that business union consolidated through the marriage of Madruga and his youngest daughter. But not wanting to reveal to Madruga his growing importance in negotiating deals for the firm, he tried to make it clear to him exactly how great his debt to him was for keeping Venâncio in his employment. An office clerk looked upon as an adversary, who would gladly see him go bankrupt rather than prosper. González knew of his deliberate time-wasting rambles through the Passeio Público, his daily visits to the Biblioteca Nacional during work hours.

Madruga finally gave him five minutes. If González hadn't finished speaking when this time limit was up, Madruga would pitilessly cut him off, launching into a defense of his friend. In his opinion, an excellent employee who, despite his peculiar habits, was suited to the job.

"What's more, you pay him a mere pittance. So why are you complaining?"

And without pulling his punches, Madruga criticized his behavior. González proving constitutionally incapable of identifying unique beings, and treating them as they deserved. This insensibility confirming that he was not cut out to have a fortune. It was indispensable, finally, to have a trick or two up one's sleeve if one was out to get people's money.

Madruga paused, giving him time to reflect. Immediately thereafter, he threatened, in a veiled way, to exclude him from his future projects if he were disrespectful of Venâncio. González must not forget that, left entirely on his own, he would not be in any position to keep up with the process of development that Brazil was going through. He had only to look around and note the expansion of the city, the new buildings that were springing up like mushrooms. The immense avenues slicing through entire districts. Poverty being banished to areas far from the center, so that nothing would spoil the urban landscape. Starting with the Avenida Rio Branco, already well on its way to becoming a stronghold of commerce and banking.

"This country is full of money, Seu González. All a person has to do is to dig into the ground or grab it out of the hands where the dough is right now. We need to create conditions that will make the money come out of its hiding place," Madruga said enthusiastically.

With the prospects outlined by Madruga before him, González began to dream of Rio de Janeiro's growing at the same rate as New York. But fearing that he'd offended Madruga, González hastily revised his opinion about Venâncio. Ending his speech with the offer of a partnership for Venâncio in the business. Perceiving, however, that he'd gone too far, he backpedaled.

"I'm referring, naturally, to a limited share. Just to perk up his morale. Who knows? He might be useful to us in the future."

González laughed to himself. He felt like an expert all of a sudden, with a talent for getting Madruga involved, so that the idea of cutting him out of his next business ventures would never enter his young partner's head.

"We'll be putting three heads together to think, Madruga. Yes, three good heads."

Madruga gave him a pitying look. He could foresee that he was going to have him on his back for a few years still. At this thought, an odd feeling of resignation came over him. Not to the point, however, of frightening him. He tried his best to master his fierce desire to call him a stupid, ignorant ass.

González had arrived in America with a heart empty of memories. As though he did not have a single story behind him. He seemed to be devoid of those memories that the most modest villages distilled over the years like honey. Without the culture that was the reward of even the rudest peasant, all of them brought up beneath the mantle of a civilization rent with historic crises and thorny heterodoxies. At their mercy, they had nonetheless inherited legends and experienced in the flesh and in the spirit the successive foreign invasions of which they were victims. Each general, each despot, each new tribe contributing, thus, to their growth. And to the eventual refinement of their palate, the enjoyment of wine, to the appreciation of which they devoted themselves, beginning with the vinestock itself. Their basic dealings with the earth evolved in the course of this gradual transition. From which there resulted an apprenticeship that forced the countryside to furnish them with the choicest viands. Which went directly from the animal pens and the tilled fields to the noble tables of all Europe.

What should destiny, however, have put in the path of Madruga, with his avid and impatient temperament, but a coarse, dull-witted Galician, who sat down and counted coins with the intention of burying them in a chest. Lacking the prodigal sense of multiplication, the heady taste for risky ventures. This close association with González representing for Madruga a sort of punishment, from which he felt obliged to free himself at the earliest possible moment.

González, for his part, did not understand the friendship between Madruga and Venâncio. Whereas Venâncio seemed apathetic, indifferent to his fate, Madruga never gave evidence of the slightest diffidence when it came to confronting bank managers or other experienced negotiators. Madruga entered restaurants with the enviable nonchalance of a steady customer. Head held high, clutching his cigar, he immediately went for a dish he'd never had before. Ever eager to broaden his culture.

When González hinted at his puzzlement at the alliance established between the two young men, Madruga blustered:

"If it weren't for Venâncio, I'd make terrible business deals. He's my daily ration of dreams. The dreams I don't have time to dream anymore. Venâncio is now in charge of dreaming in my name."

On inviting Madruga to dine at his house González considered himself obliged to extend the invitation to Venâncio. But to his surprise he refused, offering his usual excuse. He had lost the habit of socializing with a family such as González's. Though flattered, González hastened to free him of the obligation, before he changed his mind.

Once alone with Venâncio, Madruga insisted that he accept the invitation. He wanted his friend to be there, the better to get through an evening that would be boring, despite the placid beauty of Gonzalez's daughter, who never set foot outside the living room.

Venâncio, however, would not agree to appear at the dinner. Pleading pressing tasks, reading that he was behind on.

Madruga was annoyed at his friend's aloofness. "I know you want to be by yourself in the room so as to think about your family. It's true, isn't it, that you have a family? One you've always kept hidden from me?"

Venâncio flushed. And began to pace about the office, displaying an uncommon diligence. He hated Madruga at that moment. An intruder and a traitor, who did not hesitate to throw ashes and refuse in his face when such an act suited his purpose. Nothing made Venâncio more indignant than having his feelings brought to light, thus making them public. Or being made the object of innuendos such as that. At the same time, he reproached himself for not being more careful. The truth was that he had not seen Madruga right there, close by, as he reached his hand out to the mailman and took the letter from the May harvest. Which was what had occasioned that sly remark.

"It's not what you think," Venâncio said evasively, a self-conscious look on his face.

Madruga was eager to intercept at least one letter. To get to the mailman first and be handed Venâncio's correspondence. Thereby having time to examine the letter, the postmark, to take careful note of the name and address of the sender. Even though he didn't gain access to the contents. He'd be satisfied just to touch it, to breathe in his friend's origin by way of it. Not to speak of the pleasure of being able to hand the letters of those months over personally to Venâncio.

He could not understand how Venâncio controlled his anxiety in the long months of silence, when Spain was closed to him. As though life, intending to punish him, kept him from receiving news of those mysterious beings.

In those months Venâncio gave no apparent signs of suffering. His routine remained unchanged. And Madruga never saw him hurry out to meet the mailman or look at him with envy because of the letters that came from Sobreira. Between Venâncio and his people a strange covenant had been concluded, with which he was in complete accord. One whereby his affective world hung suspended in the intervening seasons. And feelings, having lost their impetus and acceleration, could not be a cause of suffering for the one who was in Brazil or those who remained behind in Spain.

An old man now, Venâncio's white hair accentuated his swarthy complexion. And his nose, slightly hooked, made him resemble a keen-eyed eagle. He could easily pass for a Semite. Especially when he outdid himself in genteel gestures toward Eulália. More and more at peace with himself, he did not react to Grandfather's frequent attempts to bait him by calling him a gypsy.

Till Venâncio, at table, suddenly showed a lively interest in that errant people. The only one in modern times to move all about Europe with uncommon skill and ingenuity. And a people who, as a result of this lifestyle, merged with other peoples. Thereby contributing to the reinforcement in the popular soul of the seeds of imagination.

"What was the gypsies' real contribution to Spain? Of what use were they to us?" Madruga challenged Venâncio as they were eating.

Eulália seemed surprised by her husband's aggressiveness. Throwing a political subject onto the table for discussion, for no reason. She laid her fork down on her plate and asked permission to speak. We all heard the firmness in her voice as she advised the two men to drop the subject of gypsies, once and for all. Not only were they living in the south of Spain now; all of Andalusia was strongly impregnated with their pleasing presence. They smelled of red carnations and bitter oranges.

And with a certain languidness, perhaps motivated by sudden fatigue, Eulália proposed that they go back to Galicia, an inexhaustible subject after all, and moreover one common to the three of them. Even Venâncio spoke of that part of the country as his.

"Perhaps Venâncio was born in Galicia and has been pulling the wool over our eyes all these years," she said with a smile. Understanding why Venâncio would have preferred us to imagine him as a wanderer, traveling all over Spain from a most tender age. Thus accounting for his acquiring an accent that immediately set him apart from all the linguistic nationalities of that country.

"Nobody can tell what part of Spain Venâncio was born in. Doesn't that make him the one Spaniard who has freed himself of the tyranny of so many different languages?" Eulália weighed the question, her head swaying from side to side.

Eulália was pleased to deliver this vocal solo at a table where everyone present stubbornly fought to get a word in. Suddenly something made her uneasy, as though she had alighted on stony ground, with enemies on the lookout.

"Are you all right, Eulália?" Venâncio looked closely at the woman as his eyes assured her that she needn't worry about him. On that pleasant Sunday, nothing could offend him. Immediately thereafter, Venâncio went back to chewing down his food, visibly bored. Even leaving his fork suspended in the air for a few brief moments before allowing it to fall back down. By this swift gesture seemingly collecting bits of apparently scattered information.

Madruga stiffened on seeing the intent look on Venâncio's face. He sensed that something of grave concern to him was about to take place. Was he going, perhaps, to answer the question put to him?

"And what could be expected of a people that has been ruthlessly sacrificed throughout its history? And that bore on their foreheads the stigma of persecution and defeat? A people that suffered more than the Jews. Since they didn't even earn humanity's admiration. Tell me, Madruga, to what other people was the Pragmatic Sanction, issued by King Carlos III, applied? A cruel and relentless decree, whose specific aim was to put a legal end to the gypsies in Spain."

Venâncio had unhurriedly brought his speech to an end. Whereupon, picking up his knife and fork again, he gave signs of a sudden appetite.

I looked at Grandfather. Madruga could not sit still in his chair. Food no longer interested him. Everything paled in Venâncio's presence. He felt him invade the terrain he had coveted since the day they arrived in Brazil. How often he had suspected Venâncio's gypsy origin, but only now had the first proof been forthcoming. At least he took the vehemence with which Venâncio leaped to the defense of that people to be a strong indication. Giving evidence of up-to-date knowledge on the subject. Though none of this was cause for surprise in the case of Venâncio, a man of impressive culture for an autodidact.

Venâncio appreciated the fresh grouper, cooked only moments before in salted water with a few cloves of garlic, a dish of which he was especially fond. All he did was add a slight trickle of oil. Which brought a tender smile to Eulália's lips. Madruga was now eating impatiently, wanting explanations. Venâncio went on talking, with no thought of showing off. Aiming his remarks at the Pragmatic Sanction already mentioned, whose secret intent had been to exterminate a fervent and colorful people. And as Venâncio expanded on the subject, Madruga eyed him warily.

At the end of the afternoon, after Venâncio had taken his leave, I accompanied Madruga to his study. Sitting in the leather armchair, he suddenly revealed his hurt, the offense that, as a Spaniard, he considered himself to have been a victim of, from the moment that he had learned of such a decree.

"Can it be possible that there existed a state with a power of imagination so great as to anticipate the extermination of a race, without even resorting to public executions or staining its hands with the blood of the victims? Do I belong, then, to a country that conceived this diabolical plan, merely to annihilate and revile this people? Is this true, Breta? Or is it an invention of Venâncio's, to leave me utterly confounded?"

He was scarcely moved by compassion. Grandfather's face took on a frankly hostile look as he demanded the whole truth about Venâncio. He could no longer bear not knowing his friend's secret. He had at all costs to master the essence of that decree in order to understand how much it had affected Venâncio's upbringing. As though through the interstices of this law Venâncio might begin to tell him stories about his persecuted and scattered clan. And if he wished to be faithful in the telling, he should be prepared to pass on to him information as to the forms of life adopted by his family. Details such as the type of tent they used for shelter. Almost always set up near the river. Where, at night, there rang out the sound of furious guitars and profane songs, which demanded of the singers a pitiless vocal range. Because the words mattered less than the melody. And this in turn because they divided the words into syllables, each syllable forming an endless musical phrase. So that the sound would never die away. Since its nature forced them to prolong the high keening note until it became unbearable. Though at the risk of rupturing their hoarse, tortured vocal cords. The only way found by them to ensure the deep sadness and despair of their laments.

Immediately thereafter, Venâncio would begin to speak to him of his maternal grandparents. Driven from their tent during the night, as they slept, by a flood that brought to their doorstep the muddy waters of a tributary of the Guadalquivir. Without one living soul of the neighboring village coming to their aid, despite their cries. After so many years, that accursed decree still kept the hearts of those inhabitants bound fast.

Hurriedly, the grandparents and the other members of the tribe gathered their few belongings together and put them in the cart. Then taking to the road, astride faithful donkeys. Doubtless related to Pegasus, that famous animal of Salvador's. And because they heard the loud call of a mysterious voice, they headed toward Galicia. From there they were driven back across the borders. Which gave them time, nonetheless, to appreciate the landscape. This quick visit affording them the opportunity to make further sallies, never a success. But thanks to which they learned the secrets of the region and how to get the better of the vigilantes. As they also learned the language through the insults heaped upon them by everyone, the moment they turned up. Insults that proved to be very useful, whenever they had to beg for bread or read fortunes. An engrossing task, since the lines in the peasants' hands were smudged from field work.

Madruga paused. He tasted his cognac absentmindedly. He seemed feverish, lost in conjectures. My attempt to break in on his thought proving fruitless. Then he went on with the story, as though Xan had taken his place, were speaking for him. Xan in person, inventing the travels of Venâncio's family, which, after all the effort put forth over so many years, saw itself rewarded. For at last it reached the estuary of Pontevedra, the most beautiful of them all. And once they were there, they decided to travel along it, from one end to the other, without anyone, happily, barring the advance of that bizarre troupe. Till at last they chose the old port of Bayonne as a resting place. Attracted, doubtless, by the haughty grandeur that some of those houses, within sight, still possessed, so in accord with the gypsies' own hauteur. In the eyes of Carlos III an intolerable arrogance.

Those gypsies did not know, however, that countless vessels, men-of-war, sailing ships had set out for America from Bayonne. Impelled by gold and, also, by the spirit of adventure. For what Christian, Levantine, Asiatic did not, in those days, find himself tempted to found a city, to come upon islands, isthmuses, capes on this new continent? On which no one before them had ever set eyes?

Those men left Bayonne in sudden dread. Despite their trust in the viability of a culture which, among other things, included arms, seeds, and the compass. As the boats drew away from the shore, Bayonne seemed even more beautiful to them. Perhaps because of the feeling of melancholy that that parting inspired in them. And was it not to that same delightful port of Bayonne that the first news of the discovery of America arrived?

In fact, after celebrating the great feat among themselves, the Spaniards were eager to bring the glad tidings to Isabella and Ferdinand. Both should be informed immediately of the existence of the earthly paradise, now the property of Their Majesties. And so they set out to reach Spain as quickly as possible.

Destiny decreed, however, that even though the authorities maintained superb Arabian horses and horsemen, in continuous relays, in the port of Seville, awaiting the first boat returning from the excursion to the new lands, whereupon the news of this discovery would be brought to the ears of the Catholic Sovereigns, lo and behold, the other boat, of lesser tonnage, charged with the same mission, anchored much earlier in Bayonne, favored perhaps by the winds and the captain's skill. And so, the news that this America in fact existed spread throughout Spain, like an epidemic, from Galicia.

An achievement so memorable that it soon transformed Bayonne into a proud and elegant town. A status that it enjoyed up until the reign of Philip II. When the King, a sovereign of ashen and cyclothymic soul, judged it prudent to disregard the advantages for his kingdom of that trade port, known to be a nest of intrigues and autonomist rebellions.

Madruga paused at suitable moments all through his recital of the facts. Thus proving himself an instinctively careful storyteller. So much so that he merely hinted at details that might serve to persuade his hearer. He even took the trouble to sow doubts, for the express purpose of dispelling them later on. Thereby adding substance to conjectures that seemed flimsy in the beginning.

Madruga was now anxious to find out how long Venâncio's family had camped in Bayonne. Had they settled there for good, and Venâncio left from there to take the boat in Vigo, or had they been driven out of that port?

And also, what grand gestures could be expected of a port whose status the King had lowered? An embittered people lived there, which had never reconciled itself to the loss of its wealth of bygone days. When the streets and the taverns were invaded by a human whirlwind. Hordes of adventurers came pouring in from everywhere. Men without a name and without a past, whose one merit was to dream of America, with its gold, its Indian aphrodisiacs, and the fountain of youth.

Madruga's excitement moved me at times. With a gesture, however, I suggested that he calm down. After all, what right did he have to trace before my very eyes a path that Venâncio might never have taken? Above all since he never referred to Bayonne or even mentioned Galicia as a home. And, if this family fabricated by Madruga in fact existed, Venâncio behaved as though he had erased it from his heart. A family that in the past existed only in the months of May and December.

"But if Venâncio were to decide to tell us his story, grandfather, where exactly would it begin?"

No one at the dinner table that day doubted Venâncio's legitimate indignation at the decree. A feeling that was communicated to Madruga and the other guests. All of them sensitive to words that made Madruga see that the pair of them had come from two peoples severely chastened by the caprices of despots. While the gypsies had suffered internal exile, the Galicians had been prey to the kings of Castile. Those august sovereigns who through continuous incursions had cast the Galicians into a cold and forgotten dungeon of history, so that, stuck fast to those walls, they would come to know the tedium of centuries.

Did Venâncio perhaps sense that Madruga's ambition was to be the herald of his memory someday? Being obliged, in order to do so, to appropriate his family antecedents. Whereupon he would confess to Venâncio, with mingled pride and pain: Thus far, I have depended on you to get my story told; now, however, I will tell your story too; and we shall be free of each other only when Breta, in the future, frees us of this mutual responsibility, and begins to speak for us.

Back in the apartment, I looked at objects with the feeling that they did not belong to me. All of them chosen indifferently and brought to this place simply to furnish it. And the answering machine, for its part, gave out messages recorded in tense voices.

I returned the calls. Invariably the caller and I spoke of Brazil. All parties on the alert against collective disasters. No one would confess to having sold his or her soul. Fantasy was our daily bread. The fantasy of dropping out of our own destiny. With the excuse that we preached national redemption in bars, living rooms, beds. And put the finger on public officials in Brazil as torturers. Wasn't it true that they were the ones who set reality in motion for us? And aren't they also the ones who stop up the cracks in the walls of houses in the working-class districts and in the Southern Zone so that the laments of reality don't creep in under our doors, and therefore we needn't bother to think about them?

I tore up letters, invitations, announcements of useless meetings. It's a form of social climbing that doesn't appeal to me. The one thing I'm in a hurry to do is hear Madruga, before he dies. Without Grandfather's roots, which are slowly dissolving, I won't be able to lean my face against Brazil's hairy, sweaty chest. To auscultate the sounds, which are the rasping rattle of the perishable language of love.

I see myself in the mirror. And make no attempt to escape bygone memories or recent ones. I track the scent of certain recollections about my body. I know how tender the eyes and the bodies of others can be, before or after passion. And over an equal period of time, full of boredom and violence.

I don't want a permanent body in my bed. Someone who nails me to it with a hammer, using affection as a pretext. Why not make desire divine without making love sacred? I'm satisfied now with the emotion that has no name and no assurance of continuity. What is more electrifying than the adventure of entering another's body like someone boarding a boat and following the trade winds for a first ocean voyage? A voyage fated to be suddenly interrupted. By a polite farewell. Whereupon a new cycle of desire begins, which oscillates between having and losing. An endless fountainhead, whose basic counsel is to forget one's fellow creature, with exquisite melancholy. Am I perhaps imitating Miguel? Or am I acting out of a lack of faith?

Back in Leblon, Grandfather received me glumly. "Let's go to the study," he said.

I accepted the aged cognac. We very nearly killed the bottle. He waited for my face to turn red; he was an excellent observer. To dispel all doubt, Madruga placed his faith in bodies on fire. He always urged me to turn even difficult moments into a ceremony.

"Let's talk, then, about that damned royal decree," he said.

"It may well be that Venâncio has betrayed himself by speaking up about the Pragmatic Sanction. But there's no way of knowing, grandfather."

Madruga was in a hurry. He didn't have all that many years left to discover the truth. Perhaps the available information was scanty. His suspicions being based only on his friend's swarthy face and his natural tendency to live apart, to care little about material possessions. As though he were still living in a tent.

"On the other hand, whatever became of Venâncio's wanderlust?" Madruga said dubiously. Being at a loss now to explain Venâncio's sedentary life. Rarely leaving Rio de Janeiro, whiling away his days in his house on the outskirts, watching the trains go by from the window.

"Maybe he exhausted his nomad spirit on his first Atlantic voyage. Whereupon he decided to thwart the wanderlust of his race. By holing up in one little corner, fleeing the temptation to move about. Can that be why he's so droopy and dull-eyed? And why he's spent years of his life roaming round Cinelândia? Isn't it true that Venâncio has wasted half his days on this earth in the Biblioteca Nacional? And might that not be the formula he hit upon to travel? Through books?"

Madruga removed a postcard from the album. There they were, two young men walking down the Avenida Rio Branco, around 1923. Beneath their feet, the tiny stones of a Portuguese mosaic sidewalk. Both wearing new suits, straw boaters, and two-toned shoes. Resolute and happy.

"Venâncio and I are the same age. I don't know why, but I have a feeling we'll die in the same year. In the same month. We're going to fight with death to see which one of us will go first," Grandfather said, his voice filled with emotion.

I went over to him, determined to impress upon him the harshness of contemporary life. So he wouldn't forget evil facts.

"The Pragmatic Sanction, grandfather, was the exact equivalent of our Institutional Act Five."

Madruga was alarmed at this reintroduction of a subject that again brought all his fear to the fore. The fear that threatened him with the loss of his granddaughter. To the point that he had scarcely slept at night during those months, without anyone to talk to. Afraid I wouldn't return home. Expecting at any moment the news that I'd been taken prisoner. He wanted desperately to forget this period. But what right did he have to do so, if the others, the dead and the survivors, couldn't forget? And does anyone who has survived merit absolution?

The collective temptation has always been to forget tragedy. When memory, in defense of its dramatic intrigues, turns violent acts into mere starts of fear, whose origin is very nearly indetectable. But is there anyone who has ever once been lodged in a house of horror, of the many scattered about the country, run by various security agencies and even by the armed forces, who has not easily blotted out the memory of events? Even though, as they were about to leave, free once more, their torturers mended their heads, using for this purpose a thread lubricated with blood, shit, hopelessness, and pus.

"Isn't it an exaggeration to compare Institutional Act Five with the Pragmatic Sanction?" Madruga asked.

"Perhaps. In any case, grandfather, historical facts end up being close neighbors. The one leaning on the other. One need only leap over the wall to the other side. And after that, it's not quite clear what the borderline between them is. The written laws seem at first to be mere formal requirements. In the beginning all of them promise to be harmless enough. The pretext for passing them is the defense of the collectivity and the interests of the State. And then when it comes time to apply them, they show their true face. At which point there is no longer any borderline between life and death. And the citizen is thenceforth dependent on just one thing, the arbitrary decision of Power. To which he submits and which he sometimes even applauds, as though the State were giving proof of its mercy."

Deep in thought, the two of us tried to fathom the feelings of President Costa e Silva in the period just before his signing of Institutional Act 5. He had doubtless followed the routine set forth in the official agenda. Since the decree had been drafted and everyone agreed as to what it said, his signature would be a mere formality. One he could no longer get around. But can he have weighed in those hours the consequences of an act that ran a knife through the Brazilian nation? Was his conscience in any way troubled, keeping him from sleeping, making him pant for breath, making his food less appetizing than it had been? As though he suddenly heard the first faint strains of old age?

Costa e Silva signed IA-5 with a firm hand, as the record shows. His hands did not fail him till a year later, at the first signs of the thrombosis that cut short his dictatorial presence in history. And the month chosen for the act that gagged Brazil was December, just before Christmas.

The minister Gama e Silva informed the country, via the national radio and television networks, of the terms of the aforementioned act and also of Complementary Act 38, which decreed the adjournment of Congress. A reading of the provisions in a solemn, slow voice, such as to leave no lingering doubts concerning the powerful designs that lay behind them.

Following this ceremony, Costa e Silva rested for a few moments before going off to bed earlier than usual that night. We may reasonably suppose that he forbade all access to his private apartments. And that, covered with shame, he drew up a last will and testament in which he expressly forbade his name, from that day forward, to be linked to the dictatorship and to that ignominious act. But the contrary may also have been the case: who can tell? As dawn broke, was he aware, amid a certain boredom coupled with a sense of pride, that through that very act he entered History? Even though it meant entering through the gate of suffering and ignominy? Too vain to resist the temptation of being on intimate terms with History, of being one of its favored guests. Caring little about the social costs of his entering the textbooks, in the form of a brief footnote.

"And what about Carlos III? Was he a horse-racing fan, like Costa e

Silva? Or did he prefer hunting parties? What were the passions he cultivated?" Madruga said distractedly.

"The Pragmatic Sanction anticipated Institutional Act Five by very
nearly two centuries. To pinpoint it exactly, it was drafted on September
19, 1783. And as far as Spain was concerned, Carlos III was brought up
from the cradle to reign over it as king. With the enthusiastic approval of
the Court, with which he learned to share certain privileges."

Carlos III had long since been put on his guard against gypsies.
There was great mistrust of them, and grave reservations concerning them.
Beginning with the disquieting fact that no one knew what their roots
were or where they had come from. They had simply crossed the Pyrenees
and gone on into Spain. Leaving disorder in their trail in the villages they
had visited. The moment they arrived, they set up their tents on the riverbank, coming forth to bathe in the nude, without the least shame. To the
scandal of their Christian neighbors, who did not accept that unruly tribe.
Whose close proximity obliged them to take precautionary measures.
Such as barring their doors to them, taking in their livestock, guarding
against nocturnal raids. Above all they began to keep a close watch on
their wives and unmarried virgins, whose virtues were clearly threatened
by that presence.

The Spaniards, moreover, did not tolerate the easy laughter of these
people. Able to laugh for no discernible reason. And to give signs of a
carefree happiness that came over them without so much as a drop of wine
or brandy.

The gypsies went about in bands. And when they came in through
the front gate, one could smell their body odor from the living room. A
smell, incidentally, of rare herbs and a provocative sweat, owing perhaps
to their swarthy complexion. This orgy of odors suggesting to the Spaniards that this race had unruly souls and genitals.

It was said of them that they roamed the world in obedience to a
precious sense of orientation. Which led them to travel indescribable dis-
tances. And though they came from Hungary to Spain out of intolerable
laziness, they had nonetheless not gotten lost.

Time and space, to them, belonged to different categories than those
which were an article of faith with Christians, who adhered to a rigorous
chronological order. Scarcely able to set foot out of their houses so as
not to stray from the cemeteries where, in the future, they would await
eternity.

They were likewise accused of worshiping exotic gods. Which may
well have been true. Since they refused to embrace the habits and culture
of Spain. And they also appeared to scorn writing, which they themselves
did not cultivate. It was even suspected that these gypsies spread from
village to village the notion that Western civilization was dying, overcome
by the feeling that the end was nigh, precisely because it had taken up

writing. Whereas the gypsies eschewed written records; yet they did not lack a rich and dazzling lore. In fact, the only thing that mattered to them was oral storytelling, free and full of improvisations. And judged by Madrid to be inconsistent and subversive, since it left them no means of controlling their thought. The *nihil obstat* of Church and State.

The grounds, then, that would serve to lay this race low were accumulating on the King's table. And they coincided with Carlos III's growing anxieties concerning the future of Spain. A Spain threatened by dissension, intolerance, antagonisms. Excesses, in a word, that the King feared. It was necessary, therefore, to put an end to the discord and the disagreement raging in the popular classes. Though it mattered little to him that such political ferment was rife at Court, since the aristocracy, to which he himself belonged, had been purposely educated for intrigue and affairs of state, and subject to no restriction of any sort.

Confronted with such problems, the King chose to sign the decree that wiped out an entire race. He therefore took up his ostrich-plume pen, with a tip of delicate Sèvres porcelain, and began to sign the law. Suddenly the pen fascinated him more than the decree. For it had the merit of allowing a fine stream of ink to pass through the nib without spotting the manuscript. Thereby enabling his illegible signature to dry rapidly. This circumstance hastening the moment when the heralds would proclaim, not only to the people but to the civil, military, and religious authorities, the news that by reason of the new law the gypsies, almost all of them usuaries of the soul of Andalusia, would officially cease to exist as such.

Carlos III was proud of the legal framework of his decree. Its tenor simple and its grammar straightforward. And far from being inflammatory or impious, it simply took a first stand against the heterodoxy of that people, whose undeniable political ambition, though unconscious, was aimed at offering Spain a thousand versions of reality. Each of them striking a blow at vital parts of the Spanish body. So how could the King accept a system of gypsy conception, whose aim was to impose on them a reality narrated in a thousand different ways? And all of them, without exception, offending a previously harmonious civilization. The country's cultural universe could never absorb those who trespassed against its laws, its religion, and its manifest vocation for grandeur.

"Poor gypsies. Since they were unable to offer Spanish society a thousand-year womb, formed of an ovum and Visigoth, Celtic, and Latin sperm, they were subject to all the rigor of the law."

"Tell me, what exactly did this decree prohibit?" Madruga said.

"To give you an example, grandfather, it forbade them the use of their own language in any place whatsoever. They could not use it in bed, even when they made love. Or at table, when they wanted to hymn the praises of choice gypsy delicacies. Or at weddings, for ceremonies, in rituals."

Carlos III slept peacefully on that night and on the ones that followed.

Nothing troubling his conscience. His decree, laid down along Christian lines, not only stopped short of exterminating the gypsies, but also gave them the civic opportunity of becoming worthy Spaniards.

The King immediately made them a present of the Spanish language. What more regal gift could there be? A proud language, sibilant and pure. With a powerful structure, hence capable of laying the foundation for refined expressions of thought. There was no question that, thanks to the acute efforts of its writers, this language had already reached a form that shone all the more brightly as they exploited its infinite resources.

Whereas the gypsies' language sounded to any ear, and the royal ear in particular, bastard, guttural, sick, spiteful, syncopated, tattered and torn. The reason for this being the endless travels of this language throughout the world without the protection of a single kingdom, of a home with walls, and of the power of the written word.

The decree also took no notice of the habits of those people. It had been decided to expressly forbid them, even though profound knowledge of them was lacking. What was certain was that they were mysterious and promiscuous, and attacked faith and tradition. Once the gypsies were shut up in their tents, to which the King did not have access, their feasts customarily ended in splendid bacchanals.

"The King was the divider of waters. What he had not seen was placed on the list of condemnations. It is there that we find the ban of language, habits, uses and customs, and folk costumes."

Each courtier, come before the King, had described gypsy dress as his imagination dictated. While certain of them emphasized the shameful slovenliness of these people, with their filthy garments torn to shreds, others hinted that those women had greedy lips, a satanic expression permanently engraved upon their faces. What was more, they concealed, beneath innumerable colored petticoats, between their juicy thighs, forbidden practices, aimed at the sacrifice of the virtues of Spanish gentlemen.

"It is probable that the essence of the Pragmatic Sanction inspired Hitler. For the reason that the decree ended with a minutely detailed study, in doubtful cases, of the past of this nomad people. Intended to dissect their family tree. To find out who was or was not a pure-blooded Spaniard."

"In such matters, that's like stirring up a hornet's nest. The one who's looking into this sort of thing has so much information to deal with that eventually he's bound to stumble across his own origin. One, incidentally, that makes a person a bastard, socially speaking. It's like it is here in Brazil: who is there who hasn't passed at one and the same time by way of the manor house and the slave quarters!" Madruga said with a carefree smile.

After the decree went into effect, the gypsies urgently needed to forget their origins so as to acquire Spanish citizenship. After which it would be their responsibility to mate and have children who would reproduce

Spanish traits. Even though this was contrary to their genetic system. All this beginning to engender countless practical problems. Not only did they continue to be born with the gypsy biotype, to speak miserable Castilian, to have no notion as to how to behave at table, and to look awkward in Spanish dress. But on top of all that they now lacked a surname. Since as Spanish subjects they were not allowed to use family names.

Plunged into despair, the gypsies had no idea what to do to comply with the decree. Ought they to knock on the door of a villager, and ask to borrow his surname? Or would it be better just to steal one, disregarding legal complications and penalties?

Everyone chose whatever surname was convenient. Which gave rise to embarrassing situations, though they got round them by telling lies and making up stories. On the road, when stopped by a patrol, it was necessary to pass for Christian. Since that way they could escape punishment.

"You there with the gypsy face, where are you from?"

"Good heavens, sir, how can you confuse us with people like that! We're Castilians, from Segovia. The city famous for its aqueduct."

"Do you know the Saavedra family there?" the roving inspector said, beginning to lose his nasty suspicions.

"What a coincidence that you should ask. We're related, on our mother's side."

"Well then, what are you doing here in Andalusia, so far from the central plain?"

"It's fate, sir. We Saavedras are on the road all the time. That's why we give people the illusion that there are so many of us. It's just that we're everywhere. What's more, we've never lacked horses and carriages for our travels. We're a rich family, no doubt of that."

As the months went by, the gypsies began to enjoy more and more the mix-ups that resulted from these whoppers of theirs. Coming from a people who carefully cultivated legends, they now saw this repertory grow at a dizzying rate. To the point that it frightened the gypsy leadership, which considered this verbal delirium to be the most dramatic consequence of the decree.

When the Saavedra family learned, however, that their illustrious surname had been definitely usurped by the gypsies, they protested loudly. That proliferation of Saavedras offended the honor of the men of that illustrious family. The fact bore with it the nasty implication that they had impregnated countless women outside of wedlock, without, consequently, assuming the responsibilities of paternity. Quite unlike Saavedras, who had always been extremely careful with their own sperm. As careful as their servants when they polished the family silver.

The authorities, once notified, were puzzled as to how to solve this contradiction that they themselves had engendered. After all, the decree itself required that the gypsies provide themselves with Christian surnames so that the official registry and the census record could be properly kept; otherwise they risked being hurled from the heights of the Pyrenees, over to the French side. And it also recommended that they choose old family names, above which there would not hover suspicions of apostasy, heresy, and betrayal of the Crown. Families having nothing to do with New Christians, who were simply Jews who had hastened to accept, in the past, the conditions of Isabella of Castile and Ferdinand of Aragon.

And so the question arose: How to give them a Castilian rootstock, without wounding the sensibilities of the pious Christian population? Rightly offended to see their surnames usurped by that colorful, raggle-taggle people.

These problems having been taken to the King, he smiled. All that merely underscored the humanistic aspect of his decree. And guaranteed his entry into History. This for the reason that, whereas the Fuero de Monzón, a law code drafted by the purist Ferdinand the Catholic, had expelled the gypsies from Spain, his own generous decree had aspired simply to assimilate them forever. Though at that moment this race was unable to understand the grandeur of the royal act.

Carlos III had acted without hope of recompense or proofs of gratitude on the part of this people. They scarcely knew how to sit at a table, use a knife and fork, or tell a good wine from one that had turned. And above all they did not have the memory of the Christian cross firmly driven home in their consciences and their hearts.

Madruga appeared to be impressed by the particulars of the decree. He was especially alarmed at having reached old age in utter ignorance concerning it. How could he have spent a lifetime not knowing of an episode of such crucial concern to the dignity of his country? Surely there had been, on the part of the authorities, and with the connivance of historians, a deliberate intention of disguising these facts. And, if possible, omitting them altogether. So that when Spain was spoken of among them its history would be tinged with colors ever reflecting the sun's bright rays.

"Our memory is tricky, Breta. It preserves in vinegar and alcohol only what favors it. How, then, to trust it or trust even what books tell us? Or trust even what we know?"

"Do you know why, grandfather? We were brought up to forget. Everything we know has been born of betrayal. We betray facts and feelings every day. But who could bear living if one were to haul a rotten fish up to the surface of one's consciousness each day? One that stinks for miles and would compromise the whole social scheme. That's precisely why hypocrisy is a healthy exercise."

I walked over to Grandfather. At his side now, I touched his shoulder. A gesture he quickly acknowledged with thanks.

"Despite Carlos III, the gypsies are still holding out. They've proved they're stronger than the decree. There aren't very many of them, it's true.

But they haven't renounced their condition," Madruga said proudly, as though he were one of them.

The subject again absorbed our attention. We had ourselves another cognac. Madruga divided the golden liquid between our two glasses with hairline accuracy.

"There was only one way of fighting that king. Opposing him. Simply remaining a pariah in that haughty, hierarchized society. Total conversion, as the King demanded, would have wiped them out forever. The truth is that no one in Spain was about to grant them full citizenship. And why would they, the gypsies, have any reason to trust a people that took away their family names, drove them from their tents, condemned them to the worst of all exiles? The exile that does away with language, dreams, the right to forge one's own soul, one's spirit, whatever name one chooses to use," I answered Grandfather in a rush of excitement.

That study had always been a safe refuge for me. I had been going there regularly, in Grandfather's company, since the age of ten. We would shut ourselves inside it together for hours at a time. No one dared knock on the door. How often I remembered it in Paris. Most of all when I was just about to board the plane for Brazil, scared stiff at the very thought of the computers installed in Brazilian airports. Since the machines that the Intelligence Community had set up as a way of keeping tabs on every Brazilian might very well swallow me up. What if they caught me?

Miguel had given me carte blanche. I had nothing to be afraid of. Miguel and Grandfather cheered me up by arguing that I had been lucky enough not to have experienced the bitter taste of exile as so many others had. They had not, for example, taken away my nationality. Or deprived me of all legal existence, like the gypsies. Had I been spared everything then? Then why was I so upset? Shouldn't I perhaps feel indebted to the Brazilian dictatorship, since it had afforded me a pleasant stay in Paris? The unwished-for loneliness, the impossibility of returning being scarcely worth noting then? Would there be an amnesty capable of making those who had been exiled, those who had been tortured, forget the offense they had endured? And merely because the dictatorship had offered exiles the comfortable, well-trodden path to Europe, and to some the title of professor in a foreign university, ought it to decide that it had neatly settled its account with History?

Grandfather looked at me with sudden tenderness. He saw his granddaughter caught up once again in the bitter memories of 1968.

"We'd best rest for a while," he suggested. "I can guarantee that Venâncio is taking his ease this very minute beneath his mango tree, with a good book in his hand."

I pretended not to hear. We hadn't yet exhausted the subject at hand. Since Madruga had brought it up, we were obliged to pursue it.

"If you really think about it, grandfather, Carlos III was very clever.

Just as all dictators are. The fact is that despite the gypsies' heroic resistance, they were decimated in the end. What's left of them today? What's more, that was the strategy behind the decree. It wasn't aimed at liquidating them in just a year or two. The intention, rather, was to wear down their resistance, over a period of uncountable decades. Look at the strategy of Institutional Act Five, for instance. In addition to purging the entire nation by virtue of its mere existence, it in fact allowed the so-called Brazilian revolution to get rid of its troublesome enemies, blocked all access to power by the political class, and quietly gained two decades in which to act and impose its ideology. Gaining time has always been a most effective formula for overpowering the enemy. Look at the gypsies. What happened to them? They reproduced themselves more and more slowly and grew steadily poorer and more wretched. Some of them even decided to come to America, in the hope of perpetuating their nomadic way of life here. Believing that America would be on their side. Poor gypsies. They were wrong, yet again. The truth is that these Americas of ours, both the Spanish one and the Portuguese, have always devoted themselves to persecuting and condemning their best children. Have you ever noticed how the most sensitive, the most libertarian of them, have always been put to the knife? Or else thrown into prison or driven into exile, as an example for succeeding generations, killing whatever dream they might have had. Amid such an atmosphere, how could this America have welcomed a race that takes no notice of borders and laws? And yet, grandfather, who is there who doesn't fear a gypsy's copper eyes?"

After this outburst, I calmed down again. Madruga, however, kept smoothing down his hair. With visibly nervous gestures, which did not help at all to relieve his sudden discomfort.

"Can Venâncio have come from a family hounded by the terror of Carlos III? A family that stole its surname from a neighbor? And is that why Venâncio has spent his entire life guarding himself against feelings and a culture that were forced upon him, while at the same time fighting to hide his most intimate being, which an entire society has decided to condemn? Or has Venâncio, in fact, no reason to complain, since we're all subject to the same pillage, all suffer from the attacks of vampires, the depredations of the strongest? Every neighbor wants to steal our soul. While the authorities are forever threatening to haul us into court. Even if we're innocent! Is that why we live in constant fear, beneath a threat that seemingly is not concrete, yet haunts our tables and our beds? And thus become cowards, ever ready and willing to give up what has not been expressly demanded of us? In return for what? Saving our wretched little pile of money and this miserable subjugated body! I'm confused, Breta, terribly confused. When all is said and done, where do we come from, outside of a village, a house, and a country? Why are we so arrogant?

Beginning first of all with myself. And why do we live so easily with the lie that camouflages reality from us?"

For the first time Grandfather was losing his arrogance, humiliating himself before me. As though Carlos III, Costa e Silva, Médici, and all the many other protagonists were chasing after him with a scythe. Handing over to each one of them more than what they had apparently demanded.

Perhaps he was still questioning, in a pathetic tone of voice, whether it was really worth the effort to accumulate wealth, possessions, merely to have moldy, withered, strictly secondhand dreams at his disposal. His suffering, there laid bare, moved me. I felt it indecent to try Grandfather's soul with complaints and accusations. We had always avoided, after all, getting down on the floor together and stuffing our worn, sweaty clothes into the same sack. I tried to lead him back to the original subject of our discussion. I did not want to deprive him of the rules that had governed him until that moment.

"Everything we've said, grandfather, is mere supposition. Venâncio, our essential witness, may be the first to deny his possible gypsy origin."

"And why is that, Breta? Has he ceased, then, to believe in the powers of a race that once stood up to the King, and still wanders about Spain even today?" Madruga said.

Beneath the view of familiar objects, we stayed on in the study. As we consumed years and words. Wherever we were, Brazil was following us like the shadow of the executioner. Wherever we went, the country trailed along behind. All of us, the unjust and the kindly alike, represented the enigmatic substance of a people which, despite its youthfulness, was repeating the stubbornness of a Europe capable of destroying, even though it did not exploit the blood it shed. We had found an equal reason for killing here. In the name of Christianity, whose codices had been decanted amid casks of wine and belches brought on by splendidly seasoned food, we had wiped out entire civilizations in America.

Eulália knocked on the door. She had no doubt guessed that we were talking about Venâncio, and had come to defend him. With a look, she discouraged us from hurting our friend. Madruga obeyed this hint from his wife, who wove the fabric of his daily life. And rose to his feet to receive her.

"Will Venâncio be with us this Sunday?" Eulália asked.

It was a sign for Madruga to console her. She was deserving of his attention. How many times Madruga, impelled by his explosive temper alone, had hurt her. Above all when he quarreled with the world, his children, and Venâncio. Wasn't it time now to be reconciled with the fruits of the earth, since there were so few years left to enjoy them? He took her arm, at once resigned and touched. And made a move to return, the two of them together, to the living room.

Grandfather's stubborn curiosity never let go of a subject when there was something he wanted to know. Today, however, he had desisted from asking unanswerable questions. Except ones having to do with Venâncio's life. His maniacal persistence, however, had grown a bit milder with the years.

Seated now in his easy chair, he may have sensed that age had drained his voracious soul of its last strength. It was about time. Even the grandchildren were now pecking at his body with their pointless demands. And he had nothing to do with this family now. Mere hunks of flesh dragging his name and his scant memory about with them.

"I'm so tired, Eulália," and he stroked his wife's hand as she sat there beside him.

"By Sunday we'll be feeling better. So as to receive Venâncio and the family."

"Yes, more rested. And less inclined to argue," Madruga said.

That living room was the perfect setting for my grandparents. The white walls, hung with framed pictures, had seen them grow old. Both awaiting a death that might come suddenly, on a sunny day. Or would Eulália prefer a rainy afternoon? The soaking wet earth reminding her of the dreary winters in Sobreira. As, on Sundays, shut up inside the house, they waited for the platters of stew, heaped high and giving off all sorts of smells, to come to the table. At the sight of the vegetables, the garden outside, frozen, with nothing growing in it, was instantly there before her. And the animals too, killed only to furnish them food.

At this sacred hour, Dom Miguel and the family spoke in particular of the excellence of the pig, whose parts, even the organ meats, served to stimulate man's palate and his imagination. The father made a move to dish out, personally, the blood puddings, the sausages, the spareribs, the ham, the red bacon, the beef, and the pieces of chicken. And he invested this act with a certain delicate fancy, knowing that his hands were serving up bits of culture and dreams.

After the pudding, into whose preparation there had gone more than twenty-four egg yolks, of a vivid yellow, Dom Miguel invited Eulália to keep him company as he drank his coffee and smoked his cigar. Only then, his heart uplifted by nature, ash-gray and barely visible through the windowpanes clouded with mist, did Dom Miguel tell Eulália the stories to which, in her old age now, she had begun little by little to contribute ingredients of her own to strengthen them, as the one last effort that life still demanded of her.

At the baptismal font, the children received the taste of salt in their mouths, and a Christian name, proclaimed by their godparents. From that moment on, Madruga devoted himself wholeheartedly to the task of instructing them. Preferably by way of little stories, the endings of which, however, he never got around to telling. Owing to the fact that he was hardly ever home and the week went by quickly, and all of a sudden it was Sunday, with its table decorated with flowers and platters heaped with food.

Though jealous of his authority, Madruga did not want apathetic, silent children. He tried to goad them into arguing, especially when he arrived home in a touchy, taciturn mood. To his surprise, however, the children refused to say a word at such times, as though they had agreed among themselves that they should defy him.

Unlike her husband, Eulália encouraged little whims in her children, as a way of enjoying being alive and exercising their freedom. Having come by her eagerness to do so thanks to Dom Miguel, who had spent his days fighting for the autonomy of Galicia.

She also taught them to cultivate solitude, which, besides enhancing one's ability to be by oneself, had the even greater merit of making mystery a permanent part of human life. Never expecting an answer to a state that could be sporadically relieved by the presence of another, though most often it expressed itself through piercing cries of wolves on the steppes.

And, wanting them to feel the effects of solitude at close hand, Eulália divided the house into zones, named after the mountains of Sobreira. Each belonging to a different child. With the right to take refuge in it without the danger of foreign invasions. Save for one by Madruga, whose invader's instinct did not respect private territories.

Tobias was the last to receive his assigned place. After Eulália caught a look in her son's eye which seemed to her to be one of envy, yet one of distress as well. So the moment had come to give him the freedom of being all by himself. She pointed out, as belonging to him, the area around the piano. Informing the others that that territory, Tobias's now, was not subject to dispute.

Madruga was given to sudden shifts of mood. When he felt happy at table, he served his children a good wine, so that they would appreciate one of the finest human gifts. But when one of them answered him back, his blue eyes opened wide in an expression of displeasure. An attitude that failed to disturb Esperança, who, in direct confrontation with her father, forced him to give up inflicting any sort of punishment.

In summer, the house was in a constant uproar. The long school vacation turning into a series of outings and excursions. And so they would all board the train, amid much shouting and scrambling. Tobias, still a small child, began to cry at the first scream of the whistle. It had been a long time since all of them, including Odete, had gone on a trip together.

Eulália looked at the five children one by one, as though she were counting them. Had they left a suitcase behind in the station? Madruga smiled at his wife's endless worries. And the moment after regretted that they were traveling by train, instead of by boat. He dreamed of taking them all across the Atlantic. The children ought to feel the impact that an ocean with a boundless horizon has upon the human imagination.

"Nothing can compare with the high seas, children. If Brazil hadn't been in the cards for me, I probably would have been a sailor."

He turned to Eulália and laughed, hinting that she too was his destiny. Grateful for the attention, she passed him a roast chicken leg, lightly dusted with toasted manioc flour, wrapped in a napkin. Standing open in front of her and Odete was the great wicker basket, filled with choice viands.

Miguel was fighting with Bento for a seat next to the window. Madruga calmed them down by working out a system of rotation. Every half hour, the seats would have new occupants, giving everyone a chance to appreciate the scenery.

The train was somehow disturbing to Madruga. Yet at each tunnel they passed through, it seemed to him that he and his family were entering the very heart of that country. He missed Venâncio. He had insisted that he come along with them. But Venâncio, his face set in a scowl, had refused the invitation.

"I've already made that journey, Madruga. What's the point of my visiting Brazil and not ever managing to understand it?" he said in a confidential tone.

Foreseeing loneliness, Venâncio promised to come stay with them at the end of the season. In that beautiful, never-changing park, they would drink water from the same spring together.

Antônia, only a little older than Tobias, scarcely stirred on the train bench. Nor did she say a word as to what she saw, obliging her father to try to provoke from her reactions that surely existed in that little body. She was overjoyed at her father's attention. She opened her mouth, with the front teeth missing, giving him a shy smile. Then she leaned against Bento's back. He immediately spread his wings so that his little sister could loll against him. Madruga looked at his family and the scenery at the same time. He ruled over life as the absolute lord and master. Not approving of Antônia's frailty, which might cause future problems.

"This child lacks the spirit to face up to life. She lets others live hers for her. She'll also give us a scoundrel for a son-in-law someday," he declared to his wife.

Eulália was surprised at her husband's obsession with the future. As if it were not enough for him to live only the present, to be there in the train headed for São Lourenço, when they would consume each day in a quiet, refined way.

Madruga leaped out at the stations in search of turnovers, meat pies, meringues, cupcakes, corn bread. Little marvels that the poor, wretched ovens of those localities turned out.

"We'll never eat anything like this again," he said to Eulália.

She applauded Madruga's effort. Taking Miguel and Bento along with him at times. Miguel, being more agile, brought back the delicacies and the change, always the right amount. Whereas Bento would come back just as the train was about to pull out.

"Don't let the children leave the train, Madruga," Eulália pleaded in a worried voice. "They're going to be left behind there in those miserable stations."

"Brazil is a miserable country, Eulália. It wouldn't do them any harm to learn from these people how terrible poverty is. Then they'd flee it as fast as their legs could carry them. I don't want my kids to be lily-livered, to be afraid to face reality. Venâncio is right. If they don't know Brazil, if they don't sound its lungs, how are they going to win?"

To Madruga, everything turned into something to fight over. A race for victory. He couldn't bear failure. He faced the thought of it boldly, eager to escape its toils. Recoiling from the wry faces of the losers. Afraid that a son of his might turn into an object of collective pity.

The train panted to a stop. Halting at water tanks, where the boilers quenched their thirst endlessly. Or waiting an hour for the train coming in the opposite direction, with the right-of-way on the same track. The children romped about the car, and the train didn't come. Was this a sign of how late Brazil was in arriving at its destination? Unable to fulfill the vision of paradise that had been imparted to it?

How often Madruga envied Venâncio, given to constant exercises of the imagination! Telling him, almost always, of a Brazil invisible to his eyes. A Brazil that it might fall to the children to unveil. But who, among his offspring, would have the drive to tell of the land that he, in the prime of life, had chosen to live in and die in?

Esperança had bright, piercing eyes. Life was entering her through radiant orbs, with a force she would not be able to resist. Unless Madruga protected her at each and every moment. And after him, the man whom his daughter would marry. It pained him to imagine Esperança crossing the landing at the top of the stairs, returning to the house as a visitor. But wasn't that the natural trajectory? And the reason why Eulália had fol-

lowed him? Accepting, instead of the solid house at the foot of the mountain, in Sobreira, a modest house on the shore of the Bay of Guanabara,
exposed to the Atlantic winds. To be part of a continent immersed in a
culture that she was far from understanding. Involuntarily, he condemned
Eulália to a universe only roughly laid out, with irregular lines and traces,
its imagination occupied for centuries thereafter in ordering its chaos.

Moved at the memory of the woman who had followed him to America, he stroked her hand. The caress beginning at the wrist, and extending
to the ends of the fingers. Overcome now, however, by a strange anguish.
Esperança observed her father's gesture. Her firm gaze assured him that
she was keeping close watch on him. The two of them heading toward
divergent distractions and interests. Perhaps that was why they had become friends yet at the same time often locked horns.

Suddenly she changed places in the train. Unceremoniously shoving
Antônia, clinging to her mother, to one side. Madruga noted this act of
aggression. He said nothing. He felt himself to be under fire from Esperança, who was still staring straight at him. Damn, Madruga thought, the
worst of it is that this creature has more spunk than those boys of mine.

"Miguel, get us a snack at the next station," he said, to hide his feelings.

"No, father, this time I'm getting off," Esperança said, ready to bellow
with rage if Madruga refused. Meanwhile stroking her mother's arm.

Who ever saw a little girl do things like that, he tried to think.

"Just tell me what you want, and I'll bring it to you on the run. And
nice and hot, to boot."

Esperança held out her hand for Madruga to put the money in her
palm. With Miguel's eyes on him, he hesitated. Suddenly, without protest,
he handed the money over to her.

He didn't want to make an enemy of Esperança. Despite the times
she'd become his adversary, forgetting the love that bound them. Madruga
was moved by his daughter's adolescent body. Everything in that growing
body new and indispensable to the expression of the emotions that were
accumulating, demanding space in order to give its yearnings resonance.
From her body, Esperança's breasts were budding, firm and sensitive. Yet
despite her young-warrior poses, he sensed in that body an intangible
frailty that he had no way of defining.

Furious, he put such thoughts to flight. They might attract danger to
his house, aimed directly at his daughter's ardent life. Her attraction to
flames was undeniable. Everything about Esperança, surely, symbolized
fire. Her temperament and her reddish hair. He had no doubt of her mortally dangerous impulses, capable of defying conventions, of attracting
intense, uncontrollable affections. But to whose lot would it fall, then, to
govern these affections, to restore order where subversion threatened to

reign supreme, exploding through her sex, through her mouth, through a perishable heart?

A shame she hadn't been born a man. It would have been easier. For he could not see her tied to a domestic destiny through an act of brute force, the power of social convention. He'd do his best therefore to make her knuckle under and obey his precepts. Eager to be replaced someday by a stranger, who would conquer Esperança by force in bed, a terrain that emitted disturbing radiations all through the house. But what would it be like to make Esperança both happy and uninhibited? Did such a combination in fact exist? And why wouldn't his daughter give in to what usually went by the name of happiness? Hadn't he himself been the first to relinquish the freedom he had once enjoyed, thanks to chance encounters, to pickups on street corners, ever since his heart had started going off like a gun at a mere look, the minute he set foot in the house?

When Esperança was born, he wanted to call her Amparo. Up until then he had avoided giving his children Spanish names. The marks of their origin revealed by their bodies ought to be quite enough. Beginning with the way they appreciated olive oil, saffron, certain delicacies, not to mention the involuntary memories that the Spanish language, spoken at home sometimes, brought to the surface.

Eulália resisted his demands.

"Don't ask me what my reasons are, Madruga. But this daughter is going to be called Esperança."

Madruga looked closely at his wife. No other woman had ever shown him such consideration and given him such proof of her trust in him. She had not hesitated to follow him, even though he might be headed for dire poverty. They had braved the Atlantic together, as he talked to her of Brazil, all the way across. And, once arrived there, she had looked after the house, with a rather queenly air, granted, but without protest. Or merely asking that he take her for a stroll about the city more often. Though they seldom walked through the streets hand in hand.

He went over to Eulália then and stroked her forehead. From that forehead, ancestral and sensitive, there sprang forth surprising words and deeds. She never chained him down bodily. Thanks to Eulália, he was a free soul. The burdens of day-to-day living could not be laid at her doorstep; it was, rather, his own excessive ambition that was responsible for them. She did not ask him questions that led him to lie.

Moreover, sensing her husband's contradictory emotions, Eulália merely mentioned offhandedly that being on earth conferred on everyone the mortal status of a traveler. Able, therefore, to visit several places at the same time, without its being necessary to offer explanations for one's acts. She herself trailing through the house, with unusual frequency, the memory of Dom Miguel, of Sobreira, of Galicia, places in her dreams. She was convinced that, as God's creatures, they had been rewarded with fleetingness. As time flew, it lent them wings, the better to carry them along with it.

The children heard the train whistle announcing their entry into the tunnel that would take them to the other side of the mountain, as if it had heard a strange call. With worried glances, their heads jerking nervously, they looked at Madruga, assuring him in this way of their readiness to answer the summons of other heritages.

After Eulália's request concerning Esperança, he consoled her with a tender look. So she wouldn't feel defeated by his daily excesses. It was all too easy for him to go too far. It pleased him, therefore, to bow to her will. He sensed that Eulália, on repeating the name to him a hundred times a day, was doubtless confirming hope as a virtue. It would be a magnetic reinforcement, enabling her to bear a daily round of life so far removed from her dreams.

"A nice name, Eulália. She couldn't be called anything else but Esperança."

From the days when she was just a little girl, Esperança would stand at the gate waiting for her father to come home. She could feel his presence, wherever she was. Sometimes, far from flinging herself into his arms, she would assume a solemn pose, head held high. She would then turn her back to him, obliging him to follow her inside the house.

In the living room, she would speak to her father in a rush of words, with the intention of robbing him of the initiative, telling him about the family, what had happened to them while he'd been gone, before he could ask. So that Madruga would feel indebted to her.

Irritated, he would head for his leather easy chair, eager to be rid of his daughter. Esperança would tag right along after him. Surprising him sometimes with words that touched his heart. Generally having to do with her father's eyes, the most beautiful ones in the house.

And on describing Madruga's eyes with sensuous pleasure, Esperança seemed not to require his presence. Nothing interrupting the flow of her description. A boldness that embarrassed Madruga, helpless to control her feelings. Ill at ease in this situation, Madruga summoned Miguel, deliberately reviving the perennial quarrel between them. He thought it about time for Esperança to begin piling up defeats. Miguel had claws and staying power. A fact that allowed Madruga to insist that both of them train. Till the time came when Esperança would abdicate her claims, so that Miguel could take over as master of the house.

Esperança was not always insolent. If Madruga gave her a severe dressing down, she would hide in the kitchen afterward. Busy with her household tasks, Eulália would take her under her wing. Calming her as she panted for breath. Perhaps the child would learn in that way to temper her feelings, to retaliate with less brusque gestures.

In the kitchen, where she never felt comfortable, Eulália glided about amid pots and pans, forks, fruits and vegetables. But taking Esperança by the hand, she would sit her down on the stool. She would then begin to tell her stories. In a voice that grew softer and softer, with the risk that Esperança might understand exactly the contrary of what her mother was telling her. Till Esperança realized that Eulália was really talking to herself and not to other people. Taking no notice even when Madruga entered the room. Going on in exactly the same tone of voice, making no effort to lure her husband to the center of her tangled plots. Some of them apparently invented, with the taste of bread just out of the oven.

Sometimes, happy that certain of her words had hit the mark, Eulália smiled. Mainly because she'd touched Odete's heart, to the point that those eyes of hers brimmed with tears, and she relaxed her martial posture. They had become each other's shadows, and so Esperança apologized as she passed between them. But Eulália was immediately distracted, back once again in the world from which she had been only temporarily banished.

As he read in his easy chair, Madruga was touched at hearing the sound of his wife's footfalls on the floor, a sign that she was about to come sit at his side. At such moments, he said words to her that she perhaps wrote down and put away in the box where she kept her most precious possessions.

Esperança admired her mother's sense of the opportune moment. That woman had a way of interrupting Madruga's work without damaging the relationship between the two of them. As though there were a discreet accord between them to make their respective voices heard, with no intention, however, of distracting each other. Even though Madruga also liked the sound of his own voice. And from time to time picked the debris of his words up off the floor.

This discovery led Esperança to think that this was far from being a family trait. It was much more like a fate. As though she and her brothers and sisters were destined to follow the same paths. All of them equally inclined to develop, to a high degree, a talent for telling themselves the story of their own lives, as a means of believing in human existence.

Miguel had entered adolescence. He constantly went off to the bathroom. There amid the tiles, he satisfied his penis with his hand. He was certain that in his body there were various orifices and countless sensitive zones to take care of. At night, in bed, he tossed and turned. In the morning, he forgot about Esperança, ever the prodigal diviner of his acts and thoughts. Especially since she imitated everything he did. She too would stroke her own sex underneath the sheet, to the point of climax and insuperable shame.

Overcome with guilt, Miguel avenged himself by challenging his sister to new contests. Esperança agreed that he should be the one to indicate the marks to be surpassed. When Miguel won, she always congratulated him. The same not being the case with Miguel, who found it painful to acknowledge her victory.

"A pointless victory, that. In any case, I'll be the only winner in the future."

They flung themselves to the ground in fury. In contact with the dust, glued to each other, they felt each other all over without meaning to. She could feel his hard body, his superior male privates next to her panties, an unexpected bulge. As Miguel pressed to his chest his sister's heaving breasts, which reminded him of Málaga grapes.

Madruga pitilessly separated them. Depriving them of trips to the movies and outings on the beach.

"Save your strength for the enemy, you two. Don't worry, they'll soon be knocking on our door."

He decided to take Miguel to the factory, sending him out to inspect certain work sites scattered about the city. Esperança watched her enemy disappear in the distance under their father's protection. She would often refuse to speak to Miguel for several days. The reconciliation perhaps taking place on the street, on her surprising him scuffling with his pals, after school. She would run to help him, both of them bent on winning. Victorious at last, her brother thanked her from the bottom of his heart. They embraced. Esperança boldly showed off her bumps and scratches, trophies of victory that Madruga taught them to nail up in their hearts.

"I want winners in this house," he said in biting tones. "Always answer insults. Especially when they call us gringos or Galicians. Saying that we're not from here, that this land isn't ours. That's a barefaced lie. This land belongs as much to us as to those who came with Cabral. Never forget that you're Brazilians, with every right in the world!"

Madruga reviewed the contributions of more recent immigrants to the industrialization of Brazil. Especially those who had arrived, as he had, at the beginning of the century. With progressive ideas as a general rule, bearing on their backs, along with poverty, proposals for organizing labor unions, a principle of protecting the working man. Moreover, they were free of the accusations leveled against the elite. Luckily, they were not yet part of the privileged class. They found themselves in a social limbo.

"It's up to people like us to proclaim the failure of those families that go back four hundred years. Beyond question responsible for the disasters and the backwardness of this country," and he awaited his children's reactions.

In those hours of patriotic fervor, Esperança outdid the rest. She was proud of the wounds stored in her memory. She hastened to embrace her father.

"Take me to the factory, father!"

Her father consoled her with little gifts. "Things like that aren't for little girls."

Madruga resented the fact that he lacked the time to devote himself simultaneously to his children and his business. Especially since Esperança, still not resigned to being kept at home, repeatedly showed her contempt for him. But what to do with her? Humor her, fling her into a world that did not want women outside the family circle? The fact was that Esperança would never be permitted to shape reality or try to oppose it. She had inherited a world sanctioned without her support. Madruga himself had learned that this supposed reality conformed to the laws of power. Mere wishing not being enough to weaken the fabric of a social system set in place to suit the convenience of a minority.

As an immigrant, his place was in the rear guard of a country on the rise. Gradually gaining real emancipation, escaping, thanks to a stroke of luck or the activities of his children, a political quarantine that had been forced upon him. Meanwhile, his voice, raised in chorus with the voice of the man in the street, received no more space in books and periodicals than the most trivial news filler. They were merely pedestrians treading a very ordinary path, a quick route leading straight from birth to death.

He finally gave in to Esperança's pleas. As a matter of fact, he felt depressed at the time. As a herald of misfortune, Venâncio kept offering him evidence that the end of the Spanish War would not mean peace with the enemy. Merely a temporary lull in the fratricidal struggle.

"The same as would happen if you were to kill Miguel with a saber and a rifle bullet," Madruga said, voicing his fears to Esperança.

Touched by these words, she sought Miguel out. Embracing him, deeply moved, grief-stricken.

"We'll never kill each other. Do you swear, Miguel?"

Fearing he might kill her unintentionally, he nervously gave her his word. Yes, the two of them would avoid all bloodshed between them. They looked each other straight in the eye.

"What's going to be left of a country that constantly resorts to the blood of brothers to solve its problems?" Madruga would shout at Sunday dinner.

Venâncio did not answer immediately. With a vague, unfocused look in his eye, he went on identifying one object or another with the aid of Eulália, ever mindful of his frailties. Noticing the dark circles under Venâncio's eyes, Eulália alerted her husband, begging him to look after his friend. Couldn't he see that they were losing him?

His attention wholly occupied with the managing of his affairs, expanding on a vast scale, Madruga remained blind to the fact that Venâncio practically dropped pieces of his body on the floor at the end of each month. Noting his insensitivity to this state, Eulália, in retaliation, shifted onto his shoulders the entire burden of responsibility for the many children crowded together in the living room.

Madruga gathered the family together. "If on life's orders I had all of you as children, I demand that you learn to survive. And I am not referring to animal survival. I want you to build houses, projects, dreams, which exist here on this earth for the express purpose of arousing men's feelings and emotions."

At six in the morning, Madruga drove his children out of bed. He knocked on the door of those who were still asleep even though the sun was already up outside. While he demanded that they show their fighting spirit, Eulália, her hand gently resting on their shoulders, drew them toward the stories that she took to be the salt of life. The moment it was light, she dressed, eager to be off to Mass. And though she tried not to make a sound, Madruga awoke in time to oblige her to say good-bye to him. This being his way of hinting that he was aware of her daily visits to church, despite the fact that she knew him to be fiercely, arrogantly anti-clerical. She, however, acted as though she had chosen to follow another itinerary, owing him no explanation.

Esperança was excited about the possibility of helping her father. Her heart beating faster, whenever strong feelings came over her. Since any excitement made her less clearheaded, her sentences did not come out in the order intended. She could hear her own head pounding. To the point that she feared that such an access of emotion was not a form of flattery; it represented, rather, a condemnation.

"Can my heart be my greatest enemy?" she said, hastening to unburden herself to her father one morning.

Madruga was suddenly alarmed. He wanted to warn her against emotions which, if not controlled, would eventually weaken her. Lacking the courage, however, to confront temporarily immortal sentiments, he chose to say no more. For the first time he showed respect for someone who had been born to love with no safe haven, heedless of all protection. Could the beautiful, talkative Esperança be a voice announcing only the love that sought to lead her astray? He had a foreboding of the strange poison that was beginning to eat away at his daughter.

"There's a house on the Rua do Lavradio that's going to be sold at auction tomorrow afternoon. I have plans for it. So you're to go in my place and make the bids. I hope you'll complete the transaction success-fully."

She was to act as Madruga himself would. Prepared, therefore, to confront various contenders, and be clever enough to get the better of them. She must act calmly. She had more than enough time to win. To find a way beyond the ceiling now set. She was to keep her eyes open, watch how the expert bidders went about things. Masters of all the ins and outs of auctioneering, users of a mime's language almost, interspersed with deceptive pauses, with imperceptible gestures, representing nonetheless a definite bid. It was doubtless a game to fake out one's opponent. Where lying, a blank face, indifference held sway. The way poker players bluff, cards in hand. By dint, however, of sweat and a sharp eye, Esperança would little by little top the opening bids, preferably keeping close to the last figure offered. There was no need to make jump bids. Above all her face must never reflect the emotions she was experiencing, win or lose.

"It's simple, Esperança. You just have to take a chance."

Esperança went inside the house, her hands ice-cold. Discreetly, she rubbed them against her arms. She donned an ash-gray suit, kept for wearing to funeral Masses. Her coiffure, a severe topknot, made her look older. At the first call, two men hastened to bid, both beneath the keen gaze of the auctioneer, who had placed the platform and his table beneath the leafy mango tree. Feeling her legs tremble, Esperança marshaled her forces to fight for an opening. And as she prepared for the next round of bidding, attracting the attention of the male audience around her, it seemed to her that she was speaking with someone else's voice.

The yard extended beyond the area that was cemented over. Disappearing from view in the thick overgrown vegetation, the entire plot of ground being surrounded by Brazilian trees. From the house there came a strong smell of mold, indicative of walls infiltrated by water. Despite the mistreatment that the house had suffered, Madruga had no doubt foreseen a sudden increase in the value of the area.

Esperança took a deep breath, pleading with her heart, her enemy, to quiet down. But what sort of game was this that made them play it so intently? Was a house with slime on the walls worth all that much? Leaping into the fray, she made several quick bids. At her heels, she spied a fat man, wearing a white linen suit, a Panama hat. His cigar clamped tightly in his mouth, making it difficult for him to speak. His voice nonetheless capable of silencing his rivals. No one else bid against him. Only Esperança went on, his eyes trained on her now. Perhaps he hadn't taken her seriously. Esperança couldn't have cared less. She called to mind Miguel's ironic laugh, gloating over her failure on her return. He too wanting to prove to his father how incompetent his sister was.

Esperança shot back at the man the presumptive look of a winner. Despite the shadow of the mango tree, he was sweating heavily. Esperança was now close to the limit set by her father; she had practically nothing left to up her bid. The fat man had only to add one *conto* more to win. Suddenly, there was a pause. The auctioneer began the count, his hammer suspended in the air. The last bid was Esperança's. One. Two. Esperança stared at the fat man, transfixed. He nodded, withdrawing in her favor.

"Three. The bidding is closed," the auctioneer proclaimed.

Esperança's impulse was to hug the man. She contained herself, walking over to the auctioneer, her back to the fat man. Something, however, attracted her. Unable to resist, she turned to him again. Smiling this time, thanking him with a gesture. Leaning against the tree, waiting for that sign, he adjusted the brim of his hat and left the yard, followed by three men.

Summoned immediately, Madruga closed the deal. The auctioneer congratulated him on the excellent performance of so young a daughter. She had finally beaten Zico, of the Praça Mauá, the most powerful smuggler in the city and the Baixada Fluminense. For the first time ever he had seen him back down, admit defeat without taking his revenge, create a precedent. Doubtless it was his heart that had been his undoing, the same organ that so often made Esperança succumb.

Tipped off by the tradesmen on the Rua do Acre, Madruga sought Zico out. Late in the afternoon, in the ground-floor bar of the Edifício A Noite. Surrounded by actors from Radio Nacional, and composers desperate to form fake partnerships with librettists. There he was, all alone, dressed in white once again, his Panama hat pulled down low. Slowly downing a stein of beer, his back to the wall. From where he sat, he held sway over the entire place. Not one suspicious movement would escape him. At the next table, his bodyguards. He did not address a single word to them.

The minute Madruga approached the table two of the men rose to their feet. "What is it you want?" one of them said. Zico looked on, aloof and impassive. Madruga insisted; he needed to speak with the boss.

"Say what it is you want, pal, or you don't get past us."

"Tell him I'm the father of the girl at the auction last week."

As though he'd heard every word, Zico signed to the men to relax. Madruga could come speak to him.

"Are you Portuguese or Spanish? I get all of you mixed up," Zico said, chewing on the end of his cigar. And he invited Madruga to sit down and have a beer with him.

"And what kind of place is that Galicia of yours that keeps driving you out?"

The two of them alone together now, Madruga described a region that surely Zico knew nothing about.

"Some of us are light-skinned, others dark. But everybody gets so homesick they cry," Madruga said, pointing to the owner of the bar. He too might be a Galician. In which case they'd sucked the teats of animals born on the same meadow.

Zico began to ply him with eager questions.

"What's the name of that enterprising young lady?"

"Esperança. Her mother named her that."

"Pretty name. She's pretty too. I hope she'll be happy."

Madruga apologized for bothering him while he was relaxing. But he wanted to thank him for his gesture, and find out why he'd let the house go to his daughter.

Zico smiled. He offered him a refill. He'd simply been unable to resist Esperança's youthful impetuousness. Her face was so full of life; the world seemed to have been created from it.

"She beat me. Despite my fame, I'm a man who can be gotten the better of by affection, by hallowed dates and by pleasant memories. Anyone who's come down from São Carlos Hill the way I did, driven out like a dog, has no pity in his heart. Except for those who make me feel like a man, the man my mother bore and suckled."

He idly wiped the sweat from his glass of beer with his index finger. Looked at Madruga sternly.

"You know very well who I am. Never mind my biography. Even I have no need of it. It's only my enemies who delve into the details of my life. I'd rather they were the ones to tell of my adventures. This Praça Mauá here is my turf. My stronghold. But it could soon turn into my graveyard. We don't last long around here. A far shorter time than you on the outside. Just long enough to win, to determine our fate. If you lose it's because you didn't know how to win. But if they mow me down someday, or my luck deserts me, I swear I won't climb up São Carlos again. I'd sooner die. I hate the stones on that hill. We used to slip on them on rainy days. We landed nose first, wallowing in the mud like pigs."

He spoke slowly, deliberately, keeping Madruga a captive audience. He ordered the waiters around with minimal gestures. An attractive figure, who brought Madruga a Brazil moving about underground, in a light of its own. Great power was concentrated in Zico's hands, and he was proud of this. At election time he had only to say the word, and in neighboring areas votes for his candidates rained into the ballot boxes. It was whispered that he shared the spoils with a senator from the State of Rio, a frequent guest at palatial tables. As the politician's right-hand man, he ran the districts of Gamboa, Saúde, all downtown. When at times he'd invaded the outlying working-class districts he caused pandemonium among rival gangs. The police, who had their orders, allowed him to operate in ever-expanding concentric circles.

This toughness expressed the resistance of a Brazil that Madruga had thus far not frequented. Despite his having ventured into the Lapa district, having had any number of women in his bed, having a good command of cutting insults and dirty words, those popular needs that the language knew so well how to express, and having each day accumulated more property, he was unable to describe Brazil with the same authority, stemming from firsthand experience, as Zico. What did Madruga know of the historic bloodlettings that had begun with the Discovery? Was there any story, read in a book, that would have allowed him to translate the substratum of the land where he would one day die?

His children, born Brazilian, could help him very little. Who, then, would be able to hold out to him the staff of knowledge? And was the

Indian, who had been there from the beginning, the master of the intricate tracery of an inexplicable embroidery? The country, after all, that went by the name of Brazil must be somewhere. Perhaps Brazil was to be found on every street corner, listening to its children's sighs of lust and longing for home. Just because those children had had Africa and Portugal far back in their past! In that case, were Brazilians too, contrary to what was generally believed, awaiting Dom Sebastião, that legendary Portuguese monarch who would return from Africa, in order to take off at last and follow their true course to greatness, and, incidentally, continue their search for a real, concrete world, accessible to the entire population? In whose political or social charge would they finally find what conventional usage called destiny?

Madruga looked around. Zico and he could hear from time to time the exclamations of those who came and went. Not far from there, a *samba de breque* was being rehearsed. The scat singer had a well-modulated voice, his shoulders wriggling though the rest of his body scarcely moved from the chair. The thought occurred to Madruga that on every hand, beneath the people's saturnalian appearance, were the seeds of death, of violence, mingling with their much-celebrated, eternal cordiality.

He wanted to ask Zico: Tell me, where is Brazil? Where is it, when it keeps seeking help from other countries, pretending it has no identity of its own? Madruga being surprised at the circumstance of Brazil's continually choosing Europe as its air hole, at the price of stifling its own imagination. Hence not allowing men like Grandfather Xan, esteemed tellers of tales, to appear on the scene. Was Brazil fending off the future, sapping its foundations, weakening the walls of the so-called present, firmly determined to break the people's strength?

There was Zico drinking beer, sweating in his rumpled white suit, wiping his forehead with his musk-scented handkerchief, sent to him on order from São Paulo, from the Liberty district. A bullet that struck him today would ricochet and hit the breast of the senator and, consequently, the walls of the presidential palace. Zico gave telltale signs, then, of having influence. Whereas he, an immigrant, at the present stage, had as yet no way to get to Vargas.

Much time was to pass before Getúlio received Madruga. Perhaps Vargas would have to die so that his children could approach the ladder of Power. Or would those of his blood be doomed not to realize the dreams that he had set his heart on during the Atlantic crossing? Since it was not easy, for those who had almost nothing, could barely speak, and harbored the sheer, naïve illusion of Power, to pass through so many closed doors.

"If I were a woman," Zico said dejectedly, "my name ought to have been Esperança. I've done nothing but fight for my life every single day. Haven't you done the same? Each of us struggling along in his own way? And today, despite my money, I can't even set foot in the Jockey Club or the Clube Naval. As you can see, this country accepts me, provided I don't frequent certain drawing rooms."

As Zico spoke, the obstacles between them slowly gave way. Madruga relaxed. The fact that Zico was a crook, a smuggler, perhaps a murderer, did not bar him from a social order predisposed to legalize the negative aspects of certain functions. Increasingly, therefore, legitimizing the illegitimate.

Madruga envied him his antecedents in this land. The fact of having been born in Brazil, as had his father and his grandfather. As far back as he could remember, Zico's people had been in this country. Maybe since Cabral's ships. His parents, for instance, had come from Bahia, where Brazil had begun, following the immigration routes of paupers. Perhaps an ancestor of Zico's, with an irresistible vocation for parleying, had boldly paraded his talents on a speaker's rostrum in Bahia, frequented the galleries of the Assembly, made speeches on the platform set up in the Praça da Sé, burned straw huts, joined uprisings that forged the Brazilian spirit. But was Zico's discourse that of a winner or a loser? Or were the words he was now using lent him by the senator of the Republic, holed up in the Palácio do Monroe, circulating from time to time round the corridors of the Catete? Zico making use of them, then, in a mere semblance of independence. Could he foresee his own fate despite the pomp that surrounded him? How many days did he have left, what sort of death would mow him down? What projectile shot off against him would hit him square in the heart?

Zico perceived Madruga's emotion. He too was moved.

"I know nothing about your race, about those people of yours who sell me beer, food, who lend me their services. There were times when I was unjust to them. I thought they were here to strip me clean. To make this land even poorer. To tell the truth, the historical facts are a complete blank to me. I can only speak of Brazilians with no morals, traitors to their country. Who sell themselves for a handful of coins. On the other hand, however, what am I myself doing? Won't I do worse things? Is the poverty once experienced on São Carlos Hill any excuse? And what are those men doing in my name?" and Zico pointed to the next table. "Are they obeying my orders or their own aggressive instinct? A nameless hatred that each and every one weighs himself down with, smothering his own conscience. At the going price."

He concluded these remarks, exhausted. Whereupon he forcibly propelled his massive body in Madruga's direction. They were very close now.

"Fortunately this conversation is just between the two of us," he said, rather pleadingly, looking remorseful.

"I've forgotten your every word. From this moment on, I couldn't possibly repeat what you've just said. I too am obliged to forget certain things I say that make me feel ashamed," Madruga said.

And he confessed to Zico how painful it had been for him, a mere youngster still, to meet the challenge of Brazil. He had never admitted, even to Venâncio, how many times his courage had deserted him just as he was about to enter a roomful of people he didn't know. He would tremble all over, and practically shit in his underpants. He blushed easily the moment he glimpsed on anyone's face a mocking smile at his still-awkward Portuguese. He had not come, granted, from São Carlos Hill. But his long journey from Sobreira had been peopled with any number of happenstances and uncertainties. How many defeats he had silently chalked up to his self-consciousness and pride. How ashamed he had been to accept the pennies offered him by Uncle Justo, halfway down the hill, heading for Vigo.

"And he didn't even give me a farewell embrace. There on the pier there wasn't one soul to give me a last hug or weep a tear for me as I went up the stairs."

"And where exactly is Vigo?" Zico broke in, interrupting his story.

"If you don't know anything about Vigo, then you don't know where Galicia is either. And you'll have even less of an idea of where Sobreira, my village, is tucked away. One of those villages that Europe is full of. They're the places where women go on endlessly giving birth to sons to work in the fields and go off to other countries. The melting pot of America was stocked with the flesh of those men."

"As far as I can see, Esperança comes from a stout branch of the family tree."

By coincidence, Madruga was celebrating his silver anniversary in Brazil that day. Exactly twenty-five years before, he had cut himself off from Galicia, whose traditions he had come by naturally, as simply his birthright. Safely corralled in his heart now. And wasn't that exactly how Zico felt about Bahia? Both of them, then, nursing the thought, wondering what nation could lay claim to the territory whose meaning our feelings decipher without effort, without greed, without a university degree.

The bar was empty now. The waiters, not watching the clock indicating closing time, had their eyes trained on Zico. At each swallow of the ice-cold beer, the sheer joy of living invaded Madruga via his taste buds, freezing his teeth, in contrast to the temperate words of the two of them, spilled out over the marble tabletop.

After bidding each other good-bye, they would go their separate ways. They would not be likely to meet in the years immediately following. Madruga would not forget him. Not knowing Zico's feelings. Certain, nonetheless, that he was remembered still when Zico, two years later, entered the factory, having thoughtfully left his bodyguards outside. Heading directly for Madruga, paying no attention to Bento, leaning nervously on the secretary's desk.

"You may not know it, Madruga, but I've been sending customers to your factory. I'm practically your partner. A partner who has only the most pleasant memories of your other one. What better relationship could there be?"

Each December, Madruga sent him a generous Christmas basket, in care of the bar on the Praça Mauá. Filled with products from Spain that he had personally chosen. To remind Zico of the words exchanged at that meeting. Till, one December, for the first time, the basket was sent back to him. Madruga was upset, fearing he'd lost his friend. He hastened to make inquiries as to his whereabouts. A heavy silence had enveloped him. There was no doubt, however, that he was still alive. Certain people dropped hints that he had left on a long trip, from which he would not be returning in the immediate future. Madruga held on to the basket for months, feeling certain that it would eventually reach its addressee. Till finally, one rainy morning, he divided its contents up among his office clerks.

Zico's senator friend was still in the newspapers. Photographed, sometimes, alongside Vargas. Always smiling, his cigar clamped firmly between his teeth. Perhaps still smoking the same brand, a Romeo y Julieta, manufactured by Álvarez y García, in Cuba. A special satisfaction to Zico, moreover, breathing out puffs of smoke with the greatest of pleasure.

A few months later, Miguel asked his father to tell him about a legendary figure.

"Is it true that you're a friend of a bandit, a murderer? The famous Zico?"

Madruga threw him out of the room. He forbade him to label his feelings. Miguel should try to cultivate his own friendships. Moreover, he would not permit any son of his to criticize a friend of his. What could Miguel know about Zico's sensibility?

Learning of her father's reaction, Esperança turned against Miguel, who had gone to her looking for sympathy. She confronted him as though he were an enemy.

"You may sleep with women, Miguel, but you don't know the first thing about life," and she bared her teeth, index finger upraised. Immediately donning a dramatic mask that turned her into another being. An exposed being, in search of sun and the play of shadows. Acting in such a way that her father would be unable to understand her. And so Madruga likewise confronted her as an enemy. A situation that deteriorated over the years. Till the day that Bento, in the middle of the night, as Madruga was sleeping, banged on the door of his room. Madruga coming to the door, still half asleep, not thinking. Finding himself face to face with his son, all upset, trembling, telling him the truth. Madruga had never dreamed that there could exist in this world words that would pin him to the floor, a nail driven deep into the wood. He lay there in the hall, not moving, insensible. Finally Bento shook him, bringing him to life.

"Say something, father, for the love of god. Can you hear me?"

The cries and whispers spread through the house within minutes, as though flames were licking at the curtains, the floorboards, every inflammable material. Odete supporting Eulália, fallen into a half-faint. The cortege of the living arrived, attracted by the uproar brought on by Esperança's death.

Venâncio was discretion itself. Not embracing anyone, he sank into an easy chair. Unable to speak.

"Weep at least, father," Miguel implored, in tears. His hair disheveled, his clothes in disarray, he slid to the floor, gazing into empty space, begging an invisible point to spare him pain.

"Esperança, Esperança, my beloved sister. My precious heart," he kept saying, without anyone coming to his aid.

Madruga finally decided to speak, but only to order the casket to be decorated with yellow roses, which his daughter loved. He took care of no other detail. The police came, only to be sent away immediately by the company lawyers. Esperança's fatal accident spoke for itself. The Avenida Niemayer continually caused tragedies of this sort. No one could even guess where Esperança had been coming from at that speed, at that hour. From a party, perhaps, or a visit. Or simply taking the air, wanting a bit of diversion, or fighting the insomnia that had recently plagued her. Was it no longer possible to die in the middle of the night without awakening suspicions, bound to cast their shadow on a family such as Madruga's, so highly respected by the community? Did they not know, then, that he had come to Brazil to bury his dead too, and be buried himself one day? And what other proof of love to offer Brazil, if not the sacrifice of his own family first of all? Madruga little by little yielding up to death parts of his flesh, substantive portions of his dream!

"And to think how beautiful she was! She could easily have been Miss Universe. Do you all remember Yolanda Pereira, that Brazilian Miss Universe, in 1930? Or was she Miss International? It doesn't matter. The fact is that, years and years ago now, she turned into Brazil's idea of perfect beauty."

"I knew Yolanda. And I too think that Esperança was prettier. All the groups kept making up their own versions."

Madruga bore up through the wake, now seated, now standing to receive people's embraces. A tearless, drawn face. Every so often, he disappeared into the bathroom, followed by Bento. Once the door closed, Bento tiptoed over, wanting to hear what was going on inside. He seemed to hear cries from his father, muffled by his handkerchief. The traces of tears, washed away with cold water. The moment his father unbolted the door, Bento vanished.

Unable to control himself, Miguel kept covering Esperança's hand with kisses. He embraced Venâncio, asking him to come with him. Once outside the chapel, he bent down toward his father's friend.

"Tell me the truth. Do you think I contributed to Esperança's death? You needn't spare me."

Venâncio didn't know what to say. He tried to calm him. "Did I fall short of the mark, Venâncio? Did I fail to give Esperança my friendship and loving concern? Can I have been a crass, selfish male, who kept a tight rein on my sister's freedom, standing in the way of her pleasure, her right to her own life? Did I too, along with my father, lock Esperança up in a prison we built especially for her? Oh, God, what a bastard I am! I of all people! I who am permissive, dissolute, who burn with passion, who curse every hour that I'm not in bed making love? Can Esperança at least have pardoned me?"

Venâncio enfolded him in his arms. "It was a terrible end, Miguel. There is no way to change Esperança's fate or anyone else's. The one thing left to do is resign yourself to the loss of her."

Miguel tore himself from Venâncio's grasp. Sílvia arrived upon the scene, tried to take him in her arms, to stay with him. But Miguel pushed her roughly away.

"Leave me alone. I don't want anyone to be with me." And he dashed across the Rua General Polidoro, heading for the corner bar.

Madruga felt someone grasp his hand. He looked and saw Eulália, pale and shaking, clinging to him. He had completely forgotten about his wife. She was weeping as Odete held her other hand. Both these extremities were now occupied. Husband and wife finally looked at each other. A gaze so painful that they embraced compulsively, not wanting, in fact, to see each other. And thus joined together, they had no idea how they might manage to separate. Till Antônia came to her parents' aid.

"Sit here with us, mother," and she handed her over to Luís Filho. Eulália's son-in-law drew her over to the sofa, held her glass of water as she drank. He also slowly dried her face with his perfumed handkerchief. Luís Filho's scent could be detected from a long way away. He nonetheless did not neglect the visitors, who filed by one by one to present their condolences. He listened attentively to each and every one.

"We're grateful for your presence, Governor. We can always count on Your Excellency's invaluable support. We were certain you would not fail us at this difficult moment."

The crowd passed through the rooms, spilling out onto the adjoining walk all the way to the entrance, opening onto the street. The gate, a fine piece of wrought ironwork, was imposing. The letters at the top of it did not hesitate to spell out the end: *Requiescat in pace.*

"Poor Esperança! What will be left of her now?"

"And of us, who live on each day of our lives?"

"Despite carnival, Brazil can no longer hold up beneath the weight of tragedy."

"But with Kubitschek in Power, we'll do a better job of attending to this country's wounds. He's a developmentalist. And a generous humanist as well."

"Mark my word, this man is also going to leave us in debt forever. Especially if he persists in the madness of building the new capital there in Brasília. That's completely insane."

"On the contrary, a new country ought to change capitals every hundred years. It's an outlet for the tensions both of power and of the people. And it also means a complete turnover in administrative personnel. A clean sweep all round."

Venâncio stood watching Eulália. She was wiping away her tears with a linen handkerchief, continually replaced with a fresh one by Odete. From time to time, yielding to a dramatic impulse, she would go over to the coffin. She would discreetly lift her daughter's veil, gazing for long moments at Esperança's face, spared in the disaster. In that farewell it seemed to take on aspects that would sustain her in the future. Esperança had not lost her amazing look of youth. That face was not contracted by pain or fear.

Each time his mother approached the coffin, Miguel followed in her footsteps. Only with Eulália's aid could he bear to look at Esperança inside the casket. When his mother withdrew, he too disappeared. Inexplicably divining the moment when his mother would go to Esperança. As though their two intertwined hearts emitted twin signals, drawing them to Esperança, whose death was taking on an illusory appearance, a nightmare from which they would free themselves after a long night's sleep.

Venâncio approached. Eulália waited for him to speak. But being persuaded of his embarrassment, she took the initiative.

"This is the second child that God has taken from us. But what can we ask of Him, if his will is unfathomable? When Bento died, it was easier. He was a baby, just getting used to life, and us to him. With Esperança it's different. The love I had to give her I gave to her, whole and entire. It was a love that would never grow greater. And it wasn't that she was the child I loved most. Exactly why does this sort of graduated scale exist in the face of death, I wonder?"

Venâncio tried to speak. He could keep silent no longer. He thought of embracing Eulália, but contained himself.

"I have always been close to the two of you at such moments. As though I were burying my own children."

To hide his emotion, Venâncio looked at Madruga in the distance. Standing, surrounded by Bento, Antônia, and several friends. He had aged little in the last years. A good-looking man who was taking great pains to conceal his sorrow and his feelings. Determined not to die with his daughter, not to be buried at the same time. Venâncio detected his despair, however, his slightly stooped body. But there was no way of helping him. Of sounding his heart. Madruga had never admitted to a pain that he would not be able to overcome one day. Or an error for which he would feel himself to be entirely responsible.

"Why didn't I help Esperança," Eulália said all of a sudden.

At the sound of Eulália's voice, Venâncio directed his attention toward her once again. Eulália then repeated the sentence.

"There was nothing you could do, Eulália," he answered.

"Perhaps I'm excessively occupied with things that are God's and forget human passions," speaking the words as though before a mirror reflecting her face. "Esperança sometimes used to say, mother, it was all a mistake, but if I did the wrong thing it's because I wanted to be admired, I never accepted my lot, forced on me by Father. But where can I find Esperança now, Venâncio, to help her? Is she alone, there in that place, do you think? Oh, my daughter, what miserable fate is this that stuffs you into a coffin amid flowers and red satin!"

Venâncio was moved. What could Eulália have done to prevent the accident? A car that goes out of control and crashes into a wall. The smell of the sea creeping into Esperança's nostrils, as she glimpsed, for the space of a second, and thanks to the light just dawning, the Atlantic Ocean, so dear to his heart and Madruga's. Moreover, were it not for this sea, would the two of them still be together, mourning that death? A death no one knew anything of. It being impossible for anyone even to say whether Esperança had managed to utter a few words before closing her eyes forever. Or whether she preferred, in the face of the last second left her, to concentrate only on the irreproducible project of realizing her own death.

"Do you mean to say that Esperança no longer wanted to live?" Venâncio said, fearing the effect of the very words.

"On the contrary. Esperança's defect was that she wanted to live more than we do. She lived intensely to the very end. Proving to Madruga that she wasn't afraid of going to meet her fate. That's why I ask myself, At what moment did I fail in my prayers? Or weren't those prayers sufficient in God's eyes?"

After the priest officiated at the Mass with the body lying in state, Madruga, with a gesture, ordered the casket closed, and stood apart, watching the preparations. The heat was stifling. Bending down over Esperança, Eulália repeated the name of God, heard only by Odete. And she was already walking away when Miguel vehemently kept the employees of the funeral home from putting the lid on.

"Wait five minutes more. It's early still. Please don't close her up in there. She loathes being in the dark, being cooped up without enough air to breathe. Esperança, my sister," and he fell into convulsive sobs. No one could tear him away. He resisted with the strength of a bull.

"Let me go. I want to be with her. I'm staying with Esperança."

Eulália went to her son, put her hand on his shoulder. "Let her go in peace, son."

Miguel looked at his mother, lowered his head. And seizing the lid, forgoing all help, shut Esperança up in the dark himself.

The funeral procession went down the main avenue. All of them following along behind Esperança, about to lay her away in the depths of the earth. To Madruga, however, it all seemed endlessly slow. An act that unleashed different emotions. Each one mourning his beloved dead, and afraid of dying too. Venâncio was weeping, at once for Eulália and for Esperança perhaps. He could not tell the living from the dead. And who could understand a mystery that made one and all weep ready tears. Enveloped in a feeling easy to reproduce yet likely to be soon forgotten.

With firm step, furious, Madruga strode on. Judging the pain he felt to be a useless burden. He halted before the grave, following the ceremony intently.

"And what pain do we really deserve?" he asked Venâncio after the ceremony was over.

At the cemetery gate, another line of people offering condolences. His friends hurriedly scattering down the streets, in search of fresh air, trying to erase death and its exotic retinue that drags all of us off. Bento hurried his father along, wanting to take him home.

"Let's go, father."

"I want to be the last to leave," he said firmly.

The children formed a wall around Madruga and Eulália. A man of humble mien approached, hesitating to speak to them. Dressed in a threadbare white suit, impeccably clean, hat respectfully in hand. With the gesture of an old friend, he placed his hand on Madruga's shoulder.

"I couldn't let you down at a time like this, Madruga. Do you remember me?"

Madruga looked at him distractedly. The next moment, he raised his hands to his face, completely taken aback. Thinner now, the man had undergone changes. The two of them, however, looked at each other intently. A gaze that excluded the others. No one could understand their feelings. Madruga, however, flung himself expansively into the man's arms.

"You came, Zico! You who were always so fond of my daughter. You thought she had a nice name! The name Eulália dreamed of."

"I wept when I saw Esperança's name in the papers. I wept more than if it had been my own death. I couldn't not come. I hardly ever leave my burrow. Because nobody knows where I'm hiding out these days. Maybe I don't even know myself. Everybody thinks I've died. Maybe even you thought I was dead and buried."

"Ah, Zico, my daughter's passed on. Gone to live the death that should have been mine. Yes, it's true, I'm the one who should have died in her place."

"Esperança didn't die, Madruga. Man's hope never dies, isn't that what we used to say when we were young? Or thought we were young?"

"Come see me one of these days, Zico. That would please me so much. Now especially."

"I can't promise, Madruga. I'm still struggling not to have to go back to São Carlos Hill. I've lost everything, but I'm determined to hold on to my last shred of pride. I'd rather die than set foot on the first of those stones," he said dejectedly.

Madruga embraced him once more. "No, if it's left up to me, you won't go back. I won't allow it. If you climb up São Carlos once more, it would be as though I were burying my daughter yet again."

He gestured to Luís Filho to come over. They were going to take Zico home, wherever that was. From that day forward, Zico was in his care. He was to lack for nothing as long as he lived.

"I was beaten, Madruga."

"I lost too. Is there ever a winner, I wonder?"

Back home again, Antônia insisted that her father eat something. With his daughter's voice assailing his eardrums, the disturbing thought suddenly came to him that he had lost his elder daughter and was left instead with Antônia. A dreadful thought, which he immediately banished. As though in apology, he embraced her. Obediently, he sat down at the table. So as to quiet his vague sense of uneasiness.

"Where's Eulália?" he said as he slowly chewed.

"Mother's in her room, with Odete."

There was a silence. Madruga's spoon halting in midair. "And where's the little girl?" he said, not looking at the others present.

"At Bento's. We'll decide what to do later, father," Antônia answered.

Miguel arrived, without Sílvia. He preferred to keep his own company. He looked well groomed now, just out of the bathtub. Only his red, swollen eyes betrayed that he had been weeping. He immediately asked about his mother, whether they'd called the doctor. He made as if to go see her.

"Don't go up, Miguel. She doesn't want to see anybody, not even Father," Antônia said.

Bento entered the room. "Don't worry, father. We'll take over. Breta's quite all right there at my place. You must rest now, sir."

"And what about Venâncio, where did he go off to?" Madruga shot back, visibly irritated.

"He went with Tobias, who's looking after him. We must care for the living," Bento answered sharply.

Madruga eyed him sternly. "Nobody's died in this house, you hear?" This thundered in a furious tone of voice.

Bento apologized. He had only been trying to help. Moreover, they were all deeply distressed. They loved Esperança, after all, and it would take time to get over the loss of her.

"What do you know about Esperança?" Miguel shouted wildly at his brother.

Antônia tried to intervene. "Do calm down. This is no time for arguments."

With apparent serenity, Madruga's gaze swept the room, eyeing each of his children.

"I've lost my daughter forever. I shall take this pain to my grave with me. From today on, I shall never utter her name again. And not because I do not think of her. But whatever I might say will not express my feelings and my hurt. Nor death bury certain griefs. Speak for me, weep for me, all of you, from this day forward. Now leave me in peace."

Madruga delivered these final remarks in a slow, deliberate voice. He turned back to his plate and went on feeding himself. No one dared answer. Miguel buried his head in his arms crossed on the table. The telephone rang in the other room. The accursed telephone that had brought him the news of Esperança's death, along with an urgent summons to the Miguel Couto Hospital to take the necessary steps. As the sound of that bell struck home, Miguel trembled. There came to him the memory of Esperança climbing the mango tree in the old house in Tijuca. She looked like a monkey scrambling to reach the last branch. From which, victory hers, she made faces at him, laughed at him, as he came following after.

"That's not fair, Esperança. You began climbing before I did."

"I always beat you, silly."

He answered in a fury. "You're the one who wins now, but in the future I'll be the one. Don't forget that girls always lose."

And before Miguel could see what effect his words had had, Esperança raced down, turned her back on him, and ran off toward the house. She paid no attention when he called.

"Please answer, Esperança. Say something."

"I have nothing to say to you. Didn't you say you'll always beat me? No matter what I do? Well then, leave me alone now. I'll take my fate in my own hands. I'm the one who'll decide what becomes of me."

"Telephone, Doctor Miguel. A call from your house. Dona Sílvia."

Miguel rose to his feet slowly, his body feeling like a dead weight. He listened distractedly. Sílvia was asking him to come home. She was in need of his company. Miguel promised her nothing. Where could life be hiding so he could go chasing after it?

"Is everything all right?" Antônia asked when he came back.

"Don't worry, Antônia, nobody's going to die in the next few years." He did not hide his impatience.

"I'm your sister too, don't forget. But I don't even know why I mention it. You never cared about me."

Madruga was annoyed. "Aren't you going to leave me in peace even now?"

"And who's going to leave Esperança in peace?" Miguel challenged him.

"What do you mean by that, young man?" Madruga felt he was treading on treacherous ground, about to swallow all of them.

"Someone's responsible for Esperança's death," and he looked Madruga straight in the eye, thrusting his chest out, ready to fight. It would do him good.

Bento appealed to them to drop the touchy subject. To avoid this emotional wear and tear; they were all still alive and kicking. Madruga paid no attention. Miguel was the only one he cared about now.

"Nobody's responsible for my daughter's destiny. Not even Esperança herself. Did anyone consult her before she died?"

"Why, father, Esperança's life was hell. A hell we all made. You in particular contributed to making her life miserable."

"That's a lie. How dare you say a thing like that to me! And what did you ever do for her? Nothing. Your one thought was to fight tooth and nail for your own house, your own marriage, your own body, your own carousing. As for me, I acted in accordance with my conscience, with what needed to be done. And furthermore, I'm the one who's responsible for my house."

"That's exactly it, father. You keep answering for each one of us. You were the one who invented a false image for each of your children, and an impossible path to follow. And woe to anybody who failed to come up to the mark. And since Esperança dared stand up to you, dared disobey your orders, she was severely punished."

"Shut your mouth. I forbid you to say one word."

"Come and make me," Miguel said, wild-eyed, beside himself.

Madruga came at him. A tiger, paw upraised, sharp-clawed, about to cuff him hard. The two of them were yelling like bloodthirsty samurai swordsmen. Bento strode over to the two men, however, reaching their side just in time to step between them. To lock hands with his father.

"No, father, not today. The day Esperança was buried," Bento said, fighting against Madruga's heavy body hurtling forward.

Miguel insisted on getting in one last shot. "And what better day to settle accounts!" he roared in a choked voice, his face livid. "What better day, while the corpse is still warm, still faithful to the picture we have of Esperança," trampling the words underfoot so as to provoke his father. Anxious to be beaten, unable to live a moment longer without his father's hard cuff.

Bento was joining battle with Madruga, holding his arm. Till finally he let him go. Madruga stood there with his hand upraised, in a white-hot rage. That son of his deserved a severe lesson. He needed to mark his face, so he would never come into his presence again without remembering the punishment he'd suffered. But looking closely at Miguel's face now, he glimpsed on it the tears that his words, so violent at first, had not allowed him to see. Hatred for his son gradually giving way to simultaneous fear and affection. Slowly, he let his arm fall to his side.

"Come on, father, go through with your gesture. Hit me in the face. Come on, don't hold back. Or do you lack the courage?"

Madruga flung himself into the easy chair. Exhausted, drained of all his strength. He felt himself to be in heavy seas. Would there be a single haven that would accommodate his anguish and his desire to survive? Minutes later he raised his eyes. There was Miguel, in despair, protected by the other children. That was his family. The only one he had left, and the only one he could count on having till the end of his days. It was for his children that he had built, with bloody bricks, a house reproduced a thousand times over through the years, as proof of his prestige. But could this be the America he'd dreamed of? And had he therefore also dreamed of Esperança's burial? Had the death of his daughter played its part in his ambition?

"I won't relieve your guilt, Miguel. You too sent my daughter to her end," Madruga said, leaning his head against the back of the easy chair.

Miguel rubbed his hand across his face as though his father had branded him. And what initials now marked his face, as a memento of this battle? He sat down beside Madruga. Bento and Antônia did likewise. There they sat, all idea of time gone now. Until it got dark and they retired to their respective houses, where on awakening they would face another day. The first day without the presence of Esperança.

*T*he children buzz about my head. They are insects with broken wings, bumping into the glass panes of the veranda. Their whispers echo, but I hear nothing. What they say touches my heart less and less. They move anxiously about the house, amid papers, looks, and words, which Eulália and I give them with the aim of improving their relationship with the earth. In addition to Brazil, they have inherited a relentless ambition. Hence they have frequently done each other harm. But their feelings, today, are contrary to mine. I am not responsible for acts that they perpetrate beneath the splendid canopies from which I am simply excluded.

My kingdom is limited to this easy chair, as old as I am. The scratches in the leather make it an abundant bosom, spurting milk. I won't allow them to reupholster it. It will be buried with me. I'm an ancient pharaoh, after all. Meanwhile Eulália is willfully preparing herself to die. Odete is witnessing her difficult and exceptional moments. She never leaves her room. Now and again, out of courtesy, habit, or grief, I knock on her door. Her sense of hearing still alert, Eulália opens her eyes. She gives me a searching look, and I too do not know what she is thinking.

There she is in her lace-trimmed nightdress, chaste, immaculate, despite the smell of death close at hand. She is pure and I still love her. This feeling goes back farther than any other that I have on this earth. This woman keeps me going. When they bury her, I shall follow her straightway. Who else do I have to fight with at the age of eighty? Did I foresee, when I left Sobreira, in the middle of the night, with Uncle Justo hurrying me along, that I would ruin America with my dream of saving up money and piling up bricks? Could I also have foreseen that because of my contempt for Venâncio's poverty and his puzzlement, life would punish such pride?

Bento approaches. He's strong and steady, a helmsman. He follows the agenda rather than consulting his heart. He regularly predicts storms, anticipates fate's moves. He knows that Eulália's death will set off the process of settling the estate. The first division of the shares between us will take place while I'm still alive. My fortune will be sucked dry by those hungry, friendly mouths.

"I know this is a painful moment, father, but there are certain steps we ought to take."

He is referring to the full power of attorney that I have from Eulália. Sober and serious, he wants me to appreciate his gestures and his well tailored suit. His glasses give him an air of respectability. But at what moment in Bento's life did there crystallize the perfection with which he now handles the business and pushes deals through? Can I have been the one who produced this exemplary, cultivated, sociable, respected, powerful creature?

Venâncio is pretending to be asleep, but Bento's efficiency does not escape him. The only son of mine who doesn't love him. But I'm unable to open Bento up with a scalpel and implant in his heart the feelings that life hasn't taught him. Nonetheless, the moment he enters the house he comes to me and kisses my hand. Without this benediction, he feels he's subject to the imprudent interference of the gods. He's like an old peasant fighting bad weather and irregular seasons, all the workings of an obscure divine will.

An impeccable order still reigns in this household. Visitors arrive and depart promptly. A cold formality. All they ask of fate is that Eulália live through the fateful nights of Friday and Saturday, so that nothing will interfere with their weekends. Since they'd have to attend the funeral. The children, myself, the family firm demand their presences. No excuses are accepted in this household.

Bento incisively suggests the signing of documents that will assure him and Miguel greater participation as stockholders in the various companies. Otherwise Luís Filho, an enemy who is all ears behind the door, will follow in his wife's wake. Above all else, Bento has his eye on the presidency.

"I'll be president of this holding company yet. That son-in-law of yours is incisive. He announces his plans with a smile that costs him several years of his life."

The grandchildren are now crossing swords. I don't regret this turn of events. They're tough, they'll put up a real battle. What difference does it make who wins out? Aren't all of them of my blood?

Antônia fears her fate. She sniffs out Bento's attitudes, dogs his footsteps. To keep her close at hand, he puts up with her trailing after him. Shut up in the dining room, the two of them scream and shout, and sometimes whisper. Held back by memories of the past, they still do not hate each other enough. The last remains of a feeling that their hearts still thrive on.

Bento assures her in a firm voice of the accuracy of the estate inventory. Besides, won't Father be there, very much alive, presiding over the initial settlement?

"Father doesn't care what happens to us. It's the same to him whether you come out on top or I do," Antônia said. Red-eyed, grief-stricken over Eulália and the exile to which Bento was eager to condemn her.

Both avoided the words that would make their differences eternal. The question was not attacked head on. They asked, then, that Miguel be summoned. In the presence of his brother and sister, Miguel does not take a definite stand. He limits himself to filtering the messages that Bento and Antônia send to each other, eliminating the cruel and ambiguous sentences.

In these last days, after Bento and Antônia called down evil upon each other's heads, Luís Filho has taken to inviting his brother-in-law to lunch.

"Yours is an inglorious battle, Bento. Nobody will ever change the old man's plans. Judging by the way he bares his teeth at the two of us, he's as much your enemy as mine. We can't depend on Madruga any longer. I suspect that he despises us so as not to despise himself."

After these lunches, Bento is pressed for time. With a vague look in his eye, he debates whether he should go see his mother or feel out my weakness. He thrusts papers at me.

"The only signature I need give you now is the one on my death sentence."

Eulália wasn't dead yet, and already I was obliged to fight friends and enemies alike. There was a curse on that fortune I made, I mused as they brought me my cornmeal porridge.

Venâncio was relieved when Bento went on home. In general, he forbore to analyze my children. He was afraid of hurting me or robbing me of part of my feelings. We both lived beneath the stigma of insecurity and doubt. Well supplied with a sort of poison that miraculously kept our friendship well balanced.

"They're grasping go-getters, every one of them. Was that what you wanted, Madruga?"

"I don't know. I don't know anything. Human fate is tragic. It sheds tears of gold and affection at the same time. They love me and they love my money. They never separate the one from the other."

"Don't fool yourself, Madruga. They're going to fight over every last corner of the house. The crystal ware, the silverware, the paintings. Even the dust on the furniture."

"Maybe they're not to blame. Could I have brought them up only for the moment that the estate is settled? To act like lions and tigers? Ah, Venâncio, was that what we crossed the Atlantic for?"

He said nothing. It all happened in a great hurry. Less than ten days before Eulália fell sick, I had made an unexpected request.

"Let me have the diary, Venâncio. The diary that's in Eulália's possession."

Taken aback, Venâncio stared at me, seeking an explanation. But what could I say? It was just that I was worried about what would finally happen to the diary. When Eulália's advanced age would no longer permit her to take proper care of its yellowed pages, about to be eaten away perhaps by silverfish. Though up until then, she had been a jealous guardian of the manuscripts, to the point of defending them as though the honor of the nation lay in those pages.

I never managed to find out what had happened after Venâncio left the hospital. If he, in fact, asked Eulália to return the diary, meeting with Eulália's refusal to grant his request. Or whether Eulália, on taking the initiative in the matter of its return, came face-to-face with a Venâncio determined not to take it back. Because he wanted Eulália's children to read it someday.

Concerned about the fate of the diary, I warned him once again. "Name an heir, Venâncio! Unless you want to burn it," I said, watching his reaction closely.

He shuddered. Horrified by the idea of destroying his sole legacy. He did his best to dissemble.

"With Eulália's consent, you may hand the diary over to anyone you please. Except Tobias. I don't want him to suffer on my account," Venâncio said.

On being consulted, Eulália refused at first. She loathed speaking of assets, the settling of estates, prime concerns in the family.

"The children act as though we'd already died," she complained.

"And are we still alive, do you think, Eulália?"

"More alive than ever. We're readying ourselves to render our souls unto the Creator."

The reading of the diary had a limited interest. Although it would help to shed light on our participation in the daily life of Brazil. When all was said and done, we were only humble rebels who had resolved to brave the Atlantic in a nutshell, our one aim being to dig up gold. Since it in no way suited our purposes to go extract the precious mineral from a South African field. Only America interested us.

Eulália had to remember that if Venâncio, weighed down by the bitterness of the Spanish Civil War, had not shirked the task of describing Brazil, though from an alien, disorganized perspective, if only because of the effects of his illness, it was not her place to deprive her children of that reading of it.

"Every word of this diary was written by us," he said to her, carried away by emotion.

In the living room, Eulália raised her head to see the sea. Not managing to bring it within her view, she rose, took a few steps. Then stopped.

"And lived by us as well." And, apparently resigned to whatever fate the diary would now be consigned to, she went on.

"And to whom is it to go? To Bento, Miguel, Tobias, the grandchildren, or the women of this house?"

"Breta is the sole heiress."

Eulália wearied of looking at the sea. She slowly left the room, heading for the stairway, certain that her husband would follow her. In the bedroom, she walked over to the wardrobe. With the door open, the six boxes could be seen on the shelf. All of them made of wood that had no doubt come from trees varying from jacaranda to oak. All of them, however, gifts that I had given her as the children came into the world.

Through the years, Eulália had taken it upon herself to safeguard those boxes that bore the names of the children. There was Antônia's box, Miguel's box, a box for all of them. Those possessions kept under lock and key. No one knew what they contained. Even I didn't know. Eulália trusted my discretion, regarded me as being incapable of forcing my way inside a universe where she had woven together the precarious story of her family.

She never revealed to us how she oriented herself during this search. In what corner of the house she had posted herself, in her eagerness to record those lives. So that in the future, when the children opened their respective boxes, identifying the material inside, they would exclaim, dumbfounded: There it is! Just what I've been looking for!

I once asked her whether it was odds and ends of her children, or her own life that was distributed among the six boxes, thus making it difficult to trace the precise development of the story, the exact sequence of events. She did not answer. Instead, she thanked me once again for the splendid presents, each in the form of a box.

Eulália never gave up her discreet task of collecting objects and papers of use for her purpose. A curious whim, inclining her toward abstraction and continually placing the appearance of the world in doubt.

How often I spoke her name without her hearing. At other times, on pointing out particular objects to her, she reproved me for my obsession with things, the value I attributed to them, moved as I was by the avid desire to amass a fortune.

Hence this eagerness to testify to the children's existence struck me as strange. As though they lacked direction and were more than a little uncertain. And as though their coming into possession of their own stories depended solely on their mother. Could this have been Eulália's intention? Or did she merely act in obedience to the memory of her father, who had implanted within her the certainty of eternity?

To Dom Miguel, it was always necessary to draw up an inventory of the facts that had gone before, scrutinize them, seek the testimony of neighbors. This was so because, all of us being rigorously linked to obscure zones of the past, it was essential to shed light on them. Hence, Dom Miguel spoke out and at the same time liked to listen. As he sat for hours sipping red wine, in the shade of a tree, taking advantage of the summer weather. He downed the wine in minute swallows, with an exaggerated air of irritation, as though sandpaper in his throat were keeping him from drinking it.

Everything about that man reflected a constant sense of obligation toward Galician history, of which he was unable to rid himself even at bedtime. He was a long time, therefore, in putting out the light, lying there with eyes wide open, unable to sleep, his face burning. In the living room, the same obsession was repeated. Eulália relieved the pressure at his temples with a wet cloth. His eyes thanked her for her sympathetic help. On her rare visits, he felt happy to have her in Sobreira. He enjoyed, at these times, the daughter who had left him for America.

"Where is America, now that those four centuries have gone by? And tell me, who are you? Hasn't it come time for all of you to admit that you've heaped failure upon failure? And to think that in the past you were a hope for the world! And now you're as lost as we Galicians are. Poor America! There's no one to explore it. From Europeans to Americans themselves. Natives who sell their souls at any price. All bent on consolidating an unfeeling culture, a conventional imagination, and still-rigid political patterns. And you don't even seem to care what happens to this sclerosed universe. You act like old men, incapable of inventing new formulas for living. Ah, Eulália, what illusion do all of you have left then? The daily illusion, perhaps, of overcoming misery and tedium?"

Dom Miguel perceived his daughter's discouragement. He hastened to soothe her troubled mind. Eulália shouldn't worry. Even in the face of such a sad picture, the individual could not be dismissed as a driving force.

"It takes only one man to change the direction of History. It is better, however, if there are many. It reduces the danger of tyranny."

Having restored Eulália's peace of mind, Dom Miguel again embarked upon a defense of the political autonomy of Galicia. He lost himself then in the labyrinths of a thousand tirelessly contrived stories. Giving each insignificant detail particular import as a symbol of freedom. Tracking it down, wherever it might be. In search of memories, data, information, he doggedly dug up the subsoil of Sobreira, consisting of cellars, wardrobe chests, trunks. And then polished this or that bit of a long-sought fact or memory till it gleamed.

Proud of such discoveries, he would proceed to the village square, allowing himself to be the object of appreciation. One Thursday, especially, he turned up looking particularly pleased. He then began to favor a group with an endless monologue. Until he suddenly consulted his watch, not concealing his anxiety. With not even a glance at the public fountain, which had always merited his special attention.

The church bell striking twelve confirmed that it was midday. The men around him were surprised that he kept looking repeatedly at the clock. A gesture contrary to the patience with which Dom Miguel always allowed the Galician weeks, years, and centuries to go drifting by. He now gave signs of being pressed for time; he had to leave them.

"Stay a while longer, Dom Miguel. You haven't gotten round to the other end of the story yet," a friend said.

"Ah, how I wish I could. I have an important appointment I mustn't miss. I can't be even one minute late."

He hurried off, not once turning his head. In the bedroom, he brushed his best suit and put it on. He combed his hair, straightened his tie, redid the laces of his black shoes. Climbing into bed then without wasting time. Before doing so, he arranged the pillow to suit him, as he had done since he was a little boy. Half an hour later, when they called him for lunch, he had stopped breathing. His body lay elegantly on the bed, the very picture of reconciliation. He had readied himself with rigorous care, not neglecting any of the details, in anticipation of his own funeral.

The news of his death reached us by cable. Eulália didn't want to open it. She was certain of what it said. She simply assumed a sober pose, her head erect. Only then did she veil her face with her hands intertwined.

"God did not want me to participate in his funeral ceremony," she proclaimed firmly, leaving the room.

She did not give way to tears till she had reached the bedroom. Dry choking sobs. For long moments she contemplated the picture of Dom Miguel that was on the chest of drawers. Clutching it to her bosom as she stroked the frame. She felt herself to be inside the church of Sobreira, among friends holding a wake over her father.

I went to Eulália. She was far away, inconsolable. In repeated gestures of anguish, she held the picture at a distance, then clasped it to her once again. Doubtless unreconciled to the idea of not accompanying him to his last resting place, remaining at the foot of the grave for some time. Once again she saw herself the prisoner of Brazil, where her children had been born, far from her dead father. The implacable Atlantic separating them, this time forever.

Odete brought the children to her. She did not really see them, or feel their caresses. The family had simply disappeared.

"We'll still go to Sobreira this year. And we'll leave flowers on Dom Miguel's tomb," I consoled her.

Taking no notice of what I was saying, Eulália asked for the day's paper. She leafed through it nervously, knowing what to look for. She stopped and read quickly. I could see her lips moving. She closed her eyes, motioning to us to leave her. She was about to go out with Odete.

"And where are you going, Eulália?"

She did not answer. I thought it prudent to wait for her in the living room. And when Eulália went through the gate, seeking to abandon us, I followed after. She gestured, ordered me firmly to stay behind. I did not obey her. She insisted, in a stern voice. A taxi stopped. I got in with her.

"To Caju Cemetery, please," Eulália murmured.

The funeral wreaths were laid out along the principal entrance, adjoining the chapel. Arm in arm with Eulália, Odete led her around persons and obstacles. I imitated Odete and supported Eulália. We went into the chapel. Several persons were standing around the coffin, their heads bowed, some weeping discreetly. The smell of burnt candles filled the air. Eulália drew back for an instant, transfigured by grief. Without a word between us, we approached the dead man. It seemed natural to me now to lament death, there where the dead are buried. In their own territory, in which one can mourn for them freely.

Intimidated at first, Eulália kept her distance from the coffin. Until finally she leaned over it. Inside lay a man with a mustache, an ash-gray tie, his face veiled by a wisp of tulle, his hands tied together with a handkerchief. On the other side, opposite us, a little maidservant was vigorously waving the flies away. It was hot. No one took any notice of Eulália, next to the dead man, weeping discreetly. Till she leaned over farther still, amid a soft, rhythmic, almost inaudible lament. Odete and I shielded her, like shadows denying others access to that act.

I looked at the dead man. He must have been about fifty. It was impossible to say for certain. Death transfigures everything, but never rejuvenates.

Suddenly, before anyone could stop her, Eulália began to stroke the dead man's face. A familiar, delicate gesture. Without breaking the rhythm of her lament. Nothing, in fact, constraining her.

"Ah, father, what terrible sorrow it is to lose you!" she recited.

Odete, inscrutable, observed her gestures. Eulália had no need to explain her sentiments or attitudes to her to keep her always favorably disposed. Fearful of the consequences, I decided to draw Eulália away. She was going too far. I did not have the courage. I looked about to determine the possible harm done. The corpse did not appear to have an owner. In all truth, we were offending no one by this intrusion.

Daylight was fading. It would soon be dark. We stayed on for an hour longer. The only ones in the chapel mourning the deceased.

"We'd best be on our way, Eulália. Each hour that goes by will be more painful," I murmured in her ear.

She concurred. A perfect alliance was forming between us. It had been a long time since we had attained so intimate a complicity. And for inexplicable reasons, at that moment I took on Xan's face.

She gave me the hand that had recently caressed the dead man. I took it in mine and led Eulália out into the fresh air. Odete followed after. We could breathe more easily now. Eulália clasped me in a strong embrace.

"Farewell, my father, until we meet again," she exclaimed in a choked voice.

As she leaned on my breast, I furnished her the warmth she sought in Dom Miguel.

"Until that day, daughter," I said to her as we breathed in the scent of the funeral wreaths scattered about the courtyard. That dead man enjoyed a certain prestige. From the gate, we saw the sun still shining. Life on the outside.

Back home, Esperança welcomed her mother. Eulália was returning to her children, accepting her responsibilities. A vague, hurt look in her eyes. The same look I recognized in old age, this time on a visit to the cemetery of Sobreira, a place familiar to us, to which we always went. Before her father's grave, Eulália contritely brought his memory back to life after so many years. Forgetting me, Brazil, the children. At that moment, there was no one who could have brought her back to reality, which, moreover, was becoming cold and impersonal for us, for we no longer put the same construction on it as before. Or was I mistaken? Did there in fact exist someone who firmly occupied her heart, outside of me, of Dom Miguel, of her Church? Someone to whom she devoted so secret a feeling that it forever contracted to a point?

"It's getting dark, Eulália. We're going to go back down so as not to slip on the stones."

The cemetery of Sobreira, like every village cemetery, had a desolate air. Its tombs, behind the church, were seldom opened for new occupants. Almost no one died nowadays in Sobreira. We ourselves, who had been born close to the stone walls, would be buried far from there. As though it were man's lot to come into this world in a thatched hut, only to die on the opposite side of his village, in common ground amid dull, dirty panes of glass.

Eulália was reluctant to leave the graveside. I insisted. After all, I had done everything I could to please her, and we had climbed up the slope so as to bow yet again to the memory of Dom Miguel. She relented at last and we slowly made our way along the stony path. We were old and unsteady on our feet, watching each step carefully. Eulália wanted to appreciate the scenery. The line of pine trees and the wild vegetation. The gorse bushes in particular. She smiled. This was her land, the haven of her dead. She breathed in the air and held it for a time. The time of memory. A brief flash only. It would very shortly be dark. I too looked at my wife and the land. And the houses of Sobreira, rough outlines whose shadows mingled. The rooftops in the distance, their colors fading. It was becoming difficult to assign names to them, to tell who they belonged to. How to locate the houses of Dom Miguel and Grandfather Xan? Did those houses still retain within their thick walls the heat of those men dead and gone for so many years now?

"We'll never come back, Madruga. This will be our last visit to Sobreira," Eulália said.

"What difference does it make now, Eulália? Spain died for us long ago."

And under my breath, I decreed the end of that country. So that the country of my children might rise, the victor at last.

Eulália leaned very gently on my arm, a caress I was unable to return. She was showing signs of exhaustion. I struggled, then, to help her. I too had grown old, the days were swiftly getting the better of us, the years robbing us of life and giving us nothing in return. Eulália was right. We would never again return to Sobreira. We had begun our farewells. But what to do in this land, when we were losing it at every step? Wear with pride in its lap its necklace, strung from the dead and vague memories?

On our return to Rio, the family joyously awaited us at the airport. Bento was all on edge, nervously consulting his watch, looking into his briefcase, checking a certain document. Rude to his mother. Refusing an invitation to lunch at the house. Breta had gotten all dressed up, spoken kind words to us. To distract Eulália, upset at Miguel's absence.

"And what about us, don't we count, mother?" This from Tobias, expansively, to attract Eulália's notice.

Bento asked for news of Sobreira. I did my best to reconstruct a land that they accept only out of consideration for us. I was nonetheless brief and concise. The remains of my memory lay in me and in no one else. Let the children pin the receipts for their own memories on their walls.

As we were drinking our coffee, Bento tried to dissuade Breta from taking off on her next trip, which coincided with our arrival.

"It won't be for long, grandfather. A couple of months at most. I'm taking my typewriter with me; I have work to do. I'll be back soon. In a way, it's as though I never went anywhere. I have the permanent feeling that I never leave this room."

Resigned to Breta's leaving, I found myself thinking all of a sudden that the earth was slipping through her sensitive hands. Or was she in the process of getting rid of a lover? Or going to meet him? I have never known what direction her heart was headed in. When would her restless, defiant sense of destiny succumb at last to the commanding voice of an unexpected neighbor?

Breta's only marriage lasted barely six months. At the end of which she closed the door behind her without asking her abandoned husband for a single personal object left behind. She disdained even the books and the wedding presents. To her way of thinking, they belonged to her husband, who had stayed behind to keep the home fires burning. Moreover, she did not want any souvenirs of a mistake.

"I won't marry again, grandfather. I'll be the one to decide who I take up with, and for how long. That way I cast and weigh anchor as I please. I'm the master aboard my ship now, and I beach it wherever I choose."

After lunch, the children straggled out one by one. Only Breta stayed on with me. A temporarily resigned face. Whom would she ever love without this act depriving her of air to breathe, of her fierce appetite for freedom?

"Come on, Breta, now that we're alone, tell me what's eating Miguel."

When I had my children at my side, I never counted them. They were expendable pieces. But if only one turned up missing that was sufficient reason for me to go searching for him among the beans, eager to keep him from falling into the boiling pot.

"The usual infatuations. Except that this time Sílvia caught him and swears she'll punish him. I have a feeling it's serious, grandfather."

Miguel turned up two days later, under pressure from Bento, who had demanded that he be present. He had circles under his eyes and looked exhausted. The three of us shut ourselves up in the study. Bento begged Miguel to get down to business again. Certain that his father would back him up. I didn't say a word, however. Bento maintained that the company ought not to suffer on account of Miguel's private troubles.

Miguel rose to his feet, paced up and down the study. He constituted a danger, with his sharp horns, his tongue dripping saliva, about to attack. Finally shouting at Bento to shut up. When it came to human passions, his brother was permanently disabled.

"All you think about is money, Bento. You know nothing about passion. Tell me, then, what's that treasure like that's taken the place of your balls?" he said in a fury, forgetting my presence. All of us characters in a spectacle that showed man's soul floating, shamefaced, in a pool of troubled waters.

Bento did not take offense. He cut Miguel short, demanding that he tone down his language. His brother's exasperation mattered little to him, as long as he fulfilled his duties. Moreover, as an adversary Luís Filho was quite enough for him.

"Must I add your name to the list of my enemies?" he concluded impassively. "You'd better watch your step, Miguel. Especially in these ticklish moments."

"If I understand you rightly, you're shouting to high heaven that we're under severe tension. Forever deciding on the fate of this damned company. When are we ever going to have a little peace?"

"Never, Miguel. What did you expect? To make a fortune without having a worry in the world? Well, learn once and for all to put up with the tensions that come from money or else give it up. As for your sexual obsessions, they're of no concern as long as they don't hurt business. But they're strictly forbidden access to our offices and this house. Don't ever forget that, Miguel," Bento said curtly, standing up to him without blinking an eye.

Miguel turned to me for help, surprised at my silence. I looked at my son and recoiled in terror. I suddenly saw traces of lust in Miguel's face, remains hauled here from a feverish, rumpled bed. I immediately averted my gaze from this imagined scene. I didn't want to know about it. Love has an ugly, deformed face outside of the territory where it has reached fulfillment. It cannot be paraded before strangers. Why should I share Miguel's passion, when his body is forbidden me? I couldn't bear to see my son reduced to the wretched intimate functions of his penis or his bowels. It is not my place to help him, rod in hand, with a hard-on, preparing to penetrate a woman. I am repelled, it is quite true, by his lust, his panting breath, the words that come leaping incoherently from his mouth like nervous frogs, amid the wild thrusts and parries of his tongue against another's.

My son's virility will always offend me. I do not want to see myself reflected in it, nor see Miguel perpetuate some of my acts. I forbid him to demand more intimate relations with me. I forbid the world to throw in my face a pleasure that I have not asked for my children, and from which I have long since been barred.

As Miguel insists on speaking, I find it hard to accept the thought that he might suddenly open his trousers fly, showing me his pointed, erect, insolent penis, expecting me to stroke it with my hand, to explain human intensity to him. And as he goes on talking, after Bento has left us, I reach the point of detesting him, just as at this moment I detest all the evolutionary stages of a life that seeks little by little to degrade us.

Miguel is suffering. He is practically sobbing. He hurt Sílvia on revealing to her a shameless passion that he could not manage to keep hidden. In the beginning, Sílvia pretended not to notice. She had taken Irene in as a houseguest out of affection for her and because of family ties. She would be staying with them for just a few days, before going on to Europe. Recently separated from her husband, Irene was going through a difficult time. Miguel appreciated her company, and fell into the habit of coming home earlier at night. The two of them sat up drinking till all hours. As Sílvia, going to bed early, left them by themselves. Perhaps it gave her a thrill of excitement to imagine herself in danger in her own home. Or did she refuse to see that Miguel was always tense when her woman friends were around?

Sílvia clung to her illusions till she surprised the two of them glued together, all sticky and slimy, in the bed in the guest room. Miguel and Irene making love, dripping with juices and sperm.

She promptly filled every corner of the house with goat and sheep bleats, chicken cackles, wolf howls. Doing her best to cover her face so as not to see how hurriedly Miguel leapt out of Irene's body. Her husband trembled all over, his member began to shrivel, the slaver of passion ran out of his mouth, all of him primed to reach the orgasm throttled to death by Sílvia's cry.

Without bothering to get dressed, Miguel ran after Sílvia, who slammed the bedroom door in his face. He went on in, apologizing. Sílvia fled, ordering him first to shut up, or else she'd make a scene in front of the children. And to Miguel's surprise, she didn't throw Irene out of the house the next day. Safeguarding her family's traditions perhaps. Or out of pride.

Irene disappeared, taking refuge in the guest room. Sílvia did not say a single word to Miguel when he came home from work. And that night they went off to bed as though they were enemies. Her eyes wide open, Sílvia focused her gaze on one point of the ceiling, concentrating her anguish on that epicenter. Where free-floating shadows formed of their own accord. Her memory endeavoring to furnish her, against her will, elements that would revive the scene that had taken place the night before. Till she was able to see, clearly, Miguel moving on top of Irene, in an effort to reach, again and again, the depths of that body with his member. The back-and-forth movement, spreading stubborn flames, scarcely allowing them to breathe. Pleasure forced them to scream, as they awaited the final piercing howl. Their bodies enjoying in anticipation the lassitude that would come over them after orgasm, indifferent to Sílvia, still watching, fascinated by her husband mounted atop the woman who had given him refuge in her warm cunt. The spectacle, moreover, of those bodies stitched together, giving off sweat and passion, had haunted Sílvia all day, to the point that she shut herself up in the bathroom to scream too, unable to stifle her torment.

Miguel tossed and turned endlessly in bed. And being afraid of disturbing Sílvia, he got up. He gave in to the temptation to have a cigarette. He lighted it with fumbling gestures. He was no longer in control of himself. He decided to leave the room. He went to the door, hesitating a second. Finally, clutching the door handle, he turned it, yet the door did not open. He fingered the lock, failed to find the key. He pushed hard against the door again, but it would not give.

Sílvia followed her husband's movements in the dark. As he paced up and down the spacious room. Close now to the Dutch table, looking for the key, which he did not find there. Miguel glanced mistrustfully toward the bed. He chose, however, to wait a moment, which seemed to him like an hour. He was having difficulty breathing. He began to scratch his chest, as though life were stored up only in that area. The hairs on his chest reminded him of the fine hair of Irene, there in the other room with a common wall to theirs. Whom he had not seen again since Sílvia's fateful shouts.

In the silence of the room, which had its effect on him and Sílvia, who perhaps was sleeping, he thought of Irene's body once he had undressed her. The woman's immediate reaction had been to glue herself voraciously to his skin, as though wanting to swallow him up. He needed to get her off him for a few moments so as to be in a position to lick her all over, to pick up the pulsations of that cunt on his tongue.

The shape and heat of Irene's sex haunted him all day. An enemy challenging him to eat it so as to rob it of energy. In the midst of his work in the office, his sensations were divided between his desire for Irene and Sílvia's cries, still echoing in his ears. He could not erase the expressions engraved upon that woman's face, her dull, anemic voice causing him to fall silent.

In the bedroom now, locked in, the memory of Irene came to him in violent spurts. He felt like kicking the door down, going to the woman, his next-door neighbor, spreading her legs, quartering her, thrusting himself into her generous orifice, capable of expanding so as to contain all of him, though he might knead it, squeeze it, and remove vital pieces of it, which would then regenerate in the form of a lizard.

He was certain, all of a sudden, that Sílvia was spying on him, dogging his footsteps. Having nothing more, in that case, to hide from her. Which made him all the more eager to seek Irene out, there so close by, surely waiting for him. If the two of them had been caught in Sílvia's dragnet, what more was there to fear? Why should they deprive themselves of the chance to make love?

"Where's the key, Sílvia?" Miguel's impersonal voice concealed his tension.

Sílvia knew her husband's daily habits when he was home. On awakening in the morning, for example, he went directly out onto the veranda. Like his father, Miguel enjoyed looking at the sea, the level of the tide, the Pedra da Gávea, the road to São Conrado. After doing his breathing exercises, he was ready for breakfast, consisting of fruits and cereals. At table, he spoke nonstop. Eager, nonetheless, to leave them.

She could likewise predict his movements that night. In a fit of madness, he would dash straight for Irene's room, not giving a damn now about a situation he'd already dismissed as hopeless. Only Eulália could dissuade him from such insane behavior. Making him see that he ought to think of his wife, his family, his reputation. And then compensate him, in the end, with her endless stories of Sobreira, the most renowned geographical spot on that family's map.

"The key, Sílvia." His voice, harsh now, grew louder with each word. "Where have you put it?"

"Come look for it," she said fearlessly, openly challenging him.

He went over to her. In the dark, Sílvia's body had become a more or less shapeless bulk. Miguel leaned over the bed, almost able to touch her. His wife's quickened breath smelled of chlorophyll.

"Where's the key?" his voice softer now, filtered through his fingers pressed against his lips. Containing himself so as not to hurt that hard, metallic woman with cunning weapons. Were they barbs? Or keen razors?

"You'll have to fight for that damned key," she said.

Miguel began to tremble. A fact that Sílvia took advantage of to rise to her feet, pushing him far away from the bed. They were undoubtedly confronting each other openly now. The pounding of their respective hearts audible to both at the same time. Both nearly overcome by mortal rage. Miguel tried to catch a glimpse of her amid the shadows as he vowed religiously to go every step of the way to ecstasy. To have Irene in his bed, to climb up the red-hot stones of her body flung wide open.

"The key is where it should always have been," she said aloud, visibly annoyed.

"In that case, turn the light on so I can find it." Miguel girded himself for battle.

"Turn it on yourself. You're the one who needs the key, not me. I can face you in the dark."

Whereupon Sílvia moved forward, as Miguel, retreating several steps, realized that he was afraid. At that moment, he was overcome by an unexpected feeling of shame, rising up through his thighs, then stiffening his backbone.

He had to make a countermove. In one quick leap, Miguel reached the switch, turning the light on. Only then did he look around the room in astonishment. Sílvia looked like a rabid bitch, poised to attack. Everything about her implied that he had best not come any closer. She would come out the winner of any fight. Her eyes, nearly half closed, could not be seen. Her attention concentrated on shielding with her hand an object suspended from a gold chain around her neck.

"Give me the key, Sílvia," he insisted again, sparring for time. Not knowing what to do.

She drew herself up arrogantly, leaving her arms hanging at her sides, so that her husband's eye could take in all of her. So that nothing would escape him.

Miguel shrank back in consternation. Before the vision of the key adorning Sílvia's breast, above her nightdress. As though the key were a religious amulet to which she clung in a moment of distress.

Sílvia laughed in his face. A lewd, satanic laugh, vilifying him. He felt a burning pain mount in his chest, the result of repeated vicious kicks. Somebody beating him up, taking advantage of his weakness. The thought of a heart attack came to him, a portent of death. Could this be death's way of announcing itself? Well, then, let death come, he thought vindictively, not afraid of confronting his wife now. Sílvia's intentions seemed clear to him. She was simply paying him back in kind for the humiliation suffered in her own house, turning the key into the crucifix his mother habitually wore around her white, transparent neck.

How often Eulália had begged him to come closer. Not to be afraid to kiss the crucifix resting on her bosom, symbolizing Christ. Intimidated, Miguel scrupulously complied with her order. There close to his mother, he could smell the delicate fragrance that came from her skin, though he could never tell whether it was the smell of herbs or of wild fruits. After kissing her crucifix, he hurriedly drew away from his mother's bosom. Assailed by doubts, anxieties. Could her religious feeling be that strong? Or did her emotion stem from feelings he did not know how to respond to properly?

In the face of Miguel's pallor, Sílvia was incisive. "You are not to leave this room before morning. Even though Irene is waiting for you in bed, like a perfumed whore, naked, going wild waiting for the two of you to make love to each other like alley cats. Or should I have said a couple of bitches? I couldn't care less that you're here at my side, suffering, hating me, unable to bear a moment longer the desire that draws you to Irene. I'm not letting you out of here today, or tomorrow either. I'm going to lock you in night after night, just so you'll beg me, claw my face. Till you kill me, if need be."

"Leave me in peace, Sílvia, let me go. Come on, give me the key," he shouted, beside himself.

Sílvia thrust out her bosom, offering herself to him, making it easier for him to tear the key from it.

"There is only one way to get the better of me. By force or by ceasing to come to this room and locking yourself inside when the clock strikes midnight. But I swear to you, Miguel, if you don't come back to this room, to be put under lock and key by me till Irene leaves, I won't ever receive you again. I forbid you to return to our house; you will no longer be my husband." And as she spoke, Sílvia leaned on the back of the bed, finally deciding to sit down. Her face had suddenly lost its combative look. As though she were again reconstructing the scenes in which Miguel and Irene had played the principal roles, and which threatened to repeat themselves endlessly.

Miguel followed her gaze, screwed now into the middle of the ceiling, and through Sílvia, he too managed to see the recent past in minute details that at the same time excited and exasperated him. He turned his face away from Sílvia, in an attempt to extinguish the vision of Irene in the bed, panting as impatiently as a steamboat.

Miguel walked away from Sílvia, consecrated by the cross that incarnated the devil. Or was it the mission of the key to protect him, thanks to an implacable circle of burning-hot coals? Reaching the other end of the room, he glued his ear to the wall, hoping to catch sounds coming from Irene's room. In her eagerness Irene might well have decided to begin, on her own body, the practices that kept her in a state of excitement, filled with wave upon wave of ecstasy, till he came, whereupon she would resume the lovemaking brutally interrupted the night before by the sobs emitted by Sílvia's rent guts.

He was certain that Irene was demanding his presence, sending him signs, unable to wait for him any longer. If he were to delay much longer, Irene would twiddle her fingers in her vagina, nervously and rhythmically, not neglecting her clitoris, both swollen now like a live, salted oyster.

Miguel hurled himself against the door. He clawed the wood, proclaiming his prisoner's status. Without the courage, however, to break down the door, shatter the windowpanes, mutilate Sílvia.

Sílvia went to her husband. She did nothing to stop him. She felt herself to be the spectator of a drama with delayed effects. Till finally she spoke, very close to his ear, in a calm voice, as though completely unconcerned.

"I hate your mad, uncontrolled rutting. But I prefer the spectacle of your despair to offering you your freedom. As long as you stay with me, you will be my prisoner. Don't forget."

Glued to the door, faint and pale, Miguel slowly slid down the wood, falling to his knees on the floor. "Give me the key, Sílvia," he murmured in a voiceless whisper, almost begging her for mercy.

Sílvia went back to bed, turned the light out. A grave silence hovered over them. Broken by Miguel's sobs. Five minutes later, he stole across the room, his footsteps thudding on the carpet. Heart-stopping anxiety as he reached the bedside. But giving in to his fatigue, Miguel settled down in bed. He felt like an intruder in the marriage bed. Not knowing what to do, what rights he had now. The memory of Irene again invading him. Like a blind man, he crawled across the mattress to his wife. Irene was waiting for him there. And he held her close with his right arm. Feeling herself held fast, Sílvia put up a fight. Miguel naturally wanted to steal the key from her. But by brushing against Miguel's hard member, in a rapid maneuver, she drove him off, immediately turning face downward in an attempt to protect her genitals from an invasion. And with uncontrolled indignation, she pounded the pillow with her fists again and again, as if pommeling Miguel's chest.

Miguel withdrew to his corner in confusion. Not helping his wife. He reached his hand down to his member, grabbing hold of it in a fury. He felt like punishing it, extracting the sap that was poisoning his life. Did his desire need to be that intense, to the point of debasing him? Once in contact, however, with that staff, now pitiful and shrunken, he immediately recalled the bittersweet memories that had been forthcoming from that sex organ and exalted him as a man. He was suddenly proud of possessing an appendage at once vigorous and contradictory, one that subjected him to dramatic embarrassments, peculiar, moreover, to the human condition. Moved at being a man and, as such, a fickle, deceiving, loving, emotional, sensitive, sharp-witted creature, he felt himself borne upon a raft in the maelstrom of the waves. The rough sea that could take him to the island of Love. Where he would better understand the circumstances appertaining to man. And unable to bear such emotion, Miguel began to cry.

"Forgive me, Sílvia, forgive me. I no longer know what I'm doing. Forgive me my boorishness, my abuse. Forgive me everything that need be forgiven. Please."

Absorbed in her own weeping muffled by the pillow, Sílvia had arched her back in a tense curve. In this position, she was following footprints of the past long since blurred by time. Without which, however, she would be unable to put the picture of her life together. And having, unexpectedly, found what she was looking for in this probing, she broke off weeping, turning in the dark to Miguel.

"Only Esperança would have done for you. To pacify that demoniacal sex of yours!" And her words came out wet with saliva and fury.

Eulália took Miguel's box out of the wardrobe chest, beneath my attentive gaze. It was distinguished from the other boxes by the dark veins lying along the surface of the wood.

"Can it be that Miguel remembers the details of his life?" Eulália said distractedly as she laid the box on the bed. She immediately brought another, without revealing the name of the child, standing there contemplating them.

"After the diary, I must take care of these boxes," she said ruefully. "At our age we don't have much time left. And there are no warnings."

"You're the only one who knows who they belong to," I reflected, with a certain envy.

"It's not easy to decide on my own what should become of the many lives shut up inside these boxes. But if I die first, promise you'll decide for me?"

Her sad eyes feared that I might fail in this mission, carried away by dark passions.

"No more of that, Eulália. Those boxes have already served their purpose. They're more ours now than they are the children's. What can bits and pieces of lives that we ourselves decided to preserve mean to them? We may well be choosing the least representative samples."

Eulália rose to her feet with difficulty. To go look for the diary. I never knew, in those years, where she kept it. Venâncio himself would not be able to locate it among her belongings. Venâncio, however, had not let a detail such as that concern him. His sole pride lay in having condemned me to exile, having kept me from reading a single page of his diary.

My presence embarrassed Eulália. I unintentionally robbed her of the passwords with which to open the doors of her delicate heart. But what final lesson had I still to learn? Feeling abashed, I left the room with faltering footsteps. Sensing that Eulália would immediately follow along after me. Regretting having mistrusted me. But what had Venâncio written to deserve such care? Had those manuscripts perhaps made Eulália suffer, feeling her friend's painful impulses as though they were her own?

In the living room, I was not pressed for time. We now had, Eulália and I, all eternity at our disposal. I was certain that she would take it upon herself to bring the diary personally. Since she had always been a prudent, punctual lady. But if she happened to be delayed, and I was no longer there to receive it, we had no lack of heirs fighting tooth and nail for the privilege of destroying every last trace of our passage on earth. Breta would be the only one to fight for the preservation of those remains.

Distracted by such thoughts, I did not notice when Eulália came into the room. The curtains half drawn, countless shadows huddled together in the corners, near the paintings in particular.

"Here the diary is. You may consign it to anyone you please. Except that you may not read it. Unless you consult Venâncio. Even though it's been with me, it belongs to him," Eulália said gravely, standing there. Reluctant to sit down beside me, avoiding sharing confidences.

The diary was wrapped in yellowed tissue paper, but Eulália had not sealed it. She was still standing there, not moving. I suspected she was waiting for my thanks. But I owed her nothing. Though Venâncio did; he was in her debt.

"It's too late now. Even if Venâncio asked me to, I wouldn't read it. What is there I still need to know in order to leave this life with my soul at peace? All I want is to bring a few dead people back to life in my poor memory. To have Xan at my side especially."

Eulália came over to me. Leaning on the back of my chair, she stroked my hair very gently. The unexpected gesture moved me. Eulália bent her body in the same way as I am now bowing before her, in bed, ready to die. Amid medicines and liquids brought by Odete, as the children come and go, I am offering her, then, the dubious solace of my presence. What more to say to her? Tell her that I shall soon follow her? And is the certainty of being able to count on eager followers enough for the person who is breathing his last?

Lying prostrate, she appeared to be sleeping. The doctor assures us that since she is weakened by her unshakable will to depart, it is a question of hours or days. Gently, she opens her eyes, turns them toward me.

"Ah, Madruga, you remember the months of November in Galicia," she suddenly said, amid sighs.

Bento held my arm. He helped me remember those months of constant rain, the wet afternoons, gradually growing shorter. The dramatic portents of winter on every hand. Eulália and I were moved in our adolescence by the pine needles, the chestnut leaves stirred by the north wind. In Sobreira the close formation of oaks, which from earliest times had witnessed Druid ceremonies, steeped in pagan fervor and ritualism, were an imposing sight.

November was the slack season. The peasants, resting after the harvest, had little work to do save to butcher the animals disemboweled at dawn, the entrails of which were immediately washed in the waters of the river, down by the mill. The wind, at this time of year, had already pitilessly stripped the trees bare. No one doubted that Saint Martin's summer, the golden season of feasting and merrymaking, was over.

Eulália motioned to me.

"How I miss Esperança! I'm sure she'll be the first to greet me."

And she waited for me to reward her with the name of her daughter, which had not crossed my lips since her death. Esperança had erected between the two of us a wall of silences, words cut short, suspicious glances. Eulália at times warily lamenting the loss of Esperança, I at times taking to my heels to avoid all show of emotion. How often I wanted to protest, but I chose instead to bite down hard on my tongue.

As I sat on the edge of the bed, we discreetly crossed swords. Eulália directed a feeble look my way. Thus offering me a bridge to cross, spanning obstacles and shattered memories.

That woman had always been generous. Nonetheless, holding my tongue, I did not speak my daughter's name. I had prison bars in my mouth, imbedded at the roots of my teeth, below the gums. I thought then, My god, help me to help this woman die. Unable to explain to myself the nature of that feeling that continually expurgated the name of Esperança.

Miguel knelt at the bedside. Holding tight to Eulália's hand, in a familiar gesture. And awaiting her wishes, he said unaffectedly, Ah, Esperança, my beloved sister, whom did I love more than you, or more than Mother?

Having given vent to his feelings, his face shone once more. He was almost smiling. Enjoying Esperança's warmth once again. And in the face of that sister restored to life, Miguel squeezed Eulália's fingers. She protested gently.

"Be careful, Miguel. Don't you see you're hurting Mother?" Antônia tried to pull him away.

Miguel resisted that sister, who was part of his parents' legacy. She was being handed down to him along with the furniture, the money, the stocks, the power. He had not been able to choose those of his blood freely. He looked at Antônia, who was aging, whereas Esperança remained eternally young. Death had preserved her youth. So that no sign of decline was visible, not a single wrinkle. Time had not snuffed out the dazzling brightness of her face.

Miguel irritated me. It seemed, at times, that Esperança took possession of him, speaking through his voice. Miguel bringing me, therefore, the persistent reminder of my daughter, which pursued me everywhere. Except in Breta. As though Esperança had held the passionate memory of herself in abeyance in her daughter. In this way allowing me to love Breta without fear, not needing to banish her from my presence. Esperança gave Breta over to my care, so that my granddaughter might emerge, piquant and powerful.

"Rest, Eulália. You mustn't let your emotions get away from you," I tried to calm her.

Ridiculous words, those! What good were they now? Did Eulália have any need to hoard her emotions in these last days of her life? And what was I in fact offering her, if I refused to speak the only name she was waiting to hear in order to die a peaceful death perhaps?

On leaving the bedroom, I inspected the scene one last time. Yes, the entire family was there, in battle array. Prepared to feed en bloc on my body, my possessions, my memory.

In the living room, I found Venâncio. Tobias had settled him in comfortably in Leblon. He had brought his clothes, whatever he needed. So as to stay with us, as Eulália's fate was being decided. He kept me company, almost without moving. On one of these afternoons, I informed him of Eulália's decision and mine to entrust the diary to Breta. Who better than our granddaughter to look after such belongings! Well versed in stories of human adventure and misadventure, both personally and professionally. Nothing, therefore, likely to escape her.

In the beginning, on receiving the diary, Breta was completely taken aback. She hadn't known that it existed. And above all that it had been in Eulália's keeping for so many years.

"The diary is yours, Breta. Like everything else that will be in your hands someday."

She clasped the diary tightly. She seemed deeply touched. She then leafed cautiously through the first pages. Not daring to read any further in my presence.

"It's as though it were your diary, grandfather. And Eulália's too. The diary of all the old people left behind in Galicia. And the diary of those Brazilians who never took up a pen to speak of their deeds."

I awaited Venâncio's reaction. He approved of the choice. Though he would rather have seen the diary destroyed. He couldn't fathom who could possibly be interested in the saga of a man who had been content as he grew older to garner trivial and shallow experiences.

"Life has strange whims, Madruga. It forced me to read thousands of books just to fool me into thinking I was acquiring knowledge. When I already knew at thirteen what I know today. We had an instinctive wisdom back then, crude yet at the same time more confident. Because we weren't forbidden to see the world."

Talking was a drain on Venâncio's strength. The hours dragged by and that suited Eulália perfectly, since she was never in any hurry to get anywhere on this earth. She always acted as if she'd already arrived where she was going. Even if she hadn't yet started. Or her stopping-off place didn't exist. The look in her eyes assuring me that wherever my ambition might lead me, I would in fact not get anywhere. It seemed to her that, while time went by, our lives dragged on and on, without point or purpose.

They kept bringing us fresh news of Eulália. There were signs about the house that she was still alive. Everything was back to normal after the initial scare. The children no longer wept as they had earlier. Even Miguel dried his tears and left.

I went upstairs to the dressing room, made over in the last year into my bedroom. In the shower, as the warm water pelted down, I carefully soaped myself all over, as though taking my leave of my body. The shower did me good. I then looked around in the wardrobe for some clothes that had long been stored inside. Taking my time doing all this.

On my way back to the living room, I went by Eulália's room, but I did not knock. I went very cautiously down the stairs. On the veranda, the children were taking in the sea breeze. Breta noticed nothing different about me. It was a question of time. Minutes later, she came out of her drowsy stupor.

"What's that you've got on, grandfather? Why are you in mourning?"

That black suit, made to order for the Mass on the seventh day after Esperança's death, had been carefully laid away over the years. As had the tie, the shoes, the hose. I never wanted to burn them or get rid of them. They would be of use to me on another occasion.

"What's wrong, father?" they all said. Annoyed at my acting this way. Almost throwing me to the wolves.

Miguel warned me of the dangers of such an attitude. And Venâncio prowled round my chair, coming within a hair of crossing swords with me. They were all adamant. Unable to understand that our ties were beginning to slacken as it came time for Eulália's departure. She was the one who had stitched us together with stout thread and an artful needle.

"If Eulália has made up her mind to die, why shouldn't I dress in mourning? You'd better get used to seeing me in black. Eulália herself will see me in these clothes."

Breta held my hands tightly in hers. I could see her eyes brimming with tears. She was giving way to such visible emotion for the first time in front of the family.

Can this really be necessary, grandfather? she seemed to be pleading.

Was she moved by her grandfather or by the discovery that she too bore death in her body?

"It's indispensable, Breta."

She drew away. Venâncio fixed his gaze resignedly upon some point in the ceiling. He distracted himself by stroking his leg with a slightly trembling hand. Perhaps he was trying out a gesture to prove to himself that he had the strength to be present at Eulália's farewell.

Luís Filho fought the hands of the clock with exemplary skill. Not one of the timepieces in his collection had ever failed him. Nor had he, whatever the circumstances, been unfaithful to them, in his obedience to schedules.

In ten minutes, Dom Mariano would receive him. Luís Filho having successfully stormed the inaccessible doors of the bishop's see in Brasília. To do so he had planned his trip to the capital down to the last detail. From his careful choice of a dark suit, worn relatively seldom, of a discreet tie, to the care he had taken to be several minutes ahead of time for the meeting also noted down in the bishop's appointment book. And as the secretary was about to announce him, he revealed, with particular pride, his full name, an illustrious one, as it happened, by way of the maternal line as by the paternal.

Bento had been opposed to Luís Filho's going to Brasília. Determined to undertake this mission himself. Madruga had not allowed himself to be swayed. Though Bento insisted, persuaded of his ability to solve the problems stemming from the gradual invasion, by squatters, of holdings that were part of the fazenda, situated on the banks of the Araguaia, belonging to the group. An invasion that had reached alarming levels, owing to the negligence of the administrators responsible for these holdings, and to the lack of interest on the part of management in drawing up a plan for agricultural use consistent with the urgent needs of the region. As a consequence of this de facto situation, it had become impossible to evict the squatters without the intervention of federal forces or of the groups involved.

Madruga immediately expressed his admiration for the adroitness with which the squatters, urged on by those in higher echelons, had acted. While at the same time voicing his severe disapproval of how management within his own group, in the hands of incompetents, had handled the affair.

"Since the day I came to America, I've always paid attention to business. And now the lot of you indulge in the luxury of throwing our patrimony out the window. Where will we end up if things go on this way?" he said angrily.

Refusing absolutely to let Bento be in charge of the negotiations. To deal with the intransigent power hierarchy on the other side or with the bishop of the Upper Araguaia himself, astutely remaining in the rear guard of the movement to expropriate the land. Or confront Dom Mariano, an eminent prelate of the modern Brazilian Church, a past master at settling fracases in camera, charged now by the minister of the Interior, in a discreet move, with lessening the pronounced differences between the bishop of the Upper Araguaia and the Madruga group.

"You studied under Santiago Dantas, but you failed to inherit his political genius," Madruga snapped, in retaliation for the trouble that Bento had caused him.

Bento did not answer back, however, though his father had wounded his feelings by questioning, in a moment of anger, his impeccable service record, the success with which he had been managing the various businesses, ever since his father had taken to holing up at home for longer and longer periods at a stretch. And, determined to overcome Madruga's resistance, he hid his resentment.

"Dom Mariano made it clear that the matter should be kept within the family. And not taken before the courts, at least not at this stage. And so, if I don't go, who will? Miguel refuses to. And Tobias is even less willing. He's sided, on principle, with the squatters. So where do we stand, father?"

Bento calmed down. His father couldn't replace him. Madruga, however, took his time before handing down his decision. When ordinarily he settled questions by firing off answers seemingly straight from the hip.

Bento pressed his point. "Ever since I took over the presidency, business has been booming. Isn't that enough to satisfy you, father?"

His forced smile did not pass unperceived by Madruga, who headed across the living room toward the veranda. With measured pace, following an inner rhythm. Yielding to a process that over the years had been eating it away, his body no longer responding as it once had. Finally, with a gesture, he signed that he was about to speak.

"I shall not do you the injustice of failing to recognize your merits. Even our adversaries confirm your high degree of competence. The fact remains, however, that thus far your only negotiations have been with the technocrats who have appeared on the scene since the Revolution. Heartless bastards, with neckties round their souls and their imaginations, tied with a good tight knot. And who suck the country dry like octopuses, governing by decree. Nobody knows where these people came from, who they are, what responsibility they will in fact assume for the future of Brazil. No, don't interrupt me, Bento."

Madruga rose to his feet once more, with deliberately exaggerated movements, which always irritated Tobias in particular, absent at that moment. "And nobody knows where they came from because they lack a clearly traceable history with which the country could identify itself. They are men with only the shakiest administrative experience, with the further disadvantage of never having been tested in the halls of Congress. Hence they have never reflected on the spirit of the law, whose practice can only be justified by service to the community. That's the truth of the matter, Bento. They've been our associates in countless undertakings, but you'll grant me that they're corrupt. Careless of the honor of Brazil, having apparently not even been born here. The worst of it is that they've succeeded in planting the roots of a recently developed consciousness, utterly devoid of moral and ethical resistance. A dangerous code, full of pitfalls. They have no scruples, Bento, and don't think twice about putting their interests above the idea of a nation. It was with that crop of bastards that your generation learned to negotiate, to get ahead, to pull strings. With the Church it's different. With two thousand years of political wisdom to fall back on, this institution has always given proof of great cleverness and a consummate ability to get around any and all obstacles that the State and society have placed in their way."

His father's lecture on morality annoyed Bento. He couldn't bear to listen to him a moment longer. And for the first time he interrupted him with a certain sharpness in his voice. "The clergy wasn't immune to corruption and collusion either, father. Or even to bribery. Perhaps they deal in coin that goes by some other name. I assure you, however, that it's currency of recognized value in any international market."

Madruga shot him a reproving look. Not for cutting him short, but for his unforgivable naïveté, for his inability to choose examples that fit the circumstances.

"It's a problem of language, Bento, and of the way language works. It's not a question of ethics. Your observation is puerile and provincial. That's not how bishops and great statesmen regard themselves. They are not bound by the usual canons. And that's what you've failed to understand. That's why you lack the tricks of rhetoric and the verbal flourishes needed to pit yourself against Dom Mariano's ancestral shrewdness. He's doubly shrewd, moreover. Because he's a son of the Church, and because he comes from a family that goes back to the Empire, at times pro-slavery, at times abolitionist. From the cradle, from the manor house, Dom Mariano and his family controlled the birth of Brazil. Nothing escaped them. They took an active role in all the political processes of Brazil. That's the sort of man you fancy you can stand up to. Do you think you can say the same thing about yourself?" he said ironically, wanting to put an end to the argument.

The question of land, a constant subject of Church councils, was of particular interest to Dom Mariano. He had publicly allied himself with the current of opinion favorable to the disinherited, who found themselves deprived of the minimum property needed to survive with dignity. In his public appearances, however, he left room for the possibility of dialogue with various social sectors. Thereby attaining immediate access to the top authorities in Brasília. The minister himself had appealed to Dom Mariano's good sense, subtly pleading in favor of the lands belonging to the Madruga group, urging that a solution be found. Taking the liberty of informing him then that the family had approved of his name being put forward as mediator, in view of his powerful moral authority. In the minister's presence, Dom Mariano agreed to serve in that capacity, setting the meeting for Friday.

"Very well, then, father. If I don't go, who will go in my place?" Bento could scarcely control his disappointment.

Madruga had recovered his patience. He gave his son a kindly look. "I repeat that you're perfect for verbal tussles with this modern Brazil that's sprung from a dubious dungheap. But the battle right now requires a Brazilian whose lineage is the equivalent of the bishop's. So that the two factions, face to face, their jaws twitching, pit themselves against each other without apparent bloodshed. Aristocrats are accustomed to communicating in whispers so that their subordinates will not hear their secrets and their strategies. But don't get the idea that they control themselves merely because they're well bred. They're even cruder than we are. They just don't admit that they're betraying their own traditions, always more powerful than ideologies. Hence they're cynical and they're smart. Simply because time is on their side, inasmuch as they believe in dynasties, in inherited rank. Hence the family ties between them never dissolve, nor their family trees disappear. They know exactly where they came from and where they should go to safeguard their privileges. And when they suffer casualties or losses, they trust in the seesaw of History, ever prompt to correct deviations. And that's the family that Dom Mariano belongs to."

"You still haven't mentioned the name," Bento persisted, in a low voice, all but drooling at the mouth. "Say the name, father. Who's going to represent us?"

"Is there any need after that explanation?" Madruga wearily took up the gauntlet.

"Yes, there is. It's up to you and not to me to say the name," and he served himself a straight whisky with trembling hands.

"As you like. Luís Filho is our man. He's to see Dom Mariano next Friday. Under the aegis of the Brazilian episcopate, and with the blessing of Rome. And mine as well."

After this effort, Madruga let his attention wander, forgetting Bento. Mindful of the fact that he had come from far away, from almost the beginning of the century. And bearing on his heart a shield with the figure of a lion, representing boldness, with an olive branch, meant to attest to his perseverance, and an eye, through which he was duty-bound to examine various simultaneous realities, without thereby losing sight of his central goals.

His fortune had not been a matter of chance. Behind it lay work, above all the mark or the stigma of intelligence, that terrible breath of air that relentlessly sweeps the earth above and beyond all its borders. How many nights he had gotten through, by shutting himself up in his study to read. Or by doing accounts. He was not afraid of standing up to his children. The one thing they beat him at was technical, theoretical questions.

"Luís Filho isn't one of the family," Bento shot back, as an argument.

"He's in our service, through Antônia. And he has what's of interest to us. He's an elegant cynic, with four hundred years of Brazil in his soul and his penis. He's dominated and corrupted this country for centuries. It wasn't we recent immigrants who brought about this state of affairs. There hasn't been time enough to get our paws on the Brazilian spirit and destroy it. Though we may get there yet. Meanwhile, Dom Mariano and Luís Filho are the beasts of the Apocalypse as far as Brazil is concerned. Never forget that, Bento, if you really want to take over this country."

Luís Filho took a discreet peek at his watch.

It reassured him to have it there beneath the cuff of his English shirt. Dom Mariano liked timepieces too. Before going off to Brasília, Luís Filho had informed himself as to the prelate's tastes. A frugal man, indifferent to pomp and circumstance. But proud of resisting worldly temptations.

At ten on the dot, Luís Filho stepped through the door. Dom Mariano greeted him gravely, crossing the room to meet him. Tall and thin, his long fingers commanding gestures of extreme elegance, as though he had carefully fitted them into his meticulously framed sentences. He affected, however, not to notice the striking figure he cut. Luís Filho observed the caution with which the bishop escorted him through the vast room. Pointing out to him the view of Brasília from the window. The wondrous brightness of the capital made the public ministries in particular stand out, symmetrically aligned, unfailing indicators of Power. The bishop then halted before a commode from Minas, in the top drawer of which, carefully opened, lay part of his collection of watches, in sharp contrast with the pale green velvet serving as a lining.

"Even if there weren't a single item on our agenda, we would have a great deal to talk about, Doctor Luís Filho," he said, immediately demonstrating his awareness of his visitor's predilection for watches. The latter was said to possess watches worthy of figuring with distinction in international catalogues.

Dom Mariano went on slowly. "In my family, we have long devoted ourselves to admiring time." He paused for a few moments, observing Luís Filho, who in turn was appreciating his collection. "And how to prove our esteem and our perplexity as regards time if not by preserving, among our belongings, a number of these pieces, which, naturally, are not comparable to a single one of those that make up the magnificent collection of the Emperor Maximiano," and he made an imperceptible gesture in the direction of his interlocutor.

Luís Filho felt called upon to speak. The dialogue must be begun without a single false move. "I am pleased to note, Your Excellency, that our families, over several generations, have had an appreciation of time, while not forgetting the merits of great craftsmen. Those creatures with magic hands who, in obedience to irresistible caprices, perfected the most dramatic object that human inventiveness has ever conceived. And because this inventiveness spans birth and death, and the other stages of man, I often ask myself, Your Excellency, whether watchmaking is not a work possessed of a spiritual end. Whether in this effort, on the part of all of us, to translate time correctly, there is not a mystical perspective which escapes the limited dimensions of a simple object."

The last words of Luís Filho's sentence coincided with the offer of a chair, directly in front of the bishop's table. So that each might scrutinize the other without the least impediment.

After trying out his own seat, Dom Mariano went over to the commode housing the watches and appeared to be concentrating on a detail imperceptible to Luís Filho, returning immediately to take up the subject under discussion once again. And as though he were eager to make amends for an attitude that might appear to be a mark of discourtesy in men of their ilk, he hastened to applaud the concepts just formulated by Luís Filho.

"The invention of the watch, above all the watch with a mechanical movement, revolutionized the concept of time. In temporal terms, naturally, as regards the life of man on Earth. Inasmuch as time, by comparison with the conception we have of God, is imperceptibly consumed, thereby completely disobeying human laws. I am even of the opinion that a watch is simply a modest pendulum, with no future within the divine perspective. If, let us say, it is up to the watch to keep track of a time that never overlooks a single human minute, by the same token it is up to man to disdain those pleasant minutes that thus accrue in his favor, when balanced against all of eternity. Doesn't it seem to you to be an absurdity, however, for men of faith, such as ourselves, to devote ourselves to preserving such rare objects?" Firmly seated in their respective chairs, Dom Mariano and Luís Filho pondered their pronouncements with extreme reserve, their eyes fixed on each other.

"It's an apparent contradiction, but not an essential one, Dom Mariano. For what other instrument save a watch marks the very time that makes us grow older and destroys our pride, revealing perfectly the misery of our human condition?"

Luís Filho downed the first swallow of the coffee brought on a silver tray by the uniformed servant. Rapidly reviewing the course of the conversation. He sensed that in the next minute, as indicated by his wristwatch, Dom Mariano would establish the rules of the reality that would govern them after the coffee break.

To his surprise, the bishop put off beginning the fray, taking out of his pocket a watch of exquisite workmanship, dating perhaps from the twelfth century. Luís Filho examined the numerals and the hands, covered by an enamel lid with, as a central motif, Cleopatra reaching her arm out for the serpent brought to her in a basket of figs, sneaked past the Roman guards by her faithful Charmian.

The watch was nestling now in the palm of the bishop's hand. The delicate workmanship of the piece fascinated Luís Filho. The rich detail revealed the vigilant Roman, standing apart from the scene, on that clear long-ago day, as bright as the one in Brasília, and the draperies falling behind the canopy, on which the languorous body of the queen reclined. There was nothing to indicate the tension of her imminent death.

Knowing that he was being watched, Luís Filho returned the bishop's look of unqualified admiration for the richness of the piece. He perceived, however, that mere appreciation was not sufficient. The prelate was asking him for an explanation as to why Cleopatra should be the central motif of a watch worn permanently by a Brazilian bishop.

"Each century erects its own mental architecture, naturally. Hence I see in the scene an allusion to the haughty indifference with which the queen confronted death. Moreover, I personally have never regarded Cleopatra as being bent upon dominating men through passion, or given to Roman sentiments, and a prisoner of them, as history has always led us to believe. The queen was scarcely lascivious. If that were a true picture of her, she would not have fought for the administrative autonomy of her country," Luís Filho said, carefully noting the effect of his words on the bishop. "By her last gesture, the queen endeavored to overcome the stringent limits of history and her own power, both of them restricting her progress. Rather than lose Egypt, which was her dignity and even her right to luxury, she deemed it more worthwhile to sacrifice her life. Trusting in the judgment of time, which in the end rules human destinies. And here we are, even today, discussing a queen who would have been fatally buried on the flood plains of history had it not been for her last gesture of defiance toward Roman power. And no other place, moreover, better lends itself to a reflection on Power than Brasília, where we now find ourselves, the seat of the most absolute power ever known in Brazil, since colonization."

"Of temporal power, if you will allow me to correct you, Doctor Luís Filho." The bishop smiled for the first time.

Luís Filho crossed his legs, straightening the crease in his trousers. Discreet, unhurried attitudes. He left it to the bishop to set the rhythm of the conversation, which he intended to follow.

"Forever temporal, Your Excellency. The watch again underscores our transitoriness."

"Apropos of time, Doctor Luís, I suggest a trip to contemporary Brazil. Or perhaps an archaic Brazil?" Dom Mariano pondered, the smile gone. Impenetrable now, the discrete veins on his forehead showing.

"It would be an honor to travel in your company, Your Excellency. And in that case, we could not do better than to visit rural Brazil. The fazenda in the Upper Araguaia, for example, at which we can put up for a few hours," Luís Filho hastened to say, certain he was offering the prelate the courtesy due him by being the first to bring up the delicate subject. And before Dom Mariano could answer, which would have been contrary to his predictions, inasmuch as the least sign of facial contraction had been banished from the bishop's countenance, now motionless, Luís Filho bent forward across the table with a certain persuasive grace.

He made a point of recognizing, without question, as part of his speech now being delivered, the prelate's broad authority over any subject pertaining to Brazil. His ecclesiastical career was more than familiar to him, in particular the humanistic imprints that he had long been leaving on great national questions, so that in his company now, he would have the opportunity to review ideas for which he had fought in the past, and which might prove, in the course of this meeting, to be inflexibly anachronistic.

The fact was that they were both confronted with a situation bound to engender discord. Yet persuaded that by common consensus they could clear up the resulting conflicts of the parties involved. The fazenda in question had long belonged to an enterprise of a family nature, which had expanded in various sectors, thereby engendering wealth and jobs. Through an excess of zeal in its undertakings, it had unfortunately neglected to draw up plans for agricultural development in the Upper Araguaia. Especially since it was important not to lose sight of the fact that such an area required investments that were not likely to pay off in the short run. Moreover, the type of cultivation that those lands would need had to be given careful consideration. For this reason alone the soil could not be put to immediate use to fulfill social aims. And they had already been thinking along these lines when the recent incidents had taken place. The lands invaded by the squatters in systematic fashion, it being evident that they were obeying a superior authority. Despite the emergency situation, at no point in time had the Madruga group thought of having recourse to federal forces or resorting to violence. Instead, they proposed to the squatters a formula of compensation for the labor invested by them there, in tacit recognition of certain rights. And the agreement was taking shape satisfactorily, when the bishop of Goiás, Dom Antônio, persuaded them to demand that the owners turn over half the lands to them, with the title deeds officially recorded, without the levying of taxes and fees on the beneficiaries of the donation. A demand regarded as nonnegotiable on the part of the company, which led to the suspension of the dialogue, threatening to bring on unwanted federal intervention in the case.

"In view of this impasse, we have come to Your Excellency in the hope of reaching, through your wisdom, a fair social agreement." Luís Filho delivered these words as though he were scanning verse in Latin. He was fond of using certain rhetorical devices, at once pleasing and anachronistic, when he spoke, as a pretext for embroidering upon timeless sentiments.

Discreetly, Dom Mariano glanced back and forth from his watch to the door. At that moment, there came a knock. With an air of satisfaction, as though everything were turning out exactly as he wished, Dom Mariano made a point of answering the door himself. Before doing so, however, he turned to Luís Filho, who, disconcerted, did not understand the reasons for that interruption.

"We were so absorbed in our examination of time that I didn't have a minute to inform you of the visit of Dom Antônio, our bishop of Goiás. I am certain that you will approve of his presence among us."

Luís Filho's heart shrank. An unexpected hot flash rose to his head, threatening to spread throughout his body, immobilizing him. Realizing the risk to himself, he promptly relieved the tension by doing discreet exercises, flexing his legs underneath the table. He did this several times, till his blood flowed freely once more. Those minutes that Dom Mariano had given him, while occupied in receiving his fellow bishop, had been his salvation. He was forced to recognize the skill with which Dom Mariano had placed his barbs, doing everything possible so that they would not cause his adversary pain. Luís Filho identified with the prelate. He too had been brought up not to yield to an enemy's pleas. He had chosen to pit himself against a man of his class. Both would know how to behave in the face of sudden storms.

Recovered now, Luís Filho awaited the usual introductions. He knelt swiftly before the bishop to kiss his ring, affixed to a solid worker's hand. He was a thickset man with a pronounced bald spot, older than Dom Mariano.

"A great pleasure, Your Excellency. We have been eager to meet Bishop Dom Antônio, so zealous in the spiritual defense of his prelacy," Luís Filho said, looking at Dom Mariano out of the corner of his eye.

As they seated themselves, Luís Filho rapidly reviewed events. No doubt he had good reason to reproach himself for not noticing another chair next to his, a clear hint that a third party to the discussion might well appear.

Dom Mariano welcomed them, praising their Christian spirit, beneath whose auspices they would seek the necessary solutions. He had before him Luís Filho and Bishop Dom Antônio, side by side now. He appeared to be pleased to have them under his strict surveillance.

Dom Antônio, for his part, speaking in a tiny voice that could scarcely be heard, promptly placed himself under his guard. Eager to de-contaminate the atmosphere, he chose him as referee. Thereby protecting the interests of his prelacy.

The exchange of politenesses threatened to go on for some time, as meanwhile Luís Filho hesitated to offer his testimony, he being in point of fact the injured party. Aware of the tactful rules of the game, Luís Filho again rehearsed, before Dom Antônio, what he had already said concerning the fazenda. Then finally he declared himself in a position to absorb serious losses on condition that they did not encroach upon the inalienable right of ownership. He was pleased to inform them at this time of the interest that the intelligence community, the highest echelon in the table of organization, was taking in the case. To the point of convincing them that Brasília would refuse unconditionally to put up with social convulsions resulting from insoluble differences. For that very reason the Madruga group, out of gratitude to the authorities, was firmly resolved to spare them difficulties of any sort, including those of a legal order, which invariably ended up being exploited by the foreign press, ever eager to blacken the image of Brazil.

Luís Filho expatiated without interruption. His listeners wearing masks so that their faces would not be visible. Dom Antônio, however, a simple sort from the country, appeared to be vulnerable to these contradances in camera. For his eyes soon tired, and blinked now, betraying his tension. To get his second wind, the bishop looked to Dom Mariano to back him up. Dom Mariano did not say a word, however, so that not even his bishop would gain advantages thanks to his inattentiveness.

With an eye to his own strategy, Dom Mariano divided his attention between the two men, so that the two of them would fight over him and dissipate their energy in this additional battle. Weaving with certain gestures and words a net ready and waiting to ensnare anyone before it at the slightest careless move.

Thin and ascetic, that man would condemn anyone who delved into his soul. His emotions apparently circulating in peripheral areas, under severe control. In the service of the Church, Dom Mariano served his own family, an almost natural prolongation. In Brazil, four hundred years before, his family had actively participated in memorable civic campaigns. From the territorial expansion of the country, to the long period of the Monarchy, followed by the Republic. Not to mention the successive revolutions, which had constantly altered the physiognomy of Brazil. This family invariably displaying a perfect sense of opportunity for conciliatory virtues, as the bishop himself chose to emphasize.

Luís Filho fell silent. So as to give Dom Mariano the chance to lean away from the back of the imposing chair. Though his elbows were leaning on the table, this did not keep him from making use of his hands, placing one palm against the other from time to time. And he looked so sorrowful that he suddenly seemed an old man. Determined to take on the appearance of age in order to justify the belief that an ancient carcass better fitted the image of the Church linked to times immemorial. An undoubtedly atemporal Church, which viewed historical records as being fated to pass through the filter of her implacable perpetuity and tradition.

"Your presence, Doctor Luís Filho, meets with the permanent eagerness of the Church to deepen its ties with all sectors of society. The shepherd's voice makes itself heard in all human circumstances. The pastoral activity of the Church has never kept itself apart from man's sorrows and joys. Wherever God's creature is, there the Church is found to imprint an ethical dimension upon that to which the social seeks to give expression. Hence, since the agrarian question is a fundamental matter for the life of the Christian of our day, we pledge our entire support in this regard. The drama of the squatter, that disinherited victim of fate, touches our heart and our conscience. It is our opinion that a reformulation of agrarian policy is urgent, in order that conflicts of this sort may be avoided. Brazilian society cannot continue to be insensitive to those moral duties. And less still the Church, which is responsible for the salvation of the soul, threatened with being led astray beneath the deluge of wretchedness. Faithful, then, to this social doctrine, at no time has it been the intention of our beloved brother Dom Antônio, bishop of Goiás, to go beyond or to abuse the duties of his office in his dealings with the most wretched Christians of Brazilian society. I am cognizant of the fact that he has confined himself to hearing, as an exemplary case, those parties who regarded themselves as having been injured and who in their despair had no one else to turn to except his spiritual authority. He naturally calmed the tempers of the squatters, so that they might reflect on the actual situation as men in a quite different state of mind. On no account did he suggest concrete demands to them that they had not already thought of making. In the final analysis, the squatters are lambs of God, and as such possessed of intelligence and common sense. Thanks, then, to the intercession of Dom Antônio, along with the squatters and your administrators, a tragedy has been avoided. We are thus indebted to him for this service lent."

Dom Mariano again leaned back against the jacaranda-wood chair, the handiwork of a master joiner. He raised his glass of water to his lips and swallowed a few drops. He then launched forth again.

"You may be certain, Doctor Luís Filho, that there is no need for the Church to depart from its spiritual trajectory, even if moved to do so by temporary circumstances. What is incumbent upon it is to exercise the virtue of preserving the dignity of man, should this dignity be injured or impugned."

Luís Filho was not surprised. He was well acquainted with the ideological posture of a certain faction of the Church, which had decided to opt for political militancy in social affairs. Though disguising the import of his speech, endeavoring to varnish it over with a strictly spiritual content, Dom Mariano was visibly endeavoring to protect his position as adjudicator, freeing it of suspicion. Taking care, nonetheless, not to undercut Dom Antônio's authority.

As Dom Mariano spoke his last words on the subject, Luís Filho realized immediately that the losses would far surpass what the firm had projected. They had studied the situation carefully, from various angles. It was definitely not in their interest to be involved in legal proceedings dependent upon a system of justice close to paralysis, which took years to deliver an opinion, as meanwhile, amid deaths and acts of violence, the squatters would end up making further inroads into lands that today were free and clear. Not to mention the fact that the board of directors was eager to preserve the image of the Madruga company as a Brazilian group serving the country and sensitive to the social changes demanded by changing times.

Luís Filho was counting on the delicate situation of the Church, obliged to take a stand on an inflammatory matter, practically establishing an internal body of laws, which would apply to the case at hand and to similar ones that would arise. By the terms of which the Church would of necessity improve the lot of the squatters, yet not strike a direct blow at the institution of private property. Not losing sight of its solid, compact hierarchical structures, on which it depended for the impeccable training of its leadership, as well as its diverse applications of social doctrine, at present the subject of violent contention within the Church.

Through his family upbringing, Luís Filho had learned to carry on a debate without losing heart, even when he found himself defeated by his opponent's argument. Examining more closely what might appear at times to be insignificant. Inasmuch as obscure material was often of great value for the light it shed on aspects of a question that would come to the surface only in the form of shadows and veiled hints. Dom Mariano, for example, undoubtedly sided with the moderate wing of the Church, and yet he maneuvered with a sure hand among the radicals, frequently backing their arguments, so that as a consequence he had now earned their confidence. On the other hand, he cleverly avoided antagonizing the princes of the Church, safely shielded by a conservative vision of society.

Dom Mariano's dilemma, which was perhaps his own, immediately projected Luís Filho to his grandfather's fazenda, in Minas. Where in the mornings, during holidays, there arrived, along with coffee, corn bread, maize cake, manioc flour biscuits, and Minas cheese, peons eager to tell of their adventures.

To a certain degree, Dom Mariano's Church resembled those men on his grandfather's estate. What they recounted did not coincide with the real intention of their stories. In them were imbedded countless elements never spoken of, hence invisible to the naked eye. So that there existed between the appearance of the story and its meaning a space that imagination shaped, to suit the taste of teller and listener alike.

Dom Mariano left off speaking. There formed round about him a circle of silence fed by his lofty authority. Without his abdicating, in the meantime, the right to express himself again. His verbal space was indestructible. Perhaps he intended to measure Luís Filho's resistance.

Luís Filho was willing to have his mettle, his boldness tested. Perhaps Dom Mariano had misjudged his handshake, affectionate and firm. Squeezing harder than he should have. Though the warmth went out of it immediately. Dom Mariano wanted him to be a supplicant. Prepared to suborn the representatives of the Church. Or did that pause warn him of the fact that, coming from so great a distance, threatened by grave losses, he ought to alter his course, conciliatory thus far, appealing instead for more direct aid? He must be cautious, however. He was crossing swords, after all, with the most arrogant institution in the West, the only one to harmonize power and faith. In danger, Luís Filho secured his position, so as to exhaust Dom Mariano's strength.

"Let us not scruple, Doctor Luís Filho, to eliminate the obstacles of a practical order, which arouse human society's undue concern," Dom Mariano finally launched forth once again, without apology for his long silence. "I therefore speak in the name of collaboration. Let us not involve ourselves in any way in matters pertaining to common justice or the federal sphere. We know you to be of good faith, however, which encourages us to continue. We have here the example of Dom Antônio, carrying on his apostolate in a region devoid of resources, contemplated in all its wretchedness and social injustice. What does he ask for? Only peace, an integral part of his pastoral activity." Pausing anew, Dom Mariano seemed to be goading Luís Filho into interrupting him to ask questions. In the face of his silence he rewarded him with a kindly look.

"We appreciate that you are freeing us of the need for exhaustive explorations concerning the present pastoral activity of the Church." And he gave an almost imperceptible sigh that betrayed his tiredness.

Luís Filho noticed his weariness, boredom perhaps. He felt called upon to speak, on pain of blocking the negotiations.

"As you very well know, Dom Mariano, I come from a family that, in practice as in dogma, has always exhorted the Church to fulfill its age-old mission, and vowed to further its principles. I can say the same for the Madruga group. I thus am availing myself of the privilege of excepting Your Excellency from setting forth more clearly a thought only too well known and admired by us. As a citizen aware of the facts, I am in close agreement with the positions you have taken, those also taken, moreover, by a responsible clergy, in view of the Council of Puebla, and the choice made there again confirmed by the wretched of the Latin-American continent. In this regard, therefore, Dom Mariano, it is most unlikely that our paths will diverge. Hence we place ourselves under your wise guard."

Luís Filho immediately searched Dom Mariano's impenetrable face. He had turned all the way around now, toward Dom Antônio, after expressing his thanks for Luís Filho's words with a wave of his hand.

Urged to participate in a more active stage, in which numbers, figures, values, and hectares played an intimate role, Dom Antônio immediately gave proof of his competence. At no moment having recourse to a single written notation. Only at the end did he add that the squatters were demanding much less than half the fazenda.

"If Your Excellency will permit me an aside," Luís Filho said. "They're asking for exactly half the area."

Dom Antônio unconstrainedly accepted the correction. And with unfailing politeness allowed him to put in other incidental remarks from time to time as he went on setting forth the squatters' demands. He never once lost his patience. Luís Filho perceived the danger. He wanted to question him as to his ideological positions, linked in the majority of cases to partisan interests. He had knowingly headed the movement, at the time of the invasion. And when they were already close to agreement, he had continued to urge the squatters to repudiate any proposal that did not grant them total control of the lands. Face to face with them now, however, he was all sweetness and light, eager to make concessions.

Dom Mariano took over again. It seemed to him the proper moment to set forth a proposal in two different versions that could be reconciled to suit the interests that both represented. Without losing sight of Dom Antônio's account of the matter, at the risk of seeing the negotiations fall through. In his opinion, there was no way to give up the fazenda, or even cede half of it. But neither was there any way to get out of meeting certain of the squatters' claims, all of them having been substantiated at this point by their labor. Even though an accord at this juncture would represent losses for the Madruga group, in the long term it would mean total possession of the remaining domains. The squatters themselves would be the first to defend and keep to the limits resulting from the present agreement.

Dom Mariano turned to the bishop of Goiás, as though assured of the automatic approval of Luís Filho, whom he had not even consulted. "I am certain that my esteemed brother will persuade the higher echelons to respect to the letter the agreement that we have just sealed. Can Doctor Luís Filho and I count, then, on your valuable intercession when this case is finally adjudged?"

Dom Mariano smiled now. Perhaps he was remembering, by a rare association, that his Church had been born in the catacombs, thus growing amid whispers, secret councils, danger that counted for nothing when the aim was the destruction of the Roman Empire. An exhaustive exercise that had taught them how to handle, at one and the same time, the force of the revelation of Christ, the winning of the state of grace, and the perverse essence of power.

"Will you have coffee?" Dom Mariano immediately rang the little bell. His every gesture was calculated. He was well aware that his slightest word had intimate ties to the realities of the country. He belonged to an institution that never renounced its temporal fulfillment, its furious attraction to the world. How could they fail to lure the human flock into God's pastures?

Dom Mariano's body, with not an ounce of fat on it, appeared to disdain succulent dishes. His eyes swept the room, inspected the two men. Not distracted by the world's visible signs; prepared to intervene in it. And that attitude fascinated Luís Filho, for it escaped his control. With what pleasure he watched the prelate rigging the human game, without fear of having his vestments or his soul set on fire. Setting up rules that seemed straightforward, yet in practice invariably fleecing the players. Dom Mariano nonetheless declared himself to be impartial and just, scarcely caring who won and who lost. As if there were no such thing as winners and losers, to the benefit of friendly human coexistence.

Claiming to be interested only in facts of a social nature, Dom Mariano juggled values, numbers, hectares, with hairbreadth precision. Until he arrived at the exact share of land that, in the name of justice, ought to belong to the squatters. Only then did he eye Luís Filho, as if to say that he would tolerate no opposition. In the face of any sort of negative response, he would give up his role as mediator.

Luís Filho perceived that the meeting was about to come to an end. Either they accepted the losses announced by Dom Mariano or they would be obliged to have recourse to the law.

The bishop was now acting as though they had already reached an agreement. Even going so far as to congratulate Luís Filho on his skill as a negotiator. Earthly life depended on judicious agreements such as this one in order that God's commandments might be carried out. And the solution arrived at aided and abetted both parties. Immediately, after discussion of the details, which lasted no more than ten minutes, Dom Mariano rose to his feet, bringing the meeting to a close. He insisted on showing them to the door himself. Giving Luís Filho one minute more of his attention, as though awaiting his pronouncement.

"I believe, Dom Mariano, that the solution pleased God, whom we both serve," Luís Filho said, smiling.

Bento congratulated his brother-in-law in a curt, cool voice. While Madruga wanted a detailed picture of Dom Mariano. Delighted by the cleverness of that aristocrat in whom there was still something of a village priest. Administering the life and the soul of his parishioners. For whom such a thing as secrets did not exist. And under whose guardianship lay any and every matter of faith. Never neglecting, therefore, the duties of bed and kitchen. These being the ingredients he used in order to keep his parish under his thumb.

Bento was eager to discuss a plan for the immediate development of the properties, but Miguel cut him short, being interested in Dom Mariano's private life. Luís Filho doubtless knew of items that would lend color to the story of the bishop's doings.

"We know nothing of his intimate life. He keeps it under wraps," Luís Filho replied.

"That's even better. That way we keep the character all of a piece. I don't know why, but I was reminded of Grandfather. If it had fallen to Dom Miguel's lot to negotiate the autonomy of Galicia, he no doubt would have acted the way Dom Mariano did," Miguel said thoughtfully.

Madruga did not want to disillusion him. Or damage the image that Eulália had woven, over the years, of a man important enough to have lent another configuration to reality had he not been so busy telling stories. Or assuring her that the splendid past of Galicia could never be tracked down now. Despite certain words, still current among them, telling them that they must trust the future.

On learning of Miguel's comment, Eulália was moved by this homage to her father, buried in Sobreira. In gratitude, she summoned Miguel to hear stories that unfortunately he already knew. They were part of a repertory that had been exhausted. In his mother's presence, however, Miguel pretended to be wonderstruck. He wriggled about in the chair, giving visible proofs that the story held him spellbound. As Eulália blushed to see this son so exquisitely sensitive to a reality fostered in the past by Grandfather Miguel, whose name he had inherited.

Eulália knew nothing of the negotiations that had gone on in Brasília. The family wished to spare her. To her the Church was an institution entirely devoted to its own destiny. To which being on earth meant a fleeting, transitory journey. As such, concerning itself exclusively with the soul. That strange territory that collected thorns and bitter herbs to lock away in a drawer. The priest's one aim being to train man to take on eternal life, once he had disentangled himself from the torments and temptations of this earth.

At dinner, a feast in Luís Filho's honor, Eulália stayed on in the living room after coffee, contrary to her habit of retiring at an early hour. She seemed happy to have Miguel at her side. He for his part was all smiles, thanks to that woman's incomparable charms. Nothing was troubling him that night. Till the moment that he caught sight of Breta, at the other end of the room, and blenched. Suddenly overpowered by the memory of Esperança, who seemed to be present.

Feeling her uncle's eyes on her, Breta was intuitively aware of the reason for that intent look. She prided herself, however, on taking Esperança everywhere with her, so that one and all would fear her shadow. As long as she lived, no one had the right to erase the memory of Esperança. Above all Miguel, who despite his jovial air was beginning to show signs of age. His hair was already turning white. A fact that spoke volumes about life and death.

Miguel went over to Breta. And, in a sudden gesture, kissed her forehead. Breta did not fight her uncle off. Esperança was receiving her brother's caresses in her place. A transmission of affection that nonetheless made her voice catch in her throat. She saw herself incapable of reciprocating. How to draw closer to Miguel, if she was not Esperança?

From a distance, Bento reproached Miguel for his excitability. Miguel accepted all his brother's reprimands, in the certainty that his brother envied him his freedom. Roaming the streets, yet inclined to put up a hard fight in meetings of the board of directors or labor unions. And when his attention wandered, Bento was always the first to pass little notes to him, to nudge him with his foot underneath the table. Once they were by themselves, however, he read Miguel the riot act. He should watch his step, ease up a little; excesses would be the ruin of him yet.

"Your heart can kill you too, Miguel. Life is going to pin the donkey's tail on you someday. When you least expect it, you won't have the strength left to live so many lives at the same time."

Miguel thanked him by giving him greater power in the firm, while at the same time not bending to his will. As soon as he got up out of bed, at a very early hour, eager to be free of Sílvia's heat, which permeated the room, he went directly from the house to the office. The doorman's deference as he ushered him into the elevator bordered on the ridiculous.

There in the office, if he happened to catch him looking contrite, Bento was disconcerted. Not knowing how to deal with feelings as plain to see as a broken bone.

"What's the matter, Miguel?" was what he usually said, not knowing what to do with his hands. He would straighten the knot in his tie and, very rarely, smooth down his hair as well. With gestures less natural by the day.

With everyone gathered together in the living room, Madruga sensed how at odds with each other his children were. He felt sorry for them for having so many years of hard-fought struggles before them still.

With Breta, he talked of men like Dom Mariano. What breed did he belong to? And Dom Miguel, Grandfather Xan, what plan had they gone by? Breta pitied her grandfather. Exhausted, however, by the dinner they had had, she looked around and spied the frail figure of Eulália on the little family horizon.

"There's no use grieving, grandfather. We won't know one thing about these figures. Whether they're alive or dead. In the end, the words we say are like shipwreck victims. They take our dreams to the bottom with them. So then, I ask you, where do the dreams we're forbidden to dream go?" and she stared intently at her grandfather.

"To Sobreira, straight to the cemetery," Madruga said slowly.

Antônia and Luís Filho came over to say good-bye. Madruga permitted them to give him a farewell embrace. Breta observed the uneasiness with which they all went their separate ways. And it seemed to her altogether fitting dramatically that she should belong to that flock. Only Madruga had wide-open blue eyes, threatening to fight off any dream.

*T*obias aspired to play a leading role in the student movement. He returned with a swelled chest from his daily visit to the building housing the National Student Union. Suffering from the illusion that he belonged to a class capable of determining the ultimate aims of Brazil.

At the dinner table, amid verbal eructations, he dissected theories based on recent episodes in Brazilian history. Obliged to listen to him, I let him talk on for the first few minutes while I enjoyed my food. Then, unable to bear his speechifying any longer, telling him to knock it off. He immediately took offense, forcing Eulália to calm the two of us down with simple gestures. We buried our noses in the food before us, and only our jagged breathing betrayed our feelings.

In the living room, Tobias was eager to lock horns again. To accuse me of not understanding a country that I had arrived in without resources, with empty hands, my heart bent only on pursuing the perverse alchemy of gold.

"It would seem, father, that money is your only god."

His freshly shaven face, shorn of its adolescent beard, made his tender years more apparent still. "It's thanks to that money that there's food on the table in front of you. And you eat very well, if I may say so. It's also that god who finances your entire life. And the life of all your cronies. Because the lot of you are nothing but snobs, thinking only of setting this country to rights," I snapped crossly, with a wave of my hand to dismiss him and be left alone.

"And what did you expect? That we'd do away with the bourgeoisie? Where we all came from? Without your money, there's no way to stage a revolution," he shot back in an insolent tone of voice.

"We agree on that point, then. Except that, despite all your fancy theories, you lack popular support. And who's going to trust students, brats who still wet their pants! What have you done so far to deserve people's trust? How are you going to prove that you're any different from the old pols, a bunch of bastards whose one ambition is to have a strongbox stuffed full of bank notes and dabble in political intrigue, with no moral principles whatsoever!"

Being forced to put up with Tobias, I went over to the bar. I poured myself a white port, slowly bringing the glass to my lips, hoping to calm myself.

Tobias was unstoppable. Like a chatterbox rebelling against his own father, a born freebooter, following in the wake of an authoritarian elite, seated on the throne of power for centuries. Determined in practice to do away with the setting up of any sort of platform from which the people could reflect their reality and give voice to their natural rights. Pursuing a doctrine of repression, structured like a war machine to block popular advances, automatically closing in on itself to protect itself against progressivist wedges seeking to penetrate it.

"You're talking, Tobias, as though history followed only one pattern. As though it were immovable and monolithic. Well, I'll give you an example that contradicts all that. The mere fact of the arrival of immigrants, at the beginning of this century, played a crucial role in the formation of the Brazilian trade union movement. And in the formation of the Communist Party as well. Yet they were mere humble immigrants, like myself. Except that they were a bit more politicized. And for that very reason they were defeated and expelled from the country. What's more, I've never seen you mention them. Or admit that they contributed to the march of history. They helped nonetheless to change the mind of the worker, who was living in the blackest situation imaginable."

"I realize that, of course, father. But I can't look back. If I do, I'll turn into a pillar of salt. I need to drain every last drop from the present situation. Immediate political action is the spearhead of history. And what makes history move on. Because history is an old matron, sitting in an easy chair. We need to push her out of there, out of her comfortable position. It's up to us students to set fire to events, which in turn will speed up history," he said with fervor.

Eulália ordered coffee brought, her way of trying to make the discussion less heated. Odete looked at Tobias out of the corner of her eye. I had long noted the fascination my son held for her. Perhaps she was contemplating making him a member of her pantheon of heroic figures, among whom Eulália was foremost. In general, creatures within the periphery of her dreams, capable of imitating virtues crystallized in Getúlio Vargas and Chico Alves, her undisputed idols. To the point that on hearing Vargas's speeches on the radio, Odete took on a sort of arrogance, which made her feel free virtually to ignore those present.

The pet phrase "Workers of Brazil!," which the President addressed, in his gaucho accent, to the laboring class, had the merit of provoking discreet tears on her part. The remainder of the day going by with Odete's attention elsewhere, far removed from household tasks at hand.

Eulália, however, applauded this behavior. She had been the first to encourage her to create heroes. Maintaining that by so doing Odete would have a gallery of saints to compete with her own.

The coffee kept me going. I crossed my legs, straightening the creases in my trousers.

"I nearly killed myself laying all that money aside. And I always put in an honest day's work. I'm proud of that. You ought to feel the same.

What's more, I'm not a member of the elite, as you accuse me of being. Our family arrived here only recently. It hasn't had time to take an active part in the making of the history of Brazil," I said in a gentler voice.

"I disagree with you. Ever since I've been born, I've been part of the history of Brazil. So I refuse any sort of passive role. You're the one who's trying to evade the political responsibilities that are your rightful due. Listen, if you live here, and have a Brazilian family, you too are answerable for the outrages committed."

Tobias had confidence in his political future. He ascribed to himself a talent for moving successfully someday through the treacherous quicksands of Brazilian politics. Long under the domination of party bosses, of the right and of the left, super-cunning wolves, whose greed made them masters of the electoral sheepfold.

He was lost in flights of fiery oratory now, my presence completely forgotten, his expansiveness accompanied by gestures. He kept fingering various objects on the table, moving them from one place to another.

"You needn't break the crystal ware before the revolution," I said sarcastically.

He did not smile. He was born humorless. He fueled his obsession by switching off immediate reality.

"Unfortunately, it's the same picture as ever, repeating itself yet again. The generation that today gravitates round the decision-making power is made up once more of men who bow to the country's moral defeat in return for small personal favors. Brazil's backwardness doesn't weigh on their consciences. So they can readily justify the fact that Brazil is capitulating to foreign capital, in the name of a strategy for the country's development."

He frowned with a professorial air. Calling my attention to new political circumstances that had suddenly arisen in urban centers as a consequence of the electoral process. Not being so much a matter of Kubitschek's victory in the presidential campaign, as of the effect being engendered among the people by the practice of democracy.

"This victory must be made to mean something. And we must liquidate once and for all those parasitical classes that are keeping the office of power from remaining empty. That is to say, a vacant place made up of breaches through which the people can succeed in choosing their own destiny. But for them Power has a prior owner, and engenders its own succession. The whole democratic process is simply a façade to fool the people. Whereas in a radical democracy power ought not to have a master, but instead a seat which is temporarily occupied. And which by nature would be transitional, ever-changeable."

Noting Odete's look of admiration, he blushed. Immediately drawing himself up to his full height, however, he shrugged. His serious face seemed to be overburdened by a weight of care. Everything was drawing him away from there. Doubtless toward the speaker's platform, from which he would send forth his fiery discourse in time to come. And so it was that he finally realized that I had left him standing there all by himself in the empty room.

In the mornings, Tobias attacked the newspapers. Confident that the history of Brazil was parading past him in print, at the mercy of his passionate reflection. Offering him the opportunity of deciphering the truths of the facts, once the latter had been subjected to his ideology and his imagination.

Tobias was infuriated by administrative peculations, ever on the increase and never brought to book. He demanded a clean soul, without a trace of blood or passion. Like kosher food, after the rabbi's attentions. His apostolate wearied his brothers, who stole off without further ado.

"I was born a year before the National Student Union was founded. I am exactly one year older than the organization itself," he said, failing to note how irksome his radicalism had become.

In order to please Odete, whenever she was near at hand he cited the name of Getúlio Vargas, the late-lamented dead man. At this reference, Odete's eyes opened wide, but then she immediately stared down at the floor so as to preserve her modesty. Not being bold enough to encourage Tobias in my presence. Meanwhile Tobias, being of unstable temperament, had already sallied forth in defense of another leader. Kubitschek this time, recently honored by the people at the ballot box, but now threatened with the possibility that he would not be allowed to take office.

And then forgetting all about Odete, who kept inventing little tasks that would keep her close at hand, Tobias would leave, his bookbag over his shoulder, announcing that he would not be home to dinner. It was his day on duty at Botafogo beach. In recent months, the headquarters of the National Student Union had become a home to him.

Tobias's aimlessness and irresponsibility irritated me. I lost patience with him.

"It's a shame you don't have it in you to pursue a political career that would take you to the top. I never see you with a book in your hand. All your culture comes from a newspaper. Like mine. What's more, you seem to be a flitting butterfly, heading nowhere."

In the face of these phrases, Eulália sensed that storms were about to break. Her sudden pallor kept Tobias from replying, his most immediate concern being to protect his mother. He then put forth the effort to approach me. He sat down self-consciously at my side, feigning reconciliation. My son's ingenuousness disarmed me. I wanted to protect him from himself. Making him see that, whether he liked it or not, old pols and the military would in fact be the real agents of the transformations which the country would undergo. Hence, in the first decade at least, popular cries of protest would be of no avail, even if wrested from the people by hunger and a thirst for justice. Those men were the only ones in charge of events. And thus the same abyss as ever between history as recounted by them and the history that the people thought they were living would continue to exist. This difference corresponding almost perfectly to the effects of a religious schism, since despite the fact that religions fell apart, they nonetheless exerted every effort to see that beliefs compatible with their own pressing interests made their appearance, to take their place and take over their power.

"What is there that is real behind a given political event?" I tried to argue, both of us calmer now. "The case of General Mamede, for example. What made him hold forth at the graveside of Canrobert, engendering this accursed crisis of the moment? Can that be where the coup began, beneath the cloak of rhetoric? And as for the Branti letter, was it or was it not apocryphal? And did Café Filho feign illness so as to keep J. K. from taking office?"

Tobias tensed, faithful to his canonical postures, which rejected alternate versions of the facts. As an ardent champion of truth, he ascribed to it a crystalline tenor, before which falsehood and all doubts gave way.

"Falsehood and truth are flour from the same sack, Tobias. Especially for people like us. What do we know of the cunning contrivances born of an act of faith? Nothing multiplied by nothing. And do you know why? Because the decisive moments of a country ordinarily come about through conspiracies. And people like us are not given access to palace intrigues, coded messages, or anything else. Our ignorance is so great that it makes us vulnerable and powerless to act. For that very reason I intuit that in the political realm full power can be attained in one way only, by the very act of plotting against power. And it is precisely because of this transcendent act that power expels us from its antechambers, dismisses us altogether. And proclaims our uselessness. This line of reasoning, Tobias, would have it that power alone is in possession of the facts. Or else is in a better position to determine the historical truth of the human heart. Outside the inner chambers, Tobias, history gets lost. Or else it becomes legend, recounted by Grandfather Xan."

"Do you mean to say that history doesn't exist? Even when it's recounted? Is it all a farce?"

"It exists, certainly, but for those who are making it. And even more so for the person who writes it. Just take writers, for instance. They invent a story, but that story has to jibe with people's collective aspiration. If it doesn't, it doesn't work. Xan and Dom Miguel were noted storytellers. But I ask you, can their stories possibly have been an absolutely rigorous reflection of corrupt political reality?"

Tobias was palpably indifferent to the evocation of his ancestors. In the role of permanent vassal of contemporary history, the only thing of use to him were events taking their course, fleeing the past. Even political praxis that did not engender a social transformation clearly perceptible to his own eyes appeared to him to be an unnecessary illustration, a sort of archaeological configuration almost.

Among other things, he was convinced that the man of his time must be intimately acquainted with the immediate challenges, without delegating complementary functions to coming generations. It was all the more necessary, therefore, to mend social wounds promptly. As for the leftovers of history, into the garbage can with them. The task of confronting events long past with those in progress he regarded as the occupation of a parasitical intellectual out to halt the march of history. His vocation was to situate himself in an age of fire, hence subject to being reduced to ashes. His youth poisoned by the fresh winds of a reality doomed to be polluted by the appearance of facts to which he did not have access, and to whose interpretation he subordinated his imagination.

In Eulália's presence, we temporized. We were also surprised at the lack of the tensions that had always set limits to our living at peace with each other. Perhaps in homage to Eulália, I forced myself to charm my son, to give him the memory of Xan as a gift.

"Grandfather died without forgiving me for not helping him to die. He told Ceferino, my father, that he would like to come back to life, just so as to be able to tell the story of his own death. He no doubt planned to make an epic out of it. Someone had told me that Grandfather Xan kept complaining of being short of breath, not being in good health. But at the time I wasn't able to leave Brazil. It wasn't as easy for an immigrant to travel then as it is today. First of all, a person had to save up all the money. So I couldn't go see him. Even knowing how hurt he was that I'd taken off as I had. He never understood why I didn't say good-bye to him, choosing Uncle Justo instead to take me to Vigo. Even so, he firmly believed that I'd arrive in time to close his eyes. He used to say proudly, there in the tavern, that his grandson Madruga would be the first to announce his death and lay him out in his funeral garments. Being careful above all to cover up certain shameful things that death dumps on the remains of a man. I remember having written to Father: 'Can it be that Grandfather, with nothing to hope for except this, wasted years of his life telling me stories? If so, can he have thought that I would stay in Sobreira for the rest of my life listening to him, while life there in Brazil went down the drain? I believe that, despite the conversations with Salvador about America, Grandfather never thought I'd cross the Atlantic, carrying a knapsack and many illusions on my back. But to me, father, what was even worse than not having been present at Grandfather Xan's funeral was the discovery that I lack the gift of going on with the plots he taught me. And I have no guarantee that, in the future, when I marry, a child of mine will come into this rich inheritance.'"

Xan's illness lasted two weeks. Lying in bed, his strength draining away, he allowed people to come visit him. Immediately getting rid of them, after a quick inspection. As though searching for a face that never came. Seeing his anxiety, Ceferino distracted his father, so as to keep him from mentioning the name of his grandson, in far-off America.

In the beginning, Xan humored him, until he could contain himself no longer.

"I was right not to trust that Madruga. A real scoundrel. When he took off to America, he had every intention of not returning. Today he's a man so busy making money he's never going to find the time to bring me back the legends he promised," Xan said with labored breath. Despite Ceferino's taking his hands in a firm grip, so that his father would fight for his life for at least two days more.

But Ceferino's effort was to no avail, for upon these words Xan simply closed his eyes and lay motionless. His sudden death rattle frightening Ceferino, who shouted for Urcesina, in the kitchen preparing lunch. When Urcesina, in alarm, came to help her husband fan away the last fires from a dead man, Xan opened his eyes.

"I haven't died. I still have a few days left. It was just an experiment to test my body, to see if it obeyed me in the hour of my death. To prove I'm able to outwit death. Now that I've gotten a leg up on her, let the witch come close my eyes. She's up to her usual dirty work. She's been spying on me for years from behind the door. Death thinks I haven't seen her sneaking up on me. But it's a happy error. I've finally felt her breath. She just wanted to hear my stories, you see!"

He paused, and then went on. "Ah, Ceferino, who's going to succeed me? We can't really count on that Madruga. So our family is going to lose its last storyteller."

The Mass with the body lying in state brought even neighbors from other villages flocking. That night, in the tavern, many glasses were downed in Xan's honor. Sitting in front of a piece of paper till far into the night, Ceferino worked himself up to announcing Grandfather's death in writing. Everything in life was a pleasure to him except writing. A pen was a most unfriendly instrument. He was better at other equally delicate matters, such as squeezing cows' udders and Urcesina's breasts. This latter act, incidentally, had never produced a single moan of pleasure from either of them. By common accord they acted as though they had caulked the door and stopped up the lock of the room. They no doubt made love hurriedly, hard-pressed by weariness and the sense of sin, which blanketed all of Sobreira. Blushing for shame, the women were both annoyed and embarrassed as their husbands went about putting their gigantic cocks inside them in the darkness of the bedroom, under the heavy covers.

Ceferino's letter arrived in Brazil on Palm Sunday. Preceded, thus, by heralds, green fronds, applause, and the memory of Pegasus, the little ass who was a friend of Salvador's. As I read it, holding it in my hands, I was afraid that my sweat would blot out the words written in ink. The announcement of that death opened a great wound in my chest, despite my father's urging resignation on me. The hour had come at last for Xan to bid a last farewell to an earth that he had celebrated by way of words and an insane love. Forever puffing on his straw-paper cigarette. The fact was that in his last days Xan had lost his nimbleness. He dragged himself about Sobreira leaning on his shepherd's staff, a long-ago present from Salvador. A shepherd's staff that stood behind the door for many years, awakening manifest fits of jealousy on the part of his wife, Teodora, who threatened to throw it into the fire. Meeting with violent protests from Xan. She must never dare, under any conditions, render a patrimony unusable. One, moreover, that enriched his memory.

"Memory is a pilaster, woman. It's what a wise man leans on so as not to lose his balance. I'd be in a bad way without it," Xan said.

"What damned memory are you talking about, when all it ever did was ruin our marriage! How many years is it now that we've not even been husband and wife to each other?" Teodora shouted.

"You're wrong, Teodora. Our marriage was destroyed by the stories I kept telling for years, without the courage to live a single one of them. We bled ourselves every day, without even noticing."

When I finally arrived in Sobreira, after being gone ten years, Ceferino was deeply moved. He was lavish in his praise of his son's ready-made suit, meant to prove to the neighbors that I'd come home with money in my pocket. Under protest from Urcesina, Father dragged me off to the cold, dank-smelling bedroom. Winter had left traces there. He took my letter, the one sent after Xan's death, out of the drawer, and gave it back to me.

"Before Urcesina pries into every nook and cranny of your years in America, and tries to contaminate you with a melancholy that's going to kill her yet, I want you to have these mementos of Grandfather Xan." And he handed me the relatively heavy leather pouch. "They're yours. Xan confessed to me that you were the grandson he loved. And he even left you the little Socorro farm, where there's the oak tree with that name."

Tobias interrupted the story. Scarcely able to contain his impatience. He had work that had to be done. "I respect your recollections, father. But you must decide once and for all whether you're staying in America to fight those reactionaries who are destroying Brazil, or going back to Galicia."

I looked at Tobias and for the first time didn't berate him. Perhaps I had failed to pass on to him, from early childhood, a sort of truth, warm and secret, which emerges only inside a home, beneath the protection of friendly walls, as the food at table consecrates the sad silence. A truth so discreet that it is no more than vaguely insinuated in one's ear, in a comfortable bed, beneath clean sheets. But America did not allow me to look after my children. Hence Tobias, in retaliation, showed a marked aversion to his own origin. And at the center of his authoritarianism, of a rather naïve stamp, lay his dramatic inability to share his father's emotions.

"How to speak of revolution, if you can't even understand a wise man such as Grandfather Xan? You're nothing but an incompetent, Tobias. No good at life or at rhetoric."

For days he did not come downstairs for dinner. Always absent at the times of day when I was around the house. I warned Eulália of a probable break. Miguel begged me to be calm. His brother had no way to work off his excess of energy.

"That's easily solved. I'll give him a pickax and send him out to the cross-country highway, where we're carving out the map of Brazil. It'd be curtains for us if we had to depend on that lazy nincompoop."

On Sunday, Venâncio suggested that I take a forced rest in São Lourenço or in Spain. As he saw it, I was a bundle of nerves, victimizing my own children. Tobias in particular, my favorite target. The very son most alert to reality.

Though furious, I avoided getting into an argument with Venâncio over Tobias's behavior. After all, I was the one whose word was law in that house. I thanked him for his advice, however. But I couldn't follow it. Those were the very days when Senator Silveira was doing his utmost to obtain government contracts considered indispensable to the soundness of the business, now growing by leaps and bounds. Though the contracts were due to be signed any day, there were details still to be settled. We were convinced that Kubitschek would not hesitate to expand the highway network, not only to generate wealth, but make it spread throughout Brazil, thereby constituting a new cycle of exploitation of the hinterland.

The alliance with the senator had begun shortly before the Revolution of '30, in the former Bar Adolfo, amid the noisy chaos of the Rua da Carioca, as we were drinking beer together. One which soon grew more solid still thanks to continual proofs of friendship. Both of us knowing the other to be possessed of an iron temperament, conjoined in the senator's case with a subtlety indispensable for wheeling and dealing in politics.

Our meetings were sealed with a hearty embrace and the sharing of a noble wine. Almost always in the Pérgula at the Copacabana Palace Hotel, where he had become a permanent guest, since he had never wanted to set himself up in an apartment in Rio. In summer, he cut a striking figure in his impeccable white suit and Panama hat. From his dress he might easily be taken for a Northeasterner. But his height and his fair hair and complexion betrayed his Italian origin, on his mother's side. Both of us recited our family sagas as a proof of affection.

"Though you may not like it, Madruga, we must broaden our network of collaborators in the ministries, and be more generous with them. Bureaucrats are now the products of a more refined school, and they have expensive habits. Someone is going to have to pay for them," and he gave a smile, which I promptly returned.

The sun that afternoon was invigorating. Though we had to stick to business. He suggested that it was time for us to forge ahead on new economic paths, in order to keep up with Brazil's rapid awakening. This suggestion meeting with my agreement, I began immediately to supply him with information whose source was the Banco do Brasil, which was on the point of granting charters for the opening of new banks. Bento and Miguel pressing me to enter the financial market. "That's where the money is, Silveira. Its apparent function is to offer services, allocate resources. In practice, it determines where money should be invested and what to do with outside credit. With a relative amount of reserve capital. Without immobilizing our capital in undertakings that provide a slow, gradual return."

Silveira hesitated. It struck him as a risky proposition at that juncture to fight with the Ministry of the Treasury for entrée into a specific, hotly disputed area. One false move, and we'd be taken to the cleaners.

I thoroughly disagreed with his argument. Given the financial volume of our investments, our business deals required a bank with which to operate, in order to protect us from the rear. And one that was sufficiently strong to finance part of the real estate developments and the heavy earthmoving business, the latter undergoing rapid expansion. Not to mention the textile industry, a recent takeover.

"We can't stay tied to government credit forever. It's slow to spawn, especially in periods when the waters get riled politically," I said, fired with enthusiasm.

The children were right. If we didn't act we'd lose our economic backing, becoming dependent on ever more costly credit that we had to beg on our knees for. With the bank, we'd have subsidized interests and credits.

"We'll operate with private savings, and invest them where they'll pay off handsomely. Profit margins are something we can't control and political payoffs are unpredictable. Though still in our favor, I trust."

"And what if the minister turns us down? I've reasons for not putting my prestige on the line just now. Next year things will be different. One refusal and I'd come up against a whole run of those negative answers we always have to put up with during a term in office. We'd best not tangle with the devil right now. Our stick's mighty short," Silveira replied.

"It's not a question of prestige, Silveira, it's a necessity. In three or four years cartels, conglomerates, are going to be set up. Brazil will be more and more involved with foreign capital, right here, under our very noses. In the future, a charter will be worth a fortune and carry enormous political weight. Right now, after the change in administration, there's an opportunity in the midst of all the euphoria. Kubitschek will change the entire face of the country in short order. And woe to anybody who can't adapt to new times. As the carrousel goes round and round, many a fortune is going to get thrown off. Good people, who never gave up an outmoded style of doing business. Those fortunes won't be able to stay on the dizzying financial merry-go-round or face up to the new demands of the market. Whereupon we'll be ending a chapter of the country's economy. In the new cycle, you'll see how the rural world will come to play a less important role. Banks, I'm certain, are going to spring up like mushrooms. It'll be the way it is in the U.S. Because bank is synonymous with city, with urban concentration. And Brazil is destined to be another urban country in the coming decades."

"Are you out of your mind, Madruga? A country can't do without agriculture, without cattle! That's where fortunes are made. Who's going to move capital out of landed property? There was a coffee crisis, I grant you. But in order really to colonize itself, Brazil is going to have to hack out trails into the interior."

"You, being a gaucho, are attached to wide-open spaces. But ever since he was a little boy, Kubitschek has dreamed of Paris. And now he dreams of Brasília, which to him will be the same thing. He's mad about capitals."

Silveira hesitated. Kubitschek couldn't use inflation as a prop, not even on the pretext of speeding up the development of the country. Taxes had to be kept at a reasonable level, so as to avoid speculation and a disorderly market. In that way the country would get round the problem of interference in its domestic affairs by international financial organizations, the cause of political conflicts incompatible with the slow, painful process of democratic consolidation.

"Don't fool yourself, Silveira. Despite the old-fogyism of any number of politicians and businessmen, Brazil has just taken a historic leap forward. And it's now on a forced march to another sort of future. This man is not a dyed-in-the-wool opponent of progress. Nor is he a great landowner. He's literally a high-stepper. So we can't sit on the sidelines, or get caught up in the short-term economy. The time has come to sail out into rough seas," I insisted, in a great burst of enthusiasm.

With the figures laid out before him, the senator's eyes had the same lustful gleam as when his gaze followed, as it generally did, some woman stealing past nearby tables. As lavish as a prince with his mistresses, he enjoyed the reputation of keeping them shut up in a harem, though he had no time to spare to visit them.

"I envy you, Madruga. You have women and forget their names the next day. Nobody captivates you for very long. A moment's whim doesn't cost you dearly. I'm different. I have the mentality of a filing clerk. And none of the talents of a memoirist as consolation. I demand a copy of their police dossier and make them stay home waiting for me, so as to enjoy a love that's all make-believe. Women are my perdition."

Silveira seemed pleased to worship sex with such conviction. Never failing, however, to visit his wife periodically at his fazenda in Cruz Alta. Where she lived because of problems impossible for her to get around. Though he offered no details in this regard.

"Well, I disagree. You're very much mistaken, my friend. Your one passion is really politics. Women are merely accessories to this extravagant sentiment. They act as the frame of a classified work of art."

Silveira laughed, as though he agreed. He could not imagine removing himself from palace intrigues. His life revolved round strategies planned with the one aim of keeping him close to power. With the dramatic certainty that a single slip on his part would suffice to deliver him into the hands of enemies incapable of calm consideration and forgiveness. He had chosen to move from out on the pampas into areas of government that would assure him of the role of protagonist.

"The day will come when I'll be obliged to retire to my fazenda. From that date on, however, I shall begin to pray for death, for her not to disappoint me, because I'll be in a hurry to go. Death to me, Madruga, is not the sudden suspension of biological functions or the mourning that precedes funerals. It's nothing like that. To me, death is plunging into anonymity, seeing doors close in my face. With a gentleness a thousand times worse than if they had sealed it shut or nailed it up all round. Have you ever seen the smile of an aide-de-camp, a mere bootblack, advising you to come back next week? And when that next week comes, hear the same thing again? It's at that precise point that your death begins. Because, from then on, a long line of flunkies, the lowest of the low, down to the ones who serve the coffee and dust the tables, start to remove your name from agendas, audiences, ceremonies. After that happens, your name never appears in print again. Or at most in your obituary or death notice. At such times, then, a person begins to wonder whether life is of any use. If in fact it's worth the trouble to prove to this rabble that we're still alive, that we haven't been declared dead. And for that reason, Madruga, I don't hesitate to state that the worst misfortune is absolute obscurity. The fatal burden of a sort of silence that casts us into the dungeon."

Silveira's confession moved both of us. Without a word, we drank the red wine, whose bouquet, unusually intense, climbed over the sides of the crystal glass.

"This wine has the scent of a female. Don't you think so?" he said all of a sudden, breaking the silence. Or masking the confession that had brought a bitter taste to his mouth.

Silveira's cheeks turned red, then immediately after that I noted that he was livid with fear. I also sensed that if a feeling of loathing spread through my body like leprosy, causing me to abandon my plans out of fear, I ought to interpret this fact as a warning that death was on my trail.

"I believe that death announces itself to every man in a different way.

To me it would be when my heart dried up, when it didn't leak oil anymore, and reality appeared to me to be merely a picture hanging on the wall that I was forced to look at all day long. Until I could no longer tolerate that ever-repeated scene, its deadly sameness."

"Well then, a toast to this most inventive death!" Silveira said.

Tobias and I finally met in the living room. Suitcase in hand, he announced that he was off to São Paulo, to participate in a congress sponsored by the National Student Union. Though they had very few resources, the moment was right politically for the organization to pressure public opinion. In his face was the pleasure of defiance.

"So you've decided to be a professional haunter of the halls of learning, is that it? An eternal repeater who can't get along without his student status? The one thing you haven't gotten around to is asking me to finance such events," I said testily, not wanting Tobias to go off on his travels happy and carefree.

"And that would be none too much for you to do. After all, what have you given this country in return for everything you've received?"

In the face of my attack, Tobias's jowls trembled, making him look like a baby. Nobody would be coming to rescue the two of us, all alone there in the living room, free of Eulália.

"I gave sweat and passion. What more should I have offered? And even if I'd wanted to give more, would I have been allowed to? Did anyone ask me for anything more? Listen, Tobias, institutions were set up in such a way as to bar us from participating in them. Mere physical existence on this continent does not necessarily make us citizens. And even if we happen to have voting rights, marking a ballot isn't a real expression of our will."

Tobias paced restlessly up and down the room. He had set his suitcase down, as though he'd given up his trip.

"Anybody who doesn't believe in voting is for dictatorships. If a country votes regularly, it puts a different face on things," he said in exasperation.

"What we see are elected officials fulfilling agreements we didn't sign. Using our patrimony to bargain with. Invariably by way of secret protocols, a farce staged for their benefit and against ours. Their honor is furthered at the price of sacrificing the honor of the people. Isn't that so? Just look at General Lott. All it took was one sleepless night for him to accept the considered advice of General Denys, to the effect that it was best to carry out the planned military coup in order to forestall one staged by others in the putative rebel group, equally eager to take on the appearance of legitimate democratic rule."

"And wasn't that precisely what happened?" he interrupted.

"Suddenly the would-be insurgents, headed by President Carlos Luz, boarded the *Tamandaré*. Did they do so for the pleasure of sailing on the

Bay of Guanabara? Or were they counting on the Second Army, from São Paulo, and on Jânio Quadros, to attack the port of Santos, and subsequently take over the country again? Or by taking flight were they merely seeking to hoist the flag of desertion or resignation? Where is the historical truth? Which of these fabrications can be true?"

"It would seem that on the pretext of justifying the argument that the truth has neither face nor a fixed domicile, and that those who hold the reins of power are all alike, you're going to end up defending exceptional regimes."

"Not at all. The fact is that I no longer have any illusions, Tobias. What we invariably see is the hallowed use of the coup for democratic reasons, on the pretext of furthering the rule of law. When did a single voter, either you or your neighbor, authorize the general to send troops into the street, thereby violating the Constitution? With or without reason. How did the general face up to an act that concerned the entire nation? He simply summoned the military command, and in its presence recognized the urgent necessity of unleashing the coup, before a surprise attack could be mounted."

"Have you forgotten that thanks to General Lott, Kubitschek and Jango were able to assume the office of president and rule the country?"

Uneasy at seeing him standing there before me, ready to attack me, I pointed to a chair. As we sat there, side by side now, I looked intently at his liquid green eyes. That gaze seemed to disown me. Tobias and I had lived shut up in a seashell that left no room for affection. Wresting from each other a deadly energy, directed toward enemies. My heart suddenly contracted with grief for a son incapable of feeling admiration for my story. One who loved only Eulália and Venâncio, who exacerbated his dreaming!

As we lay in bed at night, Eulália tried to calm me. "Tobias is young, and he's suffering. But this is the moment in his life to protest. In a few years, his heart will lose its ardor, fall silent, and no longer echo within him. It's as though the world didn't listen to us and we failed to hear the world."

That voice seemed to me to have an affectionate ring, and I stroked her hand. But I had Tobias in my sights. He must be punished for his lack of a sense of responsibility, be brought to heel. The boy dissipated his energies, whereas Miguel and Bento had proved themselves to be real bird dogs. As for my daughter, gone from the house for almost ten years now, her rebellion took the form of dramatic signals, broadcast from wherever she might be, in the certainty that I would hear her cries. Even though Eulália hid her periodic visits from me. And even though Odete went off to Esperança's with little parcels. Obeying Eulália, following instructions meant to save Esperança. As meanwhile Miguel stealthily spied on Odete's every move, lacking only dagger in hand, hoping to gather information in return. In answer, Odete breathed out in his face the odor breathed in moments before in Esperança's house.

In the study, looking for the check brought by Bento, I rummaged through the drawers, finding nothing. Carefully examining, one by one, each scrap of paper.

"Did you see anyone enter my study?"

Eulália shook her head. Only Odete remembered that Tobias had been there, looking for magazines to read. He had carefully shut the door behind him when he left, however. I worriedly went through the drawer again, exactly as I had the day before. I remembered the urgent haste with which Bento had approached me as I was reading in my easy chair.

"All I've come for is to give you the check from Medeiros. It's not the size of it that counts, father, but the sheer pleasure of winning. We can discount the costs."

I paid little attention to what he was saying and tossed the check in the drawer. Eager to return to my reading.

"It's a check with the name left blank. If you like, I'll fill it out right now," he remarked.

I searched through the writing desk again, with Eulália beside me this time.

"It's not so much the value of the check, Eulália. But it can't have gotten lost here in the house. If it isn't here, someone took it."

Eulália leaned against the wall, her face pale, her hand on her breast. I hastened to her aid. She was scratching her face now, so hard as almost to injure her delicate skin.

"Forget the check, Eulália. It's of no importance."

Her bobbing head signaled, however, her refusal of my request. Her life was hanging in the balance, painfully suspended from her body. Everything about her reverberating with a magnitude quite unlike her usual discretion.

Odete immediately provided remedies, lying everywhere about the house. Ever since her arrival in Brazil, Eulália had been in failing health. Making me swear then that I would not tell Dom Miguel that he had a daughter as frail as the quail annually downed in the Galician mountains by the Sobreira hunters. For that reason, when we visited Sobreira she always walked proudly erect, her head held high. So that Dom Miguel would interpret her haughty posture as a sign of perfect health.

Dom Miguel was so delighted at this sight that he took her for a walk in the countryside. Pleased to show off that treasure which went by the name of Eulália, whom America had thus far spared, despite its destructiveness. Hence he could state, with all due gratitude, that Brazil had dealt well with his daughter. Though that was a land in which he would never set foot, since he had no time left to come to love another country in addition to his own. His whole heart had been won by the prestige of Galicia.

"No one is more sensitive or more clever than my daughter Eulália! She has braved the swamps and the fevers of the tropics, all for the benefit of the family," Dom Miguel said.

Hovering watchfully over Eulália, Odete cast a reproachful sidewise glance at me for having wounded her mistress's feelings. We tried to take her to her room.

"I want to see the children," she protested.

Eventually they all arrived. Eulália greeted them, giving every appearance of having recovered. At table, the food was too heavily salted. One dish after the other. Could life too be that hard to swallow?

As they sat over coffee, Tobias arrived from São Paulo. Battered and bruised, unshaven. He had not been expected to return home that day. Eulália went to him.

"I prayed that you'd come now, this instant. I even asked God to demand a sacrifice of me. I would be prepared to offer it, since you've come."

Tobias held her close. "What's happened, mother?"

"Have you any idea why I'm suffering such pain?"

Protectively, Miguel went to his mother's side. "What's happening, father? Why didn't you let me know?" Miguel wanted explanations.

His face pale, Tobias drew away from his mother. Wanting to dissolve from a distance the mystery of her face, so opposed to everything he believed in.

"Was it on your behalf that I came? Was it you who called me, then, and I obeyed your call? Ah, my dear mother!" and he began to weep convulsively.

Eulália enfolded him in her arms, as though she were a woolen coverlet protecting him from the cold.

"If you came, son, everything is solved. Let us go out onto the veranda," and she began pulling him along.

I was deeply upset, panting for breath. Yet I could not shirk my duty to know my sons. To rake their breasts with my nails, to examine mercilessly an interior peopled with veins, blood, and passions. Could they be so alone in the world that they found it necessary to betray me? To betray me as I was betraying the world, my neighbor?

"I must speak with Tobias alone," I said to Eulália.

"No, Madruga. No more discussions. Leave him to me." She placed her frail hands on my shoulder.

Rage drove generosity from my heart. Unbearable suspicions hovered over that son. I could not live a single minute longer without freeing him of blame.

"I cannot accede to your wishes, Eulália. This must be handled man to man. Come with me, Tobias."

Miguel redoubled his forces protecting his mother. "Father, do as Mother wills."

In the living room were Bento, his wife, Antônia, Luís Filho. And who else? I had no idea where Esperança was. Life had swallowed her up. At that moment, Miguel reconciled vigor with gentleness, an inheritance from his mother. Yet he confronted me boldly. I felt myself surrounded by enemies at that point, despots usurping my rights. Life flowing without control, irregularly. A mere mask, or death announcing itself?

I demanded that Tobias free himself from his mother's protection. He pushed Eulália away, took one step forward, shoving aside Miguel, who was standing in his way.

"That's enough, father. We'll have it out right here, in front of everybody. You've had it coming. I took the check, but I didn't steal it, despite what you think. I merely expropriated something that belonged to you. I acted with all due justice, beginning with your own house. What did you expect? That I'd break open your neighbor's strongboxes? I chose instead to break down your door, and I don't regret it in the least. And for your information, I didn't spend the money on myself."

Moving as one, as though they'd planned it, Eulália and Miguel grabbed my arms as I struggled to get at Tobias. The other children surrounded me. The entire family, those of my blood. Witnesses to the tears I shed. I finally allowed myself to be chained down by them. A trap that cunning enemies had woven to immobilize me. Suddenly, unable to contain myself, I let out a howl. I'd gotten an arrow in the chest at last, a deep wound; the blood gurgled.

Tobias made no effort to escape my gaze. So I visited all of him, down to his very bowels. Did my son's expressions vary in accordance with my desire or according to reality? I do not know. The pale surface constituting Tobias's face seemed unfathomable to me now. Nothing in the world was familiar to me. I felt myself driven from a house made by me, with the bricks of my effort, whitewashed by my greed, my savings, my folly, my sensuality, the powerful desire to accumulate more and more. Victory affording me dividends, as it chopped me to bits.

My voice sounded hoarse; the scream had ruined its timbre. Or was my heart readying itself to vomit up cruel words?

Round about me, unfocused objects, unreachable even though I stretched my hand out toward them. Life too I was unable to touch.

"If I had had my way, you'd have died, Tobias. Before you'd even been born," and everybody heard the clearly spoken words that eliminated a member of the family like themselves.

Miguel tried to cover my mouth. "For the love of god, father, don't you ever say that again."

With bowed head, Eulália seated herself in the armchair. And slowly slid her hand down her body to her belly, where Tobias had been begotten. Owing his birth to my wife. That life so recently denied by me.

I looked at Eulália and her pain left me drained. I feared the consequences. I knelt down beside her.

"You are not to blame, Eulália. We are not responsible for our son's madness," I tried to console her. But she had taken leave of me, erected a wall between us.

Finally she spoke. "God will punish us yet more for all our pride."

I rose resolutely to my feet. So that the family would hear. "Don't involve your god in this affair, Eulália. I cannot and will not be punished. It would be unjust."

She knew that I had always been submissive in the face of this sort of threat. We had both come from a region where magic had implanted itself; it was persuasive. In Galicia, human power had met with strange presences, archaic feelings, curses. We all suffered from incomprehensible influences, and we earned our daily bread in accordance with arcane agreements. When these alliances failed or faltered, how often a house, labor, an arm, friendship were lost. The gods were implacable in the face of human challenges.

Eulália's voice came again from the shadows, a fluted sound.

"Tobias was the only one who brought me happiness, from the day he was born. And he still does, today and always. And is life not full of temptations and enticements to corruption? Who is there who knows nothing of them?" and mortified, Eulália continued to rub her hand against her belly. As if to guard against the violence of a husband who had threatened to interrupt the pregnancy whereby her son Tobias had come into the world.

Tobias tumbled to the floor alongside her, pretending not to see me. He searched for Eulália's hand, his fingers intertwining with hers. Together they stroked that belly. For many years he had not touched the region from which he had been born, toward which his own body slid downward after suckling at Eulália's breasts.

Miguel was moved by this scene. Or were his eyes gleaming with envy? With unseemly haste, I rose from my chair. My body was on fire. I didn't want Tobias about.

"Don't worry, father. If I died for you today, you too have ceased to exist for me. I'm Eulália's son, and nothing can erase that truth," he said, on his feet now, making as if to leave.

"Where are you going?" I forced myself to say to him.

"What does it matter now?"

"I haven't driven you from this house, Tobias. Despite everything, your place is still here."

"You'd have done better to drive me out. What you did was worse. You banished me from life."

Very early the following morning, Venâncio's note arrived, addressed to me, though what it said was for Eulália. It expressed concern for her lot, for the mother who had seen her son depart, not knowing where he was going. He then stated that though his house was a modest one, he was in a position to put Tobias up for an indefinite period. He had flung the doors of his house wide open for him, because his heart belonged to that godson whom Eulália and I had so generously given him, and at such an opportune moment, on the very threshold of the Spanish Civil War. He had never before explained, or even confessed, how much this act of friendship had come to be the most gratifying memory of his entire life. A life, as he himself hinted, that had had only a meager share of heartfelt feelings and joys.

It was necessary, however, to report that Tobias, put out of countenance by melancholy, refused to eat anything but the hot soup he had brought to his bedside, this being the one dish capable of making brothers of the rich and the poor. Who, in his moments of misery, has ever turned down soup prepared by a friendly hand and not regretted it later?

Amid such phrases, however, that were politeness itself, Venâncio begged us not to appear at his house. With the exception of Eulália. His godson's state required absolute solitude; for some time yet he ought not to meet with his family. Venâncio was of the firm belief that he had aged considerably in the space of just a few hours, owing to his concern about Tobias, in his capacity as godfather. "If life devoid of emotions can be a torment, when, on the other hand, it is guided by those emotions that soon crystallize round grievous hurts and cruel words, it becomes unbearable."

Miguel wanted to pack Tobias's valise himself. To choose books and papers that would be useful to his brother. He went about it discreetly. At the same time suffering as though it had been he who had been driven out of the house. During that week another son had been born to him. Nonetheless, his mind far removed from this event, he devoted his entire attention to Tobias's problems.

From the hallway, I saw Miguel in his brother's room. Standing at the door, I hesitated to enter. Tobias's odor had contaminated his belongings. Miguel sensed my presence without even turning his head.

"You may come in, father. Keep me company for a little while," and he went on gathering books together.

"I can't. I have things to do."

In much the same way as Eulália, Miguel cast a net and baited a hook so as to alert the fish, make it eager to bite. Speaking to me gently.

"I feel so lonely, father. Everything has changed so much. Our house grows emptier by the day. What's happening?" he said, overcome with emotion, lashing his breast. What he was feeling must have burned like fire.

It was hard for me to go one step farther. The walls of a house know more about us than we do ourselves. But even they would say nothing after our deaths. Everything is lost when one has as a witness a cold surface, made ironically of bricks removed from a furnace.

"I don't know, son. We're growing richer by the day. We're coming to be on more and more intimate terms with the powerful and with our enemies. Exactly as we dreamed of being. But who will relieve the pressure in our chests?" I said, before at last entering Tobias's room.

I had not set foot in there for years. It was foreign territory. What talks had Tobias and I ever really had together? I had never asked him in what region of his body life set him to trembling. Why he had decided to antagonize me with his disgusting passion and his radicalism.

That scratched writing desk had been with Tobias ever since he was a small child. He had never been willing to give it up for another. The chair covering, a Gobelin brought by him from Paris, was one he had chosen himself. Bought when he went with us on a trip. In the tapestry factory, he was fascinated by the work the women were doing, skillfully setting down unusual scenes, such as this one of the hunt.

At the time, he seemed happy. All he said was: "These women have magic hands. And they're not like Penelope. They never undo the work they've done."

The episode passed unnoticed by me back then. There was the Gobelin, however, as though fresh from the tapestry works. That chair had welcomed Tobias's feverish body. A son practically unknown. The only things I knew about him were that he attended the university, went regularly to the National Student Union, to Venâncio's house, on the outskirts of the city. And what else had I collected from that life fortuitously begotten by my sperm?

"Tobias will be back someday, father. Everybody always returns home eventually. It's part of our destiny," Miguel said, from afar. Off on a journey from which he excluded me, forbidding me to follow him. I gave a quick bob of my head, to attract his attention.

"Not always, Miguel. Sometimes life doesn't give us a second chance. Or time to take the path that leads back home."

"To whom are you referring?" he said nervously.

"I'm not thinking of anyone. Should I be?"

Ill at ease, he hesitated to go on. Something troubling his conscience.

"I'm thinking of Esperança, father. What's more, I think of my sister, so far from us, every day. Sometimes I knock on her door. She doesn't answer, knowing it's me. I even think that I can hear her ragged breathing, her nose pressed against the wood. Can it be possible that she doesn't want to see me? Doesn't want to see us? Can't see us? Speak, father," and he sat down disconsolately on Tobias's bed.

"You'd best go home, Miguel. Your wife must be worried."

"Don't play dumb, father. Where is Esperança? Still in the exile decreed by your will? Hasn't the time come to have her here at home with us?"

The children made their escape, leaving trails of destruction in their wake. Meanwhile, my chest burned. Above all because Miguel, speaking of his sister, accused me of having gone too far. As Eulália, speaking of the same subject, warned that a man's honor lay in the hands of God, the only one capable of legislating in such a delicate matter.

"I am going to confess to you, father. I've written to Esperança. She returned the first letters to me. I smiled at the time, seeing her pride. She's right. Savage and cruel, always, as you are. Who else does she resemble besides you? She's never like Mother, who's more like a sheared lamb, gentle and tender. But after the fifth letter, she began to keep them. Not meaning thereby that she'd read them or that we're finally in touch with each other and that therefore she's listening to my tearful pleas for her to come back, in spite of you, our lord and master with the austere face, willing to destroy your children, accepting the bloodletting. Perhaps Esperança is wreaking her revenge on me by this silence. And what better revenge could there be than to leave me in doubt? Suspecting that she's letting the letters pile up, still sealed, covered with dust, on her night table. So as to look at them in fury, before going to sleep. As she takes one last look at them, it strengthens her resolve and she turns the light out. How am I to know, father, if she reads those letters or not? How can I bear this torment?"

"Be still, Miguel, I don't want to know anything about this whole business," I said in a threatening tone.

I turned my back on him and went over to the window. To look at the leafy trees, creatures with a memory and a notion of time. The gardener was pruning away the damage done to the flower beds by the grandchildren. Everything round the lawn was flourishing.

Muffled sounds from Miguel reached my ears. Had he mentioned the name of my daughter? She had plunged her sword into my breast, and to even the score I wounded her every day. Trying each week to dole out to her the exact dose of poison that she should take.

From the window, I turned to look at Miguel, prostrate on the bed. "Do as you please, Miguel. But spare me. I'm not taking back what I told you. If my children want to live their own lives, I'll live mine."

Miguel hastened to my side. "That's not true, father. You're keeping Esperança from living. You're a ghost who tortures her each day. Even when Esperança looks at Breta's face, she sees you."

"That's enough, Miguel, that's enough, I said," heartsick with pent-up emotion. I could no longer bear Esperança's stifled cries, Miguel's despair, these children all conceived without originality. During those months I could not bear human passion.

"Stop running away, father. What right do you have to go on punishing Esperança?"

"My right is the exact counterpart of the humiliation she's caused me. And don't talk as though you were blameless. You too cursed Esperança, punished her when you felt betrayed. Have you perhaps forgotten?"

Miguel squeezed my shoulder. His fingers, faithful and forthright, spoke for him. That hand of an impassioned bear was crushing me. He relaxed his grip, however, and let me go.

We were looking at the garden now. Eulália and Odete were walking toward the gate, to the car, standing with its door open. The chauffeur hastened to take Odete's basket, a visibly heavy one. Odete alongside Eulália, in perfect step with her. Neither ahead of the other. I wanted to shout, Wait for me, Eulália, we'll go together. Not a sound came out of my throat. Miguel rested his face on my shoulder. A gesture from his adolescence, never repeated.

"There goes Mother," Miguel said. "The usual routine."

"In the morning, Mass. As for the rest of the day, I know nothing about it."

"It's easier when a person doesn't know, isn't it, father?"

Embarrassed, we drew apart. But with our eyes still riveted on the two women, who had gotten into the car. The two shadows seated, seen from a long way away. The car began to move, picked up speed, till we lost sight of it. Heading toward the beach, to meet Esperança, who was waiting for them.

Miguel demanded my presence that Friday. At the usual bar, where we ordered the same drink. He was attentive, wanting to please me. He had the waiter bring some hot cheese canapés. Then he stroked my hand with such feeling that he appeared in others' eyes to be my lover.

Miguel had been wanting this meeting since the week before. As I kept putting him off, he sensed that with Eulália's and Madruga's approaching death the rest of the family risked being eliminated. Including himself, whose name, memories, and estate I shared.

Miguel seemed sad. His children constantly defying him, his marriage to Sílvia a failure. With the further aggravating circumstance that Sílvia insisted on his sharing her bed, on his daily presence beneath their common sheets. Forbidden to touch her, he was nonetheless forced to smell the odor of her, to stay out of the way of her unexpected movements during the night. Obliged also to court her, giving her public proofs of his love.

His fingers are now clutching the glass. Naturally confusing it with a shapely leg or the wrist of a princess. Sitting there at the bar, we both know we are on opposite sides of a frontier. We deserve no pity. Especially since we demand a passport, proof of identity, of anyone moving through our domains. When confronted with life, we are cynical and polychromatic.

Miguel is the uncle I love most. And yet I keep wounding him. Each year I deal him a dagger blow and he scarcely notices. Because I lack Esperança's skill. A woman warrior with a helmet and sword who left deep furrows in his chest. Miguel comes tagging after me hoping that his niece, suddenly transformed into Esperança, will restore his self-confidence by means of this poignant memory. Miguel cannot do without the unconquered pride of a dead woman in order to live.

He forces himself not to speak of Esperança. Fleeing from the last remaining shadows of his sister. Paradoxically, however, without Esperança he is nothing. His own face in the mirror becomes opaque. And when making love he fails to penetrate the other's body with a sort of fury that makes him spit out, along with his orgasm, an agony anchored in him since adolescence, when he felt the first craving for victory. For a victory that was worthwhile only when he defeated Esperança.

"What will happen to us after Eulália's and Madruga's death?" he said, trying to play on my feelings.

"We'll bury them and go home."

Miguel hid his uneasiness with a smile. "You're like Esperança at times. She was forever surprising me."

"What's the use of repeating such things, Miguel, when I don't know anything about Esperança? She's a stranger to me."

I forced him to look at me. Miguel averted his gaze, his eye caught by the blonde at the next table.

"Didn't you hear, or can't you bear the truth?" I paused. Then began again. "We're a family of hypocrites and liars."

This time, Miguel was irked. "We only lie when the truth is painful. Or we have no idea what it is. But how dare you speak of the damned truth, Breta, if you've decided to write, decided to speak of human passion? Isn't creation, more than anything, an act of despair and of absolute reconciliation with falsehood?"

He paused. His mind was far from me, from the blonde, from the atmosphere suffused with a reddish tone.

"Look at Mother, for example," he went on. "She needed to invent a god that would make her forget this earth. Has she spent her life telling me stories of Grandfather Miguel just to have me as an accomplice? Thus forcing me to repeat them, to live in accordance with values predicated on hers? And hence to renounce my personal life? And all to further the life of stories, the spellbinding illusion of stories?"

I quickly stroked Miguel's long fingers clutching the glass. And immediately assumed my previous position. He pretended not to notice my affectionate gesture.

"Tell me, uncle, who was Esperança? What was my mother like?"

Miguel smoothed his rumpled hair. His lion's head suited him. He was edgy, sensing a rifle aimed at his head. Chained to the table in the bar, he would perhaps have preferred to be in bed, mounted on a female, absorbed in acts wavering between anguish and pleasure. Who could this man be, spying on me as I drifted by?

"Esperança liked to play when she was certain that I was close at hand. It was the same with me. I would venture out into the public square and the streets all by myself, certain that Esperança would waylay me on my return, immediately demanding an account of my exploits, furious because I'd won and she'd lost by having stayed home. Our competition consisted of finding out which of us had in fact been banished from the face of the earth that day. Defeated, that is to say. We were eternal outlaws, fleeing our own selves. I, from Esperança, so as to come back to her. She, from me, so as to meet me at the first possible moment. Whereas at home objects, the hiding places Mother gave us, familiar faces came between us. Not to mention our dead, whom Father and Mother insisted on bringing to the table to eat with us. Mother even went so far as to say on a certain occasion:

"'If Dom Miguel were here now, he'd lay his knife and fork down on the table, as a sign of displeasure at this stew.'

"I remember that Father found her comment odd. Especially since stew was Dom Miguel's favorite dish. Perhaps that was his reason for remarking, 'May I ask why, Eulália?' Mother seemed distracted, as though Madruga had failed to interrupt her train of thought. She cast a quick glance round the table, to see if any of her children were missing. And included Venâncio, an obligatory presence on Sundays, in this count. There he was, sitting in the same chair, wearing the same suit. Never any other except one that had been her father's. The same color as always. A present that Venâncio found it so hard to accept that it took him ages to get round to wearing it. He didn't give in till Eulália insisted. That day, then, Venâncio had taken great care to look his best. He had gone to the barber, had a haircut and a very close shave. And he'd made a point of asking the barber to sprinkle his face with a lotion made right there. A mixture of fragrances conveying brief illusions, all of them bought in the city. Ah, Breta, how happy those Sundays were! But where are they now? And where are we?"

Overcome with emotion, he bowed his head, almost as if to apologize. The waiter brought him another drink automatically. Immersed in his confused memory, Miguel forgot to thank him. Nor did I interrupt him. His restless body, with its feverish balls, endlessly active, felt the need to plunge to the bottom of his heart, there to rescue Esperança, gone down with the ship.

"After a few seconds, Mother came to. She stared at Madruga, who glared back, in violent disagreement with his wife's observation. Personally, he had approved of the stew, the vegetables dotted with gobs of fat but retaining the necessary firmness. But it was not only Father who was eyeing Eulália. We too had left off eating, watching her. Mother, after all, had nursed all our hopes. Even Esperança, who always hung on Madruga's every word, stopped chewing, wanting to hear Eulália, about to speak again. I don't know why, Breta, but all of a sudden I felt jealous of my sister. I suspected that she was acting as she was just to oppose me, to challenge my affection for Mother. She knew very well that I was Eulália's favorite son. Who else did Mother recount the most secret plots of Sobreira to? Talking to me by the hour of Grandfather Miguel, whose name I had also inherited. The famous Dom Miguel, whose life seemed to be justified only by the stories of Galicia, which he personally had saved from oblivion. Of that Galicia that Mother transformed for me into a domain at once magic and abstract. It both exists and does not exist. But now, after all these years, I have the sensation that time, that gnawing animal, is slowly killing me with these memories."

Confessing seemed to make Miguel feel ashamed. He hung back, reluctant to proceed. Perhaps he felt he had gone into too many details not properly evaluated.

"Please, uncle, go on."

"The truth is that it's something of an effort to listen to Mother now. She doesn't perceive that she's repeating stories she told me five years ago. When she talks to me of Dom Miguel, she's also making a desperate effort to bring him back to life. But everything escapes her grasp. That's why she offers me so many portraits, not one of which is true. But I don't say anything to Mother. I don't correct her. I don't even suggest another character to take Dom Miguel's place. A more believable sort perhaps. But then again, where would that get me? I know as well as you do that telling stories takes imagination. Thanks to the powers of imagination, I was able for many years to believe in Dom Miguel and the mythology of his land. What's more, it's through imagination and illusion that I convince myself that Brazil has walls, a roof, and leaks everywhere. It smells of mold, despite the sun. Because of Eulália's stories, I'm forced to admit that I've done nothing to confer life on my country, that it's existed solely to serve me. I'm part of that contingent that's a disgrace to the nation. Is there a single innocent in this country? Can I exempt from blame the worker who's a prisoner of the Volkswagen assembly line?"

Miguel showed no interest in listening to me. He would resist even a chance remark. The only things to relieve his tension were alcohol and words.

"Finally Mother decided to explain the fault she found with that stew. The basic problem was the smoked ham. Who had ever seen a ham that hadn't hung for at least eight months from the kitchen ceiling, exposed to the smoke from the wood stove and the steam of all the food cooked on it during that time? That alone would be reason enough for Dom Miguel to turn his nose up at it. Grandfather was finicky about details. He always wanted everything at exactly the right time, the precise hour. Therefore ruling the house and the persons in it with a strict hand. What was more, Dom Miguel began to exercise his authority over all of Sobreira the minute he set foot outside. Madruga had always known of his father-in-law's power, even before claiming Eulália as his wife. Despite this, he stood up to Dom Miguel, so as to win the woman who would one day be our mother. It was a duel between two despots who reached an agreement in the end. Father remains an authoritarian to this day, however, though he's admittedly a generous man. I sometimes wonder which of us inherited his gesture of opening his hands repeatedly, letting an abundance of gifts, money, pieces of bread fall from his fingers. You may add, perhaps, that Madruga also shed blood, his own and that of others, his aim being to increase his powers. And that I do the same, simply to be respected. In which case I will say that you are quite correct. Right this minute I want this waiter to be happy with my tips and my despotism. Because that way I free myself of the need to speak to him. Nothing outside of a curt and indifferent good-day. Madruga, if he were here, would act differently. Amid all his screaming and shouting, he resorts to the affectionate gesture. He ends up being loved by workers and office employees alike. And so I ask you, who in this family inherited the dazzling soul of that old man we call Madruga?"

Miguel had doubts about his father. As though he would like to forget the side of Madruga's nature that made him a hunter. Or how many plants and animals he killed for food and profit. And after sating himself, he turned to hoarding. Far in excess of his real needs. Only in that way, with trunks and flour sacks filled to overflowing with gold and silver, would Madruga be able to drive scenes of poverty from his memory. The terrible pressure of winter in Sobreira, when, harried by rain and December's north wind, he shivered in his bones with cold.

In his old age now, Madruga wore a denture, like any mortal. He no longer had the strong canines that I had appreciated in the yellowed photographs. Those teeth that by dint of so much rending of human flesh had little by little devoured part of his own heart.

Today, Madruga's teeth and weapons are matters of controversy. Beginning with Bento, who, in the effort to imitate him, added the use of resplendent shields to his father's resources. He dresses with the correctness of a prince, and fences with great cunning, without fear of running his sword clean through his enemy's body and finding it suspended in midair.

I look at Miguel and try to bring Madruga's image to life in him. But I am unable to pull this feat off. Madruga is irreplaceable. Because, from his earliest days, Madruga tackled the tasks before him with blind confidence. Demanding that Ceferino and Urcesina take him to the fields, almost from the moment he left the cradle; he had no time to lose. He immediately fondled the plow, taking a strange sensual pleasure in the gesture. Certain that the land would provide abundantly for him. And always there came to him from this same earth the renewed comfort of a stomach warmed with soup and corn bread. As, leading the cows to secluded places, he practiced on the mountainside a certain bravery that would enable him to confront obstacles. The first of all of them would be to arrive in America with much the same feeling as an explorer who had intuited the route to the Indies.

When the ship put out to sea at last, leaving Vigo behind, and they confronted the Atlantic, out of sheer nervous excitement Venâncio and he launched into a spate of storytelling. Venâncio took it upon himself to make a mark with his penknife on the old leather trunk for each day gone by. Without this practical detail breaking the flow of dreams unleashed in him the moment he looked upon the ocean for the first time. Indifferent therefore to the mistreatment dealt out on board. A behavior different from Madruga's bawling at the top of his lungs.

"What do these English think they're doing? We're not slaves and neither are we the Invincible Armada, which they destroyed thanks to a great stroke of luck. These buccaneers are arrogant and heartless. They despise folk who enjoy sunshine practically the whole year round."

Venâncio smiled ironically. "And who told you we're not vassals? Wasn't that why we fled Spain?"

They had not yet won the status of free men. Venâncio couldn't vouch for the truth of his statement. Even though he sympathized with Madruga. Nonetheless, he needed to warn him of the perils of America. So that Madruga would not lose, after the first ten years in Brazil, the radiance present in his face at this moment. When it came right down to it, Venâncio admired his capacity to reach the height of indignation at so young an age. Capable of defying the English and the Atlantic itself.

On the sixth day of the passage, Venâncio was terrified by the fury of the waves washing over the prow of the English ship. Making it for the moment a bark as frail as Columbus's vessels. The English crew redoubled its efforts to overcome the crisis. Lacking, however, the spirit of the Iberian seafarers, in the days of the Discovery. Those men full of agues and distempers. Overcome by malignant fever and intense curiosity. And for the very reason that they had been laid low by the evils of a day, they discovered America.

In the grip of his power of recall, Venâncio grew even more expansive on the tenth day, unmindful of Madruga.

"For a long time, my family roamed the world, bearing few belongings on their backs. Till finally I was born in a wretched house, with whitewashed walls and blue windows. Yet I never left off dreaming."

With Venâncio beside him at the rail, Madruga caught his first glimpse of the Brazilian shore. This event taking place at the beginning of the century. And as the ship drew closer, they had a better view of the row of low houses, the palm trees, the port, the city with its look, still, of a colonial capital.

Madruga disembarked with martial step. Despite the little knapsack on his back, stuffed full of old dreams. He and Venâncio belching forth countless illusions.

At first sight Brazil seemed to him to be an immense iron pot into which there were being thrown black beans, scraps of pork, poverty, lust, fearlessness, red-hot pepper, and bits of magic come from Africa and the Iberian peninsula. And not a soul at hand with the courage to dip a spoon in this huge caldron, to keep this exotic food from scorching and the people from starving for centuries to come.

In the Praça Mauá, on the way to the boardinghouse, Madruga was suddenly uneasy. "Well, Venâncio, are we here as Spaniards or as Arabs, who dominated us for eight centuries?"

"Neither one, Madruga. We've eaten so much of that damned English mutton during the voyage that we've lost our nationality. And we haven't had time yet to carve out another country to replace the one we had. Who knows? Maybe someday we'll be something we can't even put into words yet."

Before entering the boardinghouse, and confronting its pudgy owner, Madruga turned to Venâncio:

"Well, I say we'll be Brazilians!"

Venâncio dodged Madruga's specific questions. Not having added, in the following decades, any further information concerning his past. He had become, on the other hand, a creature of habit. He would arrive unobtrusively in Leblon, on Sundays especially, after braving the train and the bus. Inhaling the city's acrid fumes.

Of late Venâncio felt out of place in Madruga's house. He fell into a moody silence, despite the garden and the sun pouring in from the Cagarras Islands. Perhaps because of Bento's presence in the living room as Venâncio was leaving. Bento greeted him punctiliously. The two of them harboring a mutual distrust. Bento, however, hid his feelings in front of Madruga and Eulália. So as not to admit to the aversion he felt for losers who took Venâncio as their model.

Bento had the habit of straightening his tie with a studiedly solemn air. Especially when he reflected on the euphoria characteristic of Power, capable of overflooding the nature of the person who exercised it. Therein lay the most fecund human source that could be called upon. And the loss of it meant an irremediable failure.

"As I see it, Bento is a flash in the pan as a speaker. He can't resist dazzling rhetorical effects."

"An intellectual is a self-important sort. He picks over humanity's leftovers, just to suck on the bones. But how does he have the nerve to proclaim himself an interpreter of human folly, if he spends his life shut up in his office? Always withdrawn from dirty, shabby reality. That's why I have my doubts about the imagination of the contemporary artist. And I don't hesitate to say that the primacy of imagination today lies in the hands of Power. It's a legacy of the orbit of Power."

Luís Filho joins Bento, as though he couldn't do without him. He goes on with the same line of argument.

"Bento is right. Artists are no longer the only ones who possess imagination. It's Power that enjoys an extravagant imagination today. As an example, we need only look at the dictators of Latin America, to confine ourselves to this continent. And it's from this crushing Power that the most concrete evidence of imagination emanates. Even though it's a sick imagination. Be that as it may, it's this Power which in practice infects all of society. As a consequence making ideas fructify, training them, pruning away the ones that are against their interests. And clever enough to camouflage the origin of these very same ideas. Creating the impression that they have arisen as a result of society's decision."

I interrupt their debate by leaving the room. On my return, Bento backtracks. As does Luís Filho. They do not hesitate to compliment me on mere banalities. But I resist this attack. I will not allow myself to be fleeced that easily. Nor will I turn over part of Madruga's fortune to fatten their bellies. Or that of the offspring they took such great care to father. As though they were modeling life in marble.

In the bar now, Miguel demands that I pass judgment on Madruga. But whenever I try to restore his image, I betray him and me. I'm not trustworthy, since there are no calm and legitimate sources of reference.

I'm afraid I haven't sounded Grandfather's insides with a depth gauge. Just as I haven't surrendered to him down through these years. Secrets occupy my every moment. My own soul has no way of disclosing itself. It barely touches me. I am mortally secret. My lungs breathe in conflicting feelings, whose roots go down to the damp soil of blood and passion.

As I wait for emotion to surface in its raw state, confirming that I know nothing.

Madruga is comforted by the fact that I am sketching a pencil portrait of him in the future. Preserving some of his features in this drawing. So that the curious will ask me for details.

"Who is that old man with the burning eyes, the furrowed brow, the worried face?"

I will give out information only very slowly. "He was born in Sobreira. A village at the end of the world. He was baptized, or given the name, Madruga. Under that name, he formed a family: us." But I will make Madruga and Sobreira endure only through my imagination. If I'm persuasive when the time comes to describe them. So that they won't disbelieve the village and Madruga. But for this task I need at least three years. That's the only way I can lend credibility to Madruga and his luminous crossing of the Atlantic.

The waiter poured us generous drinks. Miguel hurried him up so he'd leave us alone again. Anxious to hear what I had to say to him. He had launched an investigation knowing the answer beforehand. His aim being to extort the name nailed to his conscience.

"What is it you want, Miguel? Do you want me to lie? To name you and Tobias Madruga's heirs? When you're only pastiches of Grandfather? And all we have left is Esperança! Are you satisfied now?" I said impatiently.

He seemed grateful. Indifferent to the attack he'd undergone. His attitude forcing me to mount another invasion.

"Now that I've given you Esperança's name, tell me something in return. Who it was who picked me up at Bento's house, after the funeral. Who took me to my grandparents'?"

Miguel straightened in his chair, set his drink down, ready to spill the information.

"After the funeral, Father remained in the living room for several hours. Then he locked himself into his study, where he had a bed set up. He came out for urgent calls of nature. The servants were the only ones he laid eyes on. Mother and he saw each other again at the seventh-day requiem Mass. We pounded on his door, begging him not to give way to despair like that. He never once answered. And when he returned to the living room after the Mass, he asked us to avoid the name Esperança in his presence. He had promised himself not to utter it either. And he kept his promise. If we so much as mentioned Esperança, his face contracted. With hands upraised, he would chase away bothersome flies that no one could see."

Miguel paused. He took another swallow of his drink.

"Mother did not leave the bedroom except to go to church, in the company of Odete. She looked at us with a distant gaze. She saw nothing with clear definition. At no time did Father and Mother help each other. They behaved as though they were strangers to each other. Venâncio tried to help them, but he was afraid the name of Esperança would escape him in Madruga's presence. He too was plunged into despair. Sílvia brought me bowls of hot soup, guided the spoon to my mouth, taking care of a hurt child. One night I escaped Sílvia's watchful eye and stole off to make love with a stranger. Furiously, for I was demonstrating a passion that faked real feeling. It all seemed scarcely believable to both of us. A few days after the Mass, the family gathered in Leblon. All of a sudden, Bento squared off with Father. Yes, he was the one, I remember well. And the others, as though by intuition, went to his side as one. We all pounded on the closed door of Madruga's heart."

It took Madruga some time to open. He had cotton in his ears. Indifferent to the fate of the granddaughter still at Bento's. A situation that had to be remedied. There had to be a future for that orphan creature, nine years old, with wide-open eyes, who kept herself cooped up in her room, continually ripping blank pages out of her school composition books, in a constant show of anxiety and depredation, to which they must put an end.

"And how is Breta now?" Venâncio said, waiting for Madruga and Eulália to speak, determined to hear them out on the subject for the first time.

"She doesn't ask one question. Only her eyes seek to fathom the meaning of her mother's death. At times, she leans against the wall, strokes the surface, drawing from it a sort of sap that might help her. It's urgent that we bring her to this house. Otherwise we'll be killing her," Tobias said.

Madruga was unmoved by these sad details. That granddaughter seemed to him a stranger, whose birth had brought him nothing but grief.

"Can you possibly not want to know her even now, father?" Antônia did her best to arouse his curiosity.

Madruga did not answer. His stubborn silence rivaling Eulália's. Miguel moved about the room, finding it difficult to breathe. Till he could contain himself no longer. Standing before the sofa, an imposing figure, he claimed Madruga's granddaughter for himself in a loud voice. If her grandparents did not want Breta, he would bring the little girl up.

"That's how it is, father. She's coming home with me. Perhaps Esperança's daughter is more mine than she is all of yours."

Bento disagreed. He thought it shameful that the grandparents should reject their granddaughter, even if she had been born beneath the impact of shattering grief. Breta ought to be brought to Leblon, even though Madruga did not want to lay eyes on her or have her at his table.

Miguel insisted on taking Breta over. The discussion between Bento and Miguel became heated, the two of them shouting, oblivious of Eulália's presence.

"The child's not going to be a Cinderella here," Miguel roared. "I'd never agree to that."

"How could you dare to think of Father and Mother acting like that toward a grandchild?" Bento defended them.

"At this point, I have the right to imagine anything. I don't want Breta subjected to Father's indifference. Punished with one of his implacable looks."

Tobias called upon Venâncio to prepare to take Breta. He would know how to care for the child, give her mother's milk, offer her honeyed words.

Miguel drained his glass. He ordered another whisky. He had interrupted his story. He found it difficult to go on. He immediately demanded my testimony. I could perhaps confirm the facts, if by chance I remembered. He was afraid he was betraying my story. Injecting foreign elements into it, abandoning the ones that were most to be trusted.

Miguel's challenge distressed me. I immediately began to remove the obstacles long since settled to the bottom of a dark unconscious, covered with dust and debris. How to learn my own story without the testimony of someone other than myself! Miguel, my grandfather, my uncles, for example? After all, it is passersby and neighbors who shape our faces and our words, adding what is missing.

I still had the vague memory, however, of having wept for hours or even days after being told that my mother would not be coming home again. I was then taken to a bright-colored room, which I refused to leave. I didn't even want to go to the little public square that my mother used to take me to every day.

Moreover, it was in this same square, usually, that Eulália met Esperança. As she embraced her mother, the daughter always had the illusion that Eulália was about to pass on to her the message awaited for so many years. The dream of returning to her father's house, even without trumpeters at the door to herald her arrival. The only thing required was proofs of respect, never of humiliation.

Eulália freed herself from Esperança's embrace, on the pretext of handing over the parcels she had brought. And beginning then to speak of an obscure daily life, almost without mentioning the names of her husband and children, she unwittingly banished Esperança from it. She made even less mention of Miguel, who came to see her every day. A tense devotion, since in addition to insisting that his mother go on with Dom Miguel's stories, he kept asking her in roundabout ways for news of Esperança, being satisfied with slender threads collected here and there.

On seeing certain gestures of her mother's, Esperança left the bench where she had been sitting. She walked over to the trees, circling the leafiest of them again and again, her mind far away from her mother, from Odete, and from her daughter. Knowing that Breta, in a few moments, would come running after her, fearing she'd been forgotten. Which caused her to decide to return to Eulália, waiting for her on the bench. Before Esperança yielded, however, to her daughter's pleas she would demand a kiss from her. Her arms enveloped me like tentacles. I felt her rigid, heaving flesh. Meanwhile, ill at ease at the tortured energy that Mother discharged against me out of love. I freed myself from her. And the harder I pushed her away, the more she resisted. Mother growing weaker in this struggle, while at the same time she hurt me. Were these petty resources we were using?

Back home, in Botafogo, Esperança bathed me, anxiously changed my clothes many times a day. She wanted me to be beautiful, to smell of perfume for any visitor who might chance to knock at the door. Visitors who did not appear till late at night. Mother received few people. Several of her friends seemed to like her for what was in the refrigerator. They would go directly to the kitchen, flinging themselves greedily on the cold food, noisily spitting out the chicken bones on the plate. Then leave, having a great many things to do.

Some nights Mother left me with the maid or a neighbor woman. And because she'd been gone so long, she was doubly affectionate the next morning. She bought me magazines. She read Monteiro Lobato's children's stories to me.

"If you want to get to know Brazil better, all you have to do is read about the mischief that Narizinho and Emília and Pedrinho get into."

"And how big is Brazil, mother? Promise we'll go visit it someday soon?" Wasn't that what I asked Mother one rainy day?

It rained so much that water came in through the windows of the apartment there in Botafogo, a long way away from Leblon, with no danger of Mother running into neighbors, relatives, friends, the Spanish colony. Every so often Esperança had the place repainted. Always white. She was afraid it was beginning to show its age.

"We'll get to know Brazil someday, just you wait. Someday everything will be the same as it once was, Breta. Do you remember São Lourenço? Well, Brazil is like São Lourenço. The same people, the same way of talking. Do you remember the little goat slowly trotting up the hillside, pulling you in the cart? That's how it is with all of us, slowly going up to the top of the mountain. Not knowing where we'll end up."

Esperança sometimes beat on doors. In torment. Without my understanding her brusque gestures, her few scattered words. Complaining of the difficulties of being a woman alone.

"They're punishing us in the right place, my girl. Right in the heart."

After baring her sorrow, she remained in the living room for hours. The lights of the house all on, even the one in the hall, as though beaming messages, so that everyone would know she was home, waiting for help. But was she so dependent on the kindness of strangers, or simply on a pair of eyes regaling her with vain words and caresses?

She would give a start when the telephone rang. Whispering to the maid, I'm not here. Or else ask, When are you coming? But were those really Esperança's words?

Eulália stole into the apartment. Once she had settled herself comfortably, she handed parcels to her daughter yet again. Esperança always opened them in a hurry, to be rid of them. Or of Eulália. Immediately putting away in the drawers the presents that had come from a family we were not allowed to set eyes on. As meanwhile Grandmother seemed to be elsewhere.

As for Odete, she never caressed me, not even in the public square, as she kept me amused. Nor was Grandmother overgenerous with her kisses when we met and parted. Only Esperança was effusive. She swept me off my feet, hugging me to her. I flattened her breasts, but felt her warm, generous contours.

One night, Esperança didn't come home. It was barely light out when they took me out of the house, wrapped in a blanket, still drowsy. After I'd been put in another bed, they brought me warm milk, stroked my head, so I wouldn't notice a reality that had protruding edges, capable of hurting and shaming. I asked for my mother in the days that followed. Several voices assured me that Esperança was off traveling, that she'd be gone a long time. For there were pleasure excursions and, also, other travels that a person never came back from. Through the fault of the rough sea alone, of the indescribable horror experienced amid the salt waves, the fish, devouring indivisible pieces of flesh in the darkness. How, then, to return from a journey made beneath the aegis of terror and of fear? Should I have told them at the time that they were all mistaken, that my mother had gone to São Lourenço, a pleasant archipelago, from which she would return with her soul rejuvenated?

With a gesture, Eulália calmed Miguel and Bento down. She ordered someone to open the living room curtains. She needed the sea breeze. She made them see immediately that the matter in question lay in her domain, a woman's womb that had borne that family without ever asking for anything until today.

"Isn't it true that I demand nothing of you?"

There was no need, however, to consult Madruga, at her side, much less the children. The decision she made would be her own. And so, from that day on, she would offer refuge to her granddaughter, who would come live with them in Leblon.

Madruga listened attentively to her. He did not want to rob her of the right to speak. He was not always able to rule the life of that house as he pleased. Though it was painful for him to lose. Unlike Eulália, for whom defeats were merits earned for the other kingdom. She had somewhere to go after death. Whereas things were difficult for him. After exhausting all the resources of this earth and having only exile, loneliness, boredom left him, what would he do in his old age? Venâncio himself went so far as to confess to him, as though sharing a secret, that dreams were only clay and air, something at once organic and vaporous.

Entering Leblon, brought there by Miguel, I didn't recognize the house. My memory not revealing to me a single detail retained by chance at the time of the one visit there, before I was three, in Madruga's absence.

I stumbled along, feeling myself to be in a tunnel without light, without help. Miguel squeezed my hand. He wanted me to feel in familiar surroundings in that house. Nothing should be strange or unfriendly to me. And so he offered me belongings, perfumes, clothes, space.

"This will be your room. Yours alone. Look how big, how white it is. From here you'll see the garden and the orchard. And it will be forever, Breta."

Uncle repeated "forever" in a way meant to placate me. As though he were assuring me of the freedom to build, in the future, my own walls, roof, a family, finally, that would nearly explode from the accumulation of gas.

And, at each visit, Miguel brought me new toys. Replacing the ones that had been left behind at Esperança's. Few memories of my mother were to remain. Tobias and Venâncio had taken charge of dividing up Esperança's belongings, once Miguel had refused the task, forbidding Bento to fill in for him. On the pretext that his brother was predatory, with little taste for reconstructing memories, to him a burden that one ought to shed.

Madruga observed from a distance the arrival of that intruding granddaughter. Abstaining from gestures directed solely toward her. But not wanting to call attention to his rudeness, he addressed me in the second person plural, including the others present. And offered me tasty tidbits, after serving the adults. In retaliation, I hid in corners, so they'd have to come looking for me. Till they found me. Whereupon Eulália, with words of affection, handed me over to the housemaid.

At school, Miguel answered for my behavior. He would leave a meeting on receiving word that his niece had picked a fight or burst into tears. He would take me home, not leaving me alone. We would go out into the garden, intent on choosing which tree we'd sit beneath. He liked the breadfruit best of all.

"I don't know why, but to me it's the tree that's most Brazilian. It's as though even our odor came from the pulp of its fruit. Just smell, Breta!"

In the living room, he sat me down beside Madruga. Ill at ease and embarrassed, Grandfather just sat there, saying nothing. The look in his eyes condemned Miguel. Miguel met his father's gaze squarely, to force him to pay a little attention to his granddaughter. I, however, did not say one word to him. A silence appreciated in the beginning, though it eventually made Madruga uncomfortable. He took it to be an act of rebellion.

"So then, we've yet another rebel in this house! It's going to be very easy to predict this young lady's future," he said sarcastically.

Eulália contradicted her husband. She did not permit this sort of insinuation. He was offending her and the family. Their granddaughter had come to all of them to be a daughter. They should offer her a haven safe from storms. Above all because she was Esperança's daughter. Now that Breta was there, they had Esperança back with them.

"Nobody has returned to this house, do you hear, Eulália? She's never come back to us," Madruga said in a loud voice.

Miguel flew into a rage. He would not put up with such behavior. If his father persisted in this attitude, he wouldn't come home anymore.

"What children do you have left that you can count on? Can't you see that you're losing us by fighting Esperança? Do you think you can punish her even after she's dead? And by what right, father?"

Madruga turned to look straight at me. Without my returning his gaze. He insisted on prolonging the encounter; I was turning into an appreciable adversary.

One morning, in my room, Eulália combed my hair so gently that I threw myself into her arms. Grandmother said, very softly, Oh Esperança, when will we meet again!

On seeing her mistress's emotion as she held me trembling in her arms, Odete hurriedly brought her sugar water. Thereby stemming the tide of affection that had bound us together at that moment. Grandmother allowed herself to be lured away by Odete. She laid the golden comb down on the dressing table and went to her room.

Left by myself, I buried my head in the pillow. As he walked by in the hall, Madruga hesitated for a moment before the door left ajar. And then entered. It was the first time that he had set foot in my room. He looked at the small objects that had followed me from the other apartment. He pretended to ignore Esperança's portrait, framed by Miguel, in the place of honor, on my night table. Miguel constantly inspected the estate his sister had left behind. He would not allow one thing to disappear. He answered for it for eternity. But what sort of time and space ruled his life, and his heart, that ardent flame? Those burning eyes of his, whose very gaze seemed to make his sex rise like a kite!

Grandfather's firm step practically made scratch marks in the floor. Leaving traces of his passage. Giving proof of an arrogance that Venâncio always condemned in him. Madruga leaned over the bed. I didn't move. I held my breath, waiting. Even though I hadn't consented to his presence. Madruga was certain that Esperança's daughter knew him to be in the room. He waited for her to give him the finder's reward. His granddaughter, however, was reluctant to pay the homage due him for having come to visit a room that he had always done his best to ignore.

Despite himself, he felt a thrill of emotion. He was breathing slowly and regularly, without my appreciating his sacrifice. There he was at my side, giving me the rare opportunity of offering him my apologies for the mere fact of having been born without his permission.

With my head buried in the pillow, I traversed a cave, reverberating with light and giving me back the echo of words and scenes in which Esperança held me fast in her arms with the mortal strength of a tiger. And from this cavern came the warning, to guide and protect me, that my grandfather should speak first.

Madruga stirred uneasily. That quiet seemed intolerable. He must trumpet abroad his granddaughter's insolence. Despite his second thoughts, I heard a faltering, unsteady voice.

"Are you all right, Breta?"

A voice that, doubtless, Grandfather had borrowed from his neighbor. One I paid no attention to, as he had seen for himself.

"Are you listening to me, Breta? It's me," he insisted, without identifying himself.

I said nothing. Prepared to demand his recognition of existing family ties. Hadn't he acted like an enemy thus far?

The silence began to unnerve him. He touched my head lightly. Concentrating, I sized up the moves he'd made. Grandfather's affluence began to scare me. He loomed up before me, like a mandarin, a maker of days and of lives, whose hands formed reality, made of soft bread, into different shapes.

"Answer, girl, can't you see I'm here?"

Grandfather did not hide his irritation. I could feel the pressure of his fingers on my skull. All alone in the room, we were sounding each other out. Both dimly aware of the feeling of outrage that bound us. I for my part would have sent that man to the wheel to torture him. He for his part wanted me in the gutter, driven from the house built by his effort. These emotions taking their course till his chest ached, and he left the room, slamming the door. Without ceremony, he was abandoning his granddaughter, leaving her destiny in her own hands.

In the living room, Miguel heard him out. Madruga refusing to accept the trouble caused by his granddaughter. Showing no respect for the person who had taken her in, despite being put off by her childish ways, her painfully adult eyes.

"She's Esperança's daughter all right. She's as brave as you are, father. She's going to fight you with weapons Esperança didn't have," Miguel provoked his father.

Madruga contained himself. All he had in that house were enemies.

He had produced sons who spread discord among themselves and who, fortified by the food supplied with his money, were continually turning against him.

"It's a good thing I never included you in my dream of conquering America. And when I went to Uncle Justo to ask for help, you didn't exist. Nor had you been born yet in my first thirteen years in Brazil. It's the only one of all my dreams that I keep out of your reach, untouchable, free of the presence of all of you." And he immediately immersed himself in pleasant reminiscence, as though he were speaking with Venâncio of their respective sagas.

Miguel was touched. He loved that man, and yet he often was exasperated with him, whenever they came round to the subject of Esperança. For a long time now reality had been training his father to follow the interwoven paths of life and death. He himself had begun his apprenticeship. The slave of memories and an inordinate intensity, he was finding everything a trial to him.

At dinner, Grandfather scarcely greeted those present. Over coffee, with Eulália's approval, he invited me to accompany him to his study. Seated opposite each other, we were about to begin a practice that in the future would become a sacred rite. Madruga offered me a port, sweet and mellow. I tasted it with a look of marked pleasure on my face.

"Where I come from, we have the habit of drinking and telling stories at the same time. That way, we keep track of the weeks and the years. Till we reach old age."

He interrupted his explanation, his eyes fixed on the large photograph hanging on the wall. Then he turned round to look at me. Then again staring at the photograph. He seemed to be looking for a face resembling mine among the others in the group. He was in no hurry. Determined now to keep his granddaughter with him, for years if need be. Thus defeating Esperança and his offspring. All of them monsters with well-tailored suits and friendly gestures.

Madruga felt himself translated to Sobreira. Immediately remembering Grandfather Xan, who had laid claim to him since his birth. Xan had always wanted this grandson of his to be held spellbound by a kind of storytelling that there was no way or reason to end. And Xan managed to win him over to such a point that, even in America, Madruga constantly invoked his name, bearing with him wherever he went the memory of his grandfather's thorny plots. And when Ceferino sent word of Xan's death, by letter, Madruga felt a wound whose bleeding could never be stanched open in his chest. Everything, then, proclaiming his inability to repeat those same stories that in Xan's hands grew and grew. As if he'd added yeast to them. While at the same time he ruled his stories with a conductor's baton, now speeding up the tempo, now slowing it down. If he detected signs of boredom on the part of a listener.

After his grandfather's death, Madruga discovered that Xan had decided to wreak his vengeance on his faithless grandson. And in a radical way. By cutting him out of his right to the stories of Sobreira. And all because Madruga had accumulated a pile of money with the same greed with which Xan had hoarded plots.

He had the impression, in those days, that Xan's ghost breathed in his ear: He who hoards money loses the right to stories. You must choose, my grandson, between the freedom to tell stories and clinging to gold.

Madruga pretended not to hear this warning in those years. He refused to believe Grandfather Xan's distant whisper. He was certain that one day he would take up Xan's habit, that of entertaining people with endless stories. Perhaps in the future he would be a Xan reborn, despite the bright gleam of gold lighting his face. After all, why should a storyteller cloak himself in the mantle of misery, of the false appendage of modesty, merely to ensure his credibility? What independence would this teller of tales have if he depended on a plate of food from those who heard him? On a neighbor or on an authority, prepared to prune his story, refusing to accept the direction it was taking?

Madruga could feel that the moment was a delicate one. But he wanted the complicity, willing or not, of his granddaughter, who was not responding readily. Insensitive to the warm atmosphere in the study, to his words, to the port, sipped in the part of Iberia it came from as a proof of friendship.

Madruga's blue eyes fascinated me. His face stood out amid the books and photographs. Handsome, severe, well dressed, he was doubtless better-looking than Grandmother. And more intense than Uncle Miguel. The handsomest one in the house.

Madruga showed signs of impatience. He wanted easy victories in matters of the heart. He had no time to lose. And what if he should die on Monday, without having first made a conquest of his granddaughter?

"I allow almost no one to enter this room. And do you know why? Because it's my lair. My secrets and my treasures are here," he murmured amiably, trying to draw me closer to him.

I freed myself and went to the window. The darkness did not permit me to see the plantings, always splendid. I was becoming as familiar with the garden as if I had been born in that house. Everything attracted me. Mother had preceded me in every corner. And where had she walked in the garden? Had she had a favorite tree?

Miguel had been very clear. Wherever I went, I was exercising a prerogative of mine. Everything in the house belonged to me.

"Your mother is part of this house. She belonged to these bricks and to the warmth given off here. There is nothing here that Esperança has not felt, touched, nothing that was not born of her will."

Moved, Miguel stepped up his pace, scattering all over the house, to my confusion. "No strong emotions, Breta. Let's have some sherbet," he proposed, pretending everything was all right.

Enter Sílvia all of a sudden, sniffing about. She gave me a light peck on the forehead. Perhaps she saw me as an obstacle standing in the way of her happiness. Her face never reflected an unheard-of joy. She paid attention to what she wore, however, her dresses going far beyond my wildest fancy.

"I'm free now, Breta. For whatever you like," he went on, in high spirits. Handing himself over to my care.

"I just don't want you to stop loving me," Miguel laid his heart bare one rainy day, his face somber, as though he'd been weeping. A moss-green sweater protected his attractive chest, the muscles standing out in bold relief through the fine wool. His eyes examining the house, his parents, his brothers and sisters. All of them listening for the telephone, whence their salvation would come. And why was he arguing so much with Bento, so methodical and such a disciplinarian? Perhaps Bento was asking him to be continent, more dedicated to the business.

"You're asking the impossible, Bento. And besides, it's better this way. You couldn't stand it if I were successful," he said ironically.

"Don't be funny, Miguel. It's time we made a bundle. The great fortunes will be made from Kubitschek's development plan. The money's floating in the air. And it will soon be shifted from the countryside to industries, banks, earth-moving. Don't forget that Brasília's in the offing."

Bento was excited at the prospect of an empire befitting his inordinate ambition.

"Don't worry, Bento, it's in the cards for you to die very rich. With a first-class funeral and few tears. A procession of enemies following along behind the casket."

Madruga had an iced guaraná punch brought to the study. He served me impatiently. He was afraid he'd lost that elusive granddaughter of his, sitting there before him, saying nothing. What would it take for that girl to admire him?

Madruga opened the bright-colored box. He chose a cigar, squeezing it gently between his fingers. Striking the match, he brought the flame to the tip of the cigar with extreme caution, burning only the first circle. He inhaled the smoke and exhaled it with elegance, forming round rings of ashes on the cigar, without cracks or creases. His assurance charmed me. A man able to master a cigar was likewise prepared to discipline the days, the future, each dawn so uncertain for a girl still fearful that the beings whom she esteemed would be taken from her.

All his attention focused on the havana, Grandfather had forgotten I existed. Perhaps he didn't want me around any longer in his precious den, where words echoed with perfect musicality. Anxiously, I left my seat, heading for Grandfather's easy chair. We were now so close that we were sharing the same air. He pretended not to see me. I discreetly breathed in the smell of his skin, of the cigar, of his grizzly hair. His blue eyes followed me with a sidelong glance. As meanwhile I did not flee from the area within their range.

That uncomfortable situation could not go on forever. Taking courage, I touched his arm. Grandfather trembled; I could feel his bloodless arm. I had unwittingly invaded a territory where Grandfather's life defended itself. He turned his tense face far away. I squeezed his arm tightly. I needed to put an end to that silence.

"Grandfather, tell a story for me."

Madruga looked me straight in the face at last. We eyed each other intently. He frowned, doubtless remembering past scenes which hurt him, for his face contracted. For a few brief moments he wanted to banish me from there. His body, however, gradually relaxed and he smiled. He smiled as though he had taken on the form of Xan, it being up to him now to choose precisely the right story with which to establish a habit to be firmly fixed between us, from that moment on. He no longer saw himself condemned only to riches. Wasn't it a fact that Xan had once named him his heir and most faithful listener? Sobreira was still alive in his heart. He felt again the same pulsing excitement as when he crossed the joyful, brooding waters of the Atlantic, immersed, back then, in innocence.

"Let's begin a story right this minute, without any set time for it to end. Do you promise to hear me out till the end of my life?" Madruga said, deeply moved.

I leaned my head on his shoulder. Grandfather's chest responded with strong palpitations. Snuggled up there, it would be easy to hear him. Grandfather exercising with me the gratifying function of being Xan and the young lad Madruga at one and the same time. Certain now that the Atlantic crossing had been worthwhile, despite the path carpeted with dead men and disenchantments. Nothing could deprive him of the right to tell his stories too.

"From today on, Breta, I will also be Grandfather Xan. Are you willing?"

After appointing Odete the guardian of her jewels, Eulália awaited death. She imagined it to be solemn and lacking in ample resources. Her serene face in sharp contrast to the bright-colored nightdresses changed by Odete every six hours.

On completing the seventh day in bed, without death having exacted from her the encounter with God, Eulália grew anxious. Not protesting, however, against the life that nourished her with false sap. Fearful that such distress, though modest, would trouble those moments conducive to contrite silence.

She did not want to leave earth with words and acts that would express a lack of resignation. It had always been part of her pride to behave as though she had not suffered at the hands of adversity. Otherwise, she would not have been able to prepare herself for the place that God intended to set aside for her.

The family filed past her bed every day. Venâncio lost in a deliberate, painful silence during the visit. Giving signs of wanting to follow her, the moment she closed her eyes. Nothing reconciling him with human fate. The family's low spirits did not serve, however, as consolation to Eulália. Her gaze reproved them for the oppressive weight of their sorrows.

In that week, long and hot, Madruga's soberness was accentuated by his black suit and tie. And it was in this garb that he confronted his wife. Eulália looked into his blue eyes, dull now. They had lost intensity, no longer gleaming as before. Old age and affliction had shorn Madruga of his arrogance.

Eulália said nothing to him about his mourning attire. Her husband was right to anticipate a widely announced fact. And therefore to adopt a habit that would guide his life in the coming months. As her widower, he ought to dress appropriately. Especially since it was well known that Spain was deeply attached to the custom of mourning the dead with weeping and wailing, incense, candles, and interminable rituals.

Madruga appreciated her discretion. Both had always intuited that reality provided weapons to harm and resources to heal. Perhaps for that reason Eulália was deaf to her children's pleas to resist the pain. She merely thanked them for their more and more hurried visits. Evidence that they were becoming inured to losing her.

The doctor gave her routine examinations three times a day, begging them to spare her. He had very little to do, inasmuch as Eulália had decided to die in her own bed. Since it would not be given to her to breathe her last in Sobreira, in homage to Dom Miguel.

In the beginning, Odete was violently opposed to the two nurses hired to relieve her at Eulália's bedside. Till Bento calmed her down by providing a folding bed for her in his mother's room to make it easier to keep watch over her.

On leaving the room, he lightly touched her bound hair. As she bowed her head so that Bento could feel the firmness of that hair, once come from Africa.

"Don't worry, Odete, we'll take care of you. You'll lack for nothing, no matter what happens."

Odete was moved. This son of Eulália's had always treated her with deference. Never once forgetting to send her flowers on her birthday.

Odete was on her guard, however, against Antônia's visits. Concentrating on her mother, Antônia pretended not to see her. That death, continually deferred, made her anxious. As though the flame of that life had been passed on to the family, strengthening all of them.

Antônia was torn between the pain of losing her mother and the necessity of standing up to Bento and her brothers. Displaying a more and more exaggerated sensitiveness toward them. Moreover, in the past, her mother had observed that immediately after Esperança's funeral Antônia had adopted a more elegant carriage, walking with her head held high, very nearly risking a fall. And like her father, she avoided all mention of Esperança, as though throughout her life she had been Eulália's and Madruga's only daughter.

Even now, at the mere appearance of her brothers in the room, she nervously rose to her feet. And, looking at Eulália lying on the bed, she thought of the inventory and the acid silence that had fallen over them. At each visit, she insisted on bringing her mother little plush animals as presents. Perhaps suggesting that Eulália go back to her childhood before dying.

Eulália held the animals for a few minutes, just to pick up their faint warmth of a stable, where those beasties had been eating straw. She smiled discreetly, thus dissuading her daughter from freely expressing her emotions.

In the garden, Bento mercilessly roiled Antônia's insides. Confirming that the dividing of the inheritance in that family would be painful. His sister could be certain that he was spoiling for a fight, with Luís Filho as his adversary.

Antônia mewed in answer, knifing her brother with tormented words. They were all in debt to Luís Filho, more competent than her brothers. Bento smiled.

"Breta too will decide in my favor," she said, as she crumpled a handful of leaves gathered from the ground.

Antônia entered the room, determined to awaken her mother, who appeared to be sleeping. Eulália owed her a favor before dying. So let her fulfill her maternal duties.

Odete was adamant, turning a deaf ear to Antônia's arguments. Prepared to ward off all threat to the repose of that woman who had generously watched over her destiny. Thanks to Eulália, she had come to know a country, there in Europe, that she had never dreamed existed. And it was Eulália also who had told her forbiddingly difficult stories, full of thorny problems sometimes, but always with a glorious ending, exactly the right one. And the very figure of Dom Miguel, always so austere, coming little by little to belong to her, as though there were no distance between the Celtic race of Eulália's father and her African origin.

"Mother, I need to talk to you," Antônia insisted, leaning over the bed. Despite Odete's efforts to keep her away. "Leave me alone, Odete, it's urgent. Mother needs to help me."

Odete asked her to leave, but Antônia stood her ground. She bared her teeth at her, ready to fight it out.

"Wake up, mother, there's something extremely important I must tell you."

With closed eyes, Eulália turned her head in the direction of a voice that sounded distant, intangible.

"Who's there?" she said, in an effort to come back to the reality of the objects and persons squeezed into the room, which she must leave so as to go to meet God.

"It's me, your daughter," Antônia said.

The lids of Eulália's closed eyes trembled, her face bathed in beaming light that suddenly restored her youth.

"Esperança!" she whispered.

Antônia drew back, startled. For several moments not knowing what to do. Odete hurried to Eulália, gripping her hands now.

"Yes, yes, here we all are," Odete said.

And without mentioning names or explaining situations, she repeated the phrase once again, as she cast a reproving glance at Antônia, impelling her to live the role demanded by her mother.

"Answer, Antônia, do as she wishes," Odete muttered, concerned about Eulália, who was simply delirious or dreaming because there were certain matters with no solution that she had not settled. It thus being her daughter's obligation to free her of these obstacles.

"You're mad, Odete. I'm not Esperança and have no intention of taking her place."

Eulália stretched out her arm, wanting to cling to someone. Antônia found herself on the receiving end of this gesture.

"Esperança, my daughter, you've come back at last," Eulália said again, her words synchronized with the gesture.

Before Antônia could correct Eulália's misapprehension, Odete decided to fling her body between mother and daughter, keeping Antônia from coming any closer. Antônia took note of her intention and threw herself upon her, attempting to draw nearer to her mother's face. In this mutual struggle, the two women locked hands, testing their respective strength, both of them possessed by a rage that even Eulália's presence could not calm. At no moment did Odete yield ground that would allow Antônia to triumph. As for Antônia, she wanted only to retaliate, to take her revenge at last upon this woman, now grown old, who had stolen her mother from her.

The fight went on discreetly, the contenders not wanting to disturb Eulália, who, with closed eyes, appeared to be waiting for Esperança to speak, after all the many years of silence.

"I'm thirsty," Eulália said.

The unexpected request surprised the two women, almost on the point of collapsing atop the invalid. For a few moments, Odete was at a loss as to which one to deal with. Whether with the enemy who had pinned her down, or with the woman whose needs she had always cared for. It grieved her, however, to think of a Eulália crying out for water, with parted lips, baring perfect teeth. A set that, to her and Eulália, had seemed beautifully matched in those years.

Without hesitating, Odete shoved Antônia away, freed herself from her grasp. In search of water.

"This nice cool drink will do you good. Then I'll bring you a cup of tea."

Her discomfort somewhat eased, Eulália slowly opened her eyes. And gave Odete a grateful smile. Only then did she rivet her gaze on Antônia, ignoring the hurt she'd caused.

"Mother, help me," Antônia said, bursting into tears.

Eulália looked at her daughter as though really seeing her for the first time. Turned to a statue of salt by her contemplation. Antônia had certainly put on weight in recent years. She was no longer young. On the other hand, she had a family living a life of its own, independent of her and of Madruga.

"Help me, mother," Antônia begged once again.

Eulália noted Odete's distress at the turn of events. With a mere glance, she tried to calm her. Only then did she turn to Antônia, prepared to lend her an ear. Her daughter, sobbing, was unable to explain. She had always felt herself to be a stranger in that family. Born into a tribe that rejected everything she offered. For that reason alone she had counted on Luís Filho's protection down through the years. Thanks to him she had discovered the pleasure of accumulating possessions, of hauling them inside the walls of her room. As she heard the sounds that told her that her husband was beginning yet again to weigh each bar of gold on an imaginary scale.

She had no lack of reasons for finding fault with all of them. The whole family had failed her. Even Eulália. The fact was that her brothers had never forgiven her for living on after Esperança was dead. They doubtless thought that she should have died in their sister's place. And they punished her each day of her life for her failure to have done so. How often Eulália, coming to her to embrace her, undid this gesture on the sudden appearance on the scene of Miguel, as ever so handsome, so ardent, embracing her son instead of Antônia, uttering to him the words that her daughter had anxiously awaited. And even though Eulália, after embracing Miguel, rewarded her with a gentle gaze in her direction, the world loomed up before her, opaque and self-contained.

At such times, sensing how she was suffering, Luís Filho made her reveal her secret. Whereupon Antônia gave loud voice to the contempt of which she had been the victim. Who in Madruga's house loved her, after all? In the face of this dramatic situation, her husband rose up in arms in her behalf. Immediately, however, she begged him to take a more moderate stand. It was necessary to protest without ever breaking existing ties. They had to think of their children's future. Hence they should by all means avoid any irreversible clash, from which they might emerge with grave injuries.

She yielded readily to her husband's thought on the matter. The only being able to guide her footsteps, to lend fresh strength to her reality. She emerged from these conjugal lessons with her spirit renewed. Reappearing, tough and indignant, before her mother, nearly tearing the door down.

Whenever she saw her daughter in that state, Eulália took the initiative and spoke first. "What's the matter, Antônia?"

"Everything," she confessed repeatedly. Not at all ashamed of revealing to her mother her extreme weakness.

Eulália immediately forgot about Antônia's problems, in her opinion insignificant by comparison with her own losses, represented by Bento and Esperança. And also Dom Miguel, who had died back in Galicia, without his daughter to weep for him. What else could hurt her more than life had set out to do?

On seeing her mother distracted by her household tasks, Antônia began complaining again. "Bento lords it over all of you. Just as Miguel does. What's going to happen to us, to my family?" she said, watching for Eulália's reaction.

Her mother immediately mentioned her own ignorance of business matters. "You'd best address your pleas to Madruga. He can always come up with solutions to problems." But Antônia, on hearing her father's name, answered back at once. He was someone she regarded as unbending, a man who had in fact garnered a certain amount of experience, but unfortunately had chosen himself as his only reference, which had made him the poorer over the years.

Eulália disagreed with this opinion. Especially since she held her husband in the highest estimation. Not to mention the fact that life and suffering, allied, had transformed him, above all in middle age. To the point of calming him down as never before. Didn't she find him more contemplative, giving himself over at last to dreams that had had their origin back in Sobreira, even before he boarded his first boat in Vigo?

With these thoughts in mind, Eulália gradually shed more light on the life that they had had in the first years of their marriage. In the beginning, for example, they had had to face up to the fact that money was scarce. Carefully saving every penny, so that everything around them would prosper. Especially since they soon had a family. Was Antônia forgetting that it had been God's will that they have five children in eight years? Five mouths begging for food, clean sheets, and care!

Tobias had come long afterward. As for the first Bento, he had not thrived. He had had to be given back to God, not long after he was born. The pain of losing him was like having a limb amputated. That was why she wept in secret, so Madruga would not see the sorrow embittering her heart. As she begged God, in her prayers, not to lock her heart up tight. And to let the words and deeds that were her handiwork be even more generous and freed of all resentment. Life made it our duty to grow with the taste of gall in our mouths.

Odete straightened the pillow, lessening the discomfort of Eulália's long week of lying in bed.

"And what can I do for you now, daughter? For any of you, for that matter."

She stretched out her hand to Antônia, but before her daughter had time to take it, Eulália laid it lightly to rest on the impeccably white sheets. Almost without moving, thus seeking a silent, easeful death.

"You can still do a whole lot, mother. Talk with Bento, with Miguel. Intervene on Luís's behalf, on mine. Keep vengeance from being wreaked, stave off a struggle between brother and sister. And all for money!"

Antônia immediately turned her head away, not wanting to see her mother cut up into a thousand pieces by her accusation. The silence in the room made her uneasy. It struck her as odd that Odete had done nothing to get her out of the way. She looked at her mother. Eulália's face was serene. As though she had not heard her daughter, deeply distressed now, anxiously awaiting her reply.

"Odete, I need you," was all Eulália said. Then asking her for the tea she'd promised.

Antônia inspected the room and the furniture carefully. She calculated the number of nights her father and mother had slept there, shielded by an enigma never shared with the children. An experience she did not think it possible to repeat with Luís Filho. Life very soon spent itself, being made of fleeting, inflammable sentiments. Gaining energy only through the movements of an enemy like Bento, eager to do her harm.

In those years of matrimony, Luís Filho had confirmed her belief that daily life was nothing but an eternal search for provisions. And they had made their wealth multiply to the point that they had no time left over to look after it. She having been appointed the custodian. Of what and of whom? The children gave her quick pecks on the cheek, in a hurry to leave the house. Driven by the urge to succumb to the black magic of reality, from which she had been banished.

She need weaken in her struggle against her brothers only one day, and immediately Luís Filho's protests came raining down upon her head.

Savage words accusing her of incompetence. Or harsh words; couldn't his wife see that there was not a single minute to be lost in a battle begun years before, when they had the advantage of being able to count on known enemies?

In a fit of weeping, she would seek out her father. Madruga would put a stop to the dizzying flood of tears. He would shout to Bento to come take his place at Antônia's side. Alone with his sister, Bento swore he'd defeat her, without mortally wounding her. All he wanted was to have her and Luís Filho under lock and key. Lacking for nothing, wallowing in comfort.

"Isn't affluence enough for the two of you? You still want power as well? The power belonging to our family, Antônia? Can't you see that Luís Filho is of another blood, of a race which has always held us in contempt, and which even humiliated you? And that the hour has come to take our revenge?" Bento insisted.

"And my children, Bento. What am I to do with them? What side will they end up on?"

"On the opposite side, unfortunately. They're Luís Filho's sons and heirs. As long as he's still alive at least." Bento did his best to be conciliatory.

"That's a lie, you'll never forgive them. Even after Luís Filho is dead. They'll always be the adversary's children. The other blood. Never Madruga's blood."

Odete raised Eulália's bed with the crank so that she could see her daughter at her side. Eulália again stared intently at Antônia.

"Don't ask anything more of me, daughter. All I have to give you is what I've put aside in my life. The rest, life has already given you far more than enough of. And may God preserve what you already have."

After uttering these words, she drew Odete to her, worriedly clutching her hands. Odete shouldered Antônia aside and bent down to her mistress's face. And, for the first time, she was aware of the smell of something beginning to rot coming from that mouth. Odete shuddered. Could death be bearing down, at full speed? Odete discreetly opened her mouth to breathe in Eulália's odor, swallow it, and feed herself on the last signs of life of the friend whom she had kept such close company that she would have no idea how to tell her own story now without also including Eulália's. She could almost say that with a mere sneeze of her womb she too had given birth to the children of that woman from Spain.

Eulália felt weak on that sunny morning, the light filtering through the half-drawn curtains. Odete feared that death, by order of that woman, an ally of the gods, would come to seek her out in the next five minutes. To her surprise, however, Eulália's eyes flew open, aiming perhaps at recovering part of a past on which not enough light had been shed thus far.

"Call my remaining children, Odete. I must hurry."

Rejected by her mother, Antônia leaned against the wall. Everything appeared to be taking place in accordance with an age-old agreement to which she had not been a party. One concluded without her knowledge and consent. It had taken her a long time to detect the outward signs of danger, afoot at last and affecting the surface of the world and her house.

Her back to the wall, Antônia watched her mother as she awaited the arrival of her brothers. Who were in fact staggering into the room. It was hard to say which of them had been the first to obey Eulália's summons.

Madruga was the last to enter. Solemn, still in mourning, ready for the funeral rites, in all probability during that week. Or else dressed for his own death, thus sparing his children from having to struggle with a defenseless body.

"You came too, Madruga?" Eulália was overjoyed at his presence.

"Didn't you want me to come?" He stroked his wife's face, reconciled to events.

"You're right. How could the children be here without you?"

Before her children, Eulália always placed particular emphasis on her husband's noble gestures, so that in the memory of the family his most difficult traits would not wholly outweigh his others.

"Our journey has been a long one, Eulália. The thought even came to me that it might never end," Madruga said.

He looked at his children scattered about the amply proportioned room. Madruga had always fought for a space vaster than his dreams. In everything, moreover, he demanded excess, immoderate abundance. Odete, however, confined now to one corner of the room, acted as though she were in a wretched, airless cell.

"That's the very reason that Father and your Grandfather Xan never approved of traveling. Even though they dreamed of it. Father used to say that the best journey was one made round a cane driven into the ground, preferably near a tall rock or peak, from which to contemplate the Galician meadows and mountains. On the other hand, if we had obeyed them, we would never have crossed the Atlantic. And how, then, could we be gathered here today, speaking this language of our children, which we too now love?"

Eulália seemed tired now. After having been so free with her words. As a general rule, when her speeches were lengthy, they had Miguel, Venâncio, and Odete as listeners. She did not like to have more than two persons about her. Out of timidity perhaps, or because she considered everything to be changeable and temporary, and only the last journey would comfort her.

The silence that followed made everyone uneasy. Broken, finally, by Odete's footfalls, as she suddenly stepped past Madruga, the children, pushing Breta aside as she knelt at her grandmother's side. Alongside her bed, Odete awaited her mistress's orders. Eulália noted her emotion, but she was unable to spare that black woman, born a slave, who had not failed her even as the world threatened to fall apart all round her on her death.

"The boxes, Odete. The time has come for the boxes."

The words were uttered with an effort. As though Eulália were suffering on letting go of objects in her possession for so many years. Odete was deeply distressed. Could this really be what Eulália wanted? Might she not be mistaking the symptoms?

"Is the senhora certain?" she said. The boxes now taking on a bewildering meaning.

Madruga came to Odete's aid. For a moment he supported her as she made her way to the wardrobe. He too could not bear the thought that the hour had come when his wife would prove to him that no one had the power to bend her will, to rule over her, to love her and be loved by her.

Odete let go of Madruga's arm. And, indifferent to the gaze of Eulália's children, went on across the room toward the wardrobe. A wardrobe to which Madruga had never had access. By common agreement, Eulália and he had shared the spaces of the house, avoiding needless collisions. Both took into account the friendship still theirs, peopled with shadows and intense memories.

Odete opened the wardrobe but did not immediately reach for the boxes set in a row on the shelf. There was an elegance in her gestures, practiced to perfection in the years shared with Eulália. Taking just one box at a time, she deposited them on the bed, where Eulália could see them and thus easily point to them.

Miguel shielded himself behind Bento. He did not want to be the first one chosen by Eulália. He was afraid his mother would unveil his life from an intimate, unbearable perspective. Or that cruel, depressing messages would leap out of one of the open boxes. Perhaps his mother had set down on paper impressions that she had not dared to formulate in his presence. Remarks in some way imprudent and disrespectful, which she had been unable to make to Miguel so long as she had him at her side. On pain of making her son blush, and consequently come to avoid her eyes and her company.

Divining her son's thought, Eulália raised her frail hand toward Bento.

"Your box, Miguel, is to my right. It was Odete who determined the order of their placement."

Miguel stepped out of Bento's shadow, flinging himself toward the bed. Kneeling at his mother's side, he kissed her thin, wasted hands again and again.

"Mother, I beg you, stay with us. Don't go, I need you." Weeping, he stroked her cold face. Eulália's warmth was draining away, without Miguel's being able to transfer his own fever to her.

"Dom Miguel was luckier, son. He put no one to any trouble and dispensed with farewell ceremonies. God willed that it be the contrary with me. And He granted me the time to distribute among my children the only belongings that I have to leave them." Eulália had a vacant look in her eye. Not even Miguel entranced her as he once had.

Bento drew closer. He wanted to be seen. Antônia did likewise, both fighting to be the one their mother's finger would point to next. They eyed each other coolly, but they felt ashamed. Eulália, who had always preached charity to them, was now a source of discord. Neither Miguel nor Madruga being able to spare her from witnessing her children's confrontation.

Eulália took no notice of the episode. Her entire attention devoted to the rest of what she wanted to say to them.

"Madruga is leaving you a fortune. It is what he has always wanted. A dream that cost him sweat and many disappointments. I, however, can give you only the past and the memory of each one of you. And even this in only a modest way. Who am I to dispute with God the right to create the story of others?"

And ceasing to point out the box belonging to each individually, Eulália asked them to take them themselves. Each of them would find his or her name written on the inside of the cover. Her eye falling on Tobias, she thought it best to offer him an explanation.

"I've not forgotten you, Tobias, not ever. Your box weighs less, has fewer keepsakes, only because you were the last born." And she smiled discreetly, pleased with her observation.

Tobias took his box, estimated the weight of it before setting it down on the floor. Turning toward his mother, he enfolded her in a long embrace.

"My fate, mother, was always in your hands." And turning around abruptly, he left the room. Madruga tried to stop him, but his son pushed him away. His father was offended. If Venâncio had been in the room, Tobias would have acted differently. Moreover, before answering Eulália's summons, he had pleaded with Venâncio, in the living room, to come upstairs to the bedroom with the family.

"We've been together all these years, Venâncio. Why keep your distance now, when we're losing Eulália forever?"

"She's always known where I was. And counted on my friendship and my dreams," he said slowly.

Venâncio scarcely moved in the armchair, waiting for them to tell him, at any moment, of his friend's end. Whereupon he would rise to his feet to go see her. Closely participating in the preparations set in motion by her death. Going, thus, to meet the family engaged in examining the havoc that that loss would begin to wreak. All of them learning, however, to erase her immediately from their lives, so as to come to remember her, in the future, with a pleased smile. Or with tears that would deprive the living of nothing at all.

Madruga sensed that he had failed once again to be of help to his son. Tobias had naturally sought out Venâncio, in whose arms he had wept since he was a little boy. He must no longer delude himself; he was unlikely to win that son back. There was no emotion that would make them forget the quarrels, the shouting matches, the misunderstandings of the past. Both had counted on a long life in which to destroy each other.

Tobias would doubtless weep at his funeral. A sorrow alternating with relief. Since his father's disappearance offered him the sensation of an unbridled freedom, outside the social realm. Tobias never again needing to fear that on the outbreak of a quarrel his father would banish him from his presence.

Madruga now eyed his children clutching their respective boxes. Torn between their eagerness to take possession of their treasures and their anxious desire to flee from unpleasant discoveries. Without setting foot outside the room. There was still one box to be handed out. Esperança's, fought over by everyone.

Breta noted how the family coveted the box that Eulália had kept for all those years, lacking the courage to reduce it to dust. It was taking her time, however, to come to a decision. With distraught gaze, she looked about for guidance. She began to perspire, forcing Odete to wipe her face continually. The devotion of that helpless black woman, claiming no ownership of persons or objects, diverting Breta's attention from the box. Breta knew Odete's intimate secret, and never revealed it. She asked herself, however, whether Eulália had ever suspected the dramatic loneliness of a woman who had only her to love.

Madruga refused to offer his wife suggestions. He had gone too far in the past and life now wearied him. Absorbed in Eulália, he pondered what other emotions his wife could demand of them that they had not already demonstrated in that long week of waiting.

The scent that Odete dabbed on her arms with a bit of wet cotton revived Eulália. She was ready for her last rite. Her gaze, steady now, had no need of others' witness.

"Perhaps Esperança's box belongs to Madruga. My husband, however, is mortal, and he will soon follow me." She ceased speaking in order to catch her breath. Signaling to Breta to come closer.

"Your mother was beautiful and wild. Esperança was like a Galician gorse bush. With flowers and thorns at the same time. Affectionate and prickly." And as Eulália spoke she pointed to indicate to her granddaughter that the box was hers.

Visibly moved, Breta approached the box. What could there be inside that could possibly explain her mother's life? She ran her fingers carefully over the surface of the smooth-textured wood. She felt that she was caressing Esperança herself. And as she was thus absorbed, oblivious of her grandmother, Miguel's strong, hairy bear's paw of a hand covered hers.

And those finger bones were so ardent that they imparted to her body a fervor at once unbearable and pleasurable. Their two hands, mounted one atop the other, mated, seemed to be pouring forth lava and semen, indifferent to the witnesses present.

Breta was suddenly alarmed by Miguel. No longer able to tolerate being weighed down by heavy sighs and spattered by vulgar words. Her mind firmly made up, she barred his access to the box. Miguel took offense. Deprived of that property, he went to his mother to complain.

"Is it really necessary for us to reexamine her box, mother? To bury Esperança a second time?"

Eulália paid no attention to him. Concentrating on Madruga, who felt the weight of her gaze. Obeying his wife's command, he sat down on the chair next to the bed. There was a matter not yet settled between them, and they did not have much time.

Madruga had a presentiment that Eulália would not get through the night. He must, then, render account to her. And do it before she demanded her due.

Eulália's silence commanded his admiration. A pride only to be expected of the daughter of Dom Miguel. There she was, implying, on her deathbed, that they could no longer escape the crystal-clear truths of the heart.

Those two old people, locked in an implacable struggle that excluded their descendants, disturbed Bento. He tried, then, to help his father. He put his arms about his sagging shoulders for a moment. But he immediately took the gesture back. And began self-consciously to fidget with his tie, in an effort to rid himself of a feeling about to make him burst into tears, which always frightened him. He envied Miguel, who had learned to weep easy, even enjoyable, tears.

"I know very well what you expect of me, Eulália," Madruga muttered in a scratchy voice darkened by cigars, whose taste and fumes had little by little laid down deposits several layers deep in his throat.

Eulália made no move to make his task easier. She acted, however, with perfect courtesy, since by refusing to touch his heart, she was placing her victory in jeopardy. She wanted her husband to think of the dead. Preferably forgetting the living, such as herself, with only a few sips of breath left.

Madruga stirred restlessly in his chair. His eyes fixed on Esperança's box on the bed, likewise the object of the fervent gaze of Breta and Miguel, the latter having begun to fight for possession of it once again. His son's graspingness distressed him, but also distracted him. What was the use, after all, of such greed! He turned to his wife. This time she was embarrassed by his gaze riveted upon her. Her eyelids fluttered, in an effort perhaps to awaken his pity.

His wife's increasing weakness grieved him. In a few minutes or hours, there would be nothing left to do. And unable to bear the agony, he clung to Eulália's hand.

"No, I beg you, wait, Eulália. I'm saying, I'm uttering, I'm speaking my daughter's name. Please, wait, don't leave me now. Give me a little more time, I need time to call upon my courage, Eulália."

Slowly, she turned her face away. She could not heed his plea. Another summons, much louder, occupied her now. She had no way to care for the living. And his wife's furrowed brow seemed to show him the path of courage.

He bent down to his wife, squeezed her fingers, so hard he perhaps hurt them, though Eulália did not protest. His wife's silence, sparing him her pain, helped him to speak the name so many years asked of him and always denied her.

"Ah, Esperança, my daughter Esperança. Tell me, Eulália, will I one day be forgiven?" And weeping convulsively, he noted no sign of relief on Eulália's part. As though she had not heard him. He feared, then, that he had touched his wife's heart too late. In despair, he held her tightly; he thought she had died.

His weight was crushing Eulália. Odete tried to pull him away. He resisted. Bento undertook to raise him to his feet. Face to face with his son, Madruga's eyes questioned him. Bento grasped his hand.

"Is she still alive?" Madruga said.

Bento nodded. Their mother was still with them, despite more and more feeble signs of life. And he pushed his father, weak and tottering, toward the door. He must rest. Madruga gave in, leaving the room in his company.

The other children, their attention distracted by the state Madruga was in, did not notice Eulália's almost imperceptible sign that she was about to speak. Until she suddenly emitted a harsh, almost stifled sound, "God be praised. He has finally spoken his daughter's name."

Antônia rushed headlong to the bedside, the better to hear.

"What was that, mother? What did you say?"

Breta looked at Odete's indecipherable face turned toward Africa, safeguarding forests and treasures. She had not stepped away from that bed for a single instant. She was certain that Eulália's last words were still echoing in Odete's ears. Breta did not stop to question her, her attention riveted on her grandmother, still breathing. Sustained by a minimal breath of life. The bitter thought came to Breta that her grandmother did not really want to die, as she had been proclaiming. Despite her cool, elegant air of detachment, she was clinging to this earth with surprising appetite. Did she perhaps owe this hunger to Odete, bent on keeping her among the living for a while longer?

Breta clasped the box to her breast and pushed her uncle aside. "I'm very sorry, Miguel, but this box is mine."

Miguel admitted defeat. Humiliated, he crept to his mother. Listening to her chest. Eulália was alive. He smiled. He had lost Esperança's box, but gained his mother for a few minutes more. Suddenly he called Breta to him.

"What will our story be like, do you think? Our story told by Mother?"

Breta did not answer. They all heard Eulália's muffled, almost rhythmic breathing. Their eyes followed each of Odete's movements to keep Eulália with them. Till Miguel impulsively seized Odete by the wrist, pulling her away from his mother.

Odete was frightened. She shrank back against the wall, not understanding what was happening. Miguel strode over to her. Within a step of her, he made a threatening gesture:

"Let her go, Odete. It's time," he said angrily.

*T*obias would see clients out, foreseeing the moment when they would dispense with his services with a mere glance.

His feelings hurt by the frequency with which such things happened, he would draw himself up proudly, attempting to prove to the client that he too could forgo the relationship quite easily. Yet his rumpled clothes belied his arrogant attitude. And then his shoulders drooped as a deep depression came over him.

At such times, he hastened to Venâncio's. The two of them would sit in the yard looking at the mango tree. From which there always came a gentle breeze. And mixing countless cups of coffee and sugarcane brandy, Tobias would begin a cycle of condemnations that drew into its verbal vortex Madruga and the social system, in his opinion the only factors responsible for the downfall of an idealist as thoroughgoing as himself.

"I chose the wrong profession. Or rather, I'm living the wrong sort of life. To get ahead in Brazil today, you have to be a toady and completely corrupt. I can't bring myself to be either the one or the other. I definitely don't have a mercenary soul," and he let himself be carried away by histrionic flourishes that delighted Venâncio.

Venâncio would go to the kitchen, grab the frying pan, let the oil heat. Then fry slices of pork sausage, to which he added crushed garlic to season the nicely browned skin. He did all this in a hurry, so that his godson's tongue wouldn't get all twisted from drinking on an empty stomach.

His godson's anxiety escaped his control. In general it was connected with the historic circumstances prevailing in the country. Whatever the headline in the day's paper, it disillusioned him, affecting his outlook on life for hours after he'd read it. But Venâncio, being attuned to Tobias's thoughts, would speak up, encouraging his tendency to couple his life with events that had a bearing on the fate of the nation. Thereby pricking his conscience.

Tobias had only to declare himself a total failure, practically beating his breast, for Venâncio to come to his aid. He helped him to be unhappy on that quiet afternoon, the two of them together in the yard, listening to the cackling of hens on the other side of the wall. Both mindful, however, of the reasons that had so readily brought on feelings of depression and discouragement.

Tobias had withdrawn from partisan politics after his all too obvious fiasco in the National Student Union. He had been unable to keep a single friend from those days. He had had a falling-out with all of them, leaving him with a bitter memory of them. His career warmed up, however, when a number of mothers asked him to defend political prisoners, victims of the repression that became the rule from '68 on, especially during the Médici administration.

This intimate contact rekindled his wrath. He could not bear the stories the mothers told him of the tortures inflicted on prisoners. He woke up in the morning aching to rescue those jailed youngsters from such terrible misfortune. Counting on Venâncio to help him wage this fight, lending him the courage to continue to battle the authoritarian State, despite the suspension of constitutional law throughout the country.

"Good show, Tobias. They're heroes who vindicate these dark times. I'm certain you'll manage to save at least a few of them. That's how it was in Vargas's time. Though many went directly from a prison cell to a coffin."

Venâncio always forbore to measure the degree of his godson's inertia or intransigence. Having identified with him, he went to visit him downtown. Having a coffee in the corner bar beforehand, so as to catch the sounds of the city. Remembering the times when he lived in Cinelândia.

Tobias sat him down beside him. Confronted, however, with the maelstrom of that office, with its old furniture, its peeling walls, the shelf piled high with books, Venâncio had the strange feeling that life was going down the drain. At which point he plucked up his courage, thanks to the pride his godson aroused in him. Tobias's moderation, in permanent contrast with Madruga's free-spending habits. It never occurring to him that Tobias might call upon his father on finding himself in dire poverty.

But whenever this happened, Tobias flagellated himself as a form of punishment, giving himself over to nocturnal wanderings that might last for an entire week. And in order to exhume his ghosts, he chose the company of whores and pimps, whom he called sisters and brothers. He returned home only when he had drained his anxiety to the dregs, eager to have a bath after frequenting filthy boardinghouses and bathrooms. He then dressed himself with care, proceeding immediately to Leblon. With the feeling that he lacked the essential ingredients to feed his passion.

He went directly to his mother. He clung to her in close embrace.

"Pray for me," he said in an anxious voice, without further explanations.

It was difficult for Eulália to imagine him in danger. Although every soul was always a prey to discord. And so, to Tobias's disappointment, she confined herself to asking after her granddaughters. Eulália's serene face skirting, with consummate skill, subjects involving Amália. While at the same time she spared her son the need to account in any way for his future, which she foresaw as one without illusions, and one which Tobias would not like to talk about.

That face of his mother's, as impervious to distress as to the wind, offended her son. His words then came to him in a rush, in evident rebellion. Each one intended to flesh out a narrative that would lay bare to his mother part of a reality unknown to her.

"You live in a bell jar. You know nothing of the Brazil of today. We must beware, mother. This country is swarming with monsters. Even our neighbor, who deserves our respect, may be nothing but a torturer. A man who practices torture with the knowledge of the constituted authorities. Unfortunately, we don't even have the names of these people. They're experts. They do their work wearing hoods. Or else they kill their victims so that not one of them will describe their faces. We must grant that they're competent. They know how to wrest moans and piercing pain from terrified, defenseless creatures. They're real artists, bent upon knowing the human soul through torture."

"Please, my son, you must not suffer like that." With repeated caresses, Eulália dried the sweaty hands of that son who would not surrender to dreams nor yet make his peace with reality.

"Ah, mother, what kind of country is this that you and Madruga gave us? When you chose America as a home, as you are fond of calling Brazil, did you also foresee these murders?"

Abandoning himself to his mother's caresses, Tobias flung himself upon her neck. She gave him refuge for some time. Till he was warmed. Then, wanting to show an interest in his activities, she thrust him away.

"And how is Aléxis, that young man you spoke to me of? I sometimes pray for him. I don't know how his mother survives so many sudden scares, so much suffering."

Tobias again set before her, in detail, facts long since past, giving her the impression that they were new developments. He lacked the courage to confess that he had been dismissed from the case. He told his mother that, very soon now, he would be freed. He was actively pressing his case.

"Someday, son, we'll overcome all these evils. Man can't continue to torment his fellow," Eulália said, with a sigh of relief. Perhaps considering the matter closed.

Tobias was constantly annoyed by this mother who had made herself the prisoner of the rosary and dreams. For whom reality, no matter what appearance it assumed, had as its end the encounter of man with God. Never having seen her curse the name of God. A sort of faith which he, personally, execrated. He had no reason to applaud that god, ever unmindful of the human horde, who rewarded the unjust and the intolerant. The last time he'd visited the Monastery of São Bento, though the Gregorian chant had cast its spell upon his spirit, he had felt cold and disconsolate there in the middle of the nave. Immediately making his escape.

Confronted by that son cut off from dreaming of eternity, Eulália redoubled her efforts to show her affection. She had fruit juice and cake brought him. Tobias chewed, diverted by his mother's gestures. Reciprocating by holding off the telling of any story that he was about to relate. In general, dreary, pessimistic ones. Purposely not telling her that, not far from Leblon, on the other side of the Rebouças tunnel, on the Rua Barão de Mesquita, certain men, in every way resembling her son, were at that moment shoving a bottle up the anus of a woman they'd just caught. A penetration that from the first cruelly tore the edges of the narrow circular opening, meant to expand only enough to expel human feces, the source of which, incidentally, was the products of the earth. Till they ended up shoving the bottle all the way inside the woman's body, rending the bowels and veins essential to her existence and her dignity.

His mother helped herself to another slice of cake. Tobias was upset. He did not dare confront her with ignominious details. On pain of expelling the basic matter of her fantasies. He did not want to destroy her faith. From childhood he had been accustomed to seeing his mother's life taking its course parallel to her dreaming. As though they were inseparable.

"Like oil and vinegar, right?" he remarked ironically.

Eulália beamed, overcome by a beauty difficult to grasp.

"It's only in the beginning that oil and vinegar are foreign elements. But once they've been beaten, over and over, with a wooden spoon, they eventually blend together, son. You've seen carefully dried lettuce sprinkled with that kind of dressing, haven't you?"

This sentence reminded her of her father. Dom Miguel's appreciation of familiar images, drawn from everyday life in Sobreira. He being always careful to make his thoughts concrete, by way of homely objects, within everyone's reach.

"Above all because the rustic is the perfect, original model, daughter. The most finespun thought was in fact born in a stable."

And, as proof of what he said, on dealing with any subject going beyond appearances, Dom Miguel immediately related himself to animals, to garden vegetables, and to the dishes gracing his Sunday dinner table. Everything being in perfect harmony with his idea of immortality.

Eulália abandoned the memory of her father and looked about the room in Leblon. As though surprised by the presence of Tobias, tense and strained, there before her. Whereupon, to cut the visit short, she stroked his hair.

"Be careful, son. But whenever you're in a tight spot, don't hesitate to call on your godfather."

Venâncio didn't always manage to calm Tobias down when he came to see him. He sometimes recommended, as a simple panacea, that he watch the direction events took.

"In a week's time, everything might very well take a turn for the better. Be patient, Tobias."

His godson scorned a virtue regarded as indispensable to saints. Yet at the same time having to be imitated by mortals. A virtue that called for acceptance and resignation. Doubtless commanding total obedience. When reality, for him at least, was harsh and uncompromising, sticking in his craw like a crushed bone.

"I have no faith in patience, godfather. It's in the service of dictators. It's the weapon of the resigned. I've never admired saints or anyone who renounced life in favor of heaven. I prefer a hell that offers no enticements."

In the circumstances that obtained, he admired the young people who went underground, even though their sad end could be predicted. They would all end up in Brazilian dungeons, guarded by implacable men in uniform, cheap shiny suits or red pelerines.

"Are they really pelerines? Is that how they parade about the Place des Vosges? Or don't the tropics admit of such eccentricities?" Tobias said in a tone of voice that was relaxed now.

Venâncio did not appear to be listening. He had now embarked on other subjects. Plunging into the past without asking Tobias's permission.

"When I got off the boat in Rio de Janeiro, back there around 1913, I was greeted with suspicion. As though I were an outlaw, a murderer. Brazil was ashamed of its own origin. And quite obviously hostile to foreigners. Perhaps because it wished to combat the vices handed down from the Colony, the Monarchy, and the Old and New Republics. There you had a society that had always been parochial, mistrustful. Opposed to new ideas. Having always kept people from bringing in unfamiliar philosophical and political ideas. Despite this prejudice, however, these ideas managed to make their way off the boat concealed in crates of salted codfish, hidden amid silk petticoats and bottles of French perfume. But always smuggled in. Not being able to be aired in public."

Tobias went to make fresh coffee to revive his godfather's spirits. He urged him to go on. He might be able to reconstruct what had unexpectedly been lost and simply evaporated in his memory. Wasn't it all part of the realm of imagination now?

Venâncio went on: "The damned Jesuits, the backward Portuguese, and the Brazilians created a perfect capillary system. So that nothing would weaken the solidly carpentered social structures. In the last analysis, the transition from the Monarchy to the Republic did not cause a radical break. Even today we are simply a people nostalgic for an anointed emperor to plot our fate and answer for it. But Madruga and I, at the beginning of the century, arrived in Brazil in a contingent of immigrants of great historical importance. Among our number were anarchists, who chose to live in São Paulo. Have you ever given a thought to the significance of these groups in the labor movements, indirectly spawned by them? Don't forget that besides olive oil, Parmesan cheese, and ordinary people, Italy also exported rebels to this continent in wholesale lots. As an example of this, we have Argentina."

Venâncio poured himself another coffee, without sugar this time. He wanted to taste the bitterness of the fruit. He closed his eyes as he took the first swallow.

"It's really better with sugar." And he smiled faintly. "As soon as we arrived, Madruga and I took up lodgings in a modest boardinghouse, near the port. The moment we'd set our knapsack and suitcase down, Madruga dragged me out to look at the shop windows, to walk about the streets. I felt that people were eyeing me mistrustfully. Wherever we went. I pretended not to notice. Even back then I thought they were all hypocrites. Dressed in heavy suits, with long drawers. Where in a climate like this had people ever worn morning coats and gaiters? No one was dressed for the summer heat. The men were wearing English cashmere, high collars, and to top it all off, vests, practically smothering them to death. Top hats, bowlers, or straw hats were swept off their heads at exactly the right moment, simulating good breeding they didn't have, and they even trod the ground in buskins. They were ridiculous. But enough of that. Let's get back to what I was saying before. So, amid all these popinjays, I felt like a supernumerary. Tied fast to a merry-go-round spilling out illusions at every turn. Do you know what I did to combat this wretchedness and the dampness of my room? I went to the Passeio Público and the Biblioteca Nacional. Whereas that go-getter of a Madruga killed himself working in González's flophouse. I wasn't meant to get rich naturally! Your father, on the other hand, made a bundle, carrying both me and his money about on his back. That's really true. I'd stuck to Madruga's hide, so to speak, like a leech. Just to be free and dream."

"Yet Father always says that, thanks to you, he made a fortune. Because he himself avoided dreaming, as Grandfather Xan had advised him. And he didn't want to betray the memory of that forebear of his," Tobias said.

"That's an old, old story. I know it well. The fact is that my freedom had a price. Madruga breathed in my stead, and I went along with that. To the point that, sensing those feelings, he came to tell me of his triumphs. Perhaps to humiliate me? All I know is that from hearing so much talk of figures, buildings, fake partnerships, I eventually grew indifferent to victories of this sort. They didn't appeal to me at all."

Venâncio now began carefully going back over Madruga's early adulthood. His ability to consume energy, like a fireworks display. Nothing dismayed him. A smile on his face even when he was beaten. Sometimes punctuating his defeats with thundering words. Never uttered in Eulália's presence.

That youthful portrait of Madruga, reconstructed from memory alone, brought him intense nostalgia. Whereupon he felt he'd been too hard on him. Best to summon him to the suburbs and ask him to confirm the facts he'd recounted. It wasn't right to hold forth about somebody else's life without the knowledge of the interested party. Or not to emphasize, in due detail, the pleasure that Madruga's strident laughter, whenever he wanted to amuse him, gave him back in those days. His free and easy way, for example, of speaking of the black woman, of African origin, in whose bed he was learning marvelous things. And whose body, again according to Madruga, bent in sinuous curves like a rush.

In those days, when Madruga came back at dawn on Sunday morning to the room that the two of them shared, Venâncio would hasten to breathe in the odors brought back from that black woman, which violently assaulted his nostrils. And as Madruga slept, he, Venâncio, lying sleepless, would suffocate his desire amid frantic fingerings and spasms of relief.

"Sundays were always a holiday. We wandered through the downtown streets and eventually ended up in Cinelândia. Pleased to be wearing clean shirts, high collars we'd starched ourselves. The streets stank, though; you could see feces in the clogged gutters. So as not to spend money, our amusement consisted of ogling the sly mulattas balancing baskets on their heads. They were plump, with firm hips, their eyes veiled and dull. As we approached, we breathed in the smell of their hairy armpits. My body grew tumescent then; I felt a dangerous heat climbing up my legs. I had never seen a body like that! But then too, what bodies had I known before? Just as I was beginning to take concrete notice of the places where dramatic reality was hiding, Spain expelled me, at the age of thirteen. And at the very moment that I was leaving, they injected in my veins the order to grow or die."

Venâncio fell silent. Intimating with a gesture that he hadn't yet finished what he had to say on the subject. He went to the bathroom. He relieved himself and splashed cool water on his face.

"Perhaps because of Madruga's sensuality, which made it easy for him to pick up women on the street, I asked myself questions, beneath the sheets at night. Worried about my turgid flesh and my adolescent dreams. Would my dreams of that time be in perfect harmony with my dreams to come in the future? Dreaming, of any sort, is always sudden and terrifying. How easily any confounded dream puts the simplest reality to flight! Even this reality consisting of beans and rice, or a good cup of coffee with milk and bread with butter. Maybe that's why Madruga would shake me by the shoulders on Mondays, to wake me up. Finding he'd already made coffee. Liable to come out with sudden solemn pronouncements, he was. He once said, even before he was married: 'What I eat, you'll eat too. You'll lack for nothing, Venâncio.' Was it on account of that sentence that I never lacked for food on the table, I wonder? And even owed my life to him? That may well have been the case, yet all I ever did was to project Madruga's shadow, instead of my own, on the walls of this house."

In the months of June and July, when it turned cold, Venâncio served his godson hot soup that he was fond of calling stone broth, as was the Portuguese tradition. As soon as the water boiled, he tossed a few vegetables, some nice pork sausage, a few bits of ham, into the pot. And to give it flavor, he didn't forget the smoked bacon. And also adding leftovers from the refrigerator.

It pleased him to see Tobias there in front of him, blowing on a heaping spoonful as children do, as he wiped his nose, perennially runny from a head cold, with the back of his other hand. The train whistle then reached their ears there in the living room, coming from a scene in the background that appeared to have been painted in great haste.

Though he had lived in that working-class district for many years, the neighborhood was changing without Venâncio's noticing. The street had the same houses and the same trees as always, though much older now. Only the neighbors replaced each other in relays, amid hurried farewells. No doubt worried about the furniture and the crates lying exposed on the sidewalk, like human viscera. Sometimes a smile foretold a move to a more genteel address. In which case they made a point of carefully noting down the new address on a bit of brown wrapping paper, which went straight into a drawer already stuffed full.

The new residents usually painted the façades of their houses pink or blue. Venâncio followed their first steps, confident still, with a jaundiced eye. On reaching the newsstand, on the corner, he perked up at the sight of the headlines.

"Tell me, Seu Cristóvão, when is it that you're going to discover America and set us slaves free?" Venâncio would say to him, when he woke up in a good mood.

These words, a long-standing joke between them, were greeted by Cristóvão with affection. Venâncio looked on him as being the probable bearer of the news of his death, once the stench coming from his house reached his nostrils.

In recent years, Tobias had been going through a grave marital crisis. Amália refused to divorce him, however, being quite satisfied with a legal separation.

"Our ties are unbreakable, Tobias, and that's because our interests are permanent," his wife said mockingly.

In the final stage, Tobias stopped attacking her, putting up with her insults. He recognized her merit in having brought up their daughters lovingly and well. Not to speak of her eagerness to please Bento, showing up at each and every company ceremony.

Bento sent for Tobias. He took him to task for his absence, in an impersonal voice, as though he were an employee of his.

"Any day now, people are going to forget that you're Madruga's son."

Till finally Amália sued for divorce. Tobias left the house for good, and invited Venâncio to come live with him. Using as a pretext the fact that, being together, they could argue about Brazilian defects from breakfast on. There was a great deal to say about this strange Republic which united and destroyed feelings that both of them perhaps shared.

"And since when does Brazil need us to describe it? It has no lack of writers, politicians, sociologists to do just that. And why would it be described by us of all people, seeing that we're failures?"

"Nobody understands Brazil less than that professional rabble. They're theoreticians, and they lack originality," Tobias said.

Venâncio wriggled out of the invitation, without fear of having offended his godson by making such a remark. Even Tobias unabashedly assigned himself a place on the roll of losers. Moreover, both of them understood failure, in which they included themselves, as the genuine impossibility of adjusting to a society whose ethical, moral, economic, and social order they vigorously fought. There being nothing left for them to do but camp out in dark zones of the country, from which they could witness everything, without running the risk of being swallowed up by iniquities beyond number. Personal sacrifice was worth much more to them than integration with Madruga's universe.

"Father was always impatient with me. He never gave me time," Tobias said, all upset. "Sometimes he was hard on me in the name of nothing more than false patriotism. He wanted me, above all, to respect the holy name of Brazil, the flag, and the national anthem. I sang the anthem, stammering and stumbling. Forgetting whole verses. Have you ever seen a single Brazilian citizen who could sing it all the way through? At first I applauded Father, despite my fear of him. In the end that patriotism made it easier for me to locate Brazil on the globe at school. And consequently to locate myself within this country. Except that, beginning with what my father and my teachers drummed into me, I came face to face with a cruel country that salted live flesh, cut off heads, cretinized a people by starving them. That's why we have so many imbeciles. The majority of those on the throne, incidentally. Hence it was this Brazil that I later came across on street corners. An ugly, toothless country, which began to skin me alive. I gradually grew bitter and stony-hearted toward it. And then the inevitable happened. My difficulties with Madruga and Brazil began to accumulate, fused now into a single person. And the misunderstandings grew so enormous that they resounded all through the house, and all through my heart in particular. I did not have a single safe preserve left me. I began to spy enemies, my own and the people's. Everywhere, even in the vaginas of whores, burbling syphilis and repression with each climax. Especially after that damned Revolution of '64. A dictatorship that grew stronger at the expense of the loss of my sovereignty. And I speak of sovereignty as though I were a country. Aren't all of us several different countries at the same time?"

Spurred on by Tobias, Venâncio went over his memories of the months just prior to the outbreak of the Movement in '30. There was a feeling of revolution in the air, which gradually began to take on concrete form. Once the interests of Washington Luís and Antônio Carlos collided head on. The delicate balance of power between Minas and São Paulo then going down the drain. Whereupon Rio Grande do Sul, which had always kept silent about the practice of trading off interests, sized up the situation and seized the opportunity that presented itself. Vargas would be able to solve the impasse. By leaping from the state government to the federal. Thirsting for vengeance, the gauchos lost no time in arriving at an agreement with the leaders in Minas. The great step leading to the creation of the Liberal Alliance, which gained Venâncio's sympathies. Despite this hope, Júlio Prestes won an easy victory. The economy meanwhile became a destabilizing factor. President Washington Luís's financial reform risked causing a steep decline in the price of coffee. And what with the bumper harvest, prices in fact began to collapse. As did the Old Republic. The holdovers from earlier political movements led by army officers beginning to demand that another page of history be turned over by force. Especially since the Alliance was the defender of the rights of the proletariat, which at that juncture found favor in the eyes of young lieutenants. But with the defeat of Vargas at the polls, a certain perplexity set in. Until the conspiracy was hatched. And Luís Carlos Prestes, falling out of step with what would eventually become the Revolution of '30, lost his chance to be a guiding force in the march of history.

The conspiracy gathers strength, wins followers, finally comes to light. The President is removed from office. And here comes the victory train from Rio Grande bringing Vargas and his men in its coaches. They stop off in São Paulo, amid a delirious crowd. Vargas proves to be one who fulminates, in his decrees, in his passage through the city. In less than twenty-four hours he arrives in Rio to assume power. The Palácio do Catete has been scrubbed and swept clean to welcome the new lord and master. And Vargas assumes power, hails the multitude from the balcony of the palace. There is a veritable carnival in the streets.

In the downtown bars, he and Madruga ordered beer. Everyone was pulling for the Alliance and its followers. Or rather, for the image of Vargas. The pulse of the man in the street had to be taken, testimony favorable to the movement recorded. The moment had come at last for Brazil to fulfill itself as a nation. Might not the Republic of dreams, envisioned by Brazilians new and old, be emerging from that November of 1930?

"Even foreigners were celebrating. We who were done an injustice by the despicable Adolfo Gordo Law, passed by Congress in 1907. Whereby any foreigner suspected of endangering public order could be expelled from the country. Particularly those immigrants who were most enlightened and most politicized. Immediately called rabble-rousers by the press and by their adversaries. As though we all wanted to forbid the existence of the State or create free communes and do away with private ownership.

"In a few months, certain voices began to lose their grandiloquence. The Communist Party had only to call upon workers to stage the Hunger March, and immediately the police forbade the demonstration, using force against groups of factory workers. Slowly introducing repressive methods into the social body. Then the Labor Union Organization Law was passed, prohibiting the propagation in labor unions of ideologies held to be sectarian. At the same time making it mandatory that public authorities or police officers be present at any labor union meeting.

"In Cinelândia people were now mistrustful as they drank their draft beer and their Malzbier. With veiled, sad eyes. There were no more civic celebrations. In the years that followed, Vargas's despotism took clearer and clearer shape as, in an effort to avoid crises whose origin lay in a social fabric worn thin by poverty and resistance to progress, he did not hesitate to use harsh police methods to put a stop to the activities of dissidents."

"And yet this is the same Vargas who put a new Electoral Code into effect, instituting the secret ballot, and thereby substantially diminishing the power of the oligarchy, and also came out in favor of the right of women to vote and hold office. What's more, he established the principle of equal wages for equal work," Tobias said, not intending his remarks as an outright provocation of his godfather. They rarely disagreed.

And as proof of his goodwill, Tobias went to the refrigerator to get his godfather a beer. Venâncio allowed himself to be catered to. Each of the two was the other's audience.

"I lived the Movement of '30 from the moment it was born. I did my best to sniff out its origins and the first signs that it was falling apart, which, by the way, were extremely subtle in the beginning. It can even be said that it was not till '37 that Vargas came straight out and proclaimed himself dictator. Though we had hints that he was headed that way. Certain measures are clear proof of bad intentions on the part of the person who takes them. So it was that the Revolution of '30, which came into being to heal and revolutionize the country, served to spread the dark stains of Power and of the State, and consequently to destroy rights belonging by birth to its citizens. It widened even more the unpardonable breach between State and People. The people, once again, meaning nothing to the State. Forced to abdicate its role as participant in and co-author of a nation. Vargas wanted to be the father of his country, and he succeeded. Thanks to his charisma, the labor laws drafted by Collor, and the implanting of the idea of nationhood, he became a paternalistic dictator. But unfortunately he did not scruple to pass on formulas for wielding absolute power to his successors. Getúlio more or less taught the military dictatorship of '64 certain indispensable rules for the exercise of power outside the law. Since when has it been necessary to station huge numbers of troops and police vans in the major public squares to control the people? All the latter-day dictators have learned from Vargas, who was a past master at this. It's becoming even easier today, since I don't see anyone in this country fighting openly for utopias, which, moreover, are regarded as an absurdity. I've never seen so great a country with such a petty dream! What a sad thing! Isn't it quite true that we defend a utopia in our green years, and loathe it once we've grown up? And isn't it also true that death seems more real to us with each passing day? And if that's so, what keeps us from more profound reflections still, favoring an esthetics of life rather than an esthetics of poverty, of a gross, purely transitory hedonism? Why is poverty being prettied up by the communications media, which refuse to recognize its legitimately disturbing social setting? And why does poverty itself, covered with shame at its own degrading condition, not place the blame on those responsible for it? Ah, Tobias, it's just as well that I haven't long to live. I can't bear to see Brazil go on this way."

Madruga kept offering Venâncio, again and again, an apartment in Leblon. But Venâncio refused to leave his working-class district. There in his little house, he felt himself to be part of a reality of concrete, palpable dimensions.

"To the winners—the working-class districts," Venâncio said jokingly, draining his stein of beer, now lukewarm.

"We'll confront Madruga and his successors with the spectacle of our poverty." Tobias offered his toast in the same spirit. Immediately adding, in a bitter tone of voice: "But what pride are we entering a plea for, godfather? And what sort of vanity must we be willing to answer for?"

"There is only one sort of pride, Tobias. The pride of surviving. Of being alive. And no one can cause us to doubt that we've lived. Or accuse us of not being here, in this backyard, drinking beer."

From the veranda, the waves seem to spatter ferocity and salt in my direction. Feeling restless, I go back into the living room. I think I see certain shadows projected on the walls.

Venâncio scarcely says a word. His attention entirely occupied by Eulália's state as she lies resolutely dying in the bedroom. He is unwilling to give up hope. And he no longer bares his face to me as he once did. He hides his wrinkles and his feelings.

And to think that we arrived in America together! The two of us aboard the nefarious English boat, after an endless crossing. During which, unable to sleep, we whispered back and forth about the future. How many times Venâncio held my head so that I could vomit without staining my clothes.

The meals we were fed out of cans were unsalted. Prepared with the deliberate intention of offending our sensibilities, of arousing our hunger and our indignation. So that we would arrive in the new land wild with rage and uncontrollable.

We spent hours leaning over the rail, watching the waters of the Atlantic, which to our eyes looked different each day. Thus making it impossible for us to memorize or guess by what routes these waters had come our way and what shore they were headed for.

After disembarking, Venâncio and I decided to stay together, pitting ourselves against everything that was forcing us to separate. Our story in Brazil began, then, on the same day. On a Thursday, to be precise, in the year 1913. And from then on, he was always present at the events that followed one upon the other. From Eulália's arrival in Brazil, after the wedding. To the birth cries of the first child, Esperança, born at home, while we sat nervously drinking red wine in the living room, hearing not so much as a murmur out of the stoic Eulália.

The one thing Venâncio would have no part of was my business ventures, though I described them with the greatest enthusiasm. With heartfelt vehemence, he repudiated a world that exalted money rather than imagination.

No one is more familiar to me than Venâncio. I know his face better than my own. While he describes my gestures with unerring accuracy. Yet we are not readily palpable. Venâncio in particular fiercely guards his privacy. He resents it when I show excessive interest in him. Forgetful of the fact that he serves as a framework for my story. But can it be as simple as that?

He is constantly hanging about my house, my table, my children. What is he after, what is it he wants within the orbit of my power? Can he be so perverse, so dissolute, so mendacious that he forbids me to describe his life, letting me in on no more than a few insignificant details? Does he perhaps envy me, though I for my part esteem him?

Deeply pained by Eulália's death agony, Venâncio does not hide the feverish gleam in his eyes. In her pale face there is a little night lamp burning for him. That is where his emotions have always led him; he had to track them down. Something I have never done. I have preferred to chase after money and women. To Venâncio's disapproval, his reserve being a continual source of irritation to me, from the time we lived in the room at González's hotel.

González had assigned us to the same room in the beginning. Shut up there together, we made plans. Saturday nights were promising. On that night especially, I urged Venâncio to come to the Lapa district, near the hotel, with me. Someone from the old country had told me about a cabaret there.

Venâncio didn't want to go out. He preferred to stay home reading. He was ashamed to share certain experiences with me. For some reason, his face would turn red as a beet, and he would practically stammer.

Though I was all by myself, luck smiled on me. As I entered the cabaret, a good-looking black girl ordered me to follow her. Attracted by her color, I obeyed, my heart in my mouth. We went up two flights of stairs in the old house, where apparently she lived. The wood creaked with each step we took.

She closed the door and gave a friendly smile. She began taking off her clothes in a very natural way. A naturalness that was not simply practice. She had arrived in Brazil before I had. So she had harmonious gestures, bespeaking familiarity with the land. Her race was of ancient extraction, consequently exuding an ardent, almost arcane secretion. Her genitals had landed in Brazil from the shores of Africa. Thus she had reason to suppose that her sexual pleasure was the exact reproduction of what her grandmother had once experienced in the slave quarter.

I too had ancient genitals to offer her. Native to the Iberian peninsula, where they had taken on vigor and vitality. There thus existing the possibility that, in the past, there had been a chance encounter between our ancestors, from which we had come into being. And this from the moment that a primal ancestor of that black woman had decided to row up the stream of history till he reached Spain. Coming, however, upon a febrile, ghost-ridden Spain, he had gone on to Basque country, then followed a riverbed that entered Galicia, arriving in Sobreira. He had stayed there just long enough to have an erection of his virile black member on meeting up with the privates of a green-eyed peasant lass, who placidly allowed him to enter between her thighs. Whereupon, on going beyond the shallow surface of desire, both experienced the pleasure that dwelt in the depths of their bodies.

I was awkward in bed. An adolescent steeped in memories and alien habits. Eager to unite the liquid of his passion with a woman's. Thus bringing about, in perfect confluence, the union of the probable histories of our forebears.

The woman's back was topographically impeccable. I trembled with the caresses that gradually unfolded until the denouement was reached. Climax found me anointed by her heat, born in Africa, in the heart of the world. We had been firm and aggressive in the hour of love. Did I give her a taste of the lash because I had strayed on the path of her sex, from which I was expelled by her mucous membrane, thereby forcing her to search for me far outside her body? And, by reason of this imprudence, whereof I alone was guilty, had I cried out to high heaven against her, being certain that she was still my slave?

Back in the room, Venâncio noted the dark circles of exhaustion under my eyes. He brought me a glass of milk. I sipped it slowly, determined to visit the woman again. Her eyes haunted me all week. On Saturday, she greeted me with surprise and modest reserve. Not mentioning my lack of experience. The only things that left a favorable impression on her were my clothes and the lavender I had rubbed on my body.

Each Saturday the black woman's breasts grew fuller, more exciting. And her face, a generous one, told stories without the use of the spoken word. The intensity of the pupils of her eyes forced me to contemplate where they had come from, and where they would go, after me.

Till the day she told me gently not to ask for her again. She was returning to Bahia for good. Sitting on the edge of the bed, wearing a dressing gown embroidered with forget-me-nots. Outside of the act of love, she behaved with shy reserve. Nothing betrayed her emotion. Save for a slight flutter of her eyelids. On bidding her farewell, I kissed her hands again and again. She had expanded the world of my senses. She had handed over to me a fortune destined to be dissipated in everyday living. And all so that I might gather together in the future acts and words to transcribe the various states of the body. This thermal nature of mine, blowing hot and cold, would not forget the pleasure that had been forthcoming from her thighs, beneath the watchful gaze of eyes emitting sudden flashes of light and signs of an Africa held in slavery.

From the living room, I hear the telephone ring. It is Bento, keeping zealous watch over my health. I answer him with half-truths. He is now located in a plush downtown office. An entire floor has been set apart for his own use. But this morning, despite the luxury that surrounds him, he is no doubt spewing out fear and arrogance. He has taken little pleasure in his magnificent house before leaving. The reason being that he is about to confront at last the box of Eulália's that has been given him. Sitting in front of him at this moment, on his desk.

Bento has been reaping victories for years now. Not content with mere crumbs that come his way. His fighting spirit is his future epitaph. Nothing fills his heart, not even his family. Each time he mounts his wife, he does so with a certain loathing. As though his body lacked zones capable of penetration. For this reason, Bento cuts Miguel short. He forbids him to speak of his love affairs. Life in a pure state is threatening to him. Especially when it bleeds.

More often than not, Miguel goes straight on. "Would you rather I talked to Luís Filho, then? Or is it money you'd prefer to talk about? Can it be that even the whole of Brazil isn't enough to satisfy your ambition?"

Bento shut himself up in his office. After giving his secretary strict orders that he was not to be interrupted that morning. Even if he were to give her orders to the contrary.

"Whoever it is, I'm not in."

The secretary couldn't believe her ears. Bento had always been more than available to people with power. He was at their beck and call, at any time.

That box weighed heavily upon his heart. Eulália, however, had pressed it upon him. It was his inheritance. A legacy that Bento would willingly have renounced, had it been up to him.

Intimidated by the object, he cautiously removed the lid. He seemed to be letting ghosts out, or strange itches. The only thing that came his way, however, was a familiar odor. It called to mind the perfume his mother had worn in his adolescence. For a few moments, he breathed in that scent that had survived so many years of being shut up in the box, just to assail him in his maturity. Had Eulália acted as she had with forethought? So that this perfume would become her most imperishable remembrance?

Irritated by this provocation on his mother's part, he slammed the lid of the box shut. The scent, meanwhile, had impregnated his hands, everything round about him. He ran to the bathroom, turned on the faucet, allowing the water to splash out onto the marble bench. He soaped his hands, scrubbing them with the nail brush. He returned to the room, free of the perfume. On sitting down at the desk, he drew back in fear. The odor was lying in wait for him there too.

Bento resolutely opened the box and emptied the contents out onto the desk. Carefully avoiding looking at the small objects and papers piled up in front of him. He hurriedly divided up the contents, dumping them inside three manila envelopes. He struck a match and held the flame to a stick of wax, letting a few drops fall, thus sealing the envelopes. And on the outside of each of them he wrote, in capital letters: TO BE OPENED AFTER MY DEATH.

Distractedly, he signed them "Bentinho." The diminutive Eulália used to call him by when he was an adolescent. Till he begged her not to call him that again.

"I'm not Bentinho, mother. Don't humiliate me that way. If my name is Little Bento, how can I ever come out on top?"

He left the room with a martial stride. The secretary tried to stop him. She had an urgent message for him. He waved her away, striding on to the elevator. Clutching the packets, which were burning his fingers. Once out on the street, he quickened his pace. Rapidly covering the distance that separated him from the Home Savings and Loan Association of Brazil.

In the underground vaults of the bank, standing before his safe-deposit box, he relaxed. He resumed habits temporarily abandoned. Serenity, for instance. And on burying the envelopes at the bottom of the box, he felt strong and indifferent once again. Certain that he could withstand remembrances of Eulália, gathered together without his permission.

Thus disengaged from the past, he seemed to smile. Safe now from such temptations. He did not believe that there existed inside that box a single detail that would make it easier to understand either himself or his country. He considered himself capable of overcoming nagging memories. And, consequently, of becoming a skillful teller of his own stories. Thus stealing from his mother the gift inherited from Grandfather Dom Miguel. Because he would grant no one, Eulália above all, the privilege of telling them. Only he had the means of organizing their trajectory. Moreover, he intended his stories to spend themselves gradually and wind down to a close in his own person.

While Eulália had been banished from reality at an early age, he was part of an elite that rejected the dank and musty national memory, so often a hindrance to the arduous task of developing a country.

"What Brazil needs is Itaipu, nuclear power plants, Carajás, Jari. For that we can do without all this traffic with the past, which never constituted a lesson certain to apply. Who ever consults the past when making a decision about the present? Despite historians and hallowed analogies, mistakes too are repeated. History is in its proper place in books, on the shelf. It's something for specialists. It serves to sustain the rage for interpretation of the various Marxist schools. To carry out a great national project, we have no need of the verbal hocus-pocus of politicians and artists, who refuse to face up to the reality of statistics and debts. We entrepreneurs are the ones who have contributed to making Brazil the world's eighth greatest economic power. And this despite its foreign debt and its burden of social entitlements. Isn't that the way Socialist countries go about things? Can a modern society be built without such entitlements? You know something? We're the ones who planned this recent advent of the country on the economic scene. What did Brazil amount to before the Revolution of '64? It scarcely had a fiscal policy. There were no revenues coming in; the public coffers were practically empty. The Ministry of the Treasury was a mere ornament," Bento declared roundly, in permanent disagreement with Miguel. He accused him of being out of step with the urgent needs of his time. Since there was no possibility of confusing his point of view and the interests of an entire nation.

Miguel was moved by his own oratory. He had tended to be emotional ever since he'd been a little boy. For that very reason, his eyes were swollen as he left Eulália's room. Feeling comforted nonetheless by having witnessed the distribution of the boxes. Eulália had pointed out the one that was his with a feeble gesture; he had very nearly failed to notice it. He had then kept a tight grip on the box, as though it were a treasure. Grateful to his mother, who had accumulated those modest belongings with the intention of enhancing their reality, of passing on to her children the vision of her stories, brought into clear focus by her efforts.

"Here is my box, father," Miguel said. "To me, it represents a lesson in freedom."

He immediately regretted his remark. Sensing his father's possible frustrations with regard to memories of Sobreira. While in a certain way Eulália had succeeded in keeping Dom Miguel's stories alive, his father might very well have failed to glorify Xan's. On reducing his stories to silence, he had buried his grandfather in the deepest, most wretched pit. And all for the gold and silver he was going to leave his children.

Miguel looked tired now. But he was still the handsomest of the male offspring. Esperança and he had been resplendent in their early years. Particularly so on the afternoon I surprised them having tea in the Confeitaria Colombo. I had come there by chance. I halted in the doorway. All eyes were upon them. They were sitting at the table directly beneath the great crystal chandelier. I too was suddenly overawed by that harmony.

Miguel took his leave. Having had another cup of coffee first. Still staring at the box lying on the easy chair. He stirred the sugar in as though muddling his own destiny with the spoon. I noted how eager he was to be by himself, to shut himself up in his study at home. Which was out of bounds to Sílvia. He would hole up there to discover the secrets of the box.

He barely greeted Sílvia, reading on the veranda. What was more, they seldom spoke to each other. Except about business matters. Miguel kept her informed of certain obstacles, fearing a sudden death that would rob the family of vital information. Even though the sons were already in the company. And quite used to the cold jealousy reigning between Miguel and Sílvia.

Shut up in his study, Miguel summoned the memory of Eulália. Of her yellow, emaciated hands carefully pointing out the boxes to their respective owners. Each of them in possession of their destinies confined in such a small space for so many years. Their mother perhaps wanting to tell them, as she returned their belongings to them, that they were about to be, for good, the owners of their lives. Or was their mother's gesture meant, as seemed most likely, to suggest the existence of a number of different paths worth venturing forth upon? But if that were so, hadn't this sign come too late? Hadn't all of them, without exception, ruined their lives? Hadn't he himself traded the stories of Dom Miguel, a fanatic restorer of the foundations of Galicia, for free transit through palace corridors? Always acting to further the interests of an oligarchy to which he in fact now belonged? Can Eulália have perceived that even Miguel had allowed himself to be corrupted by success? Hence passing lightly over the moral sense of her stories. Or by seeing him so attentive always, and thus capable of reproducing her stories, did she judge him to be safe from petty realities, from every sort of moral corruption?

After the crisis between Miguel and Sílvia, Eulália had come to his aid. For an entire afternoon she had kept him at her side, having servants bring endless dainties she knew her son could not resist. Not even forgetting to have nice warm cracklings brought, though they didn't go with all the rest. And before he left, she seized his hand, about to pass a message on to him.

"Even if we no longer know how to tell stories, because we're forgetting them, or because they apparently have nothing to do with us, nonetheless, Miguel, they remain hidden in our hearts. All set to surprise us at any moment. And for that very reason no story ever really dies. All that ever dies is the person who tells it."

In the midst of that crisis, Miguel came to doubt the effectiveness of Eulália's stories. Or those of anyone else willing to bow before the facts thus linked one to the other, in such a way as to hold a roomful of listeners spellbound. But with the passage of the years, feeling the repercussion of certain stories within himself, even when his thoughts were elsewhere, he began once again to believe that these modest, relatively fascinating little stories had a subversive substratum. Because they had a way of suborning the conscience not only of the person who told them, but also of the persons who heard them. Perhaps for this reason, even in his adolescence, on yielding to the pleasure of wandering about the streets and chasing women, he had refused to put Eulália's teaching into practice. Afraid, doubtless, to yield to the prompting of his own imagination, Eulália's, and Dom Miguel's. As though foreseeing their devastating effects on his daily life. Putting them into practice or living according to their dictates would have meant breaking with the structures of his present life. Casting his lot against the family's fortune.

In the face of this threat, and those that Esperança had taken it upon herself to voice, he indulged himself in sexual pleasures with unbridled fervor. Sex becoming his modern odyssey. By means of it, he ventured, like an explorer of the hinterlands in days past, into the immense, untamed interior of the bodies of others, eager to experience that day's unknown.

Before him was a rich vein to be proved with his prospector's gold-washing pan, though there were no guarantees that he would find nuggets at the bottom of it.

He trembled before the box. What was there inside that might come pouring out and make him suddenly turn violent? Impel him to head down a path leading to social ostracism? Or was precisely the contrary true? Instead of the box revealing to him a life shot through with intense, unbearable colors, might it produce, among the objects it contained, evidence that Eulália herself, without the knowledge of her children and her husband, had succumbed to mad passion?

Miguel blushed at the idea. A white-hot ardor mounted upward through his groin. He felt like flogging the cursed unconscious that kept pouring out trash and mad dreams. Harrying him now, perhaps, so as to cast a dark shadow over the genuineness of the love his mother bore him. But what sort of feeling was it that had made her single him out from all the other children? His box therefore weighing more than the others. It appeared to be filled to overflowing with keepsakes. Owing, surely, to Eulália's waking in haste of a morning, anxious not to let a single detail regarding her son escape her. Or was it his imagination that led him to suppose that his mother's love for him necessarily excluded the others?

Such a suspicion made him feel ashamed of himself. He then drew the box toward him, hugging it to his chest without removing it from the table. He did not want to feel its weight again. He must decide what to do with it. Before Eulália joined the legion of the missing.

At the same time he could not bear to live with the truth. No matter how little it hurt him. He was particularly incensed at the thought of a truth perhaps betrayed by Eulália. She who had taught him that human love was sweet. And for that reason he had surrendered eagerly to stray vaginas, with configurations he could not describe. How many of them, however, had ever come to have a name, a face, a life story?

Suddenly, on an impulse, wanting to hear his own voice, he shouted fiercely: I'm an impostor. So loud a roar that it reached Sílvia's ears, in the nearby television room. She immediately knocked on the door. Insisting that he declare himself beaten or in desperate straits. Miguel imagined his wife with her ear glued to the door, suspecting him of being up to no good.

"It was nothing, Sílvia. I'm all right," he said, driving her away. He did not want her around, her of all people, the woman for whom he constituted a hostile shadow. Whose trail Sílvia had devotedly followed in the past, guided only by the slender threads and bread crumbs that this same shadow, who was Miguel through and through, let fall on the ground as he went. Without his wife being able to stop him.

In their daily clash of wills, Sílvia, spurred on by the spirit of vengeance alone, sometimes attacked him. Repeating the same words yet again.

"Only Esperança could have overcome this passion of yours. This white-hot flame of yours."

"Shut up, Sílvia. What do you know about physical passion? About an act of which nothing remains save a gob of mucus, slime you rub into your body, just to rid yourself of memories and filth." He too wanted to hit home. In the certainty that Sílvia was hiding her face in her hands so as to keep scenes of Miguel making love to her cousin from coming back to her.

Despite Sílvia's shrewdness, trying to drive him to despair, she did not succeed in laying bare the nature of this whirlwind of emotion of his. Or the layers that went to make up his possible secret, which he himself cautiously skirted.

At times, professing pride in this gypsy fate, Miguel swore that he had never belonged to a woman. A tramp, nothing more, on the lookout for tragic sentiments, fleeting emotions, to be cast aside next morning.

The box gleamed. Odete had polished the wood with a flannel cloth, foreseeing that the day they would be distributed was close at hand. She sensed intuitively that as soon as Eulália was ready to leave them, she would proceed to empty out the wardrobe chests.

Miguel stroked the lustrous surface. Following in Eulália's footsteps. His mother had passed that way, in modesty. She who had always proclaimed the impermanence of human beings and of objects. Nonetheless, without realizing it, she had succumbed to pride. Having failed to perceive that, on pleading for the continued existence of the belongings in the boxes, she was opposing the destiny that God had traced for men. That of coming to earth with complete detachment, so as to take leave of it like one who had not even walked upon it. Had Eulália not observed the commandment of obedience and humility?

Miguel lit a fresh cigarette from the butt of the one before. He found it intolerable to criticize Eulália, now that she was dying. He felt himself to be a coward and a liar, disguising his own feelings by accusing his mother. And all out of fear of the box. He began to tremble, then fell into a fit of convulsive weeping. He leaned his forehead against the table, wanting to feel the cold of the wood. The table reminded him of the coffin that would receive his mother. Elegant and sober. His mother's imminent departure made his heart ache. Perhaps life was not within his competence, he thought then. As he repeated over and over to himself, Farewell, Eulália, farewell, Esperança.

For a long time now he had not felt the presence of the two women this strongly. At the very moment that one of them was taking the other far away. Leaving him behind, charged with the responsibility of not losing sight of them.

Sílvia knocked once more. Tired of keeping her ear glued to the door, picking up sounds from her husband.

"What's the matter, Miguel?"

He did not answer. She persisted. "Please, let me help you."

After waiting for a few moments, Sílvia crept back down the hall. Miguel had humiliated her yet again. Making it clear that he was banishing her from his life. She shut herself up in the bedroom, slamming the door so hard that he would hear. His ears pricked up now for every sound in the house, Miguel made the most of this opportunity. He hurriedly wiped his face, grabbed the box, fled from the house like a thief.

In the car now, he picked up speed. He drove quickly across Aterro, the viaduct, with the box on the seat beside him. He stopped on the Rio-Niterói bridge. It was cold when he opened the door. Facing into the wind, leaning over the parapet. Just long enough to dump the contents of the box into the sea. Free in space, they looked like a flock of fat birds. His eyes did not follow them till they fell into the water. He put the empty box back into the car and turned around at the tollgate. Anxious to keep the box hidden far out of sight of everyone. Nobody would be able to touch it. Not even he. Only Eulália, if she came back to life. Whereupon she would immediately ask to have the box back, so as to fill it once again with the mysteries of someone else's life.

Miguel too was growing old. He was past fifty. A man attractive still, still feverish. What could this son tell me now that I didn't already know? And what was there I could tell him that would serve as a letter of emancipation? And yet I loved him, with a dry love that made us cough. Both embarrassed by gestures and words about to surface, which we choked back down.

"Be careful, father. Bento and Miguel are going to attack us again," Antônia said, standing in front of me in the living room, rousing me from my torpor.

Antônia was all in favor of reprisals. To guard her rear, she had Luís Filho, who let nothing get by him. Urging her to shed tears, but keep an eye out at the same time for her brothers' every move. A conjugal sermon so effective that she kept sounding the alarm even in the hours preceding Eulália's death.

"And who's going to protect Breta from being mistreated by Bento?" she chattered like a magpie.

Breta had just arrived. She gave her aunt and her brood more or less the cold shoulder.

"Don't worry about me, Antônia. You'd best think about Eulália. Have you opened the box she gave you?"

Embarrassed by the question, Antônia didn't know what to answer. The fact was that she'd put the box away in a closet, with no intention of opening it. There would be time enough for that. She had practical problems, or more important ones, on her mind now.

"Be careful what you do with your own box, Breta. It's going to give you plenty of headaches," she said sarcastically.

Antônia had gotten along nicely in life thanks to my fortune. She never hesitated to use her daddy's money as a way of getting her husband into bed with her. Her face doubtless dripped gall and anxiety on receiving Eulália's box. She would rather have received her brothers' boxes, so as to get her hands on their probable secrets. She had no respect for her own life, already profligate enough in and of itself. The box would no doubt represent one more burden for her. She had long been lost in intrigues, both within the family and without. Though she was not clever enough to look out for her own interests without Luís Filho.

That daughter was born weak. The strength that should have been hers fell to Esperança. Or was it my drive and power that had made her frail? Luís Filho had done the rest, having had years and nights to knead the sensitive areas of her body, so as to make them work in his interest. Her breasts and belly had become opulent thanks to much modeling by her husband's hands.

In her excessive devotion, my daughter comes to the house every day. She can't live without seeing us. She takes care of me, of Eulália, of Luís Filho, of her children and grandchildren. I detect in her the smell of grief and jasmine. Or am I perhaps no longer clear about details on the eve of my death?

As far as I know, Antônia awaited her turn to receive her box at Eulália's bedside without moving a muscle. Her feeling of rejection, instinctive and exquisite, forced her to stay on for the distribution of the boxes. Before she received hers, Eulália made a comment.

"Perhaps these personal effects will disappoint you. They are so modest! The rest you'll have to wait for after my death."

She freed herself of Antônia as though she had killed her at that instant. For those who are dying, the survivors too have already departed. Passing on was the one expectation left Eulália. With the certainty that Antônia, on examining the objects in the box, would not think them important. Perhaps she would search about for some precious ring that Eulália had forgotten was inside.

Shadowy forms stirred in the darkness of the living room. As he came in, Miguel turned on the lights. He kissed me on the cheek. He smelled of salt air. And he moved about restlessly.

"Before we've even seen Mother to her grave, I've gone about burying my memories. I've reduced to dust the story that Eulália wrote just for me," he said suddenly, heading for the veranda.

Tobias approached, beneath Venâncio's watchful eye. He didn't want us to ruffle each other's feathers. He had been through the painful trial of saying good-bye to Eulália. It was as though he were seeking help now, anticipating the arrival of Amália at any moment. A meeting that was always hostile, since the woman autopsied him like a dead bird. Of value for its down and its rare coloration.

My daughter-in-law will come to see me, after the end. And on the pretext of speaking of the good old days, she will recall Eulália's jewels, and what happened to them. Thanks to her prodigious memory, she will make detailed claims. On the other hand, she still has, even today, the beauty that Antônia lacks. She has always made me bow to her charms. Generous with her whispered allurements and melting embraces.

To all of Venâncio's pleas that Tobias needs peace and quiet, and therefore to be rid of her presence, she has a ready answer.

"Tobias has exactly the peace he needs. What more does he want? I'm only looking out for my daughters' inheritance. And my daughters are his daughters too."

There were four of us in the living room now. The two children, Venâncio and I. Some more sensitive than others. We feared the moment when we would learn that Eulália was dead. Who would weep the most copious tears? And who would forget her first?

Miguel was drowning himself in coffee. I sensed marks that had gone deep, in his heart and on his face. One's children grow old too, and this was my vengeance.

"What's going to happen to all of us after Mother's gone?" he broke the silence.

"My life is already written. I've nothing more to do," I answered curtly.

Tobias watched me closely, without the courage to fight with me. Venâncio was protecting him. In that particular contest, he would come out the winner. Tobias was his son now. He had only my name and blood. Aside from memories and resentments. The remainder of that human territory belonged to Venâncio. But this defeat did not hurt me. Just as keeping the other children for myself no longer mattered to me. By deciding to die, Eulália suddenly seemed to me both clever and hostile. Leaving me faced with all the responsibilities of living. A life to be swallowed daily, along with coffee with milk, jam, Minas cheese, and warm bread.

Before heading for the living room, after the boxes had been given out, Venâncio had gone with Tobias to have a look at his old room. There before the box lying on the bed, Tobias gave vent to his feelings.

"Our family doesn't dream anymore, godfather. Especially now that Mother is going to leave us."

"But there's not a single family that dreams, Tobias," Venâncio tried to console him.

Both were weary in the face of the long list of their failures. Venâncio, however, was always noble in defeat. Above all in his old age, his shoulders straight, his hair carefully combed. Counseling Tobias to be patient. In the end, living as the two of them had was a much more difficult business than it was for those who had reasons to smile.

"All Mother did was select memories and keep them in this box. But why didn't she consult me beforehand, to see if I approved? Did Mother have the right to collect fragments of my life, the way people collect butterflies and mount them on a pin stuck through their brains?"

Venâncio frowned. As a warning to his godson about the use of words that might offend Eulália. He had a duty to protect her from human hurt. Eulália's life had been spent comforting sheep and souls. As though she had been born to retouch the blackened image of humankind.

As he described her, with great emotion, he slowly slid his hand over the coverlet of the bed they were sitting on. Aware that in a few hours Eulália would have yielded up her last sigh. To hide his grief, he bowed his head. Not even his old age weighed as heavily upon him.

Tobias opened the window. Before doing so, however, he wrote his name in the dust on the pane with his thumb. He had not visited that room for years. Though it was now neat and clean, the furniture and the walls betrayed its lack of use. Everything in that room brought back painful memories. How many nights he had buried his head in the pillow to stifle his rage at Madruga! Yet without the courage to abandon that house, his father, and his fortune.

Upset at the thought, he turned to his godfather. "And to think that the word *fortune,* in Portuguese, has other meanings, noble, stirring ones. Unhappily, almost all of them fallen into disuse. Who in Brazil uses the word *fortune* as a synonym for chance, a lucky turn of the cards, destiny, setbacks and reversals? Or the expressions *good fortune* and *ill fortune,* in the sense that Camões used them? And all because the damned capitalist system has taken such firm root in the last two decades. A system that doesn't spare even words. Merely to utter the word *fortune* nowadays is to invoke economic power. Money is destiny, the only one there is."

Tobias spoke the last words with his back to his godfather. He deliberately kept his distance. When confronted with an obstacle, he invariably asked his godfather to spare him a few moments, so as to allow him to tune the instrument he was scraping away at.

Venâncio gave him the time he needed. No more than five minutes went by. Only then did he approach Tobias once more. He went over to the window.

"Eulália's boxes had nothing to do with putting aside fortunes. They were only for collecting keepsakes. All of you may think they're the naïve heritage of a religious woman who belonged to another time. When all Eulália wanted to do was to save the life that her children were carelessly spending. Thanks to her, they can go to the boxes and recover the time lost. If it weren't for her, who would ever tell the story of this family?" Venâncio said.

Whenever Tobias spoke harshly, he immediately regretted it. With gestures that only Venâncio read correctly without reproaching him. Simply sharing with him the soup or the stew he happened to be eating at the moment. Tobias always took pleasure in the plateful of hot food set before him. Certain that he was entering Venâncio's heart, merely by eating meat and vegetables cut up by his godfather's own hands.

They walked back over to the bed. They seemed tired. Tobias looked closely at Venâncio. He had done very little for that old man. Except assure him of an abiding love. A sentiment that his godfather gratefully accepted, his mouth half open, baring his set of false teeth. Ugly and threatening to fall out. Ill-fitting and impeding his speech. In the beginning, Tobias raised a fuss. He wanted to take him to the dentist to be fitted for a decent prosthesis that would fill out his face again. Venâncio, however, saw no reason to worry about his appearance. Oldsters were by nature out of step with time, which kept robbing them of their bodies and their days at a swifter and swifter pace, without so much as a by-your-leave.

Tobias looked attentively at the box again. "Mother looked out for us, after her fashion. Even when she seemed to be distracted. From the time we were little, she gave us presents. The best one of all was the hiding places she offered us all over the house. She was the one who chose the places she thought were right for us. I, for instance, was assigned the hiding place underneath the grand piano. And each secret cubbyhole received the name of a mountain in Sobreira. She took such pride in those hills that they seemed to be towering peaks in the Andes and the Alps."

Venâncio too eyed the box on the bed separating him from his godson. He did not dare touch it. Not even once. He was afraid it would burn his fingers.

"It must be made very clear, Tobias, that Eulália did not love Sobreira alone. She loved Brazil too, from the moment she arrived here. I'm a witness to that. It was just that her love for Brazil was so patient and generous that it left no room for criticism. And so I was obliged to be most reserved and circumspect when I was with her."

"I never noticed, godfather. I always found her absorbed in thoughts of Sobreira and God. How could I have imagined her to be fond of Brazil as well? Perhaps that's why whatever love I still have for Brazil is so confused, so extreme. I don't know whether it's love or hate. I do know that I'm more ashamed than proud of it. I'm only deeply moved by it when I see the ugly, toothless, shabby people I come across in the working-class districts, in the trains on the Central and Leopoldina lines, and the neighborhood round the Praça Tiradentes. I have the illusion then that they're the only innocents amid the gang of thugs murdering this country each and every day. At times like that I ask myself if I'm not as great a criminal as those traitors in Brasília. What's the good of this fever, this rebellion, if I don't lift a finger, if my apathy is chronic, very nearly lethal? Everything I think and do dies stillborn. What will I have left, now that Mother is dying?"

He hid his face in his hands, sobbing quietly. Not reconciled to losing his mother. Thanks to whom he had kept alight until now the flame of a false youth. He was knocking, empty-handed, at the door of his fortieth year. Suddenly he flung himself into his godfather's arms, weeping. Venâncio slowly stroked his hair, unable to free him from the fury of his siblings and Amália. The latter with an eye on the inheritance, all set to ally herself with Bento, whom she admired. With no intention of placing obstacles in the path of a vast corporate enterprise whose modest beginnings went back almost seventy years.

His equanimity restored, Tobias reached for the box. A fine piece of workmanship, it was closely joined, its cover decorated with a row of triangles of different colors set in relief. Once it was open, he saw various objects and papers stuffed inside, in such disorder that he could not even estimate the value of the contents. A disorderliness reminiscent of his own life. Thus reminded, he slammed the box shut. Leaving in the air the trace of a perfume that instantly invaded Venâncio's nostrils. He drew back in alarm. Forcing his mind nonetheless to call up memories. What perfume was this?

His senses thus alerted, he suddenly remembered Eulália's perfume. The one she had worn during the Spanish Civil War. Till the day of official surrender, following the victory of the Nationalists. From that date on, when she greeted him on Sundays, the same scent never again was there, beneath his very fingertips. It was a perfume so intense that sometimes it lingered with him till Monday. And when he took a deep breath of it, an odd indolence came over him.

What was more, Eulália's personal style gradually began to change after the rout of the Republicans. She took to wearing more sober dresses, tightly cinched in at the waist. At the same time she drew her fine hair back into a severe knot. A transformation that Venâncio, an attentive observer, interpreted as a sign that her deepest pity had been aroused by a war that for three years had inflicted horrors on the Spanish nation.

That recent patrician touch suited her well, however. And doubtless it would have pleased Dom Miguel, had he been alive. A Galician of arrogant mien, unabashedly spending hours at a time absorbed in stories that Eulália stored up little by little in her memory, with the intent of passing them on.

Those years had been trying ones. The disasters of war brought aftershocks in Brazil, among the Spanish colony in particular, settled for the most part in Rio and Bahia. And largely inclined to believe that order would be restored in Spain through Franco's stern rule. Acting as guarantor of strong institutions capable of upholding Christian principles.

Though Eulália did not openly declare herself a Republican, she supported Venâncio's views, letting it be known that a Republican victory would have been closer to her heart's desire. All of this out of sympathy for the war victims. All of them neighbors and brothers.

Tobias looked over at Venâncio. To see his reaction as he pushed the box away. Venâncio, however, neither indicated his approval nor pleaded with him to open the box again. He had no right to urge Tobias to plunge to the depths of himself, by way of Eulália's belongings. As much as his godson, he feared the devastating effect of such an examination. He had spent his life almost as one with Tobias, hence what was inside the box might very well be, to some small degree, his own memory.

"I don't want to know what's inside," Tobias decided. "My story is childish and unimportant, despite Mother's diligent effort to enrich it. The time has come for me to refuse to put up with any more lies or pointless memories."

He placed the box on the red rosette in the center of the carpet. In a certain way he was relieved that his mother, and even Venâncio, lacked the cleverness to put his story together.

"For a very simple reason, godfather. A person who's a failure has no story. What's more, I'm an insignificant failure. I have nothing to offer the imagination of anyone seeking to express genuine pity for one man's aborted efforts," he said angrily.

Venâncio rose to his feet, stiff and proud. He did not want to remain in that room. His godson had shut himself up in a capsule, exactly as he himself had. Wanting never to be found. And by so doing granting no one the right to love them. Could this be the proper thing to do? Merely to pass unnoticed, with no feelings of affection, one's heart harried by a stubborn loneliness?

In order to survive the Civil War and personal crises, he for his part had resorted to keeping a diary. Forcing himself to record, amid chaos, the life that escaped his grasp, forever impalpable. He even managed to invent a country, with words seldom logically related. And a century to which he could not belong, as well. But as the entries accumulated, he noted that the act of writing, even in an amateurish way, corroborated his belief that despite his mean and miserable life, there was still something left, the rough outline of a dream with which to occupy himself.

Pursuing this aim, he went farther and farther afield with each page of the diary. Till he went to the hospital. Where he stood up to Madruga, refusing to accept his presence. Madruga did everything possible to get the upper hand. And in all their years together, they had made no substantial changes in the battle they had joined. The difference was that he now understood the nature of certain feelings. Though inherently fatal, those feelings had stubbornly refused to let go their hold of the skin of those who had proved to be to their liking for so many decades.

Tobias knew nothing about the diary, and therefore nothing of Madruga's decision to hand it over to Breta. That granddaughter who, ever since childhood, had believed that a person's story could be told in the form of a book. Nonetheless, Venâncio felt that he was betraying his godson. Or depriving him of an inheritance that was his, by right of love. He never wanted Tobias to know how much, trusting life still, he defended it in writing, as meanwhile he howled under his breath.

Tobias was appealing to him now. Venâncio felt sorry for him. His pleas were useless. He had no way of answering them. Or even of helping him.

"I too have no history, Tobias. Perhaps for the same reason as you. But there was once a time when I thought it possible to tell any and every story. Even my own."

Tobias did not answer. He headed for the door, walking round the box on the carpet so as not to stumble over it.

"What about the box?" Venâncio said.

"We're leaving, godfather. The box stays here. I'll come back and get it someday."

In the living room, there were four of us in our respective easy chairs. Four men waiting for news of Eulália. Resigned to the slow passage of time. Fearing the dawn, which sends the world circling round again. We would then have to rinse out our mouths, flush out the bitter taste accumulated during our deathwatch.

I complained testily of the smoke from Miguel's cigars. He went on puffing anxiously. Each of us kept mouthing clichés, to which we were all addicted. Of all of us, only Eulália had won peace.

Miguel crossed the living room, taking small steps. Not venturing very far. Anyone who stayed away for very long would be forgotten forever. Was that the only reason we put up with each other?

I thought about Breta. Where could she be, in possession now of Esperança's box? With a false majesty, I had designated her heiress of my soul. In obedience to a dense, dark Spanish spirit, like Goya's sinister figures, in the antechamber of death. Can we who come from Spain be a happy people only when confronted with the convulsions that precede death? And was that the one reason why I chose Brazil as my country to live in? A land that mixed together, in a peculiar form and in the wrong proportions, a bit of poverty, confetti, serpentine, carnival sperm, ardent cunts, a lazy faith, endless embraces, a boundless triumphalism! Meanwhile framing feelings in palm trees, dunes, and sea breezes. Life carved up by rivers without end or beginning. Each insuperable, preventing anyone from breasting the current and reaching the other shore. Can the tent of dreams be on the other side? Was this the Brazil that received me in those years, expecting to expel me from its warm insides with a kick in the behind, to peals of laughter on every hand? A country that will leave me pale and wan, so that this decline will be mentioned on the pious day of my funeral? Is this what this country prepared for me, then, in these nearly seventy years of life? Is that all? Is this the recompense, is this the reward? My God, I don't want to die!

I left Grandmother's room after the distribution of the boxes. I wanted to be alone. Antônia, however, followed me out into the winter garden.

She always confronted me like a skittish animal. Quick to conceal her spite. She did not want me to be a formal, declared enemy. But her heart is a pendulum, it oscillates. She attacks and makes up, swathed in a cloth that binds her limbs and her soul.

When she asks for help, all Luís Filho does is bring her into line again with a mere look. She trembles, since if she has followed the path of folly, her husband will surely make her pay for it.

Now that we are by ourselves, her gaze is pleading. She hasn't the heart to weep. Her presence depresses me.

I decide to get even with her. "Why not cry and get it over with? Do you think you have to have my consent?"

Antônia set the box down on the table. She fixed Esperança's daughter with a stony gaze. Her sister's death hadn't helped her in any way. Esperança had had the bad taste to leave a trail of nasty memories behind her, and a daughter as well. Just so she'd be remembered. She didn't want people to forget her. Esperança had always ridden roughshod over other people's freedom. She didn't give a damn about Antônia, who from the time she was just a baby kept seeking her out. It was as though Esperança didn't even see her. They fought for years. On edge, permanently on the warpath, running spears through each other.

Of marriageable age herself, Esperança parried Antônia's disapproving gaze as she walked arm in arm with Luís Filho, a suitor out to make a match for money. Besides putting up with Madruga's arbitrariness, would she be obliged to defer to this sister too?

"Why are you looking at me that way, Antônia?" Esperança was saying. "Can it be that you're jealous, or afraid of living? When are you going to rule your own life?"

Esperança turned her back on Antônia, indifferent to the pain she was causing her. Nothing mattered now. She was certain that her father would see through her that morning, having caught on that she was sneaking out at night, meeting her lover. Maybe he would drive her out of the house. He would not tolerate his daughter's transgression.

Antônia did not suffer insults gladly. And followed hot on her sister's trail. Meeting up with her, she tried to scratch her face, damage a noxious beauty. She could not bear Luís Filho's radiant gaze the moment his eyes fell on Esperança. As her sister's body glowed with the knowledge that she was admired.

Antônia prepared to attack. She polished her words so as to deal her a mortal blow.

"You are the shame of our house. And you are going to drown in grief and despair." And Antônia repeated the word *despair* like an echo. Till Esperança ordered her to calm down, though Antônia did not obey.

Esperança went to her sister, seizing her by the wrist, taking her prisoner. Ordering her to look at her. Even if it were for the last time.

"Life owes me only what I have not yet done. Quite unlike you, who will only have this idiot of a Luís Filho as your man. Know that God is with me, in everything I do. Eulália's God has always bowed before those who were not afraid to face life. And scorned the lukewarm, like yourself. People with no appetite."

Esperança let go of Antônia's wrist and marshaled her forces to laugh in her face. Confronted with the virulence of her words, her sister gave way. It was easy to defeat her. Until then Esperança's victory had stemmed from the boldness with which she defined her feelings, made her meanings clear, gave names to the sensitive areas of her body.

Despite her anger, Antônia lost her head, not daring to stand up to Esperança. Esperança marked her sister's retreat without gloating. Whenever she had bent Antônia to her will, she hastened to return her to her original cage.

"You may go, Antônia. I never wanted to keep you prisoner. If I make you stay with me, you'll end up stealing my life."

Antônia shielded her face with her hands. As though afraid that Esperança would attack her, raking her face with her nails.

"Don't cry, Antônia. I'm going now. And you're free of me," Esperança said, touched by her sister's frailty.

Esperança too suffered from her father's more and more severe punishment. Mistrusting his daughter, Madruga had long been on the alert for evidence of her misbehavior. He would never forgive certain missteps.

Esperança was afraid and anxious. She expected Madruga to arrive at any moment. She had no desire to make her escape. He entered the living room, his face somber. Greeting no one. Avoiding looking at his daughter.

Eulália came to her husband's aid. He seemed to have collapsed in his armchair.

"What's the matter, Madruga?" Eulália said.

"It's unfortunately true, Eulália. Our daughter has brought only dishonor to our house."

"Don't talk that way, I beg you." Eulália was weeping now.

"We're losing our daughter, we're losing our daughter," and Madruga trembled as though taken by fever.

Miguel came over to his father. "The whole thing's a lie, father. You don't know what you're saying. Nobody knows."

Unable to speak, Madruga motioned with his head to Miguel. And made a gesture banishing Esperança from the living room. Miguel looked at his father, then at his sister. Torn between the two. Confronted, however, with Esperança's silence, he lost his self-control. He went to her, seizing her by the shoulders.

"Come on, confess. Don't hide anything from me. Is it true, Esperança?"

She looked straight back at him, without answering. She had lost her fear of her father, or of anyone else. Everything seemed banal to her, without grandeur. At stake was an honor consisting of nothing more than a ruptured hymen.

Perceiving his sister's arrogance, he came at her, slapped her face. Livid, Esperança neither replied nor retreated. She merely looked at him in such a way that he could not help seeing her features drained of color, the rage emptying from her breast. Everything within her assuring him that his blow would not remain unanswered. She would fight him till the end of her days.

Frightened, Miguel drew back the hand that had punished Esperança. His body burned. He hurriedly beat at it to smother the flames. But why did he feel his sister and his own life escaping him, once he had desecrated Esperança's face?

Madruga and Eulália hurriedly left the room. Miguel did not notice that he had been left alone with his sister. His surroundings seemingly a matter of indifference.

"Forgive me, Esperança, forgive me," he suddenly shouted to overcome his sister's apathy and his own anguish.

Esperança ran to her room and locked the door. Her fate was now being decided between Madruga and Eulália, in the next room.

Sitting on the edge of the bed, Eulália embarked upon a defense of their daughter. Not raising her voice as she pleaded her cause. Yet her dress was wrinkled from having repeatedly rubbed her hands against it. She spoke of their daughter as a direct descendant of Xan and Dom Miguel.

"She's our blood, Madruga."

"What blood are you talking about, Eulália? What kind of blood is it that disgraces us and shrouds us in grief?" Madruga bellowed, not caring whether or not the whole house heard him.

The words echoing through the walls reached Esperança's room. She took them all in. Knowing that her father wanted to brand her with a red-hot iron, burn an obscene epithet into her flesh. So that everyone would stone her.

Her mother pleaded with her husband for silence. He must hear her out. She could not allow him, taking mercilessness as his rod and his staff, to wreak yet another insult upon her womb, which had brought Esperança into this world. That daughter was one of her finest creations. Her birth had been a prodigious feat of God and of nature. And her daughter's sin was a mere human episode. Had Madruga forgotten that sin, despite its being of the stuff of drama, vanished in the eyes of the penitent? Who was he to judge, if they had all come into the world with the task of freeing themselves from temptation?

"She's a tramp and I do not forgive her," Madruga drowned out Eulália's voice.

At each of her father's imprecations, Esperança reeled about the next room with tottering step. Till at last she flung herself on the bed, stifling her sobs in the pillow. For a few moments she willed her body to be still, her rebellious body overcome by desire. A desire crying out for the freedom to love.

"Stop shouting, Madruga. Don't you dare call her that in God's presence." Eulália trembled, slipping halfway out of bed. She beat her breast to relieve the pain.

Blind to his wife's suffering, Madruga moved about the room impelled by hatred alone, raging without considering the consequences, the fact that they could hear him in the hall, the whole house in an uproar. And that Esperança, not far from there, was picking up the message that she was being turned out of the house.

"And she is never to appear in this house or in my sight again. I'm afraid of what I might do in the future. I don't trust myself anymore, Eulália." Madruga's eyes stared into space.

Clutching her rosary, Eulália knelt in front of the bed, forbearing to use the prie-dieu next to the window. And as she recited the Hail Mary, full of grace, Miguel pounded on the door, what's going on father, please, open up, the Lord is with thee, blessed art thou among women, Miguel insisted, trying now to knock the door down.

Inside the room, Madruga steeled himself against the invasion. At that moment spurning even his friends. In all truth, the whole world was his adversary.

"Get the hell out of here, Miguel. That's an order," he roared.

With her head bowed almost to the floor, Eulália went on, blessed be the fruit of thy womb, as Madruga knelt at her side, closing her mouth firmly, don't go on, woman, no fruit of that womb will be blessed, I don't want any fruit of that womb.

"I don't want that womb in this house anymore."

"Please, father, open the door. If you don't we'll knock it down," Miguel insisted, backed by Bento.

Eulália tried to remove Madruga's hand, to no avail. Speaking in a lower voice now, he said emphatically, Don't ever ask that she be forgiven,

Eulália. Never speak of forgiveness for her, he repeated, as Miguel, impelled by the terror of losing Esperança, shut up in her room, moved to the other door. Begging her, in a loud voice, to let him in. He needed urgently to see his sister.

Esperança did not answer. Just as Madruga paid no attention to Bento, demanding to be let in. Till finally, Eulália, hearing Odete's voice at the door, took heart and pushed Madruga's hand away. He stepped back. But perceiving that he had subdued his wife by force, if only for a few moments, he who had always made every effort to protect her from everything and everyone, and especially from his fury of a raging bull, he felt such shame and despair that he fell to the floor in tears. Such a wild fit of weeping that the tears flowed as one with those of Esperança, in the next room, overcome by the same infectious anguish as her father. Madruga's flood of tears, far from being cathartic, hence capable of teaching him to pardon her or readmit her into the bosom of the family, consisted of grunts, spasms, and inexplicable feelings. From such a source there lay ahead for Esperança a hatred that would be extinguished only with the death of one of them.

This paternal rancor set off an entire train of nervous events: it commanded her to obey, to pack her suitcase, to leave the house, to turn her back on all of them, to look for another place to live, other bodies, other traditions. And finally, to cease forevermore to sink deeper and deeper roots in that house that till then had been her home, her memory, her spirit, her language.

"Open the door, Esperança. I need to see you," Miguel begged.

Madruga strained to lift Eulália to her feet. She had not moved for a long time. Trembling, she held back; she could scarcely stand. With difficulty he raised her up. He too ached all over. He felt that they were burying him in that room, depriving him of sunlight, of life in the streets. Even Eulália, pale and helpless, couldn't give him a hand. The two of them had been defeated by Esperança.

He settled his wife back in the bed and opened the door. Face to face with Madruga, Bento was frightened. Not knowing whether to dissuade his father from taking some sort of vengeance or join Miguel in an effort to knock Esperança's door down.

Odete seemed oblivious to events. She came into the room unhurriedly. Looking for Eulália, to take care of her. She immediately brought her medicine, sugar water, to calm her. She avoided looking at Madruga, acting as though he were not present.

Leaning on the chest of drawers now, Madruga found himself staring into the faces in the photographs before him, mounted in silver frames. Among them he saw one of Esperança, still a little girl. On horseback, in a defiant pose, his daughter was practically warning him to watch his step. Since she would never deny her vital impulses to please her father. A man who, merely because he had braved Atlantic monsoons, the realm of Atlantis where thousands of legends had been buried, thought he had the right to silence her, to weaken her body and the impulses that had led her, since childhood, to leap over walls, climb trees, fight, rebel against the narrow confines of her feminine condition.

On the chest of drawers there was also a recent photograph of Esperança. Visible in the background was one of the fountains flanked by ornamental lions in the park of São Lourenço. Esperança had insisted on being taken there, claiming she wanted to bid her adolescence farewell. Madruga had been puzzled by the request, when there were so many other places she hadn't yet visited. To his surprise Esperança came back with Eulália before the date set for their return, looking thin and depressed. And at the table during lunch, there was a vague, feverish gleam in her eyes. Miguel made several joking remarks about it.

"I'm not the same as I was, Miguel. So don't fool with me anymore," Esperança said.

Taken by surprise between one forkful and the next, Miguel turned to his father for support. Madruga paid no attention to him. And even Eulália, who always stood up for him, failed this time to come to his defense. All those at table preoccupied by their own concerns. Only Miguel, worried about what Esperança might do next, felt threatened by the changes taking place in his sister. She had the air of a traveler determined to take off at any moment. By boat, by plane, or on foot. With no fear that a gale would tilt her wings or capsize her craft.

Miguel poured her a glass of guaraná, but his sister did not offer him her usual prompt thanks. Something strange was undoubtedly happening to her. He looked at Madruga and Eulália. Lost in thought, they had noticed nothing wrong. On the alert now, he set out to discover who had robbed him of Esperança's gaze, continually fixed on him, following him everywhere. He had grown used to exploring the world with his sister close at hand.

"What's the matter, Esperança? Where was it you went, that makes it so hard for you to come back? Or is it that you don't love me anymore?" he said pleadingly, once the two of them were alone.

"You wouldn't understand, Miguel. I feel I'm losing everyone in this house. It's just a matter of time."

Madruga walked away from the chest of drawers, dogged by the memory of the photographs. All that must be erased. Reaching the bedside, he could hear Miguel's pleas in the distance, outside his sister's door. And the thought came to him then that his son would pound on that door forever. And that his effort would be to no avail. That daughter had made life a bitter thing for them. He himself had the taste of blood in his mouth, mingled with saliva. On the other hand, he had done everything possible to make her life bitter too.

"Can that be true?" Eulália suddenly invaded his thoughts, denouncing his plans to take his revenge.

"And why not? If I could love her that much, I have an equal right to punish her," he murmured, close beside Eulália, drowsy now from the medicine.

Bento begged Miguel to take it easy. He was still pounding on the door, harder than ever, but Esperança did not open it. His sister's weeping, audible through the door, assured him nonetheless that she was alive. Esperança's pride was keeping her from killing herself. She would abase herself first, dragging her family down with her, just so that her father, wherever he might be, even in bed with a strange woman, penetrating her with his strong, steady member, would never be able to forget her. Thus obliged to recall, with the most intense bitterness, that his daughter, at the price of a painful dispossession, had finally won the right to engage in acts resembling his own. She too had heard life finally declare, in an apotheosis of sound and fury, which bed it was in.

Antônia's footsteps echoed in the hall. She was parading her perplexity amid the tumult. Without the courage to invade her parents' bedroom. Or help Miguel. She had always fled the visible marks of passion. No intense feeling had ever lured her. The violent hues of tragedy or drama, so much to Miguel's and Esperança's taste, had the opposite effect on her. They made her want to vomit.

She could not resist, however, her desire to win out over Esperança in her parents' hearts. Her turn had come at last. She entered warily, without a sound. She saw Eulália lying with her hand on her breast, watched over by Odete. Madruga walked from the bed to the chest of drawers, drawn by the photographs. Looking at them from close up, he retrieved the images that had leapt out of those portrait photos collected down through the years. As though he were bidding farewell to an era in which it had been easy for him to be happy.

Antônia noted the care with which Madruga removed the photographs of Esperança from their silver frames, bought in Portugal. Madruga and Eulália had never gone to Galicia without setting foot in Portugal, the traditional neighbor, sharing the same soil and the same annual rainfall. To do so they had only to cross the bridge linking Tuy to Valença do Minho. Crossing back with pleasant memories, presents, and silver frames for family photographs.

Antônia saw how her father, in a slow gesture, in which there was a repressed fury, threw the photos on the floor, just to have the pleasure of trampling them underfoot. And he ground them beneath his heel, in such a way as not only to rip them to bits but to demonstrate to Esperança, wherever she might be, that she must leave the house. She no longer belonged to that family. And he went on with his task, not noticing that Eulália, her eyes open, trying to gesture and to speak to him from the bed, succeeded only in freezing into a still more solid block the silence and the immobility to which she felt herself irremediably condemned at that moment.

In evident defeat, Eulália lay her head back down on the pillow. It was not in her power to save Esperança. Suddenly it seemed to her that her daughter, on the verge of parting from them, was leaving them a perfumed memory, from which they would never free themselves. But then too, what other child of hers had been as vivacious, as daring, as unruly, hailing life with a boldness at times excessive in her eyes, though surely to Madruga it must have represented the perfect guarantee of his continuity, his succession in the making?

Madruga had been quick to learn ways of protecting himself in the presence of strangers, advancing and retreating in response to the varying pressures his enemies brought to bear. Less flexible at home, he honed his power on his children, whose reactions, dictated by affection, he foresaw and forestalled. With the exception of Esperança, who invariably defied him, undeterred by the fear of punishment.

"I won't allow you to proclaim my defeat, father," she sometimes said.

When that happened, Madruga rose to his feet to emphasize the physical difference between them. In answer to her father, Esperança also rose to her full height. Though she was of lesser stature than he, the intensity of her gaze equaled his. The two of them shared the same indignation.

He burned to advance on that creature, to tame that wild daughter, so like himself. Whom did he love more than her?

"You're going to learn yet to obey, Esperança. If not me, your father, then life itself. It's life that's going to teach you. And pay close attention, because life never spares the headstrong."

He immediately felt insecure. By describing his daughter, hadn't he defined himself? Wasn't he equally intractable, equally intolerant? Could he even count the times that Eulália had demanded that he be gentler, that he allow the children to discuss the reality he had decided was best for them?

Senator Silveira came to see him. He seemed to have a compass that guided him to Madruga, especially in times of trouble.

"What's happened, my friend?" Silveira said. "Why such a face?"

"In the beginning, the hard part is bringing up the children, providing them with milk and bread. Later on, it's the tough fight to keep them at home, under our guard. So that nothing spatters them with mud or thrusts a knife in their breasts. When it comes to girls, it's even worse. You have to marry them early and well." He buried his face dejectedly in his glass of wine.

"You Spaniards are too dramatic. Signs and omens, grim situations are your meat and drink. The minute you mention the word *life,* you bow to the dead and to ghosts. As though you were foredoomed to confuse them," he said jokingly.

Madruga went on gravely. More and more preoccupied by Esperança's rebelliousness.

"Don't fool yourself, Silveira, a child can sometimes be the disgrace of a man. A man of principles, especially."

He was ashamed of such confidences. But he had always counted on Silveira's kindness. The senator never asked him pointless questions or rude ones. Madruga confessed that he was remiss. By going after money, he had sacrificed his family. Obviously kindness, innocence, freedom could not be reconciled with the belligerent gestures, the strategies that had to be employed in climbing the social and economic ladder.

"The truth is, Madruga, that we're still in the caves. We kill our children every day with slow-acting poisons. As we do our friends and enemies. We don't know how to draw the line between them, in the hour of our greed and our absolute power. Hence I feel myself to be both villain and victim, the two roles in one person. The one thing I ask is that when someone decides to kill me dead as a doornail, he do it with a precise thrust, straight to the heart. And that he take me by surprise, so I won't see where the murderer's hand came from. And die without knowing who it is I owe my death to. Whether to a friend or to an enemy," the senator said.

Madruga poured the senator another glass of wine, both of them feeling oddly ill at ease. Immediately, however, Silveira brightened, overcome with political passion. He was never one to spare himself; he wanted to be everywhere at once. He was deeply distressed that Brazil escaped his grasp. Brazil, to him, was simply a setting for politics, within which he circulated with breezy offhandedness.

Silveira very often journeyed to the South nowadays. Not so much to visit his wife as to pay tribute to Getúlio Vargas, in exile on his fazenda in São Borja. Joining the President, he sounded him out. Getúlio kept his guard up, emitting ambiguous signals interspersed with long pauses. Silveira nonetheless foresaw that, without his enemies' knowledge, Getúlio was plotting a comeback. Smiling at the mention of those who were anxiously fighting over his political heritage, as though he'd left it up for grabs. When he knew full well that the heart of the people still belonged to him.

He had put on quite a lot of weight. Perhaps he was making up for his loss of power by consuming raw meat and maté. He confessed that he had endless days at his disposal in which to meditate. To help fill them, Silveira provided him with information for him to reflect upon.

"I'll bet anything on Getúlio's political resurrection. Nobody knows human passion, in political terms, as well as he does. Since he makes a game of intrigue and ambition, who can resist him? He has the Brazilian soul in his pocket. Nobody can escape him, from north to south. Getúlio is the very image of the father in power, just what the people want. Crafty, hard and soft at the same time. And with every day that goes by, he becomes a more powerful myth. It's his enemies who are enthroning him. And everywhere the sense of loss is spreading. Nothing is worse than mythical orphanhood. Those who think they've settled accounts with Getúlio are badly mistaken."

Despite his boundless loyalty to Getúlio, Silveira had not yet been dismissed from offices in the arena of power. For which he was paying a high price. He woke up in the morning with a frog in his throat and his breathing irregular. With a quick swallow of cane brandy, he treated his vocal cords and his life to a simultaneous pick-me-up. He felt feverish as he watched the years go by. Asking even Madruga not to show up on his birthday. It was not only the horror of physical decrepitude, but also the inconceivable fear of not making it through the crucial doors of the Brazilian Republic in the next few years.

"Power tempts my brain and my cock. But between power and orgasm, I choose the former. Sex is a passing thing; all that's left of it is a stain on the sheets. Whereas power lets me dream every dream imaginable. What's better, a dream or a cunt? What's the matter, Madruga? Am I scaring you?"

Madruga had paled at the memory of his children. He had to keep a close watch on them. Especially Esperança, whose only power perhaps was to provide an outlet for restless corporeal impulses.

"Do go on, Silveira."

"The truth is that power is guaranteed to give us the evil and indestructible illusion that the world is ours, that nothing is forbidden us, that we must risk everything. It's as though we were immortal," he reflected moodily, awaiting his friend's understanding.

As if this were a message of some sort, Madruga proposed a toast to a life running full speed ahead on power and sex. After all, wasn't that what both of them were after? And as he looked over at his friend, he was disconcerted. He seemed to see Esperança in Silveira's place, with an insolent smile, determined to proclaim her independence.

After her father had trampled the photos underfoot, Antônia did nothing to prevent him from attempting now to tear them into such tiny bits that in the future no hand, however patient and skillful, could possibly put them together again. Nothing should be left of those times. As he went on flinging the remains of the photos to the floor, Antônia, on her knees now, picked up the discarded scraps of paper. In her face was the visible satisfaction of seeing Esperança's body thus destroyed. The memory of that sister who ignored her when she passed her way. Despite Bento's having begged Esperança, Pay a little attention to Antônia, as though he were saying to her, Pass a little of your beauty on to our little sister, who was born lacking in certain attributes.

Without hiding her haste and her irritation, Esperança smiled at Bento. What time did she have for those who allowed themselves to be tyrannized by a mediocre, enslaving daily round of life! One that did the work of fire as well, its flames devouring objects and sentient beings.

Bento was scandalized. He reproached her for her arrogance, a masculine virtue, befitting men destined to lead the nation. Miguel, however, coming to Esperança's rescue, disagreed. She immediately fell into a rage.

"I'd rather die than have to endure you and Bento any longer. You're nothing but a two-man death squad. All I want is my freedom."

Miguel felt insulted. What freedom was Esperança talking about, when she depended these days on brutal gestures, threats, and accusations to justify herself? Did she envy him his sort of freedom? A privileged life that allowed him to visit brothels, where he chose women to his liking. Then, once in bed with them, he heard the rumble of their bowels roiled by his member, attacking without mercy, taking a pleasure that became more finely tuned as it resounded in his body like an echo in a room with perfect acoustics. It seemed to him that his convulsive, rhythmic penis was chasing a hare, at once the woman and orgasm.

"Don't talk to me of freedom as though you were a boy. Where have you been, Esperança? I know you've been lying to Mother," he said without conviction.

He had no idea what she had done to disgrace herself. She had doubtless sneaked out over the walls just to go meet her schoolmates: movies, the Confeitaria Colombo, pistachio sherbet. His time being all taken up with his studies and his father, he hadn't been able to keep as close an eye on her as before.

"I go wherever I please. And don't keep asking me questions. I'll never explain. You'll be the last to know about my life," and she glared at him defiantly, hoping to wound him so deeply he wouldn't sleep that night. Nor the following ones. Till finally, badly upset, he'd begin following her, and therefore not be able to pursue his own life, his new pleasures.

Miguel blushed. "What do you mean, Esperança? What are you hiding?"

"You're a fool, Miguel. Your body is going to occupy your entire life. Just because you were emancipated by Father. You'll forget all the rest."

Odete insisted that Eulália drink the glass of hot milk. Eulália paid no heed, her attention attracted by the thoroughness with which Madruga was reducing the photos of Esperança to bits, as Antônia, with rare diligence, continuing to clean the carpet, disappeared with the remains. In a hurry not to leave the slightest trace of her sister in her parents' room.

Madruga finished his task. He looked about the room, apparently not seeing Antônia kneeling on the carpet. And he went over to the bed, sitting down alongside his wife.

"Now that we've lost our daughter, her absence will be less painful to bear." A strange grief pervaded that man, reminiscent of an oak firmly planted on a hillside in Sobreira.

Eulália made no effort to reproach him. She averted her gaze, staring into the distance. They would have difficult years before them still. Best, then, to spare him. Without his noticing, life was already beginning to torture him. In short, her husband would grow old shorn of fundamental joys.

Eulália inspected her body. She felt suddenly mutilated. Parts of her were missing. Madruga could not help her. Venâncio might, if he were there with her. There came to her the memory of Venâncio's indignation when confronted with an act of violence. He very nearly went to pieces. He had entered into a permanent alliance with certain causes. After the Spanish Civil War, for example, his wrath had been focused on Vargas. Until the dictator's fall.

At those Sunday dinners, Venâncio cut up his chicken leg as though he were dissecting a human member with his knife and fork. Forgetting to eat, he would begin condemning the violence to which Filinto Müller's minions subjected prisoners, whose crime consisted of their opposition to Vargas's dictatorship.

"Eat, Venâncio. Who ever heard of bringing up things like that at the dinner table?" Madruga reprimanded him, busy pushing vegetables and potatoes from the edge of his plate to the middle.

"I don't have your appetite, Madruga," Venâncio said mockingly. "When Vargas has just sent Olga Benário back to Germany. Prestes's wife. Even though she's pregnant, knowing before the fact that the Nazis are going to kill her."

"It's a revolting crime. What's a worse crime still is that in practically no time nobody's going to remember it. And when people talk of Vargas, he'll be praised for starting up the steel industry and other nationalist projects. And someday we'll see Vargas and Prestes on the same platform!"

Involved in business matters, Madruga left politics to Venâncio. Though he didn't approve of his coming to the Sunday dinner table with the intention of robbing him of a peaceful conscience. To hide his annoyance, and head Venâncio off in another direction, he made a special point of hailing the accomplishments of Brazilians, Portuguese, Turks, Italians, people like himself scattered throughout the country, with the necessary driving force to move Brazil ahead. And this amid an awareness of the country as a nation, visibly expanding now, thanks to Vargas's enthusiastic prodding.

"My fear is that the entire cycle will be repeated, Madruga. And that dictatorships will be defensible since they bring progress. At whatever price. Regardless of the social costs."

"But aren't you the one who argues in favor of a country's economic independence as an essential condition of its freedom?'"

"There's no such thing as economic independence without political and cultural independence. And what sort of freedom are you talking about?"

Though still a little boy, Tobias was excited by the discussions between his father and Venâncio. He immediately asked for explanations.

"Is Brazil a colony then?"

"What kind of nonsense is that, my boy?" Madruga shot back, furious. Darting a glance at Venâncio, accusing him of being responsible for his son's forwardness, which he had every intention of nipping in the bud.

"You don't know what you're saying. Try to earn your independence by studying and working. Only in that way will you be helping your country."

Venâncio put his arms around Tobias, signing thereby that the boy was under his protection. Madruga bristled at this affront. After all, Tobias was his son. He too had been conceived in the marriage bed, with Eulália. But fearing to offend Venâncio, and fearing that Venâncio would not return to his house, he went off to his study. A sudden falling-out of this sort was part of Sunday dinner.

Miguel's knocks on Esperança's door echoed through the house. Overcome with anxiety, Madruga held Eulália's hand tightly as she lay in the bed, drawing energy from her. And thus united, they listened to that violent, rhythmic pounding, Miguel forcing his sister to let him in.

Eulália made as if to get up, but Madruga would not allow her to. Odete again urged Eulália to drink the milk. At which point Bento, without consulting his father, tried to pull Antônia up off the floor, to oblige her to go with him. She resisted, awed by her father's courage in not going to help Esperança, despite Eulália's grief. Bento finally pulled Antônia to her feet by brute force, keeping her from witnessing the fight going on between their parents. He then closed the door, not wanting his father to suffer on hearing the words exchanged between Esperança and Miguel.

As the noise coming from outside died down, Madruga noticed that the door was closed. He could no longer hear the children's voices as clearly as before. Troubled by the silence, he turned to his wife, who was weeping softly.

"Don't cry, Eulália. I can't bear to see you suffer. It makes me feel as if I'm about to die," he said, continuing to stroke her hand.

"We've already begun to die, Madruga. Unless we save our daughter. Don't be cruel, go to her, Madruga, please. Don't let her leave the house, I beg you. Ask of me what you will," she pleaded now, her hands clasped together.

"No, let her go. Esperança always complained of my abuses. She's free now to indulge her follies. Her destiny is hers. It was she herself who chose," he said severely.

Eulália clung to Madruga. For a few moments it seemed to her that she was speaking not to her husband but to Dom Miguel. It had always been easier for her to put before her father all problems arising from human passion, whose solution lay solely in the human heart.

"You don't know what you're saying, Eulália. You don't know Esperança and me!" He looked at his wife with profound dejection. Never again would he and his daughter renew an alliance that until that day had been sustained by harshness and fury.

Madruga had the impression that he heard a loud noise inside his chest. As though the walls of the house were falling down, dislodging father and daughter. Both naked now, wounded, counting only on rage and pride to put them on their feet again. Only with rage and pride would they build their respective houses, keeping their distance from each other. The two of them surely lost, out of overweening arrogance. The result being that she could never come begging her father for the forgiveness whereby he would agree to keep her at home if she accepted her eternal bondage. Esperança remaining among them only on this condition.

Madruga knew that at that moment Esperança was waiting for him in her room, waiting for him to plead with her to stay, despite the increasing electric tension between the two of them in the last months, when at times they had scarcely looked at each other, and exchanged only a few rare words at the dinner table. And he knew also that his daughter, impatient at his delay in knocking on the door of the room, consulted her watch, swearing to give her father just thirty minutes to decide, at the end of which she would know what action to take. And yet, this period having elapsed without her father's giving any sign of being in favor of his daughter's remaining in the house, Esperança immediately imagined him shut up in the bedroom with her mother, plotting in silence acts of vengeance and perfidy against her. Ready to put a permanent halter on her. There remaining no other course for her to follow except to take the only dignified way out, that of abandoning the house, despite Eulália's possible tears, despite the pleas now being addressed to her by Miguel, inside her room at last, now that she had opened the door.

"Who's the man? Confess, Esperança!" her brother shouted at her side as she slowly went on packing her bag. Interrupted as he shook her shoulders, wanting to punish her.

To Miguel's surprise, she let him have his way. Perhaps taking pity on her brother's suffering, apparently more intense than her own. Because, despite being shaken, she continued to lay out her clothes with meticulous care inside the bag, filling the empty spaces, folding the blouses with a certain pleasure.

"You can send me the rest, Miguel," she said sadly. "Above all the picture Mother gave me as a gift. That's the one thing I'm taking with me," and she pointed to the oil painting, a portrait of Dom Miguel.

"Who's the man, Esperança? Who ravished you?"

Miguel stepped aside. His sister could now finish packing her bag. Bento tried to overhear them from the hall. Without suffering, as Miguel had. He faced up to his sister's leaving in a straightforward way. The house would be less tense without her. And consequently, there would be more pleasant discussions at table. Esperança's insubordination somehow provoked in all of them the obligation to confront their father, to contest his authority. Wherever she went, she brought discord. And in the street, she awakened lust.

A lust to which she responded with pleasure or rage. Now offended, now impelled to win a freedom that she could not define, except that it brought the taste of honey to her mouth, and a certain giddiness. Amid such appetites, and impelled by a dark, mysterious feeling in her heart, Esperança sensed that certain rights would be assured her only through the vandalism of sweeping father, mother, and brother Miguel out of her life. All those who would silence her body.

"Who's the man?" Miguel insisted, rapidly stroking her face. She trembled with emotion, but responded immediately. She remembered Vicente.

She had met him at the gym club, at a Saturday dinner dance. She had not expected him to ask her to dance. She left the ballroom so as to make it harder for him to carry out any assignment he'd been given. He seemed not to mind. He invited her to go back to the ballroom with him. She obeyed with a mocking smile. But the man's furtive expression, just as he was apparently about to leave her, attracted her. Exactly like herself, Vicente's *modus operandi* was to be unfaithful to persons present and to events of the moment. Both of them volatile. But with tense bodies, their hands intertwining for a second, whereupon they immediately drew apart.

"You're coming with me," he said, not explaining where they would be going.

"Since when do you have the right to order me around? I refuse to have another despot in my life," Esperança shot back.

Vicente was taken aback by the young woman's forcefulness. Until then, he had been in the habit of intimidating women and receiving in response evasive gestures, shamefaced blushes, hesitant flirtation, which at the same time excited him. Esperança, however, came at him like a woman warrior skilled at wielding weapons and libertarian words. In answer, he clenched his teeth for fear of losing face.

Only at the end of the dance did he say: "Perhaps we can get to know each other better tomorrow, which is Sunday. Palm Sunday, as it happens. In the churches priests give out blessed palm branches to hold at bay beings such as ourselves who are possessed of the devil."

He was a man of rare gallantry. He went out of his way to please her, picturing, before the fact, how he would blacken the destiny of both of them. Esperança concealed the inner tumult that he aroused in her. She agreed that they should see each other, that afternoon, in the Praça Antero de Quental, on the corner of the Rua Ataulfo de Paiva.

"If I don't show up by five o'clock, it means I've run away from you," Vicente said.

He seemed to her to be quite capable of such a mad act. But she agreed that she herself ought not to flee from someone who might shape her destiny. She smiled at this assertion, to all appearances a forewarning. Surely the two of them had met in order to form, in the future, a pair of enemies.

"Love also devours, did you know that, Esperança?"

She was certain of it. Because of the feelings she saw scattered throughout the earth, and also because of the answers that her body itself offered her, especially at night, when desire stubbornly mounted her thighs as she fingered the entrance to her sex, determined to follow dark, damp paths never before traversed.

She liked his name. But she avoided repeating it aloud. The moment had not come. And if she came to love him someday, she must see to it that any sort of faith was banished from this feeling. But why? she thought in distress. As if her life had been found wanting, the pendulum bob of the scale never in the right place.

"Who's the man?" Miguel whispered again, warned by Bento to speak in a low voice. Had he forgotten that Eulália, who had taken to her bed in sorrow, would overhear anything they said aloud?

Miguel was distracted now by Esperança's method of arranging her belongings in the valise. He noted how easily life fitted into it. In fact, she didn't have much to take with her wherever she might be going. It was like death; when someone passed on, everything remained behind. There was no way to ensure objects of a future, not even those most dearly loved. The certainty that almost all of our inheritance was expendable troubled Miguel. Perhaps for that reason he now spoke gently. His sister nonetheless shielded herself beneath the carapace of an ancient tortoise, moving in turbid river waters, taking no notice of his presence now.

"Where are you going, Esperança? Let me at least take you there!"

She left the room, followed by Miguel. She refused to let him take her valise. She was in good enough form to carry that heavy a weight. She halted, however, on the landing outside the door for a moment, just long enough to imprint the room on her memory in one last farewell look, visibly moved.

"I'm coming with you," Miguel went on.

She slowly descended the stairs. At no time did she glance toward Eulália and Madruga's bedroom. The two of them, shut up in there, doubtless had no need of farewell rituals. And so, who and what was there to say good-bye to? Reality had a tough armor. Where she was going, she had no need of Miguel, of Bento, or of anyone else.

Out on the sidewalk, she hailed a taxi and it stopped. Miguel patted her gently on the shoulder.

"Please stay." His voice was no longer in any condition to roar convincingly.

"Oh, Miguel. For how much longer will we be brother and sister on this earth?" Esperança said feelingly. And she gave him a swift embrace. "We're separating here, now, from this point on. Perhaps I've gone too far. Perhaps all of you have been much too cruel. How will we ever know? Whose fault is it?" she asked as the taxi driver put her valise in the trunk.

She waved at Miguel from the window of the taxi. The house, built by Madruga, threatened to survive them. Splendid, strong, surrounded by a garden that flowered each morning. She would never come back home; that was almost certain. And the excessively bright afternoon glare kept her from seeing Madruga's face, hidden by the curtain, watching the vehicle in which his daughter was setting out to seek a course that no longer concerned him. Without meaning to, moving his right hand just slightly, he nodded. With his back to Eulália, who was not in a position to appreciate the gesture.

Eulália, for her part, concentrating on her husband as he gazed out over the garden, suddenly understood that they had reached the stage of absolute uncertainty. They were losing Esperança, merely because they lacked the courage to assume the attitudes that their daughter would demand of them in the future.

"Don't go on with this mummery, Madruga. Esperança has left, has she not? Departed forever?" she said, devoid of the energy to rise in haste to her feet in time to stop the car, which immediately rounded the curve and could no longer be seen, not even by Miguel, out on the sidewalk, in tears.

Bento knocked on their door. "May I help you, father?" Eager to announce Esperança's departure.

"Leave me in peace, Bento. No one can help me now," Madruga said testily, burying his head between the wide-open doors of the wardrobe as he pretended to put his belongings in order. Bento drew back, his feelings hurt. He had come to help his father, and once again he was banishing him. Esperança had run away, but was that any sign that Madruga had lost every last one of his children?

Madruga went over to the bed, his face impenetrable. His wife wanted to reveal her pain to him, to proceed with her most secret confessions. That man had never told her the truth. She too had avoided full confessions. She spoke only with God. Though with vague words, full of scorn, lies, fears, fantasies. All loose thread straining to shed light on human thought.

"If you have the will, there's still time for us to save Esperança," Eulália said, her hands joined in prayer.

Eulália's innermost depths, laid bare before him, shocked Bento. No less stubborn than his father, he refused to excuse his sister. Hence his father ought likewise to resist his mother's importuning.

Madruga assumed an affectionate pose. He sat down on the edge of the bed, looking at his wife. His gaze grew more and more distant, however, as though it had followed the trail of Esperança's taxi, seen a stranger opening the door, eager to take her to bed, where they would repeat acts first performed long before, to Madruga's profound displeasure. And it might well be that his daughter and the stranger had taken up lodgings in that very refuge, until such time as they had exhausted the relationship. Whereupon, jaded, their skin withered away from so much pleasure and tedium, each of them would take a different room, occupied by another protagonist. Thus keeping the series of subterfuges and deceptions going.

Madruga closed his eyes, fleeing the memory of Esperança's body penetrated by a man whose lust set him a frenetic rhythm, capable of plunging them into an intolerable delirium.

"I am not forbidding you to see your daughter, Eulália. But I do not want her in this house, sitting at our table, ever again. The doors are closed to her," he said, lacking the courage to look his wife in the face.

Outside, glued to the door, Antônia was sweating, beside herself with anxiety, trying to catch what they were saying. She needed to see them to make sure of their real feelings toward Esperança. Were they rending their garments, as a sign of grief? Or did they want to be alone at this time, bent only on wild caresses?

Hiding away in the kitchen, Antônia had not seen her sister leave. Hugging the cold tiles, she had covered her ears, fearing she might come by information concerning Esperança that would mortally wound her. In a quick visit to the kitchen, Odete, disconcerted by her presence there, had tried to drive her out.

She paid no heed to Odete. In the expectation of losing her sister, she was torn between pain and joy. Everything appearing to her to be contradictory, disparate. She could not forget that Esperança had always wounded her. In a way, she had become a clouded mirror in which she saw unwanted parts of her own being. She felt herself to be ugly, by comparison with Esperança. Hence, certain of suddenly inheriting portions of Esperança's beauty and grace, she pursued her, like a vampire, ready to drain her of energy. She could assume no other being than that of her fellow.

"Confess, Breta, who else did your mother really love, outside of herself?" Antônia cried out on the veranda, pointing to Esperança's box, in my possession now.

The box that had brought Esperança back to her. As on that day when her sister had left the house, and she had never seen her again. There remaining, in her place, a hatred of her sister, the desire, never realized, to denounce my bastard origin, lacking a father's name. I saw how tempted she was not to look. I remembered Miguel then, holding me close, after Esperança's death.

"Your father was always off rambling. He reminded me of a tumble-bug. Immediately after your birth, he wanted to register you, but since he was married, he needed the consent of his wife, from whom he had just been separated. And your father's wife never gave her permission. He shouted, protested, begged, and came out the loser. Everything conspired against him and Esperança."

During this confession, Miguel kept cracking his knuckles. He suffered on reliving painful events. He spoke of Esperança with parched lips.

"What's my father's name?" I insisted. "Mother never would tell me. Just once she asked me, teasingly, What name did you want? We both laughed, as though it were just a joke. And Esperança covered me with kisses, not wanting me to be sad. She swore to tell me everything on my next birthday."

"And it's just past, right?" Miguel forced a smile. "Your father's name is Vicente. And as I've already told you, he was an adventurer. He had a fazenda in Mato Grosso. The forest was his home. Till we lost track of him. That's all I know."

Antônia looked exhausted from having let fly at me with her darts and her venom. Through the door, I saw Grandfather in the living room. In full mourning, on the alert for news of Eulália, who had not died yet. And knowing nothing of the friction between Antônia and me.

I ran my fingers over the surface of the box. Inside there surely must be at least a note that would fill in the empty places in Esperança's life. Then after that, who else to go to for help in fitting together the story of Esperança, who had given birth to me, all alone, forsaken? Was it amid desolation that the world had wanted to receive me? Whom did my mother have for company when I was born? Had Eulália dared to stand up to Madruga and remain at her daughter's side for two or three days, to help the contractions along, to aid that body about to expel a creature? Odete and she caring for Esperança in this way, folding the little pagan's baby shirts, and the bulky bundleful of diapers? And did Miguel, in the face of the irreversible fact, run to Esperança's, knock on her door, both looking at each other in such a way as to blend into one their gaze and the strong embrace that they would have liked to exchange amid self-conscious blushes and embarrassed exclamations?

"I have no illusions as to your feelings, Antônia. That's how it always has been, since the day I came to this house. What difference does it make now? The only thing that matters is that you're eager to have Esperança's box. You've wanted it to be yours, just for the pleasure of erasing all trace of the memory of your sister, whom you've always detested. But first you were meant to read the letters, to examine the objects Grandmother kept. Only in that way would you come to know your own story better. And efface the shadows of your own shabby, pointless life. Have you happened to notice that up to now you've only lived under someone else's tutelage?"

Mortally wounded, Antônia came at me. "You bastard, you interloper, what are you doing in this house? What are you up to? What more do you want here? Aren't you satisfied to have stolen everything, even my inheritance?"

She had aged, in those moments especially. A body with rolls of fat and unwanted wrinkles. I imagined her naked before Luís Filho. Puffed up with ambition, bloated with surfeit, what did he do then? Did he go ahead and embrace her, plunge deep inside her? Or between one page of the newspaper and another did he merely pass his hand across his face, thereby freeing himself of the obligation of making other gestures? That one gesture serving him as pale comfort.

Unwilling to share the same air with me, she breathed in with a vengeance. Very nearly fainting. Finally sliding all the way down the easy chair and kneeling, exhausted, on the floor.

I felt sorry for Antônia, the fallen enemy, badly beaten. Remembering Esperança, whose last photograph, taken only months before her death, I have on my desk. Her face, slightly in profile, seems to accuse us, leaping out of the frame of the photograph. And yet, despite her proudly jutting chin, her arrogant pose, she has allowed herself to show a certain gentleness, around the eyes especially.

Suddenly, this same photo of Esperança, taking me by the hands, guided me to Antônia. I knelt down alongside that woman who was growing old without the pity of her husband and her brothers. Not one of her children was trying to give her back her lost youth. Even if it meant telling little white lies.

"Antônia, are you listening?"

Her eyes slammed shut. They would have to be pried open. And her sobs drowned out my voice.

"Antônia, I'm here beside you," I repeated.

I began stroking her. Her arm first, then mounting to her shoulder, her neck, and finally her face. She slowly bowed her head, yielding to the caress. Her body obedient to a hidden desire that was coming to the surface now. So I went on, my fingertips sliding gently across her forehead, her mouth, round her eyes. There were wrinkles there, the furrows that impoverished her. Reparations would have to be made to give her a golden age.

"It's I, Antônia. We've long owed it to each other to meet like this."

She flung herself into my arms, her eyes closed still. She did not want to see me.

"Ah, Esperança! Ah, my sister," she whispered.

And on speaking her sister's name, as though she had succeeded in sending the dead to the very bottom for good, her body, till then tense, relaxed, immediately unsealing her eyes.

"It's you, Breta!"

She frowned. And as evidence of her displeasure, she passed her hand over her face to erase the marks of my fingers. Unhurriedly, she rose to her feet, with surprising gracefulness. For the first time Antônia took on a certain beauty.

Standing there, she smiled, pleased at finding me kneeling at her feet.

"I'll leave you with your box now, Breta. You may be sorry once you open it. Knowing Esperança intimately won't be a comfortable experience, I can assure you," Antônia said with a bitter expression.

Slowly, she made up her mind to leave the scene. I had time to see that, as she made her exit, she went on stroking her own face. She appeared to take back, discreetly, the gestures that her sister had deposited there, through her daughter.

Tobias constantly asked after his mother, to assure himself that she was still alive. He wandered from the living room to the garden, and from the garden to the bedrooms, some of them empty now. No place was the right one. He moved about restlessly, his face drawn from the sudden onslaught of unexpected memories.

He finally sat down next to Venâncio, who had moved into his old room during that week. He looked at his godfather, forcing himself to speak to him. He wanted to find out precisely what motives had brought Eulália to America, to end up dying now so far from her home country. It was hard to believe that this journey had taken place because of her father alone, urging her on to that adventure. Or had it been her god who whispered the order into her ear? Or had his mother merely given in to her own ambition, to the desire to brave the wilds and forge her destiny? An ambition, however, that his mother did her best to hide from everyone, using God and her faith as disguises? In that case, he himself had inherited from his mother the same unbridled ambition, merely trying to conceal it out of consideration for Venâncio!

Tobias was distressed. How dare he judge his mother in this way, trespass upon her deathbed! Was his resentment of Eulália that great, just because Miguel had always been her favorite?

Distraught, he drew his godfather aside. Like someone who was about to reveal a grave secret to him.

"Am I envious, godfather? Whom do I envy in this house? My brothers and sisters or Madruga?"

Venâncio straightened the locks of hair that had fallen down across Tobias's forehead. That long week had begun to wear them down. A few days more, and they would be making painful confessions. This outpouring of words must be stopped immediately.

"I don't know, Tobias. I too have some difficult questions to ask myself," and he went off toward the garden.

Breta then took his place in the living room. Tobias drew back in fear, out of self-protection. His heart was easy to read, even though relatively sluggish. That niece, barely ten years younger than he, at one moment stroked his hair, then looked at him with gimlet eyes the next. Wanting the empty places in his repellent story. So as to make of it a spectacle that would save her book, even though its lower key did not fit with the rest of it.

"Here we are, naked before you. Are you satisfied, Breta?"

She smiled. Assimilating her uncle's aggression. Or that of anyone else who wanted to settle accounts with her.

"It's still a fascinating picture. How many days is it that we've been prisoners here? Madruga, Eulália, and their offspring, all scratching about in the dungheap. Is that what you want me to say?"

"I beg your pardon, Breta, I didn't mean to offend you. The fact is that people like you are vampires. Just because you write, you think you have the right to pry into other people's lives," he said cuttingly.

Tobias didn't trust writers. That race that made such a show of their rebellion against the real world, yet were pleased to allow it to continue to be immutable and cruel. Just so they wouldn't lack raw material for their factories. Otherwise their creations would never attain to metaphor and invention.

"I think you exaggerate. At best we have a disturbing gaze. And I sometimes wonder whether it's not cross-eyed and myopic."

"Don't be modest, Breta. Everything works in your favor. Without any effort on your part, life offers you reasons to write, each and every day. Even I can suddenly enrich you, if in a moment of weakness I tell you a secret. And isn't a profession that never turns away from human suffering an ill-intentioned one?" He extracted from his voice a sharp bristle that had offended it.

He felt better now. He poured her coffee out of the thermos jug, with friendly gestures. She sipped slowly. Then she rearranged her long hair. She had caught it up in a sort of topknot, which she let down now. This gave her more freedom of movement, though she looked older. Perhaps she wanted to unburden herself of certain things that had been bothering her since her younger days.

"You've forgotten to mention that I'm not the only one in the family with an eye for the human comedy. The difference between us is that I put everything I can down on paper. Outside of that, we're all active participants and observers. Take just this week. Which of us has absented himself from the intrigues, the conversations, the silences that have followed one upon the other, once Grandmother fell ill? And isn't all that a feast about which one either writes or doesn't write? And always on the pretext that behind our acts there's a motive to justify them? All we've really done is shed tears and unravel Eulália's probable secrets before she takes her leave of us. Precisely those secrets that death sometimes leaves scattered all about. I, for instance, know what I want from Grandmother. I want to wrest from her the dark parts of Esperança that I'm still missing. And what about you? What is it you want to rob her of?"

"The right to have given birth to me," Tobias said angrily.

Breta pretended not to hear. "You too will have to answer your daughters when they ask you questions about Madruga and Eulália. And what, in the final analysis, their own origin is. And though such a function may not fulfill the demands of a written text, it nonetheless obeys the same narrative principle."

She was patient. On lighting a cigarette, she watched the smoke as it rose, about to disappear like a swift-moving cloud.

"What's such a drag is having too many books, too many histories, and the whole thing a con game. We urgently need to produce other histories, setting aside official pronouncements, distorted analyses, colonialist propaganda. For five hundred years now, we've been manufacturing an authoritarian version of reality," Tobias said.

"And who besides the artist is able to lance and drain the most hidden feelings, penetrate inaccessible crevices? If you want to capture a slice of reality and, hence, of History with a capital H, you must turn to the writer. Just look at Machado de Assis. Who affords us better proof of the reality of Brazil at the end of the nineteenth century?"

"We're traveling along different paths, Breta. In a country of illiterates the effectiveness of art is limited. The truth is that we're the offspring of bandits, cutthroats, marauders. Either we break those degrading links once and for all or we assume for good the role of a people of thieves. But since I still believe in the children of misery and oppression, the hour has come for us to force our way into history. With a capital H or not, even if it means using violence. And striking the balance of reality without pity or mercy."

In the half-light of the living room, Breta sat back in the easy chair. She would rather think about her grandmother. Now there was someone able to rid herself of worldly goods. She had long since given up all outward display of luxury, passing on its symbols to her children and grandchildren. Keeping for herself nothing but a few elegant dresses, the wedding ring on her finger, and a bit of makeup on her face. Preserving round about her, however, a subtle aura of fire, never to be extinguished.

One afternoon, Eulália summoned her granddaughter to her room, from the veranda of which, to the west, the universe, lit a glowing red, could be seen. For a few minutes after Breta's arrival, her grandmother remained silent, as Odete, handy with her knitting needles, watched them out of the corner of her eye, apparently satisfied with her inspection.

The room smelled of fresh flowers, gathered in the garden of the house, practically at the ocean's edge. Eulália put her cup back down on the tea cart, customarily brought to her with little plates of toast and sweetmeats. And turned her attention to Breta.

"Only God really knows how to tell stories, Breta." And she blushed as though she had revealed a very personal secret, thereby placing herself at the mercy of another's discretion.

Her grandmother served tea with Oriental gestures. And nibbled at the toast as if, unlike other mortals, she had never had human flesh between her teeth.

Breta grew uneasy. In her adolescence, God had struck an answering chord in her heart. Until she had noted that he was dictating a text to her that lacked words consonant with human reality. And she for her part failed to see why she should complete a text, defective in itself, with equally defective words.

With such words, however, her grandmother foresaw for man the destiny of fragmenting everything he recounted, since he was prevented, in advance, from revealing the end of a story. Inspired by a conscience which she used as if on loan from God, she surely meant that history did not in fact exist. And what was more, that we ourselves existed only on account of our painful accommodation to one and the same stage set, on which, from the beginning, we had been engendered.

Eulália's unshakable religious belief was made up of examples which, without the slightest haste, she paraded past her children. In exactly the same way that she slid her rosary beads through her fingers. And perhaps because she observed this earth with eminently indifferent eyes, she did not shy away from revealing an apparently banal fact. For Grandmother, everything was temporary. Very shortly she would be obliged to rid herself of the burden of house and persons.

Prompted, however, by such observations, Breta pondered the fortune of unbelievers or of those who, abhorring reality, held the gods responsible for human creation. All of them forced to endure the martyrdom of living a personal history worth nothing in their own eyes.

The vigil that night, as on the ones before, brought Tobias and Breta a gentle torpor. Altogether untouched by the lot of that woman who, from her bed, served as the intermediary of their feelings. And had even led

Madruga to anticipate being in mourning. As though he could not do otherwise. Since readying himself for solemn moments to come had always entered into his expectations.

Madruga was different from Eulália in every way. While he had fathered a family that would strengthen his ranks, Eulália had made it hard for her children to take their place in the contemporary world. Especially since she had provided them, from earliest childhood, with the solid figures of Dom Miguel and Xan. Bent on keeping them following on behind the family, despite the many long years since she had buried them. Those old men thus owing their afterlife to Eulália, who, at night, sprinkled fresh water on their memories.

"Were Mother's efforts useless? Has she at least succeeded in getting just one of us to repeat the stories of Dom Miguel and Grandfather Xan with absolute fidelity?" Tobias remarked.

And pouring himself a neat whisky, he thought, with a thirst for vengeance, Come on Breta, answer. Wasn't his niece so filled with her own importance that she'd taken up that same damned calling?

To Breta it was natural that Eulália's heirs should fail to reproduce her voice. Just as Xan and Dom Miguel had failed in their respective testimony. For centuries a succession of errors and frustrations had been on the march. Anyone who told a story confronted the fact that narrative disintegrates and dissolves. And perhaps it even owed its excessively luxuriant nature to the inherent possibility of capturing part of the chromatic kaleidoscope of human sentiments.

"You're looking at me, Tobias, as though I were the only one to be held responsible for this task. When each one of us is master of his own story. Even Eulália, who has been so devoted to the memory of Dom Miguel, is now occupied only with her own death." She paused quizzically. "Well, aren't you going to pour me one?"

After handing her a whisky, Tobias paced about the living room for a time, visibly nervous. On his way back to his chair, he stopped in front of Breta. He put his hands on her shoulders. And in a pleading voice, he suddenly whispered to her: "Pretend you're my mother."

Deeply upset, Breta closed her eyes. She had not given birth to that man and did not know how to save him. What, exactly, was within her competence and what was not? Instinctively, she withdrew into the depths of herself. She appeared to be a snail, retracting into its own form, composed of eccentric circles, each leading to the next, in a descending scale. To the node, where the whole thing ended and there was no way left to hide. What would Eulália do in her place, if she weren't reciting the Credo at this very moment?

Breta's silence forced Tobias to detach himself from her. In his heart of hearts he was grateful to her for not having answered his pleas. He must prepare himself for the loss of his mother. Perhaps he would never hear her voice again. Or when he saw her again, in the morning, only he would be part of the world of the living. It being up to the others to make the funeral arrangements, to place Mother in her box, suffocating her with roses and carnations. Death testing human competence yet again. As Eulália tried to test the degree of mercy of her god.

"Grandmother had faith in the things she told. She used to say that a mere story can save a soul. And that soul's country," Breta said, helping Tobias undo the knots of emotion.

Recovered now, Tobias answered. "Even though someone tells a story, Breta, or takes pleasure in hearing it, nothing makes us forget the crushing reality of the facts and our misery. Before we at last reach the shore of a river that will bring us sleep and forgetfulness. This being so, we won't even see the spectacle of the animals leaping about in the muddy waters as they are greedily devoured by piranhas."

On returning from the garden, Venâncio joined them. He was cold, and poured himself some coffee, still piping hot. He did not want any cognac. And on being informed of what they were discussing, he showed no interest. What he might have to say was of little importance. Only heroes and great writers, after all, produced enduring stories. And he had no doubts as to his fate. He would immediately disappear like smoke on the horizon, leaving no proof that he had existed. His footprints, like everyone else's, were useless and vain. Who in that house, in fact, would survive that last dramatic flash exposure? Assuring himself of a frame in which to endure as a full-length portrait?

He examined the living room, the silver bric-a-brac, the pictures enveloped in shadow. Everything was familiar to him. He had frequented that house for years. But what had been the use of all those visits? Had he forged any other ties, outside of those with Eulália, Madruga, Tobias? They were all strangers. Even Odete persisted in slighting him, denying him the charity that should presumably exist on those obligatory Sundays. Moved perhaps by simple jealousy, an excess of zeal toward her mistress. Or by the ambition to be Eulália's shadow. And, as such, with access to Eulália's most personal belongings.

Moreover, when Eulália received her box as a gift from Madruga, she charged Odete with the task of polishing its wooden surface. And of removing the dust that periodically accumulated on it, even inside the wardrobe chest. Eulália told Venâncio of this decision, as proof of her trust in Odete. And perhaps for that reason Venâncio, in the years that followed the Spanish Civil War, would have liked to ask Odete if, inside the celebrated box, there still remained a little of the perfume worn by Eulália all through the strife between Nationalists and Republicans. His curiosity about the scent being justified by his identification of it with a period of the war when Franco's victory did not yet appear to be clear-cut. How often Eulália and he, on the veranda in Tijuca, had talked of this till night-fall, as Madruga toiled over his paperwork.

For Venâncio's sake, Eulália, overcome with bitterness by the defeat, poured the contents of the vial down the washbasin, so as to rid herself of the memories that the perfume roused. Thereby protesting the insane institutions about to be set in place by Franco in the Spain of Dom Miguel, an iron-willed opponent of tyrannies. There not being, in the event, any other version but that one.

Immersed in these reflections, Venâncio remembered how Eulália had always been at once gentle and fearful. Till the thought came to him, with horror, that Eulália might at that moment be entrusting Odete with the task of destroying the contents of her box the moment she closed her eyes.

Worried about the state his godfather was in, Tobias interrupted him, in flagrant disregard for his silence. "Now that Mother has distributed our boxes, to whom did she give hers?"

Venâncio stared at his godson as though he were seeing a stranger.

"Ask Madruga. He's her husband." He shrugged impatiently, then left the living room.

"What did I do, Breta? All I did was mention Mother's box!" Tobias said forlornly.

The last time Odete had cleaned the box, she had followed her mistress's instructions. Eulália had asked her to eliminate all superfluous objects. Those that, by chance, she had little by little collected on her way back from church. Eulália, however, made one exception.

"Just keep the three notes. You know which ones they are."

She seemed eager to rob her own life of all the hard evidence. As though she recognized that she had gone too far in those years. Tempted, surely, by vanity, she had stuffed the box too full of useless memories. Going against the logic of her feelings, which had always inclined her toward parsimony.

"Isn't it true that we're born in poverty, and that the Lord will welcome us in our condition as paupers?"

She awaited Odete's nod of agreement, which never failed to be forthcoming. Odete had learned the rules of everyday life through her eyes. And so, many a time, Eulália was moved to embrace her, to repay her for her fidelity. Even though she should rightfully have begged forgiveness for Odete's having sacrificed her life to serve her.

Thanks to an exclusive devotion, Odete dispelled her fears. She therefore asked no questions as to what to do with the notes. Moreover, she remembered them well. Each of them stemming from a particular circumstance. All of them, however, had yellowed with the years.

The first note bore the date 27 October 1927, and nothing else. It made no mention of the fact that on that October day, to the mournful sound of the bugle of a foreign sailor, the waters of the Atlantic had opened to receive Bento's tiny body. The son born in Galicia through Madruga's deliberate choice, resulting from his anxiety to escape the punishment prescribed by the Celtic gods for those who, like himself, had fled their guardianship very early.

This gesture of Madruga's, moreover, on his return to Galicia with his family, was regarded by Dom Miguel as an act of homage to his person, of stern and aristocratic origins. A man who, mornings after eleven, set out on his strolls along the paths of Sobreira, haughtily wearing atop his head one of his eight hats brushed daily. Certain that he was being admired by the women, carefully protected by the jalousies at the windows so that their nervous, voracious faces would not be seen.

To Dom Miguel, there was no other reason that would justify Madruga's confronting the commotion of the boat crossing with two small children save the pleasure of knocking on his door and forcing a smile out of him. His son-in-law thereby restoring to him a happiness he was lacking.

For a long time a feeling of failure had haunted Dom Miguel's house and Sobreira. In the tavern as in the fields, he seemed to meet only anemic creatures. And when he now told his beloved stories once again, not one of his listeners interrupted him, even if moved by the generous intention of objecting to a detail. In recent years, no one robbed him of one word, using it to make a good story of his own even better. And so it was that at that moment there was not a single soul in Sobreira inclined to usurp another's imagination, as a way of ensuring that the trajectory traced by Galicia would give the impression of continuity.

Dom Miguel suffered for several reasons. Because of his lack of successors. Because of the downfall of Galicia, subservient now to the sad and desolate Castilians. Because of the cities of Galicia, petty, arrogant, and insecure, whose inhabitants, ashamed of their own origins, had given up Gallego, adopting Castilian instead as their native tongue. So dramatic a repudiation of their origins even leading them to look down on country people when they came to the city bringing them eggs, smoked hams, fresh turnips, and spoke only Gallego. Dom Miguel's chest ached at all these many outrages. He felt himself to be a Don Quixote defending the mythical territory of the corrupted Galician soul.

"The country of Galicia no longer exists. It was murdered, and the country itself assented to the crime. Ah, if only Gelmírez were still alive! Ah, if only we were fearless and still certain in our hearts that one of our number would come back and build a new Pórtico da Glória!"

In those moments of high enthusiasm, Dom Miguel, in the tavern, would raise the goblet of blood-red wine on high with both hands. Through this gesture, he felt the limits of the profane being surpassed, himself becoming a Druid priest dealing with symbols instituted among

that people in the past. And this in the sole name of the belief that it
behooved them to transcend all limits in a land as archaic as that. And why
should a race with such beginnings fear criticism and misunderstandings?
Wasn't it a proven fact that in the course of millennia the different human
clays had blended together so they would all be Christians and pagans at
the same time, without embarrassment? Since only when man possessed
those two powerful awarenesses could he better understand his life on
earth!

Madruga seriously tried to preserve his father-in-law's illusions. But
invariably he headed up to the mountains with a thoughtful expression on
his face. Dom Miguel was thus able to see that there was no joy in that
newcomer from America.

In the beginning, he feared it was his daughter's fault. He thought of
intimating to her that she should sit beside her husband, pay more attention to what he recounted. Might he not, at times, take on the role of the
late-lamented Xan? The subject, however, was a delicate one. Between the
father-in-law and the son-in-law there was a polite agreement that they
would never confuse Dom Miguel's stories with those belonging to Xan's
repertory. Madruga always loudly proclaimed that his Grandfather Xan's
bold spirit as a storyteller had been unbeatable.

Eulália noted the two men's lack of esteem for each other, and chose
without hesitation to side with her father. Madruga noted her choice without being disappointed by it. He too had secret loyalties. And though his
life had been conjoined with Eulália's, he never forced the doors of her
heart. Or placed the key of his own breast at her disposal. A key sometimes spattered with saltpeter, very nearly rusting it.

Aboard the boat still, after the fatal event, Eulália shut herself up in
the cabin. In one more day the ship would anchor at the Praça Mauá. With
her nail scissors, she cut up a sheet of letter paper. Sobbing, she wrote: 27
October 1927. To mark the day that they had lost little Bento, barely three
months old, on the way to America, his new home. By thus deserting
them, the son bequeathing to his father and mother the task of living in
his place.

With the letter pressed to her bosom, Eulália then prayed to the Lord
that the death of her son would not affect her belief. She had lost her
country and her father, but her faith had remained. That crystalline material that, if not carefully handled, might suddenly shatter into a thousand
shards. Each penetrating her body, perfusing her with doubts, lies, and
uncertainties. Above all slowly burying itself in her still-swollen breasts.
The breasts that little Bento would never eagerly suck again.

For years she kept this note next to Dom Miguel's photograph, inside
her bag. Till one Saturday afternoon when Madruga arrived home dead-
tired and downcast. He nonetheless showed her the wooden box, with
beautiful carved work and a little lock. It was a present meant to make up

for some harsh gesture of his. Sitting on the bed, before giving her the box, Madruga lovingly stroked it for some time.

"When I was a boy, I dreamed of having a box to hide chips of wood, papers, round river pebbles in. No matter what, but far from Urcesina's watchful eye. I wanted to keep my secrets safe. But nobody ever thought of giving me a box. Not even Grandfather Xan. And now it's too late to realize that dream. What good would it do me? It seemed to me, though, that this would please you, Eulália. It's yours, and I'll never open it," Madruga said with circumspection.

Eulália was delighted with the box. She fondled it knowing exactly what she would do with it. Wanting therefore to be left by herself in the room. Madruga suspected the reason for his wife's sudden tenseness. He asked her no questions, preferring to take his leave of her. Eulália then summoned Odete. In her presence, she took the note out of her bag, depositing it in the box. That note had the permanent ability to bring little Bento back to her. The truth, however, was that, try as she might, she could not remember his face. Know for certain who he had looked like, Madruga or herself. What she did know was that it tormented her to carry the note with the fateful date around everywhere with her. In church, especially, she was afraid she was defying God by a gesture considered to be rebellious. As long as she kept the bag in her lap, the prayers she recited did not sound all that contrite. She ought to get rid of it immediately, handing it to Odete or abandoning it on the bench, as though it weren't hers.

In the beginning, she collected certain objects in the box. She would feel them first, in the palm of her hands, as though they were live game. Odete herself surprised her cutting off a lock of hair with white in it, just to put it away in the box. Both of them were embarrassed, and said nothing about it. Till Eulália, ashamed at having stored away a lock of hair as though it were a precious belonging, threw it into the trash. And, as punishment for such vanity, for a time she would not allow herself to look in the mirror. She barely retouched her face, guided by intuition and familiar gestures.

Odete, however, followed after her with slightly moistened cotton, to remove the excess of powder. An attention that Eulália rewarded by stroking her hand. A mark of affection so dear to Odete that, in less than thirty minutes, she again acted in such a way as to merit the same treatment, which only Eulália could offer her.

With the years, Eulália's interest in the box declined. And the note referring to Bento became a gentle reminder. And though she had resigned herself to superior designs, she never stopped praying that that note would be the only one of its kind to occupy the box. But God did not choose to answer her prayers, and one day the news of Esperança's death was brought to her. Her car had smashed into a retaining wall along the Avenida Niemayer, in the middle of the night. At an hour which the family made no effort to determine exactly, so as not to embellish with details an obscure and painful death.

As soon as they returned home, after the seventh-day Mass for Esperança, Odete laid paper and a fountain pen down on the night table, as Eulália followed her every gesture from the bed. It took her some time to discover what Odete wanted. That woman had never offended her. Of admirable reserve, she deserved every credit.

She forced herself, then, to go over the events of that week. After Esperança's funeral, she felt Madruga's firm arm supporting her only one other time, when they got into the car in the garage to go to their daughter's Mass. During the ride to the city they did not speak to each other. Both forgoing consolation.

Till the seventh day, Madruga shut himself up in his study, practicing perhaps secret acts. The fact was that Madruga, bereft of recent memories of his daughter, was not resigned to his lot. He slept and ate right there, with the door always closed. At no time did he seek out his wife in their bedroom. Eulália herself was grateful for his absence. She could not have borne to see him creeping down the hall, knocking on the door, only to show her a shattered face, with deep circles under the eyes. They were right to choose an individual territory where, with unrestricted freedom, they could discharge their most painful feelings.

Odete took Madruga's place in Eulália's room. In the mornings, very early, she disappeared to the service area, from which she returned looking neat as a pin, her manner impeccable. And so she helped Eulália to live.

As a balance in her favor, Eulália had her memories of Esperança, whom she had often visited. Without their relation ever becoming an intimate one. Both paralyzed by an exacerbated sense of modesty. And also because the moral contract that Eulália had entered into with God did not accord with the reality of her daughter. But on reliving Esperança's radiance during that week, for the first time she felt tempted to ponder whether God might not have preferred that she abandon him, the better to care for human matters, among which her daughter was included.

In visits to her daughter, whose mood swung from despair to boredom with the greatest of ease, Eulália felt her mystery, without being at all surprised, since she considered it to be inherent in all that is human. Except that she did not understand Esperança's excess of zeal in assuming the lot of a woman warrior, which led her to engage in an exhausting and useless battle.

In this week too, amid bewilderment and doubt, Eulália asked herself whether, in a way, God had not heeded Esperança's will. Always deeply distressed in the last months, avoiding looking her in the face. And with her hands constantly thrust in the pockets of her skirt or her pants, so that her gestures would not betray her nervous tension. And, each time she sat down or stood up, incapable of choosing a comfortable position.

All of a sudden, Esperança told her of her unexpected change of jobs, a fact that kept repeating itself periodically.

"To preserve my dignity, mother. Isn't that sufficient reason?" she justified herself to Eulália, who was surprised at her instability.

Her daughter had plans that would enable her, very shortly, to do without the money that Eulália very carefully left on the table so that they would lack for nothing. A ritual staged within the family circle each month, under Esperança's watchful eye. Despite this material security, Esperança's nerves grew shakier and shakier. She had trouble sleeping, and time went by before she knew it. Beginning early in the morning, being divided between Breta, studies, and work. If on the one hand she had inherited a rigid sense of discipline from Madruga, at night she thumbed her nose at the clock and considered herself free at last. Coming home at all hours. Sometimes, before lunch, Esperança had, amid intense beauty, deep circles under her eyes.

Gripped now by remorse at the very thought that her daughter had spent herself like an early dawn, Eulália went on reviewing the facts, merely to please Odete.

Once they arrived at the church of A Candelária, she seemed to lose the notion of time. She was dragged away from the altar without having been able to pray. The lines of people waiting to offer condolences stretched beyond the sacristy. A parade of faces making her memory run riot. It would take a long broom to sweep down any event that could be told with pen and paper.

"What is it you want, Odete?" she said with a slight edge of impatience. Weren't her tears enough, her sleepless nights, her body almost without slits to breathe through? Giving scarcely a sign of life in those days. All she would eat was a few spoonfuls of cornmeal porridge, and that only because Odete forced them down her. What other proofs of pain, then, was that African woman going to demand of her?

Odete's silence led Eulália to try one more time. As though it were a duty to understand the vague hints of that modest woman, whose coming into the world might have brought humiliation to her family, already hard-pressed by poverty.

Discreetly, Eulália joined her hands, appearing to be praying. Suddenly, as if aided by prayer, she discovered Odete's intention. She must submit to the sacrifice. Once more in life, feed her box, Madruga's gift, with her own vitals.

Aware of her duty, she took up her pen. On setting it to paper, she stopped, too weak to go on. This happened to her every time she found it necessary to have recourse to a pen to record intimate feelings. Because of her father's influence, she mistrustfully banished the world of writing. At no time had Dom Miguel ever aspired to the destiny attributed to written words. And with burning pride, he had clung to oral discourse. To him, only spoken words, sent flying through the air by magical sonic propulsion, went straight to the heart. And from there radiated human truths.

From her earliest days as a child in Sobreira, Eulália's education, despite the powerful presence of God, had centered round the spells uttered by the human throat. Many times, in the half-shadow of the bedroom, she would place her ear against the wall to capture the strange whispers that came to her, on rainy days particularly. Human voices in pain, doubtless, that did not allow themselves to be seen.

With her eyes, she called on Odete for help in that hour.

"Yes, Odete, you're right. Only God knows the ways of the heart. I have surely sinned through pride, without having even noticed."

She bowed her head over the paper and slowly wrote: 19 June 1956. A week before. The interminable wake, Miguel in tears voicing the name of Esperança. At this memory, Eulália hastily folded the note. She had nothing more to add.

"You may put it away in the box, Odete. From now on, Esperança will be in little Bento's care. This son has long since grown accustomed to death."

And she was about to give the pen back to her when, with nervous gestures, she asked for more paper. On being granted her request, Eulália ran her fingers over both sides of the sheet of paper. She finally folded it, without writing a single word.

"Blank, Dona Eulália?" Odete said in surprise.

"That way, I won't forget my destiny. As soon as I close my eyes, have them write the date of my death on it. It's a task I can't take care of myself."

She handed the sheet of paper to Odete, and began simply to appreciate the delicacy with which Odete opened the box again. It would not be hard for a son or a neighbor to fulfill so simple a request. In the end, the note would symbolize her gravestone in Sobreira. But if, occupied with tasks having to do with the inheritance, the family should forget the request, it made no difference. For the one who was really right was Dom Miguel, when he assured her, with a circumspect air, that the spoken word, despite even the will of the heirs, survived being forgotten. Because, even without their realizing, they would be the first to cause to circulate among themselves the words actually used in the family. At table especially, as they ate soup, the words and the expressions of dead grandparents, parents, and brothers and sisters would inevitably surface beneath the rush of hunger, nostalgia, and intense feelings.

"In all truth, Odete, only God deserves to survive," and she sighed mournfully.

At the sound of the telephone, Breta armed herself against the stubborn voices that had interrupted her reading of Venâncio's diary. It was Antônia, insisting on talking to her. And once she was convinced that it was her niece, she spoke of how much Breta had hurt her in the course of the argument between them, after the boxes had been handed out. She then declared that there was much that remained to be said about Eulália's legacy in the form of boxes. It was best, however, not to discuss the merits of it at that moment. Her only reason for calling was that she wanted to hear Breta's voice.

"Haven't people ever told you that your voice is exactly like Esperança's? Talking with you, it's as though Sister had come back to life."

Shortly before phoning Breta, she had accompanied Luís Filho to the door as he left for work.

"What's wrong now, Antônia?" he said, immediately putting her on edge.

She voiced yet again her inability to reconcile herself to Esperança's premature death.

"This time it was Breta, taking Esperança's place," she said irritatedly, forever deprived of her chance to avenge herself for the harm her sister had done her since they were children.

Calmer now, Antônia feigned indifference to the dividing of the estate that was more or less under way, even though her mother was still alive.

"I can well imagine how Father feels when he hears your voice, Breta," she said finally, before hanging up.

Breta got the message. Her aunt was accusing her, yet again, of being, even today, an intruder in the family. Whose mere presence brought up a memory that they were all eager to forget. Because Esperança had never done anything, in her brief lifetime, except hurt Madruga and give birth to an illegitimate daughter.

Madruga, at times, showed signs of resentment when he came upon some lingering trace of Esperança in Breta. Pricked by this reminder of her, he would turn beet red, not knowing what to do with his hands. In a few minutes he would disappear, muttering vague excuses to his granddaughter.

In his study, Madruga would begin thinking long thoughts about this family. He found it difficult to describe his children, even to himself. His pronouncements about them, growing more hesitant as he took pity on the whole bunch, deprived of the rules that governed his existence. Had he fathered a family devoid of the sparks of passion? A dead tribe in that case?

During one of these cold wars, Breta knocked on his door. He overcame his resistance and welcomed his granddaughter. And to Breta's surprise, he suddenly spoke of the exile he had lived in since his arrival in Brazil.

"And may I ask what exile you're speaking of?" Breta confronted him resolutely.

Madruga found it difficult to pin down the exact nature of his exile. It was not easy to prove that Galicia, so inherently attractive, had persuaded him in the past to absent himself from Galician reality, in favor of paradise on earth on the other side of the Atlantic. Or even to acknowledge that he was a mere satellite of Eulália, who constantly spoke of the sort of exile to which every man condemned himself from the moment of his birth.

"The exile I'm talking about lies in man's soul, Breta. It never abandons him, even in his sleep," Madruga said, on a melancholy note.

Antônia was not the only one to cause Breta distress in those days. Tormented by the idea of death, her uncles secretly invoked Esperança's name. Madruga himself, bowed down with age, seemed to drag behind him, through the long halls and the gardens, glued to his skin, the shadow of his daughter.

During the previous month, as though foreseeing that Eulália would be leaving them shortly, Miguel had Breta meet him again at the bar. On the pretext, this time, of having in his possession several notes of Esperança's, written in her adolescence. Remains of an era prior to his sister's break with Madruga.

Esperança herself, in an untimely gesture, had taken it upon herself to offer them to her brother. An offer that, far from pacifying him, aroused Miguel's suspicion that Esperança had in her possession other even more meaningful notes.

This suspicion once aroused, he began to spy on her, in his eagerness to discover where she was hiding her notes. Not losing sight of her, especially when he saw her with pen in hand, scribbling away. Esperança, however, on being so closely tailed, shook him off in a series of rapid maneuvers, with Miguel ending up losing her trail.

But when the final showdown between Esperança and Madruga took place, Miguel went straightway to his sister's dresser drawers, after banishing Antônia from her own room. And then, before Madruga decided to do the same, he began hastily ransacking the objects abandoned by Esperança in her desperate hurry to leave the house. Till finally, between the pages of her *Dom Casmurro,* he came across the note that completed his collection.

"Listen, Breta. It won't be long before Father and Mother will be leaving us forever. I tremble at the mere thought of the hour when their coffins leave the house at almost the same time, for the same family vault. And so a terrible lot is about to befall us, sitting alone and furious in the living room, each of us spying on the other, foaming at the mouth and vomiting gall. You're perhaps the first one in the family to confess you never want to see me again, and will be my enemy from that day forward. But before this happens, Breta, I've decided to organize part of my papers, beginning with my sister's notes, in my possession for years now."

"And why haven't you ever spoken to me of them before?" Breta said in annoyance.

"There was no reason why I should have. They were mine alone. I was the only one to read those notes. But I've decided that your turn has come. Isn't it true that you're the one who's inherited all of Esperança's follies?"

The conversation, begun on a friendly note, took an unexpected turn. Both eyed each other like enemies, swallowing hard. Miguel had a disheveled look about him, perhaps because he hadn't yet shaved.

Breta stared at the envelope, which Miguel slowly laid down on the table, next to the glasses. All of a sudden, the envelope having been exposed to public covetousness, Miguel began to fondle it once more with trembling hands. It was difficult for him to let go of what belonged to him.

Miguel's sensuality, even when he was holding a plain manila envelope, made Breta still more annoyed. Being already offended by the moral judgment pronounced on Esperança by Miguel.

"And do you happen to have an heir who'll take good care of your miserable follies? Or who will remain with you at the hour of your death? Are you counting on your children or Sílvia? Or on your countless paramours? One thing is certain," she said in a solemn voice. "Don't count on me. My inheritance runs out with Mother and Madruga."

She rose unobtrusively from the table, carefully noting the effect of her speech. And, confronted by Miguel's puzzled face, she thrust her arms out toward him. He immediately understood the meaning of this gesture, and without hesitating, deposited the fat envelope in her outstretched hands. Breta left, not bothering to say good-bye. At the door, she embraced a journalist, as though nothing had happened.

Back home, she gave vent to the distress caused her by the notes and her having wounded Miguel. For a few moments she felt tempted to destroy all the notes at once. Written, as she could perceive immediately, in a nervous, adolescent hand. If she burned them, however, wouldn't that be burying her mother a second time? Though by so doing she would be forewarned and on her guard against a phantom pursuing her, demanding vengeance.

With the papers spread out before her on her worktable, it was impossible to destroy them. And though racked with the hot and cold shivers of intense emotion, she began reading Esperança's every word.

Those juvenile outbursts afforded a glimpse of a sensitive conscience in open conflict with a family and a social milieu. Her determination to thwart the family's plans, represented by Madruga and Miguel, and overcome her condition as a woman. Though Esperança had not managed to arrive at a precise definition of the limits of her wishes. Or to dissociate herself from the effects of an ever-growing ambition within herself.

Through her use of a certain poetic language, one could discern the almost pagan impulse compelling Esperança to deliver herself over to practices at once fervent and contradictory. In an attempt to pacify the world of dreams, and her own being.

That adolescent, carnal and firm, loomed up before Breta without seeking her permission to remain. And, strangely, she did not have a face that would allow Breta to retain a memory of her features. Suddenly gripped by a feeling of loss, Breta ran to look for the photograph of her mother in that phase and propped it up in front of her, against a pile of dictionaries.

She observed that young woman. Despite the years that had gone by, her beauty had not lost its enduring gift for contemporaneity. Of a daring and flexible cast, it kept itself up to date at all times. And the contractions glimpsed in that face began to strike Breta very forcibly. To the point that she felt repelled by the emotion that that dead woman inspired in her.

Nonetheless, Breta wanted to hold her in her arms, to listen with compassion to the pulsing of a body of a priestess who had placed herself beneath the sign of passion for protection. This being seen clearly in the last note, of which Miguel had spoken, whose import, as it happened, was starkly dramatic. As though Esperança had written it as she palpated her body, in her eagerness to make intense use of it.

". . . Father threatens to punish me if I give myself over to the pleasures of love. He is my torturer. As my revenge, however, and in proof that I am mistress of my fate, at night, in the bedroom, I slide my fingers down to my sex and let myself go. I make the most of Antônia's being sound asleep beside me, so as to penetrate myself and hit the mark exactly. Everything within my body dilates then, so as to be vanquished. It is the most poignant of defeats.

. . . God will surely forgive me. He has always loved those who have loved desperately. A person has only to read the Bible and sacred books. In them feelings are on fire. Father himself never freed himself of passion. His face bears marks of fire, and, like a sorcerer, his body was burned in the public square. He is a bull with life's initials carved into his hide.

. . . Mother takes me to church. I hate the smell that comes from sacristies, the odor of a sanctity approved by men. And also the smell of sin. The old women, in black dresses, pray in despair. They too loved in the past. They were beautiful, young, and cynical. And so they mastered amorous practices stored today in the holds of their memories. They beat their breasts again and again before the crucified Christ, so as to forget the ecstasies of the past. Climax and wet thighs. Convinced now that, in order to go meet God, they must purge their bodies of all trace of love. To them, God is dry, unable to ejaculate. There they sit, fat phantoms that won't teach us the supreme knowledge of love.

. . . now, if God gave us these intense genitals, it was not so as to keep them locked up in a wardrobe chest. But to make good use of them. This being so, I will no longer tolerate the absence of pleasure, of the other sex. Mother's stories, about Sobreira and about Grandfather Dom Miguel, can only rein me in for a few months more. Miguel himself, who listens to her with an innocent, pious air, is a hypocrite. He constantly locks himself in the bathroom, coming out looking pale and superior. Is that the face of lust? Lately, he passes by me, coming in off the street, with a strange female smell, which is my smell too. And that's because woman's nature becomes inflamed and discharges worms and juices.

. . . I swear I won't feel bashful or ashamed of my body, when I surrender to love. Despite Madruga and his partisans, who force me to accept an inferior and submissive reality. Like all kings, they are despotic, and despise unruly people like me. I have a feeling that, in the future, they will decree an early death for me, merely because I'm opposed to premature defeat. . . ."

Miguel phoned, in pleading tones, the following morning. Regretting having handed over spoils that would lead her to rend her garments or wear tardy mourning for her mother. He insisted that they meet in the bar.

Breta was an hour late. Spared protests from Miguel, who kindly offered her a chair, after extending her a formal greeting.

Both were reluctant to be the first to speak. She passed up ice for her whisky, offered by the waiter.

"You still remember everything those notes say," his niece opened.

Miguel nodded his approval of Breta's laying her cards on the table from the beginning.

"I never freed my mind of those notes. Esperança's words haunt me even today. They give me no peace. Tell me the truth, Breta. Do you think I'm like Esperança?"

In a lightning-quick move, he seized her hand, twisting her fingers. He gripped it tightly so she would not escape him again.

Breta allowed him to take refuge with her. Her feet too felt leaden. She did not want to be alone. The two of them would have to put up with each other for the moment. She tried to make her voice sound gentle, not the trumpet blast of the avenging angel.

"Mother had more courage than you. She did not hesitate to commit sacrilege and trespass on forbidden territory. She trod, all alone, nothing but skin and bones, the sacred soil of Eulália. And without fear of going against the will of African gods, syncretic gods. So she bled like a sacrificial animal. She was spared nothing. And as if such deeds were not enough, they demanded her life and Esperança acceded. Because it was part of the game. She was different in every way from you. Whereas Mother had wings, you used crutches. You've always used Madruga, Eulália, Sílvia, money, your endless females as props. I'm sorry to be baring my heart like this, Miguel. It's because I really love you. You were the one who took me out into the garden of the house in Leblon for the first time, so I'd know it. I didn't have permission to visit it, to know Madruga, my grandfather. Of all of you, I knew only Mother, Grandmother, and Odete. The others were ghosts. Maybe that's why you surrounded me with attention. And when, one time, you kissed me, as the two of us were sitting under the mango tree, I noticed you were crying, because your tears ran down my face."

Breta took the phone off the hook. She wanted to concentrate on Venâncio's diary. From those yellowed leaves there rose a faint perfume. She breathed it in, again and again.

She plunged into its pages, left breathless as she read. Convinced that Venâncio, on the pretext of speaking of himself, had chosen to follow the path of imagination. To that end, journeying, with undeniable license, particularly at the beginning of the book, through the nineteenth century. From which he returned, with gloomy predictions, to take his place in his own century. And always with exemplary lack of respect for any sort of chronological order or continuous sequences.

Breta noted that time, in Venâncio's hands, readily evaporated, becoming fixed only when he had recourse to a memory at once commonplace and precious, whereby he ran years and even centuries together, altogether at random.

Nor did Venâncio hesitate to take Madruga with him to that century. And, incidentally, with visible discredit to his friend's character. Here and there were phrases that were pitiless imitations. Thorny, bristling with rancor, aimed at pricking Madruga's honor. Accused of chasing black women. Forever sniffing about them, and always for a base motive. Certain to get what he was after. That race had no way of defending itself, whether in public places or in the jungle.

On one of these hunting expeditions, Venâncio surprised him with an erection. Embarrassed by the fact, Madruga hid his privates with his hat. An unpardonable shamelessness to Venâncio, despite Madruga's explaining that he would only come to know Brazil, and heighten his own feelings, by copulating with a black woman.

Venâncio suspected that this confession concealed Madruga's preference for the bosom of the black woman, waiting for him with her legs apart, driven, rounded up, like a head of livestock. Ready to offer him a pleasure that for her was a sort of expiation in the face of the shame suffered by her people at the hands of the colonizers. The one reason for the woman's allowing herself to be defeated in the presence of a gigantic, active, industrial phallus, a power station and an imagination factory.

Out of compunction, Venâncio corrected this assertion on the following page: ". . . that's not the way it is. I prefer to believe that imagination has always been on the side of the vanquished. Oriented, however, toward a scattered and gratuitous production, which defeated peoples are in the habit of wasting, with extraordinary, voluptuous abandon. Hence the supposition that the Brazilian imagination originated in every corner of the earth. And went so far back in time that it even played a part in medieval pilgrimages. Tucked away in the sacks and the hearts of pilgrims. Participants, these, in a movement which, on intensifying the powers of imagination in Europe, popularized life and democratized knowledge.

. . . this same Brazilian imagination, which confuses and excites me, risks, however, becoming thin and pale through the pressure of poverty. Which Madruga approves of, blinded as he is by the memory of his poverty in Sobreira. This past forcing him to take his revenge. To imprison us, with iron shackles on our feet, so he will be the one and only winner. As he bursts with laughter, boasting of his own success."

The feminine figures in the diary were veiled in mystery, especially in the beginning pages. They had, so to speak, a transitive mode of inhabiting the earth. As though they were about to take off somewhere. But where? How far would they take that stoic pose?

In the pages that followed, those women, with contradictory lineages, suddenly narrowed down to a single one. Of such a nature as to inspire Venâncio to practice carnal discipline, and keep his distance from any other back that pitched and rolled as gently.

Breta was suspicious of that woman. It might well be Eulália. Curious, she tried her best to refresh her memory, to recall Venâncio in the past. Unfortunately, her few remaining recollections of him were vague. Concentrating on Madruga, she had never paid any particular attention to him. It always seemed to her that everything about Venâncio drooped, including his suits. From his body hung miserable testicles, lacking use.

It was as though Venâncio wore armor so no one would touch his privates or any other part of his body. By means of this isolation automatically cutting himself off from his condition as a contemporary. Which had naturally made it easier for him, back in those days, to abandon the dramatic circumstances of his own time and plunge into other stages in History. Thereby succeeding in inventing for himself a dubious nineteenth century in order to relieve the temporary delirium overtaking him after the Spanish Civil War.

In the diary, Venâncio was worried about the Sunday dinners. As though Eulália and Madruga might forget to invite him in the future. The invitation was repeated each week, however, usually in Madruga's metallic, booming voice. Even so, Venâncio's mind was not at rest.

At the appointed hour, he would knock on the door, not forgetting to bring with him wildflowers fresh with dew. From the other end of the room, Eulália appreciated the yellow, violet, white tones of the flowers. She remained where she was, waiting for Tobias to hurry across the room to greet his godfather. He took the flowers and brought them to his mother, who was already heading Venâncio's way to welcome him. She immediately arranged the flowers in the pitcher, with water to fill it already at hand. And after the men had drunk their aperitifs, she herself, followed by Madruga, took Venâncio by the arm to the table, where a long line of serving platters was set out, meeting with everyone's approval.

". . . Eulália insisted that I eat. She finds me thin and exhausted. I very nearly asked her if any son of Madruga's will have the gratifying memory of having buried me alongside his parents. Or do they merely intend to return my coffin to one of those Spanish villages with stones, goats, and not a single smile? To a Spain that impressed upon me the feeling of sacrifice and guilt. Needing, as always, a born scapegoat.

. . . Madruga also urges me to get some nourishment. He sings the praises of food and drink. I'm temperate in my habits. I look at my godson, so little still. Perhaps, with the years, he'll be tempted to discover the taste of failure. The same failure that intoxicates his godfather. I shall do nothing to keep him from breathing the same air. Why deprive him of the crystal-clear idea that failure has its everlasting glory? But, if that is so, why does Madruga, taking pity on my lot, leave gifts at my doorstep? Even though he apologizes later. Forever inventing excuses, thinking he's pulling the wool over my eyes. Since for a long time now he's been betraying me so as to get his hands on more money. I'm nonetheless the only one to record exactly how far he's climbed. Each time he makes it up another flight of steps, he confirms his victory in the mirror of my face."

Breta settled herself in a comfortable position in the bed. Concentrating on the diary, at her mercy now. The only one in the family able to thumb through Venâncio's confidences, to make whatever use of them she cared to. Venâncio himself had not been opposed to her grandfather's decision. He even seemed to have written the diary with that end in mind. And for that very reason he had never, in all those years, asked Eulália to return it. Or said to Madruga: Let's throw the diary into the fire, let's free ourselves of the past once and for all. Had Venâncio aspired, at some moment, to a limited immortality, despite his much-vaunted modesty?

Venâncio spoke of his body from a perspective that came close to being Calvinistic. In the diary he allowed himself to succumb to no process of eroticization whatsoever. He could apparently keep his memory from storing up amorous practices to be displayed every so often at some later time. His body was therefore not the sum of all desires dreamed of and fulfilled. Merely a palpitating reserve, with dark hiding places and glaringly obvious frustrations. Through which to drain off, as quickly as possible, any sort of nagging desire.

Some of his scribblings also expressed the urgent desire to loosen, someday, the bonds of a fierce conscience that gnawed at his heart, forcing him to turn his every thought to the Spanish Civil War.

During this period, after those nights interrupted by brief interludes of sleep, each dawn served only to confirm the advent of the Spanish tragedy, now unfolding. Before breakfast, he hurriedly made his way to the newsstand to buy the morning papers. They bore the figure of Francisco Franco on their front pages, because of his unbroken series of victories. Spain had turned into a human dump heap, with Republican and Nationalist corpses piled up in the public squares, in full view of everyone.

He sipped his morning coffee in the bars of Cinelândia, pained at the memory of a native land that had allowed itself to be divided among fanatics, saints, heretics. All inspired by perverse theologies, contemptible flirtations, and an imperishable ignorance.

On each street corner, Venâncio thought he saw the dark clouds of tragedy gathering. He felt he was witnessing bloody battles. The same ones doubtless raging at that moment on the soil of his homeland. Unable, however, to keep some sturdy Aragonese, somewhere, from thrusting his bayonet between the ribs of some unwary Sevillian. So telling a blow that the Sevillian didn't have a moment's time, before breathing his last, to remember his village, his house, the family table, his brothers belching happily.

". . . Eulália is upset at the way the war is going. And its effect on me. She is the mistress of my heart, in the sense of forgiving me the confusions that so deeply distress me, in the shadow of her house. Without ever losing her patience. All she says is: Come next Sunday. I promise you a smoking-hot plateful of food and the warmth of friendship.

And she also says: It doesn't matter what they do to our people, using doctrines and black passions as their pretext. We will never allow ourselves to be annihilated, Venâncio. Even if thousands die in Spain, at the borders in the Pyrenees, on the shores of the Mediterranean, the Bay of Biscay, the Atlantic, all those dead will one day be redeemed by our memory."

All of a sudden, Venâncio showed his fear at having gone too far by setting down a phrase diametrically opposed to Eulália's way of thinking. Since he was deeply disturbed, his handwriting instantly lost its firm contours. Immediately thereafter, however, the sentences reordered themselves. The text became balanced. It seemed impossible to him now that Eulália should fail to approve of his ideas. She was, after all, the daughter of Dom Miguel, a man of genteel birth whose sympathies, out of principle, lay with the products of labor in the fields and Galician history. Above all a devoted follower of Priscillian and Gelmírez. And, therefore, someone who tirelessly perused old books. Some of them purchased in secondhand bookshops in Pontevedra and Santiago. Others, stored in trunks, having come into his hands through a family inheritance.

These books, accounts of great deeds in the region of Galicia, presented their material in a style so captivating, as a general rule, that Dom Miguel, once attracted to their sphere, simply abstained from living the epic of his own time. This lack of congruity with the modern era arousing serious fits of resentment on his part, however. Leading him, time and time again, to preach, from a simulated pulpit, frank discord among men. In retaliation against a society frontally opposed to his memories.

Even though he did not know Dom Miguel, Venâncio was delighted by his untimely fits of rage.

"And what did this gentle knight say, when he felt angry or offended?" Venâncio asked as they were enjoying their Sunday repast, based on a Galician recipe.

Delighted to talk about her father, Eulália turned as red as though she had drunk several goblets of wine in a row. She paused briefly, however, taking care not to betray Dom Miguel's universe.

"Father's every moment was spent remembering our heroes. And in order to devote himself to this function, he took no notice of chattel or harvests. He even impoverished us. But the only thing he cared about was imagining what heroes really experienced, what books never record. Father was no lover of books. He had a great mistrust of them. As he saw it, books lacked reality. And therefore failing, naturally, to recount the essential. And for that reason, Father wore himself out in his effort to do just that. He maintained that the product of imagination did not reproduce itself in the same way as cherry trees, which have a set time to flower. Moreover, Father had against him the fact that any one episode that he might narrate had undergone a number of different versions, all having to be taken into consideration."

In the diary, Venâncio's doubts persisted. As did his fear of resorting to self-serving lies. Not informing that woman who moved almost silently, followed by Odete, of the existence of his ledgers. Not showing the same solicitude toward Madruga. He frequently returned to the attack. There hovered over Madruga the accusation that he preferred his own verbal vortex, which he kept running on and on in top gear, to Eulália's effusions, whenever his wife launched into a description of Dom Miguel's narrative power. Full of tricks, Madruga always managed to wriggle out of testifying in favor of his father-in-law's veracity.

". . . Madruga always wanted to keep me from breathing freely, from the moment that History caused us to coincide in time and in space. And he forced us to sail on the same English boat, which made us eat humble pie we soon threw up. On board, furthermore, I soon learned, between the arrogant crew and the capricious ocean waves, that the essence of any power exerts itself upon a legion of victims. Represented at that moment by us, obscure immigrants, penned up like cattle in the holds of ships.

Madruga applauded the predatory acts of the English. It would soon be his turn to live on intimate terms with power, to give forth his own signs. From the beginning, I opposed the ethic which, on the pretext of the wretchedness endured, assumes the right to take revenge with the same arms and the same immoral principles.

... in direct sight of the net and the harpoons launched by the myrmidons, represented by the English and Madruga himself, I confessed to Eulália, losing no time, having once landed in Brazil:

'I'm a wounded whale incarnating the spirit of good. Wholly different from Moby Dick.'

... moved to pity by the animal that had come to the shore of Brazil only to die, she rubbed ointments on my ribs, after removing my shirt. And in order that we might not remain alone in the room that had as witness the marriage bed, where Madruga and she lay together with various ends in view, Eulália summoned Odete, the slave bought at the Valongo Market. Beautiful and dissolute, this slave is jealous of me. She looks on me with contempt, her gaze knife-blade keen. She watches my every move, fearing that I will rub my naked chest against the breasts of the one who, suddenly, reveals herself to be a lady of lovely forms and a mistress of fiery passion.

... but what right have I to passion, if I abandoned it because of the pressure of a polar chill that mounts up through my anklebones till it meets my tiny penis. Numb and frail, I expel useless drops of semen. Whose origin is a member initially shy and withdrawn, which, to my surprise, grows, since I fear its rebelliousness and its undisciplined ways. Hence I think it wise not to betray my human condition. Especially since the body aggravates our misery."

Despite Venâncio's visible care to keep to himself the intimate details of Madruga's and Eulália's married life, that testimony forced Breta to undergo a confrontation with her own family. Yet she could only regret the sporadic nature of the notes. Some with dates, though many with no connection to time. It sometimes seemed to her that Venâncio had decided to lump all the troubles of a single month together in just one episode, even though that risked making a chaos of the connections between them.

There were other aspects that fascinated her as she went on reading the diary. Especially Venâncio's speculations concerning Brazil, as a general rule quite arbitrary ones. On this subject, unfortunately, Breta had difficulty following his line of thought. For the reason that Spain, when mentioned, readily lent itself to being a metaphor for Brazil. And as if that weren't enough, Spain was by nature well suited to conferring an allegorical role upon this tropical country. Thereby risking becoming the mirror in which Brazil saw itself reflected.

And as though this were not already enough of a mixture of genres, for which Venâncio was responsible, between the lines was a quite evident parodic tone. Moreover, to underline this intention, Venâncio, following Cervantes's lofty example, constantly accused the inhabitants of Rio de Janeiro of trailing through the streets of Marrecas, Ouvidor, Assembleía, and Lapa the dread feeling of being in the service of an exaggeratedly carnivalized reality. The only way that they had found of forgetting a shabby, dimensionless daily round of life.

These observations culminated in a particularly querulous tone. With Venâncio aware of being the favorite target of his own divided soul. This being the case, so long as he did not manage to reconcile within himself those two diametrically separated countries, his memory tended to dissolve, causing his emotions to drift out of control.

Without further ado, Venâncio vented his wrath against the Portuguese and Spaniards of the period of the conquests. Leaving it explicit that he could not forgive them their expansionism. And, with a compulsive sweep of his paw, he demolished the epic feats of the conquistadors, heaping scorn on their fantastic adventures. And, in referring to them, he was ascetic and linear, sending them packing with brief, not at all lush résumés.

On the slightest pretext, he would suddenly introduce the conquistadors into his reflections in the diary. Presenting them as fearless but unjust. With what coldness they burned a fleet anchored on the shore of the American continent! First off, so as to make their soldiers out to be pitiless creatures. And then, to make them nostalgic for a Europe to which they would not be able to return unless they plundered the treasures of American civilizations. The high command had foreseen that it was indispensable, for the triumph of their undertaking, for men to begin to dream of Europe in the same way they had once dreamed of the new continent when they were still living in their Spanish and Portuguese villages.

Nothing was to hold them back. Hence they excelled in the use of extraordinary resources. Not to mention that they proclaimed themselves, out of pure pride, the bearers of a gospel whose ultimate aim authorized them to decimate entire races, if necessary. Since these plumed peoples acted with attitudes considered disrespectful in the face of sacred images, especially those of a baroque nature, whose draperies were rendered in multiple carved folds. Those saints which, comfortably installed in niches and altars of the West, were the object of worship and homage, in the form of endless prayers and candles with lighted wicks that resounded, and lasted all through a long dawn.

With what indignation Venâncio mentioned some of those barbarians from the Iberian peninsula, whose names constituted a historic frontispiece. Giving special emphasis to those who, in their eagerness for gold and conversions, mowed down entire civilizations with the blades of their swords. Counting before the fact on the stamp of approval of History, which, in the person of its researchers, unfailingly vaunted the merits of this maritime adventure.

That gaunt Venâncio moved Breta deeply. She wanted to seek him out, but what would they say to each other? How to remove the obstacles and reach a lonely old man, with doors and windows closed, with only the wind mercilessly whipping his heart?

Alone in her room, Breta picked up that man's howls and laments. Venâncio's Brazil reaching her in great gushes. It beat on her door, miserable and threadbare. The violence of its contrasts, from north to south, forcing her to reflect once again on her own ability as a writer to reproduce such a reality. And whether, in fact, she had the right to try to capture it.

These doubts, whenever they occurred to her, threatened to gnaw away the pillars of her calling. Pillars, these, solidly based on the certainty that it was necessary for art to go all the way to the bottom of the human heart, in an attempt to bring to the surface a more and more representative sample of its painful and elusive passion.

Could it be that this Brazilian reality, in which we participated and from which we were at the same time excluded, barred any sort of record? Or because this same reality was so fleeting, so miserable, was it perhaps not worth trying to put one's ink-stained fingers in its wounds?

Breta breathed deeply. She needed to restore her confidence in the implications of her work. In and of itself, it was justified, so long as it acknowledged the existence of an essence or a mystery whose absolutely indefinable nature far transcended the oppressive circle of merely visible facts and episodes. In that case, it becoming imperative to lance reality's wounds, to exaggerate its extraordinary grandeur and cruelty. Wasn't it necessary to go all the way, even with no promise of returning? Wasn't it worth the cost, then, to take the plunge, this minute?

Calmer now, Breta noted that Venâncio's language became more rigorous when he turned to the nineteenth century. Amid the props of this era, he felt more secure. This century being, perhaps, no more than a metaphor coming from a deeply troubled heart, swaying back and forth between Madruga's ambition and Eulália's dreams. A woman breathing the advantages of eternal life into his ears.

In dealing, however, with the plain and simple facts relating to the first years in America, Venâncio refused to admit that Madruga had afforded him a soft life. Including giving him hours off each day to go to the Biblioteca Nacional and the Passeio Público. When, though aware of these visits, Madruga forbore to upbraid him for his mistakes or for failing to fulfill obligatory tasks.

Remaining in the background, Madruga provided him with resources, without his even noticing. While Venâncio made a point of giving a wide berth to a reality fostered by an unjust social system, from which he reaped no benefit. Thereby preserving his independence, even though every so often Madruga's somewhat shady business deals contributed to it.

The diary now had as its epicenter the Spanish Civil War. Very often Venâncio related this war to events taking place in Brazil. As though Spanish reality could be underwritten only by way of certain immediate correspondences to Brazil. These connections giving rise, however, to a very confused picture of the two countries.

Venâncio's status as a displaced person, emphasized throughout the diary, involved him in one personal difficulty after another. Breta identified with that trajectory punctuated by dramatic effects. She too always sensitive to the human passion that constantly prowled about her house, threatening to devour part of her heart. To which everything yielded. Since nothing existed save the life of others. Her own life not being enough for her.

Breta interrupted the reading of the diary to visit Eulália, who had now begun to die. The gloomy atmosphere of the house was reflected in Madruga, sitting in the living room. His strength drained by the long wait, he looked at his granddaughter without greeting her as usual. Perhaps because he remembered that Breta had spent the afternoon reading Venâncio's diary.

But he asked her no questions. It would be tactless to remind her that the book was available to her thanks to his personal intervention. He was convinced, however, that that diary, devoted to personal outpourings, emptied itself out in an impenetrable symbolic language, consonant with Venâncio's manifest scorn for concrete reality, from which he haughtily tried to absent himself. There not being, therefore, much reason for Venâncio to occupy himself with him or Eulália.

Madruga accepted the freshly filtered coffee. His face more serene now. At the first swallow, he was transported to a veranda overlooking a strange landscape. The unexpected fantasy seemed agreeable and he reciprocated with a smile. Of brief duration. Then, in sudden alarm, he began to fear that Venâncio, allowing himself to be carried away by biographical concerns, had involved him in his various accounts. Perhaps having even adulterated the facts about him, especially after the first trip to Brazil.

"What's the name again of the English boat that brought Venâncio and me to Brazil?" he asked, to test his granddaughter.

"Have you forgotten, grandfather?" Breta said teasingly.

Blushing for shame, he straightened in his chair, precluding any sort of familiarity on her part. And then he began to speak of Eulália's illness. He felt himself to be, however, the victim of an injustice. When he had handed the diary over to his granddaughter, he had not expected her to pass on to him in return any information concerning the book. He was indignant at the idea that he would act in his own interests. Woe to anyone who accused him of invading Venâncio's redoubts or of suborning Breta. Moreover, the dull, sordid daily life they were caught up in held no secrets. The only mysteries he respected were the ones that always enriched Xan's legends.

"When I gave you the diary, it was to make of it whatever you liked. And I repeat again now that all the papers that have accumulated in my drawers and files belong to you. Anything inside is yours. After my death, seal the door of my study," Madruga said, stern-faced.

Breta kissed her grandfather on the forehead. The unexpected caress touched Madruga. He loved his granddaughter best of all. She had not changed much in those years. She had embraced him stiffly, showing the same constraint once they had arrived home. Her long absence from her country had made his granddaughter forget people and objects. She felt herself to be among strangers.

Despite the marks left by exile, her blue jeans, her see-through blouse, and her bright eyes assured her of radiant youth. The same youthfulness as Eulália when he had seen her, for the first time, in the square in Sobreira. A meeting that was a turning point in the destiny of both. Prepared, however, to overcome his granddaughter's animosity, he hurriedly took her to the study, where, with strangers no longer present, they laid down their arms as usual.

They started with tea, then went on to whisky, straight. Only then did Breta begin to talk.

"If I hadn't become a writer, grandfather, I was going to be a tramp. One of those creatures who wander about the streets, with no fixed abode. My feet covering every inch of Brazil. Only that way would I come to know at close hand the misery and the naïveté of those anonymous faces, scattered far and wide in those vast spaces."

Hearing this confession by his granddaughter, Madruga regretted that this dream had been doomed to failure. But he thought, with relief, that it had at least been dreamed. And then he saw himself back in Sobreira. Sitting on the doorstep, as there wafted his way the sweet smell of cows and cow dung that always made him feel at peace.

"Grandfather Xan also offered me the same destiny as a wanderer. Except that I was thirteen and not smart enough to seize upon the chance. I spent my free hours thinking about America."

The family devoted its energies to bidding Eulália farewell. The presiding spirit was that of tying up all loose ends. In hushed voices, the children divided up the accumulated belongings and resentments. Eager to see what share would fall to each of them. In the company of Breta, Madruga watched the grandchildren line up, forming a fierce Praetorian guard.

"The only way of uniting them is to prove to them that their stories, taken individually, aren't worth a thing. And that they'll make sense, or will one day be told, only if this saga is enriched through the presence of all of them. Unfortunately, nobody is going to be able to convince them of the truth of this. Except Grandfather Xan, if only he were alive. Because whether these children like it or not, they're part of the same tribe," Madruga said, devastated at his own prediction.

"What tribe are you talking about, grandfather? Your own?"

"I don't have a tribe anymore, Breta. My little flock dissolved with the death of my two children. I've finally learned that the only tribe that can withstand tragedies is the one made up of an entire country. Brazil, for example, is a tribe."

"It's what's left of Xan's people, Dom Miguel's, Sobreira's," Breta said emphatically, to keep her grandfather going.

"Eulália and I have already begun our good-byes. Sobreira now seems to me to be tiny and extraordinary. I can hardly remember my village. I have no more than vague memories of it. The only things that stand out are a few old oaks, and the rooftops, that gleamed in the November rains when seen from the mountain."

Breta couldn't explain to her grandfather that by including him in his diary, Venâncio had not meant to offend him or defile his image. Despair alone had led him to embroider a story whose truthfulness was irrelevant. The one thing that mattered was self-preservation. Having written the diary to free himself of the insanity that was already wreaking its havoc. A madness overcoming him amid the death rattles of the Civil War, though Madruga had not noticed the symptoms.

Eulália herself had not suspected the existence of a diary to which Venâncio was attached, as to a relic. Only much later, on realizing what had happened, did she come to regard the diary as an object precious to her. She wrapped it in tissue paper, with special care. Perhaps that was why there rose from its pages a sweet perfume, absorbed from the cotton soaked in essential oil that Eulália glued to the inside of the cover.

As she looked at Madruga, Breta did not feel that she was betraying him. She had always been faithful to him, since early childhood. How often she had gone so far as to make a personal sacrifice simply to protect that man, whom she would succeed. The idea of this inevitable succession made her uncomfortable.

"I think you were wrong about Venâncio, grandfather. The only gypsy in this house is me, not him," she said teasingly, to relax the tensions in the living room.

Madruga suspected that his granddaughter's secrets did not come out because she had always wanted to spare his feelings. And to continue to be loved by him. Breta would never risk impairing his affection, at whatever price. She was different from Eulália, who had burned the bridges that would permit her return to her father's house. The two of them identical, however, in their discretion.

Thus far, Madruga did not know whether Esperança had spoken to her mother of his visit to the square, on that Thursday morning a few days before his daughter died. As for Odete, the one witness of their meeting, perhaps she had said nothing about it out of devotion to Eulália. In order to chase away all cares threatening to disturb her mistress. Thereby keeping Eulália, overcome with grief, from leaning back against the walls, pale and wan, as though living were a painful burden.

Home once more, Breta wandered about the apartment. Feeling cold, she huddled up in the poncho from Peru, a present from Mário. Through that fine piece of craftsmanship, the diligent hands of the remaining Incas bore witness to the last traces of their culture, cruelly debased in the past.

Breta remembered the Indians that she had seen wandering about the streets of Lima. Some of them dirty and reeking of coca. Blank-faced and impassive, they seemed devoid of energy. As though they had been banished from the last several centuries. She, however, was not taken in by this picture. On the contrary, she thought that there existed a burning instinct of revenge in the unconscious of that people. From them there came the mute and permanent outcry against the white man, who besides burying their history had destroyed their arcana and their cities of gold.

Perhaps that was why they vilified themselves each day, their one intention being to exorcise the eternal white colonizer through their abject presence. So that white society, despite having robbed them of their gods, their myths, their dignity, would not forget that, thanks to the resistant sperms and ova of their race, they still had the ability to reproduce themselves forever. More and more of their blood was entering the veins of the whites, commingling with their arrogant bloodlines. In the end, this ravaged genetic patrimony was the last manifestation of pride on the part of those ancient royal rulers.

Breta went to the kitchen; she was hungry. Despite the protection of the poncho the cold mounted through her bare feet. She ate with gusto. Food always served her as a measure of reality. And as a means of taking stock of human displeasures, among which was included the memory of Esperança. She refused, however, to cling to her mother's despair as her only model. Using it to retaliate, to attack everyone. She went on thinking, violent thoughts, as she listened to the sound of the cucumber in her mouth being ground to bits: anyone who tells a story runs the risk of ceasing to live.

In her room, as she listened to music, the passion expressed by Schubert brought her, for a few moments, a feeling of anguish, corresponding to the agony that Eulália was no doubt enveloped in now, like a soap bubble about to burst.

She banished the thought, drawn once more to the diary, lying on the night table. There was still a great deal to discover. She felt deeply touched to be able to enter Venâncio's sad universe once more. As she made her way through its pages, however, she sensed that she was about to encounter a bitter, necessary confession.

At each respite offered by death, Eulália went on to reciting the *De profundis clamavi ad te, Domine,* trying to repeat what the priest had said to her a short time before, on granting her absolution prior to leaving her in her family's hands. Still not satisfied, Eulália went on to recite, with long pauses, the *Domine exaudi vocem meam.* Till it seemed to her that she had said enough. God could not demand of her what was beyond her strength. It had fallen to her God to organize human time, to ease woman's encounter with death. Death was, indeed, a pandering, cruel witness. Eulália's *De profundis* was most moving. *From the depths I cried unto Thee, Lord, Lord, hear my voice.*

My wife's faith was inimitable, and I envied her. I lacked precisely the sort of faith with which a man sometimes sews his life together in such a way that not one thread will come loose. She, however, closed her eyes rather gently; I saw her mouth contract slightly. And her sigh had nothing of the force of Galician winds. But it was surely the last of a well-nigh endless series. She took her leave of us as she had lived: discreetly. Making her way through houses, countries, years, her mind elsewhere. Even the wild waves of the Atlantic had not disturbed her composure.

During the deathwatch for Eulália, we repeated certain gestures, some of them vague and faint, that we had gone through before, at Esperança's funeral. My daughter had heretofore been our dead person, passed on to eternal glory. We had mourned her death, as it happened, in that very chapel. Everything was more restrained this time. We had lost our theatricality. Life had quieted us down.

I don't know who dressed Eulália in that silk dress, which I had casually admired at the last Sunday dinner. Her coiffure was impeccable, her face retouched with only a trace of makeup. In the first hours at least, she did not have the usual pallor of the dead. Odete had doubtless followed orders given her some time before. As rigor mortis had not yet set in, she placed in Eulália's hands the rosary, come down to her from her great-grandfather, which she had brought with her from Spain. The beads looked worn from having passed for so many long years through the sweaty, aching fingers of Dom Miguel's family as they prayed. The women always more inclined toward prayer than the men, perhaps because they had a bosom ready to pour forth a sweet milk, as an offering to the god of their choice.

"Men know very little about women. They don't understand the creatures whom, historically, they invented," Breta said on one occasion, speaking very softly.

In this subtle way, Breta was extolling Esperança, without mentioning her name. In her eyes, her mother had done no wrong. I therefore carefully sidestepped an argument on the subject. Esperança's shadow haunted us during these hours. Why was that?

When all was said and done, who had that daughter been? Had she sacrificed herself because of my cruelty in never allowing her a freedom that violated my own? But who had freed me? Didn't I too have reason to rebel against Urcesina, when now and again she cut the bread at table in wrath, though she apportioned it justly?

Wasn't it, then, the usual human practice to dance the ring-around-the-rosy of mutual accusation? Not even forgiving the dead? And in this vortex, I too railing in my old age at the children and grandchildren trying to place stumbling blocks in my way no matter where I turned? All of them eager to win power sooner, more than willing to discredit the use and exercise of my memory. The last skill we can call on to clothe the scenes of the past in a happy, emotionally satisfying carnality. Thanks to which reality, for a few short moments, is subject to miraculous reconstructions. Whereby life itself is restored, a remote awareness of what certain ardent, youthful moments in the past were like.

From a very early age, Esperança had proved willful. And therefore capable of leaving home without even sending us a message. A note at least to the next-door neighbor. And so I walked through the streets fearing that I would suddenly come upon her swollen belly, her eyes of a drowned woman, always opened wide whenever she detested something. She had blue eyes like mine, as though she had deliberately stolen them. To make herself a successor prepared to betray me. And in fact she did betray me, by giving herself over, without scruple, to wild, unbridled freedom. To the bondage of the flesh. From the moment I discovered her crime, I never wanted to see her again. But making it clear to the children that that woman should lack for nothing, not even the superfluous.

Though Eulália disapproved of my behavior, she willingly took checks to Esperança. Some of them much too generous, deliberately so, meant to corrupt my daughter.

Esperança promptly sent them back, thus thwarting my plans. What I really wanted was to sully her life, so that her pleasure, in bed, in the public square, in restaurants, would never bathe her in its radiant glow.

"Don't overdo it, Madruga," Eulália pleaded. "Life will punish us yet for this impossible puzzle we've made of our feelings."

To calm me down, Eulália counted on my ancestral fears. From a very early age, in Sobreira, they had taught me to interpret the language of thunderclaps, floods, fire. Certain elements being louder than others. But then, how else would the gods speak if it weren't for these signs? Yet I indignantly rejected my wife's warnings. And now, at this late date, she was invoking the aid of death, which threatened us daily. What to do but defy the gods at every step?

Breta had lately been choosing selections of Wagner for me. In that music was an ultimatum to life and the imaginary. Woe to the man who does not surpass himself, the solo voices and the chorus decreed. Though attractive, that land of heroes and myths did not promise generosity. By contrast to Grandfather Xan's myths. All tending to promote charity.

Breta prided herself on having identified the crucial point of my encounter with the hard-breathing German. "What you applaud in Wagner is the authoritarianism of conscience and imagination. Only those races that proclaim themselves an elite set such standards. But those are unfair criteria, grandfather, because they show nothing but contempt for the dregs, for the remnant, for misery. They form rigid societies. Completely different from Brazil, a tousled, toothless country. But the day is not far off when we will make ourselves heard by other peoples. Using, however, in order to do so, an ample and unrestrained language, expressing the quintessence of the people's heart."

While Breta moved at times in a mechanical way, Esperança never could resist imitating the movements of lions, she too roaring in obedience to the thunder within. For years my daughter clenched her teeth, sealed her lips so that not a single shout for help would escape her, much as she rebelled against her father's silence. Her father's supposed indifference. Esperança having little idea that my heart would suddenly begin to burn in the middle of the street, forcing me to take shelter beneath the marquees, to go into a bar, to hurriedly drink a cup of coffee, at the mere memory of the hours my daughter was spending with strange men, there in Botafogo. Those scoundrels who came to her door one after the other, without my being able to seal it at a distance. Or seal her sex, her desire. To stamp them with our family's signet. And then, overcome with despair, I would burst into the house, looking for Eulália, who was almost always in the living room. She sensed instantly the origin of my anxiety. Ever fearful of my impatience, which spattered all about in the form of impiety. As to that end I employed words and engaged in acts that it would have been better to have left inside secret drawers and rusty coffers.

In the face of these omens, Eulália proceeded with caution. As though I might hurt her. When in truth it was the children against whom I vented my wrath. She then brought me a port, whose smoothness came to me as a messenger of peace. Of what use, after all, was carnage that all of them survived, their memory crushed to bits in the great bloodbath? As I took my first sip of port, she seemed grateful. The flavor of grapes crushed by anonymous voices, by our Portuguese neighbors on the other side of the Minho, gradually calmed me. As though Xan, at my side, were saying, There's not a single slow, sad afternoon that can hold out against good wine and a good story.

Smelling her body at a distance, I went over to Eulália then. She must not have perceived my anxiety, the desire to creep inside her body so as to become her, if only for a few instants. Thus enabling me to wrest from her the fresh memories of Esperança that she was safeguarding, having met her that morning. For wasn't it true that they saw each other on certain mornings, when Eulália was caught unawares by her daughter and her granddaughter?

Esperança's words found shelter with Eulália. The two of them sprinkled each other with fake holy water. Eulália always set aside half of what her daughter told her. A poignant confession would have upset her, troubled her prayers. When face to face with her mother, Esperança had long since ceased to be able to hold that woman in the palm of her hand.

Though they spent hours together, Esperança did not mention a single member of the family by name. Avoiding comments that would betray her interest. Though Miguel was a source of worry to her. She sometimes fled the square on seeing a car stop nearby, a man striding excitedly toward her. Miguel might very well try once again to wrest from her confessions buried in her compassionate breast. The same ones he demanded from her before Esperança left the family. Insisting on her complete repentance, once she had abjured innocence, covered the family with shame. His sister should punish herself, go to the pillory, like a slave. Esperança answered, however, by attacking her brother, raking his face with her fingernails.

"Never come near me again, Miguel. Don't make me hate you," she said, prepared to lose him.

He drew back. With nothing to prop it up, the false front formed by his body, separating him from his sister, collapsed. "Do you mean to say that you're banishing me from your life? Speak, Esperança!" His voice sounded hoarse; the cords of his neck were plaited together like a braid.

"If it's to humiliate me, never seek me out again, Miguel. Ever since you've been my torturer, I've been prepared to kill you. And I forbid you to come looking for me." Her chest hurt; inside it was a rolling of drums beaten by the king's enemies. The king was Madruga, on the other side of the river. There on the opposite shore, cutting her off from the water, trees, the future.

According to Eulália's sparse descriptions, her granddaughter was tiny, with huge dark eyes. She had not inherited Esperança's blue eyes. Nor did she appear to be my granddaughter. I heard her out, frowning. When she had finished revealing certain of her soul-searing secrets, I rewarded her by threatening to leave the house that very night.

"I don't want to hear another word, Eulália. That daughter drapes us in mourning each and every day. I have long since banished her from my heart."

I slammed the door behind me, not returning home till late that night. Eulália never asked me where I had taken my anguish.

Eulália's casket was red and black, personally chosen by Bento with great care. From the moment Eulália was placed inside it, Odete never left her bier. But I did not see her weep a single tear. Her neatly pressed Sunday dress was no doubt homage paid Eulália. Certainly both had decided beforehand what rituals were to be observed. The meticulous performance of a ceremony uniting them for the last time.

Bento devoted his attention to comforting Odete, who, he presumed, felt lost amid strangers and funeral wreaths. She should lack for nothing at this moment. He looked after her as though she were Eulália's widow. As for Venâncio, he was more discreet. From time to time he went over to gaze at Eulália's face, returning immediately to his place on the sidelines. The entire family put in solid performances, though some gave more evidence than others of a talent for crying. Miguel, for example, no longer shed as copious tears as he once had. After Esperança's death his weeping had never been the same.

Breta touched my arm. "You'd best get some rest at home, grandfather. It's going to be a long night."

Nothing could keep me from Eulália's wake. Though the excitement, the food, the hot coffee, and cane brandy from an ancient still would all be missing at a big-city wake.

Luís Filho and Bento were fighting over the right to receive the flowers and the condolences of the personages present. Since I'd made it big in Brazil, they were all there, from any number of different worlds. Coming to pay their respects to an immigrant who had never told them a single story of Grandfather Xan's. They knew nothing of my past, of my ancestors. I knew nothing of their origins either. A mutual ignorance, owing to our fate as pawns of history. All of us together on this earth, hurriedly passing through. Lives tightly caulked, so that no one would get inside them. Every one of us a damp cell.

The battle had long since begun. Luís Filho rushes over to the governor, fat and impenetrable. His soul hiding underneath his white suit. He addresses ashen words to us, expresses a passing interest in the corpse that is our property.

"Dona Eulália comes from an old Galician family, rural nobility, as is evidenced by the coat of arms proudly displayed at their country seat even today. A pious woman, of unswerving religious faith." These details furnished by Luís Filho, feigning grief.

Expressions of condolence follow, one after the other, breathed more often to the children than to me. Though I am the patriarch, the possessor of the fortune, cliques have already formed. Supporters of Luís Filho, Bento, Miguel. Antônia begins to cry, but her husband brings her back to reality with a gesture. She does not have the right to let her attention wander. From this moment on, the race for the estate, the fight for possessions and power is on.

Depressed by this spectacle, I hurriedly bade Eulália farewell. After all, we'll be seeing each other again very soon. She was always wise and prudent. Since the day we landed together in America, embracing Brazil at almost the same time. Our children born of this embrace.

The one thing left for me to do now was to witness Venâncio's farewell to Eulália. He merely stroked her hands, not daring to go farther. Whereupon Tobias suddenly came over, forthrightly taking hold of his godfather's head to press his lips to Eulália's brow. Demanding that he give her a farewell kiss. One last one. Had there perhaps been others? Eulália and Venâncio were so discreet that I had never once caught them exchanging so much as a caress. At times it troubled me to think that Venâncio's feelings for Eulália were akin to my own. A woman who grew old along with us, at our side, while we were so intent on living our own lives that we never even noticed.

The kiss appeared to have embittered Venâncio for the rest of his days. He glared at his godson in white-hot fury, threatening to sever the ties that bound them. He hesitated, however, not having the heart to punish him. And overcome by emotion, they hugged each other in a long embrace.

Drawing away from Venâncio, Tobias looked my way. And feeling abashed at not having offered me a single sign of his affection, he brought me a cup of coffee, which I politely refused. There was no need for him to feel upset; there would be more than enough time for him to comfort me in days to come. Though he was surely only dimly aware that he had already renounced his power in favor of Bento, Miguel, Luís Filho. Whom he was now begging to lend him the strength that he had allowed to be passed on to them.

At that family reunion, Esperança, Breta's mother, was missing. Were she still alive, her place in the funeral chapel would have been alongside Miguel. Being the oldest child, she would now be wrinkled and white-haired. Yet with the same ability as ever to hold her own in verbal duels with friends and enemies.

And surely she would have said to me, Oh, father, we will never be the same after this event, meaning Eulália's funeral. The same words that she had uttered in the square, when we had met in Odete's presence after the many years that we had been absent one from the other. I had not been able to resist the temptation to go to the square that morning. Fate took me to the place where my daughter was in the habit of going, accompanied by Breta, still a little girl. Owing to the influence of Eulália, who exhorted me to see Esperança, or at least make the acquaintance of the grandchild who had visited our house, some two or three times, taking advantage of my being off traveling. Or attending a lunch of some sort, returning late at night, with the smell of wine on my breath, my hair slightly out of place. Ruffled by the hands of some strange woman, thus giving it a certain naturalness.

In the month of December especially, Eulália urged me to see Esperança. I kept refusing. "It's no use to insist, I won't go. I have nothing to say to strangers."

"She's not a stranger, Madruga. She's your daughter. Your very own flesh and blood. The only child who has your eyes. The eyes of your father Ceferino, of your grandfather Xan. Can you have forgotten the law of heredity?" And she looked at me as though she didn't believe my explanation of why I had come home at such a late hour.

I hadn't even told Silveira about this mistress. I'd been going to her place for two years. My only commitment being to ask if she would be free the next Thursday. Her answer was sometimes no; she would be off traveling for a month. I missed her at such times. I liked using her body with my eyes closed, lending her faces from days long gone, brought back to life by a moment's passion. No transport of the senses, in all those years, had had the power to banish Eulália, since she was the only one to talk to me of Xan, of Sobreira, of the Atlantic, to confirm my story. In the end all women became forms of vegetation, magnificent trees that I climbed seeking the unsurpassable tremor of leaves and branches, rooted in sex.

That mistress stood up to me boldly. Amid ardent words invoking names that were not mine. Which freed me to imitate her. Both agreeing that we should obey our needs. She was nonetheless fond of describing my body as that of a boy, thereby restoring my youth. At times I was upset, overcome by the sensation that my grandfather Xan, my father Ceferino, my dead were penetrating her in my place, that I was lending them my member to satisfy themselves, half intimidated and half perplexed by those remains of life. Rocked like a baby by dead men, I nonetheless bucked and capered on the body of that woman. I gloried in the advantage of being alive. When I fell exhausted at her side, however, everything seemed strange to me. Especially that arrogant member, whose magnificence was over and done with now, and which had no knowledge whatsoever of the language I needed most in order to be on closer terms someday with my lost daughter. Lost because of acts such as these. Esperança had not wanted to give up her body either, and hence had dramatically rejected the disciplined body that I forced upon her. She kicked out against my will, determined to choose her own loves, according to her appetite.

On learning of Esperança's transgressions, Miguel rebelled, cuffed his sister. I forbade the two of them to kill each other, however. To see to it that they did not, I pretended that she had died. I did not want to get overexcited. I readily grant that life excited me. Money, construction projects, the power I was gradually mastering.

In bed, the woman stroked my hair. "You aren't here. Only your body has visited me. Fortunately I didn't notice it at the time."

I smiled at her helplessly. Once the last embers of our pleasure had died, our bodies were cold. I got out of bed, my nerves on edge. It had been a hard day. "You needn't see me to the door. Stay in bed. I'll be back again someday," I said to her. She shook her head, intuitively sensing that I would never return. We had lost our spontaneity.

The following morning, I decided to take a stroll in the public square. I didn't think I would run into Esperança and Breta at such a late hour. I looked carefully about for trees that would serve as a prop to hold me up in case I was overcome by intense emotions. I went on apprehensively. After all, this was my daughter's square. To my right, sitting on a bench, Esperança was waiting for me, as though she had foreseen that I would be coming.

We looked at each other for the first time after our long separation. She had not changed. The same rigid body and proud, beautiful face. Who does this woman, who is my daughter, take after? I thought, on seeing her rise to her feet, as one does when receiving visitors. I was her visitor.

"I had an idea that you'd be coming. And that we would meet in this very square." She hid her embarrassment, rubbing her hands together. I appreciated her generosity in coming forward, in speaking first.

A short distance away, Odete was playing with a child whose back was turned to me. I could not see the little girl's face, just her hair and her body, a tiny one indeed. Odete pretended not to see me. She was there on Eulália's order. Her acting as a witness made me uneasy, and to restrain her, I went so far as to pay her compliments. She turned her head away without giving me any assurance that she would be discreet about this meeting.

"I don't know why I came. All I know is that I've come."

"Mother always comes. Perhaps you've arrived in her stead," Esperança said, with a sharp edge of irony in her voice. Was she making fun of me after trying to kill me?

"I know I've come, but I've nonetheless not forgotten how badly you hurt me. The thousand deaths you caused me."

"I've done nothing that I wouldn't do again, father," and she ran her fingers through her hair, like a comb, a familiar gesture of hers that she had not abandoned.

"How dare you speak to me that way, after all these years? Will you admit, then, that you haven't repented, that you're not ashamed of the life you're leading?" I shouted at her.

Esperança drew back. She felt the full force of my insult for a moment, then recovered. "What do you know of my life or of my dignity? Come, tell me, what do you know of my pleasure or my fight for life? You always wanted to dominate me because I'm a woman, and therefore owing you absolute obedience. But I was not born to obey or to be submissive. I want a life that's crystal-clear, or agonizing, or whatever, so long as it's mine. I want to walk on my own two lacerated, bleeding, proud feet. You, father, came to America in the same spirit as the conquistadors, out to punish Indians and women, even white women. To punish them by taming their genitals, making them a submissive sex, meant only to bear children," Esperança roared in pain.

I too was unable to control myself, after all the years of torment. "Come, beg my forgiveness, this very moment," I insisted, hating that woman there before me, capable of spreading her legs for nameless males. My body ached; only my tongue moved in search of words to decimate her.

"I've already told you. I'd rather die than surrender. I'd rather lose you forever than humiliate myself before you. Though you were dying in agony before my eyes," she said in a loud voice, walking round and round the bench, now eyeing me steadily, now looking about for her daughter, not far from there, fearing she might be overheard. At a single glance, I saw that Esperança had aged. Her beauty had turned into a hard, frozen, implacable set of her face. I detected in her the same gestures that I used when I was out to demolish my adversaries.

"Beg my forgiveness. Mine and your mother's. Mine and your brothers' and sister's," I went on spitefully.

"I'd rather see all of you dead. I'd rather lose you forever. Anyone who wants to humiliate me doesn't deserve me. I'm not afraid to stand up to them, father, because I've nothing left to lose. The price of my freedom must be set by me and not by you, Miguel, and all the rest of this family."

"You've made me grow old during these years. You've been bent on killing me during these hard years. Why, will you answer me that? What is it you're seeking revenge for?"

"Say my name at least, father. Speak my name, just once. Or have you forgotten that it's Esperança?"

Her voice was softer now. I had only to make a friendly gesture and she would fling herself into my arms. Or was I deluding myself?

"I'll never speak your name again. It's a vow I've taken. I intend to be true to that promise till I die," I said, immediately appalled at the dramatic tone of that utterance. I sounded like an old peasant invoking the vengeance of the gods.

"In that case, we have nothing more to say to each other. You'd best leave me. If in your eyes I'm already dead, you've died at this very moment in mine. I shall delude myself no longer. Once I have no family, I'll kill each one of you within me. There won't be a single one of you left, I swear to you. Even though I destroy myself in this holocaust," and she began to walk away, without saying good-bye.

"Wait a moment. I haven't dismissed you yet," I shouted, moved by diabolical pride, Lucifer in my soul, all the demons, a pitiless heart, wielding knives, scythes. Where had I come from to employ such cunning words?

Esperança returned to the same spot as before, attracted by a center invisible to me. There was no indignation in her eyes. She appeared to be moved, bathed in a serene grief. She felt humiliated, beaten. And I have not forgotten the last words I heard her speak.

"Oh, father, we will never be the same after these events. Only death will teach us now. Since life did not give us time to correct our mistakes," and she swiftly turned her back on me, taking Breta with her.

Eulália's funeral procession proceeded down the alley of trees, at the slow pace set by Venâncio and me. Halting at the burial site where the gravediggers awaited us. Figures who, luckily, did not allow themselves to be betrayed by emotion, they had divested themselves of the feelings that shadow the unburied. It was a profession that called for prudence. Bento supervised the ceremony; it must betoken surpassing richness. Surrounded by this pomp, there followed the gentle Eulália, whose countenance, hidden from our eyes, might well be gazing into the face of her god. In accordance with the faith for which she had sacrificed her life. Outside of this god, who else existed for her? What did children, life, love, a man's swollen member, even her own moist privates mean?

Venâncio clutched my arm. He frightened me by repeating a gesture of seventy years before as, from the deck of the English ship, Vigo grew smaller and smaller, till we lost sight of the city. The boat transported across the waters two wretches whose only patrimony was their fragile and perishable lives.

Venâncio demanding of me tears, anguish, a feeling of loss. A proposal I turned down; he could weep in my place. And so I named him proxy for my emotions, obliged to experience unbearable feelings in my stead.

"With Eulália's departure, the two of us are losing our homeland and our family in one blow," I whispered so that no one would overhear us.

Venâncio clutched my arm again, his grip surprisingly strong for an old man's.

"Eulália was the only family I had. I never had any other," he said, and averted his eyes.

Why was that man sharing confidences he later would regret? Jealous of such dark sentiments, I felt an urge to provoke him. Now that we no longer had Eulália to separate us when we tangled with each other.

"What about the letters in the months of May and December, during our first years in Brazil? There were always three letters for each period. Or was it four? After the Civil War, however, not a single one arrived from across the Atlantic. Why was that? Had the senders died or were they merely reduced to silence? Was it easier for them just to forget America?"

Venâncio let go of my arm. To my surprise, not having him at my side was painful to me. I felt cold and lonely. Insensitive to my state, he walked over to the other end of the graveside, joining Tobias, who held him close. Venâncio was again withholding information from me. He was avoiding the truth even in the presence of Eulália's casket. The only living being who could have gotten his story out of him. Occupied as she was, however, with her mystical realm, she never went to the trouble of asking him questions. Of taking an interest in human plots.

Antônia approached, followed by Luís Filho, who was bending over backwards to be polite to me. I wished I had died in Eulália's place. From now on, I would have to try even harder to put up with them. Those amorphous, spineless creatures left me cold. But wasn't Antônia the only daughter I had left?

Back home again, I opened Eulália's wardrobe chests. There in her dresses and her polished shoes she lived on. I gave Odete orders to empty the chests out. Everything belonged to her by natural right. She moved like a robot, incapable of following my orders.

"You can clean out the wardrobe chests some other day then. This house, after all, will be yours and mine till our deaths. And we'll have more than enough time left us to take care of such things."

My heart touched, I went over to the woman. That proud, steadfast black African, who always treated me as though I were a stranger. Her stubborn love for Eulália immediately brought my wife back to the room, to the entire house. When we wanted to have Eulália among us once again, we had only to summon Odete. But Eulália's spirit ought not to be disturbed. I too was preparing to leave.

The family promptly dried their eyes at the mention of practical matters. It was decided that the house would not be divided as long as I was alive. They were willing to wait.

"Be patient a little while longer. I haven't died yet, but the Black Widow will soon be coming to fetch me," I snapped at Luís Filho, who, his vest unbuttoned, pestering me with questions, wanting information, was affecting an informality that my presence had never before prompted in him.

Even when he kept silent, Luís Filho clearly felt an antipathy to my origins. Contrasting them with his own. Above all when I talked to everyone of Sobreira, of work in the fields of Galicia, the reward for which was thick calluses on one's hands from wielding a hoe or a hatchet. From endless tilling of the soil with a primitive plow hitched to amiable cows. Whereas he had been born sucking the nipples of a nobility in decline, but still harnessed to power. Thus cutting the working class off from opportunities rightfully theirs. Despite the fact that the workers had gotten the better of them thanks to their superior manpower, they had ended up corrupting us every time we sought their aid. Or instructions as to how to use silverware at table, or what new habits ought to be inculcated within the home, the school system, an upwardly mobile society. With what elegance those aristocrats took down their pants in salons, without fear of their rude backsides offending us. And when we rebelled against this supremacy, they flaunted their illustrious surnames, their dexterous handling of knife and fork. A practice which, in truth, was the precise counterpart of our skill at exploiting the land, the same land that had been feeding them for centuries.

Venâncio's approach put Luís Filho to flight. "Luckily, he detests me. You, unfortunately, don't have that kind of luck. These heirs keep moving in closer and closer. About to smother a person at any moment, to take one's easy chair. Will they be in that much of a hurry to bury us?" Venâncio said testily.

I appreciated having him on my side in the fight against Luís Filho. But only for the moment. I was doing nothing to rout Luís Filho. Money had corrupted me as much as it had him. And he would be my heir, so as to perpetuate my estate. As the legends that Xan had once imprinted upon my soul vanished.

"And what about the legends, Venâncio? Who's going to recount them, someday, so they won't disappear?" I threw up my hands, painfully, my rheumatism having settled in my nerves. Each day found me with fewer signs of life. My memory was going; certain names did not come to me as readily now as they once had.

Miguel gave evidence of a certain pity for the old man who sat in the same easy chair for hours at a time, wanting to see the ocean in the distance.

"There are fewer of us every day, father. I can't bear to see the family disappearing," he said, overcome with intense emotion.

An odd family, this one. With a gift for loving and hating symmetrically. Every one of them, with the exception of Tobias, gravitating round material possessions, forefinger upraised to warn off the others. The lot of them able at times to be tender, especially when begging for favors. All of them incapable of spinning plots out of the legends left behind by Gelmírez in his political primacy. Even Breta, being Brazilian, showed no interest. She laughed on coming to grips with the difficult character of Dona

Urraca, who, despite the rules of courtly love, doubtless fornicated with a splendor that would reflect her power. The queen's every move took into account the eternal conflict with those who sought to restrict her power and bleed her royal house. Stories and suppositions that Xan and Dom Miguel invested with sovereign dignity so that they would be remembered. The result being that now he mixed them all up, owing partly to the workings of the chaos that memory is, with stories pertaining, for example, to José Bonifácio, to the Emperor Dom Pedro I, or even to Dom Sebastião. This last a myth that had landed in Brazil with the aim of impregnating the people with new desires, or of coupling them with a fruitless hope, which led them to neglect to fight their enemies and instead await the king's return.

Breta visited her friend and oppressor daily. Not neglecting her grandfather, especially after Eulália's death.

"Like Xan and Dom Miguel, I too fear that Brazil will be wiped out. I fear they'll steal our language and leave us a carcass good for nothing but echoing useless sounds. Did you know that languages die too, grandfather? There was even someone who bore witness to the death throes of one. A Celtic dialect, spoken in Scotland, which died just at the turn of the eighteenth century, in the mouth of a woman well along in years, and perhaps toothless. And it was said that she spoke a few words on her deathbed. The very last words that a language uttered before dying, as though it too were a person about to depart from this world forever. What words do you suppose they were?" Breta said.

My granddaughter had become the only being making the banner of life flutter in my breast. And why not use that image? Wasn't life an unfurled banner that might tatter in the wind?

"Swear, Breta, swear," and I could not go on.

"Swear what, grandfather?" she said.

"Of this whole family, the only one I have left is you. Swear that you'll save yourself. Even though they leave you all by yourself, and you can't bear the loneliness any longer." And I turned my eyes away from her.

That afternoon, Breta felt compassion for her grandfather, defying the family by way of his difficult temper.

"Nobody can manage to keep a careful enough watch on life to save himself, grandfather. What's more, it makes no sense to save only oneself," was what Breta said.

My granddaughter was right. But she ought not to forget the reasons for my grief. In my old age now, and after so many years in America, I had lost access to Grandfather Xan's stories. They were becoming very hazy in my memory; I remembered almost nothing now. All I had left were loose threads; it was impossible to end the stories properly with them. Had memory betrayed me, then, just because I had given up the dreams that Xan taught me to cultivate, even at the price of poverty? Was that why

Xan, aware of such risks, stubbornly fought to remain the best storyteller in Sobreira and all the country round?

"Don't torment yourself, grandfather. There will always be someone in the future who will tell Grandfather Xan's stories. If they deserve to survive, that is. If they turn out to be really indispensable to humankind."

Breta took my hands, held them for some time. The blood flowed back into them, life returning to them.

The thought came to me then that Breta still had an innocent face. Whereas my own face bore witness against itself. Everything I said now would necessarily be doubted. Because I had dared mix words and feelings with gold and silver. My gestures no longer mirrored that fervor that has deep roots in those who know how to tell stories with a sincere heart.

"A storyteller needs to be truthful, isn't that so, Breta?"

Breta approved of her grandfather's stealing certain of her ideas. After all, ever since I'd been a youngster, I had wandered through the streets plundering what was fresh and lush. Challenging the powerful in this conquest. How many times, in the beginning, Silveira and I considered suspending our agreements. In 1932, however, we sealed a definite friendship, which lasted for decades. Till the day they divested him of senatorial power, Brasília having decreed that he was washed up politically. He phoned me with the news. I noted his embarrassment as he made every effort to hide his despair.

He wanted to meet me in the usual place, the Pérgula at the Copacabana Palace. Catching sight of him there in front of me, I noticed that keeping up appearances was of special concern to him in his old age. His hair was dyed and he hadn't yet given up those impeccable white suits of his. I had arrived first, and as he came to join me, head held high, he had the air of an emperor. He deliberately avoided looking about him; he was beginning to be ashamed of his new status. Fearing, surely, that people would no longer fawn upon him as they once had.

"How ironic, Madruga. I don't know if they're being so cordial on my account or if it's because I have the pleasure of your company. You've unintentionally robbed me of my last illusion of power."

I was unable to put him at his ease. I too was melting away like a wax doll. Only if my memory could have brought back the figure of Xan intact, and his world too, left far behind now, would my spirits have been lifted.

"At a certain point in life, Silveira, we have no more enemies except ourselves. I have no one I can blame. I myself destroyed my dreams and part of my family," I confessed, so that he would not be the only one to feel defeated.

We had ordered a Reno white, a recent vintage. A Spätlese, a new type that braved the most inclement weather, the grapes being picked in the very last days of the season. Any miscalculation, even by just one day, and the harvest was lost, ruined by rain.

"What are you thinking of doing now, Silveira?"

Despite his fastidiousness, his hair coloring had not been properly applied at the temples. His eyesight was bad, but out of pride he would not allow a professional to dye his hair.

"What I've always said I'd do. Go back to my fazenda in Rio Grande. Nobody in this city or in Brasília is going to watch me turn away in humiliation from the first door that's slammed in my face. I'm certain that today, for example, I've knocked on a door for the very last time in my life. I only got them to open it out of respect for my memory. For what I was in the past. But I've just used up all my reserves. I mustn't push my luck any farther. In the future it won't do me any good to have been a Senator of the Republic or a conspirator. Someone whose ears caught the whispers of Juscelino and Jango, and Getúlio's death rattle. They're all dead, and I'd best follow their example."

Silveira withdrew into himself, neglecting to inspect the neighboring tables, as had always been his habit. His unexpected timidity touched me. I wanted to show him I sympathized, to mention how I too was suffering. But he wouldn't let me get a word in. As though he were holding forth from the podium for the last time.

"Power is a trap, Madruga. If you take one minute off to rest your rear end on the floor, you run the risk of being swept out with the trash. That way the country gets rid of the men it's used to make its history. And the new history then gets made by those who begin their climb to power by knocking down their predecessors. It's a massacre that's useful and never-ending. Because when you get shoved off the landing, there's a secret law that says you half survive. Well then, so be it. I learned long ago that life isn't just a banal matter of breathing in and out. It's something that implies constant claims on a person, and a series of predatory acts. I was once a hunter, Madruga, as you were. We've both hunted, not to ensure anything so pointless as our survival, but to accumulate a stash and share it. We were driven by a dream and by passion. And what do we have left now? Who are we, my friend?"

"We were men who were experts in the past. But today we're men who are beaten. And that has to be enough for us, Silveira." And I raised my glass as a toast to that.

"Right, a toast to the life left to us. Each of us imprisoned on his respective veranda. You, for instance, will see the ocean, your beloved Atlantic, from your very own house. As for me, I'll bury my gaze in the desolate pampas. There's a loneliness there that's impossible to overcome. And when they bring me my maté, I'll pretend to be reading or reflecting on past glories. Even in this last exile I'll have to make everyone believe I'm a powerful man, able to hand out crumbs and fat plums to peons and neighbors, thanks to my fortune and my pull as a former Senator of the Republic."

"As your reward, Silveira, you're invited to attend my funeral."

We both laughed as though trying to attract the attention of the people at the other tables. So they'd appreciate the meaning of our presence in the Pérgula at the Copacabana Palace.

Breta tried her best to banish my loneliness after the loss of Eulália. Refraining from any show of tenderness toward me when the other children were present. On finding myself deprived of her kind attentions, however, I would head for my study, sure that she would come following after. Once inside together, we looked long and hard at photographs, of the dead and certain of the living.

"You have to look for the right language. Pity the writer who makes the wrong choice. Above all you have to write in the most important language, the one the country is producing then and there. If Montaigne had written in Latin, nobody would remember him today. The same happy lot did not befall Francisco Sánchez, a philosopher pursuing the same line of thought as Montaigne. Having little faith in the advances being made in his time, not understanding the new direction that History was taking, he urged the use of scholarly Latin. Thereby underestimating the magnitude of the seismic shifts taking place among the various peoples newly aware of their identity, all of them demanding the use of their own everyday language."

Breta rose to her feet. Her face reflected the risks she was taking with every word she wrote. Assuming through this alliance a total, ethical obligation.

"This week we've buried Eulália. In a few months my hour will have come. Sometimes it's a true language that's buried and sometimes merely a style suffering from hardening of the arteries. What difference does it make, Breta? At each and every moment life is full of individual and collective mistakes. In this great circus, only heroes escape. They've been circumcised by grandeur. They, I grant you, soar above the ephemerides. But can that be just, Breta?"

Breta preferred to believe that we were simply transient, volatile creatures. Each of us the possessor of a violin with delicate strings, though subject to jangling, unpredictable discords. The sound they produced would be perfect only by virtue of a carefully planned series of accords and treaties that reflected collective interests. There was only one winner, history itself, whose account was balanced daily. History being the deciding factor in determining what merited preservation. Anything and everything vital, by its very nature, to its own survival.

"We're all losers, grandfather. History is cruel, and the only thing that singles out the winners. Yet, to our relief, what is this history but the people restored to life?"

The hour was late. I ought to have been going off to my room. I rose to my feet. Breta insisted on accompanying me upstairs. Perhaps she wanted to put me to bed, tucking me in with affection and pillows. So that, in the morning, I would pat the covers, expecting to find Eulália beside me once more. And what sort of illusion would seeing her again be?

We went slowly up the stairs. At the door of the room, before going inside, I felt a dizzy spell come over me, but Breta did not notice.

"Ah, Breta, where does the human heart lie?" I said all of a sudden. I paused for a moment. "So, then, did I go off, conquer the waters of the Atlantic, endure humiliations, just so you, my granddaughter, would tell our story someday? Xan's story, Dom Miguel's, Eulália's, Odete's, the story of all of us anonymous dramatists who don't know how to write?"

Her heart touched, Breta hugged me. So hard I feared for her fate. At times, she seemed frail and vulnerable to me. Emotion is always a passageway that narrows like a funnel and transports us to an unforeseen and dangerous place, I thought, thus confronted with her fervor.

"Leave me now, Breta. Please," and I cast her from my body.

"You're right, grandfather. I think we're going too far. I too need to be free of you for tonight," she said hurriedly, then immediately recovered her composure. She no longer seemed to be there, her thoughts far away. As though she inhabited a universe that was gradually casting us out on the pretext of writing our story.

Breta poured herself wine. She savored the taste of the grapes, as though she had personally gone to the trellis and picked a cluster still warm from the afternoon sun.

She remembered her father's note. The only memory left her of that happy-go-lucky man, to whom she owed sperm and nothing else besides. In the note he had written, perhaps as a way of defining himself:

"It's a thankless life, and I'm taking my revenge on it by going on the bum. So to hell with all of you. There are no traps that can hold me. I'll gnaw right through every one of them, Vicente."

Death had sneaked up on him, not giving him time to draft a farewell letter to his daughter, whom he had never seen again after her first birthday. Without Breta's ever being able to find out whether, at least once, in the midst of the battle he had joined with Esperança, he had leaned over his daughter's cradle with the hopes that this last sight of his face would linger in Breta's memory.

She took another sip and offered a toast, aloud: "To the memory of that father, an unknown soldier. But who asked him to choose the swamplands of Mato Grosso to die in? And so, I repeat with him: To hell with all of you!"

The reading of the diary, in which she was again absorbed, was exhausting. It forced her to take notes, occasioned by Venâncio's verbal sensuality. So often immersed in endless emotion, just below the surface of words.

"Eulália hinted that I am taking too many trips in these last months.

'Is it necessary for you to know Brazil all that well? At the very time when the fate of Spain is being decided?' she said, with veiled gentleness.

Eulália has little idea that I'm lying. How many times, instead of taking off somewhere, I merely go down the seawall of the Praia do Flamengo to contemplate the foreign boats sailing by, their flags billowing in the wind. Carrying crews doing work in secret, like leaf-cutting ants. Hurriedly launching harpoons and casting nets into the sea, determined to haul into their holds those treasures and maps that have resisted the corrosion of salt water. The bottom of the sea lives on dead men. And the live ones feed on their remains.

Eulália knows so little about me! She knows nothing of the existence of my family. Nor does she know that, beginning with the first month of May of the war, my mother's depression grew even more severe. She had always been a melancholy woman. Her body seemed to be steeped in poverty and ignorance. Life weighed heavily upon her from the day of her birth. Her dresses, full of mends and patches, were evidence of this. And her hands, scraped raw from grubbing in the earth. My mother, in fact, could no longer put up with reality, which she knew only as something miserable and threatening.

How often she wept as she wrote me! I could tell because the paper was stained. I could almost hear her harsh, rough voice. Like her emotions.

That was when Mother, all of a sudden, begged me to be discreet when I spoke of the Spanish Civil War. She forbade me to reveal the news of this tragedy with the lightness of some mere passing emotion. Mother placed all her faith in immortal sentiments. Perhaps she was preparing me for the letter that would follow. In which she wrote: tears mean nothing. And then, two paragraphs later, she abruptly announced: Your father has disappeared. They say he was taken prisoner by the Nationalists, but I don't believe it. Why would they jail the body of a man grown old before his time, if the misery he lived in was already a prison?

Mother bemoaned the scarcity of food in those days. Even the potherbs were spindly when they came up. They turned their backs on people. But on the second page of the letter, she declared: Your father is indeed in prison, and not far from here. The person who told us that also said that, as punishment, he's slowly dying in solitary confinement these days. With nothing but rats and the stink of his own shit for company. It's a Francoist prison, with prisoners who have committed every sort of crime.

There are some there whose only crime was to curse the war, when they'd had too much to drink. We're hoping though that your father can escape, once they take him back to the main cell block. Because the bars there are flimsy and the jailers few in number. Almost all the men in the country are at the battlefronts now, enjoying the pleasure of killing off their neighbors and their enemies armed with rifles and bayonets.

In the month of December, in another letter, Mother added: Our race, son, has always loved the meadows, the mountains, scorching hot nights. Your own father would rather have died than be in a cell where there is no singing, no wine, no revelry. They say that in these months your father has taken to talking to himself so much that they roughed him up and beat him. And they also say that the more they thrashed him the more he sang. He took great satisfaction in humming away as though he were running a bayonet through his torturers' heart."

Venâncio's mother wrote him as though they were not separated by the Atlantic. And as though her son were her nearest neighbor, and thus up on what was happening on the other side of their common wall. Which saved her from having to pass on the cruel details. Telling him next to nothing, for example, about how his father had broken out of prison, in the middle of the winter, after having been subjected to rigorous punishment. Stripped of his clothes and flung naked into the prison yard. Exposed, thus, to the cold that penetrated his body through the joints, in full view of the guards and the other prisoners. All of them able, then, to see his thin, ugly thighs, his shamed penis, that modest appendage deprived now of passion and tenderness. A humiliation so painful that he had not hesitated to make his escape, ready to die in the rigor of winter or suffer even more severe punishment, should he recover.

"At the end of this letter, surely out of commiseration for her lonely son in America, Mother enjoined me to grieve to the depths of my soul, saying: Let us pray for your father, for if he hasn't died yet, it is only a matter of days. If he doesn't die of pneumonia, he will not escape his enemies, who will capture him again."

At times in the diary, Venâncio forgot what his father's fate had been. And what had happened to his family, which had split apart following the disappearance of its head. Beginning then to write about Andalusia, a region of rare lyrical intensity. His reason for this being to hymn the praises of poets and of *cante jondo*. Without at any time indicating the exact place where he had been born. Taking great pains to surround himself with a mystery indispensable to his understanding of the world. Thereby rejecting, with visible pride, any inquiry into the biographical details of his life.

But in the month of December Venâncio recorded in the diary, without further preamble, the probable death of his father. He suspected that he was no longer alive. He minutely examined the May and December letters, hoping to discover the truth.

The transcription of certain sections, some of them obscure, afforded him a glimpse of the family's despair during that long period. The reason, perhaps, why the facts did not always agree. Because the statements that were available to Venâncio conflicted. Though the voices of his mother and his brother and sister never faded or dissolved.

The family had no idea of the father's fate after his escape from prison. Till they received an official report to the effect that the man had not been located until the last day of that severe winter. The Guardia Civil had scoured the nearby mountains, the houses, the caves, finding not a single trace of his passage. Nor any remains of his body, torn to pieces and eaten by wolves. Animals prevalent in that area. Jealously devouring intestines, buttocks, breasts, human thighs with their sensitive canines. As though the whole pack of them had made a pact with the peasants to add to the cruel legends about them that had circulated for centuries and that all of Spain spread abroad.

The police finally gave up on his father. Certain that he would be found dead, at the bottom of a precipice or an abandoned well. Unless the Republicans, impelled by barbarous instincts, had taken that unfortunate creature, bearing strong signs of madness even before his capture, back to his cold dungeon. This act being aimed at keeping Franco and the Nationalists from making known what the vile and disrespectful Republic was capable of. In view of what they had done to that man, whose illness improved thanks only to an impious and perverse ideology, whose core could engender collective madness.

The report on his father, held to be insane, wounded Venâncio deeply. Night after night, he muffled his weeping in his pillow. And in order that Madruga, in the office, wouldn't notice his swollen eyes, he hid in the shade of the trees of the Passeio Público. Tormented by what he had inherited from his father, threatening him with insanity.

He feared at each instant that he would rupture the sensitive cords of his heart, succumbing to his father's stigma. Obliged now to consume his days in perpetual vigil, probing the advance of the insidious madness.

"Only now do I discover what I have inherited from my father, in the form of symptoms that move me to compunction and cause me to look upon humanity wild-eyed, my heart in tatters. Up until now, I had attributed this agony merely to the consequences of the civil war. And also to the chemical incompatibility that I have long felt with regard to Brazil and Spain. Since I do not form part of these clever nations. But was my father always a madman, as the Nationalists wish to make us believe? Or was his precarious equilibrium destroyed even before he escaped from prison? His madness stemming from the blows on the head, the tortures to which he was subjected for more than a year. Hence, in this unbalanced state, finding it better to expose himself to the winter cold, without clothes, than to go on coexisting with his torturers. He chose to go to his death. Certain that life, without dignity, offended him and the myrmidons at the same time. Having understood at this moment, through a supreme act of generosity, that to free his torturers of his presence was likewise to free them of guilt. For my father did not wish this crime to weigh upon humanity. A fault so apocalyptic that it could be redeemed only in this way."

From the window of the apartment on the Avenida Beira-Mar, on whose walls were projected the shadows of his disintegration, Venâncio stood gazing at the Bay of Guanabara, increasingly obsessed by the telescope. Through which he could reach the nineteenth century, in which useless lessons had been invested. The same lessons that had been responsible for the bankruptcy of his century. In the one century and in the other, he felt circumstances blunting his scruples, leaving him to drift helplessly.

With this painful prospect before him, it seemed to him that his mother's letters would never arrive. His mother, however, a woman of stern character, kept to the rules established between them to write to each other twice a year. She did not go back on this agreement even under pressure of heartbreaking emotional crises. Or when they lacked bread, having nothing but crumbs left. Come what might, she held out. She took up her pen to write only in the first week of May and December.

And it was not only food that was scarce now. His mother felt her life growing scantier. Her legs were getting stiff, her mouth was dry, her heart in anguish. In the mornings, everything was painful to her, beginning with the thought that the months were drawing near when she must fulfill her duty to write to her son, exiled in America.

To get this chore over with, she scribbled words, sad ones usually, without faith. She then went to the post office, with the letter and a peseta in hand. Haughtily, she deposited the coin on the counter, in exchange for a stamp bearing, before the advent of the Republic, the effigy of the king.

After the well-nigh endless wait, Venâncio received the December letter of the year 1942. Brought to his door by the postman, still protecting Venâncio's interests. That same week, González had invited Madruga and Eulália to dinner at his house. Without including Venâncio in the invitation. A fact that Madruga would not accept. He demanded that Venâncio be present at the meal. If his friend was left out, he would never sit down at González's table again.

"If it weren't for Venâncio, who would confirm the dreams Grandfather Xan taught me back in Sobreira? If Venâncio didn't take care of dreaming in my name, how would I have the time to earn these few miserable coins?"

After bending González's will, Madruga announced to Venâncio that they would all dine together. But with brusque gestures Venâncio refused the invitation.

"And may I ask why?"

"I'm very busy."

"Is it perhaps because of the letter that arrived for you this morning? Or do you think I didn't notice?"

Madruga took pleasure in hurting him, resenting his secretiveness. While at the same time his curiosity banished any feeling of pity for his friend.

Venâncio withstood Madruga's attack. Not giving him any information. Madruga knew nothing about him. He didn't even know if he had a family. Or who wrote to him in those years. So Venâncio made no mention to Madruga of his father's disappearance. Or conveyed to him the fear he felt at the approach of the months of May and December, ill-omened ones usually. His mother liable at any moment to confirm that they'd buried his father. Which might come, however, as a blessing to the whole family, free at last of that penance. Since endless misery should be punishment enough.

". . . I haven't died yet, son. God made me a strong woman. But all I want is to settle accounts with Him. I don't have the heart to go on living, what with all the cruelty there is here in Spain. This is no place for the living nowadays. Whoever wants to can live in my place, if they have the courage.

Maria is around all the time, keeping an eye on me. She and her husband. Seeing how feeble I am, she brings me a little weak coffee or a bran soup. Trying to force me back to health. The truth is that we're having a terrible time of it. It's only Maria's odd jobs and her husband's that keep us on our feet. And the money you send, which is taking months now to reach Spain.

As for that other son of mine, an ingrate, I've no news at all of him. Maybe he's afraid to share his poverty with us. And as for me, I don't know if I'll write to you again. This silence not meaning that I've died. Just that I don't feel like saying anything. I've no words to explain why I'm tired of living. Your father hasn't died yet, I'll tell you that right away. But it would be better if he had, so we could at least bury him with kind and gentle hands. Better for him and for us. He was a young man once, and good-looking, though none of my sons turned out to look like him. Even if all I remember of you is your face as a youngster. I've never laid eyes on the man you turned out to be. I've never asked you for a photo, expecting that you'd sense my curiosity and my heartache and send me one on your own.

It's only as the years have gone by that I've understood that your not wanting us to see your face as a grown man, with a beard and much older, meant that you had no intention of coming back to see us. You decreed our death, and we yours, especially that day when we saw you off in Vigo, on that freezing-cold morning. None of us went to the pier to say good-bye. We thought our parting would be easier that way. Can we have hurt you deeply because of that? Our race, after all, has continually been accused, for centuries now, of overdoing things when we weep, when we sing, when we dance. It was time to contain ourselves, to be, for the first time, as sober and responsible as northern peoples. We'd grown tired of being part of our own people, ever burning with passion, carrying things to extremes, being illogical, and thus depriving us of so many advantages. . . . Mother did not write in those words. But it was what she meant, using especially poignant words. I merely want to add this comment, out of respect for myself and for my own story. Since I fear that this diary will fall into enemy hands someday. But can these outpourings be of such value as to arouse the greed of enemies?"

At times, driven by the ebb and flow of events, Venâncio lost control of himself. Swiftly seeking shelter then amid the walls of the nineteenth century, where everything seemed more agreeable. Thus free, for a few moments, of the Spanish drama, whose tangled net of cruelty and bloodshed cast him to the bottom of his own heart, where he saw miasmas, seaweed, reptiles floating.

Certain phrases, without attribution, came spilling out all of a sudden. Despite Venâncio's scrupulous habit of citing within quotation marks. Breta found one of them particularly moving: "All of you are the beginning of my country."

Whose words could they be? Breta regretted that they were not her own. So as to send them to Madruga, along with a bouquet of flowers, as a token of gratitude. She owed her birth in this sun-drenched and proscribed America to him. A fact she would never get over.

Breta turned back to this phrase. She did not believe the words were Venâncio's or Madruga's. Both had come from a worn-out soil, from which nothing more would spring. Myths and an eagerness to flee the borders that hemmed them in had been all they had left.

She went on skimming through the pages of the diary, skipping a number of them altogether. She would soon find out. Finally, in the middle of the dramatic story of Venâncio's father, she came upon what she was looking for.

"Madruga got up from the table before the meal was over. He has always acted on impulse. Toward family especially. At such times, the deep wrinkles that furrowed his face betrayed both his arrogance and his grave concern.

'What was that you said?' He made a move toward Esperança, on her feet now.

I noted Madruga's caution. His daughter was unpredictable. She might very well accuse him of being neglectful or indifferent if she found him distracted or if he left the room without spending time with the family. Anything served her as a pretext to do battle with Madruga.

With equal caution and calculation, Esperança moved toward her father. Keeping in the shadow of his imposing figure. In the midst of this prudent skirmish, she tossed her long hair falling loose about her shoulders. She had an acid, intense beauty. Our eyes burned as we looked at her. She was not yet fifteen. But already she had parted the curtain to expose to our view a vast, threatening horizon filled with intimations of her outrageous conduct to come.

'All of you are the beginning of my country,' she repeated, in a firm voice.

Madruga wavered, at once deeply touched and caught off his guard. Mistrusting his daughter's intentions. She was out to extort something from him. Perhaps to trap him.

'Have you forgotten that Brazil began four hundred years ago?'

'As far as I'm concerned, it didn't begin till you arrived, father. When you got off the ship at the Praça Mauá. So today Brazil is only twenty-five years old.'

Esperança blinked her eyes, slowly and seductively. As though we were the clear mirror in which she was looking at herself.

Madruga sensed the danger. His daughter's hunger for freedom threatening him, prowling about the house.

'Don't you think that a country as young as that deserves total independence? The right to walk out the door as often as it pleases, to go live in the open?'

Esperança appreciated symbols. Obviously intending to use them as a weapon against her father. He saw what she was up to. He must answer in kind. Otherwise, in just a few days' time, his daughter would ask for the key to the house. Refuse to stay in her room. All in the name of an immortal youth.

'Unfortunately youth is wrong more often than it's right. It's foolish by nature. It's far worse when it's a question of a country. A young country has no laws or solid institutions. Just a useless vitality. So it ends up being curbed through an excessive authoritarianism, simply to avoid chaos. And there you are, talking as if a wild and unruly country was something praiseworthy. Is that what you want?'

Esperança faced up to her father with spirit. She was never afraid of him. 'Europe is old, father. And Brazil runs the risk of growing old without ever having been young. All I want is a land where there's room for invention, for the imaginary. What's the use of coming into the world if it's merely to be the slave of countless laws, decrees, instructions, social conventions? If it's impossible to find even one place to have whatever adventures you please! A person has to be an adventurer, father.'

'You don't know what you're saying, Esperança. You know nothing of the practical advantages of a political regime, actively using its powers to the fullest. And doing exactly the right thing. That's what a mature Country means. Don't you realize that there are countries that have a basic constitution that's more than a thousand years old?'

'How awful, father. Countries like that aren't for me. I don't want to depend on compasses as absolutely precise and inflexible as that to guide my footsteps. I prefer to follow the stars, and rough calculations. Moreover, even the saints had a sense of adventure. God loves adventurers. Just ask Mother if it's possible to win sainthood without passion, without the spirit of adventure!'

Esperança flung Eulália's name in her father's face to defy him, to upset him even more. So that Madruga would summon Eulália. And have her enter the fray with the same fervor she devoted to her favorite saints. To whom she rendered humble tribute before the altar each day.

'Go on, father, ask Mother,' Esperança said incisively."

Venâncio unexpectedly broke off the episode. Leaving Esperança's question hanging in the air. Breta quickly leafed through the following pages. Anxious to discover Madruga's reaction. A silence concerning the subject hovered over the diary. Nowhere, moreover, did she find any further reference to Esperança. While Madruga's and Eulália's names were mentioned more and more frequently, Esperança's had disappeared, had simply been banished from the diary. She preferred to think that Venâncio, as scrupulous as always, had regretted including Esperança in his account without her express permission.

This way of going about writing frustrated Breta. Even knowing that the diary represented a therapy for Venâncio. And that he had kept it with no concern for its literary effect. She sensed, however, that she would soon find what she was looking for in the events that followed. Since Venâncio, freer of fear, of the boiling wake left by certain rare events, now returned to that same letter from his mother, though he did not transcribe it in its entirety.

The diary, moreover, was becoming more concrete, as he described the misery of those years. Venâncio emphasizing that his family had in no way grown mean-spirited amid all the wretchedness of the time. There was even evidence that compassion was still alive in the hearts of his mother, her daughter Maria, and her son-in-law.

His mother and Maria, indeed, had devoted their free time to collecting their neighbors' table scraps, usually fed to the pigs. With these leftovers, his mother made a garbage soup, immediately taken to the asylum, the walls of which adjoined the house that they were now living in, following the disappearance of his father.

Though his mother stirred the soup in the pot, and thought of man's fate as she breathed in that aroma, she shied away from taking it to the asylum. She could not bear the sight of the mental patients wandering about the yard, the majority of them doomed to die in less than a year.

Maria respected her mother's decision. She sensed her fear that suddenly, without warning, a grave break with reality might happen to her as well. In those days, after all, madness was tracking the entire community. And were this to occur, her mother would be forced to end her days in that musty house, which, when the wind blew from that direction, sent a disgusting smell their way.

Maria, however, on being entrusted with this task, was pleased to note the inmates' gratitude for her presence, despite their glassy eyes and their aimless wanderings about the yard. On returning home, Maria seemed exhilarated. She spoke of them as persons who were part of the family.

As a protest against such disrespectful behavior, the mother bared her shriveled toothless gums to her daughter. If she had had her way, she would already have fled the house and life at one and the same time. She did not dare ask Venâncio to increase his quota of sacrifice. Her son in America depriving himself of everything so as to support his father. It was not his fault if Spain, in a fit of madness, murdered its best men. In the streets and in bed, the survivors had faces spattered with blood and shame. In those days it was indecent to be alive. It represented an act of cowardice and connivance with fascism. One was morally obligated to cross the country's borders and never return to Spain.

Tuesday was the day the mother collected potatoes at the neighbors'. She cooked them with the skins on, urging her daughter to take them to the asylum while they were still hot. So that the inmates would have a festive lunch. According to Maria's description, they clung to each other and dragged themselves about the courtyard, as though they sensed their own degradation. All of them in tatters, their faces wrinkled, their eyes hard as oak wood, and given to tears.

"... suddenly Maria burst into the house shouting. She ranted and raved, no one being able to control her. While out in the street she had already begun ripping off the kerchief she ordinarily wore to hide her hair. She had also aged during this period. What was more, the entire nation had.

The husband, hurriedly summoned, fell to weeping and wailing.

'Another one in the family who's gone mad. This one doesn't even have the excuse of having been tortured.'

For that was precisely what my son-in-law said, wanting to weigh me down with yet another burden. I saw exactly what he was up to. And that's why I ask: When will our differences with the world end? When will we have at least a moment's repose, son? Time to get a little meat on our bones and peace for our souls!

Maria seemed furious. She beat her fists against the wall, screaming and shouting.

'I can't bear life anymore, mother. I can't bear any more, I swear.'

Her husband, the neighbors, and I insisted that she tell us the truth. Wanting her despair to have stemmed from a concrete fact. She refused to believe that madness had taken possession of her as an inheritance from her father. Had her father really gone mad before he died?

Calmer now, Maria accepted the warm milk they poured down her throat. Somebody had contributed a bit of sugar, to quiet her down. Only then did she add:

'If you're so anxious to find out what happened, go to hell and leave me in peace.'

It was then that Maria's husband . . ."

With his mother's letter in his pocket, Venâncio wandered about the city once again. Wanting to disappear, to pretend to be off on a trip. Not to see Eulália. Or even Madruga, who observed him closely, trying to detect signs of grief in him. To trap him into revealing how many members of the family he had lost in the war.

Venâncio could not bear Madruga's affluence as Spain was going up in flames. And had Brazil, protected by distance, escaped the Spanish Civil War? Wasn't Brazil a vulnerable character, sacrificed on the altar of greed and injustice?

He had a feeling that Eulália was reprimanding her husband. "Why are you neglecting Venâncio? Can't you see he doesn't need himself as much as he needs us?

"And who hasn't aged in these years, Eulália! Which of us hasn't suffered, hasn't grown uglier? What to say of Venâncio, a man of dogged pride!" This from Madruga, refusing to heed his wife's admonitions.

On the Passeio Público, Venâncio fingered his mother's letter in his pocket. He then went back to the nineteenth century, even without the aid of the spyglass. This time visiting Valongo, with Eulália. But indignant at blacks being sold at public auction. Despite his being temporarily immersed in that century, his mother pursued him even there. Despite her not remembering his face. He hadn't seen her since he was thirteen. Yet the woman imperiously demanded tears from her son. The reason why, in her letters, she provided him with details that would keep him from being happy for a single moment. Venâncio did not have the right to suffer less than they, back in Spain. Even his sister looked like an old woman now! The husband keeping her in his bed only as an act of mercy and out of a fear of loneliness. In Spain, people nowadays didn't fuck the way they once had.

"Mother set the mug of water down on the table. She too helped her daughter, her eyes staring into space.

'What's happened to Maria? Has she gone altogether mad?' the husband asked, rebelling against fate. Life threatening him with yet another burden, on top of the run of bad luck he'd already had.

'He was her father,' someone said.

'What do you mean, her father? Don't you know that Maria's father died before the end of the war? We buried him ourselves, as quickly as we could. With no time to provide him with a gravestone with his name and date of birth,' the husband said, wanting the neighbors assembled in the room to give him a hearing.

The neighbors were not convinced. Hunger had whetted their tragic instincts. Bloodshed and intrigues conjoined had not only aroused them but also provided them with abundant evidence of life. Indifferent to the man's remarks, they stampeded off to the asylum close by. And immediately, confronted by the guards, they felt themselves to be momentarily indestructible. Their voices were thorns in their throats.

'What father are you talking about? Who is this man? Bring out the madmen, we want to see them,' the neighbors shouted, followed by Maria's husband, holding them back.

'Come on, bring out the ones who can still walk. The only ones we'll excuse are the ones who are going to die during the night.'

Clinging to the bars of the gate, men and women alike seemed to be elated at a drama that took their breath away. They went wild, frantically scratching their chests, their testicles, their buttocks now. The one thing they did not want was for the unburied to be handed over to them out of a spirit of revenge.

The director came to the gate, with an escort of nurses. He was wearing a cavalry uniform and impeccably polished boots. His gaze almost failed to register the ugly crowd in rags, mingling with the inmates. With a mere gesture, he reduced them to silence.

'At the first scream, I'll hand you over to the Guardia Civil. I won't allow riots and demonstrations in a public institution, in Generalissimo Franco's charge.' He did not raise his voice, being certain that he could make himself heard.

All of them fell back, a long way, in utter terror. Those soldiers with their three-cornered hats, khaki uniforms, black capes, had death in their hands and in their eyes. Anyone who gazed upon them had best prepare to die. Left in their trail were dead and maimed. It was they who had dragged García Lorca up to the mountains destined to be his Calvary. Rumor had it that they had shot him in the ass three times. A sodomite must get his in the place where he betrayed society, the gunslingers of the Guardia Civil muttered, with boundless hunger for moral justice.

The director, in a monotonous voice, now prescribed rules of conduct that were to apply both to the asylum and the city. Without such rules a country ran the risk of moral decadence, of enslavement by the Red Doctrine. Only in this way would the new political order established by Francoism be maintained, irrepressible, incoercible.

'Those of you who have a madman at home, don't be frightened. You need only denounce him or bring him directly to me. And don't listen to what your heart tells you. It was our hearts that gave out on us as we fought the Republican advances. We came close to turning Spain into a Communist country. Don't forget that we must purge Spain. There are more madmen in our country than we suppose. And beneath their cloak of madness, they're nothing but traitors and counterrevolutionaries. Though they look healthy enough, they are the living debris of what remains of the nefarious passage of the Republicans among us. Franco named me to free you of these people. The sole aim of the new regime is to purify the nation, to preserve Christian dignity. Now tell me what happened.'

Beret in hand, Maria's husband respectfully stepped forward.

'My wife often visits the asylum, sir. She is very charitable. And her name is Maria. Except that today she came home yelling and screaming and tearing her hair, as is the habit of country people and of our race. Without a demonstration of this sort meaning any disrespect toward the authorities. Our grief is not sober and solemn, as is the case with you gentlemen. That's why they scattered us far and wide in the past, because of all the uproar we caused. A judicious measure, moreover. For if you gentlemen had not taken us by the hand and taught us, where would we be now? Up until the time of Carlos III, all we knew of life were intense, riotous feelings. But, as I was telling you, sir, it was only because my wife started screaming that the neighbors were convinced that Maria's father was confined here, when the truth is that my father-in-law has long been dead and carefully buried.'

The director consulted with the inspectors in a low voice. The matter having aroused his interest, he looked like a pointer catching the scent of Republicans.

'We're going to solve this mystery. We may have a political case on our hands. Someone who's been declared dead so as to escape being condemned. But who has swelled the ranks of the enemies of Franco Spain.'

Paco, a nurse whom the director trusted implicitly, approached. Skinny, with prominent cheekbones, his hooked nose almost resting on his lips.

'This afternoon I brought Number Five out to the yard for a walk. He hadn't seen the sun for months. I thought it would do him good. We walked about slowly, till we reached the gate at the entrance. Through which a woman came, carrying an oil drum. The minute she saw us, she dropped the whole thing on the ground. It had potatoes in it, and they got covered with dirt. And she began to scream, My father, my father, with her face contorted and her body all hunched over, almost squatting. I couldn't make her shut up. Control the patient and her at the same time. The guard came to give me a hand. When she saw him, she went off sobbing, not even bothering to pick the potatoes up. But at no time did Number Five give any sign that he recognized her. He just glanced at her, returning immediately to the center of himself, to his deep, dark circles where he gives you the idea he's lived forever. He's never going to come out of there, sir, out of that hole, full of circles and slime. God's gotten hold of that one forever. Maybe because he owed God some sort of penance. The man's record is a total blank. It doesn't give his name or where he came from. We don't know if he's a Nationalist or a Republican. If he fought for us or against us, during the war. And we also don't know whether this might be a case of feeding an enemy. But we're forced now to put up with him till the end. Even though that end is near, sir.'

And he gave the director a winning smile. Slowly rubbing his hands together, thereby promising him to carry out his job with relentless efficiency.

After the group dispersed, my mother was convinced she had her husband as a neighbor. He was still alive, though in a lamentable state. Affected by his loss of reason. Dementia had overcome him for good. And according to Maria, he was so thin you could see his bones, without an X ray. Not having died, perhaps, only because of the few potatoes and bread crumbs his wife had taken it upon herself to send to the asylum.

'Up till now my husband has owed his life to us. And God, for his part, has tried to punish us by this terrible revelation. We were the ones who helped feed those poor unfortunates, all of them sons of a wretched country. What in heaven's name is left of Spain? Do we have one man who's still alive? Or was it only cowards, madmen, and kings buried in the royal crypts who were spared?"'

As the diary went on, certain quotations in Galician stood out. Through Eulália's influence, surely, since she never abandoned the task of spreading that minority culture for the sake of which she had been prepared to memorize the epic achievements of Galicia. From the time she was a little girl, she heard Dom Miguel reciting centuries-old poems to her. Thus implanting in his daughter ballads that risked disappearing from human voices.

"'In short, Eulália, they will translate our songs and ballads into Castilian and we will never again call them to mind. So let us hasten to recite: *'sedíame eu na ermida de San Simón / e cercáronmi as ondas, que grandes son; / eu atendendo o meu amigo . . . !'*

'Is it a song of disdain or of love?' Eulália asked her father, being unable in the beginning to tell the one from the other.

'Non, é cantiga de amigo, a perfección lírica en finxida boca de enamorada. Escoitade: "Tardei, mia madre, na fría fontana, / Cervos do monte volvían a augua."'"

Venâncio had grown passionately fond of the Galician lyric poets. Pero Meogo, Don Denís de Portugal, Martín Codax, Mendiño. As meanwhile he wondered who, in Brazil, denounced poverty and encouraged dreaming. Castro Alves, surely, following a tradition of heartfelt, spirited, epic writing. Though the lyric poets attracted him, he also was critical of their individualistic tendencies, their incessant homage to love. Forgetting misery, countries torn apart, blood flowing down the sewers.

Back home again, after his sleepless night in the Passeio Público, Venâncio transcribed into the diary: "Despite her son-in-law's pleas not to make such a dangerous visit, my mother refused to give up the idea. In anguish, she wanted to see my father, who would die in the next few days according to what Paco the nurse reported. Moreover, she could see no immediate danger, since her husband would surely not recognize her.

'We'll be careful. Nobody must know that we were Republicans,' Maria said, siding with her mother.

'Yet another reason not to go. If they discover that the old man escaped from prison, they'll kill him before death comes for him. And end up nabbing all of us.'

Visibly frightened, the son-in-law pointed out the consequences if they went ahead as they planned.

'We're going anyway. Father's madness will protect us. But if you're afraid, don't wait for us. You're a free man. You can flee this house if you choose.'

Mother ached all over just thinking about seeing that first and only man ever to take her to bed, where in the beginning they had joyously made love, till affection turned to sadness. She accepted the warm milk brought by her neighbor, a woman ever-generous in tragic moments. She dressed for the visit with great care, as though she were going off to meet her sweetheart. And slowly walked the short distance between the house and the asylum, leaning on her daughter's arm.

The guard stopped them at the gate. It was not a visiting day. They persisted, claiming they were there at the behest of the director, who was interested in the fate of Number 5. Because the women had the idea that he might be a former neighbor of theirs, said by his family to have disappeared. And whose presence in the asylum, the evening before, had caused the daughter, overcome by emotion, to start screaming, to call him father, to invoke the image of her own father, buried years before in a distant city, in a distressing ceremony, of which the two women retained a painful memory.

The guard let them past, going off immediately to arrange to have the patient brought to them. The mother, deeply upset, clung to the cross on her breast, seeking to summon the necessary strength to see her husband face-to-face. She then had recourse to her ancestral gods, preserved in brine in the depths of her heart, beseeching them to enable her to endure this trial without screaming or fainting or giving way to other excesses of emotion. And as she prayed, the man arrived on the scene, practically dragged bodily by Paco the nurse. With trembling hands, he shielded his eyes, barely able to bear the light of day. Any sort of life hurt him. Reality had long since expelled him from its center of agony.

Standing there before the two women, the man paid particular attention to the mother. She saw the look in his eyes and controlled her own feelings. She did not want to bring disgrace upon the family by allowing herself a loving gesture. Nor did she have the right to embrace the man with whom she had slept for so many years, whose body she knew as well as she knew her own when she washed herself in the tin basin.

The man gave no signs of recognizing them. Or else, perceiving the danger weighing heavily on their shoulders, he repressed his own emotion. Or can he have disguised his own feelings simply to safeguard the last breath of life still left him? Dispirited, lost, did he nonetheless cling to life? That entire family being disposed to invent a dramatic lie to shield its existence, wanting to extend it for a few months more. They did not want to die, despite extreme privation, cold, and disillusionment.

'Can we bring this poor man the clothes we still have that belonged to my husband, who died in his trench defending the fatherland against Communists?'

Having uttered these words, Mother wanted to die. Ashamed of committing such villainies. She had thrown everything away, once and for all, even the world that the Republicans had promised her. She had behaved toward her husband exactly as Peter had toward Christ. They were all traitors. And able no longer to bear the human condition, she began to weep convulsively, beneath the worried gaze of the guard, the nurse, and Maria. Perceiving the danger, however, she flung herself into her daughter's arms.

'I'm so sorry, Maria. He could have been my husband. I'm also thinking of the poor woman who is weeping for this man, not knowing where he is.'

The more my mother pressed her daughter to her bosom, the more she felt that she was embracing her husband. That dull-eyed man at her side, who five years before had left her bed and been presumed dead. He, however, remained unmoved by his wife's grief. Being not at all attuned to so many human tribulations, he was satisfied to transport his body, consumed by insanity, from one corner of the world to another. The wrinkles and marks that pitted his face and extended down his neck were no doubt lodged everywhere in his body. He could not have many days left to live. Perhaps because he sensed that the end was near, the man drew closer to the women. His body gave off a smell of urine and mold. Standing next to them, he tapped them lightly on the shoulder. As though thanking them for the trouble they had taken to come there.

And he whispered, so that only they could hear: 'There is someone who has left, never to return. We'll miss him forever. But who knows? Perhaps a stranger will tell you his story, once you sit down round the table to listen to him!'

Only then did he leave, with tiny footsteps, not asking permission of the nurse, who followed him immediately."

At this stage in the diary, the sentences became concrete. Venâncio had abandoned the nineteenth century for good, and turned to his father.

His handwriting was small, nervous, and hurried now. Making reading difficult. Breta grew tired. She threw the sheet off and went to the window. It was almost dawn. She ached all over. She returned to the middle of the room, next to the chest of drawers. She opened a drawer, flinging the diary inside. She felt no need to consult it in the next few days. Though she would certainly go to it in the years to come. The diary was part of her life now.

In the kitchen, she made herself fresh coffee. The aroma it gave off was agreeable. As were the words with which Venâncio had ended his testimony. Shortly before handing the diary over to Eulália and putting himself in the care of the Spanish Benefit Society.

". . . Madruga's visit was unexpected. He came without being invited. And did not hesitate to speak his mind about the state of my psyche, in his opinion precarious. After he had left, I decided to keep his prophecies from coming true. By seeking hospital treatment. Simply because I don't want to cause Eulália distress. So I'll go visit them this Sunday. And sitting in my usual chair, I'll eat what they offer me. Madruga's table is always well laden. He pulls his guests' souls in through food.

Little Tobias, sitting beside me, will ask questions. I suspect that in the future he will help me to die, clinging to my hand.

It's best that everything end this way. Tonight I will also seal this diary for good. I am thinking of entrusting it to the care of Eulália, a kind custodian.

As for my mother, she will never write me again. She too sealed her life. For the good of all of us. This way I shall never again suffer the bouts of fear that the months of May and December brought. She and Maria have bidden me farewell. They intend to leave for a distant village, far from everything. They could not bear to stay there in that house and hear the laments of the mad in the asylum next door. Because amid all the cries coming from there they couldn't tell which of them came from my father. Perhaps forcing himself to talk back and forth with them through the moldy walls.

After coming to this decision, they were never to see my father again or have any news of him. They too needed to look for ways to live out the rest of their days and make arrangements for their coming death. Especially since they were still dreaming of a garden, with hens scratching about in the yard. Maria's husband was preparing to bury his clumsy hands in the earth and speed up the germination of the corn and potatoes. And this expectation served them as consolation to enable them to confront the rigors of different whereabouts and new neighbors. Best, then, to say good-bye for good to the son, now settled in Brazil. If in all those years Venâncio had not wanted to come back for a visit, he doubtless had good reasons.

Eulália will have the book tomorrow, before dinner. As darkness falls,

I will go to the hospital. One thing is certain: Madruga must not be able to read these pages. The diary is unpretentious, but impenetrable. But perhaps another question is appropriate here: Have I succumbed to vanity by setting down these notes? Or do I simply want Eulália to take notice of me?"

I arrive in Leblon as usual. I am wearing a mask and am not observed. Madruga and Venâncio are occupying their respective easy chairs. After Eulália's death, Venâncio stayed on at the house. Nobody wants him to go back to his place on the outskirts of the city, leaving Madruga alone. Both are acting in common accord and talk less and less. Madruga accepted my kiss, but avoided my eye. He is waiting for me to make the first move. He is wary of my present strength. And is afraid to yield to my new demands.

Madruga does not mention Esperança's box. He prefers to ignore the probable treasure buried inside, thanks to Eulália's zeal. Grandmother left us quietly, without making a great show of it, a week later than the time she had stipulated.

Madruga points to a high-backed chair. He wants to have me in front of him. To see his aquiline profile, I will have to move to a different place. His eyes follow me. My voice gives no hint that I am the possessor of Esperança's box and Venâncio's diary. This is a matter of indifference to Venâncio. He trusts our agreement that I will keep the diary out of Tobias's hands. He knows nothing about it. He would surely feel betrayed and rejected by his godfather if he found out.

I am the only one to know what is in Esperança's box. The modesty with which Eulália went about collecting objects, papers, photos, and dried flowers in particular. She did not want to carry things too far, however. So that Esperança's life would not weigh too heavily on her heirs. During the night, I fondled the objects. Without names or definite origins.

Human life had turned into as great an enigma as inanimate objects. Esperança's sole remains were myself and the box. Nothing else was left of her. The flowers especially fascinated me. I have no idea where they could have been gathered. In Sobreira, by Grandmother, or in São Lourenço, one of Esperança's mythical realms? Esperança's delicate, tapered hands had personally gathered some of them. Others had been contributed by Eulália, to please her daughter, forever observing life amid discord and flights of passion. That daughter gave proof of a dark and alarming life of the senses.

Wherever I turn, traces of my mother haunt me. A strange one, this family of Madruga's and Eulália's. Immediately after leaving Galicia behind, both of them took great pains to collect evidence that they had in fact arrived in Brazil. They lived nowhere else but there. Hence their children should appreciate what there was in their home, signs of the new continent, brimming with vitality.

A young girl still, Esperança listened to her mother's sad voice, telling her about Brazil. Eulália being determined to retain the images of a country that seemed to escape their grasp simply because they had arrived there less than twenty years before. Unlike Madruga, who, being an optimist, embellished the house with concrete objects, multiplying at the same rhythm as his fortune. Eager to prove to them that Brazil was no mere abstraction, a Portuguese invention, pure and simple. And he had such firm confidence in the future that he had amassed bricks, walls, roofs on that sun-drenched shore. He'd even bought a splendid burial vault in São João Batista Cemetery, with room enough for the entire family.

"What's wrong, Breta?" her grandfather asked, overshadowed by her presence.

"Nothing. Tired, that's all."

Madruga's cross-examinations would go on as long as he had time left. "Ever since Eulália died, it seems as though everybody in this house is lying," he said, speaking in a falsely casual tone of voice.

Venâncio sat listening to him. As the afternoon drew to a close, they exchanged a few words. And consumed a few more drops of wine as well.

"Lying doesn't do anyone any harm, grandfather."

"That's what I think. I've lied so much myself that I no longer know when I'm telling the truth. Do you have any way of knowing?"

I went to the window. Ever since I was little, whenever I've felt restless, I've glued my face to the glass, distorting my features, my nose especially, as I looked out at the garden. The trees in particular fascinated me. How long had they lived among us? This time, however, the sight of the garden failed to calm me. Everything was suffocating, it seemed to me. I did not see myself as having the right to ask Grandfather for explanations. To ruin his last weeks of life. His last two years. I would never disown him, for reasons known or unknown to me. I ought not allow the memory of Esperança to deter me from fulfilling my keen desire to love Grandfather, to understand his miseries.

"Tell me, Breta, is love able to forgive because it loves or because it has forgotten?" Miguel said recently, clearly referring to Esperança. He too had punished his sister. Out of love, jealousy, spite? Who could say?

A heavy hand touched my shoulder. I thought it might be Tobias, who was in the habit of coming at that hour to visit the two old men. I turned around cautiously, expecting to find a strange face confronting me. What I saw was a tall, imposing Madruga, as though he were standing on a platform. His blue eyes had a bright youthful gleam in them.

"If only I knew what there is in Esperança's box!" he said hurriedly, immediately averting his face. The second time in twenty-five years that he had uttered his daughter's name. And because he had at last retrieved that resounding, once beloved name, he looked at me again, ready to repeat it in measured tones.

"Esperança, Esperança, my daughter, where are you?"

I feared for that man's life. I hastened to save him. As though I were Esperança, I leaned my head on his frail breast. He was no longer the strong man he had once been. He had nonetheless forced himself to go meet a granddaughter who was threatening to run away. Fearing he'd lose me even before death punished him.

"Stay with me always, I beg you," he also said.

Now that Eulália had died and he was obliged to live with the doubts engendered by Venâncio's diary and Esperança's box, Madruga seemed less proud. For a few moments I was tempted to hurt him. I had reason enough. Esperança forced me to make a fist so as to push him away. To what lengths would Esperança's memory go in pursuit of her plan to attack the old man whom she called father? Wherever she might be, would she be pleased if her daughter assumed the role of avengeress?

There before me, Madruga appeared to be reconstructing, despite the years that had gone by, the moments of a morning when Eulália had left him very early. She had dressed hurriedly, without addressing a single word to him. She had been awakened by Odete by means of signals, taps on the door of the room, which only she heard and understood.

"If you're not going to Mass, Eulália, then where are you going?" Madruga was aware of a sense of urgency, his wife trying to exclude him from her secrets.

"God is waiting for me at the usual hour." So saying, Eulália stole out of the room.

His wife was lying to him so tactfully that he had no desire to follow her. Invading each other's territory had never been their way. Despite their living under the same roof and their having come to America together, their individual spaces were marked off by a wooden partition.

Out of sorts with Eulália, Madruga summoned Miguel to his office.

"What's up, father?" Miguel said, confronting a stern-faced Madruga.

"That's what I want to know. What's been going on in this house?"

"Mine or yours?"

"As long as I'm alive, there will be only one house. Mine, to whose rule you and your children are subject. What's happened to my family?"

"It's still alive," Miguel said caustically, at the risk of putting his father in an even worse mood.

To Miguel's surprise, there was no reaction from Madruga. As though his father wanted to extract his mysteries, introduce himself into his heart, on the pretext of restoring law and order in the family. It had been a long time since his father had asked him questions revolving round the subject of the house.

"And where is Mother?" Miguel said.

Weary of these evasions, Madruga did not answer. Instead he went back home. There he found Eulália, who had changed her clothes. She gave him a smile, her usual affable self. Unlike Odete, whose pallor was a certain sign that Eulália was upset. Eulália accepted her husband's prying into her affairs. He nonetheless did not question her. His pride did not permit him to extort information from his wife.

At the lunch table, they all chewed in silence. But Madruga, finding the food too heavily salted, refused the dishes offered, contenting himself with thick slices of Minas cheese. Eulália did not defend him. Immediately threafter he excused himself and left the table. His tiredness allowed him not to stand on ceremony. He needed to rest by himself in his room.

To calm his wife's anxieties, Madruga claimed he was in a hurry to get to the office. He had a heavy day ahead. He wouldn't be back till dinnertime. Eulália noted that he too was hiding the truth.

She allowed herself to remain in her suite, listening to Odete repeat, several times, in the same nervous tone of voice, the story that she had told her very early that morning, as she passed on to her the message from Esperança, who wanted desperately to speak with her. The reason for their having left in such a hurry. But Esperança was not home when they arrived, nor did she turn up later, though they waited till noon.

"I haven't spoken to you of this meeting before, Dona Eulália, because the two of them, father and daughter, looked at each other with such bitterness that I was afraid. It was the first time I had ever seen a father and daughter fight like that, before my very eyes. And the eyes of anyone else looking on."

Eulália nodded, her emotions divided between Odete's words and the fear that they inspired in her.

"Let us go back to Esperança's again. To find out what's happening. I need to see my daughter at close hand. I'm so afraid, Odete! A fear I can't explain."

Esperança received her mother in tears. "You've finally come, mother. I didn't want to upset you. But you must know that Father is my enemy. As are Miguel, Bento. Who else in this family ought I to accuse of being my torturer?"

"What really happened, Esperança? Tell me, daughter."

Eulália allowed her daughter to take her to her bedroom. She noted, deeply touched, the small objects on her night table. The books, the medicine, the photograph of Breta.

"And to think that even my daughter's name was meant to move Father's heart. Breta. From Brittany, mother. One of the last territories of the Celts. And all for nothing. He never sent me a single word through you, to lead me to believe that he might at least regard his granddaughter with respect. And for that very reason want to meet her! What right does he have to feel so indestructible, so far above the powers of this earth? Am I obliged, then, to punish him, to teach him a lesson, once and for all?"

Esperança flung herself on the bed, hiding her face in the pillow. Hovering at her side, her mother embraced her, taking her in her arms as she had never in her life embraced Madruga. He was the man who came to her when he desired her. The two of them shy and retiring in their love play. In the very first gestures above all. Because Madruga was afraid of offending this wife of his, Dom Miguel's daughter, so partial to lyric poetry, to stories that, once her father had embarked upon them, seemed endless.

"Madruga is a generous man, daughter. And his feelings are still hurt, even today. He doesn't seem to understand other people's failings. Perhaps because he came to America when he was still just a youngster, with no fear in his soul. Or if he was afraid, he hid it well. I've never seen that man back down. Or his resolve weaken. I suspect he's made a pact with himself, promised himself that we'd never see his frailties. But there'll come a day when he'll realize his mistakes."

"It'll be too late by then, mother. I'll have punished him severely, and beaten my pillow with my fist."

"What do you mean by that, Esperança? Speak to your mother. I'm here beside you."

"Poor Mother! Didn't you too abandon your children? Didn't you exchange us for God?"

Filled with remorse, Esperança clasped her in her arms. She felt how frail the woman was. Her mother was growing thinner and thinner, with white hair that she did not tint. Wanting visible marks of time when she looked in the mirror. Thus anticipating, through her own ruin, the timeless journey that she was one day destined to make. If Dom Miguel had died with courageous unconcern, having carefully arranged to do so, she would act with equal forethought.

"We will all meet again someday, daughter, I am certain of that."

Lost in thought, Esperança did not hear her.

"Miguel is more honest at least. He glides along the walls of buildings like a snake, hoping to catch sight of me. Sometimes he sits cooped up in his car, watching me as I walk by. He doesn't dare speak to me, because I immediately turn my back on him. I pretend I don't know him. To tell the truth, he's a cowardly male who didn't help me when I needed it most. Even though he was the brother I loved the best."

"Don't be unfair to him. Miguel would do anything for you."

"That's not true, mother. He helps me, the way you do. He sends me presents. He always knows where I'm working; he tails me. But he's never sent me words of affection at the right time. It's as though Miguel had my letter of emancipation in his pocket, and won't let go of it, out of a perverse intent to keep me dependent on him. He's a colonizer and a pirate, a buc-caneer. And he hates women, mother."

On her feet once more, she headed toward the living room, rejecting Eulália's fond caresses. She didn't like herself when she was tender and lovable. Life had made her tough.

"And where is Breta?"

"In school, happily. I need to be alone. I don't have anyone I can talk to or ask for a helping hand. Miguel only toots his horn at my door during the night to remind me he's checking up on me. He's not like Father, who finally came to me. When I saw him, my heart went off like a gun. I thought he was going to take me in his arms."

"Madruga's been to your house?" Eulália was surprised at a version contrary to Odete's.

"No, he'd never come here. He didn't want to take the risk. Not know-ing who he might find in my house. Even today, if he had his way, I'd wear a veil and tunic and live a cloistered life. It was in the square. Breta and Odete were with me. Didn't Odete tell you?"

"She mentioned it to me only today. Up till then I didn't know a thing about it," Eulália said, uneasy at the direction the conversation was taking.

"It happened just last week. The day Odete came to bring me the clothes you gave me. He approached me warily, hesitantly, but I noticed immediately how hard his face was. He's aged a great deal in this time of separation. He seems a different man, a stranger to me. There was nobody I could ask to send me a photo of Madruga in those years, as proof that my leaving had been a severe punishment for him. That might have given me great pleasure."

For Eulália it was like staggering down a hill to a quagmire from which she'd escaped thanks solely to family life, which safeguarded her from the passions. Her deep distress, in turn, made it almost impossible to discern her exact words.

"Please, Esperança, don't speak of your father that way. What good are all this hurtfulness and resentment?"

She moved closer to her daughter in an effort to keep her from vent-ing her feelings, to change the subject.

"And why not speak of him? If I don't speak of you who were my torturers, of whom will I ever speak? Who knows you better than I? Be-cause I want you to know, mother, that he came to the square without so much as looking at Breta, who was playing a short distance away. And he didn't even offer me his hand. Perhaps, for imperceptible seconds, his eyes were pitying. He then drew himself up to his full height, because pride and his overbearing nature have always gotten the better of him. Once again he had a fortune in his pocket, in his eyes, in his head. He immediately demanded that I beg his forgiveness, after all the years that had gone by. Never, I swore. He will never hear me plead for mercy. Odete, a long distance away from us, did not move. I don't know if she heard what we were saying. She was naturally eager to know what was going on, just so she could tell you later. But tell you what? That Father had come to me? But what feelings had led him to do so? What did Father want, mother?" Esperança said in the living room, her right hand clutching her throat, her breathing labored.

"That day, Odete came to my room, as is her habit. All she told me was that you were all right. For the first time she hid secrets from me. She wanted to keep me safe from harm for a few days. I suspect that for Odete I'm a crystal," Eulália said feelingly.

"To her, you're a god!" Esperança burst out, in a rage against that submissiveness, which in a certain way affected her.

"Don't say those words again. Spare me, my daughter."

Trembling, Eulália collapsed in the easy chair, next to the wicker basket full of Breta's toys. She picked up a rag doll, shapeless now from having been hugged to her granddaughter's bosom so many times. To her, Breta was a stranger. Whenever she visited them, Eulália was afraid that the mystery of that house would suddenly be disclosed. A world that her daughter had constructed with the intention of preserving it intact. To that end having left Madruga's property, without, in all those years, ever asking their permission to come back. Since the dramatic breakup between them, Esperança had returned to Leblon only once, on a lightning-quick visit, holding Breta, a small child still, by the hand. It had been difficult for Eulália to persuade her. She had taken advantage of the family's absence, all of them being in São Lourenço. Eulália had agreed to join them later. They were not to worry about her; she had Odete for company. After Madruga called her from the hotel, she hurriedly hunted up Esperança. She had firmly refused to come. She would never set foot in that house again, even for her mother's sake.

"For Breta's sake, then," Eulália insisted. "You can't condemn her to eternal exile. The house belongs as much to this little girl as to the other grandchildren. They're all of my blood."

On the visit to Leblon, Esperança took her daughter under her wing, so that she would not be frightened by the size of the house, the strange bright gleam of the crystals hanging from the ceiling. The details of that magic park, with its leafy trees, full of shadows.

"When you come to live with us, you'll know the way, Breta," Eulália said, with rare excitement.

The intimate contact of the rag doll, clasped to her bosom, made Eulália feel uncomfortable. With a rough gesture, she immediately shoved it back into the basket. She looked at her watch; she must head back home. Esperança noted her anxious haste, for which her father was responsible.

He would naturally be dining at home and her mother must be there waiting. Rising to her feet, Eulália inquired whether there was anything else
that had led her daughter to summon her so urgently.

At the door now, with her mother in a hurry to leave, Esperança
straightened, swallowed hard.

"I just needed to get things off my chest, mother. And I was homesick.
Forgive me if I gave you a scare."

Shortly before Madruga arrived, Eulália received a hand-delivered
envelope.

"How can it be from Esperança, if we just left her?"

Odete sensed how heavy the atmosphere was. Masses of air bearing
down, bringing the plague inside the house. Eulália opened the envelope
nonetheless.

"It's a note, Odete," and she asked for her glasses, always on the night
table alongside the religious books and the volumes of poetry.

She read to the end, and then immediately reread from the beginning,
her body motionless. "My God, help me to bear this moment."

After a long pause, she passed the note to Odete. "No one must read
it except you."

When she had finished, Odete handed the note back to her with extreme care. Eulália held it tightly between her fingers. Fearing it would fly
away. And that delicate life with it. But why hadn't Esperança spoken to
her personally? Was it true, then, that modesty and pride were easily confused, the two of them alike being mortal sins? she thought, unexpectedly
involved with human passion.

Suddenly, they heard Madruga coming up the stairs. Her husband's
step had never sounded as heavy as that to Eulália, as though he were
wearing winter boots. Using brute force to announce his arrival. So that
both of them would have time to disappear with the incriminating
evidence.

In the morning, Madruga announced that he was off on a trip to São
Paulo, and would be back on Thursday. Eulália was relieved. Mistress of
her own fate now with two days all on her own, out from under Madruga's
thumb. Not needing to hide her grief. He packed his bag as she looked on.

"If you need me, just call. I'll be right back." He seemed tired.

"Everything's fine, Madruga. There's no reason to worry," she said,
hiding her anxiety so her husband wouldn't suspect that she and Esperança
had secrets between them. The contents of all of them highly problematic,
being mere traces in her daughter's swift imagination.

"And is Miguel going with you?" she said, unable to contain herself.

Madruga stopped short, holding a shirt he was just beginning to fold.
For a few instants, he reviewed the house and the children in his mind.
And the thought came to him that the family was getting smaller instead
of growing. Despite the grandchildren. In all truth, those grandchildren

counted for nothing as long as he didn't know even the children whom he himself had begotten. If he couldn't get close to them, what to make of his grandchildren, born of women whose origins were completely unknown to him?

"You're right. Miguel had best keep me company in São Paulo."

He looked closely at Eulália, the one tree, as a matter of fact, that he had planted in that house with his sweat and his ambition. And keeping his face from tensing, he folded the shirt carefully. It was best that Eulália stay alone in the house, in Rio, in that country. Alone with her soul, able to retreat within it.

After Madruga had left, Odete went to Botafogo. To tell Esperança that Eulália would be coming by. Her mother did not want to surprise her in the company of strangers. To play a part in her private life. Not that she demanded that her daughter live a chaste life, but she preferred not to know with whom she shared it. Or how furiously she was fought over. Was Esperança going too far as a way of wreaking her revenge upon her father? So that the news would reach Madruga that his proud, independent daughter was leading a man's life, falling into shameful habits?

"Why such formality, mother? Come whenever you like," Esperança said. Wearing a blue bathrobe, her eyes sparkling despite her unruly gestures. Sitting alongside her mother, she haughtily offered her water and coffee at the same time. And before Eulália could get the truth out of her, Esperança began to ply her mother with questions.

"Please, Esperança, don't hide things from me. What's the matter? Why the note?" Eulália broke in.

"The note was to bare my heart to you. Or a modest literary composition. Let's not talk any more about it. After all, everything is already decided." Her tone of voice, harsh and forceful before, was softer now.

"What's all decided?" Eulália said pleadingly.

"That everything is going to stay exactly the same. That is to say, Madruga with his stubbornness and me with my defiance. We'll be enemies till the death of one of the two of us," and she turned her face away from her mother. She went into the bedroom, remaining there for several minutes. On her return, she had on one of the new dresses, a present from Eulália. Ready to leave the house now, she practically pushed her mother out the door.

"I'm terribly sorry, mother, but I didn't know you were coming. I couldn't cancel my engagement."

"Don't you want me to stay with you for these two days?" Eulália asked. "It will do us good. How many years has it been since we slept under the same roof?"

"Or heard rain falling on the roof? I remember that on rainy days your eyes always shone. I never discovered why. Whether out of happiness or sadness. Maybe because your heart ached from all the memories it was full of. You were thinking of Sobreira, weren't you? Or perhaps of Grand-father Miguel, the storyteller. Every family always has one. I pity the fam-ily that doesn't have one sitting at the table. In that case it's probably an orphan family, without a story to pass on. I know ours was different. We heard too many stories. Or ones that weren't good for us. I sometimes feel our lives are poisoned. And do you know why? Because the stories all of a sudden turned into legends. And the legends turned into tales. Tales with a moral. Madruga's and Miguel's tales, full of the very worst male traits. Now, I ask you, in the name of what principles are they trying to force rules of proper behavior on us? Can you tell me that, mother?"

Eulália tried to take her daughter in her arms. Esperança cut the em-brace short. Then she looked at her watch.

"I've an appointment with life, mother," she said with a big smile.

Eulália was relieved. Her daughter was rehabilitated for combat. And now had an austere beauty.

"If you need me, promise to call me," she pleaded anxiously.

"Don't worry. When I need you, everybody's going to know I called you." Esperança's unexpectedly evasive tone of voice gave her features an enigmatic cast.

Her daughter looked like a woman warrior with a sword and armor. Confronting Saracens over a matter of faith. And on looking back at her, almost at the corner now, Eulália all of a sudden mistrusted her daughter's words. She suspected that within that heart there was an intense desire to give up the truce by which she had heretofore been bound. She thought of Madruga and was moved to pity. Her husband did not know that Espe-rança intended to attack him with cold steel, at the next waning moon.

"What are you thinking about, Odete?" she said sadly, on reaching the car.

"Sooner or later, all houses are touched by discord." Odete spoke slowly and deliberately.

"Are you referring by chance to tragedy?"

"Where I come from, tragedy is different, Dona Eulália. It's less tragic."

"Let's go home, Odete. I want to put Esperança's note in her box. It must not come to light before my death."

Eulália's spirit hovers about the house now. We have just buried her in São João Batista Cemetery and her room still gives off a familiar scent. Venâncio wanders gravely about the house, convinced that he is thus breathing in the last traces of Eulália. In a few weeks more, she will leave us forever. Until even the objects that preserve her memory will be distrib-uted among everyone. And many of them, affected by the salt air, will soon fall apart. Madruga will give the grandchildren whatever they ask for. Keeping the easy chair and the key of his study for himself.

"Shall we take a walk through the garden?" Madruga said.

This was Grandfather's way of probing my soul, in his eagerness to discover the havoc wrought by the diary and the box. He was still sharp-witted and sly. He had always been good at gathering details and bread crumbs. As meanwhile I stole the last grains of wheat from his granary.

"This mango tree was always Esperança's favorite," I said rashly, bringing Mother's mortal remains to the surface. I had always avoided her name, sensing that the mere mention of it would bring reprisals.

Madruga's fingertips lightly brushed the bark of the mango tree. Awe-struck by the immortality of the tree. While many people had died, it had stubbornly gone on living. From the beginning, even before buying the building lot, he had been fascinated by those exposed roots, which even today continued to spread; nothing could stop them. All excited, he had then taken the family out to Leblon to show them the plot of land where he would build their future home.

Esperança rushed to the tree, putting her arms about its trunk with sudden passion. Madruga was frightened, immediately attempting to pull her away. As if to spare her suffering. Esperança suspected her father's intentions, and would not let go, clinging to the tree.

"What are you trying to do, father?" she said.

He finally confessed that they needed to cut it down to make way for the house, which was to be built in that very spot. Esperança instantly protested. Outraged, almost pleading with him to cut her down with it. She would not allow him to decree the death of that specimen of rare beauty.

"I too love trees, Esperança. But the project is all set to go. If I change everything at this point, I'll incur losses," he objected. Esperança stood her ground against her father, impatient now.

"And since when do you fear losses, father? Can't you see that this mango tree arrived here before we did? It's more Brazilian than our family is. And it's going to survive till my death!" Esperança said vehemently.

His daughter's voice sounded familiar to Madruga. Like Grandfather Xan's, permanently defending the organic life of plants, above all trees, in his opinion existences more necessary than his own as a transitory story-teller. Esperança was not mistaken. Madruga's life would be eighty years in the telling, at the maximum. Whereas that tree would be celebrated for five generations. All descended from the same line as Madruga. He finally gave in to Esperança's arguments.

"You've won this time, Esperança. But don't get the idea that you'll always come out a winner," and he looked his daughter square in the eye. She laughed in reply, wanting to tell him that whichever way he turned, he would always find her prepared to mark off the course of her own life to the very end.

"Esperança was not my enemy, Breta. We loved each other, don't forget. Even though it was a difficult love, full of challenges and lies. We were the first to mistrust this love. And also because the world distracted us too much. Never ask me if I regret having stood up to my daughter. I wouldn't know how to answer, and neither would Esperança, if she were alive. Even today our voices are weak and our arguments shaky, full of cracks."

Madruga continued to stroke the trunk, his hand lingering on the rough bark. Esperança's tree.

"Let's go in, grandfather. It's getting chilly. You might catch cold." I offered him my arm in the hope of touching his heart, of comforting him.

In the living room, several of the children had arrived. They were going through their hallowed rituals more or less halfheartedly. Not a one of them had given up gestures instilled in them with an authority that no longer depended on being enforced by Madruga's and Eulália's memory. With the children in charge, a spectacle was unfolding which no member of the family would think of not turning up at, thereby running the risk of no longer knowing what to do with their lives.

I owed them no fidelity. Certainly not the fidelity of telling them stories. Madruga remained the axis around which we rotated. Eulália's memory vying with her husband for the center of attention. As for Venâncio, foreseeing that he would not be able to bear being absent from a narrative of which he would be one of the cornerstones, he had moved into Tobias's room after Eulália's funeral. For hadn't he come in the same ship as Madruga, both of them of a mind to discover America? Columbuses of immigration? Luckless Pedro Álvares Cabrals, who, surprised in mid-voyage by an Atlantic calm, were blown to the coast by a wind driving them on to discover Brazil.

Antônia's greed prowled round the mortal remains of Madruga, alive still. She foresaw that Bento, at each defeat inflicted on Luís Filho, would summon her. Merely to lend his sister support at that time. Thus assuring her that certain rights still held good. There was more or less of an agreement between them that they would supply each other with a stock of affectionate gestures and kind words. For the first time, deceit, wrath, and envy would cease to be visible in Antônia's face. Just a weariness that rapidly aged her.

Eulália's box had not been able to save her. Or help her. It may well have induced in her the feeling of defeat. On perceiving, among her belongings, a niggardly life full of dark shadows. Without one beam of light that would lead her to pay a visit to her own soul with the aid of a little lamp. Her life entirely presided over by Luís Filho, after freeing her from Madruga. But who would free her of her husband's yoke? And if he were to die, what would happen to her? Widowhood would surely bring her no consolation. Merely a loneliness accorded an official status. Luís Filho had long since hurriedly turned his back on her in bed. If their bodies so much as touched each other, the only thing the two of them did was talk about the rapidly expanding businesses, the children all set to attack the family coffers. A mobilization of orderly troops, birds of prey.

Antônia had telephoned me again. Lacking the courage to ask me for help. She hinted, however, that life did not seem as joyful as Luís Filho had led her to believe when they were young. The children surrounded her with ostentatious luxury and false illusions, just so that they would not be bound by deep-reaching alliances.

"Nobody confides in me. Nobody. Not even my husband," Antônia said, still on the telephone.

As we left the garden, Antônia hastened to help Madruga into the house. The two of us took him to his easy chair. Miguel gave me a big bear hug, checking whether I was denying him the heat of my body. That bull with a permanent erection, eternally searching for doves sacrificed on the altar! Fearing, like Madruga, that his cock would shrivel, leaving him nothing but a fortune, and the painful memory of his mother and sister. And how would he erase so many memories?

"You're the only one who will give us continuity, Breta," Miguel said as consolation, stroking my hand.

I let him come closer. To keep him from wasting precious drops of life at that moment. The drops that Esperança gave him as a present. Even though Esperança hadn't mentioned him in the note. She had not mentioned anyone in particular. As she wrote, she tried to be impersonal toward her neighbors. She allowed them to exist, but they had all turned to dust. There remained few vectors to follow. The universe was a thankless confrere. And only she had the irresistible power to destroy her own life.

How often did Eulália read the note yet another time after the death of Esperança? Till finally she folded it, swearing to herself never to touch it again. Thus avoiding creating in her soul scales visible to God and to her own family. Yet, despite her prudence, Eulália did not want to deprive me of this heritage. She thought I would know how to wash away Esperança's bitter residues.

No new light was shed on life by Esperança's words. But they fulfilled a duty. They came down to me, her daughter, untouchable, subject to interpretations, as is the destiny of words. And the note, now yellowed with age, brought Esperança to the center of my house, crossing me with a sword.

"Life is poignant. My enemies have finally set fire to my garments and the walls of the house. I was lured into the yard, exposed to the sun, to absolute visibility. There is no one who does not see me and hurl poisoned darts at me. After all my earnest efforts, I lost my natural defenses, even the clamshell one is born with. My bones seem to be without solder. And the alloy of my blood, once effervescent, is breaking down in the face of my feelings. I no longer have lead and resistance in my favor. And I violently reject this succession of sleepless nights and more and more gasping breathing. Is that what the rhythm of my solar plexus is like as well, limping and sinister? I wish to add nothing more. As we well know, words do not correspond to feelings."

I do not take into account the moment at which Mother wrote the note, the better to follow her trajectory. Since Esperança vindictively refused to date it. It might have been written shortly before her death. Or after the break with Madruga, when she left home. Or else on the occasion of her separation from Vicente, following a violent quarrel. When Esperança swore not to let him into her house. She did not want cowards in her bed and at her table. This lesson, learned with Madruga, Esperança put into practice. Miguel himself assured me that my mother drove my father from the house with those very words.

"And who came after that, Miguel? Who else slept in Mother's bed?"

I appreciated my uncle's embarrassment. I took pleasure in taking my revenge for his cowardice and neglect. He blanched, rejecting the image of Esperança making love with a stranger. Her legs parted.

"No one, Breta, no one. Respect Esperança's memory."

I put the note away in the box. Life surrounded me with rich ingredients. Yet I was also alert to an evil dragging me every which way. I did not doubt Esperança's strong, arrogant character. Capable of extreme gestures. And therefore fascinated by vengeance, preparing herself to wreak it. To poison Madruga's last years with the venom of her death.

Grandfather, however, knew nothing of the note hidden away for so many years in the box. He did not have the slightest suspicion of its existence. I might be the only one who can make it possible for him to read those words. My desire, however, is to spare him till the end of his days. Mother punished him in my place. With one sure blow. Where she knew him to be vulnerable. Except that Mother forgot me. She did not hesitate to rob my future inheritance of a date that would have solved the mystery of the note.

All the children had gone home, leaving Madruga and Venâncio alone in the half-dark living room. I had gone out into the garden. On returning, I stole back in very quietly, and they did not see me. Entertained by the tedium that kept them company now. Any noise might have frightened them. In his old age, Madruga seemed incapable of ruthless gestures. Such as, for example, mortally wounding Esperança. But what does this matter now, if I intend to keep him company to the end? In his long day's dying. Him and Venâncio. Both of them eager for me to get around someday to writing the book about those immigrants who crossed the Atlantic in different eras, intending to cast anchor in Brazil forever. A story that has its risks, however. Certain precious pieces will be missing. After all, and I repeat once again, to whom do I owe fidelity? Nobody owes fidelity to life. It confuses us and encumbers us from one end to the other.

"Who can tell a complete story?" Eulália said once, in an effort to console her granddaughter, who had conceived the ambitious plan of converting the words spoken by Dom Miguel and Grandfather Xan into written words.

I will write the book nonetheless. And when I've finished it, I will go to Sobreira. Taking Brazilian ghosts and myths to meet myths and ghosts from that land. By then, Grandfather may have died. The threads that bind him to life are thin ones. We're almost certain to bury Venâncio and him in the same month. One ship won't survive the other. I hope Grandfather takes his leave of this earth in November. He always loved the Sobreira rains in that month.

Only after burying Grandfather, and being persuaded that he did not trick us with a fake death, will I be able to settle down peacefully in the ruined common room of Xan's house, in Sobreira. A house that keeps a dignity fed by Grandfather's money. On that afternoon, I will slowly sip my coffee. Only after that will I look in the fireplace for the old splinter of wood, to see if it's still there between the stones. If I don't find it, it will be the sign that Madruga has left us for good. Or might it simply mean that even though the chip of wood has fallen from the fireplace, ripped out by anonymous hands, Madruga has won and still dwells among us? But how is that possible, grandfather? Didn't you tell me that the sliver of wood will only remain firmly fixed there, between stones scorched by the fire, as long as you live? Why, then, should I bet on your fictitious life, knowing that you in fact left us and are now buried near Eulália, Esperança, Venâncio, all of them keeping you company?

And at that point Madruga, his blue eyes upon me, will suddenly appear in the room, making an ample gesture, capable of being shared bounteously between Sobreira and Brazil. Adopting a solemn tone in which to speak.

"Grandfather Xan did his very best to relive the stories buried in the earth of Galicia. While Eulália, Venâncio, and I arrived in Brazil with the intention of mixing Xan's stories with the ones that already existed here. But we weren't able to. We all capitulated. We've managed to make just one episode of this book. And now you're the only one we have left. It will be your task to write the entire book, at whatever price. Even if you must plunge your hand into the bottom of your heart, to pull life up out of it. A book which, as it speaks of Madruga and his story, also speaks of you, of your language, of the cruel and desolate Brazilian shore, of the entrails of these lands extending from the Amazon to the Rio Grande. I'll live in the book you're going to write, Breta. Have no fear of hurting us or even killing us. It's always necessary to kill and wound when one tells a story. Only that way, Breta, will you restore our memory, and keep it alive. As long as there is such a thing as your beloved Portuguese language."

After this speech, Madruga's shadow will soon fade away, as though it had not visited me in Sobreira. Resigned to an immemorial discretion. Absolute silence. So as not to interfere too much with my text. Granting me, finally, the freedom that he was unable to accord his family.

And when I am returning to Brazil, after taking my leave of Sobreira, I will look down from the deck on the waters of the Atlantic, certain that Madruga is there beside me. His willful blue eyes stubbornly tracking life as though he still had the duty to live it.

Odete approaches, her feet dragging in her slippers. She is bringing a tray with cups of coffee. Madruga and Venâncio are awaiting this moment. I take the tray from Odete without her protesting. She is eager, even, to free herself from small tasks and take refuge in her room, which she almost never leaves. I thus regain the right to approach those two old men.

On seeing me, Madruga smiles with an anxiety he cannot hide. He immediately calms down, however. Life no longer touches him. Venâncio, more discreet, thanks me for my kindness. I sit down with them. For how long I don't know. I only know that tomorrow I will start to write the story of Madruga.

A NOTE ON THE TYPE

This book was set in Fournier, a type face named for Pierre Simon Fournier, a celebrated type designer in eighteenth-century France. Fournier's type is considered transitional in that it drew its inspiration from the old style yet was ingeniously innovational, providing for an elegant yet legible appearance. For some time after his death in 1768, Fournier was remembered primarily as the author of a famous manual of typography and as a pioneer of the point system. However, in 1925, his reputation was enhanced when The Monotype Corporation of London revived Fournier's roman and italic.

Composed by Graphic Composition, Inc.
Athens, Georgia

Printed and bound by The Murray Printing Company,
Westford, Massachusetts

Typography and binding design by
Dorothy Schmiderer Baker